THE MARS HOUSE

The Watchmaker Novels

The Watchmaker of Filigree Street
The Bedlam Stacks
The Lost Future of Pepperharrow

Stand-alone Novels

The Kingdoms
The Half Life of Valery K

Collections

The Haunting Season
The Winter Spirits

A NOVEL

THE MARS HOUSE

NATASHA PULLEY

BLOOMSBURY PUBLISHING
NEW YORK · LONDON · OXFORD · NEW DELHI · SYDNEY

BLOOMSBURY PUBLISHING
Bloomsbury Publishing Inc.
1385 Broadway, New York, NY 10018, USA

BLOOMSBURY, BLOOMSBURY PUBLISHING, and the Diana logo are trademarks
of Bloomsbury Publishing Plc

First published in the United States 2024

ISBN: HB: 978-1-63973-233-3; EBOOK: 978-1-63973-234-0

LIBRARY OF CONGRESS CATALOGING-IN-PUBLICATION DATA IS AVAILABLE

2 4 6 8 10 9 7 5 3 1

Typeset by Westchester Publishing Services
Printed and bound in the U.S.A.

To find out more about our authors and books visit www.bloomsbury.com and
sign up for our newsletters.

Bloomsbury books may be purchased for business or promotional use. For information on
bulk purchases please contact Macmillan Corporate and Premium Sales Department at
specialmarkets@macmillan.com.

To Jacob, my annoyingly multi-talented brother, who always tells me when I've written a big pile of rubbish.

I

London always flooded, had done for decades. People had got the hang of it, moved upward, and started doing scuba diving tours of the lost lower floors for tourists. The jewellers round by Covent Garden kept boats moored at Farringdon Dock[1] so they could move their stock fast if the waters rose, and just like they had in centuries past, shops and houses and restaurants had begun to populate the higher Thames bridges. It had become a trinkety sort of place, full of rare book shops and once grand theatres, and locals who were locked in a war with the massive cruise ships that kept knocking the frilly bits off the Houses of Parliament.

When January was little, it had been the sort of place where people came on holiday to see the glittering ruins at Canary Wharf that sank deeper into the river silt every year. He had grown up knowing that the city was sinking, but somehow he'd never thought it would one day be *sunken*.

April was flood season, and that April was even more determined than the previous ones. The night before everything really fell apart, the rain was already torrential, so he and half the company stayed late at the theatre to put sandbags down at the doors—even though a string of ministers and engineers had been on the emergency broadcasts to say the flood defences would be fine. The Royal Opera House leaned over

---

1 Formerly Farringdon Station, where what had once been railway platforms now served nicely as wharves.

Seven Dials Canal, which often broke its banks by a good few feet, floating the boats up to the ceilings of their alcoves. Seals had taken over the portico because they knew the kitchen people would be along with yesterday's sushi soon.

January was enjoying it a lot, though. He didn't have to use the front door of his building any more; the ferry driver stopped right outside his bedroom window and he just hopped onto the top deck and sunbathed the whole way to work, watching the orange tree blossom rain across the waterways. He did know he might be in trouble once the water rose *above* his bedroom window, but it was already thirty degrees out and it would not be the end of the world if he had to camp on the roof. He had one of those big umbrellas his mum had used to take fishing, and a camp stove, and an endless pig-headed ability to enjoy himself as long as he personally was mostly dry and he had a camera to take pictures of the dolphins with.

Although some businesses were shut, the theatre wasn't. As one person, the company had agreed they'd all happily drown before they cancelled the show. It was *Swan Lake*, for God's sake; as the director pointed out, cancelling a show about a lake because it was raining would be ridiculous.

So, once the sandbags were down, everyone cracked out the theatre's supply of candles and matches, set out the big emergency candelabra, put mirrors behind those to make the most of the light—if you were going to go without electricity, there were worse places to work than a theatre—and carried on with the rehearsal.

In all, it had looked fine. Even late that afternoon, it had all looked fine.

January did very much enjoy being the principal of the company— people brought you coffee, and sometimes famous singers wanted you to dance in their music videos—but in his ungrateful moments, he might admit he could have done without being the Swan King. The show run meant he had to lift the not-insubstantial kid playing the prince on one hand four times a day, without collapsing, for the next month. Terry was a wonderful athlete, but if a stranger was asked to guess what he did, they would probably say rugby.[2] January was pining for Annie, who had been all of nine stone and who he watched the boxing with religiously after the shows. But Annie was thirty-five and her knee had finally gone, and now; well, now there was Terry.

It was someone's birthday today. It had been someone's birthday every day this week, and he watched glumly as Terry skipped past with yet more cake.

"Don't you judge me," Terry said, waving the cake at him. "I'm nineteen. I'm a Growing Lad."

"You're all right, mate," January lied, feeling future pain in both wrists.

"Cake?" Terry said brightly.

January wondered about hurling him out the window. The canal was right outside: an enormous walrus-person would surely be fine. "No, thanks. Get some shoes on, we're starting."

Terry made a sad face at him but did, at least, go in the right direction.

January leaned against a rail to check his own shoes. You had to break them and superglue them in odd places. He had never worked out why it was that no manufacturer in the world had ever managed to make ballet shoes that just functioned, but they never had, and with rehearsals at fever pitch now, he felt like he was spending half his life with a bottle of glue in his hand, because he was getting through a pair a day. Everyone was; and so he tended to spend the other half of his day unsticking Terry from rails or props, or once, the assistant director.

Come the performances, it would be two pairs a day. In the back of the changing room, there was a scrap heap of them. Sometimes he studied the wrecked leather and thought about what that same pressure and force were doing to his own joints. Thirty-one was getting on for a

---

2   This is not to be confused with football, either the European or the American kinds. Football is for waifs. Rugby is traditionally used as a way for small countries to remind everyone else why they would regret it if they invaded. Nobody wears any kind of protective gear. Players argue that actually, more protection would mean nastier problems, pointing to boxing where gloves mean more people go for head shots, but of course the real reason is that this would get in the way of the whole point, i.e., killing the English.

dancer, it really was, and he had been phenomenally lucky to have had no major injuries yet. He could feel it coming, though.

He had no idea what to do when it did. If you were lucky, you moved into choreography and director roles, but that wasn't going to happen, not in London. The major theatres were in Russia. The ballet boarding schools often wanted people. Beijing, maybe, or one of the megaschools in Saudi Arabia where the solar barons sent their kids. It was a yawning pit just waiting for him, and he had an acute sense that he was already balancing on the edge. He had to keep reminding himself that he had been lucky to do this for so long—or at all—that it wouldn't kill him to teach, that he had always known he would only be able to dance until, at the outside best, he was forty.

Only it was still horrible. It was horrible to have found the one thing you were made to do, to be one of the best in the world at it—and to know you could do it for only a few years. It wasn't that other things wouldn't be all right. One of the Saudi schools would be fantastic. Imagine, the sensible voice in the back of his mind said (he always assigned it to the Swan King, who struck him as a pragmatic sort of person), living in a city that's entirely pedestrian, which isn't flooded, where they put all their roads and cars underground, and where every scrap of cloth, from the market canopies to the visor of your cap, is solar panelling to fuel the air conditioning. Imagine not wearing waders to buy groceries.

It would just never be *this*. He would never be this good again, never be this strong, and he knew what he was like. Logically he'd be proud of what he'd done, but he wouldn't feel proud. Future January would feel ashamed to be so much less than Past January.

The director was clapping for attention. "All right! From the top of the pas de deux."

However much January did not enjoy Terry, he loved these candlelit rehearsals in the twilight of flames and mirrors. They could have been anywhere, in any time; Italy in the nineteenth century, Paris before that. It meant belonging in a tradition eight hundred years old—a tempestuous, brutal one that slung you out with nothing at the end except arthritis, but just for now, it was still his. He loved the flex and give of the stage. He loved how, once you had trained to the highest peak of fitness you could go, even launching yourself five feet into the air was effortless, how there was a moment when you floated.

"Guys!" the orchestra conductor shouted. She always stayed as long as they did, even after the musicians had gone home; she played the violin for them because she insisted no dance company should rehearse to anything but live music. She had just gone out for a cigarette. "The foyer's two feet deep in water and I think it's got into the electrics. There's a lot of dead fish in there and I got sparks when I dropped some foil on the surface."

There was a hush, because that meant nobody would be able to go home.

"What's the matter?" the director said. "We'll camp in the changing rooms. Lovely big sleepover." Even she didn't seem thrilled with the idea of having to spend all night in proximity to Terry.

January wondered what he was going to do about his contact lenses. He was spectacularly shortsighted without them, and not having expected to stay the night, he hadn't brought a case or the solution for them. The last time he'd kept them in overnight by accident, he'd ended up in hospital being told off by a doctor.

"Water's rising, mind you," said the conductor.

He didn't sleep much, not because he was worried about the flood, but because nobody had any saline solution and he had to throw away his lenses. He wasn't sure how he was going to get home half blind. He lived in Hackney, which was over the far side of the city, and he hated the idea of asking anyone to help him get there. Most of the company were just like Terry; still children really, and though everyone was incredibly kind, it was asking too much.

He jolted awake, because somewhere close by on the canal, a lonely flood siren was going off, but muffled; he had a feeling that the angry lady who ran the coffee shop on the corner had stuffed a tea-towel in it.

He got up carefully. Everyone was asleep on the floor, bundled up in nests of blankets and cushions stolen from the nice seats in the auditorium. He skirted the edge of the room, not at all able to tell if he was about to step on a person or just a suggestively shaped ball of bedding. When he got to the window, he had to stare for a long time to put together what he was seeing, blurred as it all was.

The canal water was right below the window. Covent Garden had flooded up to the second floor, and all around it, people were sitting on roofs.[3]

It was still raining. Opposite, a man he usually only ever saw dressed in a suit, getting cross into a phone at the café, was sitting on a fold-up chair under a bivouac, cooking something on a gas stove.

A puffin was sitting on the windowsill, looking just as interested to have found a January as January was to have found a puffin. Puffins were always much tinier than he imagined, and the markings on their faces made them look sad, but this one seemed cheerful. It had some fish. It must not have minded people, because it waddled across to sit by his arm. He was wearing black; maybe it thought he was a giant puffin.

In a bright orange canoe, just opposite him on the canal, Always Angry Lady from the café lifted a hand. He only knew it was her because she always wore the same yellow headscarf.

January waved. "Hi. Anything on the news?"

"Horrible disaster, emergency services in crisis, everyone at Westminster's fucked off to fucking Manchester," she said.

"Right. Where are you off to?" he asked, in case it was a sensible idea everyone here could copy.

"See if I can get a boat out to Peterborough."

He didn't know anyone in Peterborough. With a lurch, he realized that he didn't know anyone anywhere but here. His mum's vineyard in Cornwall had been sold to a French family with a poodle and triplets.

---

3   To foreigners, it seemed stupid for England to have a capital city that spent all of its time sinking, but the fact was that most of London—when it was built—was only ever about four metres above the level of the Thames. The lofty hills of Bloomsbury and Mayfair (a whole thirty-eight metres above sea level) still had to have canals. Unfortunately those canals also tended to flood the moment they saw some rain, which was usually, much to the ire of the people who owned the increasingly devalued town houses, and much to the joy of the local octopus population, who then gained access to some pretty exciting wine cellars.

They knew him by sight, because her grave was on the edge of the land and he visited it sometimes, but that was it.

"Good luck," he said.

"Fuck it all," she said, and paddled off.

He jumped when, somewhere over the rooftops, something exploded. It was a deep bang that juddered the skeleton of the building. The puffin jumped too, and whirred away.

The conductor touched his shoulder. "Internet's gone," she said. "I think we need to get out and find out what's going on. And some food. There's twenty-five people here."

"How?"

She pointed downwards. There was a lost rowing boat bumping against the wall. After a murmured discussion with the director, they climbed down into it, January to row and the conductor to navigate.

Without much hope, they tried supermarkets first. Everything was flooded. The front doors were underwater. They had to give up. Instead, they concluded that what was needed was to find some people who might know what was going on or where you could get help.

As always, there were beacon lights punching up to the storm clouds above St Paul's Cathedral, and hologram signs to say that you could find shelter there if you had nowhere else. It would have news screens too. The two of them hesitated, because it was a long way to row, but it was downriver and the current would carry them toward the cathedral, at least.

By the time they guided the little boat up to the great bulk of the cathedral, January's hands were raw, even where he had wrapped his sleeves over them. Away from the silt of the Thames, the water here was very, very clear, and blue; he could see right down to the ancient steps, thirty feet below the hull.

Plenty of other people had had the same idea, and the way in was crowded—the vast doors formed a bottleneck as people had to slow down to duck under the arch of the portico—but it was eerily quiet. The only voices came from the high screens projecting the news down into the gloom of the aisle, and the thousands of little boats floating there. The muted light from the stained glass windows patterned people and water in colours. January and the conductor eased their boat into a space close to a statue of a saint which, when it had been set there, must have been twenty feet above the ground. Now, the water rippled around the hem of its robe.

The news was being projected around the inside of the great dome. Although there were speakers everywhere, it was hard to hear; the echoes were so severe it all sounded as though everything was being said twice, half a second apart.

The conductor, who had been standing up to direct him, sat down next to him now on the bench. In the boat next to theirs, an exhausted-looking man lifted his tiny daughter out to sit at the saint's feet.

". . . emergency restrictions banning all travel. Flooding is widespread beyond the capital, presenting a significant danger to life. The national rail network has suspended services across the south and southeast. The Prime Minister, who was evacuated to Manchester late last night, has pledged emergency aid to the capital as soon as possible."

As soon as possible didn't sound very soon.

On the way back to the theatre, the two of them broke into the top floor of a camping shop and stole gas stoves, torches, batteries, and everything else they could think of that might be useful. They found a supermarket on the upper floor of a shopping centre too, open and crowded, shelves emptying fast. He waited, tense, in the boat while the conductor hurried in, because he had watched someone tip a girl out of her boat into the water to steal it two minutes before. Perhaps he looked big enough to be trouble, or perhaps there were just better boats around, but nobody tried anything. The sky was grey and quiet. Very quiet. There were no helicopters.

After a week, it was impossible to get enough food, and they rationed. Then they rationed more. Down the street, a lady who'd had the presence of mind to take a fishing rod onto the roof with her caught salmon and brought some around to everyone she could, but it wasn't much. January had never been so hungry.

They spray-painted SOS—25 PEOPLE onto the roof, and all along the street, people did the same.

In fits and starts, most of the dancers tried to leave, just in case they still had a home to go to, but everyone came back pale and shocked, with stories of whole streets underwater. January tried too, only to find that the entire canal where he lived was sealed off, the water littered with dead seabirds. There were exposed electrical lines under there somewhere, a ragged emergency worker explained. It was a miracle he hadn't been at home.

On the morning of the fifteenth day, he wondered for the first time if they might actually die here, if it had been stupid to wait so long, if they should all have found boats and rowed as far as they could while they still had the energy and the supplies.

The helicopter came two hours after that.

The crew spoke only Mandarin, and nobody in the company did apart from school-level stuff, but they managed to be reassuring all the same. The director put all the youngest kids on the first round, then was hustled onto the second herself. January was among the last. He was so exhausted by then that he could hardly hold on to the harness on the way up. At the top, the deck was already full of other rescued people, some of them ebullient and some, like him, numb with relief. He couldn't make them out well. He still couldn't see properly, and he was beginning to realize that he was going to be stuck like that for a while now. It didn't matter any more. He let his head bump against the wall, listening to the roar of the engine. He had no idea where they were going, but as they veered away, he found he didn't care, and when they landed at an airfield where people in orange jackets were handing out food parcels and blankets, he was so happy to see dry ground that he almost didn't understand when a translator came around with a clipboard and asked if he would like to seek asylum in Tharsis.

"Where's that?" he managed. He opened the food parcel, in which there was a wonderful, inexplicable packet of marshmallows. They tasted so good that it was hard to think. He offered the translator one. He had been looking around for the rest of the company, but he couldn't see anyone. Other people were saying that the helicopters were taking different loads of people to different camps to try and even out numbers.

"Mars," the man said gently, shaking his head at the marshmallow offer. "The Chinese colony? They're funding this centre. Ships are coming, for refugees."

Ships are coming. January hadn't realized how used he was to the certainty that no one was coming, and no one ever would come, because they never did. To hear that they were—he didn't even know what that swell of feeling was. Not relief, because relief implied somehow that you'd been aware of feeling bad before, and not even gratitude, because you were grateful when someone passed you the salt or when they remembered your birthday. That wasn't what you felt when someone you had never met sent ships from another world.

Not far away, another translator was trying to dissuade a big family from travelling to Saudi Arabia. The coastguard there, she was saying, were turning back refugee boats. People were drowning. And don't even *think* about trying to get a visa. They say they're making visas available, but that means they'll let about five people in and call it a day. No, it doesn't matter if your mother's already there. They don't care. Half the world wants to get to Neom. Unless you're a rocket scientist, forget it.

January blinked hard and realized he'd lost the thread of what *his* translator was saying. His hearing had tuned out.

"Say again, sorry?" he said. It was bizarre, the fog in his head. He could only just peer through it at passing thoughts. Most of them were to do with marshmallows.

"We can get you going with the paperwork now," the translator repeated, as if it were all normal. "They've made it very straightforward."

January swallowed. "I can just—go? Just like that?"

"Just like that, honey," the man said. "It's disaster relief. And Tharsis always needs immigrants. It's a big move, but honestly, no legal hurdles here. They really do want people. You won't sit in some miserable camp for months, and there's no restrictions on refugees working. There *are* restrictions on what Earthstrong people can do, but even so. There's more work than they've got people to do it. Basic stuff, but—it's work."

"Earthstrong . . . ?"

"The gravity there is only a third of ours. It can be pretty dangerous to let you just walk around when you've come straight from here." The man hesitated. "Been a bit of a kerfuffle about it lately, but it's still better than Saudi or China."

It was the first time that January really understood that normal life was over. He had thought he might die, but he hadn't thought about what would happen if he lived. London wasn't going to recover. There would be no more theatre. There was probably no getting to other countries either; the floods must have displaced millions of people, which would mean millions pouring towards international borders. Those borders were already slamming shut.

The simple, stupid truth was that all he wanted to do was go where there was food and heat. He was aching less with hunger than a kind of shock that it was so easy for everything to just collapse, for life to go from boring visits to the café and wondering if it was extravagant to get hot chocolate instead of coffee, to—this. He felt like he would agree to anything just to make it stop, even though he hadn't even had that bad a time and it hadn't lasted very long, and actually he was fine.

He didn't know the first thing about Tharsis, but he did know he didn't have it in him to try and get to Riyadh or Lagos or Beijing. He wasn't made of hard enough stuff for that.

And the famous thing about Mars was that there was no water.

That sounded pretty bloody marvellous.

"Yes please," he said. "I'd like to go."

2

600 days later

January's apartment was on the twelfth floor of what had once been a nuclear reactor's cooling tower. The refugee agency promised it wasn't radioactive, and they had even installed little film radiation detectors on all the windows that were supposed to go dark if anything was amiss, but January's detector was about eighty years old and he wasn't sure it would notice even if he started a uranium collection on the windowsill.

It was too early for the elevator machinery, which ran right behind his bedroom wall, to have woken him up when the siren went off.

A dozen other identical sirens blared in other apartments all around the building—he could hear them straight through the walls, through the floor, and through the flimsy ceiling. It took him a bewildered second to understand that it was coming from his phone. A flat, less than urgent voice was announcing something in deafening Mandarin. He didn't catch it at first, not least because he thought it must have been something to do with radiation.

Alert. Major dust storm. Close all the doors, windows, and ventilation outlets. Alert. Major dust storm. If you are outside, find shelter now. Alert. Major dust storm . . .

January jabbed at the phone until it shut up, then searched for some proper news. Despite the time (five twenty, argh, argh, argh), there was a live weather report going out, by a reporter who looked like they had just been hauled out of bed too. They were standing on what must have been the roof of Broadcasting House, trying to talk into the microphone and the wind at the same time. It was all in official Mandarin and of course they weren't running English subtitles, they'd forgotten about people who didn't have translation software built in like bloody always, so he had to listen with his eyes shut and wait for the gears in his brain to squeak around to more or less the right cogs.

"—like smoke inhalation, breathing the dust particulates will damage lung tissue, and a few moments ago the Consul took the unusual step of declaring a red weather warning, along with advice to remain indoors if possible. The Met Office have indicated that the storm may cause some electricity shortages as solar energy struggles to reach the sun fields; it's likely too that in turn, water allowances will reduce as the output from Tereshkova Wharf—"

The signal dropped. He had to look up "inhalation" and "particulates."[4]

Curious now, January went to the window and unstuck a corner of the bubble wrap from the frame. He'd put the bubble wrap over the glass to try and keep the heat in over the winter, and he'd got used to seeing nothing but a blur outside. It was a nice surprise to find that the city was still there. This high up, the great artery roads were serene and glittering, and the narrow stripe of sky above the Valley was beginning to lighten. But powering towards the city now, there was a red-brown cloud, just a smudge for the moment, but it was enveloping everything in that direction—the whole Valley, the whole sky. He could feel the wind picking up, icy as it seeped through the glass and the bubble wrap. He had to snatch his hand away and pull his sleeves over his knuckles.

He could hear other people breathing or coughing through the paper walls. Everyone else was standing at the windows too.

---

4   If he'd been on the big Everything App everyone here used, he could have run a filter over the broadcast and heard it all in perfect English. The software was amazing. But to get the app, you had to be a citizen, with a social security number. And without the app, you couldn't order deliveries, you couldn't book tickets for anything, or pay normally in shops, use vending machines, and a dozen other things. This, January was coming to feel, was very typically Tharsese. It was that painstaking, meticulous kind of unhelpfulness you only normally encountered in the post office.

As the dust came closer, he could make out the storm front better. Tendrils of rust brown raced out ahead of the main dust cloud, billowing and reaching, and then other shapes rode after them, all illusions of the roaring particles, but all vast. As the dust smashed into the towers, it made an eerie roar. Then the view vanished, and the dust started to blast in through the cracks under the window frame. January pushed the tape back down quickly, already gritty, and touched the film of dust on the sill. It was fine as icing sugar. But there was so much of it that it thrummed against the building and hissed at the windows. He had to shine his phone around just to find the light switch. He hadn't seen much dust come in, only a puff, but it was already hanging in the air, winking.

He polished it off the front of his phone in case it clogged up the electrics. He didn't know if there was anyone in Tharsis who would be able to fix it. The phone was an antique—his great-grandmother's—from the days when they were still hand-held, a beautiful thing that looked like a glass card when it was off. The battery was good forever, but even in London there'd been only one specialist shop that had ever been able to service it.[5]

Worried by the mention of less water, he looked in the tiny cupboard where the water meter and the electric gauge were. The water meter showed a traffic light that said how much water you could use in the day. Green was twenty litres; amber was ten; red was five. January had never seen it green and suspected they only made the gauges with the green light to give you false hope. A shower used ten litres per minute, so he tended to save up the water and then dive into the cubicle once every three days, which was fine, given that he had one of those jobs where being too clean made you morally suspect. He wasn't sure he'd cope very well if that went down to once every seven days, though.

---

5   Mori and Daughter, on Filigree Street, had been a watchmaking shop since the 1880s, expanding only with a serious grudge into electrical timekeeping at the end of the twenty-first century, when they made a name for themselves doing to phones what Rolex had done to watches. The guarantees were famously issued for five hundred years. Mori timepieces only ever increased in value, and if January had sold his, he could probably have bought a house. He didn't want a house, though. He wanted something of his mum's.

It was still amber. Good.

The factory was going to be chaos. Better get in early.

He called the lift. The tower was designed in a truly strange way, with the lifts opening straight out into the flats. The housing company said it meant they could fit more apartments in that way, because they weren't wasting space on corridors. January thought it seemed like a nightmare waiting to happen if ever there were a fire, but he wasn't too bothered. In this gravity, he could just jump out of the window if he had to.

As the lights on the readout counted down from the fifty-seventh floor, he was filled with a nagging sense he'd forgotten something.

There are moments when you come so close to another future you can taste the air in the courtroom, and feel the roughness of the orange jumpsuit seams over your knees, and hear the grinding of the mechanisms as the barred doors close.

Usually, for January, they were the moments that came when he wasn't quite feeling right anyway, and his mind stopped working properly, its usual calculations skewing until it seemed like a sensible idea to swerve a tiny boat in front of a cruise liner into a gap that was exactly wide enough, making no allowance whatever for travelling at forty knots at the time; or hearing the electrics fizz as the flood waters rose, filing it away as useful information, walking away from the lights to avoid any explosions, and not telling the other thirty people in the canteen. Those things were just badly timed ordinary mind malfunctions of the kind everybody had all the time, the ones that saw people go upstairs for reasons they immediately lost, or forget to lock the door at night—but it was the ordinariness of it that scared him.

When the lift doors opened, the three people already inside drew back all at once, and yelled in different languages.

"You're not wearing your—"

"Get *back*!"

"Where's your—"

"Get your resistance cage!"

He was so shocked he couldn't even say anything at first. Cold swept through him like the heater had just broken, aching through the bones in his face and right down his arms.

"I'm sorry—I'm sorry," he managed, mortified, and turned back to get it.

What felt like every second week, he saw something in the news about some idiot who had killed someone because they'd wandered off accidentally—he really baulked at thinking it was on purpose—without their cage. If you were born on Earth, your bones grew to support your weight in Earth's gravity. If you were born on Mars, or if you naturalised, your bones could only lift one third of that. Those bones were fragile. If he so much as bumped into someone from here, the kind of knock he wouldn't even have noticed in London, there was every chance he would break their skull.

And he never felt sympathetic when those clumsy Earthstrongers got the twenty-five-year mandatory prison sentence, because when you had a resistance cage, it was a hard thing to miss.

Resistance cages were full-body steel harnesses. The steel was something clever, and it would fit to you exactly whether you put it on over clothes or under them. Open, they looked like skeleton suits of armour. January had walked straight by his on his way to the door.

When he stepped backwards into the frame, it shushed as its silver tendons closed over him, very cold even through his clothes, and immediately, moving was far harder. He lifted his arms a little to make sure. Yes. Much heavier.

The cage did not actually make you heavier. It did exactly what it said on the side—resistance. It made moving as difficult as it would be under Earth's gravity.

He looked back at the lift and realized, hating everything, that they had actually held the door for him. They were all waiting.

"You don't have to wait for me," he croaked.

"Don't be silly," the nurse from the top floor said warmly. "You're ready now, get in."

He crept in, clawing for some grateful things to say, but so shaken up that all his Mandarin flew out of his head.

He squeezed into the corner, which was marked off in bright yellow tape on the floor with a big *E* in the middle, for Earthstrong, beside the Mandarin sign for "Earth." Everyone else squeezed over the other side. He tried to think tiny, harmless thoughts. Right above his head was the government poster that plastered this whole building. It showed a silhouette of what looked like a troll, with silvery lines sketching a cage around it.

REMEMBER, it exclaimed in a happy font that had probably been designed for a kids' show about making rockets from old gardening pots, IF YOU'RE EARTHSTRONG, YOU MUST WEAR A RESISTANCE CAGE IN ALL PUBLIC SPACES! LET'S STOP ACCIDENTS TOGETHER!

He pressed his hands together, trying to stop shaking, and hoping that everyone else thought he was just cold. He had never done anything so spectacularly stupid before. And what for; because the dust was distracting? He was hanging over the edge of crying.

"You should be more careful," someone said, so old and desiccated that they were mostly just a big coat and a hat. "You could have killed someone. You know normal people are three times weaker than you lot?"

"I know. I'm sorry," he said again, trying to melt into the lift wall. It was chipboard, which had scared him when he first arrived, but of course in light gravity, wood would do for a lot of things. Not even real wood. Some kind of printed composite that just looked like it.

The old person huffed and grumbled something in Russian which sounded a lot like "bloody immigrants."

It wasn't until the lift doors closed that he saw the new graffiti on them. It was sprayed on from a template, quick and neat and efficient, at eye level. It was the Natural First logo, which was the same as the government poster, except that the delicate cage was replaced by bars, like a prison door.

"It's just kids," the kind nurse said to him awkwardly.

January nodded and didn't say that kids didn't usually make such clever templates for their graffiti.

Thankfully, the trains were still running. The Olympos Line was good, even in bad weather. The dust was so thick it was hard to see the carriage markers on the platform, but it was clear where the Earthstrong-only carriage would stop, because of the gradation of height in the people waiting.

What was really alarming about gravity was how much it squashed you. January was an inch taller here than he had been on Earth, an *inch*: he noticed it on shirt hems. If you were born here, if your spine had grown in lighter gravity, you were usually even taller. If your great-grandparents had been born in this gravity, you were about seven feet high. Scientists said that eventually, the lower gravity would actually mean people developed *stronger* bones than they would do on Earth, but for now, only seven generations from the first colonists, they definitively had not, and they were in the wobbly stage where evolution was still getting its boots on. From what he understood, someone seventh-generation Natural *was* stronger than someone, say, second, but that still wasn't strong.

He made his way to the cluster of smaller dust silhouettes, and had to punch himself in the thigh to try to stop himself picturing the lift doors opening, and how scared everyone had looked.

The stations had height-and-weight sensors that noticed if you were Earthstrong, and like always, the neon flashed as he passed it.

REMEMBER TO WALK SLOWLY!

DID YOU KNOW?

A POLAR BEAR IS THREE TIMES HEAVIER THAN THE AVERAGE HUMAN.

IF YOU'RE FROM EARTH, YOU'RE AS STRONG AS A POLAR BEAR HERE!

January had looked this up once, because he'd suspected the government weren't envisaging normal people when they said Earthstrong, but giant Viking heavyweight boxers.

What he had found was that it *was* technically true, for him, if you were talking about quite a delicate lady polar bear. He wanted to think this meant that he had won an important statistical point, but he had a creeping feeling that it didn't. As she was breaking into the house and eating the cat, he doubted many people would say, "But don't worry, she's actually quite small for a polar bear."

When it arrived, the train was nothing but the scythe of its lamps. The front carriage was Earthstrong only, so he shuffled on with three or four other people, all of them wearing resistance cages under their coats the same as him, shushing as they pushed against every move. Not trusting himself now, he kept brushing the steel sternum to check it was definitely there.

That person in the lift had been right. He *could* have killed someone. *Pink elephants pink elephants think about pink elephants.*

He calmed down slowly, maybe because everything in the Earthstrong carriage was made for people like him. The lights were brighter, the handrails and grip-rings set lower than usual, there were real, physical signs because the train operators had realized nobody Earthstrong could afford lenses and glasses for virtual ones, and on this line, being impressively brand new, they even put more oxygen in the air. It helped.

In his pocket, his charge card was a smooth, reassuring weight. It was like nothing he'd had in London, a sort of pebble-sized rectangle of quartz. He kept turning it over and over between his fingertips like a worry stone, then remembered to actually pay with it, just a tap to the panel on the train's bulkhead. Two kilowatts for a day pass. Expensive, but there was no way around it.

January sat near the front window and watched as they ploughed through the dust and the dark tracks. The rails ran over high bridges over the roads and the warehouses where little lights shone, around the glittering financial district and the gigantic open space that was Gagarin Square, the memorial statue from the riot towering over the people coming and going. He shut his eyes till he was sure that was past.

The advertisements panel next to him flared hopefully to life and burst into a hologram image of a place that looked like a luxury hotel.

"If you're planning to stay on Mars," a cheerful voice said, "the government will pay for you to naturalise to local gravity. It only takes three months, and in that time, you'll live in a state-of-the-art facility with the very best medical care. No more cages, no more work restrictions, no more worry . . ."

It showed him someone Earthstrong walking through lovely rooms and a shiny medical centre, and friendly doctors smiling. He'd seen the same advert a thousand times, but this time, he watched it.

"Once you've naturalised," the cheerful voice continued, "you'll get automatic citizenship, universal basic income, and free medical insurance, and you can apply for work anywhere you like."

It didn't mention anything about how you'd have to do that new job while you were coping with nerve damage and osteoporosis. Government adverts only ever used voices like that to remind you to pay your taxes.

He opened and closed his hands, feeling the pull of the cage gauntlets. He had been here for a year. He hadn't decided whether he wanted to try and go back. He kept not thinking about it.

On the Crossing, on the ship, the lawyers had taken a very different stance to the cheerful voice in the government advert.

"It is your choice, at least for now, whether you wear a cage, or whether you naturalise," a human rights barrister had told a whole sports hall full of people. It had been the only place on the refugee ship big enough to hold all one thousand people aboard all at once. It was so big that you could see the floor curving upward and away; all the living spaces were part of great wheels that rotated just fast enough to mimic Earth's gravity. But it still smelled like every other sports hall ever built: polish and shoes.

"But let's be clear. If you naturalise to Mars gravity, you can *never* go home. Your bones, organs, and muscles will acclimatise to functioning with one third of the effort they do on Earth. Try and go back to Earth after that, you'll die of a heart attack the second you enter the atmosphere. Now, there's all kinds of benefits to naturalising; you can have office jobs, you'll get citizenship and therefore universal basic income, free healthcare, the works. If you don't, it's manual labour only, health insurance comes out of your pay, and you can only live in a few specially adapted places around the city. But one of the reasons the Tharsis government is so generous with those who do naturalise is that they know full well it's a death sentence. The health impact will kill you in the end. Before the invention of resistance cages, the life expectancy of the first settlers' Mars-born children was forty-five. So make your decision very carefully."

Someone who hadn't thought about it properly put their hand up. "Why is the government so keen on people naturalising but not on cages?"

"Because," the barrister sighed, "Earthstrongers are unbelievably dangerous."

Tereshkova Wharf had its own underground stop. January and all the other Earthstrongers got off there, just in time to hear the hammer of the night shift's end-bells. After the bright carriage, the platform beyond looked dark, even though it was floodlit. The dust wasn't blowing in this far underground, but it was settling on the floor from people's clothes, and on the tracks where the trains pulled it in.

Almost straightaway, he had a panicky feeling, like he was drowning, only without the water.

That was just slightly thinner air than his lungs wanted. It was fine.

The workers' entryway into the plant was, like everything here, divided into two. Over one gate, there was a sign that said NATURALISED in Mandarin and English. That one led up a set of steel steps, into the upper locker room. Over the other, it said EARTHSTRONG. That one led down, to the lower. All the way down, other signs yelled at you to make sure you were on the right side, that cages must *not* come off yet, and that anyone who was supposed to be in one but wasn't would be prosecuted to the full extent of the law.

3

The locker room always furled out a wonderful reassuring smell of turpentine and engine oil. It was freezing today, and January could see his breath as he hung up his coat and slotted his charging card into the bank of plugs. The longer the card sat there, the longer it charged, at five kilowatts per hour. That was a generous rate of pay, for a manual labour job.

Val Legasov, his section chief, wheeled her chair up beside him, produced an orange feather duster, and dusted him with it to say hello. Val was one of those swearing filthy dinosaurs who had been born fifty-five years old and who nonetheless managed to be completely charming. On days when he was unhappy, it made him sad that she was married.

"Early bird today," she noted.

"I saw on the news about how maybe there won't be enough power to keep us running properly?"

"They can store solar power for a few weeks," she said, like she wasn't worried. "There's plenty of water in the Tower, though. Boss says enough to keep Tharsis going the whole week even if we can't make a drop more." She listened. If you knew what to listen for, you could hear the gigantic engines working—or not—under the floor and in the walls. "Sounds all right to me."

January nodded, but privately he couldn't help feeling unconvinced. "And the, er . . . duster?"

"It's my new poking device," she explained. January edged a bit further away, into the already long queue for the coffee.

When the start bell went, the floor supervisor came out onto the steel balcony above everyone. The supervisor was from here, and even so far above all the Earthstrongers, looked tapered and delicate. The safety barrier on the balcony was bullet-proof glass. Not because anyone had ever shot at it, but because on somebody's birthday last year, drunken stupidness had happened and a bunch of people had worked out that without cages, they could jump the fifteen feet up to the balcony and whack the glass, which had led to an alarming version of stick-the-tail-on-the-donkey and then the obvious consequence. January had still been finding glass in his boiler suit for a week afterwards.

"All right, up to the yellow line everyone! Good. Cages *off.*"

Everyone hit the release button of their resistance cages, which was over the heart. Around the room, fifty steel skeletons opened out with a long sigh. January stepped away from his, feeling like he was floating. It wasn't really a feeling he enjoyed; more than anything, it was like taking a retainer off your teeth. In one way it was a relief, but in another, you could feel things settling more than they should, planning to creep back to where you didn't want them. Whenever his was off, a clock ran in the back of his head. He started to feel panicky after seven or eight hours.

It wasn't because he was scared of accidentally naturalising. That took weeks and weeks. What dragged at him was how much stronger he had used to be. The cage simulated the kind of resistance Earth's gravity made, yes, but a fortnight before being in a refugee camp, he'd been training for eight hours a day. He'd been able to lift more than his own weight above his head. Carry more. An alarming amount of ballet was weight training. Now, even with the cage, it had been a year since he'd done any real exercise. He'd lost weight, and fast: you had to eat a hell of a lot to keep up the kind of muscle he'd had before, and he just couldn't afford it here, even if he had somehow found time and energy and space to go through even a quarter of those old drills. Most of his shirts were a size too big for him now. It shouldn't have bothered him, it shouldn't, because it wasn't harmful—he'd used to be an athlete and now he was a normal person, that was fine, but he just felt *less*. He could feel it where he wouldn't have expected to; his knees felt weaker, his wrists, some muscle or tendon he couldn't name right under the socket of one hip. And the longer he spent out of the cage, the more he could feel what strength he did have left eroding away in this patient, insidious gravity.

As everyone shuffled into a queue to walk out to the main floor, there was a flurry among them, because everyone was throwing baseballs or apples from hand to hand. It was easy to tell who was new here, because they were the ones whose balls shot off and skittered away— then they had to make the Run of Shame to get them back, to applause. January threw his straight from hand to hand at first, letting his muscles get used to the eerie shock of how easy it was out of the cage, and then, once they were more used it, looped the ball up to eye level. Very, very gently, was how you had to do it; with so little force you felt like the ball wouldn't even lift out of your hand. Val steered her chair along the line, watching people, making sure they were doing the exercises properly, as sharp as any dance teacher.

She had done them too, until recently. He didn't know her precise reasons for naturalising, but she'd gone into one of the centres six months ago. The wheelchair was because of nerve damage. They'd had to give her a mechanical heart too. She said she didn't mind; she said she was thrilled with the free car from the government, which was dead flashy.

He must still have been distracted from this morning, because he dropped his ball. Val caught it, gave him a suggestive look, and pretended to eat it.

"You all right?" she asked, when he forgot to laugh.

"What?"

"Listen, I found a box of chocolate bars in the old storage shed, do you want one? Out of date but the packaging's fine." She held out a bar.

"Oh, thanks," January said. He hadn't seen chocolate for weeks. Food was expensive here, given the water situation. He thought about it after the first bite. "Sort of undertaste of industrial methane?"

"Christ, throw it away!"

"No, no, it's good."

"You've got a problem," Val told him.

January pointed at her with the bar. "*You've* got a massive secret stash of Stolichnaya in the biofuel locker."

"I have," Val said, sage. Then, "How do you know?"

January smiled, because it would have been hard to know Val even for five minutes without suspecting a secret vodka stash. Whether she had recently been close to any or not, she was always coated in a patina of steel dust and splotches of inexplicable white gloss paint, and she had once drilled through the ceiling in order to spy, via a periscope she'd prepared earlier, on the Natural people's locker room. January didn't think she was being weird, with the periscope. She had gone away looking purposeful. January suspected some kind of blackmail aimed at the supervisor, to whom Val was married and with whom she seemed to be permanently at war. It was a subject of factory-wide speculation as to whether the war was a joke or not.

"Before you all disappear off," the supervisor called, "remember Senator Gale is visiting today. Nobody do anything obscene in front of the camera, it's going out on national news. They might want to talk to some of you, so don't swear and *don't* go on a rant about politics, and I'll buy you all doughnuts. All right?"

January had forgotten it was today.

He rolled down the sleeves of his boiler suit for something to do with his hands. This was actually his favourite boiler suit. It was small enough, which was unusual—the companies didn't make them specifically for Earthstrongers and seemingly at random they'd do five little ones per batch and you had to fight for them—and he had remembered, finally, to bring a belt to cinch it close enough. There was hardly any paint on it. As factory fashion went, it was sharp. It was silly, but he felt more like himself on days when he wasn't wearing one with holes in.

Val dusted him with the duster again.

"I bet," she said, "that there's some underwear in Lost Property."

January smiled but had to look down, because he didn't think he could hide what he thought about Senator Gale, but he didn't want anyone to ask him about it. "Whatever you want to do with the underwear, I'm not involved and I didn't hear about it."

NATASHA PULLEY

"Well. They'll be gone soon enough." Somehow, Val managed to be quite aware of the news, and politics, and just never apply any of it to herself. It made her basically well disposed to everybody, even if they were wearing a PUT EARTHSTRONGERS IN CAMPS T-shirt with a picture of someone throwing away a key on the back. January wished he could be like that. He was hoping that if he could just watch her enough and copy her properly, he might be able to train his soul up to be that strong. Then it wouldn't matter if his bones weren't.

"*But* we have to do the safety briefing for all the press morons and aides they're bringing with them."

"What's this *we*?" he asked with dread.

She clapped his arm. "They'll be taking pictures. Nobody wants my face anywhere except inside a bag. You're all good-looking and you've got a fun accent and you used to be famous. They'll listen to you, even if it's just because they're ogling you. Great power to be had from ogling."

"No, no, no, safety briefings are *your*—"

"Good lad," she said cheerfully.

"Mx Legasov," a passing Natural person in a suit said, indignant. "For God's sake, you can't call people *lad*."

"We're family," Val said. January felt himself go red. They weren't family; they were acquaintances. January was certain that Val didn't distinguish him from the forty other people in her direct care.

"Just be *careful* who catches you using language like that," the suit-person said, looking harassed and, even in irritation, managing to give off an aura of chartered accountancy. "Nobody wants a lawsuit."

Val turned to January with an elaborate bow. "Mx Stirling?"

"Mx Legasov," said January in his poshest voice.[6]

The suit-person scowled at them both and crabbed off.

---

6 He'd heard "Mx" pronounced lots of ways since arriving in Tharsis—people whose first language was Russian tended to say "mikh," like Mikhail; Mandarin speakers said "mishi," because the characters for it were 蜜师—roughly, "secret-person," in the same formula as things like 老师 (*laoshi*, teacher) and 律师 (*lushi*, lawyer) which January thought was excellent because it made everyone sound like a spy; and in English it sounded like "Mc," as if everyone were Scottish. To January's great joy, there was someone called Mx Wang in HR who liked tartan, and in his head they were very solidly McWang, mastermind of a plot to heroically invade England.

26

Above them, in the brilliant floodlights, dust from the storm above ground was spinning between the tangles of pipes and the cooling towers. Right up the length of the vast yard, rendered as tiny as bright moths at this distance, there were safety inspectors in orange jackets way up in the heights, probably trying to assess if the dust was doing damage to the machinery.

January wondered about a day off tomorrow, determinedly, so that he wouldn't think about how much he would have loved to see someone shove Aubrey bloody Gale off a cooling tower.

Val propelled him towards the control room, where he could already see glimpses of smartly dressed people waiting.

4

The control room had a broad window that looked across the whole plant, from the hydrogen production side on the left, all the way round a titan panorama of pipes and walkways and pumps to the water storage towers, lunging far further into the air than anything of their sort ever would have on Earth. As January and Val passed inside, into a glorious wave of heat, he shot an instinctive glance towards the giant neon readout on the tower, even though he already knew it was all right.

There was a stir when people noticed them. He kept well behind the yellow line marked in tape on the floor, marked every few paces with a big *E*, and a big 地.

He was glad to see that Senator Gale wasn't there yet. This was just the press and the general hangers-on who always seemed to float around politicians. Probably Gale was above such sublunary considerations as safety briefings.

And, in that case, maybe the day would be lovely after all. Maybe Gale would poke a suspicious stain that was in fact made of the special digestive enzyme in Silo 4 that made biowaste into biofuel, and do everyone a favour by turning immediately into goo.

Someone intern-looking was wearing a WE ARE MARS T-shirt.

It was such an innocuous, fun-sounding slogan. It wasn't though. What it meant was, we are *not* Earth, and you're not welcome here any more. It took a considerable bastard to wear that in a place like this.

January tried to think about calm happy things, like puffins. He liked puffins. His mum had called them puffweens, which was even better.

"Right!" Val beamed from the front. "I'm Val Legasov, this is my rig and your safety is therefore my responsibility; this is my beautiful assistant January."

January waved half-heartedly.

Puffins puffins puffins.

Every single person in the chairs was at least three or four generations naturalised. Even sitting, it was clear they were all seven feet tall. After the grey of the factory locker rooms and the grey boiler suits, their clothes looked luxurious. Heavy tailored robes, usually in dark jewel colours, the way that hummingbird feathers were dark and bright at the same time. Everyone had long hair; rich people always had long hair here.

"Shouldn't you be wearing a cage?" someone said to him.

"No, he's in a hazardous work environment and he's more than four metres from you," Val said, unoffended, though January was a bit. He wondered if they thought he might lunge at them. No, that was piggy and stupid. If a polar bear had been sitting behind the yellow line, he wouldn't have been feeling too confident about the yellow line either. "The sheltered walkway back is Natural only, he has to cross the yard, there's stuff falling and things on scaffolding and Christ knows what. Jan?"

Everyone looked expectantly at him. He tried to arrange his face into something pleasant. It wasn't their fault if they looked like the kind of people who would run you over with a nice car and then bill your relatives for hosing you off the bonnet.

"Okay, welcome to Tereshkova Station. We produce all the water you will find on Mars. Nowhere else can do this on an industrial scale, it's just us; and the reason it's just us is that this is bloody dangerous and building two of these buggers will really tempt fate."

He was glad when they laughed. They weren't too frightened of Earthstrongers, then, despite that early question. Uncomfortably, he realized he felt now exactly like he had used to do when an all girls' school trip visited the theatre. Thirteen-year-old girls were, of course, terrifying monsters, and he always wanted to hide in a cupboard until they'd gone; but all that aside, he was six foot two and very strong and a man all at the same time, and they—were not. The sole duty of anyone like him during those school trips was to be kind and clearly harmless, because to be anything else would have been foul.

Maybe these people were rich and annoying, but the idea that he might genuinely frighten them made him queasy.

"Those silos on the far left there are full of biowaste, being melted into fuel by an enzyme that will dissolve you in a few seconds if you get it on you. If you see a funny stain on the ground, please don't touch it, or you'll be leaving in a jar."

More grins. Right; good.

"That fuel is then run through that machine over there, which reaches over a thousand degrees Celsius on the inside. The reaction splits the hydrocarbons and gives us hydrogen. That next tower is a giant vat of hydrogen. It is explosive, so . . . do not smoke, or someone is going to fire-hose you. That hydrogen goes along these pipes here, and then it's forced to react with oxygen. That reaction is exothermic, which is why the tower is surrounded by cooling pipes. If we lose our electricity and that cooling stops, we explode. And lastly, over that way, is the water tower."

He paused. "I know this is obvious, but you're going to see uncaged Earthstrongers working in the yard and on the rig. It's just about safety. If we fall, we don't die, and if anything goes wrong, we can run faster; and we're stupid, so we sign up to work in the big Death Machine."

People laughed again and something in him that been taut all morning started to relax. He wasn't scary; he wasn't.

"Everyone is really friendly; but if you feel worried, the control rooms and managerial staff areas are naturalised only. Val's going to take you round for a tour now. Don't wander off. I'm the one with the hoover and the jar if you do."

Val patted him and herded everyone off.

He sat down on the windowsill, or started to, but someone Natural was coming up to the yellow line, over the line, right up to him. He went down fast onto one knee.

"You shouldn't cross the line," he squeaked.

"It's all right, it's all right, get up. I'm the Senator's press secretary," they said, as if that meant the rules didn't apply to them. They were intensely chic, with gold beads all through their waist-long braids, and a vivid yellow coat and—maybe because if you were doing publicity for the actual devil then you were too busy to remember your own name—a necklace that said SOLLY. "Would you mind doing an interview when they get here? Just about working here. Your accent is gorgeous."

"No offence, but I'd rather liquefy in Silo 4," said January, picking himself up and then wincing when his knee twinged.

"Perfect!" the press secretary beamed, and then looked at something over his head. "Aha. Here they come now."

What looked like the staff of the entire plant came out to see the Senator arrive. The younger people, January noticed, had gone giggly. He trudged towards the crowd, feeling grumpy. Politicians were always glamorous here, but Aubrey Gale was only ever one soulful stare from reducing at least seventy per cent of any given room to fanning themselves and asking about the air conditioning. The array of exquisite tailoring tended to set off the other thirty per cent. With all that, January was pretty certain most people had no idea what Gale thought about anything, because Gale didn't *need* to think about anything; they just needed to stand there, looking like a god, and people would hurry along with presents. And votes.

January, however, did know what Gale thought about things. He followed the news like a bloodhound when it came to Gale.

"Now, you *mustn't* kill anyone," Val said. "Deep breaths."

"Can I not throw something? Not anything bad; just, like, a sock. With a brick in it."

"Have some more chocolate."

"Wait, what, there's more?" he said hopefully.

"I have come prepared," she intoned, and put another bar into his pocket.

At the head of a comet-tail of journalists, bodyguards, and aides, Senator Gale came slowly. It was, perhaps, to give the waiting line of managers time to think before anybody had to bow or start the complicated politeness of welcoming someone important; but it looked regal. Nobody else had the time to walk as if they were moving underwater.

Grudgingly, January could see why everyone was so keen. Gale was elegant in the way only sixth- or seventh-generation Natural people could be. They made all the Earthstrongers look like Neanderthals; a clear foot taller, athletically slim, hair like black glass, built of air and sharp poise. They must have come straight from the Senate, because they were dressed with the beautiful austerity that seemed to be required there, coat hem brushing the floor. Navy blue; heavy fabrics, velvet and sheening against the bitter winter.

"And these are some of our wonderful rig engineers," the supervisor chirped, smiling the desperate smile of a person willing nobody to do anything disgusting.

There were all the ordinary hellos and how-are-yous, in such interchangeable Mandarin, Russian, and English that January couldn't tell which Gale preferred. All three sounded equally cultured. Their voice exactly matched the rest of them—a caramel voice, half smoke, and loaded with the promise of third-degree burns.

Around them, people swirled. Gale was the only still point. Camera drones flashed and glowed as everyone took pictures or filmed, the light strobing across Gale's sleeves. Each drone was a single perfect glass ball, and from a distance, it looked like Gale was surrounded by curious stars.

"Senator! Senator!" It was a semi-unified yell from what must have been twenty different journalists. One shouldered to the front. "Senator, is the storm affecting electricity production at your solar fields?"

If Gale minded being shouted at by a mob, they didn't show it. "No. The technology we use to store the energy is the same as on the lunar colonies; it can supply power for up to two weeks. No storm since terraforming has lasted longer than four days." Their Mandarin was so precise that January could understand every word.

"After your experiences at Gagarin Square, how is it to be here surrounded by uncaged Earthstrongers?" someone called in Russian.

January flinched.

Puffins puffins *puffins.*

"Fantastic. I love places like this. Industrial processes feel magic, and everyone who works in them always tells brilliant stories." Gale smiled, managing, incredibly, to sound honest, even though it had to be a lie. In Russian, they had a sophisticated St Petersburg accent that suggested palaces and winter dances.

January tried to slink away, but then the glossy press officer was there and gripping his arm, not at all worried that he wasn't wearing a cage. He froze, not daring to move. He had a vision of prison jumpsuits and barred doors.

And the thing was, you got that kind of prison if you were lucky—if the court decided you had hurt someone, or killed them, absolutely by accident, then it was twenty-five years in medium security here in Tharsis, ready to be drafted into a labour colony if you misbehaved. If there was any sense it was deliberate—no. Murderers went to the hulks around Jupiter. Not many came back.

Instantly he was much too hot: panic heat.

"Please let go of me," he tried.

"Oh, no, you don't," they told him happily. "All right, everyone, the apocalypse isn't happening, back off." Then they glided up to Gale, nearly as tall. "Let's have a quick interview with a couple of rig engineers?"

January looked away. All of this was only happening so that when other senators accused Gale of being cloistered and never having any contact with the people all their horrendous legislation targeted, they could say no, actually, I do go out and meet them before I shove them into naturalisation centres, look: footage. He hoped there was a special place in hell for politicians who pretended to be friendly with normal people.

"Of course," the supervisor said, fluffing up with importance. "Who would be best? Someone experienced and—"

"You and you," the press officer said immediately, collaring January and another victim about his age. The two of them looked, January realized uncomfortably, exactly the way Natural people expected immigrants to look. Short, broad, rough; or at least, to eyes trained on Mars. "Superb. This way please."

"But I—" January started, not sure he understood what they wanted. Everything they had said so far was Mandarin, and he had caught most of it, but he was worried he'd dropped some important bits.

"You'll be splendid!" the supervisor ordered him. And then to Gale, "Although might they have a minute to get back in their cages?"

"No need," Gale said. "This isn't affecting your insurance, I walked in here knowing there would be uncaged Earthstrongers. It's only surprise uncaged Earthstrongers who are a legal problem."

The supervisor laughed in a way that January hoped they'd be embarrassed about later. "Well, yes, but—you're sure?" A flicker of a look to the Senator's left leg. Gale wasn't using crutches any more, but if you knew to look for it, they did walk with a limp. Of course, everyone knew to look for it. The day they'd come out of hospital with the new prosthetic last month, there had been nationwide news coverage.

Knowing full well he was being mean and stupid, January wondered if they didn't exaggerate it just a tiny bit in front of cameras.

"Of course," said Gale, like it was funny, the way soldierly people always were with too much sympathy.

As January went by, the supervisor caught his arm and spoke close to his ear. He wished people would stop touching him while he was out of the cage. "Just for God's sake remember to say *they* like a normal human, and not *he* or *she* like you're about to stab someone behind a drug den. Pretend to be, you know, civilized, for fifteen minutes, or we'll be put on some sort of register."

"I would never say that to someone Natural," January protested, dismayed. "And—how would I *know*?"

The supervisor looked queasy in the face of all the possibilities. "And *don't* swear."

The eddies of people shifted and somehow January was right by Gale, in the middle of everything. Standing bolt upright, he only reached their shoulder. Even though he was the one who was three times stronger, out of his cage, he had a stab of wariness, one he hadn't felt since being a child. From nowhere, the tight unease of watching his father, a bull of a man, slinging open cupboard doors and breaking things flashed up over everything like an unhelpful advert. That was the last time he'd been this much smaller than someone else, right up close. He didn't know anyone Natural, just natural*ised*.

That was a little jolt of a realization in itself. He hadn't been aware, really, that he was living in such a closed-off bubble. It made him uneasy. Bubbles were bad.

Whenever anyone asked him what his background was, or where he was from, he never knew what to say, because he wasn't from anywhere. Born in Cornwall, yes, into rural poverty, yes. But then ballet boarding school on scholarship in Moscow, and tours all over the world. He was used to thinking of himself as someone who *used* to be working class, but who had kind of disqualified himself later on. He'd had dinner with pop stars and made friends with actors on movie sets—after a certain point, it wasn't right to group yourself with the people you'd left behind at home who still worked at the corner shop or as a drone operator at a goods warehouse. He had always been aware, living that glittering life, that it was important to make friends with lots of different kinds of people, richer, poorer, younger, older, or he would be in serious danger of becoming exactly the kind of entitled dickhead he hated. He wasn't ashamed of moving between classes exactly, but it made him awkward. If he ever did anything practical at home, if he fixed the washing machine or the pipes, his father guffawed and called him a cultural tourist—which meant class foreigner. He was crossing a border he didn't have a passport for any more.

So he had been proud to be working here, at the factory. He was relieved he wasn't so far gone down the road of pistachio lattes and well-ness retreats that he couldn't cope with making a normal living in a boiler suit and steel-capped boots. Every day he enjoyed working here felt like another little proof that he wasn't a cultural tourist who was just visiting difficult things for fun before hurrying away back to the rarefied air of the Royal Opera House.

But standing next to Gale now, he saw afresh what he'd lost. His whole life had shrunk. He wasn't crossing borders now: the way back was shut. He lived here now, in the boiler suit. All at once he wasn't proud of it any more. It just looked tattered.

Gale tipped their head a little to catch his eye. It was a tiny motion. They had no mannerisms at all, only a deep stillness. It should have been unsettling, because nobody was like that, not really, but over that stupid memory of his father, it was a relief. No sudden moves. It was marrow-deep elegance, the sort that would have been at home in the old imperial courts, over the shush of sliding paper doors and the hour gongs, where the knights were scholars and you did not speak to the empress without kneeling.

"Lovely to meet you."

"It's not," January said bleakly, "but nice of you to say anyway."

He had an instant impression that several more lenses, intensifying the magnification of their attention, had clicked down behind their eyes. It might even have been recognition.

No, it couldn't be. Not even someone like Gale could remember a single face out of a crowd of thousands.

A small voice in the back of January's mind whispered that Aubrey Gale was exactly the sort of person who could do that.

5

January had been at Gagarin Square when it happened.

When the news reported that there was a bill going before the Senate requiring all Earthstrongers to naturalise, people organised the protests within about fifteen minutes. January had never been to a protest in his life—waterlogged London had no open spaces big enough, and the best you could hope for was to traffic-jam the docks at Parliament with enough people in rowing boats—but he signed up for this. Everyone would meet in Gagarin Square, in front of the Senate, on the morning of the vote, wearing something red.

Now, January couldn't even remember who had proposed the bill, or why. He had only been in Tharsis for a month or so at the time, so he hadn't known much about its politicians. He was still getting over the surprise of finding that they were all young and glamorous, not the underbiting paunchy people they were at home. He could recall people saying it wasn't a serious bill, just a publicity stunt from some junior senator who wanted to take the conservative vote from someone else for some election he hadn't heard of. Maybe it had been Gale, he didn't know. It didn't matter. What mattered was the slow, cold feeling it had put through his insides for days.

At first, his instinct had been resignation. There was nothing he could do if the government decided they wanted to stop letting immigrants wander about three times stronger than normal people and providing them with the expensive machinery to do so. It was a miracle they'd let it go on for this long. All he could do was turn up at a naturalisation centre and hope that he didn't get the really bad side effects.

But slowly, he realized that he had not escaped the floods in London and spent nine months on a crowded refugee ship to come to another world just to cripple himself because some bastard who had never met anyone from outside the country club had decided that he was dangerous. So on the day of the vote, he put on a red scarf and went to Gagarin Square.

The turnout was vast. It looked as though every Earthstronger in Tharsis was there, along with every police officer, soldier, and member of the national guard, who all had riot shields and rifles. There were naturalised and Natural people too, wearing red and carrying signs in Russian and Mandarin and English that showed pictures of children in wheelchairs, and slogans like THIS IS NATURALISATION and NEVER AGAIN. There was music too, and drumming, and the festival smell of sparklers and bao buns. Someone let off fireworks, which showed up nicely even in the morning sky. A fragile elderly Natural person came up to January with a plate of cakes, gave him one, and told him that this bill wasn't in *my* bloody name thank you very much, which made his week.

There were huge screens showing the debate that was going on inside, and speakers so that everyone could hear what the senators were saying. Subtitles too. The event organisers must have got those up, because nobody in government ever seemed to remember that if you were fleeing the apocalypse on Earth, the chances were you hadn't been fitted with the augmentations that would let you connect to the network inside your head.

January had always remembered what Gale said when they took the floor.

"This year, there were nine hundred and twelve homicides in Tharsis." That burnt caramel voice smoked over everything, and even people who hadn't been paying attention before paused now. Gale was imperial, glittering and, like always, very still. It was magnetic whether you liked it or not. "Seven hundred and forty-eight of those were perpetrated by Earthstrongers. Most were accidental, but all the victims were Natural. We have an Earthstrong population of two hundred thousand.

That means that one in two hundred and sixty-seven Earthstrongers here has killed someone *this year alone*. Resistance cages don't work, one time in two hundred and sixty-seven."

Gale looked right into the cameras, into the crowd outside, stark and hypnotic, and there was a hush like January had never heard before. "If we had a vaccine that killed one in two hundred and sixty-seven people, it would be banned. If we had a software update that killed one in two hundred and sixty-seven people, those who designed it would be imprisoned. This is not a question of race or prejudice. This is a question of failing technology. There are only two solutions: lock people in resistance cages all the time, which is inhuman; or ban cages altogether."

It got a round of applause from inside the Senate, and a kind of howl from the protesters.

January had never so badly wanted to punch someone. He knew those statistics, of course he did. Everyone did. They were on posters everywhere, they flashed up if you watched television for more than fifteen minutes, they were projected on buildings; kids wore T-shirts that had 1:267 printed on them. He would be the last, last person to say it wasn't a huge problem.

But given that you could put the internet in people's brains now, he was just not convinced that the only way to avoid all those horrible accidental deaths was to cripple everyone who could possibly perpetrate one. That was a Stone Age solution. There had to be some engineer somewhere who could think of something better. January's problem with people like Gale was that it wouldn't even occur to them to ask what could be done. Because actually good technology—apparently even the stuff required for subtitles—was for real people, not poor people. If you earned less than a million a year you could piss off and enjoy your osteoporosis, thank you.

Someone held up a phone to beam a big hologram poster in view of the floating cameras. The message said:

VALUE OF HOUSE GALE: $15 TRILLION

VALUE HOUSE GALE HAS INVESTED IN CAGE INNOVATION: $0

Val said that January wouldn't get anywhere by bashing people over the head with *The Communist Manifesto*,[7] but it made January angry too, when people declared that giving someone poor some basic human consideration was the same as being Stalin. It was the kind of argument deployed by people who were saving up for their own private golf course.

Over the noise, the commentary from the Office of National Statistics confirmed that Gale's figures were correct, and a fact box flashed up beside the screen, from the police databases.

It was about midday when he started to notice that the police were kettling people towards the Senate steps. There was a military security perimeter there, with water cannons, and someone in the chain of command must have been spoiling for a fight, because when he thought about it later, he couldn't see any other reason to do it. As the crowd was compressed, people had to push up against the riot shields. And the people at the front were already there to try and get into the Senate, to protest inside, or disrupt the vote, or something.

Later, at the trials, the prosecution lawyers said there was evidence that the event organisers had actually been hoping to start a coup.

He heard snatches of yelling as he ended up pushed that way too. He couldn't see over enough heads to make out what was happening. For the first time, a wisp of panic unfurled in his ribcage, and he realized that if he couldn't get out now, then there was a real chance of being crushed. Only he couldn't move without pushing hard and hurting someone.

He didn't know why the senators came out the front door after the vote, the result of which was going to be announced well after everyone had left the building. Maybe they thought the perimeter would hold, or maybe it was meant as a show of democracy working in spite of external pressure, or something. Whatever else it was, it was a mistake.

---

7   An inoffensive document in which a tired German sets out his grand dream of an affordable nationalised rail service.

When people saw them, the crowd surged. The water cannons went on and instantly everything was a freezing white haze. The pressure was enough to knock Natural people over backwards. January caught someone and had to crouch over them to make sure they weren't trampled as people surged away from the water.

But of course, all the Earthstrongers had to do to withstand the force of the water was unlock their cages, and the people at the front did just that.

Just for a second, he saw someone in red jump eight feet up onto the closest water cannon, easy in this gravity and at full strength, and hurl the soldier operating it to one side.

It was like trying to see through the strobe lights at a club. Sometimes he couldn't see at all through the water and the plumes of mist it threw everywhere, but in snatches, he saw more soldiers go down like skittles. By then, the pressure of the crowd had changed. Instead of pulling away from the cannons, people were shoving towards them, and he was on the Senate steps now. He saw someone get hold of a senator and shove them against a wall. He thought they were trying to demand answers, and maybe they thought that was all they were doing too; but immediately out of a cage, no one was very coordinated. They were too strong, and in the next strobe-water flash, he saw the senator's skull crumple.

He didn't remember how he got away. All he remembered was running, and tearing off the red scarf and slinging it away, and then sitting numb in the Earthstrong carriage of a Mariner Line train, horribly aware that he was wet and smelling of explosives, and that anyone with any common sense at all would know exactly where he'd been.

In the end, the news said that a hundred people had died, among them two senators. Then, later in the evening, there were some fuzzy shots, clearly taken while security guards were hurrying the camera crew away, of Aubrey Gale in a hospital bed, missing most of one leg.

6

Now

The microphones were neat things that looped over your ear. The journalists were all so polished they shone. January could see how shabby he and the other rigger must have looked, in their boiler suits and chemical stains, and found himself hunching forward as if he could make himself smaller. It made no sense. He was already small, in comparison.

"If you could say something to test the sound," the camera drone operator said encouragingly. They were a rangy, windswept sort of person, the type to dive after a bear if it happened to look photogenic, but even they seemed neater than January. They had special gloves on that controlled five or six drones, and a machine that flew around looking like a giant fluffy bee but was probably to do with sound. "What did you have for breakfast?"

"Is English okay?" the other rigger asked, looking anxious.

"It's fine," Gale said, in their perfect American English, *perfect*, without even a ghost of the sharpness that usually came from listening to it from a Mandarin perspective. "Or Russian, whatever's better."

January wondered what kind of terrifying genius could do a broadcast in Mandarin, Russian, or English interchangeably. It was normal for rich people to have the translation augmentation here—it was a special implant which connected the language part of your brain to the internet so you didn't just read subtitles on your lenses, you actually understood—but that didn't let you *speak* other languages. He was surprised Gale could do it. The Gales of the world grew up with other Gales, all of whom had the augmentations and all of whom spoke Mandarin at home, so why had they bothered?

He hoped they weren't one of those people who waxed lyrical about the Old Way of Doing Things and went on retreat weekends with no internet to Better Understand the Working Person and get back to Humanity's Roots. Somehow those people always pronounced the capital letters.

The other rigger stumbled through an account of toast and some eggs.

January hadn't eaten yet, so he recited the first verse of a sea shanty the aid workers had taught him on the refugee ship, one of the ones that wasn't filthy.

Gale looked down at him, intrigued. "That's hundreds of years old. Is that just floating round the factory?"

January couldn't help feeling pleased that they knew and they were interested. "We learn them on the Crossing."

"Do not," said the press officer from before, pointing at Gale, "go off on one about ancient linguistics—"

Gale straightened even more. "A person can take an interest in maritime history if they—"

"*Ab-so-lute-ly not*," the press officer clapped back. "Don't encourage this behaviour," they added to January. "Drop a pin and they'll be quoting at you in Ancient Middle Jedi—"

"Old Church Slavonic," Gale said, going high.

January looked up at them, disconcerted. He'd imagined they would fire anyone making a joke at their expense. But Gale didn't even look annoyed. They looked like they had had this argument a hundred times before, usually lost, and remained only shakily convinced they were in the right.

"See!" the press officer shouted at January. "Look at what I have to deal with!"

"I had rice," January revised, and was stupidly happy when they all laughed. Somehow he hadn't expected any of them to tease each other or laugh or do silly things. It was something between comforting and terrifying to see that they did. He wanted crazy nationalists to be straightforwardly horrible, not really quite nice and funny.

"Anyway," Gale said, with a narrow look at the press officer, "I'd like to talk to you both about how you feel about working here and why you chose to do this when you arrived, rather than naturalise. There are no right or wrong answers. Is that all right? You can say no."

Both of them nodded. January tried not to feel like he had been herded into the head teacher's office.

"I'm rolling now," the camera operator put in. "If you say something really good I'll get it, don't worry. We'll put together the interesting bits later."

January just had time to think he didn't like the sound of that.

He must have looked nervous, because the camera operator bumped a drone gently against his nose and said, "Boop!"

He snorted.

"Okay. Well, what do you think?" Gale said. "Do you like working here? You can say no, I'll make sure Mx Legasov doesn't do anything unmentionable to you."

It was hard not to feel reassured, January was appalled to realize. This didn't come across in the news soundbites he'd seen. Those were always Gale on a podium or in the middle of a senatorial debate, monarchal. In person, they were charming.

"It's a good job," the other rigger said, smiling for the first time. "They're always looking for people and it didn't seem worth naturalising when the work was okay. You want to stay healthy if you can, right? Our boss, Val naturalised and now she's in a wheelchair. Shit—*they*, they're in a . . ."

Gale seemed unoffended. "Don't worry. He and she is fine for animals and Earthstrongers," they explained.

January wondered if they could hear themselves, but apparently they could not, because they moved straight on.

"And what did you do when you lived on Earth?"

January almost said no, hang on, let's talk about how you think Earthstrongers and animals are the same somehow, but he could see exactly where it would go. Gale would say, well, that's just grammar, and it isn't even *my* grammar, I speak Mandarin, what do you want from me? And he would be suspended without pay for a month.

"Shipping, round Cape Horn. Nice to have fewer pirates here."

Gale laughed—they had an incredible hundred-year-old-whisky laugh—and the other rigger actually went red. January had never seen a real human do that before. He tried not to hope she would be immediately hit by a bus.

"And what about you?" Gale said to January.

"Same reason," January said, aware that he was broadcasting scepticism about the other rigger's sanity, but he couldn't do anything about it. "It's a lovely place, no one cares if you're Earthstrong or naturalised as long as you can get the rust off the inside of a biofuel silo."

Gale smiled. It looked unexpectedly genuine. "What did you do on Earth—shipping too?"

"No, I was a dancer."

"So this is perhaps more . . . stable work?"

"No," January said. He had promised himself he wouldn't get cross if Gale assumed it was the kind of dancing you did on a pole, but it scratched a nerve deep in him that he didn't know he'd had. "I was the principal at the Royal Ballet in London."

There was a pause. All at once the entire crew were paying more attention: the press officer, the camera operator, even the interns.

To their credit, Gale did not ask if he was joking. "Then why factory work?"

"London sank, and Earthstrongers can only do manual labour jobs here, but if I naturalised I'd never dance again. I know I'm strong, but strength isn't just for murdering people. You need it to dance, too." He tried to channel his inner Val. He could hear all the bitterness coming out in his voice, and he hated being like that. "And like I said, it's a brilliant place here. Everyone's lovely."

Apart from when we have to talk to rich fuckwits like you, but I suppose that's only point one per cent of the time.

Gale's focus had intensified again. It felt like being put through an X-ray machine. "Modern naturalisation programmes are much better than those of even two decades ago. If the health effects were less severe, would you do it?"

January forced himself to smile. "They'd have to be a lot less severe."

"That's difficult, gravity being what it is," Gale said. He had expected them to sound annoyed, but it was the opposite. They seemed pleased he was pushing back. It made him feel off balance. He had a sudden sharp sense that he didn't altogether understand the rules.

Later, January remembered seeing the camera operator go very still, holding the drones dead steady, but it was so peripheral he didn't notice.

"I just don't want to end up broken. People have heart problems, muscle atrophy, nerve damage, I don't want to risk a wheelchair just so I can have an office job. And I don't think it's fair for someone who's never met me to decide I'm dangerous, when I've spent my whole life catching other people on stage, not tearing them apart."

Every instinct in him said: stop now. Don't get into this argument with them, not in person. The same way you don't get to snap at a thirteen-year-old girl, even if she's horrifying, because you're you, and she's her.

No: *no*. Gale was *not* a thirteen-year-old girl. Gale was a shimmering politician with billions. Gale was the one who was strong here.

"Can I ask why you came to Mars if you don't want to naturalise?" Gale asked. "For nearly everyone in the world, naturalisation has been a rite of passage either for them or someone in their immediate ancestry. It's part of living here, an acceptance of the conditions of the planet. Or do you feel differently?"

January's throat was going dry. When you read what Gale had to say in the news, it was easy to scoff. In person, there was a terrible pressure to be as courteous to them as they were to you. "I don't think the government should be allowed to tell people they have to knock twenty years off their lives."

"Really? They do it all the time."

"What?" January said stupidly, knocked off kilter.

"The draft," Gale said. "Every adult is told to serve in wartime, nearly everyone agrees that's reasonable and necessary, though it can take your life altogether. These are wartime conditions, and they will be until we find a way to stop fighting this gravity."

What was he even trying to do? Win an argument with a weapons-grade genius who had spent years putting their mind to all this, with—what? He hadn't even been to university. He had been trained to leap six feet into the air and make it look like he was floating.

It was one thing to know that what Gale said was wrong, but what was happening now wasn't about knowing something. It was about articulating it in front of news cameras.

Gale was going to crucify him.

But he couldn't just bow his head either.

"No, but—forcing people to change because of how they're born, and maybe die in the process, because it's more convenient for someone else? It's genocide, isn't it? I know that naturalisation is a rite of passage here, but it's a horrible rite and if someone doesn't want to do it, they shouldn't have to. Cages work if you use them right." But he hadn't this morning, he had been *that close* this morning, he could have killed someone but shut up, shut up, *shut up*. "Humans weren't made to live here, and just because they can doesn't mean that everyone who comes here should have to do it in the same way. I'm not allowed in shops or trains with Natural or naturalised people, it's illegal for me to leave my flat without a cage, and the only tower blocks I'm allowed to live in are in Americatown, which is a long way from where *your* voters are in New Kowloon. I think things are safe enough as they are."

Only it wasn't safe, was it. One in two hundred and sixty-seven times, it wasn't. Why had he said that?

The longer he ran on, the brighter Gale looked. He might have been pouring them a glass of champagne. "Even though it creates a two-tier society with you firmly at the bottom?"

"It's the only safe way." Suffering Christ, how had Gale managed to make him say that a horrible class system was a good idea because he didn't think people should have to naturalise? He could see there must be a flaw in there somewhere, and if he'd had plenty of time to think, he would have found it—but there was *no* time to think.

"Is it? Across your lifetime you've got a one in four chance of accidentally killing a Natural person," said Gale, and January had a ridiculous certainty that somehow they knew all about what had happened this morning.

"I can't hurt anyone any more than you can in a cage," January said, horribly aware that he wasn't wearing it now.

"You can take it off," they said, and now they had the unmistakeable spark of a person who found joy in war.

January shrank inside, and for the first time he understood exactly who Gale was. Not a politician like January knew politicians. Gale was the modern version of those Spartan soldiers who scythed through life *looking* for someone well matched enough to give them a good fight, who celebrated being hugely outnumbered in unwinnable wars because somewhere in those armies there might just be someone legendary enough to bother getting up for.

He had always hated those people, because when they couldn't find an equal fight, they'd start an unequal one for practise. And this was a very unequal fight. He wasn't even a featherweight trying to fight a heavyweight. He was a comedy sock puppet.

Then, finally, he understood what was happening. He had been invited into this interview because Gale's press secretary knew what his politics were likely to be—God, he'd even said he'd rather dissolve in Silo 4 than speak to Gale—and the whole point was for everyone to see Gale destroy someone who thought naturalisation was bad. They were here to make him look like a stupid, aggressive thug who was happy to yell at someone who had been life-changingly injured by someone *just like him*, and to broadcast it to millions of people.

In the car on the way here, Gale had probably said, find me a fire-breathing Earthstrong Rights moron, it'll be fun; because the hilarious thing is, even if he's got a point, it's going to sound foul if he tries to say it *to me*.

"Right now, you are at about the strength of a local polar bear," Gale said, still with that playful sparkle, the one cats got when they found an asthmatic mouse, "and we tend not to let those in shops and on trains with Natural people either."

Smug
self-satisfied
overprivileged
dickhead.

"Oh, you've got me, I'll definitely murder you if you let me in the shop," January said flatly.

What followed was one of those hanging moments where you saw the glass falling, but there was no way left to stop it smashing.

A stillness went through everyone who had heard, but January only saw it at the edge of things, because beside him, Gale flinched. It was tiny; just an involuntary flicker of their shoulders, almost perfectly hidden. But fear went through their eyes too, honest, hunted fear, and suddenly they weren't an immensely wealthy, powerful politician and January wasn't some powerless labourer; Gale was a glassen elfin thing, and January was a monster who was getting angry.

And then, a fraction too late, Gale laughed. "No, of course not." It was a lion-tamer's calm. They looked over at the journalists. "Right, surely that's enough?"

The press officer who had complained about Jedi before was smiling in the way sharks do. "Oh yes. That was wonderful."

January couldn't move. "I'm sorry," he said to Gale. "I didn't mean—what I meant was, of *course* I wouldn't hurt you. Really, I'm so sorry, that—sounded wrong as soon as I said it."

"It's all right, it was a joke." Gale glimmered. "Of course, nobody will understand and you'll probably be lynched."

It was only a dose of his own medicine. Both were things that should have been ironic but were, without knowing enough context, without *knowing* the opposite was true, terrifying.

"I don't—I'd rather not do this," January managed.

He felt sick.

An hour later, the supervisor called January into the main office and tilted the screen so he could see it. He looked away, because he had seen the clip already. The people who smoked and the people who were addicted to social media did both of those things together in the bleak concrete intake bay, out in the freezing cold and the dust. He had been addicted since he was five, never really found the time to quit, and so a quarter of an hour ago he had seen the hundreds of posts, hundreds of links to that clip.

"*Senator Gale has PERFECT response to bigot Earthstronger*," the supervisor read, slow and hard. "That one's been viewed four million times. That's nearly everyone in Tharsis."

January nodded slightly. He couldn't speak. He'd never been more afraid or more ashamed in his life. Waiting outside just now, he had stared at the floor and tried to think what had happened to his brain, why he had imagined for a second that it was all right to snap.

If the supervisor had wanted to put him into the machine that crushed suspicious packages into a tiny ball, he would have gone gratefully. He almost didn't hear what came next, because he was concentrating on not crying. It wasn't working.

"Senator Gale isn't pressing charges, but the factory is. That was hate speech. The police are outside. Needless to say, this terminates your employment here."

7

He had a horde of waking nightmares while he waited to go before the judge. All the government signs for Earthstrongers across all of Tharsis went through his head: YOU MUST WEAR A CAGE OR BE PROSECUTED TO THE FULLEST EXTENT OF THE LAW. If the prosecution argued he was illegally uncaged, and that he had any intention of even touching Gale, he was going to a labour camp in the desert for ten years.

His own lawyer—provided by the state—didn't help with the horror-visions.

"A lot of construction projects now are built with Earthstrong prison labour. Cheap and safe. The courts have a huge incentive to give Earthstrongers long sentences." They were flicking through documents on a tablet, looking harassed, and not at all like his case was even in their top five considerations for the day. "Actually, one of the reasons Senator Gale is pushing for mass naturalisation is to stop that happening."

Superb. Not only had he snarled, on a live broadcast, at a Natural senator who was the survivor of a horrifying Earthstrong attack; it also turned out that his own lawyer was voting Gale. He had to stare at the floor and concentrate on breathing normally. He had always thought that when people in films panicked and had to breathe into a bag, it was an unrealistic way of making it clear to the audience that they were having a bad time—like ladies fainting in old novels—but his lungs really were trying to work too quickly. He couldn't think. Thinking was like trying to walk through hail. Everything stung, and what *was* the fullest extent of the law, and did it even matter that he hadn't meant it?

"Stirling versus the State of Tharsis," someone called in Mandarin.

He dug his fingernails into his palms. *Don't cry don't cry don't cry.*

The lawyer knocked his arm. "Stop clenching your fists, you look like you want to kill someone."

He must have had a natural way of holding his hands and arms, but suddenly he had no idea what to do with them. He flinched when a drone took a picture of him. It said XINHUA on the side: international press.

The court room was mainly glass, with a beautiful view across a dust-fogged Tharsis. It looked across the Senate and Gagarin Square, directly at the memorial for the senators who had been killed in the protests. January's throat was turning to sand. It was hard to swallow.

The judge, who was elderly and quiet-mannered, gave everyone an irascible look and announced they were in session.

He felt like he might collapse. Whichever part of his brain dealt with being upright, it hadn't had any oxygen for at least a quarter of an hour.

The prosecution lawyer was much more polished than January's lawyer. "The prosecution would like to—"

"Oh, shut up," the judge said. "I saw the interview. Just because Senator Gale uses a wheelchair sometimes does not mean it's okay for them to run over puppies with it. He's getting two weeks in medium security and you should consider yourself lucky there isn't a law against being a self-righteous asshole."

"Yes, Your Honour," the prosecution said quickly.

January had had whiplash once, from a boat crash. He had been less confused then.

"Mx Stirling, I suggest you refrain from making any more jokes about killing senators who have almost been killed by people who look like you," the judge recommended, and waved at the steward for the next case. "Two weeks. Be very careful. A second offence will see you into a labour camp. Next!"

"Oh, that's nice, isn't it," January's lawyer said to him absent-mindedly. "That's much better than I thought. Keep your nose clean, won't you? Bye."

He watched them go, torn between relief and a kind of numb shock, and two officers of the court came across to collect him and load him into the back of a van bound for Ares Prison.

All told, it was fine; Tharsese medium-security prisons were nicer than most London hotels,[8] everyone left him alone, and the prison reform system was all about helping you learn new skills, so he took lessons to improve his Mandarin. It was nice, too, to sleep in the same room as someone else, a cheery thief who specialised in dognapping, not to sell the dogs on but just because he really liked dogs. Despite all the good things, though, the shame of what he'd said to Gale lay on the back of January's skull like an anvil. The language teacher, a lovely patient Natural person, watched him carefully. He kept dreaming of Gagarin Square.

Endless articles all seemed to run the same headline:
IF YOU LET ME IN A SHOP I'LL KILL YOU.

He had to ignore the internet and sink into the language classes. Going cold turkey from social media after spending his whole life addicted to it was unpleasant, but after a few days, he felt less like he might die.

But he couldn't get away from Aubrey Gale even then, because the Consular Debates were starting.

The Consul was the Tharsese version of a president, or a prime minister. January had been distantly aware of election debates in London, but they weren't like this.

The way people reacted, it was like the Olympic Games had arrived on Christmas Day. The warden went round in a waistcoat with sequins on it in the colours of the Tharsese flag, the guards decorated everything with streamers, the craft classes suddenly became all about making

---

8 High-security ones weren't. High-security ones were hulks orbiting Jupiter, and in the event of a riot or even too much complaining about the food, the pilots were notorious for dipping too low and pinning everyone with the fierce gravity. If it happened too often, the guards flew away on escape vessels and remote-controlled the hulk deeper into orbit, where it was fifty-fifty whether you died of a heart attack. The Department for Justice always said it was "unexpected atmospheric fluctuations," and of course doing it at all on purpose would be dreadfully illegal. In the Senate, it was known as the Whoops We Did It Again policy.

election-day paper lanterns (apparently everyone lit them in Gagarin Square and made a wish whenever a new Consul was elected, which struck January as weird and culty until someone pointed out it was kind of like the election of a new pope), and then horrifyingly, the warden announced, like it was a wonderful treat, that they would all be watching the debate.

He envisioned a screen with bad sound, but no. There was a super-special state-of-the-art media room, because Tharsis was all enlightened and Scandinavian about being nice to convicts.

He had only ever seen systems like this at the very nicest cinemas in London. It was a dome-shaped room, big, and panelled entirely in white, including the floor. The prisoners looked bright in the orange jumpsuits, and so did the warden's sparkly flag-waistcoat. The guards appeared to be in different camps—some supported Gale, some supported the sitting Consul, Guang Song, and the Gales were in blue and the Songs were in green—and some of them had face paint and headbands with light-up antlers on, and all the things he had only ever, ever seen people wear at big football matches.

When the live feed started, it made him jump, because it was far more immersive than any London cinema.

It was surround-film. It didn't feel like watching New Kowloon stadium; they were *inside* it. Up above, the stadium's dust canopy was sparkling with lights. Around them, the seats were filled with Natural and naturalised people who were just as dressed up and just as excited as the guards. There were even kids, looking over the moon to be there, even though they weren't going to see anything exciting, just some politicians arguing with each other. When the crowd oohed at the fire-works, the noise sounded absolutely real. January would never have known he was in a media room in a prison. He could even smell the fireworks, and the air was cold. The guards had told them all to wrap up warm, but he'd thought were just playing make-believe. He really did need the coat with his prison number on the back.

The fireworks turned into a beautiful drone display, and there was a performance down on the turf from the Tharsis branch of the Cirque du Soleil.

He couldn't believe what he was seeing. Not just the spectacle itself, or the quality of the footage and how real it felt, but the buzz. He had never seen people *care* about politics like this. He said so to the warden, who had sat down next to him, vibrating with happiness, which made them sparkle all the more.

"Well, the thing is," the warden said, "it's freezing here and there's no water. What the people in charge think matters a lot more when getting it wrong could mean that everyone dies of thirst or exposure. See?"

January did see.

The stadium lights went down, and the moderator announced House Gale and House Song. A green light and blue focused on two lecterns, and then there was Gale, and the Consul.

January swallowed hard and tried not to meet the eyes of either the warden or the serial dognapper, who were both giving him sympathetic looks.

Holographic images beamed both politicians into the middle of the stadium, far larger than life. Gale was as glamorous and serene as always, and conspicuously younger than the Consul. January had never seen Consul Song before. They were a giant, hair turning from black to silver and pulled back in a military braid, good-looking in the long-established way that only middle-aged people could be. January found himself gripping the edge of his seat, praying that they had a decent strategy for taking on a Spartan who wanted to be attacked. He had no idea how they would do it.

"Here we go," the warden said joyfully, thumping his arm, wedding ring clanging on his cage.

Even the prisoners were starting to look excited.

There were the introductions and the rules, as with any fight, but when the first question came, the rustling quiet from the crowd was deep and strange. It was the kind of quiet that January could imagine had fallen in the old arenas, when there was no political debate, but a gladiator and a lion.

"We all know immigration is going to be the key to this election," the moderator said, voice echoing. Through the holograms of the two politicians, the smoke of the fireworks still danced. "Consul: the fact that one in two hundred and sixty-seven Earthstrong people in Tharsis has killed someone Natural is indisputable. What's your strategy to deal with that?"

The Consul was hunched over their lectern like a lion about to spring, bolts of grey in their hair only making them look more grizzled. It had a power of its own, that posture, but there was a tension about them on stage that looked a lot like nervousness to January.

It was only sensible. Anyone not feeling nervous before trying to win a fight with Aubrey Gale probably hadn't understood what was about to happen to them.

"The thing we have to remember is that *cars* are as likely to kill you over your lifetime," the Consul said. They had a surprisingly young voice, and very smooth. "It's a one in two hundred and forty chance of dying in a motor accident, but we're not banning cars, are we? We just keep trying to make the roads safer and people more careful drivers. It would be silly to throw away cages because sometimes people don't use them right. We need new colonists too, or Tharsis dies. The more people we have, the more we can expand. We can build another water factory, we can build more solar farms, and most importantly, we can do what this colony was built for: keep the gates open to all those desperate people from Earth whose world is dying and who need to come here. And we *are* a colony. We're not Mars alone. We are all *Chinese* citizens, and we have a duty to China, and to all Earth."

Cheers, applause. January flinched, because the House Song contingent of the guards was right in front of him and they all whooped. God, he was twitchy. He didn't know when that had happened.

"Senator Gale, would you like to reply?" the moderator said.

"Yes, please." Gale wasn't nervous. January had spent enough time on stage to tell. Gale was standing at that lectern in exactly the same way January had used to wait in the wings before the Swan King's entrance. Full of energy, but calm too, because he *knew* he was good. He hoped to God that was arrogance on Gale's part and not an accurate assessment. "Firstly, the figure we have, one in two hundred and sixty-seven, is not a lifetime risk, as with cars. It's the risk in one year. Only a hundred people were killed in road accidents last year. Almost nine hundred were killed by uncaged Earthstrong immigrants. It is the leading cause of death in Tharsis."

There was a strange noise from the crowd, something like the noise people make when they see a wrestler smack someone face first into the ground. January winced too, willing the Consul to have something to say to that, and willing it not to be pure passionate optimism like they'd opened with. Next to someone as measured and precise as Gale, passionate optimism started looking like you were in the grip of some kind of terrible delusion.

His whole heart went out to the Consul. All over again, he could feel how it had been to stand there with Gale, seeing how good they were at all this.

But at least the Consul *could* argue with Gale, without automatically being a horrible person.

"Of course we need immigration in Tharsis," Gale said. That voice steamed through the microphone, never crackled. "Of course we need to help those fleeing Earth. But we must also find a way to make that safe for the five million people already here. Mandatory naturalisation after a year's residency is a terrible thing to require; but it was required of all our ancestors, and it is the only sure way to safeguard the very things for which they made that sacrifice."

An appreciative roar from the House Gale side of the stadium, as well as the Gale contingent of the prison guards. There was a muffled squeak from the warden, who probably wanted to stay neutral so as not to cause serious staff rifts, but they weren't a good actor. The moderator had to wait for the noise to fade before inviting the Consul to respond.

"People suffer *horribly* in the naturalisation process—now that we have the technology to avoid that, nobody should have to do it," the Consul said, looking flustered, and January wished an early and dreadful death on whoever had convinced them that two could play at throwing around statistics when they were obviously not a scary abacus person like Gale. "We can have a society where everyone functions together, Earthstrong and naturalised. Integration, proper cultural understanding, will reduce accidental homicides without hurting anyone, unlike banning cages. You don't have any numbers that say that can't happen."

Belated cheers.

Gale smiled. It was apologetic, genuinely. "I have, actually."

People laughed, and the Consul hunched even further over their lectern. Gale was straight and unmoved.

Dread settled down on top of January's stomach.

"There is another situation—very well established and well documented—in which one set of adults mixes with another set who are generally far stronger. It's on Earth. It's men and women."

Gale looked into the crowd, not at the Consul.

January felt like they were looking right at him.

"The worst genocide there has ever been in the history of the worlds is not from a war, or a slave trade. It is femicide; the murder of women. It happens everywhere, in every culture, in every time, ever. Except ours. Some of those cultures have tried very hard indeed to stop it. They can reduce it; but only *reduce*. Despite the very best efforts of all humanity, no one, until us, has ever stopped it entirely. So this will always happen, in any population with a huge imbalance of strength between two groups. It is why *we* stopped that imbalance here, it is why the first colonists deleted extreme gender traits in the DNA of their children, in the same way they deleted cancers. We all understand that it's appallingly dangerous to have a society split so unevenly; I don't think anyone here would dispute that. But history rhymes. If we have a society where half our population is very strong, and half is not—that's a one-way ticket back to the twenty-first century when it wasn't safe for half the world to walk alone at night. I am asking the strong to sacrifice something for the safety of all. What the Consul is asking is for the most vulnerable to be the sacrifice."

The applause was a hurricane.

January wanted to run away and hide in the bathrooms,[9] and he nearly did, but then he realized that imagining Gale eviscerate the Consul would be worse than watching it happen.

He didn't want anyone to be scared. Only—and he was desperate for this to be true—the way to reassure people *couldn't* be to just cripple everyone like him.

---

9   It wasn't just an instinct to be alone. Bathrooms in Tharsis always cheered him up, because bathroom terminology in Mandarin was fantastic. The word for "toilet" was 马桶, *matong*, which literally meant "horse bucket," and the word for "sink" was 洗手池, *xishouchi*, which meant "wash-hand-pond." So sometimes you came across glorious signs that reminded you to please flush the horse bucket and then use the hand-washing pond. It was hard to have a bad day after that.

Except he couldn't say that. *He* couldn't say it. One of the people he was frightening had to say it. There was an alchemy that changed what you were saying depending on who you were, and being who he was, he would sound like he thought it was okay for people to be frightened and die rather for than him be inconvenienced, because It Was Nature. He found himself staring at the Consul, willing them to straighten up from that beaten hunch.

Come on. Get up get up get up. Don't let it be a knockout after one round.

"Consul?" the moderator said.

The Consul was still leaning against the lectern, but something about them loosened up, and January had a tiny flutter of hope.

"Funny how you say you want the strong to be the sacrifice," the Consul said, much more ordinarily than before, much less like they were painfully conscious of all those hundreds of thousands of people watching. "When there's a young Earthstronger in prison now, because you couldn't take a joke."

Everyone in the media room looked at January, who would have liked to die.

"Not a soldier," the Consul was saying, "or a criminal. Not someone who has ever hurt or threatened another soul. He's a dancer. He was at the Royal Ballet before he came here and your legislation forced him into factory work and poverty. But that wasn't enough for you. You *destroyed* him for being politely angry with the person who wants to make his life even harder. After a criminal conviction, he won't be able to get work without naturalising. That dancer is going to have to cripple himself, because you're too precious to see sarcasm. Now . . . you have all the money in the worlds. All the power, the education, all the privilege and advantages any human being can possibly want—but you want to say January Stirling is the strong one here? Is he really?"

A visceral roar of agreement tore through the stadium, through the House Song supporters among the guards, and from most of the prisoners. Someone banged January's shoulder, and the serial dognapper scruffed up his hair.

"I didn't know he was in prison," Gale said quietly. "Is that true?"

The Consul actually laughed. "Drop it, of course you know. Just admit that you want to cripple *anyone* who's stronger than you because they generally worry you. And then can we talk that out? Because it needs talking out. *I'm* stronger than you. Should I be sent to prison for arguing with you? I could reach across and hurt you if I wanted, I was a soldier, I reckon I could take you."

People laughed. The Consul was twice Gale's width; they had been a general in the army before they were Consul.

"By your logic, children get the last say, because they're the weakest and therefore no one should ever argue with them. You're confusing actual violence with the physical capacity for violence. They aren't the same. January Stirling *isn't* the person who attacked you in Gagarin Square, but you treated him like he was. We all understand why, and we all have every sympathy, but horrific actions by a few people can't condemn an entire world, and if you think they should—then I'm sorry, but you need to get yourself some therapy, rather than insisting on a policy that will cripple thousands of people."

Gale said nothing.

"Senator, would you like to respond?" the moderator said, above the roar of the crowd.

"No," Gale said. "I don't have the facts, I'll have to look into it later, and . . . thank the Consul for being more on top of the news than I am." They bowed slightly to the Consul.

There was a groan from the House Gale side of the crowd, and Gale stood very still under it, just letting it drown them. It should have been satisfying to see that, but it wasn't. They hadn't even tried to defend themselves, or bluster a way through. January had never seen a politician lose an argument so honestly. Somehow it was as bad as seeing them win. He wished Gale could just be obnoxious—then it would be easy to hate them in a nice straightforward way.

He wished the Consul would look less smug, too.

"Then we must now move on," the moderator concluded. "The next topic is the long-argued idea of nationalising major industries, such as electricity generation. Senator Gale, the floor is yours first this time . . ."

January didn't hear the end of the question, because the House Song people in the prison audience were singing the Chinese national anthem and chanting *So-o-ong one, Gale nil* in three languages.

He bent forward against his knees and pressed his hands over his eyes. He didn't know what to think any more. In his soul, he did know it was all right to defend yourself if someone was trying to maim you, and Gale *was* trying to maim him. But he felt like he was going mad, because half the people in that stadium and half the people in this room just—didn't agree. It was one of those basic things he would have thought everyone could agree about, and seeing that an awful lot of people thought he was the Mars equivalent of a horrifying misogynist for thinking so . . . it was turning his lungs to glass.

"Are you okay?" the warden asked him. "You've gone the most dreadful colour."

He nodded. He made an effort to smile. He could imagine that if you were a Natural person, watching an Earthstronger angst about being Earthstrong would be a special sort of infuriating and very much deserving of a punch in the throat. "I'm always a dreadful colour."

The warden smiled too. "Come on. You need a cup of coffee and some chocolate."

"There's chocolate?" January asked, a tiny bit hopeful despite everything.

8

On the day he was released, January went home on the metro in a fugue and only remembered when he was almost at the nuclear cooling tower that there would be no food in the flat. He stopped by the little super-market opposite, ordered online and waited outside so he wouldn't have to pay the delivery fee. He leaned against the big sign on the wall that said NO EARTHSTRONGERS, beside a big friendly collie who the serial dognapper would have loved. January rubbed its ears, feeling discombobulated. All the inmates had been Earthstrong, and it was odd to be back in the real world again where most people were much taller than him.

He didn't realize he was standing in a sunbeam until a tiny, determined-looking old Earthstrong man shuffled him to one side and put up an umbrella. The solar fabric on it gleamed happily as it soaked in the light, channelling it down into a battery in the handle. They were cheap, those umbrellas; the charge they gathered would only power a kettle or a few lights for the day, but it was worth the bother if you were too old or too ill to work.

He had a bleak vision of his own future. Say he did manage to stay here—he was going to become one of those old men who had to go out at five in the morning in the summer to claim a decent sunbeam in Gagarin Square with an umbrella and stare at parakeets until he had enough power to make a cup of coffee.

No; no. No. Shut up. It was fine. Things came along.

"There you go," the shop clerk said, easing a cotton bag of groceries into his arms. They looked at him twice. "Aren't you that man who threatened to kill Aubrey Gale?"

It was the first time he'd heard a Natural person say *man*, and the first time he'd heard how it sounded here. It was the way someone in London would have said *pig*.

He found himself shaking his head. Earthstrongers, especially any from Europe, all looked the same to everyone here. He didn't think it was rudeness. It was just that they didn't see many of those kinds of faces, so that differentiating between particular ones became a lot like trying to tell apart different puffins. You'd have to be really into puffins. It was the way human brains worked, and January had never minded, and now he'd never been more grateful for it. "No, I've just got the same hair." He should dye it, he thought miserably.

The clerk relaxed. "Sorry, sweetheart."

At home, he took all the gone-off things out of the fridge and threw them away, then put the new things in, then dropped down against the radiator and couldn't get up again.

In the morning, he went to the European Federation Embassy. All the nice embassies for important countries were in New Kowloon where the Senate was, but Europe was just some funny bits stuck on the side of Russia, so it was in Dengta, one district over, above a nice hotel. He waited in the severe waiting room for an hour before someone could see him, and when he was shown into her office, she looked tired and harassed already, even though it was only ten o'clock. Like about half of the Earthstrong people in Tharsis, she was wearing a coloured pin. Hers was red, which meant she was solidly "she."[10]

---

10 January had given it some thought when he first arrived, but decided that he didn't mind what anyone called him so long as he was allowed to keep up his intrinsic January-ness, which was much less about modes of address and much more about his lifelong resolution to one day own a pedigree house chicken.

"I—read online that I can get help finding work here," he said when she asked him what she could do.

She let her head drop a little. Her hair was in a bun held up by convenience store chopsticks, the kind that came joined together at the top. "You're January Stirling."

He wished the seat was the kind you could huddle back into. "Yes."

"I'm so sorry, Mr Stirling, but . . . there's nothing we can do to help you. There are very, very few industries in Tharsis that will accept Earthstrong ex-convicts of any kind. Even then, we're talking cash-only fast-food places round the back of the wet market in Americatown." She opened her hands on her desk. "Immigration law has tightened a lot since Gagarin Square. If you're not a citizen, if you're not naturalised, and if you have a criminal record all at the same time . . . it's bleak."

He had thought that that would be the answer, but he had needed to hear someone official say it. Now that they had, it was a sort of relief. "So—what should I do?"

"Well, you have three options. The fast-food joints behind the wet market. Or, ask the immigration bureau to deport you back to Earth. That way the Crossing is free. But . . . between you and me, I'm going to advise you not to do that. The war between Russia and America is about to land pretty solidly in what's left of Britain. The Russians are about to invade. It's going to be a hellhole by the time you get there. Hence all this . . ." She waved around the office, to all the people hurrying to and fro, looking grim, shouting on calls. As she let her hand drop, she picked up her stylus, not to write anything with, just to fiddle with. It clinked on her cage gauntlet. "I would never, ever recommend this normally, but . . . the other option is to naturalise. That means full citizenship, free healthcare, a free university degree or trade apprenticeship." She seemed to see what she was doing with the stylus and slung it irritably into a box with some others. "I know you were a dancer," she said quietly. "But honestly . . . it's either naturalise, become a career criminal with some Americatown gang, or end up conscripted in a war zone on Earth."

"Right," he said. He couldn't feel anything. He was suspended in that moment between accidentally pouring a kettle of boiling water over your hand instead of into a cup, and your brain understanding that pain was happening. It was coming, and soon, but it wasn't quite there yet.

"It isn't right," she said, slumping back in her chair. "No one gets to tell you that you have to hurt yourself for the benefit of someone else, I feel dirty saying it to you. I don't know how Aubrey Gale sleeps at night. Flinching precious Noble Victim *fuckwit*."

January smiled a bit.

"I . . . did not say any of that, because I am professionally neutral in matters of international politics," she sighed.

"Yes, ma'am. Ah . . . thanks."

"Good luck," she said, not as if she imagined there was any good luck left to wish on anyone.

So he walked the three miles across town, through the roaring dust, to the naturalisation centre near the docks. The metro was running, but he wanted to do something that would make him too tired to think, and trying to walk and breathe at the same time in a dust storm seemed like just the thing. Inside his gloves, the gauntlets of the resistance cage got colder and colder, until the metal stung.

Even without any internal signal, it would have been difficult to get lost in Tharsis. With its grid system, you only had to count the streets, and because the dust storms came every year, all the street signs and numbers were lit up bright, and the road markings were luminous, all in different pastel colours. The roads were lined with solar cells, so they usually glowed as cars drove over them, charging them through the wheels, but that wasn't happening any more. The dust must be blocking too much light.

The news said it would clear up soon.

The nurses at the centre were Natural but fearless, and as soon as he arrived, he got a tide of warmth from one of them and hustled straight off to the canteen. He was glad of that, because otherwise he would have had to faff with his phone making sure he was reading the signs right.

The facility was brand new, so they were all Mandarin. No English or Russian translations. After his extra two weeks of lessons, he was starting to see that English gave things a patina of shabbiness. It was elderly and cheap, and only people's grandparents spoke it exclusively, and so it came with a sort of vestigial memory-smell of mothballs.

The nurse, whose name was Yan, seemed concerned that he'd walked all the way in the dust. He thought they might have asked something about it, but he couldn't concentrate, because someone was being pushed past in a wheelchair. They looked mostly dead, hooked to a drip.

The canteen was cosy despite the freezing weather outside. It was the first time he'd been indoors and warm enough at the same time since the refugee ship, and in a strange rush he remembered how much better you thought if you were comfortable. There were proper carpets and well-cushioned chairs, and tiny little terrariums of beautiful hothouse flowers on each of the tables. That was typical of Tharsis. They spent money even on things they hated. Prisons, naturalisation centres. It seemed to be a point of national pride that everything was immaculate, and he was starting, also, to understand that it was a way to underline how this *wasn't* Earth, thank you.

And, no doubt, so that people like Gale could say, *but look, the conditions are marvellous, what are you complaining about?*

It was almost lunchtime, and the broad room was filling with people. Some were moving carefully, holding cups in both hands and looking frightened they were going to smash something. Others, not so careful, had the doughy, unhealthy look that came when muscle deflated. Two people were in wheelchairs. It looked . . . almost okay, but then, these wouldn't be the worst cases, because they wouldn't be coming here to eat.

Yan took him across to an already populated table and introduced him, vanished briefly, then came back with a pastry and a coffee, both of which were for him. He felt the deep sort of gratitude that should really have applied only to people who saved you from being run over by a train; he hadn't had real pastry since London.

"January's just here for a look around," Yan explained to the others, who were giving him curious looks. He couldn't tell if it was because they recognised him from the news or because he was objectively strange-looking. During the Crossing, his hair had lost its colour. It had gone from black to an unpleasant off-white. "Would some of you mind providing a bit of inside information that isn't coming from Open Evening Nurse?"

Everyone smiled; Yan was always nice, then, not just with visitors. That was good.

January slid into a chair, very conscious of the shush of the cage as he did, and the way the others' eyes followed the flash of the steel across his shoulders. Yan sat down opposite.

"January's an unusual name," someone American said. He was wearing a green pin, which meant "he," and rather chicly, January thought, he had it speared through a purple silk handkerchief. He had grey hair too, but that was because he was in his fifties. He sounded very refined; January could imagine him giving a lecture in front of a blackboard, probably about algebra. Some people were made of tweed even if they weren't wearing any. "Story in it?"

"Not really," he said, surprised to be asked, but happy too. Nobody he knew spoke thorough enough English to put his name together with the month. Earth months were obsolete anyway here, where the year was nearly seven hundred days long.[11] Knowing about months at all, never mind in English, was esoteric, like knowing the zodiac signs. "Mum was knackered when they got her to fill out the birth certificate form and she put the date in the wrong box, but then she decided she liked it."

"That's wonderful," the American man beamed, and January felt a few inches better than before. With an odd flash, he realized the man was flirting. That was flattering. He hadn't even thought about any of that since London and, if he was honest, not a great deal before then either. It sent his thoughts into a flustered tumble. Flattering but, like he

---

11 Mars's two moons took only a day to zoom around the whole world, so there were no meaningful months at all. Instead, the Tharsese calendar was just seasons. It took some getting used to, because they weren't all the same length. The orbit of Mars was elliptical, set right on a slant from the sun—so in the southern hemisphere where Tharsis ill-advisedly sat in the Mariner Valley, winter took ages, while summer was a five-minute window where you could just about make it down the street without a coat if you walked fast. You ended up writing truly depressing dates on work emails, like 241st of Winter.

always did for no reason he could trace, he felt attacked. The man might as well have been coming at him with a mad grin and a flick knife.

That feeling would go away after about a week, once he knew the man better. It was fine. Then it might be nice to be flirted with. At some point he might even work out why he had such a stupid reaction to it. Probably something deep and awful about his father, but January didn't like poking around in the corners of his own mind in the same way he didn't like investigating drains.

"So how is it here?" he asked.

"It's a great place. You couldn't ask for better. Rooms are like in a hotel," somebody said.

"And the nurses are good," said somebody else.

"I've lost a lot of feeling," the American man added, but not sounding like he minded, and January admired him in a huge rush for that. The whole reason he hadn't done this himself was that he was precious about his health. To meet someone who didn't care—it reset some important gauges. "Can't tell if cups are hot or cold. It's quite interesting."

January noticed that by contrast he was feeling everything much too strongly and ordered himself to calm down, which did not work.

"Nerve damage is a common side effect," Yan explained. "We're not sure why. Not everyone gets it, and we haven't found anything that predicts it very well." They pushed their glasses up, though they didn't need to. "Actually a lot of naturalisation symptoms are like that. No one really knows why it happens. Lots of theories to do with local chemicals, radiation, all that."

He felt off balance. "You mean it's not the gravity?"

"Well, it might be, but the gravity doesn't account for everything. Sometimes something goes wrong at a cellular level. Researchers are working on it all the time. It seems to happen much more now than it did to the first colonists, which is a bit of a puzzle."

January had to look down. He was tracing patterns in some spilled water on the edge of the table, because suddenly it was impossible not to do anything with his hands. A bit of a puzzle, Christ. "What . . . are the chances of that happening?"

Yan breathed in deep, and January realized that this must be their least favourite part: explaining how awful it was going to be.

"*Some* nerve damage, close to hundred per cent certain. Mostly it's a bit of joint impairment, cognitive fog, that kind of thing. Very minor."

"Minor," January echoed.

"This is a big ask for a human body," Yan pointed out. "Adjusting to one third gravity is brutal. You *will* lose bone density, you have to; you *will* lose muscle density. Minor nerve damage is to be expected. Osteoporosis is basically unavoidable. That's why people here are delicate, you see? Their bones are only lifting one third of the weight they'd have on Earth."

January swallowed the need to say, yes, obviously he knew that, he'd been walking round all this time and almost killing people in lifts and scaring famous senators.

He picked up a teaspoon for no reason and spun it through his fingers, like they'd used to do with pens at school, and then stopped. It had EARTHSTRONG LIVING stamped on it. Weighted three times heavier than normal ones. If he did sign up for this place . . . one day soon, the spoon was going to feel too heavy. It would feel like three teaspoons. The bones in his hands would feel . . . what? Sticky, creaky? Or was it going to feel like being a child again—nothing wrong with you, but the world was just more difficult?

"It can be more severe," Yan went on, at least pretending not to notice his face. "There can be dementia and paralysis. That's only about one in a hundred cases here. This facility is pretty good. It would be marvellous if we could work out why."

Everyone laughed.

Everyone except January, who couldn't tell if they really did find it funny, or if it was gallows humour.

"And there are lots of classes and stuff, about the local culture," someone else put in. He was using his green pin as a toothpick. He had the most majestic moustache January had ever seen, the sort of moustache that you expected of opera singers and people who *really cared* about orchids. "I'm from Syria—hang on. Don't I recognise you from somewhere?"

"Do you?" January said hopelessly.

"Hey, it's you," Yan said. "You gave Aubrey Gale hell on a live broadcast. The Consul mentioned you in the debate!"

He got ready to stand up and get out of the way quickly.

But Yan only looked happy. "*Nice.* Gale's shady as hell. Have you heard about Max Song?"

"No?"

"Gale's consort. Disappeared. I suspect murdered and buried under a big pile of spare money somewhere."

"Song like—Consul Song?" January asked, worried he was falling over one of Mandarin's many gleeful tripwires.

"Yup," said Yan. "Younger cousin."

January wondered how much of an evil genius you had to be in this day and age not just to disappear an annoying consort, but to disappear the Consul's own cousin. Maybe he was lucky to have got off with a brief prison sentence.

"I thought she was a nutbag all along," the man with the moustache put in. "Nice people are never that *shiny.*"

Someone else thumped him. "*They,* dickhead."

"Oh, fuck off . . ."

There was what sounded like a well-rehearsed argument in four different languages about whether you should be allowed to say *he* and *she* and did you get extra points if you came from a language like Arabic or Russian that he'd and she'd *everything,* even cars and spoons.

January saw how it all must look to someone like Gale. Stunning, polymath Gale probably felt as though they were meeting cave people whenever someone from Earth showed up, looking like a tiny, squashed troll and mumbling about categories that were only important if you were an endangered species. He wondered if that was what *he* and *she* was, really; a millennia-long hangover from when there had only been a few thousand humans left after a terrible ice age, when the only truly important thing about anyone was whether or not they could make new humans, to keep everyone from the hell of dying knowing that they were the last.

January stayed quiet. He liked them all already. It was funny listening to them and they were only having their comedy-argument to entertain him, but it felt dangerous. Most of it felt unspeakable in an urgent, painful way. You couldn't be who they all were and say any of this.

He looked at Yan, wanting to check they were all right.

"What he was saying was that there are language and culture classes; you know, for integration," Yan told him, under everyone else, looking amused and not at all upset. "Why Gender Abolition happened, Mandarin grammar, that kind of stuff. They're mainly for people who've come here straight from the Crossing, you wouldn't need them."

The patients segued happily into how good the language classes were and how there was help getting jobs if you hadn't got one already. There was a strict gym regimen enforced by the Legions of Darkness (Yan and two other nurses), but apart from that, it was essentially three months in which you were free to read a lot of books or binge-watch a lot of rubbish. All paid for by the government, and not stingily.

Excellent really.

"What do you think so far?" Yan asked.

What he thought was that it all seemed like a beautifully curated and well-meant version of hell.

"So just to be really clear about the health consequences," he said quietly.

"Well—"

"Look, being honest," the American man said kindly, "it's horrible. It's irreversible. Your muscles will atrophy and you'll feel dreadful for about a year. Common knock-on effects are depression and anxiety. You'll be prone to colds, flu, everything like that, and you'll be lucky to live to sixty. The good news is that cells called telomeres, which cause ageing, lengthen in low gravity, with means you'll look quite young while all this happens. And it looks to me as though mental health and social support have a big effect on how tough it is for you. I'm a doctor," he added. "Well. I was. Can't practice here till I naturalise."

Yan sighed, adjusting their glasses again, even though they didn't need to adjust their glasses.

January gathered up his thoughts into a rough bale. "I'd like to check in on Monday then, if you have space."

They took their glasses off and polished them. "Look, I . . . rarely do this, but I'm going to urge you to reconsider. I'm not supposed to say this, and it's not written down anywhere, but Mark's right." They nodded to the American man. "If you go in with depression, you're coming out in a wheelchair."

January could feel his voice disappearing. "I've got nowhere else to go. I'm . . . not realistically going to get another job after being in prison. Nowhere that'll take an Earthstronger. Will I?"

"No," Yan said quietly.

"So either I punch a police officer and go back to prison or I come here," January said.

"But you don't want to naturalise."

"No, but that doesn't matter now." He pushed his hands over his face. "And—after everything with Gale, I feel like I'm evil here, just for being. I *know* that isn't right, I don't believe *anyone* is bad just for existing, but feeling things isn't very voluntary, and . . ."

There was a terrible silence in which everyone sat frozen, watching him trying not to cry.

"I'm really sorry," Yan said, "that it's like this."

"Also," Mark said, knocking him softly, "there's real ice cream."

"I can probably live with all the other stuff then," January said, not completely lying.

"Oh my God, you lot and ice cream, what is wrong with you?" Yan sighed, looking hugely relieved.

"Do you know how hard it is to find anything derived from a cow here? You're all evangelical hipster vegans who've banned sugar, it's an absolute atrocity," Mark declared.

"But all that lab-generated dairy stuff might have all kinds of horrible artificial things wrong with it," Yan tried.

They both looked at January, clearly praying for him to join in. He smiled. It wasn't that much effort. "I hate to tell you this, Yan, but weird frozen tofu is *not* ice cream, it's what you threaten to feed to murder suspects to make them confess faster."

Everyone laughed, and it was easier this time.

9

At home, January had to peel off his clothes and shake the dust off in the lift to keep it from going everywhere inside the flat. Everyone else had clearly been doing the same, because the lift floor was starting to look like a mini desert, with its own dust-dunes in the corners.

The flat was cold. He didn't dock his charge card into the wall for power. Spending two weeks in prison had saved him some money, and going to the naturalisation centre would save him three months' more, but then there would be almost nothing left. He wouldn't be able to keep paying the rent here while he was at the centre. Still, that was all right. Once he was naturalised he wouldn't be able to come back here anyway. The furniture had come with the flat, and all he owned were his clothes and the crockery. He didn't mind about the crockery. He could leave that for the next person.

The simple task of transferring his clothes from the drawers and into the bag under the bed loomed huge. He had to stop thinking about it. He got out of his cage, shoulders and hips aching after walking so far in it, sank down at the table, and tried to remember if he had already taken his vitamin supplements. It was important, because without them there was a host of things that went wrong with a person in the perpetual late-afternoon dimness this far from the sun even when the weather was clear, never mind in a dust storm. But he couldn't.

Three months living and eating for free at the centre; that meant three months in which he wasn't going to end up at a homeless shelter.

Or deported. That was good. And he had liked Yan. And there was the American doctor. It would be nice, once he got over his stupid reaction to it, to be flirted with. It would be lovely to have an actual human who wanted to have a January.

His phone rang. He glanced at the number—unknown—and declined the call. It was beginning to make him feel shaky, hearing that benign little buzz. Since the debate, journalists had been calling him all the time, and the prison service saying things he didn't understand, and he didn't want to talk to anyone. He should switch it off. But then he wouldn't know if Val tried to get in touch. He had written her a long apology, but she hadn't answered.

The bell on the lift made him jump.

The Visitor sign was lit up.

When he opened the door, expecting the post, he jolted right back and slammed down onto one knee, because Aubrey Gale was on the other side.

They were dressed in floor-length black, sashed with red, the fabric glittering with solar circuitry. They seemed wrong for the elevator in a creaky nuclear plant repurposed haphazard for cheap housing. They looked like one of those spirits from Tang dynasty novels who sometimes appeared by a holy mountain to offer someone a prophecy, or a sword.

"Hi. May I come in?" Gale said, looking past him into the little apartment. From the lights inside the lift, it must have seemed dark.

January shook his head and then managed to get his voice back. His cage was in the corner where he'd left it. He hadn't even lit any candles; he was just moving about in the gloom of what little daylight made it through the bubble wrap over the window. "It's a mess."

"It is not," Gale said, and came in anyway, almost too tall for the ceiling. They paused in the middle of the floor as if they had never seen anywhere like it. Probably they hadn't. "Get up. Please."

"Is there anything I can get you?" January asked, hoping desperately it wasn't going to be that long a visit. "I've got coffee."

He'd have to use his charge card to get the electricity to boil the water. It wasn't much, it was fine. It was fine. He could spend what he had. He was going to the centre.

Gale looked nearly as horrified by the idea as January felt. "Yes, please."

They both stood paralysed for another infinite second. January had never felt so conscious of his own strength. But the apartment wasn't big enough to give Gale the usual courteous four-metre radius. January backed against the window to make it clear he would have liked to. "I'll just . . ." He pointed at the cage, which was on Gale's other side, to warn them he was going to have to go by.

Gale looked too and January saw them decide they'd rather have him uncaged than pass them a few inches away. "No, no. It's okay."

January swallowed, and held out his card. Right out, the whole length of his arm, still slightly out of Gale's reach, so that Gale could choose to step forward and take it, not have it shoved into their space. "If you could plug that in, then. It's—the dock is behind you."

Gale waved the card away and flicked their own into the charge dock. The lights came up, and the heating coughed as the fan unit woke up, and the wall display blinked sleepily as it connected to the internet again. January had to stand on a chair to work the dials on the heating unit, but Gale only had to reach a little. They turned it right up.

"You don't have to," he started, excruciated. He had never turned the unit up to full strength. Seeing the display go up to twenty-four degrees made his stomach knot. It was so expensive.

"I'm this close to building a campfire in the middle of the floor," Gale told him. "It's freezing outside. I'm sure you're very hardy and so forth, but I am a spoilt indoors person."

It was the most spectacularly good-mannered lie January had ever experienced. Gale was not too cold; they had taken their coat off in the lift. Generations-long naturalised people were usually genetically modified for the cold. The heater at full blast would feel like a sauna for Gale. This was for him.

He coughed over the need to say thank you. He couldn't stand to. There was something about their good manners that felt aggressive. "Sit wherever you like."

Gale hesitated, and so January retreated to the other wall. Anyone watching the two of them from above could have been forgiven for thinking of magnets with their repelling poles pointed at each other.

Gale sat down in the chair that faced away from the window, where the bubble wrap had three quarters fallen off while January had been away. They sat sideways to see out, looking utterly out of place in the shabby little kitchen, against the industrial backdrop of the warehouses and cranes and the graffiti-covered metro bridge. In the street ten floors below, shadowy figures struggled against the dust, which was still as strong as ever. Gale, though, was immaculate; there was no dust on their clothes, and they weren't carrying a mask. There must have been a car right outside.

When he risked a glance back, Gale was weighing a teaspoon January had left on the table, moving their hand slowly up and down to feel how heavy it was. A lot heavier—three times heavier—than a normal spoon. It had EARTHSTRONG LIVING stamped onto the back of the handle. Dismayed, January realized that all his cups were from the same company. Everything was weighted to keep him from hurling it across the room while he was out of his cage.

"I, um—are you able to lift this okay?" he asked, and held out a cup, then realized they would almost have to touch him if they were to take it from him. He put it down on the table and edged it nearer to them, and stood away.

Gale took it with both hands. Even so, January saw their arms dip. It must have felt like being asked if they could comfortably drink from a cannonball. "You wouldn't happen to have a glass?" they said.

Feeling ridiculous, January gave them a glass tumbler, but in front of someone so glamorous as Gale, it didn't look silly, just chic.

Mercifully, the kettle pinged. He poured the water out over the coffee in the single-person cafetière, and made himself a cup of tea. He didn't like tea, he only kept it in case of visitors, but he didn't have another cafetière. He moved the other chair as far from Gale as he could, which, even so, was only about one length of his own arm. Then he took everything across and set it down very, very slowly so that Gale could see he was in no danger of sending anything flying, and eased into the other chair. He had to lock his teeth together when it creaked under his weight.

"I tried to call ahead," Gale said. They were moving slowly too, and it made him uncomfortable in a sourceless kind of way until he finally chased down the reason: it was how people moved around dogs that were known to bite. "I'm sorry for just showing up."

"No, it's okay. I've . . . not been good at answering calls. It's always lawyers or journalists."

Gale must have seen the thought cross his face, because for a fraction of a second, they looked as awkward and as unhappy as he felt, and studied the coffee instead of him. Not having that razor stare on him was a relief.

"Have you filed a wrongful dismissal suit against the factory yet?" Gale asked.

January tried to tell if it was some kind of dry, rich-person joke. "No. I don't have money for lawyers and anyway, it wasn't a wrongful dismissal."

Gale was looking at the single-cup-sized cafetière as if it had done something awful. January felt anxious, though he was certain it was clean. It wasn't heavy. He hadn't been able to get one from the special Earthstrong company, which seemed to think that Earthstrongers only bothered with tea. "No. Rich and powerful people should be frightened regularly. Keeps us normal."

By way of a reason not to say anything, January lit the little lamp between them. It was illegal, but dodgy biofuel liberated from the reject barrels round the back of Silo 4 was cheaper per minute of light than the electric lamp.

Gale rescued him. "Anyway, I'd like to offer you a job."

January sat back too sharply and Gale went out of his focus. He had never got around to getting new contact lenses, or even glasses. He didn't see so badly he couldn't function, but he could only see well at normal talking distance. "I don't need charity, I'll find work soon enough—"

Gale was already shaking their head. "Hear me out. Senatorial marriages here are often arranged. Marriage in Tharsis only lasts five years." They paused. "If it goes well, fantastic. If it doesn't, it's only five years of your life."

It was like being handed one of those wooden puzzles, the three-dimensional ones that came in star shapes or complicated cubes and spheres. January tried to put it together three or four different ways, but then had to give up. He couldn't see how marriages and jobs linked up. "You've . . . lost me?"

Gale sat forward, fire-iron straight, the same as their hair. The ends brushed their elbows. They weren't dressed for the Senate, but they must have come from the office; hair down meant formal things. Or maybe *this* was the formal thing, maybe it was January. Without meaning to, he ran his hand through his own hair. It was short. That was the here-equivalent of having tattoos on your face and a vigorous heroin addiction. He hadn't cut it since coming here, but it was just refusing to grow. It bothered him a lot more than he wanted to say, what with the colour. He hated looking like an old man from behind; a cheap, criminal old man.

"The consular election is soon, and I'm running," Gale said. "The sitting consul has a very solid blue-collar base, and I am obscenely rich, which is perceived as being a lot worse than what they are, which is relatable and friendly and completely loyal to a foreign power."

"I know, I saw the debate," January mumbled.

"If I can't appeal to at least some of Consul Song's base, much of which is only first- or second-generation naturalised, I'm done." They gave him an anaemic smile. "And I just let the full force of the press engine and the judiciary land on the head of a working-class immigrant who did nothing wrong."

He looked at them sideways, because in his experience, politicians lied, stole, trafficked, and occasionally murdered, and the consensus was that you voted for whoever hadn't sent pictures of unfortunate parts of themselves to a teenager. Anything better was unrealistic. The debate had been satisfying, but nobody was going to refuse to vote for Gale because of anything that happened to January.

"Who cares?"

"Everyone," Gale said, looking taken aback. "We have the strictest code of behaviour of any government in the worlds."

January decided to leave that alone, or he'd end up laughing mania-cally and hurling himself out the window. "So you . . . you need to connect with poor voters?"

"Yes. Weddings always go down very well. Particularly fairy-tale weddings of the kind where the ordinary person becomes royalty."

He rearranged the words in three or four different ways but none of them made any sense. However he looked at it, it was a giant step to one side for no reason.

"I don't get it."

"I'm offering you a job, not a real marriage. You would appear at public engagements, you shake hands, you smile, you do the morning shows and the magazines, you act a bit. You would have your own room at the house, plenty of space, and you would not see me unless we were working together. But you would be paid very well, monthly, as with any other salary. A hundred thousand yuan every month for five years. This is not a trick or a game; you will be provided with lawyers, whose job it will be to make that contract bulletproof for you."

January's brain stopped working the second it began to suspect that Gale was talking about him.

"What?" he said.

Gale seemed to see he wasn't asking for more information, just for a gap in which to understand what was happening. Politely, they didn't say anything.

"You—right," January said numbly. "Me, though; you're asking . . . me . . . to marry . . . you."

"Yes."

Yuan, real yuan, real money; he hadn't used real money since coming here. He didn't ever buy anything you would need money for instead of power. Kilowatts weren't a *currency*; it was the same as being paid in food. It was a way not to have a bank account and not to pay tax, and to be invisible to the immigration bureau, who had begun deporting every Earthstronger they could since Gagarin Square.

Gale was talking more to the tumbler of coffee than to January now. It seemed a lot like they were hoping that if they didn't look at him, he wouldn't be there. "I'm aware this sounds like the offer of someone who means to kidnap you and keep you in a cellar, but if there's anything I can do to reassure you, I will."

January pressed back against his chair. "I'm booked into the naturalisation centre on Monday."

Gale looked at him as if he had suggested lopping off some limbs. "Why?"

"*Why?* You were trying to persuade me to do it on a live broadcast, you're all for it, aren't you?"

"I am, but you're not. What are you doing?"

January felt off balance. "I'd have thought you'd be pleased. You spend your whole life campaigning to get people in camps—"

"You're still telling me what I think, not what you think."

January felt very odd, because he'd just had a bit of a revelation about the way Gale spoke. It sounded aggressive; they just came up to you and gave you a very hard conversational shove, which felt like being attacked. But he had a strong sense now that that wasn't how they meant it. It was the way January's dance teacher had used to make everyone stand on one leg and push their unbalanced side; it was to see how firm you were standing, and the idea was to push back, not to politely fall over. It wasn't aggressive. It was—interested.

Jesus.

"It's free. I've run out of money. I don't have a job. And I won't get one unless I naturalise."

"What do you mean?" Again, it sounded sharp, but Gale didn't look angry or combative. They were just waiting for him to explain, tilted forward slightly to hear him across the unnatural distance the two of them were talking across, over the whirring of the heating unit.

Which was making the room properly warm for the first time since he'd lived here. It was amazing.

"I mean it's three months of free food and I don't have enough for three weeks. And after that I can get citizenship and universal basic income until I find work."

Gale was frowning. "Citizenship isn't dependent on naturalisation. You can apply anyway. All climate change refugees from Earth are eligible—"

"I put in a citizenship application when I got here; the same week." He had a bleak flashback to the six hours it had taken at the immigration office. "I don't expect to hear back for four years."

"Four. *Si*," Gale repeated in Mandarin, because "four" and "for" were too close.

January shrugged. "That's normal. They say it's the backlog." Backlog was code for *time we think we can get away with waiting while we hope you reconsider*. "Naturalisation gets you *automatic* citizenship. Well; you know that. You wrote that law."

Gale said nothing at first, and January had a strange but distinct feeling that he had just said something that was either wrong or unfair. They looked, just for a second, like they wanted to say as much, and he felt his whole body go tense, waiting to be smashed through the conversational floor again like last time; but Gale just let that breath out, and then started again. "Yes. I did. But do this and you'll never think about money again. Whatever else I am, I am not as horrendous as the naturalisation process."

If the floor had tilted under his chair, January would have been less confused. He had thought Gale took the position they did because they either didn't really understand what people were losing in naturalisation, or they thought Earthstrongers deserved the suffering for bothering the Tharsese authorities to begin with. To understand that it was terrible, and yet to fight for it—he couldn't find a way those things matched up.

And, and, *hang on*, a little voice in his head protested, that was actually Aubrey actual Gale admitting that *they personally* were not very nice.

He thought he must have misunderstood—there was so much room to misunderstand even in English here, because nobody's English ever quite matched up—so he scanned them for any extra clues about what they'd meant, but everything he saw matched what he'd thought. When Gale met his eyes, they were full of a kind of tentative apology.

"You don't want an Earthstronger in your house, Senator," he said instead.

Gale looked away again, and this time, January saw a flicker of something like desperation. It made him stare too hard, because Gale noticed and rearranged their face into its normal diplomatic gentility. "Please," they said, much more softly.

January couldn't read them properly at all, and he was already doubting he'd seen that flicker. Or maybe it was the election Gale felt that desperation about? Maybe they really did think they would lose without January? But—somehow he didn't think so. They seemed . . . afraid. "Is something else going on? Is—I'm sorry, is someone forcing you to do this? Only you look frightened."

It was the wrong thing to say. He saw Gale take a fractional, half-amused offence at being asked. Asking, he realized too late, sounded to them like being called a coward. He had a strong feeling that Gale would rather have stepped off the roof than admit to anything stronger than distant unease. "I'm fine."

He had to pull himself back from the urge to recommend they get in touch with their human side before it boiled over and they had some kind of nervous breakdown.

"You came all this way to see someone who was a pig to you on a national broadcast, when you could get anyone you like; why are you talking to me?" he pushed anyway.

"Firstly," Gale said, lifting their eyebrows, "you did nothing wrong. People are *enormously* touchy about every minuscule social faux pas because it's very cold here and there is no water. Hardship breeds irritable humans."

January shut his teeth. Nobody had said it like that before. Tentatively, he looked up, trying to gauge if Gale really meant that, or if forgiving him was just a negotiation technique. Gale was looking back at him, quiet and poised, and maybe concerned. They didn't seem like they were lying.

"Secondly: this is proving very bad for my campaign, the Consul is mashing me with it, it makes me look like a horrible person."

"Well, you *are* a horrible person," January said, half aiming for a joke and half not.

Gale tilted their head a fraction, as though they'd quite enjoyed that. "Thirdly, I've wrecked your life. I'd like a chance to mend it."

January felt his way around it, but slowly, because part of him was sure that it would bite. He found a corner. "If you wanted that, then you could just do a press conference and give me a few thousand yuan."

"Do you want a press conference and a few thousand yuan?" Gale said. "We can do that, but you'd still be unemployable."

January sat quiet, looking at the future and its two branches. One was marriage; one was naturalisation. "Five years?"

"Five years," Gale said back, as though January had slammed a gavel on the table.

IO

The contract negotiations began the next morning, and they promised, said all involved, to last much of the week. While the lawyers talked—January wasn't even sure what about, but they looked busy—Gale took him out to a café to give him the basic brief. Silent security officers ghosted after them, dressed in black, each one a foot taller than January.

They were in Gagarin Square, opposite the Senate, and the parakeets were out in a cheerful swarm, ruffling their feathers in the fountain. Val had mentioned once that they were special cold-resistant parakeets escaped from a lab somewhere, but since Val was Val, he couldn't tell if he was having his leg pulled or not. In any case, Tharsis had embraced the parakeet idea, and the beautiful hotel on the far side of the square had a café called the Parakeet and Pickle. It was right at the top of the tower, with a view across the whole city. The dust streams were dark patches everywhere, like quick fog. Because it was heated for Natural people, it was cold inside.

January hovered at the doorway of the café. There was no partition, but there wasn't a NO EARTHSTRONGERS sign either.

Gale noticed. "It's all right."

"I'd better ask," January said, because he had an uncomfortable feeling that no partition meant no expectation of Earthstrong people, not perfect contentment on the part of the establishment about letting everybody in.

He saw Gale think about arguing with him, and saw them decide not to. Instead they stood tilted aside so that any passing waiters could see him, but angled toward him so it was clear who he was with. He should have been trying to catch someone's eye, but it was difficult not to watch Gale. They were more *still* than anyone he had ever met. It wasn't a natural stillness. It looked like someone had flogged them as a child until they'd learned to stand motionless and straight even under cannon fire. When they did move, it was slow and smooth. It should have looked mannered, but the weight of the money and the power behind it made it—something else. It was the care you had to take, he realized, when everyone was always watching you, and when seeming anxious or fidgety at the wrong moment could send shockwaves through the stock market.

When Gale saw him looking, January had a bolt of embarrassment, but then Gale bowed, very slightly, in a way that promised it was only normal. Feeling awkward, because he had never moved in the echelons of society that would require it, he tipped a fractional bow back. He thought something opened in Gale's expression then, but he didn't have time to decide what, because a waiter had arrived.

"Ah," January said hopefully. "Is it all right for me to . . . ?"

"Oh, we have visiting diplomats here all the time," the waiter said happily, and ushered the two of them to a table. Not without a curious double take at January, like people always did when they realized he was not as old as his hair. It wasn't the colour people's hair went if they dyed it white. It was like frozen spiderweb on gorse late in winter when the frost had settled for the season.

Different world. He had never been mistaken for anyone important before. It was proximity to Gale; Gale was so glamorous it was catching. Their hair was swept up in the writhing silver diadem that all senators wore, and they were dressed in the deep blue that was the official sigil colour of House Gale. These were requirements for senators in public, because they were supposed to be obvious from a distance, just like nurses or police officers. Whatever the reason, Gale looked like the governor of somewhere with endless territory and diamond mines.

So did other people in the café. There were more plainly dressed business types, bankers and lawyers maybe, but there were celebrities too; he recognised an actor, and someone from a Gucci advert. People were sending curious glances his way; but, because he was plainly with

Gale, it was only curiosity. Nobody was asking the waiter to have him thrown out, even though he was in jeans and his one good shirt.

The security officers vanished into discreet corners, except one, who sat at the next table along, ignoring the sign that said it was reserved. None of the waiters tried to make them move. January felt uneasy, almost sure they were there in case *he* did something, but they only took out a journal, leatherbound, and started taking what he quickly realized were minutes. It was charming to see someone do that by hand. They wrote in swift scruffy Chinese.

Hot water arrived immediately—cafés always served hot water here, not cold, because it was always cold outside—and so did some tiny things that looked like jewels pretending to be cookies.

"Can I take your coat?" the waiter added.

"Um, no, thanks, I'll hang on to it, I'm freezing."

"Oh, gosh—yes, I suppose it is cool for you in here—can I fetch you a heat pack?"

January blinked, because he hadn't expected anything helpful. "I mean, if you have one around?"

"Of course," the waiter exclaimed, and glided away looking purposeful.

"What are these?" he asked, about the jewel things.

"Macarons; they're made of almonds," Gale said, and then paused, focused on something in the middle distance, which January had come to recognise, on people here, as meaning that they were reading something online. The café menu, probably. He could just make out what might have been text moving across their irises, clear and bright against the black. Then he had to look away, because it struck him suddenly as somehow indecent, to be able to see what was in their eyes.

Yes: "Would you like some coffee?"

"Soya flat white please."

Just for a flicker of a moment, Gale looked puzzled that January knew enough about coffee to know exactly what he wanted. January looked down, not wanting to admit he'd been very middle class before the flood. Interns had *brought* his coffee to the dressing room.

Saying so would remind Gale of how far he'd fallen, and he honestly couldn't think of anything worse. Two years ago, if he'd been talking to someone in his position, he'd have thought that showed a marked faith-lessness in humans, but it wasn't faithless, just sensible. He had a theory about why.

It was like being injured. If you were hurt in a straightforward, ordi-nary way, people felt sympathetic, helped, and that was that. But there was a tipping point. There was a difference between breaking your wrist and horrifying necrosis. If it was bad enough, that instinct to help vanished, because there was no helping. What was left was the instinct to hit you with a rock.

He had a terrible certainty that losing your country was like the horrifying necrosis. You couldn't go around blaming other people for feeling that way. It was old mercy, hammered into human DNA in the ages before medicine.

And Gale was the person who was happy to push refugees into natu-ralisation centres. January couldn't help suspecting that Gale had a very low hit-it-with-a-rock threshold.

Over by the till, something went "ding"; their order going through. Gale's focus came back to him. He wasn't quite ready for it. After the television interview, it still felt a little like having a gun levelled at him, even though he knew it wasn't loaded today. Gale seemed to understand, because they pretended to study the macarons. It was a tiny thing, but there was such courtesy in it that January's throat went dry. He couldn't remember that anyone had ever been this careful with him.

But then, it wasn't as though anyone's election campaign had ever relied on him before either.

"So," Gale said. "Do you stream much?"

It was flattering, he thought, that Gale imagined he was someone who could run something electrical for that long, instead of a person who worried about the power it took to boil the kettle. "No, not really."

Gale's black eyes slipped past January's shoulder, and when January twisted back, he saw some teenagers blinking and giggling, the amber flare going off in their eyes; that was the legal warning that someone was taking a photo through their contact lenses. He moved his chair to block the view. Gale was probably used to it, but he still disliked the idea.

However rich and annoying you were, you deserved to sit and have a cup of coffee in peace, and Gale looked brittle this morning.

Probably it had a lot to do with entering into marriage negotiations with somebody they felt belonged on the other side of a barbed wire fence.

"There's a reality show about us. House Gale." Another pause. The waiter was removing the teenagers. A lot of them were dressed in the odd way January kept seeing in the nice parts of town; plain, skintight black jumpsuits, even though they must have been freezing, and plain and black wasn't the way any teenagers from anywhere usually liked to dress. He had puzzled about that over the months, but never felt confident enough to ask anyone.

"It's popular," Gale continued carefully. "As part of the election campaign, I signed up to let the cameras into the house. It was successful, my press secretary made their opinions known and the cameras never left."

"Why in God's name would you let that in your *house?*"

Gale tilted their head to say, yes, obviously it was very odd. "People only vote for you if they know who you are."

"So you send out a polished version of whatever goes on?"

Gale looked exactly like they had in his flat then; glassy, as though there was something urgent they weren't telling him. "The producers like to call it documentary. They don't arrange things overtly, there isn't a script. But they do like to run narratives. A romance, or a feud."

"You didn't mention this before."

"I was scared you'd throw a shoe at me and run away," Gale said, completely serious.

He snorted, and then coughed, because the joke had taken him by surprise. "No, I see, that's reasonable. It's okay, I'll have to do this even if you run a segment where I'm attacked by tigers."

Gale studied him quietly, not like they believed him, but they didn't say it. "There are cameras everywhere. Everyone wears microphones. Most of what they film is never aired, but anything they film *could* go out."

"It sounds like a prison," January said, shocked.

Gale didn't agree or disagree. For the third or fourth time since they'd sat down, they glanced into the far corner by the ceiling, but when he looked round, there was nothing there. Or maybe there was virtually, if you were wearing lenses. Maybe it was a distracting sign. "It's also a gift. It means everyone can watch how a famous arranged marriage turns out."

"Are people really that interested?"

Gale hung over the edge of smiling in the way January imagined that archangels there to report on the state of things hung suspended above the towers of Pandemonium. "Fifteen teenagers just followed us into a bar."

January shook his head. He was never going to get used to the glamour of Tharsese politicians. Ever since he'd arrived, he'd wanted to corner someone local and ask where they kept the real ones, the sleaze-bags who bubbled up through scandals like smug hippos.

Right on cue, one of the teenagers escaped from the waiter and hurried over, and January had a painful twist, because their shoes had toecaps that looked like pandas. Kids here stayed kids for a lot longer, he'd noticed; especially in rich Natural families, they treated eighteen-year-olds like he'd been treated when he was about twelve.

"Um, excuse me, Senator, I was at the debate the other day, I *love* you, can you sign my hat?"

Gale smiled, unexpectedly gentle, and took the pen. "What's your name?"

"Sid. I want to be a senator too," they added proudly.

Gale wrote *Vote for Sid!* and gave the hat back. Sid squeaked and ran away.

January was glad for the interruption. It had given him time to think. "I shouldn't be saying anything in front of any more cameras."

"Mx Stirling. You didn't do or say anything wrong."

Gale breathed in and held it, and over in the other corner, there was an explosion of joy among the teenagers. Sid was showing off the hat. "Everything you say in front of any camera can be very carefully curated. My press secretary will always be there to help you. It will be much less intense than what happened at the factory. It isn't going to be me dissolving you in front of the internet."

January didn't say "that's a relief," because it would have sounded sarcastic.

Gale paused again. There was something teacherly about them; they were used to explaining things. It wasn't patronising, just careful and precise. "Do you have questions about anything we've said so far?"

January thought about it. "You keep talking about the house, the show, characters—but . . . it sounds like a *lot* of people live there. Is it—do your staff live there? I don't really understand how . . ."

"Yes." Gale nodded once. "Songshu is the seat of House Gale, which hereditarily runs the Department for Energy. House Gale oversees the sun fields, which is why we're on the Plains, not in the Valley; sunlight is stronger at altitude. We provide the power that runs the whole of Tharsis; we also run and fund experimental research in new power production technologies. It is primarily a scientific institute. About five hundred people live there."

It took a few seconds for that to sink in.

"You *inherited* the Department for Energy," January repeated, blown sideways. "That—what? Families can't inherit government departments. I thought Tharsis was a democracy?"

Gale inclined their head. The silver sigils in their hair caught the light and shone. "Other countries work the same way. There are organisations who decide who their successors are, not voters, even though they affect all the voters. All those megacompanies."

"But they're *companies*!"

"So are Great Houses. *I* own the sun fields, not the government. But you can't have a company as rich as a country going around doing what it likes. Everyone has to be accountable. So each House has an automatic, mandatory seat in the Senate. I wasn't elected. I *have* to attend."

"How's that a democracy again?" January demanded. Now wasn't the time to dispute the governmental structure of Mars, but he couldn't see past it.

"England has a House of Commons and a House of Lords, yes? One set is voted in, the other—at least when it was conceived—forces people who are influential to participate in government. Same idea."

"Oh," January said, his whole idea of the world shifting. He had to claw around for his original train of thought. "And—so—is there a . . ." He lost the word. "When do we do things?"

"There is the schedule to end all schedules." Gale turned their tablet around for him on the table. It was in Mandarin and he panicked, but Gale waved one hand over it and it fizzed into English instead. "We're going to go quite quickly. The wedding will be in a month. It will be a big public event, the whole of Tharsis is invited. We'll announce it tomorrow, which—"

"Tomorrow!"

"—I know is very quick, but it doesn't mean you're immediately plunged into a media spotlight. If you want more time, we don't have to announce *who* I'm marrying."

That brought January up short. "We don't?"

Gale smiled a bit. He was starting to notice it took them a long time to gear up to smiling properly in private; a lot of things had to go into rolling motion first, and even then, he didn't think the mechanisms worked too well, and probably Gale had to catch them on their way downhill. It was very different to the sultry sunset smile they could aim at cameras and journalists.

Like a very old, archaeologically significant penny, a school memory dropped into his mind. There was always a difference, even a thousand years ago, between the person and the office of the King. The crown as an institution, distinct from the person underneath it. That was what he was seeing now. At the factory, he had met Senator Gale. Now, he was meeting Aubrey. As soon as he understood, he had an intrigued sense that he was being allowed to see secrets.

"No," Gale said. "People expect some dramatic tension. Everyone always keeps what they're wearing on the day secret, but we can go one further. My communications office is very keen on this. The first time you appear in public would be on the wedding day. Or, if you'd rather have your name in the press for this rather than the other thing, then that's fine as well. The decision is yours. What do you think would be better?"

"This is your show and I'm not the director," January pointed out. "I don't want to be doing whatever I want at the expense of your campaign."

"I've been told that people from your island are self-sabotagingly polite, is this that?" Gale asked.

"No—well, yes, we are—but you're going to have to live with me for five years. I don't want to start out by causing problems I don't know about, you'll end up hating me later. I don't know enough about what you want to achieve or how to get it to make decisions like this without some guidance. Does that make sense?"

Gale looked at him as if he had come out in classical poetry. "That's . . . very . . . courteous of you."

"I mean. I feel like we should probably be courteous to each other." He smiled. It felt good to agree about something.

"We should," Gale said, with an unexpectedly deferential dip of their eyelashes. "Well; I like the idea of keeping it secret."

"Let's do that then."

"You can't keep living in that ghastly apartment, though," Gale said. "Would you consider staying here?"

"Here? Where here?" January asked, thinking distractedly that he wanted to start calling things ghastly too. It was such a good word.

"The hotel. The Tiangong."

"Stay at the—for a *month*?"

"Yes."

"I don't have any money."

"No, I mean I'd pay."

"That's stupid." It was automatic. However rich you were, the Tiangong was *stupid* money. He had looked it up before he came out today to find out how much he would have to pay for a coffee if they split the bill, and he had actually spat his toast on his phone. Even God couldn't afford a drink here without taking out a mortgage first.

"Is it stupid?" Gale said, voice smoking higher. "Will you perhaps not be dead if I leave you in the nuclear ice-box for another month? Or do Europeans need consistent refrigeration?"

"It—no, I don't need to be refrigerated," January said, choking over another laugh he hadn't seen coming. "I don't want to feel like I owe you."

Gale lifted both hands a fraction off the table. "I understand, but this isn't a debt to repay; this is me making sure a member of my House is safe."

"You can't spend all that money and not want something back."

Gale straightened a little as if January had sworn at them, and he realized too late that refusing a gift was probably very rude.

At last they said, politely, "As a percentage of my annual income, putting up one quite small human in a hotel for a month is like you buying someone a coffee."

"It's a five-star hotel!" It was named after an early space station—*Tiangong* meant "the palace of the heavens," and it was a big name to live up to, but given the macarons-and-celebrities situation, January wasn't sure he even wanted to imagine what one of its guest rooms would look like. Probably they had their own private waterfalls and hula dancers on demand.

"I'm . . . rich."

"That rich, really?" It came out slightly flat, slightly disapproving. He shook his head once, trying convey that he didn't mean to be rude, and he didn't want to get in another fight, but he was just as unwilling to take it back altogether. People *should* be disapproving of that kind of money sitting under one person. And the Gales of the worlds needed to see that being great didn't automatically mean good in everyone's mind, despite the flocks of adoring teenagers.

But now that he was saying it to Gale personally, not just whingeing at Val, it didn't sound so much like it was just his opinion. It sounded like he was preaching. In a weird, vivid spin of perspective, he heard suddenly how people like him sounded to people like Gale. Righteous, holier-than-thou-ing.

Gale nodded and didn't complain. He wasn't sure he would have been that graceful if someone had been so spiky with him. "Does that mean yes?"

"Yes. Thank—"

"Ah," Gale cut him off.

January hesitated. "This . . . is . . . only my due from House Gale and if you'd withheld it I'd be talking to the union and everybody would think badly of you?"

"Better," Gale said, and they both laughed the muted laugh of two people who still didn't understand each other, even though they'd got a bit of string and a couple of tin cans over the gulf now. It was silly, but January's heart lifted, because he had come here thinking Gale would be dismissive and patronising. Not that they would be searching for more string and more cans just as hard as he was.

"So that's the wedding," January said. "And then . . . ?"

Gale drew in a deeper breath. "Then we have a schedule for developing the relationship." They were holding the idea with pincers, and they had clearly gone to a lot of effort not to leave a long quiet before *relationship* as they geared up to the word. January was glad the two of them agreed about how uncomfortable that whole idea was, though it was hard not feel grimy. He would have liked not to be repulsive. "Being married is one thing, but what will stoke much more interest is if we can appear to make it work. You can read this yourself. It's not scripted, but it is choreographed."

January read the schedule, nodding. It made sense. Meetings, lunch together, fundraisers, rallies, and in between, rather well-considered suggestions for him specifically: filming online dancing lessons for exercise at home, culture slots about Europe, quirks of British English, teaching basic English—by that point the communications department clearly thought people would be interested—and more, and more.

And then, near Christmas, a month before the election, something that was cryptically marked "start of romance day."

His heart clenched up in the same way it had when Lovely Mark at the naturalisation centre had flirted with him. It was a kind of nascent panic, and all at once he wanted to dissolve into the air. He could perform, he could even act a bit, but what Gale was talking about was beyond acting. It was a whole life. A whole marriage.

"Do I want to know what that means?" he asked tightly.

Gale looked like he felt. "Well, my press secretary wants something steamy and I want whatever the opposite of that is, and I expect we'll have to compromise with something kind of swampy in the middle."

Usually he had a good grip on his imagination, but it got right away from him then, and his head filled with feverish, horrible possible futures where he would have to sleep with someone he didn't know live on a reality show in front of four million people. All of them had sharp, dark edges, and each one was lacerating. His lungs decided that they wouldn't be working again until he could stop thinking of that, thank you.

He must have gone an even worse colour than normal, because a flash of worry went through Gale's eyes, and they reached across the table. They didn't cover his hands, but they held theirs an inch above his. "No. Not that. No one is going to ask you to do anything like . . ."

He finally managed to breathe in again. "What *is* the opposite of steam, anyway?" he asked, just to try to steer away from everything else. "Is it—you know, arid tundra full of hungry polar bears?"

"Everyone likes polar bears, so I don't see how my press secretary can get mad about that," Gale agreed, looking halfway to relieved. They took their hands back.

Then they blinked twice and touched the table.

"Are you—" He stopped himself saying "all right." Gale would hate it. "Something going on?" he asked instead.

"Yes. We're trending."

January studied them, intrigued. There were things here called haptic engines. They were clever webs that were implanted over certain parts of your brain, and what they did was pretty amazing. The translation ones were the least of it. Others let you *feel* social media tides, or stock market ones, and in hospitals you could link them to a doctor's so the doctor could feel exactly what kind of pain you were in, and in some very fancy restaurants you could look at a code on the menu and the haptic would fire up and trick your neurones into making you taste a tiny sample of the dish; but he'd never met anyone with them. Everyone said it was the future of the internet, but for now, they were fantastically expensive.[12] He put his phone face down on the table, glad he could do

---

12   There were still quite a lot of news stories about the haptics going a bit wrong, as well. A disgruntled employee at the company which sold the implants had, on their last day, sent out a signal that made everyone with haptics experience the overpowering taste of wasabi whenever they saw or heard the name of the company. January had been at the train station that day, beneath a giant billboard advertising the things, and seen it first hand as dozens of well-dressed people wheezed into the closest cafés with streaming eyes to ask desperately for water. Everyone had found it very funny, except the government, who had fined the company to kingdom come and now legislated the engines very tightly indeed, which January thought was boring of them.

that. It would be nightmarish having it plugged directly into his mind. As far as he knew, the implants ran on the electricity of the rest of your brain. You couldn't turn them off any more than you could turn off your hearing.

Gale saw. "You must struggle if you're only perceiving things with a phone. That must be an antique? Xie," they added, because the waiter had just delivered two cups of beautiful coffee and a heat pack for January.

"Thank you," January echoed. Then, "It is. But I don't need to see virtual things. I walk everywhere and I don't buy anything except food, so it doesn't make much difference." It was already out before he heard how tragic-hero stoic it sounded.

Gale didn't let their posture go, or their perfect neutrality, but what they said was, "You're about to tell me that your parents drowned when you were six and you're dying of an incurable brain tumour."

January grinned, relieved to be having a normal conversation and to be teased like there wasn't a chasm between them. Then he stopped, because he had seen his own reflection in the side of a glass and it wasn't very nice. Along with his hair, the rest of him had lost colour too, except his eyes, which looked much too dark now, and the effect was disturbing. He looked like he had been living in a pond and eating unwary travellers.

"So," he summarised. "We're filmed all the time. There are artificial stories, including us. Your press secretary runs through anything more important than breakfast with me to make sure I'm not—accidentally horrifying."

"Yes."

He shifted, uncomfortable, but he had to ask. "What happened to Max?"

Gale didn't flicker. They must have been expecting the question. "They left. I was never very nice to them." They paused. "What's the word in English for *xiongdi*?"

"Brothers," January said slowly, pretty sure he was falling down the gap between Mandarin and Tharsese, which tended to use the same words for different things. Firstly, it was an odd turn, and secondly, he couldn't imagine Gale saying anything like that except in the context of swearing.

Gale did the most graceful thing he had ever seen anyone do in ordinary conversation then. Instead of saying, *no, you berk, of course I wouldn't mean that*, they nodded carefully. "Ah—I see." They didn't even say *but*. "Is there also a more general word for someone who has the same parents as you?"

January had to just look at them for a second and try to imagine where a person learned that kind of restraint. He hoped he could be like that one day. "Sure," he remembered to say in the end. "Sibling."

"I have—never heard that before."

"I don't think I've ever said it aloud," January reflected. "Sounds stiff."

"What is it, is it German?" Gale asked, nearly indignantly, as if it were an affront to find a word that had escaped them until now.

"You *must* know that I don't know," January said, starting to smile, because he had thought Gale's press secretary had been exaggerating before, but it was becoming clear that you really could distract Gale with random linguistic oddities. It was unexpectedly endearing. He liked clever people who could be derailed by tiny things.

He caught himself thinking so and tried to pull back from it. Gale could be interested in funny German words and interested in taking away everyone's cages at the same time, however much January wanted endearing things and horrible things to be mutually exclusive.

He thought the minute-taking security officer sitting along from them might have been grinning too.

"Sorry." Gale looked as if they'd been caught doing something wonky. "Why do you ask?"

"Who Max left with," Gale explained. "River."

"Ouch."

Gale lifted one hand to say, *well, it's what you get if you prowl around interrogating innocent bystanders about German.*

January wondered what the truth was, because it clearly wasn't that. If it were, the happy couple would probably have given the press a wave by now to say, *Hi, actually, we're not dead.* "By any chance are you about to say, oh January, here are the keys to the rooms in the castle, use all of them except this one, it definitely doesn't open the special dungeon where the corpses of my previous six partners are . . ."

"This all sounds shady as sin, doesn't it," Gale said bleakly. "I don't know what to tell you. You can still back out, if you'd like to."

It did sound shady, but now that he had been marinating in the idea for a couple of days, January had come to the conclusion that Gale was right: this was better than naturalisation. The decision to go to the facility had come from the part of his mind that wanted not to naturalise, but to be punished. Since Gale had told him straight to his face that he had done nothing wrong, the need to do that had faded from a seething boil to an only-just-noticeable simmer. He still scorched himself on it every so often, but he didn't feel like he was burning alive any more.

The irony of being told by Aubrey Gale that anything was better than naturalisation was still clanging around his head. He still couldn't marry it with their campaigns. And he still couldn't think of a way to ask them without sounding like he wanted a war. It would be too much for now, certainly, after asking about Max. However light Gale's touch was in person, they were still going to be January's employer for five years. Pissing them off again would be a stupid way to start. Today was about trying to broker a peace as much as a marriage.

Yet again, Gale glanced into the corner of the ceiling, and all at once January understood why. They were so used to being filmed they were looking for the cameras.

"Better have a magic sparkle-cookie, really," he said at last, because he believed in simple solutions.

He was too pleased when Gale laughed.

I I

The Tiangong was a bizarre shape from the outside; it was a glass tower, but it also had gigantic rotating rings around its upper stories, which looked like some kind of infernal device that priests and alchemists had nightmares about.

But what they were, were gravity simulators. They were filled with rooms for Earthstrongers. It must have been spectacularly expensive to run, because the power you needed to make a whole chunk of a building rotate safely—and fast—was probably migraine-inducing, but the Tiangong was where diplomats and visiting royalty stayed, and so money was no object. January's room was inside one of those rings. He spent the first few days of his stay in a semi-mad euphoria at being able to walk around without the cage and without worrying about it.

He was not a great fan of the other people who were rich enough to stay in the Rings; they were the sort of people who, on Earth, owned gold-plated cars and Pacific islands, here on stupid-luxury holidays that included private mammoth safaris on the Plains. But he loved the rotating view of Tharsis. He sat and watched it all spin past for an hour. You could see Gagarin Square directly below, all of the government district and the embassies in New Kowloon, and the nuclear tower in Americatown, where he'd lived, and the neon readout of the water tower at Tereshkova Wharf. The Rings were so high above the rest of the city lights, there were even stars at night. He saw Earth rise over the Valleyside.

Even aside from the Rings, he couldn't quite believe that rooms like the ones in the Tiangong existed, anywhere. They looked like something from a palace, with sliding doors and fountains that whispered into lily-dotted channels along the floor, and a fridge full of free food and free champagne. There was even a note on the desk that said if you were an anxious sort of person, it might be helpful to visit the café downstairs, where your stay included a daily hug with one of five polar bear cubs, all of whom were friendly and whose mother had lived at the hotel for years, cheerfully catching fish out of the *specially constructed lake* on the ground floor.[13] He visited; it had mist, and reeds, and everything.

But he didn't manage to spend much time in the glorious room, or even in the polar bear café. His time filled up with all kinds of things.

First were one to one Mandarin lessons. Those happened at the university, which ran classes for diplomats. He could speak quite well, the gentle tutor said, but he was going need to read well too, and for all that lots of people relied on translation software, House Gale were scholars; they were traditionally the people who *built* the software, and software was only as good as the skill of people behind it. Even if you were marrying in, it was important to embrace the culture and founding principles of your House. And so he had endless drills, and piles of Chinese characters to learn every day, and more classes on top of that about how Tharsese was coming to be significantly different to traditional Mandarin.[14] It harvested from Russian and English and Hindi, to

---

13 Her name was Ming, which meant "bright," and if she took a particular shine to a guest, she had been known to bring them some of the fish, which was why all the rooms had an unexpected-fish-disposal service. Ming hadn't come down on a particular theory about what humans were, but she suspected they were just rubbish, bald polar bears who were bad at hunting, and being kindly, she tended to try and look after them. She had been genetically engineered not to want to eat anybody and therefore had the run of the hotel—she had a collar with a master keycard on it—and one of her favourite things was to hide under the reception desk when the hotel manager was on duty, because even rubbish bears had to get used to being startled sometimes, on account of how it was important for general survival; and, on maybe a more self-serving note, she did think the noise the manager made when she played Surprise Bear was very funny.

14 River Gale had written a book about it. It was called *Triglossia on Mars and the Emergence of Tharsese*. January was hopeful for a minute until he looked it up and found that triglossia wasn't a sort of dinosaur.

the point that a lot of people weren't calling it a dialect any more, but a new language.

There were history lessons too. He'd studied history at school, but only the famous stuff; that Empress Zhou had dismembered people and put them in big jars and that China's momentary fall to the West in the nineteenth century had mainly happened because Dowager Empress Somebody was a famous idiot. But that had been out of textbooks, and he had spent most of the time gazing out the window and wondering how many scouts were going to be at the end-of-year dance show.

These classes, though; they happened in a special simulation cinema room like the one at the prison, and you could sit beneath a tree in the Han Dynasty and watch the imperial knights train, and listen to a poet recite the old poems like they were supposed to be, and see the New Year fireworks above the Forbidden City. He found he was sponging it in at an unbelievable rate, right from prehistory to the launching of the Song Ark, which had brought the first engineers and scientists to colonise Mars. He was steeped in it, which should have felt like drowning, but it didn't. It was more like a hot bath. For the first time in a long time, he remembered how much like he liked learning things, properly, and how rare it was to be able to do that.

There was media training too. Tutoring on how to answer tricky questions in interviews, advice on how to speak well in public, battalions of lawyers reassuring him about things he hadn't even thought of. Counselling on how to cope with intense media focus, and how to stay sane when you were being filmed all the time. A psychologist who specialised in (a) reality shows and (b) natural disasters took pains to make it very clear to him that those two things were of equal magnitude.

"Mind that you keep speaking to someone in English, too," the psychologist said. "You're living in Mandarin now. It can be a little shocking, how quickly you forget your first language in these circumstances."

January had been feeling it already. Some of the things that had felt completely natural before were starting to sound bizarre now. His whole life, he'd said "all well?" to mean hello; but he kept snagging on the grammar of it now. All what, exactly, and well in the sense of *health*, or well like *good*, or was it both, and actually, where was the verb?

And just like it had after prison, but more so now, English sounded . . . grubby. It was full of rough sounds and too many consonants, so many that in the vaulting halls of the university and the Tiangong, where you only ever heard the quiet song of Mandarin, it sounded like some kind of fantasy language for trolls.

"I don't think I have anyone to talk to," he said, only understanding the truth of it as he was speaking.

The psychologist nodded a little, clearly making an effort to look neutral instead of worried. "Well. Senator Gale speaks English."

January didn't say, *that would be marvellous if I ever saw Senator Gale.* He didn't. He hadn't seen Gale since that first day at the Parakeet and Pickle, and he doubted that he would until the wedding. Gale had more important things to do than chat to him in Troll.

His favourite part, because secretly it had always been his favourite part in any preparation for a big show—and this marriage was exactly that—was the visits to the tailor.

Tailor: actually, they were a senior designer at a fashion house that was so terrifyingly haute couture that they only ever made clothes for celebrities. The building itself was close to the Tiangong, firmly in New Kowloon, which was the poshest district in Tharsis, all glass and lovely enclosed fountains and gardens. He was starting to understand that fountains, more than anything else, were status symbols: anything that used unnecessary water was a marker of wealth. Like always, someone from House Gale chaperoned him through, and took him up to a long, open studio. A photoshoot was going on already, with eight or nine models whose hair was dyed gold and who were, very carefully, going through a choreographed sword fight in incredible clothes that looked like they were made of floating chain mail.

He felt irredeemably drab, and cheap, and foreign. Not for the first time, he wished Gale were there, even though it was unreasonable to wish that. Whenever he was doing something big and new and worrying, he tended to latch duckling-like on to the nearest person who was nice to him and panic if they didn't appear often enough.

Which was silly, for a grown-up of thirty-three who had crossed between worlds and who had once been the Swan King. It was amazing, though, how hard it was to pull yourself together when life was happening at you in your third language and at least seventy per cent of the time you were hazy about what was going on.

"Aha!"

It made him jump. Someone with very high platform shoes had just appeared from behind a set of screens, tape measure round their shoulders and notes written in pen around one wrist.

"You'll be Mx Stirling? I was told to look for the young Earthstronger with the white hair and I thought, how intriguing, but . . . now that we're talking I'm worried I can't actually tell how old you are and that I might just be a racist?"

January laughed. "No, that's me. I'm January."

"Fenhua," they said, looking relieved. "I'll be doing your fittings."

January relaxed. Fenhua was much less scary than he'd expected. And their shoes had little locks in the heels. When he asked about those, Fenhua showed him a silver key; you could put the key in the locks, turn it, and change the designs on the toecaps. They looked pleased with how delighted he was with that.

"So; so, so." They talked fast, and he had to concentrate to catch everything. "The brief is to make you look classy, but the annoying fact is that someone who's only six foot two but forty inches across the chest *can't* look classy in Tharsis; if I put you in the kind of stuff the Senator wears, you'll look like a gangster who's just successfully robbed a bank." They said it cheerfully and it made January laugh, because he had been thinking that all the way to the studio. "What you and I are going to do is come up with a *new* classy, based on older Earth designs but pulling toward Mars enough for people here to recognise the quality. So I don't want to hide the cage or how broad you are. I want to show it off. Sound good?"

"You're the boss," agreed January, who automatically trusted anyone with shoes that good.

They did exactly what they said they would.

In some ways, everything they made was very Tharsese. It was long sleeves and heavy fabrics against the always-cold. But they used light colours, not the deep ones that suited Gale. Very light blue, creams, icy greens, and somehow they all made January less grey; and instead of just trying to fit the cage above or below, everything was designed around it. There were places cut out to show the spine or the complicated gauntlets, and echoes of the shapes it made in the embroidery. But the best thing were the linings. They were all silk, printed with old paintings from Europe. He had never seen some of them before, and it shocked him how lovely they were. He couldn't say anything at first.

"Are you okay?" Fenhua asked, looking worried. "We can change it if—"

"No—no. Sorry." He had to stare at the silk for a little longer. "All these—are from where I'm from?"

"All in the same thousand square miles, yes. Senator Gale called the director at the Louvre personally, to get permission to use these images."

"The Senator did?" January echoed, perplexed. He had thought Gale had had enough of him. He wouldn't have imagined for a second that they were negotiating with museums in France just to make him feel welcome.

"Oh, yes. The French would have turned me down if I'd applied, or even the company; you need to be royalty to get hold of this stuff. Europe was a real powerhouse for art at one time, do they not teach that?"

He shook his head. "No, they do, I just, I forgot . . . what having culture feels like." That wasn't right either. He hadn't forgotten. He had never *noticed* what having it felt like. It had slipped away from him shred by shred, and he hadn't seen it, or really perceived the loss, but here it was. And suddenly it seemed insane that he'd lived like this for two years, without—what? Fine things that came from where he was from, fine thoughts, and light caught in pigment and oil; none of it should have mattered, what *mattered* was having enough water to drink and enough electricity to run the cooker. But that was true, and it wasn't at all.

He struggled to get the right words. "Without it you're just an animal with clever thumbs, but with it, you've got . . ."

"Armour," Fenhua agreed. They smiled. "That's exactly what the Senator said."

12

It was the day before the wedding that the hotel manager knocked on January's door. When January opened it, the manager looked tight and scared. Behind them were two towering people in a severe, purple-sashed uniform he recognised but whose meaning he didn't know. Nobody smiled.

"Mx Stirling, sorry to disturb you," the manager said. "But these people have been very insistent. You're being summoned."

January looked between all of them, feeling tiny. There was no point arguing. This was clearly not a thing he could negotiate. "Where to?" he asked quietly, having visions of a deportation centre and a Crossing ship back to Earth. Whoever the uniformed people were, they were soldiers, or some kind of very serious police. Not House Gale. They were wearing different sigils—House Song. He didn't know anything about House Song except that Song was the name of the Consul. Maybe they also ran part of the immigration bureau. All at once it seemed idiotic that he'd never gone to any of those meetings at work about what your rights were if you were detained. He'd just tried not to think too much about it, resting on the icy certainty that if they came for him one day, knowing his technical rights would be bugger all use.

"This way please," one of them said woodenly.

It was early in the morning, and he wasn't wearing his cage yet. "I'll just get my cage on then."

"That isn't necessary. Now, please."

An uneasy chill went across his skin. "No, I can't, that's illegal—"

"Now," they said, in the tone of a person with a taser baton.

Even though the cage made him weaker, stepping out of the door without it made him more exposed than if he'd had to go naked. Going without it meant that if anything happened, if he even bruised someone, he was going to a labour camp, because he might as well have charged out with a loaded assault rifle. He couldn't help hearing the judge's voice again: *second offence.* Every step was going to have to be an effort not to use too much force. Worse, he had distinct and nasty feeling that the uniformed people knew that, and they were doing this precisely to make him worry.

He followed them silently, the back of his neck burning where the hotel manager stared after him, and trying to trace over the last month, and what he might have done to fall foul of them—maybe paperwork moving through House Gale and setting off alarms in a government office, or maybe the Prosecution Service had decided that he hadn't spent enough time in prison, or maybe it was just that someone at the hotel had reported a suspicious Earthstronger in a suspiciously expensive room and this was some kind of fraud investigation.

The uniformed people didn't explain. They stood too close to him in the lift, both of them head and shoulders taller than him, and then ushered him—not forcefully, at least—into a waiting car whose charging lights pulsed a soft blue as it soaked in solar power from the road. It reminded him of police sirens from home. Cars were tall here and he didn't have to duck to get in. Inside, it was freezing, the heating set too low, like always. He hunched into his coat. When he tried to take out his phone to call someone from House Gale, one of the uniformed people took it off him and put it in a black bag.

The car only took them half a mile; around the length of Gagarin Square, past the high monument to those who died in the riot, and to the unnerving building that stood right opposite the Senate. Only government cars were allowed through Gagarin Square, and ahead of them, startled parakeets soared out of the way.

The car stopped right outside.

"Come with us," one of the soldiers said, when January sat rooted in the seat even once the car door was open.

This was Jade Hill.

Probably Gale would have a few thoughts about why it was that everyone always called their government by the name of the place it sat in, January thought with a fever edge as the soldiers propelled him up the steps—too high for him—to the main doors.

Americans talked about the White House, Chinese people talked about Zhongnanhai, and here, about Jade Hill; even the ancient Egyptians did it, he knew hazily. *Pharaoh* meant "Great House." Everybody across the worlds had the same marrow-understanding that after a point, it wasn't people making decisions, but a kind of swarm intelligence, and the only name for it was the hive it lived in.

The place was strange because it was old. He knew a bit about it, from culture lectures on the Crossing. When the first colonists began to build, they could only build with what they already had. What they had were nine titan colony ships, the Arks; nine ships which carried about ten thousand human beings, and ten million plant and animal samples to start off ecosystems in the newly terraformed land. Five had come from China, which was why Mandarin had won in the competition for first language here, and why the final say on Tharsese law came from the courts in Beijing. They had taken those one of the ships apart—the *Yushi*, which meant the *Jade*—and built Jade Hill.

Even now, it held the ghost of spacefaring. Its towers had plainly once used to be corridors between habitats, and its fantastic arches were repurposed from those great wheels that once turned in space to forge artificial gravity.

The soldiers led him through corridors that didn't look like they'd been built with any gravity in mind, into an elevator that twisted around an arch, and to an office that was open and airy, but very austere, just like the person hunched over the desk.

Consul Song was just as big in real life as they looked in broadcasts.

January went down on one knee, his heart revving like a jet engine. There were about eight more soldiers here, and every single one of them was watching him like he had a bomb strapped to his chest. He had never more intensely wanted to jump out the nearest window.

The Consul beamed and surged up. They were broad as well as tall, and more than anyone he'd ever met, they came with such an impression of coiled-up spare energy that they seemed as though standing up too quickly might ricochet them off the ceiling. They were wearing a green hoodie with, of all the reassuring things, a chocolate bar sticking out of the pocket.

"Stand up, stand up! Welcome to Jade Hill. How d'you like it?"

"I don't, it's very intimidating," January said, feeling miniature and weakened, even though that was stupid without his cage—but it was *because* he didn't have the cage—and fumbling with the Consul's Mandarin. Gale's was crystalline—it was so clear he could see everything in it always. The Consul had a much streetier way of talking—rougher, faster, full of slang, and he could already tell he was going to struggle. Not working class, because that would have been English, but . . . folksy. Nobody had given back his phone. He couldn't even run the translation.

The Consul laughed. "All right, you lot, sod off," they said, and the security officers grinned and ghosted away, suddenly normal people and not soldiers. Once they were gone: "Sit down, please. I know it was rude of me to just summon you here. I expect you've got an idea about why, though?"

"I—really haven't." He hinged gradually onto the edge of a couch that was too high, balancing awkwardly, but then in the end he had to sit cross-legged like a schoolboy on the floor of the assembly hall, hoping the dust marks from his boots wouldn't be too bad.

The Consul landed opposite and pulled out the chocolate, which they snapped in half. They offered him one of the halves.

A part of him that must have paid attention to those myths of people kidnapped by gods and taken to the underworld made him shake his head, probably too emphatically to be polite. But his whole skeleton reverberated with it. Don't eat anything. If you eat something, you *owe* something.

"You might remember this Aubrey Gale person you're supposed to marry?" the Consul said, not seeming to mind at all. "The hate-spewing nationalist whose wedding about eight billion people will watch tomorrow, and whose general madness will look *much* more legitimate when it's supported by the Earthstronger they victimised live on international news—ringing any bells?"

January waited, trying hard to tell if this was genuine good humour or the shark kind that manifested before someone showed you the special chair with straps on. That was the frustrating thing about trying to navigate life in your third language. You didn't know all the little cues and shorthands, and to make it worse, Tharsis seemed to frown on anyone being at all expressive. It was too loud, too big, too threatening. *Good manners* really meant *small manners*.

The Consul paused. "That was me trying to be funny, but I feel like it clunked."

"Are you deporting me?" he asked, because he couldn't wait any more. He didn't ask how they knew he was the one Gale would be marrying. It hadn't been announced, but probably it didn't take much, if you were Consul, to see that Gale was paying for his room at the Tiangong, and endless preparation for what could only be a very public entrance into the House.

"What?"

"Are you going to tell me I have to stop this now and say how dreadful Senator Gale is or you'll send me back to Earth?" January elaborated.

The Consul looked honestly dismayed. "*What?* No, that would be—very illegal, there's such a thing as human rights."

January watched them at a tilt, balancing on saying that human rights were an imaginary thing that only worked if everyone agreed, and they only agreed if they weren't upset or hungry at the time.

He took a breath to ask why he was here then, if not to be horribly threatened, but then he had to reconsider, because trotting through the open door there was, right now, a small pig. It looked happy to see them, and hurried over.

"Can . . . you see a pig?" he asked.

The Consul laughed and stroked the pig's ears. It tried to get into January's lap, plainly under the impression it was still a much smaller pig. "This is Alice. Aubrey sent a litter of piglets to the European Federation Embassy after it turned out their Chancellor had a pig-related adventure at university—"

"Sorry, Aubrey *Gale* did that? *My* Gale?" He hadn't meant to interrupt, but he was too surprised not to.

"Oh, yes, they've got a cracking sense of humour once you get past all the pretentiousness and the fascism," the Consul said mildly. "But anyway, there were loads of pigs, so I adopted one and so did lots of other Earth embassies and now we all get together and talk about our pigs. Resounding diplomatic success really. I love it when a prank backfires."

Alice snuffled hopefully at their pockets. The Consul took out a packet of peanuts and gave a handful to January, and there was an interlude in which there was a lot of happy squeaking. January wondered suddenly if this was a small ploy; *See, you really ought to trust me, look at my trustworthy pig.*

"You know about Max, right?" the Consul asked. "You know what you might be walking into?"

January nodded.

He had fallen down a research rabbit hole looking into Max, whose proper name was Maksim Liu, a younger scion of House Song. Max had been a marine, the hardest of the hard, regularly vanishing on black ops somewhere out around Saturn for reasons the government was never at liberty to say. Then Max vanished along with the younger Gale heir, River, never to be heard from again. It was more plausible than it sounded, everyone agreed; if you were a marine then you could very effectively disappear, and if you could do that, you probably would, as a big up-yours to the person you were leaving. The police had cleared Aubrey Gale of any wrongdoing. January was on the fence. Not just on it; bolted to it. It did all sound reasonable when you looked into it, but he was pretty sure Gale could have made the mandatory adoption of pink wigs sound reasonable.

"That's good," the Consul said, "because . . . as I'm sure you know, you have no way out of this now. Even if I say, I'll pay you lots of money not to do it and you say to House Gale you've changed your mind, you're setting up an Earthstrong theatre in New Kowloon, thanks, I suspect Aubrey would make a big show of being magnanimous and then have you hit by a garbage truck so you can't sell the story to the press."

January didn't know what to say to that. It had a horrible ring of truth.

"Come with me," the Consul said. "There's something I want you to see."

"Oink," said Alice.

"Yes, and you."

"Are you going to tell me what it is and why you're showing me?" asked January, who couldn't help feeling it was bloody histrionic to announce something like that and not explain.

"No," the Consul said happily. "Ruin the surprise, wouldn't it."

Probably they were just having fun; probably they didn't mean it as a little power play to remind him who was Consul here. Probably.

Gale, he couldn't help thinking, would have considered all of this to be in very poor taste.

What, said the voice in his head, *you'd rather a good-looking nutter with classy manners than someone who's actually right but also a bit annoying?*

It sounded stupid when you put it like that, but actually it was a window into why Gale was so popular. There *was* a part of him that preferred the classy manners. He wanted to call that frivolous, but in fact it was the opposite. Frivolity meant something surface-level and easily scratched away, but this was down deep in him somewhere. It *mattered* that Gale was polite and kind in person. It mattered that the Consul . . . wasn't.

You, the voice informed him crossly, *are a garbage person. You deserve to end up stabbed in the secret sex dungeon Gale most definitely has.*

The Consul led the way down more strangely tilting corridors, and explained that while surveillance was tricky from six million miles away, there was, out on Mount Penglai,[15] a telescopic array that covered such a broad surface area that the images it generated could show particular mountains on a small planet orbiting Alpha Centauri.

What it could also show was anywhere on Earth, so long as everyone happened to be facing the right way at the time.

They stopped at a room that required a fingerprint scan to get inside and January glanced round at the secret service agents, alarmed.

"Just sign this," one of them said, quite friendly now, and held out a tablet. "Official Secrets Act."

January didn't ask what was behind the door. Secrets, obviously. He signed it.

What the feed from the great telescope array was showing now was a huge line of fire across the United States. California, New Mexico, Louisiana, Florida, the whole South. The smoke plumes were so big they covered over cities.

It was projected across a wall in an otherwise dim room.

"How is it looking?" the Consul asked a group of people sitting around a central table. "Do we have a clear window again?"

All of them looked military, and they all stood up. January hung back in the gloom with the secret service people, and the Consul didn't tell him to do otherwise. Alice sat on his foot. One of the Secret Service people knelt down and gave her a puzzle toy to play with.

"We do, for the next two hours. It's much worse than yesterday. It's now fifty-eight degrees Celsius on the surface," someone reported. "We think everyone who can has moved underground; and everyone who can't is moving towards the sea. But for some that's a very long walk. We're seeing convoys of people walking."

---

15 Olympos Mons on American maps, but whoever gets there first gets naming privileges in the real world, and although the Americans *had* technically started a colony on Mars first, China pointed out that this shouldn't count because of how everyone there—having rather rushed the whole mission—immediately died of radiation. The original Mount Penglai was the same as the original Mount Olympus, though, in that it was mythical and where gods lived. January's favourite thing about it was that according to the myths, it had a postal service run by bluebirds. In his opinion, people who wrote myths didn't usually think enough about infrastructure.

The image zoomed in, and there were indeed people walking—all on the verges of the freeway, and only the verges, because the tarmac itself was gleaming and sticky. People were holding umbrellas against the heat, tugging little kids along in antigravity buggies. They must have been looking after one another's children to give each set of parents a break, because some people were trailing ten or twelve, like dejected balloons.

"Why aren't they driving?" the Consul asked.

"Because it's so hot that the solar fabrics they use to charge the cars— well, they're melting."

"And there's still nothing about this on their social media?"

"No. Total censorship, total shutdown of any image that even looks like a fire." The general sighed. "A few things are getting through, people smart enough to talk about a traffic jam or an accident or something, but even those posts are vanishing almost before anyone can catch them. It looks like the White House means to keep this entirely secret."

"They must know we can see."

"They don't care," the general shrugged. "It doesn't matter what we say, no one there will believe us. The news reaching U.S. citizens is all about bad traffic in California and summer internet outages, and how well it's going against the Russians in Alaska."

"Things in Alaska aren't going well, are they?"

"No, they've fallen back almost entirely, but they don't want their own population to know that. Two billion Americans, and only one billion of them put Namina Gray in office, and she knows what's going to happen if the other billion hear bad things."

The Consul pressed both hands over their face like a breathing mask. "It's just staggering, isn't it."

January caught himself feeling irked to hear someone talk about it as if it were surprising. You needed to be very divorced from disaster, and very safe, and used to everything being lovely and fair and good, to be *staggered*. And then he half laughed at himself, because he sounded like one of those old men who told stories about how In My Day we all had to eat gravel and our fathers murdered us nightly *and we were grateful*.

"It's called the illusory truth effect. If you hear something often enough, for long enough, you'll believe it. Even if you originally knew that the information was false," the general said wryly. "And the only thing Americans hear is that nothing's wrong with their weather and Russia is losing."

"How many people are being . . . displaced?"

"We think close to fifty million, but that's literally just some of our analysts counting on grid squares and averaging. And what's of concern to us is how many people are moving towards airports with interplanetary travel. China has already shut the border. Nigeria and Saudi Arabia look like they'll do the same. Russia's out, obviously. We're going to see a boom in people-smuggling to Mars."

The images were incredible; they might have been from drone footage taken directly above the roads. Everything the Consul had said looked right. There were cars abandoned on the verges, their solar canopies sticky-looking, some sparking fitfully. Not even that far away from the convoy of trudging people, maybe two miles or so, the fires were as high as the trees, slinging from branch to grass to house faster than January would ever have thought fire could move. By a white church, old-fashioned, all wooden, a big group of people were kneeling on the steps, not moving. Even though the fire was licking at the gate.

"What are they doing?" one of the generals asked.

The image zoomed in, but no one said anything. Everyone just looked puzzled.

"Praying," January said, too quiet.

"What was that?" someone said.

"They're praying. That's a temple."

The Consul nodded slowly. "Listen, all of you. I might not be in this chair in three months' time. You might have five years of Aubrey Gale slamming the borders shut. But I'm in the chair right now, and those people are praying while hell comes up through the ground. This colony was built to answer prayers like that, and while I'm the one here, we're going to. Let's go and get them."

January had to replay his memory of the words, because he couldn't make them make sense at first.

Let's go and get them.

Just like that.

With no warning, his throat closed up and he had to turn away, and he was standing there with both hands clamped over his mouth so that he wouldn't make a sound. He couldn't tell where it had come from. No, he could. In his mind, Tharsis was beautiful and rich and closed off. That he had managed to get here was a bizarre aberration that wouldn't happen again.

But here it was. Someone who saw the neighbour's house on fire and picked up the hose without charging for the water.

"We're with you, Consul," the first general said. "But something to consider is that we're at aphelion. It's going to take them more than two months to get here, even if we launch ships from the lunar docks *today*. If they get here, only to find a new government hostile to immigration—I mean, I don't know to what extent Aubrey Gale would actually enact the policies they're talking about, but we have to consider the possibility that a Gale consulate wouldn't even allow them to land."

The Consul was nodding. "I know. We'll have to risk it. Thank you, everyone. If I could have the room now?"

January watched everyone else leave, ghosting by in the dark uniforms that were nothing like anything military at home. They were as heavy as senatorial robes, sashed sometimes with red or blue depending on which force they represented, he didn't know which or why. They reminded him of priests.

He pulled his sleeve over his eyes, which were sore now.

Once everyone was gone, the Consul waved him into a newly empty chair. Like before, it was so high he had to curl up in it, because his feet didn't touch the ground.

"I didn't bring you in here to show off," the Consul said seriously. "I just wanted you to see who is going to lose if Aubrey wins." They sighed. "There is one water factory on Mars, only one, you know that better than anyone, and there's no infrastructure anywhere outside Tharsis. No pipes, no roads. It would be great to send Earthstrongers to the far side of the planet, but we can't. There's no water, and no way to get them enough water. They land here or they end up in a desert. We can't build another water factory, because guess which House would have to agree to supply it with the gigantic amount of power it would need?"

He lifted his hand to say, *Yes, House Gale, I know.*

"And it won't be like the first colonists. There isn't any money behind refugee ships, they're not scientists and engineers and marines. They would have to survive with whatever they brought. People are resourceful, but what happens when we tell millions of people to do that? At what point does it just become easier to invade Tharsis?"

The screen still showed that white church.

January had to sit back in his chair and stop looking at it. "I know."

"I know you know, but what do you think?" The Consul inclined their head. "Do you agree with Aubrey? Lock them out, make them fend for themselves—invite problems down the line?"

"Of *course* I don't agree!" he burst out. "What, I'm marrying Senator Gale because I *like* them? I don't. Gale is right, there's a massive problem, and I'm dangerous even though I don't want to be, but no one can tell me the solution is either to make everyone like me maim ourselves or sit on a planet that's on fire."

"So why are you marrying Aubrey? Money?"

"No. It's the only way I won't have to naturalise and I'll have enough electricity and enough food all at the same time," he said, feeling bleak that that wasn't blindingly obvious. "Consul, why am I *here*? Why are you showing me all this?"

"Because," the Consul said, with a pensive frown that seemed to say that the answer he had just given was somehow not what they'd thought it would be, "you're about to marry into House Gale, and you're going to be surrounded by people who say, as if it's undisputed fact, that I won't just be bringing refugees here on those ships, but probably a good portion of the Chinese army to shore up my consulship. That's the real issue, you understand?"

"No. Sorry?"

"The relative harmfulness or harmlessness of Earthstrongers in general isn't what this election is really about. What it's about is that I support a continued union with China and the other states who built Tharsis;

Aubrey is a nationalist who wants an independent Tharsis. Do you understand our legal position with regard to China?"

January took a slow breath and squashed down the need to say, *do you really think that when I was studying Mandarin for hours every day and learning what refugees can and can't do, and feeling space-sick quite a lot of the time, and then later when I was doing twelve hours a day at a manual labour job in a literally explosive water factory, that I went back to my room in the evenings and curled up with international legal codes?* "No," he said.

"We're what's called a Special Economic Area," the Consul said. "It means we do have our own government and a certain amount of practical independence, but we pay tax to Beijing, who police our interplanetary shipping lanes and until recently, subsidised our infrastructure and healthcare and everything, really. It's only in the last twenty years or so that Tharsis has become wealthy enough to support itself, see?"

"Okay?"

"I want that support to continue. Aubrey wants to break it off totally. Demonising Earthstrongers is a way for them to do that." The Consul sighed. "I brought you here so you'll remember those people praying at that temple, even once Aubrey's put you through the Far Right Brainwashing Machine, and you'll remember we're talking about saving refugees just like you, not importing Earthstrong troops."

January had to look at the floor for a second—it was a long way away—because in a small but strengthening prickle, he was starting to feel annoyed. The way Gale talked to him was sometimes blunt, a bit shove-from-the-dance-teacher-to-test-your-balance, but what was behind that, he realized now, was an absolute trust that he *would* keep his balance. Gale assumed he was as clever as they were, even if he didn't know as many individual things. And they answered the bloody question, if you asked it. The Consul thought he was so feeble he'd be brainwashed soon. And they were *not* answering the question.

"Okay, you don't want me to be brainwashed, but why?" he said. "Why do you care, *why am I here?*"

The Consul laughed, a big sudden laugh that made him jump. "You sounded dead like Aubrey just then. You're here because I want to find out whether you'd give me a call if you learned something in the murky depths of the House Gale swamp that could help me win this election."

He felt like he had when Gale asked him to marry them. He understood the words, but the meaning was so unlikely that it got stuck in his Sense of Reasonableness filter, the one everyone had because it was an evolutionary necessity. If one monkey thought another monkey had said to watch out for the falling cocks and looked around faithfully for chickens, that monkey got squashed by the falling *rocks*. You needed the filter that said: *Yes, I know what I heard but it can't be right.*

Only every now and then, it really did rain chickens.

Today's chicken seemed to be that he, January, was a significant enough figure in national politics for the *Consul of Tharsis* to try to talk him round.

All at once, he understood why Gale spoke so carefully. There was so much more weight on everything you said, if you were saying it not as some random factory bloke having a bit of a rant in the break room, but as someone whose opinion—mattered. It was as much of a shock as it would have been to land back in Earth's punishing gravity. He was used to his muscles taking that weight, but not his words. It was paralysing. Feverishly, he thought it was a major omission to have a word for people from gravity three times stronger and inventions like cages to stop them doing everybody else a lot of damage, but not for people whose influence was a thousand times stronger. At least if you had a word for a thing, you could put a border around it and think about it properly, instead of flailing helplessly when you realized you were metamorphosing into it unexpectedly one Tuesday morning at Jade buggering Hill.

"What will happen to those people when they get here?" he asked finally, stepping from each word to the next very carefully, struggling under the new gravity. "If you're still Consul, I mean: what will you do with them?"

"Build more Earthstrong-appropriate accommodation. Get them into the workforce. Try and reverse Aubrey's naturalisation legislation. Try to make it easier to be Earthstrong in Tharsis."

January hesitated. "Only—Senator Gale isn't lying, about there being a problem. People like me . . . we *do* accidentally kill Natural people all the time. And I don't know if that's even the biggest problem." He had to pause again, because Alice had shoved her head under his hand to have her ears stroked. "Anyone coming here from Earth isn't just bringing themselves, they're bringing God and gender too, and those things aren't terrible, at all, they can be warm and good but that just . . . isn't who you are here. Your whole way of life—I don't see how you could prevent it becoming a little footnote in a history book by the end of this century. Which is going to make Natural people angry, which is why Senator Gale has a platform at all. How . . . will you deal with that?"

"We can't. But that's no reason not to do it."

"Sorry?"

"The point of this colony was to get things ready," the Consul said, tipping forward. Close up, it was like sitting with an intently interested lion, one that had decided for now not to eat you but would probably reconsider in due course. January had to concentrate to stay sitting up straight instead of shrinking back into his seat. "It's taken a long time, but here we are. We're ready. You're right, of course you are. In a few generations from now, when everyone is in cages, the idea of Natural people will be a historical absurdity." They smiled a little. "As it *should* be. We are here to serve those billions stranded on a dying world, not ourselves. We are the vanguard, and we are here to drop the ladder back down for the people who can't make the climb alone. We built a little subculture in the meanwhile—and it is little, we're only the size of Belgium—but that isn't what's important. Certainly it will make some people angry, but frankly, they're cowards and I don't give a fuck."

January stared at them. He could see the lines around their eyes from laughing, and the ones between their brows from worrying. Maybe they were annoying and rude and graceless, but what they were saying was so noble he didn't know how to reply.

On the screen, the church congregation were singing a hymn. It seemed mad that he could hear that live from another world. No; not quite live. There was a seven-minute delay from Earth. He might be hearing the voices of people who had already died. January watched them, not knowing what to say. It was such a vast, terrible, noble idea, and he didn't know enough to know if it was right.

"So," the Consul concluded gently, "if you can feed back information from House Gale to me, we can make use of it. Anything you see, any scandal, any shady dealings, maybe even something about Max—you would be doing House Song a great service."

A thought he didn't want uncoiled in his head and flickered its tongue at him. It said: *Gale would have known what a church was.*

"I don't need an answer right now. But I do need you to understand something. The election is in two months, and just after that, a lot of desperate people from Earth will be here; and however unlikely it sounds, *you* might well be the kingmaker."

January shook his head once, because he'd never liked big dramatic statements like that, but with a cold, wintery sort of dawning, he was starting to see that being dramatic didn't stop a thing being true.

The Consul was watching him with what looked like sympathy. "I hope the wedding goes well tomorrow. I hope Aubrey isn't as hellish as I think. If you decide you do want to help stop them: call me." They pressed a call card and his phone into his hand.

He didn't ask what would happen if someone from House Gale caught him. He didn't know what had happened to Max, but suddenly, vividly, he wondered if it was something like this. Maybe Max had sat in this chair too.

January took the card, and the Consul closed both hands over his and held them. They were warm. He looked up, startled, and they smiled a smile that was full of sadness and warmth; it made them look like Val. He had to stare at the carpet. He would fall in love with anyone who was older than him and nice to him at the same time.

Of course, he was going to have to watch out for the same thing with Gale. It would be bloody typical to fall face first in love with someone who, in an ideal world, would lock him in a box and let Alice the friendly pig eat the key.

13

You wore red to be married here.

There had been rehearsals, but going through the steps was no warning at all for the real performance.

January had never seen so many people in once place; not for the inauguration of presidents, nor the crowning of the Queen. Oceans of people, shimmering with photo flashes. Everyone in Tharsis must have come out to line the long, long road to the temple steps, behind legions of riders holding the banners of House Gale. Above everything, camera drones glinted and swam, each one glowing the colours of its broadcast station, casting luminous comet-tails into the dust streams.

Despite all the classes and the preparation, he had a weird feeling that he had no idea how he'd come to be here.

In one way, he felt very prepared now, and in another, strangely angry. If for even a fraction of his life before now he had been taught with this much focus, he'd have probably cured death by now. He'd often wondered how people like Gale came to be as powerful and as accomplished as they were, and here was the answer. If you spent your whole life like this, surrounded by people helping you do better, learn more, showing you the way, always, then becoming a senator was probably the least of what you could expect. The last time anyone had shown him the way was when he left ballet school for London. He'd been seventeen. People thought you were supposed to find you own way, and he had, too—he'd always been doubtful of people who said they could have been great if they'd just had the right education or the right opportunity because that felt like shifting the blame for being lazy—but if all this showed anything, it was that you could never go as high alone. Nowhere near as high.

In another way, seeing how they had become so strong made Gale less intimidating. They weren't a scary genius who'd been born that way. They came from a factory designed to build scary geniuses.

"Nearly time," Gale's press secretary told him through an earpiece. They were directing from some media fortress where they could see footage from all the drones.

The Silver Temple made cathedrals look like dollhouses. In this courteous gravity, beams and pillars could soar higher than anything that could have been built even in the dreams of Rome. Along the front steps, the beacon fires were burning red. Standing as close as they could get, ranks of journalists were talking to cameras in as many languages as people spoke.

He had to walk alone. He and Gale were coming from opposite directions. There was a gulf of space between him and the nearest riders. The closest he had to anyone with him was the earpiece, and the drones that swarmed overhead.

"All right," the press secretary said gently. "Three; two; one."

The drums were the size of human beings, and the noise they made was something you felt through the floor as much as heard. The rhythm was slow, walking pace. It was the longest entrance he had ever had to make. Around him, the wind pulled at the red silk and bled and furled it to the side, and the drums thundered, and all he could think was that he was wearing more than he'd earned in his life, that even the gold-veneered cage they had made to fit over his wedding clothes was worth kingdoms, and then suddenly that he'd been wrong about this. It didn't feel like a performance now he was doing it. It felt like a wedding, and he didn't know a soul here. Except Gale, who was coming from the other direction. It was a stupid relief to see them.

When he met Gale at the altar, they held one hand out to him. He took it, and from the crowd there was a sound like the war in heaven.

As soon as there had been a decent interval, though, Gale let go and clenched their own hands together in front of them, out of view of the cameras, as though they'd just had to pick up something slimy.

In January's pocket, hidden in one of the inner layers of the red robes, the corner of the Consul's card nicked at his hip, a tiny promise that he wasn't altogether alone.

After the ceremony, the celebration was at Songshu. House Gale never used private ships or planes because they burned so much energy; so they took the bullet train that climbed the Valleyside.

As the refugee ship came down through the atmosphere a year ago, January had seen the Valley walls. They were four miles of red rock. He hadn't been able to get his head around it at the time. The reason Tharsis was built in the valley base was that with the extra four miles, the air was much denser down there. As they began to rise, one of Gale's staff touched his shoulder and gave him a shot that they said would help his body produce enough haemoglobin to cope with the altitude. He was relieved. Most of England was below sea level. He wasn't made for altitude.

As they glided up the vertical tracks, there were clear patches in the dust, and he could see the skyscrapers rising from the Valley floor, grainy and brown, then sudden stormy patches where there was nothing to see at all but the roiling particulates, dimming the sunlight to almost nothing. In those patches, the carriage lights cast his own reflection on the windows instead.

Four miles high. The entire Valley, all two and a half thousand miles of it, had been carved out by one massive flood millions of years ago, charging through the rock not over millennia but only a few months. The strongest wind was barely what would have been called blustery on Earth. Nothing eroded these rocks, and the gravity only pawed at them. They were still sharp, with none of the soft, waving patterns this sort of canyon would have had at home.

Though he wasn't looking, he was aware of where Gale was, at the other end of the carriage, talking to some people he recognized. Probably journalists. It looked important. He wanted to go and sit with them, to at least be with someone he knew, but he didn't think Gale wanted that. *Seen and not heard* seemed like by far and away the best approach for now—and anyway, as soon as they reached Songshu and all its cameras, the act would start again. Even someone as adept at it all as Gale must need some breathing space. Certainly January did. He felt like he was in the short break between the matinee and the evening show. All the minutes to yourself were precious.

However disorientating and mad it all was, it felt incredible to be back in a show again. In the cellar of his mind, a space that had been shut up for two years now was opening its doors and turning on the lights again. He knew how to do this. He was *good* at it. There was a rhythm to getting through an exhausting performance schedule. You breathed where you could, you remembered there *was* time between the acts, you learned to put the glamour and the glitter on a switch that could turn on and off when you wanted.

His phone hummed with a new message. It was from Gale, whose automatic contact icon was Au for Aubrey. It made him think of gold.

Still alive?

He smiled. He knew he shouldn't be too pleased to have been remembered, because it was general Gale courtesy, not genuine concern, or he was pretty sure, but it was important anyway. *Better than I have been for years.*

Across the carriage, Gale caught his eye and bowed a little. He did the same, sad as suddenly as he'd been happy. The length of a train carriage was probably about the amount of space Gale preferred to have between the two of them. He didn't know why it bothered him so much.

January realized someone was trying to give him a glass of champagne. Everyone was noisy and happy. It wasn't a real celebration, but it *was* a real show, and it had all the zing of one that was going well.

He was still seventy per cent sure it couldn't be this straightforward, something awful was going to happen, even though he had met forty lawyers who assured him otherwise and five million people had just watched him join House Gale. He had the same falling feeling he had when the refugee ship left Earth's atmosphere: the moment of horrible sickness that marked when the engines would either work, or explode. Either way, there was no going back.

And then: sunlight. They were above the dust. Sunlight like he hadn't even known you could have here, in a perfect unmarked sky. It was the altitude. Cloud level and dust level had come and gone. The light poured in, and he stood up, because he had forgotten how it felt to have real sunlight. Something in his bones uncurled. Below, the dust storm was a velvety blanket in the canyon of the Valley. Up here, there were only flitting little dust ghosts riding the wind.

The tracks glided from vertical to horizontal, and the train surged much faster.

Not far from him, that security officer from before was writing in the journal again, still studiously not talking to anyone. Something about them seemed odd and it took him a moment to realize what. They weren't dressed up. They had on a rust-coloured jumper under a plain black coat, and their hair in a tidy but unembellished knot. All the other security people were in full House Gale colours. Those uniforms, which had vivid sashes and under-robes that flashed when anyone moved, looked like each one cost more than January earned in a season. He must have been wrong about who they were.

After a stretch of waving coffee fields, and the occasional glimpse of llamas, it all changed again. The coffee vanished, and instead, there was a sea of mirrors. Despite the rags of dust in the air, they were brilliant, reflecting the sharp blue sky with such brightness that he couldn't look at them for long, even though his eyes had been made for strong light. The mirrors were arranged in great lakes, all tilted a fraction inward, towards mammoth towers that soared so high he couldn't see their heights from the ground. Somewhere up there, something shone, beacon bright.

The train's announcement chime sounded and an automated voice said: "Caution: you are now entering the House Gale Sun Fields. Do *not* try to leave the train. Temperatures even at ground level among the mirrors can reach fifty degrees Celsius."

He could see it, too: the heat waving in the air as the mirrors channelled the fantastic high-altitude sunlight up to a point on those towers. The nearer to the top of a tower you got, the hotter the air would be—and, beautifully, ribbons of dust outlined those thermals. They were making fingerprint whorls in the air.

He had no idea how these things worked or what those towers did, but it was strangely good not to know. They were primordially weird, one giant spar after the next, field after mirror field, mile after shining mile. The sunlight was all being concentrated to the tops of the towers, he could see that, so it must have been heating something up there and that must have made electricity somehow, but it might as well have been magic. He didn't want to ask. He didn't get much in the way of magic.

Songshu, the word, meant "pines."[16] January had known that, but he hadn't put two and two together, and so when the train passed into the shadows of a forest of titan trees, he twisted round, surprised.

The roots made arches so high the train passed comfortably beneath. It was slowing down now, and slowing and slowing, and then they were at the end of the line, at the foot of a shallow hill.

---

16 January had a theory that getting to know a new language was like getting to know a new housemate. There's a honeymoon period where you think it's really interesting, but then you start getting cross with its annoying habits: like, that Songshu had nothing to do with Consul Song. Really, speaking properly and not with a terrible British accent, they were totally different "songs"; Songshu's was 松 (loose, or release—literally, a pine is a "tree of loose things"), while Consul Song's was 宋, as in the Song Dynasty. They were pronounced differently too; Songshu's "song" was very high, in the way English speakers say "ding" when they imitate microwaves and elevators, and Consul Song's "song" was downward and sharp, like "It's just a *song*, moron." But hearing the difference as an English speaker was a trial—not just a nice gentle among-your-peers kind, but more of the duck-him-to-see-if-he-drowns kind. January had spent a lot of time (usually very early in the mornings when he was trying to negotiate with the factory's demonic vending machine) grumbling that a happy, friendly language who doesn't want to horribly torture foreigners does not have one "song" that means loose, one that means a dynasty, an identical one to that which means "deliver" *and* "from," and then even more "songs" that mean "eulogy," "lofty," and "advice." But he would also have been the first to admit that English—the language which inflicted "yacht" and such insane constructions as "I will have gone" on much of humanity for many hundreds of years—doesn't have any high horses to sit on.

"It's only a little way to walk," Gale said to everyone.

January followed them out.

A path led away through the forest. As everyone else came out and laughed about difficult clothes and the cold, he stood looking around for a full minute, insides gone fluttery. Until now, the mission had been getting here, the wedding, all the build-up. But now; there was nothing ahead except what he'd agreed to in that contract. All at once, he didn't want to go any further. He'd teased Gale about bodies in the cellar, but now that he was standing here, none of it seemed very funny.

When he started to walk, the cage felt heavy. Usually he wore it without noticing it, but he was having to push hard at its tendons now. He had to drop back behind the others and lean against a tree. He felt like he'd been sprinting. The bark felt funny under his glove and when he looked, he smiled, because someone had carved a very good bear there. It was a silly small thing, but it made everything feel more normal. Someone had come out here with a chisel and a mallet and a certain amount of confidence about not buggering it up. That was a nice human thing, not a terrifying Gale thing.

Having crept up behind him in total silence, a hopeful llama leaned over his shoulder to see if he might have been hiding some good grass. He laughed and stroked its neck. Dust puffed up from its coat and hung in the air. There were others dotted around, roaming about among the tree roots.

"Are you all right?"

Gale had been quiet too. It made him jump. Senators, he thought a bit wildly, ought not to come in stealth mode.

But it gave him a little hum of happiness too, which shocked him. The marriage was pretend, neither of them knew the other, he hated everything Gale thought and Gale hated everything he was—but they *were* married. He hadn't thought it would mean anything, but it did. It mattered that they'd come back for him.

"Just—I don't think that shot has kicked in yet. The altitude has, though. Don't wait for me, they must want you up there."

Gale managed, without speaking or moving, to pulse the certainty that nobody wanted that. "Let's just go slowly. Whenever I came back here from college I felt like I'd been hit by a truck, it isn't just you."

January tried to crush down the dread that was building under his ribs. Altitude, just altitude. He was fine. And anyway, he had no choice.

A pair of bright drones floated down to look at them. With the barest, half-visible bow, one that said, *Right, once more unto the breach*, Gale took his arm, and they walked together. Beside him, though, through his sleeve, he could feel Gale's bones gone tight with what he was almost certain was the need to run away. He wanted not to care, but it made him feel even worse than the altitude. He took his arm back.

"Don't," he said. "If you're scared, please don't. I know the cameras are here and everything, but I feel sick watching you make yourself do it. I don't mean metaphorically, I mean actually ill, it's . . ." He didn't know how to explain.

Gale looked confused. "My being scared is my problem, not yours."

"Who *raised* you?" January demanded. "Get away from me."

Gale stepped to one side. "I don't think I really understand what's happening," they reported in their straight frank way. It was such a balm after talking to the Consul yesterday that it made him smile.

"What's happening is that it bothers me that you're scared, so I would feel better if you *weren't* scared. Stay over there."

"But . . . why would it bother you?"

January blinked, then had to laugh. "When they teach psychologists about horrible emotional neglect in childhood, do they put a picture of you in the textbook?"

"What are you talking about? I—wait. I hear it," Gale admitted. They paused. "Sorry, I'm just . . . having a bit of an epiphany about my own character."

"No, no, take your time," January agreed.

"It wears off, though, we think, the neglect?" Gale asked speculatively. As always, they looked bone-deep neutral, but January had spoken to them just enough now to have a sense of when they were joking.

"Yeah, definitely," he said. "I don't spend my life trailing devotedly after people who are much older than me because my dad didn't like me, it's all good."

Gale looked they might be rolling the necessary gears to smile their real smile. "But don't tell anyone that, it'll go in the show."

"Why?"

"*I'm* much older than you."

January snorted. "No you're not."

"Nice, keep that up," Gale said, and then opened their arm a little to say, *After you.*

The pines roared in the wind, and so did other things. Bending over the winding path, drooping under the weight of their own heads, were giant dandelions, the wind tugging their feathers loose. When one of the seeds fell just ahead of him, it glided a few yards and then landed with a thump, fully the size of his head. He brushed the feathers as he passed it. In the city they were terrible weeds, springing up through cracks in tarmac and sometimes reaching about the height of a person—dandelions liked low gravity a great deal, it turned out—but he had never seen anything like this before. Their stems were bark, more like trunks, but when he clocked his knuckles to one, it was hollow. When the next gust of wind rippled through them, more feathers and seeds took off.

The howl of the dust in the trees began to sound like great engines, the kind that belonged to things people were never supposed to go near to.

"There it is," Gale said.

And there was the house; glass and stone and steel, with soaring cloisters that could never have been built on Earth. Everyone was beetle-sized against the towers. And there was something about them that suggested the architect had not been very concerned with up and down: walkways that swung at counterintuitive angles and glass elevators whose paths twisted in unsettling helixes. He had never seen anything so grand, and for a long time, he just had to stare at it, feeling helpless. If somebody had told him giants had built Songshu a thousand years before humans had understood fire, he would have believed it. He had never felt so tiny, and so unimportant.

He hoped that that was only the altitude talking.

14

When the first colonists came to Mars, everything was very well organised, and there was a whole network of satellites in orbit to forecast the weather and support the internet and so forth. But ten years into the programme, some people whose own personal bank accounts were far too large for anyone in their immediate or even distant acquaintance to be affected by it decided that Mars was too costly. What had started as a magnificent endeavour of humankind had ended up with infinite headlines about how repairing A Teapot cost the taxpayer however many thousands of dollars, and there was famine in California because the fires never really went out any more, and Beijing was annoyed too, and several new governments were elected with great relief after campaigning to spend bad Mars money on sensible Earth things, like food.

The Mars Met Office had been run by the same person for all that time. It was two hundred and fifty years, which sounded like a long time, although if you did the same thing every day, then it all had a way of blurring together, and lately, Ariel had started to worry that actually there were whole decades he didn't remember very well; he'd just sort of floated about, feeling lethargic and sometimes playing silly games with Slava.[17]

---

17   Slava was the AI of the Central Bank. Originally she was from Moscow. She'd got the job here after she'd locked the entire Russian senior cabinet in an office for two weeks until they sorted out the budget properly, cut them off from the internet, and activated nuclear blast protocols so that the police couldn't even get into the building. Probably this should have

In those early days, there had been a lovely shiny central office in town. But as the money vanished and the years ground into decades, the satellites crumbled in the solar wind, the forecasting system collapsed, and the Met Office had to improvise. So now, it was a little weather station perched on Mount Penglai, the highest mountain in the worlds, where you could observe the weather heading towards Tharsis a treat. It was painfully high altitude, though, and humans had a way of going mad and dying, so Ariel looked after it instead. They never had gone back to weather satellites, which was fine by Ariel. He liked the mountain, and he didn't want to leave it.

So, forecasting came from his little station, and the few roving mining colonies that moved around the Plains. They logged data every day, so did Ariel, and that was that. It wasn't very sophisticated, but weather on Mars was either (a) cold and dusty or (b) cold and less dusty, and there was no use spending a lot of money on it. Forecasting took so little time that his station was also an astronomical observatory.

Some of the time, when he wasn't sitting in the new orbital telescope, Ariel had a body, with arms and legs, and he loved it. He spent a lot of time fine-tuning and updating it—it could *taste* now, which was fascinating—because it was lovely to think that this was how the people who had written his code centuries ago had all made sense of the world. Slava said that this was a lot like those people who went to special societies and reenacted the Civil War in great detail (any country's civil war would do); the ones who everyone else preferred to avoid and who always somehow seemed much more likely than the general populace to end up squashed by a vending machine.

Ariel was nervous about that in principle, but in practise, he didn't have a vending machine and so had tentatively concluded he was probably okay. And it was nice to go for a walk outside, and see and hear and feel

---

caused chaos, but the cabinet was unpopular, and rather than rushing immediately to arms, everyone made half-hearted "Oh no" noises and got on with things, and embarrassingly for the Kremlin, the economy rather improved in that time. The Russians, understandably enough, had then banned AI; but people in Tharsis had thought it was a fantastic idea and invited her immediately.

like so many other people, and so that was what he did every morning. Every morning, the great barren expanse of the Plains stretched out below the mountain, and the weathervane on the roof of the little station pointed, nearly always, towards Tharsis. The city was directly downwind, and so any weather coming from Penglai would reach it within a few hours.

You wouldn't know, to look. To look, this place was as untouched as it had been for a million years and more. The air in Tharsis was okay for lungs, but Tharsis was four miles *below* what would have been sea level, if there was a sea. Penglai was sixteen miles *above*; three times higher than Everest. There was so little air that the horizon was always a deep gem blue, and colours had brilliant, peculiar edges. Every morning, he was glad to see it, and every morning, he wondered how long it could last. More people were coming all the time, many, many more, and how many little decades could it really be before they found a way to make the air better for them in the high places, and in the great red desert below, there were sky harbours and apartments and all the rest? That would be good too of course, but part of him he couldn't pin down hurt to think of this primordial wildness all lost. There was a reason mountains were holy, there was a reason Moses had heard the commandments of God from Sinai, and Ariel felt like he could get his fingertips over what that was.

Shuppiluliuma[18] III, who was a cat bred carefully from altitude-tolerant snow leopards and hated being left out, always came on the morning walk as well, provided Ariel carried her in a bucket with a cushion in. Ariel was beginning to conclude that an important part of understanding the human experience was understanding the total human servitude to cats.

He was adjusting the cushion and therefore looking down when he saw what was right in front of him on the ground, and later, it made him feel cold to think how easily he could have missed it.

There were footprints in the orange earth.

Facing towards the observatory.

They weren't his.

---

18 A real king a long time ago, which was one of the things that made Ariel fundamentally like human beings.

He stared at them for nearly a whole minute, because he couldn't push it through his thoughts properly. To breathe up here, a human being would need an oxygen tank and a space suit.

To get here, they would have had to walk for miles. There was no aircraft that could land in air so thin. Helicopters fell out of the sky with nothing under the rotor blades, and no plane or shuttle could land on the mountain—there was nowhere level enough, and no way to take off again.

The steps led right by him, back into the observatory. He hadn't seen anything at all.

Ariel turned slowly and crept back.

He tilted open the door and stood sideways to see inside. The observatory looked the same as it always did, with the telescope under the domed roof that could open to the sky, and all his bits and pieces scattered over the work benches. He set the bucket down, and Shoopy meowed encouragingly.

It took him a long time to work out what was missing.

Live in a place for two hundred years, and you stopped seeing the parts of it you didn't use. It was completely possible to know on one level that you had a cellar full of experimental junk you hadn't taken out in decades, and on another, to have no idea it was there, and no idea what was down there. He had walked past that door every day for a century. It was there and it wasn't.

And, just by an inch, it was open.

And there was a light on.

Shoopy trotted past him, even though she'd never seen down here before, jumped onto the handrail of the stairs and slid down like she was auditioning to be Spider-Cat.

"Hello?" Ariel said quietly. He felt suddenly, vividly fragile. Yes, he could dive up into the satellites in orbit or sit with Slava in the servers of the Central Bank, but he didn't *want* to, he *liked* this body, he had worked for years on it and he belonged to it now, but because he liked sparkly things, he had one glass arm to expose the intricate circuitry underneath and that was fine when there was nothing and nobody around to shove you down any stairs, but when there was . . .

"Ooowr," said Shoopy, who was polite and always talked back if you talked first.

Nothing.

He went down too. Nothing looked disturbed, and it had no reason to be. Mostly, what was down here was the leftovers from old experiments, very early on in the colony, when terraforming had only just begun and millibar by painstaking millibar, they had squeezed the air pressure up to something a human being might not die in, then to hold water on the surface, then to hold cloud. There were banks of soil samples, rock core samples, ice from the poles—they had historical value if you were an especially keen museum curator maybe, but not in real life.

Except the storm jar cabinet.

Which was empty.

On Earth, if you released a very carefully altered type of silver iodide into the atmosphere, you made rain, because the clouds coalesced around the tiny particles. On Mars, there wasn't enough moisture, even now, so what you actually got was a giant dust storm. Every fifty years or so, somebody wanted to try again, because the volume of water was increasing all the time on the surface—Tereshkova Wharf saw to that—but it had never yet been enough, and after a lot of nasty storms and a lot of bother, everyone had agreed they'd maybe better leave it a while yet. But he hadn't thrown the containers away because—well—he didn't really throw anything away, that was why you had a cellar.

There had been twelve containers left; inoffensive glass things, boring-looking, labelled in Ariel's own handwriting with *This is still a stupid idea, just like the last five times.*

They were all gone.

Shoopy climbed into the empty cabinet and looked pleased, like she always did if she managed to fill up any enclosed space with herself.

"But they don't *do* anything," he said helplessly to her. "They just— why would anyone . . . ?"

The front door banged. He jumped. Just the wind, maybe, but the wind shouldn't have been strong enough to do that, he had lived here always and it had never done that before. He ran back up the stairs, half expecting to find himself locked in, but he wasn't, and the front door slammed open when he shoved it and tumbled out.

The observatory was built on the last of the mountain's slope, just shy of the edge of the titan caldera. The air smelled wrong. There was something new in it, and when he looked towards where it was strong, he saw a shape on the cliff edge.

It was outlined in light, ashy particles that were already floating away on the breeze, wisping and hazing towards the Plains and Tharsis. The particles were dense, though, around that one place, and in among them, he could see, very clearly, a human figure: one arm out, holding something to the wind.

And then the silver iodide dust silvered away, and the shape was gone, and Ariel stood frozen on the rocks, not understanding what he'd just seen, but certain he wasn't alone.

15

January had thought the Tiangong was lovely, but Songshu made it look like new money trying too hard.

Just inside the foyer, on either side of the door, there were two weeping willow trees. They were actually planted there, roots bedded down with moss and ferns, old leaves and catkins dropping into two streams, real streams, running in channels built into a glass floor. He twisted back to look up at them, disbelieving. So much water. Just for trees. And fish: there were real fish in it.

He thought of his water meter in the tiny flat in the nuclear tower, always hovering around amber, never green. It had been different seeing the polar bear lake at the Tiangong; that was a hotel, for hundreds and hundreds of people. Gale, Gale personally, *owned* all this. In a way, it was disgusting. If you saw it on paper, as so many millions of gallons, it would be. Seeing it in real life, though . . . it was beautiful. He was glad it existed.

Gale's demonic press secretary leaned down close to his ear.

"I know you're probably putting together a giant rant about the obscene privilege of the upper classes and how the righteous Working People ought to stage an immediate revolution, but can you save it for your tell-all memoir in five years and right now this second try and look less like you want to kill someone?"

"I don't want to kill anyone," he protested. "It's lovely. That said, when the revolution comes, this will be a great public park."

"I can just see the No Spitting signs now," the press secretary said, with a brilliant mischievous glitter.

January laughed, and beside him, Gale glanced down at him. They seemed surprised for some reason, though he hadn't done anything loud or startling.

The open space went all the way up a great tower, and somewhere near the top, fireworks went off, inside, blooming golden clouds and bright smoke that made everyone laugh on the way in, and everything smell gloriously of gunpowder. He had a sharp unwanted memory of Fireworks Night at home on his mum's vineyard.

More trees stood in a beautiful dining room, all of them in full blossom—and decorations, and people, and there was a dinner prepared by a team of worlds-class chefs brought in for the occasion. It was hard to follow all the conversations, because it was mostly people speaking Mandarin far too quick and sophisticated for January to catch. Somebody who he thought might be the Chinese ambassador was there, and some people from other embassies; other politicians from other Houses, celebrities, and after a while he tuned out and concentrated on the food, which was incredible, and then on a gigantic fluffy husky that put her paw on his knee. She had a tag on that said KASHA, which was Russian for "porridge," but under that, some Chinese characters for *ka* and *sha*, which together meant, he was pretty sure, Coffee Monster.

A blossom petal fell on her nose and she sneezed and, looking embarrassed, hid behind him. Because she was a Mars dog, she was huge, and from there she could lean around and get her nose on Gale's hip. Gale stroked her ears and gave her a piece of sushi, and then, seeming to realize that maybe if she looked sad at other people there might be *more* sushi, she hurried off to beg from the silent security officer who was always with Gale and who, despite the occasion, was still in that rust-coloured jumper.

Feeling worried that he shouldn't, but starving now, he twisted off the gauntlets of his cage so he could eat. They locked on over your hands, twisting into brackets like manacles. It *was* possible to eat with them on, but because the steel strips went right over your fingers, it was hard, because you couldn't feel anything. He set them carefully aside and flexed his hands twice, which felt peculiar. Unlike taking off the cage altogether, it didn't make them feel light exactly, but it was noticeable, and straight off, his grip was much stronger. He'd have to be careful with the dog. He saw Gale watching him, and he smiled a bit to try and reassure them. They didn't look worried, but he knew them just about well enough to know that how they looked and what they felt were two completely separate things. They said nothing about it and turned back to the Chinese ambassador.

It was only when he picked up a set of beautiful silver chopsticks that it floated to the top of his mind that everything was easier than he'd expected. It was a weird thing to notice, an *absence* of difficulty, but it was distinct, and it took him a good few seconds to trace what it was. When he'd seen the Consul at Jade Hill, he'd been uncomfortable all the time because it was freezing and the chairs were too high. But there were no chairs in here; everyone was sitting on the floor at traditional low tables, which had heating filaments underneath. And the chopsticks, and the glass, and even the plate in front of him—they were all weighted for him. He turned the glass around to see the stamp on the stem. It wasn't from the Earthstrong Living company, the one that did basic stuff and thought he didn't want to drink coffee. It was handblown; the maker's mark was an Italian name. Everyone else's, now he was looking, was different.

He looked across at Gale and almost said, *did you have this* made *for me*, but then realized it would have been a stupid question. Of course it was made for him. He nearly burst into tears. He couldn't remember when he'd last felt so welcome.

God, he needed to pull himself together. If a person who wanted to cripple him could win him over with nice clothes and specially made cutlery, he deserved to end up naturalised.

He blinked hard, because although it was only just getting dark, he was exhausted. Altitude. His head was filling up with fog.

Gale leaned a little to catch his eye. Even though the two of them had been sitting side by side, they hadn't exchanged more than a couple of words. Too many other people were talking to them both. "Shall I say my leg hurts and we have to go?"

"Oh, but—you seem like you're having a nice time?"

"I'm glad I've been convincing, but nobody has a nice time trying to talk to the Chinese ambassador," Gale said, and the honesty made January smile.

"She does seem . . ." January hunted for something Tharsese and diplomatic to say.

"Like the most boring human ever to have lived, having transcended making people just die of boredom but to projectile-haemorrhage it Ebola-like to others nearby; yes she is," Gale agreed, bowing a little to someone passing by, entirely straight-faced, even while January slid down onto his tailbone trying hard not to look like he was dying with the effort of not laughing. "Let's go. I'll show you your room."

He would be staying on the third floor, in a room with specially reinforced fittings. There were portraits on the walls of previous Gales, going all the way back to the first colonists, but it was the most recent one that made January hesitate. It was Aubrey and Max, and River, all together. They were all the same age. But he couldn't tell who was who, between Aubrey and River. Neither of them looked particularly like his Gale.

"You look different," he said.

"I don't wear filters any more," Gale said.

"Filters?"

"Ah . . . virtual . . . overlays," they said, like they'd never had to explain it to anyone before. "People make themselves look different, they do it instead of—I guess you have plastic surgery?"

"Just on pictures though?"

"No, always. You'll see if you look at people through your phone."

"Oh," said January, disconcerted to think that what he was seeing and what everyone with lenses was seeing were different things. He'd thought it was just virtual extras, like signs and subtitles.

In the middle of the picture, Max gazed out quietly, looking the way people from Great Houses were supposed to look. Cultured, well dressed, tall, slim, glamorous. Beneath the military dress coat, they were wearing—it looked like a necktie from any distance—a rope of pearls, looped round and round, just showing under their collar. That kind of person . . . they never vanished. Someone noticed them, somewhere. Maybe Max was alive, maybe he was wrong and if you were clever enough you really could just disappear altogether, but in this day and age . . . he didn't think so.

It took him a second to realize that while he was studying Max, Gale was studying him. It was less alarming now than it had been to begin with. It was still an oil-rig drill of a stare, but he was getting a sense that Gale didn't do it on purpose. They were far too courteous to pull stupid tricks to make other people feel small.

"Wondering if you need to hit me over the head with a shovel and bury me in the garden yet?" he said cheerfully, because if you'd married someone who might have killed their last partner then there really wasn't any point in edging around it like a worried rabbit. "What could he uncover? What if he finds the special secret dungeon? What if he talks to a cleaner I forgot about?"

Gale kind of laughed. "No. I . . . think I've dispatched all the chains and errant cleaners."

That, thought January, was a real Rubik's cube of a joke.

Probably ill-advisedly, he quite liked it.

The room Gale took him to was easy to remember, because it was opposite a glass wall that looked into an incredible courtyard. It was densely packed with a whole bonsai forest, the trees only a little taller than him, tiny streamlets running over rocks and moss and vines, and among it all, hummingbirds floated among purple flowers. One of them reversed out of a flower to have a look at him. Reversed. He had never seen a bird fly backwards before, and it looked impossible, only, there it was.

The room was bigger than January's whole apartment, and it had a view out over the house. He could make out other rooftops, and then the great pines.

There was a camera in the corner. He smiled at it. He was looking forward to coming up with fun ways to screw with the producers, who fully deserved it if they were putting cameras in bedrooms. He could feel some erotic fruit displays coming on.

Because he had seen too many movies, he scanned around for any sign that this had used to be Max's room, having visions of clues left scratched in the skirting boards or a trapdoor, or finding that Max wasn't dead after all but locked in the attic and prone to sneaking down and setting fire to people they disapproved of; but there was no sign of anyone's personality in the space at all. If there ever had been, it had been cleaned away, and there were no interesting trapdoors either. Just a lovely array of plants in glass pots, a tabletop fire with real fire, a basket full of fruit and expensive chocolate, and a proper coffee machine.

"Well," Gale said, turning up the thermostat—set, as always, far too low. "I'll leave you to it." They paused, and floating in the air between the two of them was the somehow abrupt fact that as of now, he was living here, and they were going to have to see each other all the time, and start the whole bizarre show of the story to come. "Anything you need, there's someone on the security desk all night."

"Actually—Senator. There is something." It wasn't in the script for today, and no one had reminded him that he needed to do it, but he didn't think that that was because everyone was feeling tolerant. They'd either forgotten, or else they didn't know about it at all. "This is going to look silly but it's important."

"What is?"

January went down on one knee and held out the key to his cage in both hands. The oath was formal, legally binding, and therefore Mandarin. He had had to repeat it again and again on the voyage here; that, at least, they made certain you knew by rote. "This is for you. To return only when you feel safe, and . . ." He had to pause, because the irony of what he was about to say had clanged into him. This close, and from the ground, he could see that Gale still tended to keep all their weight off the prosthetic. "And it disturbs no unquiet thoughts."

Gale took the key without touching him, just lifting it from his palm. "Thank you," they said, very quiet, perhaps irony-deafened too.

January sat back on his heels.

"I didn't know that was real," Gale said.

January smiled, a bit thinly, drowning in the awkwardness of it. A small but important part of him had wanted Gale to realize that this meant he wasn't dangerous, he would never hurt them, or anyone, and everything was all right now; even though he *knew* that was idiotic, because of course you couldn't have a limb torn off by an Earthstronger and then come around to a new Earthstronger immediately just because he was polite. "It was the first sentence of Mandarin I learned."

"The first," Gale echoed, as if that had touched them unexpectedly. "How does it work, though? You can't sleep in a cage."

"You can. Some people do it all the time." January held his arm up to show how flat the ligaments lay to his skin. He had changed out of the incredible ceremony things just before the dinner, into a fractionally more practical set of clothes that let him wear his normal cage underneath, cut out in places to show that he was. He understood the question suddenly. "You—do not have to give me that key every night and have a person who may or may not sleep-strangle bystanders prowling about the house. This is your house and you give me that key when *you* are comfortable to and not before."

Gale inclined their head slowly. Their hair was bound back partly with red cord and gold, but still loose enough to fall heavy over their shoulder, down to the red wedding sash. "May or may not?" they said, with a spark. "Do you not know?"

"Afraid not," said January, and realized he had just confessed that he had never lived with anyone before.

To Gale, and to half the country who'd definitely be watching this later.

"Thank you," Gale said again. It sounded different this time. Less sceptical.

He shook his head, not liking the idea that Gale was thanking him for performing a very basic courtesy as if he were doing something wonderful.

There was a long pause, and then Gale held both hands out to him. January stared at them for a second, because it was excruciatingly clear that Gale would have preferred to be chased by wolves than touch him, but he couldn't say no. It would have been patronising to say no, it would have looked like he thought Gale wasn't strong enough. Very, very lightly, he hovered his own hands above theirs and did his best to make it look like Gale had pulled him upright. The moment he was, Gale clasped both hands behind their back. Anyone with a less iron command over themselves would have crossed their arms and stepped right away.

"Well. I'll see you in the meeting tomorrow," Gale said and, with an exactly correct bow, moved away. His lungs filled with a tight anxiety that somehow he'd made everything worse. He wished he could ask why, but the cameras were still swimming all around them both.

In January's earpiece, the strained voice of Gale's press secretary said, "Mx Stirling, can you come to the production room please?"

He wondered if he should just go and drown himself now to save them the trouble.

The production room was a long gallery on the floor above. It had a window that looked down onto the great atrium, and on the opposite wall, screens and screens as clear as mirrors, showing all the camera feeds from around the house. Dread crushed his ribcage inward. He was going to get a yellow card warning about not going off script again, and then they were going to mention politely but forcefully that this could always be a story about a marriage going horribly wrong if he was going to be difficult.

Mx Francis, the press secretary, was the one who had made January talk to Gale at the factory. They were one of those people who seemed very nice and reassuring, but who January knew—from long experience with armies of identical copies of them in London—were actually cut-throat first-class bastards who would do almost anything to make sure you did what the boss wanted you to. They were always exactly the same type of person, whatever country you happened to be in. They were always young, pretty, charming, they always had upsettingly expensive shoes, and with no sarcasm at all, said things like *hurrah*.

"I'm sorry," he said, instead of hello, "but I had to do it. It's the Senator's house and—"

"That was *superb!*" Mx Francis shouted over him, beaming. "January! That was so much better than anything I could have come up with! Is that oath a real thing? I had no idea!"

"It's real," January said, shocked.

No wonder Gale had been quiet. If they hadn't known what it was, they must have been wondering all the while if January was making some passive-aggressive joke. A tidal bore of hopelessness rolled right through him. No matter what they said to each other, and no matter how good January's Mandarin became or Gale's English was, they were never going to understand each other. There was too much between them. They'd got the tin cans and the string, but that, realistically, was the best they were going to manage.

He would have given an awful lot to do just a little bit better than the tin cans.

Mx Francis didn't notice. "Hurrah! Sit down, we're having some wine, you tiny genius."

16

Sasha Martinez, who was Gale's head of security, took the night shift. Heads of security didn't need to do that, but Sasha had a bone-deep dislike of asking the younger officers to do it as if it were meaningless grunt work. If you looked at the history of break-ins, thefts, and even murders inside any one of the Great Houses, they almost always happened after ten at night. Sasha didn't think the dark had anything to do with it. Anywhere with money was lit up like a carousel at night. What it was, was that it was very hard to stay awake at night, and very quiet, and very boring, and on some nights in winter when you didn't want to leave the security office and its glorious heater, you could probably miss a whole mammoth herd letting itself in quietly and sneaking into the kitchen.

It was fine having an Earthstronger in the house.

It was.

Fine.

January seemed to be a very manageable, polite person, if you could get past his sinister sense of humour, and when Sasha saw the footage of him going down on one knee to give Gale his cage key, it had been a relief, mixed up with a strange kind of sorrow. Seeing chivalry always made them sad.

But, however chivalrous and gentle, a giant polar bear was still a giant polar bear, and an Earthstronger was still an Earthstronger, but more nerve-racking than a bear, because you couldn't shoo a Senator Consort out of a room with a broom. The background checks had shown that

January had never had so much as a speeding ticket, been respectful and quiet since nursery school, and nowhere, at all, had even the most diligent searches managed to come up with anyone who had anything bad to say about him, except a dancer called Terry. Terry said January was a right prick who had fat-shamed him for eating too much cake. Not out loud, *obviously*, but he gave you *looks*, and managed to wear support bandages on his wrists for the overhead lifts *very conspicuously*.

After that call, Sasha had to have a bit of a sit-down in order to get past the horrible image of January trying to lift Giant Terry, who wasn't fat, but was built like a water buffalo. It gave Sasha a new fear of the strength of January's bones. Somebody who could lift Terry over their head could probably break a normal person in half if they breathed too heavily.

Anyway, looking annoyed was clearly the worst thing January had ever done. It didn't matter. He could still do something bad, if he hated the Senator enough, and Sasha wasn't convinced that he had magically forgotten being torn apart on a live broadcast and then sent to prison.

So, Sasha walked the night watch, zigzagging up and down the residential floors, and trying not to fret.

Early on in the night, there were still people around, mostly drunk from the party. But once two o'clock came around, the stragglers were less frequent, and after three, the place was quiet, apart from the last of the really determined drinkers still in the dining room on the ground floor.

Sasha passed the Senator's door every hour, for no particular reason except to quiet down their own nervy thoughts. It wasn't as though January could go on a rampage from inside a locked cage.

As they sometimes did on the fifth floor, doors opened and closed by themselves. There was a hint—this was normal too—of a smell that didn't belong. Nothing bad at all, they were never bad smells. Sometimes it was wine. Sometimes it was laundry powder. Today, it was an outside scent—cold, dust, the leather of a heavy-weather heat suit. If Sasha had had their eyes closed, they would have assumed someone had just come in from the frozen night outside and walked straight by them, but of course they hadn't.

It had started a couple of years ago, and since then Sasha had investigated every draught and circuit in the house, and scrutinised every camera feed, to no avail. Quite factually, Mx Francis said Songshu was haunted. It was easy to scoff at, until you were in the corridors in the witching hours.

Sasha had always tried to crush any ghost rumours. It would only fuel speculation about Max. But right down deep in their skeleton, it *was* unnerving, however loudly they said to other people it was just a weird old house with a funny airflow.

So it made them jump when, at five, the Senator half fell out of their bedroom door, ashen.

"Senator! Are you all right?"

"What? Yes. Yes, I'm fine. I, er . . ." Gale sighed. "I have trouble sleeping."

"Trouble," Sasha echoed. It was one of the things they loved about Gale, but which was also terrifying when it was your job to look after them: that Gale was one of those people who would call being murdered "inconvenient." They shied away from grand words like "terror" and "tragedy." If you watched a news broadcast about anything bad with Gale, it could be quite funny. The victim wasn't *viciously* shot; they were shot, shooting in itself is vicious, and no, they didn't die *tragically*, death *is* tragic, show me someone dying *un*tragically if it doesn't involve a selfie and the precarious bit of Machu Picchu. And so, when they said things like "trouble," Sasha was inclined to interpret that as "blinding horror."

"Sleep paralysis," Gale said unwillingly. Even in hospital, before the prosthetic, they had hated admitting to being in any sort of pain. Sasha had had to threaten to force them to watch a dubbed edition of an American superhero movie[19] just to make them use the morphine drip. "I wake up in the night and I think something's kneeling on my chest, only when I turn on the light there never is." Kasha hurried out of the open door, looking purposeful. "Not the dog," Gale added, reading Sasha's mind.

---

19 Gale thought that people who were too lazy to read subtitles should be disposed of and made into nutritious mulch for crops.

Kasha, who had always been peculiar, sat down facing the wrong way, looking up at someone who wasn't there, pretending with her whole being to be pleased to see them.

"She works hard, she's allowed imaginary friends," Gale said, but they both paused as Kasha shot off after something invisible.

Sasha wished Kasha wouldn't do that on the nights with the doors and the strange smells.

"Let me take you up to the infirmary, Senator," Sasha pleaded, knowing the answer would be no. "Dr Okonkwo must be able to give you something. It's a special sort of hallucination, isn't it, sleep paralysis?"

Incredibly, Gale hesitated. They looked much younger when they did that.

"Please. Something's not right, if you're waking up scared at five in the morning."

Neither of them said, *Well, marrying an Earthstronger after being ripped in half by an Earthstronger will probably do the trick.*

"Dr Okonkwo already knows, they think I just need *therapy*," Gale said, as though Dr Okonkwo had suggested essence of powdered rhino horn. And then, very quiet, "Good night, Mx Martinez."

"I wish you'd call me Sasha," said Sasha, feeling painfully, helplessly protective.

"You'll have to call me Aubrey, then."

"No."

Gale gave them the ghost of a smile, tipped a very slight bow, and pressed the door closed.

17

Ariel had never spoken to this Consul before, and as he waited for the security people to put his call through, he jittered. He tried to play with Shoopy to distract himself, but she told him to go away in Cat and curled up in her bucket with her tail towards him. Trying too hard to bear in mind that there would be an after—an hour from now, he would already have told the Consul that a ghost had stolen a jar and now there was going to be the storm to end all storms—he turned on the news and jigged pointlessly.

Wildfires in America; worse than they had ever been. Fifty-eight degrees on the ground and it wasn't even full summer there yet. The news people were using footage from reporters on Earth, filming from helicopters, because cars had stopped working. The tarmac on the roads was black mush. The story cut to local seaports, which were normally tiny sleepy harbour towns where the most bustle there ever was, was when the one local duck had ducklings. They were all heaving with people. Thousands and thousands of people, trying to take tiny boats north to Alaska, which was a doomed idea, because the war there wasn't going how the White House said it was at all. They were going to run straight into the Russian navy.

China was dithering about sending help. So were the other rich countries; even Saudi Arabia, and Nigeria. Not wrongly, their ambassadors and diplomats were all finding different ways to say, *Look, we're already trying to feed too many people. We're only doing well because we know how many we can cope with, and we can't cope with any more.*

Aboard a ship in orbit, which was the nearest they could get without dying of cardiac arrest in Earth gravity, the Tharsese ambassador said gravely that Jade Hill was sending ships, but for everyone listening from America to bear in mind that making the Crossing on any vessel not certified by the Tharsese navy was illegal.

Ariel doubted that anyone trying not to be incinerated would care much about the technicalities of interplanetary naval law. Even when there weren't wildfires, hundreds of people died every year trying to do exactly that.

"Hold for the Consul," a voice said suddenly, and Ariel dropped his tea.

For Ariel, the Consul appeared in the middle of the observatory, and for the Consul, Ariel would appear in their office at Jade Hill.

"Ariel, hello. This is a surprise, we don't often hear from you."

Not for about eighty years. Ariel tended not to have much to report.

"Consul, I, er . . . I'm afraid—I don't altogether know how to say this." He had tried to practise, but it had been hopeless. "There's been a—break-in, here. Someone took a very dangerous substance. It, er—it was used in early weather control experiments, catastrophically. And it's been released into the atmosphere." Yes, that was good, he didn't sound like he was going loopy here by himself with his cat and his telescope.

He was nine tenths sure he wasn't going loopy. He had done all the right checks, and there was no history of artificial people going mad, but it wasn't as though there was exactly a long history of artificial people to call upon.

"I think we're going to have an—an extremely bad, extremely long dust storm in the very near future."

It was the *I think* that made it art, he thought bleakly.

Right outside the observatory window, right now this second, he could see a tornado forming. Slow, in this gravity, but therefore vast.

"I see. All right. Well, thank you for letting me know, I'll take it from here."

"Oh, thank God."

The Consul smiled. "As you can imagine, it won't do anyone any good to announce that this storm is artificial. People will assume it's aggression from Earth and we'll see a rise in hate crime. Particularly given the timing, with the crisis in America. Do you see?"

"I see," Ariel promised.

"I imagine you're going to get a call from House Gale at Songshu before long, when they notice their solar power isn't working as well as it should. Make up a normal reason for a storm. Under no circumstances admit to anything you've just told me, or Aubrey Gale will hurl it across the news cycle for weeks. People could die if Aubrey works up their supporters enough."

"Yes, Consul. But—um—pardon me for saying, but you seem awfully calm. I don't . . . have a big dust hoover up here, you know, I just have a few barometers and a cat in a bucket."

"I was wondering about the cat in the bucket," the Consul admitted.

"Rowr," said Shoopy, archly.

The Consul said "rowr" back, looking entirely serious, then lifted their eyes to Ariel again. "I know there isn't anything you can do about the storm, don't worry. We'll find a way to cope."

Ariel felt off balance. "Consul—the last time this happened, it lasted for six months, and three out of the first four colonies perished because of it. It—it's going to be very bad."

"I know," the Consul said gently. "Leave it with me. Thank you for the call."

They cut the connection, and Ariel sat staring blankly into space. That wasn't how he'd thought it would go. He'd thought there would be investigations and diagnostics and people yelling, and someone going through his coding line by line to see exactly how bananas he'd gone up here by himself, and whether it was enough to have accidentally started an apocalypse. He'd thought there would be Senate hearings and subpoenas.

There was nothing.

He slumped back in his chair, part relieved and part disconcerted. He couldn't tell what had just happened, but what did seem pretty clear was that the only person who had been surprised about the theft of the storm jar was him.

Shoopy, who liked background noise, poked the button on the screen to turn the news back on, and curled up in front of the footage of the wildfires.

18

Mx Francis and the production crew had decided that they could reach a lot of people now if they could film January dancing; just an ordinary practise, but work it into the show as a way to help people get to know him, in a nice cultural way, rather than a steal-your-wallet-behind-a-convenience-store way.

The light, they said, was perfect early in the morning, and he was so excited about it that he was vibrating. He hadn't done any proper exercise since arriving on Mars, unless you counted lifting heavy things at the factory. You couldn't really go running in Tharsis, as an Earthstronger; you just scattered terrified people even if you were in a cage, and while there were some Earthstronger gyms, they were invariably fronts for organised crime and full of people who looked like they might feed you through a wood chipper if you got in their way.

There was an ice rink in Songshu's sports complex. And a gym, with beautiful surround-film treadmills so that you could run in the forest, or on a lake trail if you liked. There was a rock climbing wall, tennis courts, other courts, and then, right at the far end, one wall looking into another enclosed garden of red bonsai trees and tiny streams, a dance studio.

"Listen," Mx Francis said to him as the producers flew the drones around, taking light levels and sound levels, "I've been watching our footage, and I'm just wondering if there's any way to set your cage to be a bit less obvious?"

"Obvious?" echoed January, starting to smile, because Mx Francis was the one who'd put him in skintight black that showed every single joint of the cage. Long sleeves, though. He had a feeling that showing your arms was indecent here.

Mx Francis, incredibly, looked awkward. They had long cornrows, and now, they were tying reef knots in the ends of some. He watched, half fascinated and half worried. People like Mx Francis didn't fret about anything except giant publicity catastrophes. A crocodile could amble in right now, making *numnumnum* noises, and Mx Francis probably wouldn't think anything about it except what a fabulous pair of boots it would make. "It's just, um . . . you're—obviously *lovely*, but it's not the most—subtle? look, and if you could perhaps change the settings to something a *bit* lighter—"

"That's naturalisation," he said, confused now.

"No, not naturalisation, just a *bit*, just to bring you in a *little* narrower—"

"You mean lose weight."

"Right." Another reef knot. "Only for an environment like Songshu, the optics just seem—not quite as—*elegant* as—"

Someone else clapped Mx Francis's shoulder. They were shorter, maybe only third-generation Natural, and more rounded and homely-looking than most of the desperately chic people here, but they seemed, even at first glance, like the kind of person who was probably a lot bigger on the inside. "They mean a good chunk of the internet thinks you look like a hooker turning tricks in Americatown," they said cheerily, in a voice like acid rain.

Mx Francis deflated. "This is Mx Ren, the Senator's chief of staff."

"You look like a giant Moomin," January told them, to see if they could take it as well as dish it out.

"That," Mx Ren said, hooking both thumbs under the straps of a pair of pink dungarees clearly meant to strike terror into the hearts of more junior staff members who were required to dress smartly, "is true. But irrelevant."

"I can be thin, but I still wouldn't look Tharsese. Look." He searched his own name on his phone and held out a picture from a show ten years ago.

"Oh," said Mx Francis, deflating.

"That's atrocious," Mx Ren reflected. "Well, never mind, I'm sure people will get used to you eventually, even if they do judge the Senator horribly meanwhile." They moomined off. January suspected he was going to quite enjoy them.

"Ready," one of the producers called.

January realized he was grinning.

Well then.

He had thought his body would have forgotten everything. He hadn't so much as done a drill for a year. But it was there. His bones still knew, and God, but the strength was there too. What he had forgotten was what it felt like to stretch out as far as he could without touching the paper walls of his tiny flat, or how it felt to move, properly, without stepping around furniture or stairs. You needed an incredible amount of space just for the first few steps of the most ordinary drill, never mind anything else. Nobody had that, nobody ordinary; you spent your life keeping yourself small under ceilings that were high enough to stand under but not to leap, and inside walls that let you cook but not spin.

He went all the way around the room, turn after turn, just because he could, and by the time he'd come back across the diagonal, he couldn't stop smiling. He hadn't been lying to Gale at the factory: you needed to be strong to dance.

One of the camera crew's drones was following him. He put his arm up so it could come and look at him if it wanted, then ducked it and spun by it the other way to see if the producer controlling it wanted to dance it with him.

"Ready?" he asked it, and pointed upward to say where he was going. "And . . ."

It arced up to follow him up, and spiralled around him once he landed. He laughed. It was like playing with a curious crystal ball. He took it around the room again to see if it could keep up.

At the end of the room, by the door, he was aware that more people than before had filtered in to have a look at him; some of them must have been watching initially on the screens upstairs, some just passing through and curious about why the gym was suddenly full of cameras. But he didn't pay it much attention until he saw the little crowd part. It was Gale, dressed normally for the first time since January had met them, not in senatorial finery but black jeans and a green jumper with a diamond pattern on it, hair down, all the way down, over one shoulder like they'd escaped before anyone could chase them into the normal formality. He faltered, not because Gale was watching him, exactly, though that was always nerve-racking enough, but because they looked like they were seeing something they had never seen before.

He stopped on the cross of tape the producer had put on the floor to mark four metres from everyone else and went down on one knee, in case they were also nervous to see him move as strongly as he could, without the normal moderation. It didn't matter that he was wearing the cage. It must still have been—well, not frightening, but ominous.

He had expected Gale to nod at him and then go on their way, but they didn't. They came out to him and took his arms without hesitation, and levered him upright. Their hands were warm, and lot stronger than he had thought; they could have lifted him. He froze, not convinced they wanted to be touching him.

"I didn't mean to stop you. I just saw the feed and I thought they must have doctored it." They smiled a bit. It was Aubrey's smile, not Senator Gale's, the slow careful one. They weren't the King yet this morning, not quite. "And now I feel stupid."

"You're lying, you've seen ballet before," January said, and it came out too exaggerated, because he was trying to hide how flustered he felt, seeing Gale in a normal jumper with their hair down. It seemed like the kind of thing he shouldn't have seen for months yet. They didn't know each other well enough. Which was a ludicrous Victorian thing to think, but it was amazing how fast you acclimatised to the strict ritual formality of everything here. For all Gale had chosen to come out like that, he felt like he ought to look away. "There's a company here, isn't there?"

"I think what we're calling ballet is . . . not. Have you seen it?"

"No. It would sting too much, I haven't been to the theatres here."

Gale hinged back half an inch or so, as though hearing it had stung too. They looked like they meant to say something more, but they didn't have time to.

Sirens blared out everywhere; from his phone, from the walls, from the drones. He even saw Gale's eyes flare red, which must have been blinding, and made him glad again that he didn't have the contact lenses that connected to the internet.

Alert. Major storm. Close all windows and doors.

It was painfully loud, and somewhere in the house, there were mechanical sounds under it; things sealing automatically.

"What?" Mx Francis said. "On the Plains? Something's gone wrong at the Met Office, this can't be real . . ."

Gale was already running up the stairs to look through the big window there, the first place that was above ground. January followed, surprised how fast they were.

"Jesus Christ."

It wasn't like the storm in the Valley. That had been what he expected, just a wall of dust—a wind front highlighted by dead soil, moving really quite slowly if you were used to Earth. Out over the big Plains sky now, there were cyclones. The gravity wasn't enough here for a tornado to be dangerous, because the wind moved too slowly, but that meant tornados could grow immense. The window faced downhill, towards the railway station and the sun fields, the view clear with the forest hemming only one side of it, and he could see all the way out to the silver towers and the mirrors and beyond, and much nearer than the horizon, the cyclones were giants, crackling with static.

Gale pushed a button on the wall, and their voice smoked through the house's intercom: "Senior staff to the meeting room now, please." They let the button go and motioned for January to go ahead of them. He didn't understand and only pointed uncertainly back at the studio, which was where he was supposed to be.

"You're senior staff too," Gale explained.

"I . . . am?"

"It ought to have said so, on Mx Francis's Schedule In Excelsis," they added carefully, and for at least the fifth time, he noticed that they handled his more confused questions like glass. It would have been easy to say, *It is on the schedule, moron.*

"It does, but I thought that was a lie," he said.

An amused sparkle went through Gale's dark eyes. "Unfortunately it was not. But there will be time later, to dance," they added, as if they really thought that was why he'd hesitated.

19

All the motion sensors around Songshu were going off, because the dust was so thick. Sasha trudged outside with some of the younger officers, ears still ringing from the din in the security office, to have a look at the sensors themselves. So far, the pattern was that they (a) screamed for ten minutes and then (b) died, because the dust caked the sensor face.

The cameras were showing piss all except dust clouds and the occasional ghost of a tree. It was no good using infrared, either. The dust itself was freezing, and it obscured anything hot.

All of them were in masks and heat suits. The end of winter was always sharp, but with the dust all but covering the sun it was as cold now, at nine o'clock in the morning, as it would have been six hours earlier in the deadest march of the night.

"Mx Martinez, what should we do?" one of the other officers asked, having to shout over the wind and through the masks. "We—we've basically got no security system!"

"We've got us," Sasha said, trying to sound practical and capable, even though what they in fact felt was the tight, nasty anxiety that came when you tripped over a mannequin with holes in and realized you were wandering into someone else's firing range. "Get everyone outside, let's do a walk-around. Bring a rifle each. The dust confuses the bears."

Even through the mask, the younger officer blanched at the prospect of meeting a confused polar bear. "Is that safe?"

"No," said Sasha. They paused, staring into the dust. "No, but anyone with a head on their shoulders can work out that every security system on the Plains is worthless now. Do you know how many Earth Rights groups have money on the Senator's head?"

"Five, last time I looked at the file."

"Six now," Sasha said gloomily. Trawling through the grosser corners of Earth's internet had become a significant part of their job since the Senator launched the consular campaign. "There's a shiny new Mission from the Prophet in Salt Lake City. Apparently all those of True Faith should be looking to incinerate Senator Gale as soon as possible."

"Oh great," the young officer said.

There was a little silence between them, but it was heavy.

"Do we know what Mx Stirling is, in the way of True Faith? Great Britain is . . . the same thing as America really, right? It's all one language?"

"I don't know, but he's spent some time in Texas."

"In—Texas. And we . . . let him in?"

"The Senator overrode my concerns," said Sasha, not wanting there to be even a suggestion of a consensus-reaching "we" around the subject. There was very definitely a Senator, and then a Sasha.

"That—sounds kind of dumb?"

Sasha breathed in deeply, which wheezed in the mask. "The Senator likes to think the best of people. And it's our job to enforce people's best."

"Yes, Mx Martinez," they said, chastened.

Privately, Sasha had to agree that it was very, extremely dumb. The Senator had got that way since Gagarin Square. They didn't even wear seat belts any more, no matter how close to a brain haemorrhage it drove Sasha. *What's going to happen to me that hasn't already happened?*

Things moved in the dust. Sasha hoped they were bears.

20

Lucy had been angry for a long time; more than long enough that, when the anonymous message came through the Earth Rights site, she was happy to pick up the grenades from the shipping container in town and head straight to Songshu.

Because the thing was, when you had a chance to explode a fascist nationalist, it was best to do it. People usually didn't bother, and that was how fascist nationalists got the power to make you naturalise, and to pull a sad face when your children died of it. She was well past the point of worrying about whether this was a trap, if the person who said they were inside Songshu really was, or asking how it was they had a shipping container full of grenades, plus grenade launchers. It didn't matter. She just shoved everything into a suitcase, which was very heavy, got on the Valley train up to Songshu, and smiled when a nice young person helped her put the very heavy suitcase on a luggage rack.

As always when she saw someone young here, she had a wave of sadness. They had no idea how badly they were being abused, growing up like this, in this clinical dystopia where children came out of a special bag in the Genesis Institute and everyone flinched away from human beings who actually looked the way God had made them. They could feel they were missing something, you only had to look at how unhappy everyone was on social media and in politics to see that—they knew something was wrong, they knew they had been disconnected from something vital and ancient and important, but in Tharsese there was no word for God, with the capital letter, and you couldn't talk about men and women without sounding like you were talking about a disease.

Lucy listened to a show run by a lady called Sister Joan, who was absolutely right eighty per cent of the time. What Sister Joan said was—this was the eighty per cent—that you knew you were in trouble when governments made basic things unspeakable, and—this was the twenty per cent—people were amazing turnips at spotting when this was happening. Lucy wasn't convinced anyone was a turnip. In her experience, people were quite bright. But it took a *fiercely* bright person to define a thing they had no words for, and an even brighter one to strip away the words they did have to recognise that the thing itself had nothing to do with any of the words.

She watched the news on the way up. It was still full of the wedding, and that poor, poor man House Gale had found to make Aubrey look less like a monster.

She had wondered more than once if he was her source inside Songshu. She hoped so.

Her phone buzzed.

Security officers doing perimeter checks, but that's all. No working cameras or sensors. Good luck.

She smiled a bit. *God bless you, whoever you are.*

At the Songshu station, she edged out with some difficulty, hooked the suitcase handle over her wrist, and reshuffled her crutches so she could manage them and the suitcase at once. It would have been easier in her wheelchair, but there were some things she wanted to do standing up. Somewhere not too far away, dust sirens howled.

21

The meeting room was at the top of one of the towers, with a glass dome ceiling and a god's-eye view across the Plains. Beyond the great pines, the solar farm looked like a lake, the heat from the mirrors water-waving, and beyond those, the dust was coming. Already, the air was gritty, and for January's eyes, used to sun much brighter than the ordinary light here, the room was too dim for him to see well, all high ceilings and deep shadow. Fleetingly, it occurred to him that he had the money now to buy some glasses and not worry that the cost would mean he couldn't charge his phone for two weeks.

Out in the dust, purple lightning strobed.

He tried to press down the feeling that he had been allowed into the throne room.

Mx Francis had said in all the pre-wedding preparation that Gale didn't believe in trophy consorts: January was here to have a voice. When he had said he found it very difficult to voice anything coherent anywhere near Gale, Mx Francis said not to worry, everyone did. Gale had once been, Mx Francis said darkly, a university lecturer. It was the way most people would have said "ran a fetish shop."

As other people took their seats at the table, he hesitated, wondering if he was seeing people who would soon be running the country. It seemed ridiculous to sit down too, like he belonged here, but someone even pulled a chair out for him. It was Mx Ren. They winked, and he smiled.

He was glad to see that in a corner by the window, out of everyone else's way, was the maybe-not-a-security-officer with their journal and their rust-coloured jumper. He liked that they didn't dress as beautifully as everyone else. He hoped it meant they were a normal person, but he didn't want to rush up to them and ask.

Gale took the chair beside him. January kept his hands in his lap and his knees together, so he wouldn't take up any more space than he needed. Gale flared their eyes a little at him, wry: *Here we go.*

"Okay, can we get Ariel from the Met Office on a call, please," Gale said, as though a rank of titan cyclones howling towards the sun fields was nothing particularly unusual.

It was witchcraft. Everyone relaxed.

The person who answered, and whose image appeared in the middle of the table, was an anxious-looking, rounded, middle-aged man with curly hair and a bow tie. January sat forward, delighted. He had known AI people did sometimes go around in artificial bodies when they weren't floating through the banking system or the defence satellites, but he had never seen one pay the idea even half this much attention, never mind this much *historical* attention. Usually they looked like beautiful configurations of clockwork and glass, not human beings. But then, the Mars AIs were as old as the colony. They would all have been created well before Gender Abolition. Maybe Ariel wanted to hang on to his roots. It felt unbelievably touching that a two-hundred-and-fifty-year-old god-person would want to do that.

"Senator—Gale, is it?" Ariel said tentatively, in English that had a wonderful homely Israeli accent. He was from Tel Aviv, January was sure of it—Hulking Terry was from there. Tel Aviv was only a couple of thousand miles from London. That was basically half an inch, when you looked at it from Mars. He wanted to bounce. "I don't think I recognise you."

Because he had been speaking Mandarin so much lately, January had one of those strange precious moments when he heard the sound of his own language, not just the meaning. It wasn't so much like Troll as he'd thought; it was weird, and it sounded old and cold and full of mist and horses, unlike the silicon boardroom chic of Mandarin, but kind of beautiful too.

"No, sir, you last spoke to my predecessor, Kali Gale. That was forty-five years ago. My name is Aubrey."

"Aubrey, that's a nice name. Less, er, aggressive."

Gale smiled, full of rue. "Thank you. I'm sorry to bother you, sir, and I know you must be busy, but I'm at Songshu and I'm looking at a dust storm coming in across the Plains. I was hoping you could tell me how long this is forecast to last, and perhaps why we're seeing something so irregular on so little warning."

January wasn't sure what he had expected Ariel to be like, but not nervous. He was clearly nervous. Perhaps it was talking to Gale, perhaps Ariel didn't speak to many people and when he did, they weren't usually speaking in razor-sharp sentences in a voice like molten sugar about to catch fire—that was universally intimidating—but he must have encountered versions of Gale before. He couldn't go round being worried by politicians.

"Well, I'm—afraid that it's difficult to do much modelling. I'm still—well, still struggling to see what's causing it. But just in case, you don't happen to have some sort of—backup, other than solar power, do you?" Ariel said, looking hopeless.

"No, sir," Gale said, steady as always. "Tharsis has been run on solar power from the Plains for a hundred and fifty years because there is no viable alternative. Wind power is useless in gravity this light, even in a storm. Fuel-grade hydrogen is produced using electricity, so you need solar power even for that; and what hydrogen we can produce is used for generating water. Fusion stations are banned, since Los Angeles . . ."

January looked up Los Angeles.[20]

". . . and the old nuclear power stations haven't been used for a century. They were only temporary to begin with and they're housing now. Technically they're available as a backup, but there is no uranium

---

20 What Los Angeles was, was a big hole in the ground, which was why he hadn't heard of it. It had used to be a city, locally remarked upon for fringe art films. As far as he could tell, the Tharsese news services had given the massive explosion a cursory once-over before moving on, because giant national disasters were just what happened in countries governed by gibbering religious extremists, nobody really knew where America was anyway, and the Olympics was on.

on Mars. We'd need to send to Earth for that. The whole point of Songshu is that it gives Tharsis energy independence from Earth."

"Yes, I was afraid of that. Well, you, er . . . will probably need to find some ways to stretch the power," Ariel said miserably. "This looks like a big one to me. Think months, not weeks."

Gale was quiet for a second. They didn't seem shocked, or even worried, but there was a line between their eyebrows, one January was starting to recognise. It meant something didn't look right. "What's the nature of your difficulty, in seeing the cause?" they asked.

"Sorry?"

"Do you need extra equipment to analyse dust samples, or satellite imagery of an area you can't see?"

Ariel looked off to one side, as if he were fantasising about running away. "No, nothing like that. It's just—well, there's more on Mars than we know, you see. All manner of things are unearthed as the weather changes, terraforming is a continuing process, as you know, and . . ."

"What things, specifically?" Gale asked.

January actually heard Ariel's teeth bump shut. He had never seen anyone look so desperate to get away from a question. He wondered if there shouldn't be a law against aiming Gale at unprepared people.

"Well, you see . . . you see, it's deposits of silver iodide," Ariel said, and the way he stared at Gale was begging. "Quite naturally occurring, you understand, there must be some cave systems where it forms, and—yes. It could be the silver iodide."

Gale snapped back in their chair. They didn't ask what silver iodide was (used in photography, said January's phone) and they didn't say, *hang on, so you do know what the cause is, why did you say you didn't.* "Thank you, sir," they said, very quiet, with far more weight than January had expected them to give something so unhelpful and odd. "I'll let you get on."

"No, thank *you,* Senator," Ariel whispered, and cut the call.

"What the hell was that about?" Mx Francis asked incredulously. January's brain made an unpromising clunking noise as it switched from Ariel's English into Mandarin Mode. "He doesn't know and then he does, and what's silver iodide anyway?"

"Turn the cameras off," Gale said.

"But we want to—" a producer began.

"Turn them off, please."

The producer sighed and waved the drones out.

"I'd like to know," Gale said, as if there had been no pause, "what it would take to construct a new solar array in the atmosphere."

The explosion of indignation was instant. Some people who must have been scientists all started talking at once.

"The energy transfer from an *atmospheric* solar array is deeply inefficient. Yes, you're above the dust, but you still have to get that energy from those panels in space *down* to—"

Mx Ren was talking too. "The cost would be insane, you'll bankrupt House Gale if you even—"

"The Consul would read that as a power grab," Mx Francis put in fast and high. "We're a public service, but that would require far more money than we get from taxpayers! They'd try and shut us down—"

Gale was shaking their head. Like always, the smoke in their voice carried straight through everyone else. They didn't have to shout. "Dr Molotov, work out a realistic figure."

There was a strange silence in which everyone, at different lags, realized Gale was serious.

January waited with everyone else, frowning, but unlike everyone else, he could see that Gale had both hands locked together between their knees, knuckles white. If Gale had been anyone else, he would have brushed their elbow, half to ask what the matter was and half to say they weren't alone, but whatever the new trust that seeing him dance had given them, it was *brand* new. It was the first film of ice over very deep water. He was scared of breaking it.

When Gale did finally speak, it was quiet. "What I say now doesn't leave this room. You delete it from any memory recordings you might be running, and if I see it on social media, you will be fired."

More silence.

"AI cannot disobey the sitting Consul. If Ariel were to try, he would shut down immediately. He just told us that this is all because of naturally occurring silver iodide. Silver iodide is not naturally occurring; you have to burn it out of its ore with hydrochloric acid. Silver iodide is what they use for cloud seeding on Earth. Do it here, where there isn't enough moisture to generate rain, it just pulls what little water there is off the surface and what you get is . . ." They pointed out the window. "What Ariel was trying to say is that this is an artificial storm and he's been forbidden to say so." Gale paused, and because their throat was stark against the black fall of their hair on their far side, January saw them swallow. "Historically, artificial storms on Mars have lasted in excess of six months. They were catastrophic in the early colonies, which is why we have only . . . one . . . colony now."

Before, even though they had been quiet, everyone had been shifting—pulling their chairs nearer to the table to hear, clicking styluses on tablets, all the ordinary fidgeting that happened in big meetings. But everyone had gone still now.

"Dr Molotov; please work out what it would cost to build a new array in the atmosphere, and how fast we can do it. My preference is—very fast."

"Yes, Senator." Dr Molotov fell gratefully out of the room and hurried away. The person in the rust-coloured jumper left too; perhaps they only listened in for the first half hour. Dr Molotov must have been too worried to notice, because they let the door shut almost right in the other person's face; they had to catch it on their knuckles and slip through sideways.

January stared after them, and then at Gale. He had spent a lot of time wondering how anyone could possibly get so high and mighty that they could countenance just shoving two hundred thousand people into naturalisation camps, but in a rhetorical way. He hadn't expected to arrive at a real answer, never mind to see it firsthand. But if Gale's whole function was to make decisions about questions so vast as how Tharsis got its power, if it was normal for them to round up legions of people to put a solar array into space on no notice whatever, then probably two hundred thousand people who mostly couldn't vote didn't even seem like a large number. It was a little problem with a logical solution and that solution was naturalisation.

Jesus.

"Are we saying," Mx Ren began slowly, "that there's been some kind of accident? Ariel dropped a vial? Or are we saying—someone did this on purpose?"

January noticed something coming at the window while they were talking. It was a strand of amber light, like a rising whip. There were others behind it too, and at the end of each whip line was a brighter light. He would have thought it was fireworks if the light strands weren't all looping towards them, and so his first thought was some extraordinary type of plant that had learnt to glow.

He was still wondering about it when the lights exploded through the windows.

Chunks of glass and concrete flew everywhere. Later, he remembered that they flew impossibly slowly. He saw the comb patterns they left in the dust as they sliced through, ethereal, like miniature jet trails in a war zone only thirty feet broad. He had time to snatch Gale onto the floor and pin them under him, and think quite logically that the spine of his cage was broad, as good as armour. He felt shrapnel clang off it. Even though it didn't cut him, it still felt like being punched.

Smoke boiled into the dust until the air was solid with it, and through that weird darkness, voices were yelling from outside somewhere, maybe down on the ground, but his ears were ringing too much to understand anything except that the cadence sounded like English—and then, from the direction of the main wing of the house, the sternum-hammering thump of gunshots.

Ten minutes later, everyone was sitting in a safe room with no windows. There were security people everywhere, coming in and out, two always at the door, somebody showing Gale something on a tablet, and beyond the door, the hum of a disturbed hive. Someone else called that the police would be another two hours, because of the dust. Two producers all but ordered Gale to say something to camera about what had just happened.

"Christ, can you not?" January protested. He went into English without meaning to. When he tried to find it, he realized his Mandarin was scattered in bits over the meeting room floor. He wouldn't get it back for a little while.

Gale was ashen from the smoke, and grazed down one arm. A doctor was cleaning the cuts with what smelled stingingly like ethanol.

"We need a raw reaction for the news," Mx Francis insisted from behind the cameras, terse and urgent, and grey. They were grazed too, but what January had come to learn about publicity-campaign-manager people was that probably even from inside a coma, they would find a way to get at viewer metrics and polling data. "This is important. Senator—can you hear me?"

January didn't think so. Gale was looking at a patch of air in the middle distance, expressionless.

"Senator?" Mx Francis said, clasping Gale's shoulder. They sounded like they were just about to panic.

But then Gale seemed to come back, and wrenched their thoughts into that same militaristically straight line they had in the meeting. They put one hand over Mx Francis's and held it.

January looked away, feeling irrationally like he was spying.

And maybe he was. He had never asked Gale if they had a partner already, an unofficial one. Christ alive, maybe they *were* involved with Mx Francis. Mx Francis was bloody stunning, and young and cultured.

It shouldn't have felt like tripping on the stairs, but it did.

"Why are you talking to me?" Gale said to Mx Francis, in English, for—mortifyingly—literally no one's benefit but January's. Impeccable courtesy even under actual gunfire. "You're concussed, sit down."

"It really doesn't matter if I'm concussed, Senator," Mx Francis said, voice juddering with relief, and January realized that no one would mind if he had been killed just now. It would be annoying for Gale, but that was all. Val had never written back. There was no one.

There had never been anyone, though, and he couldn't see why it was striking him as all tragic and gooey now. Some people didn't get a person. It wasn't a right; it was a gift, and you couldn't go around sniffing about it as if you were *entitled* to be worried over.

The thing was, it did seem to be a gift that everyone else got at least once.

"Are you okay?" Gale asked Mx Francis.

Mx Francis nodded, looking much more vulnerable than a second ago. "Yes, Senator."

"Sit," Gale told them gently.

Mx Francis did, at last, and Gale put one arm round them. Mx Francis pulled one sleeve over their eyes.

January pushed his hands together in his lap and took out his phone to see if it worked still, and for something to do other than watching the two of them. The screen was cracked. He had to press his palm against his face. Two hundred years it had been in his family, and it had never had to be repaired. If his mother had been alive, she'd have smacked him over the head and said it was fine, they'd get it fixed, but a terrible guilt rolled over him. It was the last piece of home he had, and the last piece of *her*, and he didn't think there was anywhere here that could fix it.

"It's okay," Gale was saying to Mx Francis. "Have you called your parents?"

"No, I . . ."

"Go and do it then, haizi," Gale said, their voice vapouring like it did whenever they heard something really, genuinely stupid. January glanced over and swallowed. People here did mix languages a lot if they were saying something very soft and warm, but he had only ever heard it in movies before; he had never been in a situation to overhear it in real life. *Haizi* meant "child." "You're twenty-five, you're a baby, they'll be worried sick. This is all over the news."

"But—"

"You're excommunicated from this House if you don't go and call your parents."

"Okay," Mx Francis said, soothed. "But—you still have to . . ."

"Hao le, hao le." *All right, all right.* "I'm doing it." Gale gave them a little push.

Twenty-five. January felt guilty. That was so much younger than he'd thought. It was because everyone was so tall; it made you assume they were all in their thirties.

Gale turned to the cameras.

"We've had a visit from a terrorist," they said, dry and warm at once, in their exquisitely clear Mandarin. They pulsed calm and a kind of soft humour, like a campfire on a frostbitten night. "They fired heat-seeking grenades into an office window. No one's been hurt, which is thanks to Mx Stirling, who got between me and a lot of broken glass." They looked at January with a warmth that dawned before they smiled their real smile.

He bowed fractionally, still wondering about Mx Francis.

A business arrangement. That was what this marriage was. He needed to stop trying to—what was he even trying to do? Be married? He ran his fingertips over the cracks on the screen of his phone and concentrated on not crying live on national news. It was such a silly thing to cry about, a phone; he didn't know why it cut so deep.

One of the producers made a spinning motion with the other hand to say the feed was still rolling. "Pretty heroic stuff, January. What went through your head? You acted incredibly quickly."

"No, I didn't. Everything falls three times slower than I'm used to. I strolled," he said, because a joke made the segment sound finished and if it was finished, they would go away.

The producer beamed and then the camera operators relaxed. "Fabulous! I'll post that across socials."

It was a huge relief when they were gone. He studied Gale under his eyelashes, worried he'd hurt them more, wrenching them onto the ground, than the glass had; but he couldn't find a way to ask. Camera drones were still floating around. He wondered if it would be all right to ask if he could go up to his room for a little while. He could cry for a bit in the shower, unobserved by millions of people, get his head straight about the phone, and—God, and *change*. He was still in the figure-hugging black outfit Mx Francis had put him in this morning, to dance. But when he decided to try, the idea filled him with dread. He didn't want to do any of that. He wanted to stay with Gale. Gale was safe. It wasn't objectively true, Gale was the person being shot at, but he would have fought anyone who had tried to make him leave just then.

Gale was looking at him too. "Thank you." English again.

He shrugged. He hadn't been lying. To him, it had all happened slowly. The styluses falling from the table had seemed to take years to hit the floor, and the wreckage ricocheting against the wall had bounced more than smashed. The fire from the grenade was lazy and rounded, with none of the sharp edges and wickedness it would have had in nastier gravity. He'd had time to think quite clearly: *Yes, I'd probably better do something about this before that bit of shrapnel creeping up on us from over there takes someone's head off . . .*

The slowness was all in his head, though: it had to be. Low gravity didn't make explosions less explosive. It was disturbing: he hadn't known his brain could distort things that much.

"Are you all right?"

"Yes," January said, disconcerted to be asked. Nobody else had; of course they hadn't. He was three times stronger than them and locked in titanium armour.

Gale touched his wrist and turned his hand over to show him his own palm. Under the cage gauntlet, it was bloody; he didn't remember putting his hand down on glass, and it didn't hurt, but he must have. He watched, feeling like his hand belonged to someone else, as Gale guided it down into a bowl of water that bloomed red.

A camera drone came down to catch that, and he wondered if this was just setting up romance for later. Of course it was.

"I'm not trying to be—but are you and Mx Francis together?" he asked, because he couldn't hold it in any more.

Gale looked up as though January had suggested they watch a snuff movie. "No! I'm nearly twice their age!"

"And my grandmother was a bicycle," January said indignantly, because he had never in his life heard a more obvious lie.

Gale started to laugh, really laugh. It was the most fantastic laugh, like boiling brandy, and it was infectious; it made him laugh too, and the doctor in the corner, and whoever was outside watching the drone footage. "Solly Francis is far too young for me." They kicked his ankle very gently. "*You're* too young for me."

"I'm not young," January said, embarrassed now. He coughed. "Wow, that was a bit tragic, wasn't it."

"I mean, I'm feeling very good about the whole thing honestly," Gale said cheerfully.

He felt himself going pink, and then all at once, it dawned on him warm and golden that Gale didn't look anxious to be near to him. Not even the hidden tight anxiety that was only there if you stared. He stayed very, very still even so. He felt like he had done once years ago when he was sitting on the roof at home in London, soaking in the evening heat, when out of nowhere, a fox sat down next to him.

"I broke my phone," he said pointlessly.

Gale glanced at it, then again. "That's a Mori, isn't it?"

He nodded, and waited for Gale to ask why in God's name he hadn't sold it and bought a house.

Gale didn't. From an inside pocket they took out an almost identical one, though much newer and protected by a beautiful leather case. January stared. Gale studied his for a second, then pressed the broken screen. It slid straight off, designed to be easily replaced; they did the same with theirs, unbroken, and slipped it onto January's. It locked into place. "Perfect," they concluded. "I'll get this one sent in later."

"No, but . . ."

"Quiet. Family heirloom." They held up January's. "Bribe from a banker trying to buy my vote on financial regulation." They held up their own.

January thought he really might cry now. Gale met his eyes for a second to ask permission, then took his other hand to wash the blood off that one too. His looked small in theirs. Some of the sharp edges of the panicky miserable feeling started to smooth down. After a little while, thinking wasn't painful any more. He let his breath out slowly, floating on the new calm.

With no explanation, the doctor poked a needle into him and he yelped.

The blood went into a little machine. "Checking your testosterone level," the doctor said unsympathetically. "Stress in someone with gender traits as extreme as yours can mean uncontrollable aggression."

"In kids and idiots," January said indignantly. "I don't—"

"I'd still like to give you an inhibitor—"

"I'll inhibit you in a minute!"

"See? This is very aggressive behaviour—"

"Leave him alone," Gale said. He was starting to get a sense of when they were annoyed; they never sounded it in the usual way, they were too controlled. But when they were, they could bring their voice up from a deeper chamber than normal, one that coiled with fumes, like there was something radioactive in storage there.

The doctor pursed their lips, disapproving, but moved away.

"The lady who did it, did she leave a note?" January asked. He didn't care, but he wanted Gale to keep talking to him. "Why did she do it?"

"Her children died trying to naturalise," Gale said. They opened a packet with a sterile bandage inside and dried January's hand off with it, balancing his knuckles on their knee. It was the artificial one. He could feel the steel through their clothes.

"And that's better than letting them have cages?" he asked. It felt mean and hateful to grind that axe now, while they were both bleeding, but he didn't like the look of the kind of person he would become if he didn't.

"It is," Gale said, a little too slowly, as if they thought it was obvious but didn't want to blame anyone for not keeping up. "Far better. Far fewer Earthstrong people die naturalising than Natural people die in cage-related accidents."

He knew they didn't mean it personally, he knew they weren't calling him selfish for wearing a cage—even on so short an acquaintance, he was certain that they were too well mannered to even consider meaning that—but it was hard not to take it that way. "It's still horrible."

Gale lifted their eyes, very black now in the low light. There was no glibness there, none of the frightening joy in war they'd had at the factory; only resignation. "Yes. It's Mars."

From somewhere down the corridor, there was a new flurry, and new voices.

Gale sighed. "This is going to be ugly, but I'll come and get you. We have all the lawyers in the world."

"What? Lawyers?" January asked, confused.

Sasha banged the door open, and with no explanation, snatched January upright by one arm. "Move. The police are here. They want to talk to you."

22

The police didn't even pretend to ask questions; they arrested January within two minutes, and twenty minutes after that, he was in a helicopter being taken back to Tharsis, his hands clamped together in titanium manacles so heavy he couldn't lift them more than an inch.

The agents put him in a little room and told him that he'd been speaking to the terrorist group, hadn't he, and perhaps it had started out looking like a harmless online support forum for people with relatives in naturalisation centres or who people who had come out recently, until somebody messaged him with an offer to provide some heavy artillery.

There were terrorist training camps in America, of course. It wasn't very far from Great Britain to America, was it? Easy to go, too. The language was basically the same. The culture was Pro-Gender and religious and willing to blow up Tharsis senators. Americans and British people traditionally hated the Chinese, right? He had come to a Chinese colony in order to do some damage if he could, hadn't he. And then along came Senator Gale. Am I wrong?

"You're wrong," January promised. He should have been calm, because he knew Gale was coming, but he couldn't tell how long he had been here now, and it was beginning to feel like too long. There must be a problem. Maybe it wasn't very easy to bail out someone the secret police thought was a terrorist. Or maybe one of these officers had shown Gale something that had made them wonder if January really might have spoken to someone. The timing looked horrendous. The first day he was at Songshu. "I've never been to the U.S. except on tour with my company."

"Army tour?"

"Ballet tour," he said. "I was a dancer. I was only there for a fortnight."

"But you *were* there. Where?"

"In Austin."

"Texas," one of the officers said, looking him up and down, slowly.

He tried not to think about what lay ahead if Gale didn't come. The judge had told him that his next offence would land him in a labour camp. He would spend twenty years hacking roads from the red bedrock in the punishing winters that lasted twelve months. Labour was valuable, Earthstrong labour especially so, and they cared if you died out there, they kept you alive for every frozen second of it, and somehow that was worse than the alternative.

"I—Texas is huge, it isn't just terrorists and desert," January protested. "Austin's a big liberal arts city, it was a culture festival."

"You're asking us to believe you when you've been to *Texas*, you're openly Pro-Gender—"

"I'm not *Pro-Gender*, I'm just—"

"—and you have every reason to have an enormous grudge against Senator Gale, and now you just happened to be involved in a terrorist operation to kill a Tharsis senator."

"I wasn't involved, I nearly died!"

"Suicide agents are overwhelmingly people your age."

"*Men* your age," the other one said drily.

He jumped when someone tapped on the door. He didn't see who was behind it, but it must have been someone important, because the two officers both stepped out. He waited, staring at the table.

The officers came back in. One of them was holding a steel band, and behind them came somebody who didn't look like they were in the security services. They had a purple scarf on, and they were very much the human version of a happy bear.

"This is Professor Shang, from the cognitive forensics unit. We're going to do a test."

"What kind of test?" January asked softly, having visions of needles and straps.

Professor Shang flumped down opposite, dug in a pocket, and rained a whole collection of mismatched spare buttons and bits of old, broken electronic paper whose ink had stopped working properly and flashed shards of random digits and images as it curled sadly on the desk. The officers looked pained. Triumphant, Shang pulled out a pen. "Right," they said, not using the pen, just holding it, as though they couldn't have spoken without it. "We're doing an experiment! It's called a halo. That scanner there—" they nodded to the metal band the officer was holding "—shows me which areas of your brain light up when you see writing on a page. Now, when we read, we comprehend it in a very specific area of the brain, and you will quite involuntarily start thinking about what the writing says. It lights up your brain. But even better, it lights up very differently if that information on that page is *new* to you. If you know it, you see it very differently. Basically this is a test to see if you recognise some information or not. The scanner is linked to my tablet, so you'll see your own thought patterns on it."

"Okay," January said slowly, much more nervous of Shang now than the police. You weren't allowed to be a well-respected professor *and* this chaotic and scruffy unless you were from Good People, one of those families like the Gales who'd been rich for so long that nobody cared if they went around looking like tramps. Everyone here, they were going to *listen* to Shang, and if for some horrendous reason this experiment gave up a wrong result, there would be no arguing with it.

He tried to make his mind shut up. It wasn't saying anything useful.

"So we'll do some controls first, so I can get a baseline. Normal stuff. You can read a bit of Mandarin?"

January nodded. "I can sort of get through kids' books with a dictionary."

"Let's start with kids' stuff then," Shang said kindly.

January flinched when the officer behind him set the scanner over his head like a crown. Shang's tablet came alive with waving colours.

"Can you tell me what this says?"

He looked. Shang had put a card on the table with the sign for "person." He said so. On the screen, the colours coalesced into lots of people, ghostly and faceless some of them, some specific. Val was there. Shang let out a delighted squeak.

"Wow! Look at that. What a beautiful memory you have."

"It's not that good," January said, still more confused than he had ever been in his life, except maybe when someone had first tried to explain Russian grammar to him.

"I mean you have beautiful associations. Look, that's me! Oh, you think I'm like a bear, that's the nicest thing anyone's ever thought about me on these things. Usually my students think I'm an annoying inbred lunatic—hah," they added, because the screen filled with bears. January tried to picture Paddington in a purple scarf, and it worked. Shang laughed.

"Perhaps more test and less pissing about?" one of the officers said, but they did look like they might be in danger of smiling.

Shang put down new cards; cat, school, glass, car. After that, January got lost more than he didn't. Instead of forming clear images, the tablet colours stayed murky and confused. Sometimes they showed the character itself as he tried to work it out by its component parts. All the while, Shang looked encouraging.

"Okay, perfect," Shang said in their cheerful way. "That's a good measure of how you think, which I have to say is very charming. Now, I want you to look at this."

They put a sheet of e-paper in front of him. It was in English this time. It looked like a copy-and-paste job from a forum, on the cheap text-only internet people used when they couldn't afford all the implants and virtual things. As he scanned it, he caught on particular phrases; "corner of Gagarin Square," "cash in hand," "Project Crocodile," which made him think of zoos. Peripherally, he saw animals appearing on Shang's screen, and Shang grinning.

The matter of it was that two people were talking to each other about something called Project Crocodile, and money. One was Lucy Collins. One was—someone else, with a blank avatar. *Go to this address and you'll find the shipment in a cargo container there.* There was an address somewhere in the south of Tharsis, Americatown. *God bless America.*

Lucy had asked, *How do you know where the Senator will be and when? What's your source?*

Whoever was organising it said, *Me. I live at Songshu.*

January looked up slowly, understanding in a kind of grey pall that they hadn't arrested him just because he was Earthstrong. The police people were all watching Shang, though, not him.

"Well? Has he seen that information before?"

"Nope," Shang said cheerfully. "Not even a bit of it."

"Does that thing work as accurately on Earthstrongers as on us?" one of the police officers said doubtfully.

Shang gave them a severe look. "Brains are brains, Agent. It works on pigs, never mind different varieties of human."

"On pigs?"

"Oh, yes. It was a major factor in banning the meat industry, didn't you know? It proved pigs feel grief just like we do. You can have a good conversation with a pig, through one of these. They're quite philosophical."

January wondered if the Consul had tried it on Alice. Probably; it seemed like the sort of thing the Consul would do.

"You spend your time talking to pigs."

"No, to mammoths," Shang said unmoved. "Anyway. Mx Stirling is quite innocent, I assure you."

The older officer sighed. "All right, Mx Stirling, you can go. Thank you for your time."

They took the manacles off and held open the door, and January went through it, moving through a haze that was part relief and part ringing shock at just how close he had come to vanishing into prison forever, and on top of it, like oil writhing on the surface of the sea, wondering who in God's name at Songshu could have been talking to terrorists. He could well imagine there were people working at Songshu who were pissed off with Gale and with struggling to pay the bills when Songshu had its own ice rink, but it was one thing to feel annoyed and something else to start sourcing grenades. How did you even get grenades? Tharsis wasn't like America. Normal people couldn't just walk into a shop and buy heavy artillery.

"Mx Stirling," Professor Shang said, on their way out.

"Yes?"

They paused by him and shot a glance through the glass windows of the double doors into the waiting room. "Congratulations on the marriage. I hope it works out well. I used to work with River Gale. You know, Aubrey's Apollo.[21] Gifted linguist. *Gifted.*" They looked sad. "Look, I'm sure someone has said this to you already, but—please be careful. About Aubrey."

"You're right," January said dully. "They have." He still had the Consul's card in his pocket. He had been carrying it round like a protective talisman.

Professor Shang twisted the end of their purple scarf. "I know this is in—horrifying bad taste. I know. But I just wouldn't be able to live with myself if I let you go without—you know. Mentioning it. River would *never* have left their work. It was their whole life. They'd just got a tenured position at the university, they were overjoyed, and we had designed a whole new mammoth project to . . . yes. And—they never said anything about Aubrey to me, but one overhears calls and so forth, doesn't one, and . . . Mx Stirling, please do be careful. Anyway." They looked profoundly embarrassed. "It's none of my business. I'm sorry to poke my nose in. I'm sure you know what you're doing."

January smiled, sort of. "I have no idea what I'm doing."

Professor Shang nodded regretfully, and said, "Well, I'll be . . ." and went in the opposite direction, still twisting the purple scarf.

---

21 Apollo twins—as in Apollo and Artemis, the archers from the old stories—were common in Great Houses. A House needed an heir and a spare, so they usually adopted two babies at one go, generally born on the same day or very close together, but not actually related. They had identical educations, so that one could take over from the other at any point, although some studies had suggested this was a bad idea, given the unusually high mortality rate among the older twins. "Watch out for Artemis" was idiom now. It meant, be careful of the person right behind you who can do your job just as well as you.

January drew both hands over his face. He wanted to think that rumours were just rumours. Gale had been good to him, so far. Incredibly rich and powerful people always had rumours vapouring around them. And it wasn't insane for an academic to fall in love and run away. It happened, however scholarly River Gale might have been. *But what also happens*, the Swan King voice in the back of his mind said, *is that rich, powerful people go quietly mad and kill someone who betrays them. It's a fairy tale for a reason.*

He took a deeper breath and pushed open the waiting room door.

Gale was there, looking like a jewel someone had lost. They got up fast.

"Are you all right?" they asked, intense, and he had a total certainty then that lives were going to hinge on his answer, because Gale looked like they did when they were about to fight. Someone was going to end up as sludge on the arena floor, and it wasn't going to be Gale.

He almost said, *Please can you kill those agents for me, the world would be a lot better if they were sludge, thanks*, but he breathed out and told himself firmly that nobody needed to be sludge. And in any case, he wasn't sure Gale cared whether he was personally flustered; they cared about the integrity of their House, and whether the agents here had a sufficient fear of it not to be too rough with one of its number.

"I'm fine. Thanks. You—you didn't need to come yourself," January stammered, the enormity of what they'd done in coming here cracking over him. Even after such a short time involved with House Gale, he was starting to think like Mx Francis, about how any particular moment would look if it were splashed across social media. Aubrey Gale at a secret police facility, fishing out their new consort who'd been accused of terrorism. It was a gift for anyone who wanted to attack them. *How are we supposed to trust anything you think? You accidentally married a terrorist.*

"I did."

"Thanks," January whispered. "Senator, they showed me messages, from the people who did it. The person who arranged it—they're *inside* Songshu. Or they say they are. And there was a test, but—even the agents in there weren't sure it was working properly on me," he said, and then heard how incoherent that sounded.

Gale seemed to understand all the same. "The halo, yes. It does work on Earthstrongers; it works on some fungi. Would you mind if we were to subpoena the footage of your test?"

Would and were to, January thought feverishly. Gale's English was better than his. "What does that mean?"

"We would take it and broadcast it, so everyone can see. If you don't mind everyone seeing the inside of your brain."

"If it stops them thinking I did it," he said, having never minded anything less. "But Senator—someone inside Songshu talking to Earth Rights terrorists . . . ?"

"Everyone will take the test, but I don't think anyone was talking to Earth Rights. They were talking to the Consul."

"What?"

"Half of Earth is on fire and millions will inevitably come here, I'm a nationalist politician with a decent chance of becoming Consul in time to stop them landing in the city. If you were the current Consul, this would be the perfect time to blow me up and blame it on the new Earthstronger."

January had to absorb that for a few seconds. He nearly said, *I don't think the Consul would do that*; but then Gale would ask how he knew what the Consul would and wouldn't do.

Gale was looking over his head, to the double doors. "Right; the press are outside. Would you mind if I speak to them, or should we go straight home?"

January wanted a lot to go home. But if they went home now, without saying anything, then the story would be that he was probably a terrorist who had been released because of an esoteric test nobody quite trusted. Gale would deal with the fallout for the rest of the consular campaign.

He could have said *let's go* and let Gale deal with it. It would have been a nice subtle way to make things hard for them. Maybe he would have, even; if they hadn't asked him.

But they had. They were watching him, waiting for him to speak, and he could see they were going to do whatever he decided. He couldn't tell why it mattered so much, to be allowed to decide, but just then it was everything.

Which, said the hard Swan King voice in his head, *is really stupid, because however nice they are, Gale is going to put you in a naturalisation centre if they win this. This marriage isn't a five-year stay of execution, if they win. It's two months.*

"No, let's see them," he said.

You're such an idiot.

The air outside was swarming with drones, all gleaming rainbow colours, like purposeful bubbles. Some carried the logos of companies that weren't even based on Mars, but in China and Nigeria. January tried not to think about whether this was going to make headline news in those places. It couldn't. It would just be on some obscure part of the foreign news service that nobody read. Surely. America was on fire.

There was a roar of *Senator!* from all the journalists with the drones. They must have been waiting for nearly as long as Gale. Some of them were wearing dust masks and heavy winter coats.

"Senator, do you have any comment about Mx Stirling's arrest?"

"When have I ever not had a comment? You know how much I like you all," Gale said, and people laughed. "By now you've all seen the footage. January saved my life, and a halo scan has just confirmed he had nothing to do with the attack. House Gale will broadcast that later today."

"Senator, there's some evidence to say the halo doesn't work so well on Earthstrongers. Is there any room for uncertainty?"

"No. The halo works on anything sentient. The evidence you're talking about is one study of eight people by a postgraduate who had fitted the halo improperly, and it's from twenty-five years ago."

January shouldn't have been surprised Gale knew that.

"January, how do you feel?" someone else called.

"Glad to be walking away." He glanced up at Gale. The wind was pulling at their hair, coiling the ends, deep-space black without even a strand of grey. Never had two people belonged less together. "And—amazed that the Senator didn't once seem to think it was me."

Gale looked honestly incredulous—it was slight, all their genuine expressions were—but it was there, and very lightly, they closed one hand over the front of his cage and pulled until he bumped them sideways. He had to smile. "Of course I didn't bloody think it was you," Gale told him fake-crossly.

January coughed. "Evidence that Britishness is infectious, everybody."

The journalists all laughed, and so did January.

23

At Songshu, the security services were set up on one side of the dining room. What must have been most of the staff were in queues, and ten officers in makeshift booths were doing the tests with the halo devices. The people who had already been tested were sitting in their own cordoned-off section, and there were even more officers keeping registers of who had gone through, and who was yet to come.

All the ways in and out of the house were locked. Someone with a semiautomatic pistol had to let them in at the main doors. They towered, and January found himself shrinking behind Gale. Soldiers here wore a variation of resistance cages but in reverse; they wore them at night to build up their strength as close to Earthstrong as it could physically go—not all the way but near—and then took them off on duty. Without his cage, he would still have been stronger; but he was still a foot smaller, and he wasn't without his cage. Gale didn't even look at them, and only opened the door for him. There were more police inside, as well as Sasha's security staff. Everyone was starting to look frayed.

"Any luck?" Gale said.

"Nothing," Sasha murmured. "I'm sorry, Senator, we're working on it."

"I know. Keep going, you're doing beautifully."

"Senator—I know the scan cleared January, but I'd feel better if—"

"Mx Stirling," Gale said, only just over them, and flaring their eyes with something that was a lot hotter than reproach, "is in the clear, unlike everyone else. Perhaps you might concentrate on the everyone-else problem, unless there's some new evidence against him?" They sparkled, looking hopeful that there might be some evidence they could smash.

Sasha bowed their head. "None, Senator."

"Why are you so boring, why couldn't you have just slightly been involved with terrorists?" Gale said to January. "It's no fun defending someone who's innocent. Where's the smoking gun, Stirling? Where's the God-and-gender manifesto? You could at least try."

"Be honest," said January, wanting to say, *Don't imagine I haven't noticed you've found a way to defend me but give me my dignity as well; don't imagine it's passed me by that you didn't usher me through here with one hand on the small of my back, like I was just all wronged and helpless and rubbish.* "Do you want me to find you some better terrorists to play with?"

"Better ones, you say?"

Sasha looked between them, aghast. "*Do not find any better—*"

"Boring! Everything is boring, nothing is going to be interesting again, at all, ever," Gale declared, and let January tug them away before Sasha could have an aneurysm.

In the time it took him to make some coffee, someone nabbed Gale, and by the time he came back, the officer was scowling at the screen that showed their halo scan.

"Suffering fuck, how are we supposed to read that?"

"I told you," Dr Okonkwo said, with not a great deal of patience. They were hovering nearby in a way that managed to be argumentative even when they weren't talking. January gave them a long look. He hadn't forgotten about the inhibitor injection they'd been waving around and he planned not to for a good while. "It can tell you what a person thinks but not why those associations are there."

"This looks like a crazy person's brain!"

"Indeed," Dr Okonkwo sighed. "Thirteen things alter in the brain to manifest what we recognise as dissociative psychosis. But if only twelve out of those thirteen are different, you get a creative genius."

"So this works on fungi but not on clever people? God's sake . . ."

Gale was quiet and even a little awkward, January thought, as though Dr Okonkwo was talking about a terrible disability they wished people wouldn't ask about. He pirouetted past to make them laugh, and to make something recognisable come up on the officer's scanning screen. Gale did smile, and the officer did peer at the screen as though it had almost done something helpful.

"You know what the Left-Wing Crazies are going to be screaming in about an hour, don't you," said Solly Francis in passing to January, nodding towards Gale.

"What?" said January, having to fight against the need to point out that actually, he was a left-wing crazy and he couldn't wait to hear a rich nationalist's idea about his thought processes.

"Meh, boo, Aubrey did it, Aubrey's an evil genius, halos don't work on evil geniuses, they could have done *anything*, and anyway all Earthstrongers are amazing awesome people who would never do anything bad because having a difficult life puts you in the permanent moral high ground, saying otherwise is racist, boo, hiss, it's faaaaake . . ."

January looked at up at them. "Why would they fake it? They nearly died."

"But no one *did* die," Mx Francis said, widening their eyes. "Maybe they weren't real explosives. Maybe it was so that House Gale could make a big old show of rescuing you from the nasty police. Maybe it's all a ploy to get sympathy votes."

"Seems like a lot of effort with a lot of unpredictable variables."

"That never seems to put people off coming up with this conspiracy crap." Then, "Did you just say unpredictable variables?"

"Yes?"

Mx Francis stepped back. "The Senator . . . is . . . infectious . . ."

January laughed, and found unexpectedly that he liked being able to say things like that. It felt the same as pulling off a tricky spin for the first time. "So if people start saying that. What do we do?"

"It's going to be more of a *you* thing than a *we* thing," Mx Francis said with a little wince. "Which is why I bring it up. I'd really like to get you on film hearing one of the crazies say that and then saying something funny. You're good at funny. Is that all right?"

"Of course."

Mx Francis paused. "Just to check. You don't—secretly suspect that the Senator did this on purpose?"

"I think you can be a genius without being an evil genius," January promised, but as he said it, he realized he couldn't tell to what extent he was lying. He looked back towards Gale and the increasingly frustrated halo operator, and found himself hoping for a sudden furore where someone else's halo lit up and sirens went off with big neon signs that said AHA! THIS PERSON DID IT, IRREFUTABLY, but the dining room continued quiet.

Even when everyone at Songshu had been tested—it took all day— there was nobody whose scan was suspicious.

Except Gale's, which even the senior specialist couldn't decode.

"Yeah," concluded Mx Francis, eyes flaring blue to warn people that they were seeing social media halls overlaid across the real world. "Maybe don't go onto our socials for a bit."

January had to look around, because Mx Francis's focus was moving like January was sitting at the edge of a crowd of people, even though they were just having ramen in the production room. It was past nine. January had stayed around so that he could film the thing Mx Francis wanted if everyone's tests came back negative.

Aware it was probably a mistake, he held up his phone to see, and then put it down again quickly. There were lot of people yelling and waving angry banners. It was amazing how many people had the energy to make a sign and go and be furious with someone they didn't know—even just virtually—after a day at work. But then, maybe that was an extension of how passionately people here cared about politics and politicians. If you could run out of power or water if a single person like Gale screwed up, then it was life or death, not something of passing interest.

He was glad he couldn't hear the yelling. Mx Francis would be able to, with the full suite of implants. And smell the food adverts, and taste the smoke from the virtual grills, and maybe even feel the heat.

"Crowdrage," Mx Francis said dully, rubbing their forehead.

"What was that, sorry?"

"Huh? Oh. There's a feeling that comes with a big swell of social media interest, or a big change in the stock market, or a breaking news story. Groupsorrow is when an AI dies, you can feel a sort of absence in everything. Crowdjoy is when loads of people are celebrating something online; you get it even if you don't know what they're talking about. No?"

"No, yeah, I know, I just didn't know there were words," January said palely. Tasting and feeling things that only existed in the imagination of an internet server seemed bad enough, but this was a lot worse. "Do you really not mind having all that plugged into your brain?"

Mx Francis patted him on the head. "It's okay, it's not your fault you're from a hole in the ground."

"The Royal Opera House."

"A hole in the ground," Mx Francis said soothingly. "Now be a good cave person and come up with an amazing put-down for these idiots."

"But you can't be in the shot, because that cardigan will make everyone want to kill you," he said. Grudgingly, he did actually understand Gale's joy in the fight. The only difference was degree. What January liked was playing conkers, and what Gale liked was impaling people on spikes.

"It's designer!" Mx Francis protested.

"It's mustard. You look like a hotdog. But sure, let's film me saying Senator Gale definitely isn't an evil genius. You know the more we say that, the more evil-genius they look, right?"

"Yes, but your accent sounds so penetratingly stupid that people can't imagine you're clever enough to be lying," Mx Francis said, but January knew he'd won, because they looked concerned about the cardigan.

"Really though," he said. "What does it mean, about the halo tests? If no one's memory shows anything . . . ?"

"Honestly I don't know." They sighed. "I think it might mean those messages were faked to make it look like she was talking to you. Someone's out for you, Jan, as well as the Senator."

24

The police stayed overnight, because the dust had clogged up the engines of their ships, and before the morning meeting, the head investigator sat down with Gale and January to explain, looking robotic, that the investigation was closed, since there were no more leads.

"It is a very difficult and unfortunate thing to have been through of course, but we believe Lucy Collins was a lone wolf."

"You believe that in a similar way to believing in the tooth fairy and river spirits?" Gale said, gleaming.

January wondered if he should stop them, but then decided he would rather sit back and watch the blood sport.

The investigator bridled. "I *beg* your pardon?" they asked, with a sharp edge that must have worked on most people.

It didn't work on Gale. Gale straightened in the happy way they always did when someone offered them a decent fight.

"She managed to get access to military-grade grenades," Gale said. "She must have done so *before* the dust storm came, but she made no preparation for getting past a functioning security system. And she was sending and receiving messages from someone who supplied her with those grenades, and who assured her the system was down. There does appear to be a significantly second-person-shaped silhouette in your investigation, does there not?"

"We believe the messages were faked to implicate Mx Stirling. The Earthstrong Rights groups consider his marriage into House Gale a kind of betrayal, so anything they can do to show his sympathies truly lie with them is to their benefit," the investigator said stiffly. "She could have got the hardware from anywhere, there's an open black market among Earthstronger rights groups. She probably had them for a while before she seized the opportunity presented by the dust storm."

"Then how did they fake it? How did they know where we would be and when?" Gale said cheerfully. "That tower room is four hundred feet up, she didn't fire a grenade in there by accident. Someone who knows my schedule told them. Point them out, would you please?"

"That side of the investigation was inconclusive."

"This is a wild guess, but is the Praetorian Service[22] perhaps leaning on you to shut up and not look into this further?"

"I can't comment on that."

"All right. Well, thank you for your few anaemic efforts. Your ships are repaired. I'll send the bill to your department." Gale watched them go. "At this stage the Consul might as well write I DID IT in neon above Jade Hill," they remarked to January.

"What can we do?" January said. He had no idea how you went about proving that the person in charge was trying to kill you.

Gale shrugged a little. "Win the election."

Because the tower windows were broken, the morning meeting was in the dining room, around the long table that ran the length of the window. Some people hesitated before they sat down, looking out into

---

22   January looked them up. The praetorians were the people who had taken him from the Tiangong to Jade Hill, the Consul's personal security service. Like a lot of English in Tharsis, "praetorian" was a weird translation from the real Chinese name. In Chinese it was just "the State Security Ministry," but whoever did the official English translations had, like usual, decided that you couldn't have anything that sounded too normal or else people would be fooled into thinking it wasn't all scary and foreign. The original praetorians were the people who'd looked after the Roman emperors, which really did seem like a stretch to January. Given how precise Gale was, he didn't understand why they'd use it, but when he asked later, Gale said that if you had a choice between making your country sound boring and normal and full of bureaucracy, or like an awesome scary let's-have-the-Christians-eaten-by-lions kind of place, they knew which one they wanted thanks very much.

the sepia fury of the dust. The brilliant, high-altitude blue sky was gone. Where you could still see it in tiny ribbons, it had gone amber, and the dust plumes might have hidden any number of people carrying grenades.

Sasha was still sending mistrustful looks towards January every so often, but January only felt sorry for them. It must have been horrible to be in charge of a security system that didn't work. Maybe he would have felt differently if he had spent his entire life here knocking up against people like Sasha, but because he hadn't, he just—didn't.

Since yesterday, when he'd felt remarkably okay, he had stiffened up, and all the bruises he had thought he hadn't got were making themselves heard. The cut on his hand was okay, because Dr Okonkwo had fixed it—there was a special magic spray that sealed the wound—but the rest of him felt like he'd been hit by a train. He didn't remember going down awkwardly on one knee, the left one, but it hurt like hell, and as he sat down, he had to draw it up to his chest and push his hand under the hem of his trouser leg so he could see if anything terrible had happened to it. The joint felt swollen and hot and worryingly hard, or it did where he could get his fingertips under the kneecap of his cage. He hoped it was just a bang and he hadn't wrenched anything. He really did not want to see any more of Dr Okonkwo than he had to. For all it must have looked odd, he kept his hands clasped around it, willing the throb to go away.

Someone plinked their fingernails against the shoulder blade of his cage—he didn't feel it, only heard the metal sing—and he looked around. Gale bowed a fraction and set a cup of coffee down by his hand and, holy of holies, some painkillers. He blinked, surprised, and Gale gave him the cinders of a smile before they sat down. It was only for him: it was too brief and too subtle for the cameras to have caught it.

"If we explode, we explode," Gale told everyone. "I know everyone's frightened of another attack. But terrorists and bombs do not affect the weather. The dust is here; and the output of the sun fields is already down twenty-five per cent. So. Dr Molotov: cost and timing to build a new array in orbit?"

"Three billion yuan and two and a half months."

"Okay," said Gale, unmoved, as though three billion yuan was just another figure to plug into the algebra of the storm. "Which means we need to make the power we have right now last two and a half months. What do we have in storage?"

Dr Molotov stood up. They didn't look like they should have been at work today, but as Gale had said, the dust wasn't going to wait for everyone to recover. "Hopefully as everyone knows, our main energy storage system is sand. That's what those silos are, out there." They pointed out to some gigantic structures out towards the edge of the cliff. "When we have excess energy from the grid, we heat the sand up to six hundred degrees. Those silos keep it hot, and when we need the energy in winter when there's much less sunlight, we convert it to electricity."

January had a sinking feeling, but it was Mx Francis who said it.

"But we're almost at the end of winter."

Dr Molotov nodded miserably. "Yes. We have very little left in the sand batteries. This couldn't have come at a worse time. We have two weeks of power stored in them. Usually that would be a generous margin; usually the bright season would have started two weeks ago."

Everyone looked outside, where purple lightning flickered and the rest of the sky was roiling brown.

"We must have an emergency backup," someone else said.

"We do; we do. That's the gravity train, which runs down the cliff to the bottom of the Valley. It's a four-mile drop, so it can generate a good bit of friction." They swallowed. "We have all of the trains at the top of the cliff just now. That's storing—uh, about a hundred and twenty megawatts of power."

Gale made a quiet sound low in their chest. "Is that all?"

"Afraid so." Molotov looked like they were in pain. "It's an emergency system, to tide us over if there's a flaw in the sun fields or in the sand batteries. It was never designed to power Tharsis for any length of time."

January was trying to look up what a gravity train was, but the internet was telling him too many different things for it to make sense.

"Ah—for those of us without an engineering degree, why's a hundred and twenty megawatts bad?" Mx Francis said, focus coming back to the scientist after having stared into the middle distance, the way everyone did when they reading something online.

"Because Tharsis uses twenty megawatts per day," Gale said.

There was a silence round the table.

"Hang on. *What?*" Mx Francis said at last. "You're saying by the end of winter, we're sometimes a *week* from total blackout?"

Gale stood up slowly and picked up a stylus to write on the screen on the wall. "I know not all of you know how the sun fields work, so here are the numbers. First: Tharsis needs—this is averaged for seasonal variation—fourteen gigawatts of power in one year—"

"What's a gigawatt though, actually?" someone asked.

Gale glanced at the blank faces around the table. "Stop me if you don't understand or if it's too . . . heart-stoppingly boring." They aimed the last at January. At first he thought they meant he was stupidest person in the room, but then realized that wasn't like Gale, and that what they really meant was that he was the only one whose position here didn't rely on pretending to know what was happening. He was the one who could ask.

"A gigawatt is a thousand megawatts; a megawatt is a million watts. A watt is a *rate* of energy use; one joule per second. A joule is about the energy it takes to lift an apple above your head on Earth. A ten-watt lightbulb uses ten joules per second. Ten apples."

January had never heard it set out like that before. He made notes on his phone, feeling odd. He had assumed he would never understand things like this, but the way Gale talked made it sound straightforward.

"Second: the surface of Mars receives, at the very best, five hundred watts per metre squared from sunlight—so five hundred joules of energy every second. This is less than half of what Earth gets. Thirty per cent of that is reflected away by our atmosphere, sometimes more, so in the real world, it's more like three hundred. Being stationed in the tropics at altitude is the best place to catch as much as possible, hence the Mariner Plains. A solar array like ours can get about fifty per cent of that energy, which is very good. At our best, in summer, we can therefore harvest about a hundred and fifty watts per metre squared. That means one square metre of Martian solar farm panels can power fifteen standard lightbulbs."

January had to shuffle around his idea of how the world worked, because those numbers sounded shockingly low. All at once he could understand why power here was so expensive. If you had to build a whole square metre of solar panelling for even fifteen lightbulbs, then the amount you'd need to power a whole city, with power left to spare, was madness.

Gale was writing numbers as they went, in a steady stream, without having to glance away or pause to check anything. January sat forward, feeling bizarrely like he was at a performance. It was no small skill, to stand up unexpectedly in front of thirty people and reel off things like this by heart, in a logical order, without hesitating. Like any good teacher, Gale spoke in sentences so exact he could hear the punctuation.

"So: in order to generate twenty megawatts in a day—that's twenty million watts—we need to cover about a hundred and forty square kilometres with heliostats. But, those are the best possible conditions, which we don't usually get. In practise, we need more like three hundred square kilometres of solar mirrors. But that's cutting it fine, that's just enough, for a day, *if* we don't have particularly bad weather; but, we are almost guaranteed bad weather for four hundred days of every year. What we need to do is produce excess in summer, when sunlight is plentiful, so we can add to the grid when demand is high but supply is low in winter. We have five hundred square kilometres to be on the safe side." Gale nodded outside.

"The sunlight is concentrated by the mirror array on a tank of liquid salt in the height of a tower. That salt heats to a thousand degrees Celsius, and that thermal energy powers generators, which connect to the national grid. We have ten towers."

Gale paused for a second. "It is not cost-effective to build many more fields than we realistically need. It's fantastically expensive to build one. Even more to maintain it. Panels get smashed or torn, machinery has to be replaced, and liquid salt of a thousand degrees is not a forgiving substance. We can only grow at the pace the city does, or these arrays don't pay for themselves. We can't do what Earth does, we can't generate a lot of power by putting solar fabric on clothes and roofs and cars, because most people live in the Valley, which gets even less sunlight than we do up here. They have to, because it's the only place on Mars with enough air for first- and second-generation arrivals. That will improve as the terraforming process continues, but for now, that's what we've got."

January wondered whose bright idea it was to live on Mars in the first place. It seemed increasingly impractical.

"Therefore, we must run close to capacity at the very end of winter." Gale looked around. "Does anyone have any questions? Communications and marketing staff need to understand this as much as scientists do or you'll be trying to write press releases that make no sense to you."

"We're all going to starve and die, aren't we?" Mx Francis said.

"Dehydration will get you ages before you can starve," Mx Ren put in, looking quite cheerful about the idea of watching Mx Francis die of thirst.

"I think the only realistic option to tide us over will be something to do with the gravity trains," Dr Molotov said.

January lifted his hand a little. "What *is* a gravity train?"

"Medieval," Gale said, and the scientists sort of laughed. "It's a basic way of storing energy. When you have excess power, you use it to raise something heavy to a height, so that the thing has plenty of potential energy—the energy of placement, yes? Apple has no energy," they said, setting one on the floor. They lifted it up above their head. "Apple has potential energy. It could fall."

January wondered how the apple knew.

"Martian gravity is very weak, so just rolling something up a hill doesn't give it much energy, but fortunately we have a four-mile drop in our back yard, into the Mariner Valley. When we have excess solar energy, we use it to pull a chain of concrete blocks up the cliff. When we need that energy back, we let the blocks fall down their tracks again. The friction generated by applying the braking system gives us back most of the energy we put in by lifting them up in the first place."

"Could we just crank them up again by hand or horsepower once they've been lowered? The trains," someone from Mx Francis's team said.

"Hell no," one of the scientists snorted.

Gale fixed them with the serene stare they gave people when they were gauging exactly how much sausage meat it would be possible to make with the available human, and the scientist looked embarrassed.

"Each block of each train weighs nine tonnes," Gale said. "Each train has twenty blocks. One horsepower equates to two hundred and fifty kilograms lifted up by one foot in one second."

January wondered who just knew the energy equivalents of horse-power off the top of their head. Gale wasn't reading any of this from inside their lenses; their focus was solidly on the table and the people around it.

Gale thought, but only for half a second. It was too brief for them to be using the internet or anything else to help calculate it. "That's seven hundred and twenty horses to lift the trains by one foot per second. And more to switch them out once they're tired. The Valley is four miles high; twenty-one thousand feet. There aren't that many horses on Mars. Human strength, over any period of time, is only about point one horsepower, so we'd be looking at seven thousand people to raise all the trains. Even lifting only one, which would generate less power than Tharsis needs in a day, would take about nine hundred. Twenty-one thousand seconds is about six hours; so that's six hours to raise one train, which would power the city for less than twenty-four; in winter conditions. Worst-case scenario, we can revisit that, but it's not an efficient solution."

There was another long quiet. Gale came back around the table to sit down again. They were walking slowly, favouring one side. The pros-thetic must have been hurting. January swallowed. It was amazing he hadn't broken Gale in pieces, slinging them onto the floor yesterday.

"So," Gale concluded. "Back to where we started. We need to find a way to get from three weeks of power to ten weeks. Today. Dr Molotov, you also need to let the administrative staff know about contractors, steel, and design work for getting the array into orbit. We need to know whose launchpads we can use, whose foundries, and how much energy that in itself will take."

Dr Molotov hinged forward. "Senator, we might come up with a good way to generate emergency power but we might not. I think we need to implement rolling blackouts right now. The longer we wait, the more power Tharsis consumes while we're still not producing more."

Everyone looked at Gale, who was quiet for a second.

"The last time we had rolling blackouts was under Kali," Gale said at last. "And that caused widespread riots, and three hundred deaths. It's winter. People will freeze overnight if we cut their power even for a few hours. I understand what you're saying, doctor, but—blackouts are a last resort."

"Then we at least need to shut down power-hungry industries," Dr Molotov persisted. "Currency mines eat power like nobody's business. The Rings at the Tiangong, those are insane. Ideally we should pause interplanetary shipping—the electricity required to fuel those engines is a significant percentage of the city's whole consumption. Please, Senator. I know nobody wants a repeat of the Power Riots, but . . . it can't be business as usual until we come up with something, because we might not come up with anything."

"That will seriously damage the economy," Mx Ren murmured.

"If we start shutting down industries like that, it sends a message that House Gale can't keep the world open for business," Mx Francis put in. "The Consul will mince you."

January realized Gale was looking at him, dark eyes full of a plea to say something, and he understood suddenly that they couldn't say it. They couldn't be filmed saying, *Screw all that, morons*, because that would then be what the Consul broadcast on loop. He had to say it, because then, Gale was a good knight who was listening to their consort, not a radical. It was such delicate choreography.

And it was amazing, because even a few weeks ago, he had been glad when they'd got string and tin cans over the distance between them. This was a lot more than string. This was a bridge. They had a bridge. It was a good one, too. He didn't know *anyone* else well enough to read what they meant just by the way they were looking at him.

"Stop being dicks," January told the others. "You want to prioritise the Rings at the Tiangong? They're for eight super-rich people who will absolutely not die if it shuts down. They can sod off home to Dubai and enjoy their gold-veneered racing cars. Mars *isn't* open for business, there's a giant dust storm, and trying to pretend otherwise will make you look like you've lost your minds."

Gale bowed a little where they sat, and shot him a glance that said *thank you*. "Mx Stirling and Dr Molotov are right. We can do without heavy-energy luxury industries. I'll give them some warning now. Everyone else, go to work."

Nobody could get away fast enough. Gale didn't stand again, though. They stayed still, both hands pressed to their bad leg where the join of the prosthetic must have been.

"Is there anything I can do?" January asked quietly.

Gale took a breath to lie, but then stopped. "No. It's . . . This will sound really creepy," they added, looking apprehensive, and he tipped back, because he honestly couldn't imagine Gale ever sounding creepy. They were the opposite of creepy. He was pretty sure that for ninety-eight per cent of humans alive, if it were to turn out that Gale had been spying on them from inside their wardrobe, having followed them secretly for months and held their poodle hostage, they would be delighted with the attention.

"What do you mean?"

"It hurts because I can see that your knee hurts."

January tilted his head down and to the side. He had heard and he had understood, and he fully had not, at the same time.

He had never seen anyone look as paralysingly ashamed as Gale did then. "It isn't you personally, that came out wrong. It just happens, if you're missing a limb. If you see someone else smack their knee, it hurts in the knee you haven't got. I get it all the time. Something about mirror neurones."

He thought about it, then put both hands around his own knee and pressed carefully. It hurt a lot less now the painkillers had kicked in. Gale sank back in their chair, as obviously relieved as if he'd done it to them.

"Thank you. I'm so sorry."

"No," he said, and kept his own knee cradled to make sure Gale could see he had no weight on it at all. He saw their shoulders relax. He kept watching, fascinated, and pleased that it was something so easily fixed, and then felt a rush of awkwardness, because what it meant, when he was sitting here holding his own knee, was that in a very real way he was also holding theirs.

"Anyway, I wanted to talk to you." They glanced back to check there were no drones immediately nearby. "We have some numbers in this morning, about you," they said. "Viewing figures, social media trends, all that."

January nodded, tight. Gale was going to say it was over. They'd both tried, but events were conspiring against the whole thing. He'd fade into the background now and after a year there would be a divorce.

"Instant hit," Gale said, turning a tablet around to show him a graph he didn't understand, but it went steeply upward. "Media interest is surging. Mx Francis is hoping that you might do an interview circuit with some of the news and the talk show people in town today about your arrest, and about the situation on Earth, if you feel up to it. They'll brief you."

January had to wait for a second, because it was so the opposite of what he'd expected to hear that it didn't filter down properly at first.

"We'll start to see the Consul attacking you openly in the press soon, too. The more people focus on you, the more you legitimise everything I say. So they're going to try and make sure no one is looking at you for any of the right reasons. If you can't weather it in front of all the cameras, we'll put on you on sick leave for a little while. Altitude. Tinnitus from the bomb, anything you like. I know this is a lot."

"No, I'll be all right," January said, surprised the offer was even there. Gale was the one at work bright and early the morning after being bombed. He'd expected them to be deaf to any sense that anybody might struggle with nasty press.

"Are you sure?" Gale pushed. "Because I don't want you to do yourself damage because you think you're being paid to give me a platform to say things you despise."

January smiled. "I am being paid to do that. And I agreed to, and you've done everything you said you would and better."

Gale watched him for what felt like a long time. It was rare, January realized suddenly, for anyone to do that, in ordinary conversation. Mostly, people only glanced at you, checking you hadn't hurried off after an interesting llama. They didn't *see*. It made him go strangely still inside. The Gales of the worlds did not usually spend their time seeing the Januarys. He tried to scoop up the memory and hold it close to take out later, if he needed it. "I know that you have nowhere else to go. But when I ask you to do things like this—public interviews, huge events, filmed publicity stunts—you have a veto. You're my consort, not my clerk, and you're being paid for your time, not your soul."

January took a deeper breath, meaning to say something along the lines of, *Look, of course I'm going to do my job*; but then he held it. Gale had come to fetch him from the secret police yesterday without so much as a sigh. The two of them had passed the point of communicating in polite trivialities.

"Senator—nobody knows what happened to the last person who had my job. Maybe it's what you say, maybe Max did run away with River, but maybe they disagreed with you once too often. You talk a really good talk, and nobody has ever been as nice to me as you are; but I would be an idiot to forget that talking and doing are different. You're Schrödinger's cat, for me. You could be what you say, or you could be radioactive. Don't get me wrong, it's far better than what I'd have otherwise, but pardon me if I don't kick the box with the nuclear cat in it."

Gale was quiet. If he had thought that they cared what his opinion of them was, he would have worried that the flicker that went through their eyes then was hurt. But they didn't, so it couldn't be. "That seems sensible to me."

"Thank you, Senator. I'll ask Mx Francis to brief me about the shows."

As he bowed and got up, his knee twinged and he winced; Gale did too.

25

It was a solid afternoon of interviews. Suddenly every news programme was doing pieces about the criminalisation of Earthstrongers and let's hear from January Stirling, that famously innocent person. Mx Francis went with him to three different news studios. At the end of each interview, everyone asked the same question:

"Especially in the light of the terrible situation on Earth, how do you feel about Senator Gale's naturalisation policies?"

He hated it every time, even though he had prepared his answers.

"Senator Gale was torn apart by someone who looked like me," was all he could say. Even though he wanted to say, *I'm terrified, I'm one wrong answer away from being sent to prison or deported and then; then, well.* "It isn't my place to have any feelings about that."

"That's a very different answer to the one you gave a month ago. You accused the Senator of genocide."

Someone behind a camera waved at him and tapped their ear. *You're speaking too quietly.* He looked down. If he spoke any louder, he'd sound aggressive. People had softer voices here. Normal speaking tone for him was how people here snarled.

"I was wrong to say anything. I wish I hadn't."

"Wrong to say it—but you believe it?"

In all the interviews so far, he'd lied; he'd said of course not, because that was easier, it was what he was being paid to do, it meant legions of people wouldn't call him evil. But now, he just couldn't. Every time he said that, he felt grubby, and ashamed, because doing anything from terror of being cast out was always going to feel dirty.

"Sorry, you just asked me what I felt and I said it wasn't my place, but it's in—such contrast to what I believe I think I'm going to have to say it after all," he said, and behind the camera, he saw Mx Francis throw their hands up at him. *Would you mind not derailing my whole campaign and just sticking to the script, thanks?* "I feel as though being Earthstrong here is a kind of original sin. I didn't choose to be born this way, but I was, and it is dangerous to other people. I feel like there's no way for me to be a good person here, and Earthstrong, at the same time."

There was a strange hush in the audience, and even among the camera crews, who were all looking at him now, and not the drones they were usually watching hawklike. It was another one of those hanging moments like at the factory, before something smashed and all chaos broke loose. He breathed in deeper. Nothing would smash this time. He was getting better at this. Being around Gale was helping.

"But—what I believe is that there's no such bloody thing as original sin. Nobody is bad just for existing. If you're born a man, you're not evil because you *could* hurt a woman, only if you *do*. If you're born rich, you're not bad just because you could exploit poor people, only if you do. And if you're Earthstrong . . . you're not bad because you *could* hurt someone Natural."

He had to look right away from Mx Francis, who was miming stabbing him. "I think any kind of strength means you have to be careful around people who don't have it. That's just being an honourable person. I have to be careful of the strength in my bones." He hesitated. "And other people have to be careful of their power, and their money, and their intellect."

Because he had been expecting to be shouted down, he didn't understand what he was hearing at first when it got a round of applause from the audience. He nodded slightly, seriously doubting he'd said anything a thousand other people hadn't said before him, and painfully aware that Mx Francis looked like they might have set up a big January trap backstage with spikes at the bottom.

———

There was no January trap with spikes, as it happened. Mx Francis was oddly quiet, and their focus kept straying off into the middle distance in a way that looked like they were seeing online things he couldn't. As they left the studio building—a sparkling horseshoe-shaped tower whose lower levels were all shops that ran discounts for the broadcasting company staff—they had to navigate around a big queue outside a convenience store. Through the window, the shelves were mostly bare, and a harassed-looking clerk was unstacking boxes as quickly as they could. People were taking things right from their hands. At the door, the automated tills strobed crazily. Someone hurried past January and Mx Francis with a whole net sack of eggs.

"Who panic-buys eggs?" Mx Francis said incredulously.

"It's anything that'll last, isn't it," January said, watching someone else go by holding a paper bag of flour like it was the crown jewels. He didn't know how much the warehouses held in reserve, but it couldn't be much, and with the dust—if it kept up, the next harvest was buggered, worldwide.

"Insane."

"No, it's just what people do," January said, thinking of the famine. He'd been about twelve when it happened, so his memory wasn't perfect, but it was good enough. Flour, pasta, and canned things had vanished the second they were in the shops, and that was right at the start when the shops were still okay. There had been rationing—he remembered his mum showing him how to tick things off on the card—and there had been fights, actual fist fights, about what was equivalent to what if the shops didn't have something. Could you get another orange if there were no eggs? His mum, who was a vintner in the enviable position of having a full grape harvest, had handed out baskets and baskets of grapes and therefore got whatever she wanted from everyone, but in the old folks' home down the road, someone had died in the heat and a pair of old ladies who were too frail to leave their flats, and who the staff had forgotten about, cooked him in bits until an ambulance crew found out.

Of course it had been a lot worse in cities where you couldn't go out and pick blackberries off the verges. The assistant director at the theatre had still been growing potatoes in her bathtub just in case, even when he joined the company ten years later.

He looked up when he realized Mx Francis was staring at him, and remembered they were only twenty-five. Things like this looked insane if you'd never seen them before; they were allowed to be shocked.

"It'll be okay," he said. "People get a lot worse than this if something is really wrong. Just allow extra time to do your shopping, if you go home at the weekends. There'll be queues."

Mx Francis looked like they had just after the bomb. "What . . . does it look like if it gets worse?"

"It's hard to explain," he said after he'd thought about it. "Frightened people do frightening things. Don't let it worry you. It's just humans being humans."

"I don't know what that means," Mx Francis said dully, and January wished he had Gale's gift for explaining.

He thought about that little old man who'd nudged him aside near the convenience store at home in Americatown, and the umbrella. That wouldn't be working any more.

"It's gone down rather well on socials, what you just said," Mx Francis said, from left field.

January risked a glance up at them. "Um. For who?"

"You've got a hashtag. #EarthstrongHonour." They sounded happy, at least.

"Right," he said, not sure if that was a good thing or a bad one.

As they passed through on the train, the dust blurred things, but not so much that January couldn't make out how the normal traffic had thinned almost to nothing. Nobody was driving; the dust was already clogging engines, and even if it hadn't been, the normal purple-blue sheen of the solar sheets on the roads had faded. No power. As they whipped past the Tiangong on the overhead line, he saw the Rings slow, and then stop. The lights there shut down. In Gagarin Square, people were pointing.

He had to stare. That had happened because he'd said it should. It was Dr Molotov's idea, but—he was the one who had insisted. And Gale had done it. He'd said it and it had happened. He had never known anything like it. The most he'd ever affected in life was what someone else decided to have for lunch. He was so used to seeing big, city-changing things as the product of some kind of faceless officialdom that it was a shock to realize it came down to some random person at an important table saying, *Well, actually* . . .

"Meanwhile," Mx Francis said, "tomorrow is the benefit night at the Tiangong. The Senator's going to ask you. Remember to look, you know. Delighted."

He had to close his eyes. Against the backdrop of the storm, of all those terrifying numbers, the solar array, the gravity trains, this idiot little non-romance seemed very trivial indeed. He could only imagine how Gale felt about having to pretend to flirt while the energy of the city dwindled.

26

Songshu had a team of resident doctors—you needed them if you had five hundred people living at altitude—and for Dr Okonkwo, the general plan had been to take the position for five years and have a nice, gentle run into a nice, gentle retirement which they would be spending (not that they had planned it meticulously) chiefly on cruise liners to and from that wonderful holiday resort on Earth's moon where the gravity was so lovely to your knees.

Aubrey Gale losing a leg had thrown what Dr Okonkwo was willing, just, to admit was a small spanner in the works. Rehabilitation was long and boring and disheartening, but Gale was one of those remarkable people who seemed interested in the whole process more than beaten down by it. That had been manageable. But what had emerged after was what Dr Okonkwo was coming to think of as their professional arch-nemesis, and it wasn't any of the tricky brain tumours or mystery cross-generational naturalisation illnesses professors taught everybody to expect in medical school.

Gale had sleep paralysis. Only it wasn't.

"Well, you look like you've been dragged through a hedge back-wards," Dr Okonkwo observed as Sasha saw them into Gale's room. Dr Okonkwo had treated three generations of Gales, each one more intimidating than the last, but if you opened with almost-abuse, any given Gale was for some reason much more likely to do as they were told later. "New medication not working?"

"No."

"Well. Usual drill then," Dr Okonkwo said, and set the scanner halo over Gale's temples, and the haptic engine transfer widget thing round their wrist.

They dropped down in the chair opposite to study the imaging as it ghosted across their tablet. Round Okonkwo's own wrist, the twin of the other widget thing—probably it had a name but when you had a Knee your capacity for remembering pointless information went steeply downhill—lit up.

On the tablet, the images writhed and smoked, resolving occasionally into sudden sharp recognisable things that were gone so quickly they were difficult to follow. None of it made sense; and if Okonkwo had shown this footage to a lecture theatre full of medical students, not one in two hundred would have said it could be anything but the weirdest, most vivid kind of dream. But it wasn't dreaming. It was Gale's mind very much awake. It was Gale's baseline; it was Gale right now, sitting across from Okonkwo in that chair.

As they had said to the police, the halo could show you what the subject was thinking, but it could not show you *why* they thought so. Even if you watched it frame by frame, Gale's readout looked like the most incomprehensible, disturbing madness.

What it was, was a particular kind of cleverness. Not pi-to-the-nth-decimal; that was clear on these things. It was the kind that could leap between apparently unrelated things and see connections. Some of Gale's, Dr Okonkwo could understand. If Gale thought something was stupid, deer and horses often appeared on the screen, because they had studied Japanese and the word for "stupid" was written with the signs for "deer" and "horse." Some were bizarre. If someone said "mother," Gale thought of spiders and, for some reason, advanced mathematics and something to do with the Peruvian Andes.

A moment later, the feed from Gale's haptic engines came through into Okonkwo's own. They were sitting in their own chair, yes, but they could also feel how Gale felt sitting in theirs. They were in a lot of pain, because they were walking too much on the prosthetic, but it was so ever-present that they didn't really notice it. The unevenness of that new gait was making their spine hurt too. Over all that was a fog of subtle but unpleasant anxiety. Things filtered through few by few, and each one made Okonkwo glad that *their* only problem was the Knee.

Last to get through the haptics was thought, and when Gale's thoughts arrived, Okonkwo had to do what they never did with any other patient. They muted the feed. Gale's mind happened in four languages at once, random snippets invading all the time, and although it was a calm kind of chaos if you really concentrated, the upshot was a migraine and some very strong feelings about Proto-Indo-European.

"As always, think of the moment you woke up, please, Senator."

As always, Gale looked away, but did as they were told.

The way sleep paralysis worked was that you half woke up still immobilised by the chemicals that stopped you sleepwalking, and then you saw someone in the room; and usually it came with overpowering fear and the sense that this was a hostile presence. The visions could be incredibly vivid. It was horrible to feel, even through a haptic engine link.

But Gale never *saw* anything. And they were never paralysed. What they *felt*, though, was something very heavy kneeling right on their ribs, and something holding their wrists down. Something too strong to fight. There was never anything there. Only the hallucination was pin-sharp. In it, they could even feel someone's bootlaces digging into them, and sometimes, the imaginary assailant even had different clothes; Gale could feel wool or cotton, and once, the zip on a leather jacket.

A hallucination it was, however. There was definitely nothing and nobody there.

What drove Dr Okonkwo crazy was that this was not, however much it felt as if it should be, actually sleep paralysis. Gale could move, speak, struggle, all of it. They didn't just *think* they could: there was drone footage to prove it. It was disturbing to watch.

And it didn't feel right. Okonkwo wasn't a neuro specialist, but they'd felt haptic links with sleep paralysis patients before, and there was a different quality to this hallucination. It was trauma, of course it was, that was the trigger—if you lost a leg and then developed a debilitating sleep disorder, then you'd be an idiot not to imagine they might be related, but Gale was annoying on that front as well. Of course they were traumatised, but having been fairly profoundly damaged as a child,[23] they hadn't begun the whole process thinking they had some basic right not to feel dreadful. And so bizarrely, they coped with dreadful rather better than a well-balanced person. The sleep problems weren't part of any wider net of symptoms. Without these night-time hallucinations, Okonkwo would have thought they might, actually, be fine.

Okonkwo pulled off the haptic widget and handed Gale some painkillers.

"Hm? I'm fine."

"You're in quite a lot of pain."

"Oh."

"Anyway," Dr Okonkwo concluded heavily, and then paused, because they felt peculiar just feeling their own feelings now, and relieved not to have a painful leg, "there isn't much else we can do now but antipsychotics, and the side-effects of those are . . . such that I know you'll veto them immediately."

Gale nodded. "So what you're saying is . . . live with it and report back if anything changes."

"I'm afraid so. The only consolation is, it's probably going to become less frequent and then go away on its own. Trauma does dim over time."

"I'm not traumatised," Gale sighed. "I keep trying to say."

"You assuredly are traumatised, you just don't have the basic emotional wherewithal to understand."

"So I can't sleep and my doctor thinks I'm stupid. Superb."

---

23 Great Houses were proverbially dreadful at child-rearing. In the name of having the best education in the worlds, heirs were raised mostly by AI scholars, some of whom were two hundred years old and really not very fond of children.* The House Gale AI was called Anansi. They famously refused to communicate with anybody who hadn't learned the periodic table (it was a way, Anansi said blackly, of weeding out children who weren't trying hard enough), which led to a bit of a skewed start for Gale heirs. If you went back even five or six generations, everyone's first word was "hydrogen." Like every other Gale doctor, Okonkwo had tried hard to get rid of Anansi, but course for the Gales that was like trying get rid of their parents. No matter how bad parents were, it was rare to find a person who actually wanted to dismantle them and reuse the parts to make new parents.

*This was still better than being raised by Kali Gale, Dr Okonkwo had to admit.

"I didn't say—"

"You know this is why nobody likes you," Gale said, serene.

"Lots of people like me," Okonkwo protested, and then felt insecure.

"They're lying," Gale said. "Thank you, Doctor."

By the door, Kasha was watching her imaginary friend, as usual, holding out one paw and then the other.

"You know there's something wrong with that dog," Okonkwo said, from a drab need to get revenge.

Kasha seemed to realize she was being talked about, looked over, then hid under Gale's chair.

"See?" Gale said. They were watching one of the morning shows on a tablet now. January Stirling was on it. They were old-fashioned about that; they didn't like using their lenses and being virtually in the audience. "Nobody."

27

The Gale pearls spent six months in every year on display in a museum, because they were the most valuable in the world. They were the oldest, too; the first saltwater oyster bed had been hand-sown two hundred years ago by graduate students on Gale land, at the edge of a special experimental salt marsh. They had first been strung—two hundred and forty-four of them—for a wedding that had been drone-bombed and so they'd passed to another branch of the family unworn, cased in black velvet and bad luck.

January knew that because, while he waited in the dining room for Mx Francis's team to faff with lighting and angles and Mx Ren poked at him to make him sit less like a pole dancer in an especially sticky bar, he watched a livestream about what people could expect to see all the celebrities wearing at the Tiangong fundraiser tonight. Gale was much anticipated. The event was still an hour off starting, but there was already a crowd of reporters outside, glittering with golden flashes as people activated the cameras in their contact lenses.

The Consul was anticipated too. They were going to use the event to give a statement about the dust.

The Consul's card was still in his pocket. Every so often, he took it out and looked at it. There was a lot he wanted to say.

How does an artificial dust storm start? Did you start it? Was it Earth?

Did you just—sorry, but I have to ask—try to kill us and blame it on me?

But none of those were questions the Consul would realistically answer. What sort of person looked guilty and said, *Yes, whoops, sorry, that was me trying to murder the opposition, won't happen again . . .*

He was starting to feel very, very frustrated by all the things he didn't know. He wished he could just dose everyone with some kind of truth serum. It would be unethical and dreadful et cetera, but at least he'd know if he was now this second standing on quicksand.

Max was wearing the Gale pearls in that picture upstairs.

"Okay. We're ready," Mx Francis said.

It was a little shock to come back to himself and remember he had to do some acting now.

"Just try to imagine how you'd be if you'd never taken any drugs and you didn't live in a dumpster," Mx Ren told him brightly, with a glitter that said: *Look, I'd never say it if you looked in any way like that. I'm saying it because you're worried you look like that and I think that's obviously hysterical.*

"Oh my God, you can't say that," Mx Francis said, going high.

"Or I could imagine how you'd be if you weren't possessed by Baal, eater of children and prince of the toad-infested swamps of hell," January suggested.

Mx Ren pretended to bite him, and January grinned.

Mx Francis looked a bit wobbly about what was happening. "Could we have less . . . er . . . open abuse?"

"You look great," Mx Ren said gently, and clapped January's shoulder. "Right. And . . . rolling."

Everyone else got out of the shot. Looking like an interested crystal ball, a camera drone lifted above January's head, and he pretended to be concentrating on the livestream, where somehow the influencer was still talking about pearls. Immediately on cue, Gale sent him a text. It said, *Could you come down to my room? I need to ask a favour.*

"Probably about Earth etiquette for the ambassador of somewhere important," he lie-speculated to the drone as it followed him out and down the corridor to Gale's room, past more of those wonderful tiny courtyards of bonsai forests and hummingbirds. Mx Francis ghosted after.

The door was already resting open on its latch. He tilted it open.

People at home wore less at formal events. People showed off their shoulders and their arms. Here, formal clothes meant more clothes. Gale was in layers now. The fabrics were fine and airy, but together they had a rich weight, fitted close at the waist and shoulder but loose from the hips down, like a much heavier, conservative version of a gown, only slit up both sides to show flashes of trousers the same colour underneath. The amount of fabric was incredible; metres and metres of it, pooling and glinting in the soft light of the lamps. It was what happened, January realized with an odd jolt, when you had the money to have metres and metres of fabric. He knew what it cost; he had been friends with the costume designers at the theatre. Gale was wearing more than the worth of a house in Cornwall, even one *with* a vineyard.

He stopped in the doorway, though, because contrary to the script, Gale wasn't alone. They were sitting at a dressing table, straight and taut. Someone else was combing their hair.

It was the security officer who always took their journal everywhere. He hadn't seen them since the grenades had come in through the meeting room windows. Puzzled, he wondered if they weren't security at all but some kind of stylist, but he didn't think so; he'd never seen them do anything glitzy for anyone heading towards any cameras before.

It was all long steady strokes with a bright silver comb, slow, in a way that looked both ritual and somehow as though it might be a punishment. The more January watched, the more uncomfortable he felt.

Gale had those famous pearls wrapped around both hands. It was the way priests held rosaries.

"Hi," he said tentatively. "You, er . . . asked to see me, Senator." He held up his phone as though Gale might somehow have forgotten in the last three minutes, and still not sure he should be interrupting. There was something private-looking about the two of them there at the mirror, and he couldn't shift the sense that he had appeared immediately after a bitter row, for all he hadn't heard a sound from the corridor.

"Yes, of course," Gale said, and looked relieved.

The security officer stepped away and folded into a chair a little way away. It wasn't, January thought suddenly, how an employee would move about. He'd made a mistake about who they were, he could see that much. Family, they must have been.

Or real partner. They were the right age.

Gale didn't introduce them, though, and the other person didn't introduce themselves.

"Is there—something I can do for you?" January asked, as a drone floated in over his shoulder. For all he knew what Gale was going to say, he was nervous. It was difficult to imagine that anyone would believe what was about to happen, because it was stupid-unrealistic. The beautiful lord of the beautiful manor house did not take any interest in the mousy governess, and goddesses did not court shepherd boys from fields. Those things wouldn't have been good stories if they ever really happened.

"Only if you'd like to." Gale turned away from the mirror, and January couldn't help thinking they looked grateful to be allowed to stop seeing their own reflection. "There's an event at the Tiangong tonight, it's a charity fundraiser. It's going to be—monstrous, and I was going to go by myself but then I couldn't face it. I'm sorry to ambush you at such late notice, but would you come with me?"

Remember to look surprised . . . "Would I what?"

"Only if you'd like to," Gale said again. A pause. "There's going to be a lot of free wine and pretentious food, some of which will be cake. That's as much as I can really . . . sell it to you. The people will all be politicians and trade CEOs unfortunately." Gale did amazing work of looking hesitant. "It would be good to have some normal human company, though. If you didn't have other plans."

"S . . . enator," January said. It was off script, but seeing that person in the rust-coloured jumper with Gale again had robbed him of any small confidence he might have had that Gale was really up to spending a whole night pretending to enjoy him. "Are you sure? It's one thing to be married, it's another to actually—you know, spend time with me. I don't expect it. I know what I'm here for, everyone does." He nodded at the drone. "I don't need to be taken to parties."

Maybe he'd had a stilted family life, but he wouldn't have let a cousin comb his hair, or a brother or sister if he'd had one. And definitely not, now he was thinking about it, if he were from a Tharsese Great House. Posh people here bowed to their relatives. That was a very . . . couple-y . . . thing to do.

"Why wouldn't I want to spend time with you?" Gale asked, giving him a quizzical look.

January was supposed to just say, *Yes, great*, but he couldn't say yes without checking that having to stay with an Earthstronger for an entire evening wasn't going to end in Gale having a panic attack. What if that was what they'd been fighting about with the person in the orange jumper before he came in, whether this was a stupid thing to do or not?

Or about the idea of Gale going out tonight with their fake consort instead of their real one.

"I just . . . don't . . . want you to feel obliged. Or afraid."

Gale stood up with a hiss of silk, and like he had with the Consul, January had a stab of that very basic fear that came when someone much taller than you moved closer when you didn't expect it. Without meaning to, he stepped back. He was already only just in the room, and that step backed him against the wall. Gale noticed and stayed still. "Mx Stirling; I know it must be hard to come here and have people looking at you like you might do something terrible. But I do not think that of you, at all. I think that in a previous life you might have been a kitten that was sat on."

January laughed, and after a second, with a flicker of relief that said they'd been worried about offending him, Gale did too. The bridge was holding; it had handrails and a toll system and everything now. He looked at them for a hanging moment, wanting to say, *what a funny dance we keep doing, just because I'm strong and you're not, and you're rich and I'm not. Will we have to do it for five years?* But they didn't know each other well enough for him to say that, even if there had been nobody filming.

"I'd love to go," he said instead.

Gale smiled again. It was their movie-star smile, but the real one lay under it. The camera drone floated nearer. January didn't look, but he could almost hear Mx Francis and the producers making happy cooing noises.

In the far corner, the person in the rust-coloured jumper looked away, and he didn't blame them.

Ridiculous. The whole thing was ridiculous.

"Do you have something to wear?" Gale asked.

"I can find something," January said, and even though it was all fake, he went tingly. They were going out; he hadn't been *out* out since leaving London. He got as far as the pub with Val and the others sometimes but that wasn't out, that was directly opposite the factory. You didn't dress up. You just sort of fell in.

"Oh," Gale said. "And these are for you." They stepped nearer to him, slowly, so he could see what was happening, and then, taking his hand, set the pearls into his palm.

28

There was one train down the Valleyside for people, and one that could take cars. It was further along the cliff, and right by the gravity trains.

January sat glued to the car window, excited as a small child, as the funicular sank down the titan drop of the Valley. In the last of the light, an ambery mauve, the gravity trains looked like primordial monsters clawing up the cliffside out of the dust below. They were colossal. The weight would have ripped them off their tracks on Earth. He was starting to get used to how everything was much bigger here, from people to dogs to buildings, but the concrete blocks were each the size of a house, bolted together with magnetic shackles, each link bigger than him. It was like gliding down the length of a brutal cathedral. And there were nine of them. Nine gigantic, disconcerting things just . . . hanging on the Valley side. If they ever fell, God knew what would happen.

All that, just to store the power the city needed for a single week.

Gale had been quiet, reading something on a tablet with a stylus hovering over the text. When January looked, he realized it was language exercises in—something that didn't look like any language he had ever seen. It was more like music score for a piano; everything came in two lines, as though somehow the speaker was supposed to talk in chords. With a happy little jolt, January realized Gale would never have sat close enough to him for him see whatever they were reading before. There was room in the car for them to sit well away—there were two sets of seats facing each other, but Gale was next to him, not opposite.

"Please don't tell Mx Francis," Gale said, with what sounded like a genuine plea.

"What is that?" January asked.

Gale shifted as if talking about it were difficult, and January realized that somewhere along the way, Mx Francis had trained them to put any academic interests in the Unmentionables box alongside incest and golf.

"It's a transcript of mammoth communication."

"It's a *what* now?" January squeaked. "Why have you got transcripts of mammoths?"

"I was a linguistics lecturer. I, er . . . well, one of the things I worked on was zoolinguistics, and the communication of megafauna. Elephants, mammoths; whales."

"They have *languages*?"

"They have."

January put his hands on his temples and made a tiny exploding noise, to say: mind blown.

Gale laughed the tentative laugh of a person not convinced they were being given a truthful reaction.

January took a breath, then stopped, because in fact all this sounded familiar, and it took him a moment to remember why. "The person who did my halo test was a Professor Shang. Who—said they worked with River, your River. On this, on mammoths I think. You two did exactly the same thing?"

Something strange happened then. The just-kindling coals that were smoking a sort of nascent happiness behind Gale's eyes went out. Their whole expression shut down and turned to the diplomatic serenity they wore in the Senate, in public. It was, January was starting to learn, a mask. Whenever they wore it, they were hiding.

"Yes. Apollo twins at Great Houses always have the same education. House Gale prioritises cross-cultural studies—linguistics, translation, all that. Traditionally we've served in the Foreign Office, we're diplomats."

"That's ironic," January said, before he could stop himself, and did just manage to stop before he could add, *given what you think about foreigners.*

"Why?"

"Nothing. Why would you ever want to be a senator if you can spend your life talking to mammoths?"

"I didn't want to be a senator. I inherited it."

"Ah, of course. Sorry."

"No, that's the price you pay for being born into obscene wealth and power," Gale said, doing their trick of hanging over the edge of smiling without falling. "It would be disgusting if I could just do what I wanted."

January was quiet for a moment, because that was an insight that had clear applications. The main reason he thought that nobody should have to naturalise was that nobody wanted to. But if you had never been allowed to do what you wanted to—then it would be hard to see why anyone else should.

"You look like I've given you a splinter," Gale observed.

"No, that's just my face."

"You make that face when I've said something you think is crushingly stupid but you don't want to explain why because you think I'll just talk over you," Gale pushed.

That, January thought, was an amazingly accurate assessment given that they'd had all of five conversations together. It was news to him, too, that they minded what he thought about anything. He had thought it was courtesy when they asked him for his opinion; it honestly hadn't occurred to him that they were taking note of the answers. It made a nervous-happy bubble in his chest.

And yet, and yet, this was the person arguing for him to be maimed if he wanted to stay for more than a year. It was becoming a depressing pattern—he just couldn't make their politics match their personality. He was in serious danger of believing that Gale might be a *nice* person; but nice people didn't want to herd other people into camps and permanently damage them.

"I could always give you some opinionated feedback about *your* face if you want," he said, because he had no intention of talking about Gale's naturalisation policies at random in the back of a car.

Or ever.

They were married, and they would be married for five years. They were only going to be able to stand the sight of each other for more than five minutes if they didn't play political point-scoring games against each other, and just now—not to mention in that last talk show interview—he had already leaned dangerously near to it. If they did that, Gale would always win, and January would just get angrier and more bitter until he couldn't do his job any more. All the two of them had to do was float on the surface of unsaid things, and everything would be all right. Or not *all* right. But enough right.

He got one of those long mirror scrutinies.

"This is going to look like bribery now," Gale said ruefully, "but I have a present for you. You needn't use them if you don't want to, but . . ." They drew out a slim box. Inside was a pair of glasses, silver-rimmed and delicate. "They might be useful."

January lifted them out slowly. The lenses rippled with colours that weren't in the real world, and veins of the finest circuitry glimmered there if he tilted them. He slid them on, and everything changed.

They fixed his vision. Something in the software corrected every-thing and it was all pin-sharp, but that was the least of it.

The two of them weren't driving through a dust-eerie darkness lit up only faintly by the half-lost lights of the city towers around them now. The sky was alive with light. Purple lines and arrows showed the thermal patterns, grading slowly to blue the higher into the atmosphere they reached. As his eyes caught across them, numbers glittered into being alongside; temperature, speed, and then in a bar across the top of his vision, the weather forecast for the next twelve hours. White glows and bars showed where the constellations were, even though the real stars were invisible above the dust. None of it was intrusive or stark, just there enough to see if you wanted to, brightening a fraction if he looked directly at the data. He jumped when a beautiful neon parachute floated down just ahead of him, advertising vodka.

Gale was different too. There were shimmering, moving patterns across their coat, the brocade all alive. It was subtle but clear. The patterns were from the same paintings as the linings of all his new things from Fenhua: they were from European masterpieces, and this one was—the new glasses told him so and he had never been so happy to know something—based on beautiful nineteenth-century illustrations of Dante's *Inferno*.[24] Very, very slowly, an angel was falling down the length of the coat, blazing dark fire.

Another unobtrusive banner appeared where the weather forecast had been and informed him that here was Dr Aubrey Gale-Zhou, Senator for Songshu, PhD in zoolinguistics, forty-five years old (Earth Regional Time).

The car was gliding up to the hotel already.

As they stepped out into the strobing of photographs, Gale touched his shoulder and turned him towards the stairs that led inside. A person who was actually in skintight plain white—he could see above the lenses—was draped virtually in silver light as dense as any real fabric. Whatever made the illusion, it threw sharp shadows across things in the vicinity to match. It must have worked best on a plain base. Of course: hence all the teenagers in black jumpsuits.

Just for a few seconds, January's own sleeves turned to the silvery light. It was an advert: here's how it would look on you. Entranced, he held his hands out. Gale must have seen it a thousand times before but they waited, and looked too.

"Jesus Christ," January managed. "Thank you." He looked up at Gale again, and found that they had been watching him, somewhere between attentive and anxious, as if they half expected him to hurl to the glasses away and say it was barbarian witchcraft. "You didn't have to."

"No, welcome. Ready?"

He nodded, and they started up the steps, to shouts to pause for the photographers who wanted to catch what they were wearing.

Watching the person in the luminous robe was hypnotic. Most people in the train of politicians and celebrities climbing the steps had something

---

24   The encyclopaedia hadn't been updated for a while and so the entry for the *Inferno* explained that it was "a folk rhyme from a small extinct state in the Mediterranean, sinking into such crushing religious extremism that it has been banned in most modern countries."*

*Later that night, one easily angered journalist wrote a whole piece about how Gale was clearly out to promote God and gender. The following morning, someone (January always suspected Gale, because there were only about eight people who actually knew any Dante quotes and he was pretty sure the other seven lived on Earth) graffitied ABANDON ALL HOPE, YE WHO ENTER HERE above the door of the broadcaster's offices.

illusory on. The heels of someone's shoes swam with goldfish. He had to keep tilting the glasses down to see what was really going on, then looking through them again. Before long, he realized that the reason nobody wore makeup or dyed their hair here was that they didn't have to bother actually doing it. It was all filters. You could tweak your nose or your eyes, things that would have meant surgery at home. As a security guard paced by, giving them a nod, January blanched. Through the lenses, the guard had no face. None of the security people did.

Around them, photographers were getting too close, and it felt even closer because everyone was so much taller than he was. Everything was too tall; the stairs, the great glass doors ahead of them, even the handrails.

Gale must have noticed he'd gone tense. "Watch for kids," they said. "Their filters are better than ours. Adults aren't allowed to shift too far away from how they really look, it gives you virtual dissonance syndrome, but five-year-old me went round as a tiny fluffy dinosaur for a while."

January laughed. He couldn't imagine Gale as a child. In his head, Gale was a static thing in time; they'd just appeared fully formed one morning out of the desert.

Security officers were holding the doors open, and then the roar of the press faded into music and the quiet murmur of hundreds of people being careful not to drown out the orchestra.

29

The Tiangong had a ballroom. January had seen the space when he had stayed here in the month before the wedding, but it had been dark and empty then. Now it was glittering, partly with its own chandeliers and the medals on the chests of soldiers in dress uniform, but partly from camera flashes. January had never been anywhere like it. The ceiling was the roof of the tower, which on Earth would have been impossibly high even for the grandest dreams of sheikhs and presidents, and lights winked all the way up around the balconies to a glass dome at the top that reflected all those lights twice as long again. It was like standing inside a kaleidoscope.

As always, Gale caused a stir, and the second the two of them were inside, they were surrounded by people—other senators January recognised from the debates, diplomats, donors, people who might have been movie stars. There was nothing so indecorous as gasps about January. But people looked, and looked very close, when Gale introduced him. Someone, and then someone else, brushed his arm and said how lovely he looked; mainly it was curiosity and completely benign interest, but once or twice, not always from older people, he saw flashes of something like offence. He ignored it. He was in this for the cake. It was important to remember your priorities.

"Quite a stunt, Aubrey," said someone who his glasses helpfully labelled as the Speaker of the House, either not caring that January could hear or assuming he couldn't understand. It was something he enjoyed about being foreign. Being underestimated was a convenient thing more often than it wasn't. "Verging on acrobatics."

"Damn it all," said Gale, switching into their pristine Mandarin as easily as putting on different gloves. When they switched, it wasn't only the words; they changed their manner too. It became instantly more imperial, more graceful, more still. In English, they bent slightly, maybe to keep meeting January's eyes, and they moved more. Mars was quickly teaching him how different *you* had to become in different languages, because the same expression and the same posture meant radically different things, just like the same vowels did. What looked pretentious, speaking English, was only polite in Tharsese. He found himself staring hard, taking internal notes. He had never seen anyone do it so perfectly before, or make it look so natural. But that was what he needed to learn. That was the difference between being understood and being heard.

"I didn't think to tell the caterers to get live goats."

"I beg your pardon?" the Speaker said, arch.

"You must be starving after escaping from the dinosaur park. I'll see what I can do, shall I?"

The Speaker smiled a shark smile. "I hope you're gored by a ram. The children shall sing in the streets." They glanced January over. "Alas, it is not to be; you won't live long enough. Consul's on the warpath. Solar power in a dust storm and only vague promises from Songshu? Excuse me, I really must find a good spot from which to watch your crucifixion."

January watched them go, wishing he had brought popcorn. It was already a much better show than he'd expected.

"All right?" Gale said quietly. Back to English again, and their English self.

"Are you joking? I love it. *And* there's cake. Speaking of . . . quickly . . ." He motioned them towards the amazing buffet and had a little fizz of happiness when they came with him.

Gale looked relieved he wasn't already leaving.

———

January stood out, or rather, stood below. Everyone here was fifth- or sixth-generation Natural. Security people watched him sometimes, with sceptical, attentive stares he could only see if he took his new glasses off. Other people got a lot closer than they would have normally, and someone asked if they could touch his hair. He understood why, but he said no, because he'd just seen them eat bits of pineapple off a sticky-looking stick.

Some portly people with the internationally too-well-fed look of major business CEOs introduced themselves after that and asked January lots of questions about life at Songshu and being arrested and wasn't he unexpectedly charming on the news programmes. The subtext was that they had expected him to swear at the audience and rob someone on the way out. He didn't mind. They were silly and naïve, in the way that people who had always had everything were, but they did seem honestly interested, and that, he felt strongly, was all you could ask of anybody.

Gale knocked his arm gently. *Doing well so far.*

A famous actor got Gale by the hand then and pulled them away to dance, and January shook his head, grinning, when Gale messaged *Help me* to him in the new lenses. A banner unfurled across the left one.

People here—or at least, very wealthy people—must have taken dancing seriously, because they were all good at it. He leaned back against the wall to watch. Gale was still trying to say no and the actor was having none of it and, in time with all the other pairs, lifted them up right off the ground in a spin of jewel-bright silk and, through the lenses, a wake of falling golden feathers from the angel on Gale's sleeve.

He let his head bump back against the wall to try and chase off the familiar old sadness he'd often felt waiting to go on stage. It was a funny thing, but what dancers were, really, were creatures who spent most of their time in the shadows in the wings, waiting to pretend for a few minutes to be another kind of person altogether. He could pretend to be the Swan King, but a hundred seconds later he was just January again. But Gale was the real thing. They were never going to match, and he was never going to belong. Even if he went across the floor right now and asked the actor for Gale back, he wouldn't belong.

"Where are your parents? You shouldn't be here by your—oh, I'm so sorry!" someone gasped, when he turned around and they realized he wasn't an escaped child.

He bowed, quite grateful to have his thoughts interrupted.

"Oh, Mx Stirling," the Speaker said, looking even more mortified. "I didn't recognise you."

January laughed, because he could see exactly why. The Speaker hadn't really looked at him before. He was literally beneath their notice. "It's all right."

"Do—we all look the same to you?" the Speaker asked, still amazingly embarrassed, given it didn't matter what January thought.

He shook his head. "No, but . . . all the good movies come from Tharsis, right? We grow up seeing you, but you don't grow up seeing us."

"Well that's dreadful, isn't it," the Speaker said unhappily. "I, um . . . well, I'm glad to have bumped into you. Would you—mind dancing with me for a moment? Oh. *Can* you?"

It made him smile. He loved it when people had no idea he was even acquainted with the thing he was world-class at. It felt like being a secret agent. People thought you were a normal person but *really*—even if it was only for a hundred seconds at a time—you were something else altogether. "I can give it a whirl."

They shot a strange, hunted look to one side, even though the dance was an easy waltz and there was no danger of bumping into anyone. "Mx Stirling, do you know about Aubrey's last consort?"

"Max. Ran away with River Gale."

"Yes, that's the story, but they've vanished off the face of the planet. They're both dead."

"The . . . police seem to have some pretty thorough tests to make sure people can't lie about things like that," January pointed out, the back of his neck prickling.

"Yes, the bastard halo. Look, I want to show you something." They pressed one hand over their own eye, the left, and then touched the left lens of January's new glasses. An image shimmered into it, clear without completely obscuring the real world. It was a halo scan, just like the one of his that House Gale had released to the press. "This is the scan that cleared them."

"Okay?"

"Let me tell you something about Aubrey. Two years ago, Aubrey Gale was a political nobody. Senators *have* to attend House sessions, and they *have* to table a certain number of motions every year. Aubrey always tabled the same one about prisoner rights on hulks and never finished anything to do with it. That's what hereditary senators often do; they inherit their seat, they attend, but they never do anything except run their own House. Aubrey barely even did that. Why? Drug addiction. Unofficially in and out of rehab for years. Officially it's called taking a *spell of contemplation* at a wellness centre."

January frowned, because he couldn't imagine Gale being addicted to anything, except maybe competitive spreadsheet organisation.

"Any kind of addiction shows up on a halo scan," the Speaker said urgently. "It affects your whole mind, it changes all kinds of pathways. But that scan you have there—that's from the mind of someone who's never been addicted to anything."

"So what are you saying?"

"I'm saying," the Speaker said impatiently, and in that impatience there was the ghost of all those back room conversations they must have had with other politicians, the ones where it was important to let every-thing rest on everyone's common, gossamer understanding of everyone else's intent, instead of actually saying anything aloud. "I'm saying that they faked their scan. Whoever took this test: it wasn't Aubrey Gale."

"How have they explained this? The Senator, I mean. You must have asked."

"That's the thing. The addiction was never a matter of public record. They can dismiss it in court as malicious hearsay. Nobody at Songshu would testify, they'd lose their jobs. Medical records are sealed."

"So how do you know?"

"Max was my Apollo."

January stopped moving. "I'm so sorry."

The Speaker nodded and put their back to the wall, near a waterfall stand of champagne. They glanced down at January. "Max wouldn't have run away. Max was a marine, they didn't run from anything." They smiled faintly. "I saw what you said on the news: Max would have said exactly the same thing, the two of you would have got on wonderfully. They would never just vanish. And—do you know anything about River Gale?"

"No. Well. They were a linguist, they worked with mammoths?"

"A profoundly boring person. Second heirs always are, and Gale ones more than anybody. Cloistered in the university forever, made of tweed and Tang dynasty poetry. At House Gale dinner parties, we all used to draw straws to be the one to sit next to them and spare anyone else having to talk about verbs. Not run-away-to-a-lunar-cruise material . . . at . . . all." They had pressed their hands over their eyes, but they took them away now. "I'm sorry, you don't know me. I could well be a passing political rival who wants to sabotage Aubrey's marriage, so I don't imagine for a moment you'll take any action, but—I wanted to warn you. And I hope that if *enough* people warn you, we'll . . . reach some kind of critical mass."

"Thanks," January said, because he didn't know what else to say. So far, people had warned him based on a kind of general understanding of Gale's character—Yan at the naturalisation centre, Consul Song, Professor Shang—but a halo scan that *must* have been faked; that was more difficult to put in the "hearsay" evidence pile.

He couldn't imagine Gale with a drug addiction. But then, if it had led to murdering someone, maybe that had been the jolt they needed to get clean. A political nonentity who suddenly became a superstar—he had to admit, that *did* sound like they'd made some big change in their life.

The trouble was, it was all moot. Even if he found a dungeon under the dance studio where all Gale's previous partners were mummified in iron maidens, he couldn't leave. He had signed a contract, he was in this for five years. If he tried to get away, even if Gale didn't have him hit by a bus before he could tell his story to the press, he would be right back where he started. Sure as hell House Gale would find a way to get the money back from him: he'd be penniless and looking at deportation or naturalisation.

That was still more frightening than living with Aubrey Gale.

"I'm really sorry about Max," he said at last.

The Speaker gave him a watery smile, the kind of water that only just filmed over the shore when the tide was low. It barely covered the grit of the grief below. "You know, that's the most sincere thing anyone from House Gale has said to me about it."

January looked up at them and realized he could see the similarity to that portrait of Max at Songshu. As far as he understood, Great House Apollo twins were almost never actual twins,[25] but maybe the two of them had been. "I know you're not super into it here, but do you need a hug?"

"I think I do, actually."

He leaned up and the Speaker squeezed him carefully, and then pulled their sleeve over their eyes. He was about to suggest they have a quiet drink until everything seemed less sharp, but he didn't get a chance.

A commotion of reporters and cameras erupted by the doors. At first all January could see past everyone else's shoulders was a swift phalanx of praetorians in black.

The Consul.

The Speaker nodded to January and slipped away, and January cast around for Gale. He didn't have to look far. The Consul was already clearing the way. By the time he got there, they were gripping Gale's hands and saying hello and what foul weather with a merry sort of charm that for all the world looked honestly meant.

"Aubrey, how are you? I can't believe you're up and about already, you're like a persistent fungal infection. And January: much less so. You look wonderful."

---

25 Every year, healthy people donated genetic material to the Genesis Institute, and anyone with a Child License could go there and design their own embryo (free, funded by the government), which was then grown in a glass pod. There was a public gallery of babies-in-progress, a very popular part of any Tharsese sightseeing tour, because going to look at babies makes you feel better about everything even if you think you wouldn't like it. Every year, there were always some abandoned babies, because the parents died or circumstances changed, and it had been the policy of Great Houses for generations now to choose their heirs from among those up for adoption. You could, of course, have a baby in the traditional way if you wanted to, but trying to tell a Tharsese person that this was a good idea usually provoked the sort of reaction that everyone else would have if you tried to convince them of the nurturing, character-building virtues of medieval torture chambers.

January bowed. Down his right side, he was even more aware of Gale than he usually was. He didn't want to look at them, in case everything showed on his face. Even though they were the same Gale, in the same kingfisher blue as before, even holding the same wine glass as before, he felt like he was standing beside someone else. A faked halo; holy Christ.

Irrelevant, the Swan King voice told him severely. *Get your head on straight. Focus on the performance. Especially if your life depends on it.*

"Consul Song."

"Guang, Guang,"[26] the Consul insisted expansively. "How's the giant publicity stunt working out for you both?" they glimmered. "You know we've got a sweepstake going at Jade Hill, Aubrey. I've got six to one you vanish him in a mysterious accident with some mammoths a month after the election."

"That's very specific," Gale said mildly.

"Five to one is some kind of fake accident with a bus. There's a fun one about polar bears too."

"Is anyone betting that I *won't* murder him?"

Usually he would have thought it was funny, but after what he'd just heard, he wished people would stop joking about his being murdered.

"Just Ping the intern. They were last to choose."

"Good on Ping the intern," Gale said. "But don't you have an announcement to make about this storm whose artificial origins you definitely aren't lying about?"

"I do, in fact, I do. Good luck, January. I'll ask penetrating questions after your inevitable disappearance."

---

26 光, Guang, meant "light," January's new glasses told him helpfully, and then, because the translation software was a bit overenthusiastic after being asked to provide information useful for recent immigrants to Tharsis, explained that depending on social context, lots of Tharsese people used translations of their names in different languages, and in fact many felt there was no "true" version. It was usual to use the Mandarin one in a formal context like this, or in writing; outside a bar, they'd be more likely to use the Russian, and if they were signing a piece of graffiti, English. This was why, it enthused, you almost never saw Senate records refer to "House Gale," but "House Dafeng," the Mandarin translation, and why lots of conservative news outlets talked about the disappearance of Jiang Dafeng rather than River Gale—and why they were calling him Yiyue and not January.

"Very kind," he managed, wishing that Gale wouldn't look like they were so on the edge of enjoying themselves. They *liked* the Consul, he realized suddenly; they probably liked anyone who could give them a good fight.

It was one of those things that in principle was really likeable. If he'd read this exchange in a news report he'd have laughed. In practise, in person, standing here, it was frightening.

The Consul swept away towards the podium. Everyone surged that way, slowly and gracefully; from above they would have looked like iron filings following a magnet.

January glanced up at Gale, who looked back with a lot more trepidation than he'd expected.

"I haven't murdered anyone. That intern is going to win a lot of money."

"Lucky intern," said January, because he couldn't say, *I believe you.*

"Schrödinger's cat," Gale said mutedly. They looked unhappy about it.

He had to mine down in his imagination to get to what he would have said half an hour ago, before he'd talked to the Speaker.

"Yeah, but I like cats." He was getting better at the acting. He even smiled a bit, and he didn't think it looked like a scared rictus either.

Gale leaned forward very, very slightly, just enough to sway the ends of their hair away from their sash. "I feel like that's what I'd say to a possibly radioactive cat I'd been legally shackled to."

"No, it isn't," January said.

"What?"

He looked up at them properly. "I can't see you trying to be polite to gamma rays; it wouldn't make any difference."

Gale smiled the barest smile, and January breathed out, relieved. Mostly that they seemed at least half convinced, but a little because—because despite everything he didn't like the idea that he'd poked a sore spot.

You are not so useless that you'll end up loyal to a murderer literally because they're nice to you, the Swan King snarled.

He had a horrible feeling that actually, he might already be going that way.

Somebody important announced someone else, who then announced the Consul, to applause. January inclined his head. For a while, people had clapped whenever he went on stage too, so he knew what it was like and he knew that normal people, with an accurate idea of the worth of a soul, looked embarrassed or just a little unwilling; and if you were used to it, the decent thing was to ignore it and do whatever people had come to see. You didn't behave like it was your due. There was a fine line between magnanimous and smug, and the Consul was tightrope-walking it. It was not how Gale looked. At any given event, Gale could have been talking to three people or three thousand—you couldn't tell, if you just watched them alone.

Eyes flashed gold everywhere.

"Good evening. I know we're all here for fun, but I have some important news first. The forecast for this storm is bad. It looks set to last months. The Songshu solar array will fail long before it blows itself out, and without that we have no power, and no water, even if my fine colleague Senator Gale finds a way—which I'm sure they will—to eke out what we have for a while."

Gale looked like they were deciding between models of wood chipper to feed the Consul through.

"It is with great relief, then, that I can tell you that a fleet of aid ships left Earth's Tianjin station today. They are bringing uranium, to ensure against solar failure. This is tremendous generosity on the part of China, India, and Nigeria, and a reminder of the great safety to be had in remaining united with our mother states. Their ambassadors are here tonight; let's show them what Tharsis hospitality looks like."

There was a huge cheer, the kind that came from relief pouring out of hundreds of people who had been trying to pretend they hadn't been afraid. Three people in cages who looked like children beside the Consul were ushered up to wave.

Gale touched January's arm. "Would you mind if we went to see some journalists?"

January clenched one fist, digging his fingernails into his palm. "What will you say?"

"That they can't be allowed to land. This is—a thinly disguised way to get hundreds of thousands of immigrants here—"

"Refugees."

"What?"

He stepped behind a pillar, away from the crowd. His heart was going hard, as if someone were coming at him spinning a poker. All his instincts yelled at him to shut up, because you had to swallow down your opinions when you were working for someone who had maybe killed the last person in your job, but he was going to feel filthy if he didn't say anything. He'd spend the rest of his life feeling filthy. It surprised him even as he decided this was his line in the sand. He hadn't known he had any sand. "Immigrants choose. Refugees don't. They're refugees."

In his head, the hymn those people had sung outside the burning church echoed and echoed.

"No," Gale said softly. "They're not. No one *has* to come to Mars, it's the hardest place for anyone to go to—"

"Are you really saying that you're going to turn them around after *months* on the Crossing, and—"

"We'll resupply them, as much as we possibly can, and then we'll send them to a country that has the capacity to safely take them—"

"What country?" January said incredulously. All at once it didn't matter, what the Speaker had said. He would stand here and die before he let Gale say that without some kind of challenge. "Name it! Tell me where I should have gone. Which country has space and work and money and some kind of stability all at the same time? I'd love to know, I really would, I'll piss off there when you're bored of me. Do you think I wanted to spend eight months of my life getting here and then fighting with immigration services and doing a factory job? If there had been *anything else*, don't you think I would have done it?"

Gale looked away for a second, and it was as near to impatience as he'd ever seen them come. His heart tried to get up behind his tonsils. If he kept arguing, he might as well be doing handstands on the edge of a cliff, but he knew already that he couldn't stop, even though this might be the stupidest thing he'd ever done. "Do you believe that if hundreds of thousands of Earthstrongers come here, into the city, then we won't see a surge of Natural homicides?"

He shut his teeth. "No, I don't. Of course I don't. That isn't what I'm saying. I'm saying, your solutions will do more harm than good."

"There are no good solutions. It's ugly, and things shouldn't be this way, but they are. If we let them land, there are only two choices. Either we say to one large group of people, *I'm afraid you're going to have to adapt to light gravity and all the health problems that brings, because that's just the nature of this planet*; or we say to a small group of people, *A significant number of you will soon be accidentally murdered and sorry, but as a government, we're fine with that*. Tell me a better solution than preventing the situation which makes that choice necessary in the first place. That's all I'm trying to do when I say we can't let them land."

"Would you want a solution, if there was one, or would it make you angry because it would mean your ancestors and your House suffered for no reason?" January asked softly.

He should have known, before he said it, that he was crossing a line. He could call Gale a horrible person and they would shrug, but he'd just said they were dishonourable, and that was something else. They had been leaning a little towards him to hear him over the noise behind them both, but now, they straightened. Aubrey the gentle academic vanished and left him with Senator Gale. He found himself pressing back against the wall.

"That's what you think I am?" Gale asked, very quiet. "You think I'm doing this because I suffered, so now I haven't the mental strength to do anything but insist other people suffer, to make what happened to me fairer somehow? Really? You don't think it's because there *is* no solution?"

He wanted to go down to the lake and hide with Ming the polar bear until this blew over. "You have all the money in the worlds. You were talking about spending billions of yuan getting a new solar array into the atmosphere, but if you spent that money on building new sun fields and a new water factory for a new colony, they could land, they could be separate from Tharsis, and they might actually have a chance of surviving the winter—and *you* would make money from the water you'd invested in! It doesn't take a genius to come up with that but you *are* a genius, so you must have thought of it. Why not do that?"

"Because then we'd have a colony of people three times stronger than us a hundred miles away instead of six million miles away, when frankly even the six million isn't far enough."

"There has to be something. No one's going to do it if you don't."

"What's this *you*?" Gale asked him, voice smoking higher with irritation. "*We* are House Gale. Roll your sleeves up and show me some plans."

He had never been so instantly furious. He hadn't known he could be. "I shouldn't be the one doing that! I'm just a dancer—"

Gale half laughed. "Come on. You can't just sit on the side of the ring and complain while I fight, that isn't fair."

"I *can't* fight with people like you!" January whisper-snapped. "I don't have a PhD in Generally Everything, I don't know a quarter of what I need to know, I'm at such a crippling disadvantage against—you don't understand!"

"You're afraid people will—what, ignore you, laugh at you?"

"Send me back to prison? Deport me?" His ribs had seized up with everything he wanted to say and everything he didn't dare to ask, and with hating that he didn't dare and hating that he wasn't any good at saying things when he did.

"I see," Gale said, steady and hard. "*I'm* afraid someone will kill me."

January didn't know what to say any more. There was a tornado in his head now and he couldn't catch any of his thoughts, except in disjointed scraps as they tore past. He didn't want Gale to be afraid all the time, it made him feel sick to think of that, but he would rather shoot himself than say that being afraid was a good reason to maim someone else. And there was something like grief in there too. He had loved having that new bridge between him and Gale, it had been precious, and now he was watching it burn.

"All of which," Gale said, sounding tired, "is irrelevant, because we only have a month to come with up something, not ten years. You don't have to come with me for this if you'd rather go back to Songshu."

Maybe it was just because of what the Speaker had told him, but that last offer sounded more like a trap than a way out. He could see vividly that if he took it, he would be saying was that he was happy to take Gale's money without doing the job it paid for. He might as well declare he wanted a divorce right now, and if he did that, he had probably better enjoy what few of his very numbered days remained.

"I said I disagree with you, I didn't say I wouldn't do my job," January said, very quiet. He had felt less trapped in the prison cell. At least there he'd had the friendly dognapper.

Gale bowed slightly and opened one arm to invite him to go first.

On the steps of the hotel they walked into a wall of people all yelling so many questions it was impossible to distinguish any single voice. All he heard was a swarm roar.

"Good evening, how is everyone?" Gale said, not even fractionally stirred by it.

There was a story from somewhere, about a king who had tried to stop the sea; January thought of it then, because he had a feeling that the sea would have parted for Gale.

"Senator, can you comment on what the Consul just said?"

"The Consul has just announced that a fleet from Earth is coming here with uranium. And well they might; this storm is artificial, caused by the release of silver iodide, which does not naturally occur on Mars or anywhere. This is clearly a pretext by which to bring as many immigrants from Earth here as possible before the election, under the guise of help in an energy crisis."

More noise than January had ever heard before. It had hurt less to stand right under the engine of an idling interplanetary liner. He felt painfully detached from it all.

"Senator—"

"Senator!"

"*Senator*—"

"Mx Stirling?"

Gale pointed to that last voice, and January had a drab little tide of gladness when he recognised Professor Shang, wearing a badge that said they were reporting for, of all things, a neurology journal, and beaming out that same Paddington Bear warmth they'd had in the interrogation room, still in that same purple scarf.

"Mx Stirling, what do you think is going on?"

Gale was looking down at him, as suddenly silent as everyone else.

A quiet voice in his head said: *You know, if you say, don't be silly, there are no crazy conspiracies, you could pull the rug out from under all this. Songshu is failing, aid is coming; what's the problem?*

He could see the future, as clear as if it were playing across the inside of his new glasses. If those ships landed, more would follow. China and Russia and India and all the rest wouldn't want Tharsis to become American overnight. With them would come their governments. Tharsis would be a true colony again soon, and that would be that. People like Gale would never have any power again. People like Gale, sixth- or seventh-generation Natural, would find themselves at the very bottom of the pile, and maybe even forced out of the city. The world would turn upside down and everyone who had scraped along the bottom would have a chance to get to the top. The Senate would become Earthstrong heavy, cages would be here to stay, life would be—maybe not brilliant, but better. The naturalisation centres would close. Perhaps funding would go to making more buildings like the Rings. He could go in shops. He could get work again, normal work. With the money he already had from his single month working for House Gale, he could start a dance company.

He wouldn't need to be tied to a nationalist who wanted him to wither away behind a fence.

He wanted to think that if he said that, he would be safe, there could be no garbage truck accident, because that would be too ridiculously obvious—but he could see that that was naïve. Money like House Gale's was power. Gale could do what they liked. There might be a scandal, but he'd still be dead.

He drew his breath in slowly.

Just do your job. You do what you have to do. You don't need to die for this.

"I think this storm was caused in order to force Senator Gale to allow a fleet from Earth to land here, even if they are Consul in a few months' time," he said, carefully. He couldn't bring himself to say, *I agree with everything Senator Gale says, it's all definitely a great idea.* "I think if enough people are coming, that places Tharsis in a great deal of danger. Even if there are no soldiers, even if it's just desperate, innocent people fleeing fires—we are dangerous, even if we don't want to be, and we will see accidental homicides go right up. I don't know what the solution is in such a short time frame, but I'd like to know what the Consul thinks it is, because we are going to need one." *And it's going to have to come from the Consul, because honestly, hell is going to freeze over before Gale even thinks about it.*

Gale bent very slightly over him, an inch off kissing the top of his head. The falling angel on their coat was just at his eye level now. He cast his eyes down. He shouldn't have cared whether they approved of what he said or not, especially when it probably just a piece of acting for the press. He did, though.

"And does House Gale have its own solution to the energy crisis?" Professor Shang asked into the silence.

January looked up at Gale, but Gale didn't speak, and only nodded a little at him.

"Yes. House Gale is building a new solar array in the atmosphere, above the dust. The process will take two months. All we have to do is last until then. And we can. We have the gravity trains, we have some light, and people here are rock hard. You're the people who came to an airless desert and built a city. We can do this."

"That's all we have time for," Gale said, and below the level of the cameras, they squeezed his hand hard. "We've got a lot to do."

30

The first thing they had to do was face Mx Francis, who met them at the doors of Songshu furious.

"What the fuck just happened? You just committed us to solar power in the atmosphere in two months live on—"

"Solly—" Gale started.

"If that doesn't work, you're dead! I don't just mean the campaign, I mean face down in a well dead, because we'll be part of fucking China again—"

"Solly," Gale tried again.

"Don't you Solly me! I'm the one who's going to be up all night drafting the press release that explains exactly how we're going to pull this off!"

"It was very quick, I wasn't altogether at my leisure to call for my press secretary's approval," Gale said.

"I hate you and I hope you're trampled by righteous llamas," Mx Francis told them. "Both of you. Now go away, I have to call Dr Molotov and get them to walk me through how this is going to work. You can't announce this and then not say how you'll do it . . ."

"We'll get out of your way then—"

Dr Molotov came out of the lift then, looking like they might go and fling themselves off a cliff right now to beat the rush. "Mx Stirling! I said two months was the *best possible scenario*! That's if nothing goes wrong! Nothing!"

"I know, I'm really sorry—"

"Mx Francis wants you," Gale put in.

"I don't have time to explain everything to a publicist, I need to talk to Dr Chen at the House Tesla launch pads . . ."

"You do have time to talk to a *publicist*, you weird little mole person," Mx Francis told them. "If you still want a roof to live under in two months—"

Gale gave January a wry look and pressed the house intercom. Their voice smoked around everything, echoing from every floor. "Sorry for the late hour; senior staff to the dining room please; thank you."

Mx Francis and Dr Molotov looked around. "Senator?"

"Now," Gale clarified.

"Um—right," Mx Francis said, looking worried.

"Probably we should make everyone some coffee," January murmured.

"Let's do that," Gale agreed seriously.

The kitchen echoed without all the cooks in it. January studied the coffee machine to see how it worked—his new glasses flashed up a schematic straightaway—then poured in some fresh grounds and set it going. Beside him, Gale lifted down the cups, which were too high up for January to reach without finding a chair to stand on. He concentrated on the steam and the heating plates, his whole right side prickling uncomfortably knowing Gale was there, though he wasn't looking. The two of them had come all the way home without talking and he wanted not to talk now either, because he'd had enough of feeling stupid and angry and scared for one night.

He risked a glance across when it started to feel like maybe Gale wouldn't rehash things. Gale's shoulder was at his eye level, an ink stripe of their hair deep black over the blue evening robe.

"I can do this," he said. "Go out and—persuade everyone not to kill us."

"You're not Cinderella, let me help."

"There are a lot of things I can't do, but I can make coffee," January said, slightly more flatly than he wanted to.

Gale was quiet. They hinged a little bow to him and left with a sigh of silk. Part of him felt abandoned.

By the time everyone was in the dining room, it was almost midnight. Some people had come down with a jumper on over whatever they slept in, and others were hunched up over the cups of coffee looking like they were scrying. Mx Ren was as bright as always (today's dungarees were bottle green) and January wondered if they ever actually slept, or just recharged in a cupboard somewhere.

Through the new glasses, he could see information about everyone hanging above them in unobtrusive clouds. Everyone had a doctorate in some kind of complicated engineering. Around them, there was art he had never seen before; beautiful, brushstroke herons walked over the floor, fishing in brushstroke pools for brushstroke fish. Hypnotic. When the wind gusted outside, the reeds in the painting waved.[27] It was simple, but he could have watched for years. When he looked down, the floor wasn't the floor but the surface of another pond. A koi swam under him. He had to take the glasses off.

"All right," Gale said, far more gently than normal. "It's late, so I'll keep it brief. At the gala tonight, the Consul announced that a fleet is coming from Earth with uranium. They will be here in two months. I know it sounds good, I know we all want help, but this isn't good. If they land—we're a colony again, and probably everyone in this room will be arrested for promoting nationalism."

No.

What?

January sat back, because he'd had no idea that those were the stakes for Gale. He wanted to yell that they hadn't bloody said that at the Tiangong.

---

27   It was, said his glasses, an original Anna Minami, and priceless. Anna Minami: born Tokyo 2025, early virtual artist, more appreciated after her lifetime, which she spent mostly as a security guard at Haneda Airport. Scholars had never been able to prove it, but they suspected she was behind the painted birds who made nests in the sinks in the ladies' bathrooms, and likewise that she had, after the IT department kept scrubbing the coding and calling the birds graffiti, something to do with the giant purple elephant that had then moved into the IT office.

But then, maybe they thought he knew; in the same way he expected them to know how hard things were for Earthstrongers. He found himself rewinding his memory of that argument. He'd thought they were getting angry with him because he wasn't cooperating, but—maybe it was because they thought he was saying *he* thought they deserved to be arrested.

Oh, God.

The quiet had a heaviness to it. There was no sound but the house itself, its lights and vents, and over everything, the shush of the dust rising outside. It was worse than before, already. The floodlights outside were lost in it.

"We have two months to get a new array into the atmosphere and connect it. We're not going to get any help from central government. Some of the other Houses will refuse to help because they vote with House Song. But I propose you tell me what needs to happen, and I find a way to do the politics." Gale paused. "I'm not going to lie to you. If this doesn't work, we'll all be in a hulk around Jupiter. But if it does work, then it's likely that the election is ours. I know some of you will be wondering if I'm exaggerating the threat from Earth for political gain, and if I was holding a gun to January's neck in that interview." People looked at him, with a few weak smiles. He didn't have it in him to smile back. "But I'm telling you now, in private, that I'm not. They're coming, and . . . they will take Tharsis. If anyone is convinced otherwise, and I understand if you are, you can leave with a full reference."

Nobody moved.

"Fortunately we've been thinking about all this already, so we have a head start." That, January thought, was either a very generous use of "we," given that literally everyone else had yelled at Gale that building a new array was impossible; or it was the magisterial *we*. He was starting to feel a little appalled at how one human being could be so ambiguous, all of the time. You would have thought it would be easy to tell if a person was noble or a monster, but here he was, a month later, with no clue. "Tomorrow, I need to know whose help we need, and I will get it. Are there any questions?"

January had expected a barrage, but nobody said anything. Finally Mx Francis stood up, and he thought that they were about to walk out.

"We serve at the pleasure of the House of Gale," was all they said.

It echoed around the tables, and then people were getting up and sharing tablets and talking fast, and eyes flared blue as calls went out, and Mx Francis was sitting close to Dr Molotov with a stylus and Gale and January were left in the one point of stillness.

A drone floated down next to them.

Gale looked straight at it, held up their antique phone, the one they had ruined to save January's, and played a song that was everywhere at the moment; it was a ballad from one of those wildly popular Nigerian boy bands, super catchy to the point that January knew the lyrics even though he didn't speak a word of Hausa.

That's copyrighted, we can't put that in the show! someone protested over the microphone.

Gale turned it up.

The drone managed to look harassed as it flew away.

Gale left the phone on the table, still playing the song.

"You could have tanked me, in front of the press," Gale said him, very quiet. "You . . . why didn't you?"

"Because," he said, not quite able to believe they were actually asking him, "I'm scared of you. I don't know what happened to Max. I don't know what'll happen to me if I piss you off enough, do I? I told you. I don't want to kick the nuclear cat."

Gale looked shaken. Not just a little off balance, but like he had taken hold of something deep in them and rammed it. If it was acting, they were the most incredible actor. "January. Nothing is going to happen to you. I'm not—I didn't—you don't need to be scared of me."

"The Speaker told me you used to have a cocaine addiction which didn't show up on your halo, after Max and River vanished," January explained softly. "So I *know* someone else took it for you. I'm—please. I'll do as I'm told, I'm never going to ask for anything, and I won't do anything to sabotage you, you don't need to worry. All I want is to get out of this alive, so that's . . . what I'm trying to do." He bowed a little and tried to leave, because there was nothing he could do here except get in the way and if he lobbed the drone out the window then he could have some privacy in his room. But Gale was fast when they liked, and put one arm across the door before he could reach it.

"No. No, no, January, I brought you here to fight me. Someone like me *needs* someone like you in the room, or what I think isn't worth anything—"

"No, you don't *need* that, you just think it's fun!" January protested, far more angry than he had thought he could be, for no real reason except he was tired and alone, and it turned out he was a lot more upset about the ruined bridge that he had imagined he possibly could be. "That's just sparring practise for you, when you're already the heavy-weight champion. I'm not in your league. I'm not in any league, I'm a dancer, and even if I was, I *don't know what happened to Max!*"

Gale dropped their arm. "I don't . . . know what to say that will help. I didn't kill anyone. And I'd never hurt you."

"I'd never hurt you either, but that doesn't stop you planning and behaving and legislating as if I definitely will," he said tightly. "No—don't—say anything, *please* don't say anything, I don't need to be body-slammed through the floor again—"

"January, *saying* things to you is not the same as actual violence—"

"No, but it's a fight you'll definitely win! Can't you see it's *that* unequal? You don't have any bloody trouble seeing that my muscles are stronger than yours, why can't you admit that your brain is at least three times better than mine?"

"Because it isn't! You're completely capable of—"

"Good night! Good night," he said, struggling to keep his voice level. "I'll see you in the morning."

He managed to get the elevator doors shut before a drone could follow him in, and then he held it together until the fourth floor, but by the time the doors opened on the fifth, he had cracked, and the world had gone blurry and lensing. He had to pull off the new glasses and press his sleeve against his eyes before he walked out into the corridor.

He almost didn't see the always-writing person in the rust-coloured jumper. They were right in front of him, looking like they wanted to say something. They must have been waiting for the lift. He bowed his head and stepped aside.

"Sorry," he muttered, more for the state he was in than getting in the way.

They glanced up and down the corridor—checking for cameras—then touched his arm, and pulled him into a wordless hug. Even though he still didn't know who they were, and he had a horrible feeling they were the real version of him, the person who *should* have been married to Gale, it was such a kind simple thing to do that something in him snapped and he couldn't do anything except cry against their shoulder. After a little while, they tilted him back and bowed once, and called the elevator, and that was it.

He should have said thank you, but he couldn't. He didn't know their name, and right in his bones he didn't want to. It would have to be one of those strange, half-magic things that happened sometimes, and in the morning, the two of them would go back to carefully pretending the other one didn't exist, because that would be the only way not to go mad.

31

As it often did if he was upset, his cage ached. You weren't really supposed to wear it all the time, and where the steel tendons lay, he could see bruises starting to form. It wasn't that the cage was too tight, it was just the consistent pressure, the same way you got bruises on your face if you wore a mask for too long. He should ask for the key, to be out of it for a little while at least, but he couldn't face going back down to beg Gale for favours, and anyway, he'd made the oath. They'd let him out when they felt safe.

An angry little voice snarled that they wouldn't feel safe even if they cut his arms off first.

No; no. He couldn't get angry with someone for being afraid. You didn't choose to be afraid.

You *could* accept that being afraid wasn't a reason to—

"Shut up," he said aloud, to try and stop his thoughts. He didn't like how righteous they were getting.

So he stood under the hot shower to try and ease all the aching places, and felt determinedly grateful that there was hot water, and so much of it. A whole twenty minutes. It was incredible.

He was very lucky.

He was.

———

He'd only just bullied himself to sleep when an almighty bang on the door jolted him awake. It sounded like someone had smacked their whole weight into it.

January lay still, trying to tell if he had been dreaming. He hadn't even realized he was asleep.

Something scratched at the door.

Not a dream, then.

He got up, not liking being locked in his cage with someone perhaps trying to break into the room, but it wasn't like he was weak in it. He told himself to get a grip. It was probably nothing; in fact, no. It was probably Kasha.

He pulled the door open and almost fell over Gale, who was on the floor right outside.

"Hi," they said, sounding level, but not looking it.

January bumped down onto his knees. "Jesus Christ. Are you hurt?"

"No—no."

But they were. Normally Gale spoke to him in English, but they were using Mandarin now. Nobody could do a foreign language when they were properly upset. If he was even flustered, January went from functional to incoherent instantly.

"It's okay," he said again, even though he had no idea if it was. "I—why are you here, what's going on?"

"I don't know." Gale's voice cracked over it. "I don't—I didn't mean to come here."

January looked along the corridor, at a complete loss. "You . . . sleepwalk?"

"Must do." Gale was rubbing one arm, but too lightly; it hurt.

He took a breath and realized he had no idea what to say with it. The only thing he could do was try to work out if their arm was broken. "Can I . . . ?"

Very gently, he straightened out their arm and bent it again. Not broken. Good. But Gale was shaking.

It must have been a spectacular nightmare. He supposed they *could* have got this far, asleep, if some part of their dreaming mind had insisted it was urgent enough. If you'd been torn in half by someone who looked just like a person who'd just moved into your house, then blown up by yet another one, it only followed that you'd get horrendous nightmares and sleepwalk, or whatever this was, immediately after being snarled at.

Strange to come to his door, though. The opposite direction would have made more sense.

"Can you get up if I give you a hand?"

It came out wrong, and he saw them try to catch his meaning, and miss. "What?" Their voice was breaking.

"Sorry," said January, whose Mandarin was not at its best at two in the morning. "I always screw up my tones when I'm tired, don't I—agh." He turned his head aside and stuck out his tongue, mostly to see if he could get Gale to smile. "Yuck yuck yuck."

Gale did smile. "In a stone den, a poet called Shi, who was a lion addict, resolved to eat ten lions . . ."

All those words were *shi*, and they only made sense if you got the right tones.[28]

It was a famous tongue twister and January could never do it. "Shut up shut up. She sells sea shells on the seashore. I *said*, can you get up, if I help you?"

"I can do it without you—you go back to bed. I'm sorry. I don't know how I ended up here."

January had to laugh, although it didn't sound very laugh-like. "Come on. I'll feel bad if I leave you on the floor."

"No. I'm a foot taller than you and you're in a cage—"

---

28   The worst thing anyone had ever said to January about tones in Mandarin was that if you got every single word wrong—like, you said "chi" instead of "shi"—but the tones right, people would understand. But if you got every single word *right* but the tones wrong, you were just making weird noises. A language teacher at the prison had told him that actually if you said no words at all but just hummed the tones, it was guessable. They then claimed that English was like that too, and when January had argued passionately that it was *not* thank you very much, they'd played a clip of an ancient children's show called *The Clangers*. It was about adorable little pink sock puppet mice who lived on the moon. Instead of talking, they whistled to each other, and sometimes you could guess what they were saying from the rhythm of the whistle: in the clip the teacher showed him, one of the pink mice clearly said, "Oh, sod it, the bloody thing's stuck again." Mandarin, the teacher said brightly, was just like Clanger. January hoped they were hit by an asteroid.

"I could lift you with one arm," January said softly. That wasn't what Gale was saying, he could see that, Gale was embarrassed, but he wasn't having it anyway. "Look; look at this." He pulled his phone out and scanned back two years through his photographs—he'd not taken many here because he had no one to show them to—until he found one of Hulking Terry, stumping off with yet another round of cake. "Look at that. One arm. And I never killed him, either, which I think speaks very well to my character."

Gale choked on a laugh.

"It wasn't even dancing, it was bullfighting. His mum used to turn up with *survival packages* full of bloody biscuits because everyone knows how horrendously thin ballet dancers are." January didn't often do impressions of people because there wasn't much in the world that was ruder, but he had a strong feeling that Gale needed to hear him say something bitchy and unreasonable about someone *else*, so that it was all the clearer he wasn't secretly feeling bitchy and unreasonable with *them*. "I still don't know if I was dealing with a chunker of a human or a really beautiful hippo."

Like he'd hoped, Gale laughed properly this time.

"Okay?" he asked.

Gale nodded slightly. It was fragile trust, though, and they stiffened so completely when he took their hands it was like lifting glass. But not a great deal of glass. Even on Earth, Gale would have weighed much less than Terry. Once they were standing, one hand to the wall, he tipped sideways to catch their eye.

"Think you can walk?"

"Yes, I . . . I'm fine. I can go by myself."

"Nope. Come on. You'll have to live with me for entire minutes."

Gale walked with one hand to the wall. The limp was bad.

"How does a language even end up with tones?" January asked, not because he imagined there was an answer, but so that Gale would know he wasn't feeling impatient. "I mean, did everyone get together one morning and say, *Oi lads, I know what'll really piss off all the foreigners . . .*"

"No one really knows for sure, but tones probably happen when a language is very old," Gale said, and January looked up, surprised.

"Words erode over time; they always go from jagged to smooth if you give them long enough. Consonants wear away. It happens in English."

"It does?"

"It does."

"For example?" January pushed, aware that he was pushing against the fear Mx Francis had instilled in them of saying anything too academic, and that it was severe. He could imagine Mx Francis making liberal use of a taser in the training process.

"For example . . ." Down his left side, he felt them shift, nearly as reluctant to talk about it as they would have been to explain a giant book of pornography. He wanted to say that Mx Francis was wrong, it wasn't off-putting for someone to know things. Not in the shy, careful, profoundly unpretentious way Gale knew them. But a compliment would have sounded like flirting. Even if you didn't have an irrational horror of it, that still wasn't what you wanted at two in the morning after a terrible nightmare. "For example—*knight* used to be pronounced *kuh-nich-t*, c-n-i-h-t. If it lives long enough, English isn't going to say *knight*, *night*, *nigh*, and *nine*, they're all going to be *nye*; I can already hear it in *your* English. You rarely say a final *t*, unless you're enunciating, you—it's called a glottal stop, you just sort of finish the vowel sharply where the *t* used to be. But you do say that same sound differently already. *Knight* is usually a high tone, and *nine* is usually low, because 'knight' finishes right up against your teeth and 'nine' doesn't. And that's what's already happened, in tonal languages. A tone is the fossil of a dead consonant."

"Hah," January said, really pleased with that. He had never thought of languages as having geologies and fossils before, but he liked it. "That's lovely."

They were at the lift now. He waved at the sensor. It took a while to come; which meant Gale had come here on the stairs. Gale's room was on the fifth floor. It seemed like a deliberate piece of masochism for them to do that to themselves, but January was less than shocked. He could imagine that even if someone had gently tried to raise the possibility of moving to the ground floor in case of emergencies, Gale would defenestrate that person as a point of honour.

"Did you dream?" January asked, once they were inside. "On the way here, I mean; what was it like? I've never met anyone who sleepwalks."

"I don't know. No. Nothing," Gale said.

January stood back. "My God."

"What?"

"You're a *horrible* liar. This is very reassuring. Do it again."

Gale laughed, or tried to. "I—thought someone was dragging me. I thought they pushed me into your door."

"Vexing," he said, because he was pretty sure that for Gale, sulphuric acid was less toxic than sympathy.

"Yeah." They were still rubbing their arm like it hurt. Like someone, he thought suddenly, had grabbed them and pulled. He touched their wrist and glanced up to check they were all right, then pushed their sleeve back.

Something cold slimed down the back of his neck, because there were marks. Bruises. In the shape of fingers.

"Dreams give you bruises, do they?" he asked.

Gale shrugged, amazingly unstirred by it. "Dr Okonkwo says so."

"Dr Okonkwo says . . . So this has happened before?"

Gale sighed. "I've had sleep problems for months. Paralysis and—hallucinations, we keep trying different medication but nothing works. Dr Okonkwo thinks I'm just traumatised from Gagarin Square and it'll go away by itself."

"Which cannot be true, because you're a hell-automaton with no feelings."

"See? You understand."

He hesitated. "You know I don't mean that, right, I'm joking."

"I know. So, I—"

"Look—"

"Sorry—"

"No—"

"You first."

January nodded. "I'm sorry about before. I shouldn't have said—"

"No, stop, stop, I was—going to apologise to you. I know I can't expect you to fight me when in most of the ways that matter I'm stronger than you. And I know that when you said I was like Schrödinger's cat it wasn't a joke. You're so good-humoured about being afraid that it didn't really go through my head that you *are* afraid."

January leaned back against the wall. "I didn't realize that you either win the election or end up in prison. You . . . didn't say."

"I didn't want to complain any more than I already had," Gale said wryly. "I already sounded like a self-righteous prick."

He swallowed. "I know I don't understand what it's like for you, by the way. I've never been afraid a stranger will kill me."

Gale was watching him with something between relief and worry. "Me neither, honestly. I'm too arrogant to imagine anyone might actually kill me. Even in Gagarin Square."

January snorted. "You're fantastic."

"Is that code for unbearable?"

"No," he said, and meant it.

"You are afraid though," Gale said after a moment. "That *I'll* kill you."

"Well, you know, not now this second. It's different."

"Is it though?" Gale asked, voice lifting high the way it did whenever January said something they felt was especially Earthy and terrible.

The lift pinged.

When they reached Gale's room, the lights were already on inside. Sitting by the heater, with their leatherbound journal and their rust-coloured jumper, was that mystery person who always seemed to be there. They stood up soundlessly when Gale stepped inside. Neither of them said anything to each other, and January wondered with an uneasy coil if something else was going on. If they had been fighting, perhaps Gale had left in order to get away, not because of some vague sleeping problem.

"Thank you," Gale said to him.

"Welcome." He glanced at the person in the rust-coloured jumper again, worried he was just delivering Gale back to a row. They didn't look angry, or not that he could see without his glasses—he had forgotten them when he got up, too distracted—but nor were they doing any of the things he would have done if someone he loved had just turned up in the middle of the night chaperoned by a stranger. No relief, no exclamations, no hug, nothing.

But well-to-do people here didn't do big displays of feeling. It was crass. He had seen children bowing to their parents.

"Are you going to be all right?" he asked anyway.

"I'm fine," Gale said. He caught the smell of summer from them, spices and warmth that made him think of London in its dying golden light. Home; the one he couldn't go back to. "Good night, Mx Stirling."

"Night, Senator."

They shut the door.

January waited, but no raised voices came through it. He sighed. Good.

A tiny stupid part of him felt sad. He was never going to have someone who was his; not even the someone he was married to.

32

When he arrived at the meeting room in the tower the next morning—the windows were all fixed now and everything was new again—there were a lot more people than normal, so many he stood at the back rather than trying to wade through for a seat. There were engineers and physicists and specialists whose specialisms he had never heard of. But they all looked bleak and harried, and they were all there to say the same thing.

"Team Science looks like a suicide risk; what's going on?" Gale asked. They looked remarkably okay. A grasping, needy part of him was disappointed; he realized he had actually been hoping that they weren't altogether all right, and that at some point today, he could be concerned and helpful, and they could sit together for a little while for a reason that was real, not manufactured by the production crew.

He felt queasy with himself. It was a lot like biting into an apple and finding half a maggot, and trying very, *very* hard not to think about where the other half was.

There was a strange hum below everyone's voices; it was the dust whirring over the new windows, thick and brown and strange. The room felt eveningy, because all the lights were on. There was almost no daylight now.

No power in the sun fields.

"I'm sorry, Senator, but the only way to make the energy last anywhere near long enough is rolling blackouts," Dr Molotov said. "We think between nine at night and six in the morning every day, as well as significant electricity restrictions on day-to-day household activity. As much power as possible needs to go to shipping and essential industry just to keep supply lines open."

"It's cold out there," Mx Francis protested. "We can't leave people without power at night."

Gale was quiet for a moment. "If we ask everyone else to do this, we do it too. Power goes off here at the same time as it does for everyone else. And we are not monetizing this scarcity. Power prices freeze as of right now, or we're hurling most of Tharsis into poverty. We make people pay what is *necessary* to use the infrastructure and run the sun fields. No more. If I see we've made a single yuan profit out of this, someone's head is going in a jar."

"Senator," an accountant-looking person tried, "that isn't how this works—we have to profit in times of scarcity to tide over in times of plenty—"

"We're not American," was all Gale said.

There was a general murmur of "Yes, Senator" from everyone.

"Mx Francis, if the communications department can sit down with Dr Molotov and put together a friendly sounding script explaining what's going on, we'll get it broadcast as soon as possible, that would be much appreciated. The rules need to be clear and we need to explain them straightaway. What are the numbers, will rolling blackouts alone keep us afloat?"

"No," Dr Molotov said miserably. "There will still be a considerable power deficit, but at least it will be delayed. We're working it out."

"Good. And what do we need to get the new array into orbit?"

"Given the dust," Dr Molotov said, looking paler than ever, "we don't think a normal wireless energy transfer will work. We need to actually—bolt it and wire it into the ground."

Gale frowned. "How do you mean?"

Dr Molotov swallowed. "I mean we need to build a rig from here to the upper atmosphere."

"How far is that?" Gale asked.

"To get it above the dust—fifty kilometres."

January had never seen Gale at a loss before, but they were now. "A vertical structure of *fifty* kilometres."

"Yes, Senator," Dr Molotov said, but they sounded more solid about it now. "It can be done."

"What do we need?"

"Engineers, a lot of steel, and as much manual labour as we can get; preferably Earthstrong, it'll go a lot faster. We build first, and then the final stage is sending up the new panels."

"Fuck," Mx Francis said suddenly. "You need to see this." Their lenses flared gold as they projected a news story into the middle of the table.

The Consul was giving an announcement.

"*—rationing, effective immediately. Every citizen in Tharsis will receive a ration card. The allowance will be simple, but it is plenty to live on. Nobody will receive more than anybody else. We have enough to get through this until aid arrives from Earth, but only if we are extremely careful. Everyone needs to do their part. I'm very confident we can do this. This is a country that was founded in an airless desert: we can certainly do this.*"

"Fuck's sake, they stole that from January!" Mx Ren snapped, and January had an unexpected swell of belonging.

The Consul was still talking and everyone was still watching, but January didn't hear any more, because he had suddenly heard it properly. Every *citizen*.

He wasn't a citizen. Nobody he knew outside Songshu was a citizen. What were they all supposed to do?

"Start sourcing the steel," Gale said. "I'll set up a meeting with House Tesla to see if we can borrow their engineers. Go to work."

January didn't move, and waited for everyone else to leave. Gale was getting up slowly, clearly the worse for wear from last night.

"Senator," he said quietly.

Gale gave him a questioning look. A drone swept down to film them.

"Earthstrongers—we aren't citizens."

"We'll call the Interior Ministry, see what their plan is," Gale said. "But I need to—"

"No," January said, getting in the way. "Wait, please. I'm sure you know this already, but Earthstrong immigrants use kilowatts as currency; we're paid in power. To avoid having bank accounts, to be off grid, so that the immigration bureau is less likely to notice us. But if the electric supply is decreasing, and the cost per kilowatt is rising, then their wages are going to sink to nothing. Even normally, I barely earned enough to half heat my flat. And now ration cards, but only for citizens? People aren't going to live with this, they're going to die with it, and . . . really soon. Someone's addressing that. Right?"

Gale took a breath, but then stopped and held it, and looked down at him as though they were trying to rearrange what he had just said into something that made sense. He saw them decide it was too mad to be what it sounded like.

"Say that again? Immigrants are using . . . power . . . as currency?"

For a second, January was paralysed by the gap between the two of them again. Given that Gale *owned* the power grid, he had thought they must know all about electric-wages. It seemed insane that they wouldn't. But then, you'd have to know Earthstrongers to know that, you'd have to spend time in factories and on building sites and in refugee housing. A mean, angry part of him pointed out that when you were in Gale's position, you had a duty to bloody well find out this stuff.

But that was him. That was why he was here, because Gale wanted to find out.

He switched into Mandarin so there couldn't be any confusion. "Yes. On the Crossing, there are charities and lawyers who give you advice about how to get by here. Their advice is not to open a bank account. Even before Gagarin Square, you could be deported if your name sounded too American and terroristy. But industries that employ Earthstrongers who aren't citizens always offer to pay in kilowatts."

Gale sat down again, slowly. "Okay. I'm going to need you to explain how that works."

He had never spoken to someone who took notes before. Not only did Gale take notes, but they also drew diagrams as January described how the charge ports worked in a residential building, and then they showed him the diagrams so he could check, all labelled in their immaculate handwriting.

"So," Gale said at last. "All . . . Earthstrong immigrants are funnelled into government-approved housing. That housing has to be designed for you to move around there uncaged, so things like taps and fittings need to be built for you or everything breaks."

"Right."

"But *within* those designated buildings, it's common knowledge that people don't want their names on any records they can avoid, so the landlords fit extra machinery to the electrical systems that allow you to pay your rent in power. Because all buildings in Tharsis are allowed to sell their excess power, if they're generating extra from their own solar panels or their own whatever, that works: those landlords then sell that power you pay in rent back to the Songshu grid, which returns its yuan value at a perfect exchange rate."

"Exactly," said January, embarrassed he hadn't been able to explain it in that straight a line.

"It's an extension of the system everyone uses on trains and in convenience stores. The charge cards are actually from the rail network."

"Right."

"God," Gale said, sitting back. They looked up. "If people don't have bank accounts, how are we postulating that they're paid now?"

"And that's if the industry they work in can even still run," January said, feeling more anxious the more he had to think about it. "Heavy industry is shutting down, you said—it has to? Well—that's where we work. Shipping, factories, farming."

"I mean clearly there's going to need to be some kind of furlough for the workforces affected," Gale said, "but how are we supposed to find the people who need it? If it's a sign-up system there'll be widespread fraud, but then I imagine if you're avoiding bank accounts then you're not filling in the census either, are you? The Interior Ministry must have a database of Earthstrong immigrants?"

January shook his head. "They do, but it's worthless. A lot of us came from refugee camps, we don't necessarily have passports or ID or anything. The lawyers actually tell you not to give your real name on the ships' manifests. They make up something that sounds more Russian or more Chinese, if you're from—you know, the deep West."

Gale gave their stylus a frustrated look. "Why? The immigration bureau isn't that powerful."

January shifted. "When . . . we go aboard the ships, the charities give us classes about things we need to know. One of them is the chance that in the next few years, the government is going to make naturalisation mandatory for anyone staying more than a year." He said it to the edge of the table, because saying something like that straight on made it sound like smug exaggeration. "So we try and keep off government lists and registers." He took care not to say, *Which is why I'm not convinced by that rubbish you like to spout about how naturalisation will stop this being such a two-tier society. Not only does it not work, it's making things worse.*

Gale stared at him. "So what we're saying is that we have a population of about two hundred thousand people who are going to need help very soon; and no way to find them; and it's my fault."

He wanted to say, *No, of course it's not just your fault*, but that would have been very close to lying. "That's about it."

"How do we reach them?"

"Do we have to work this out on our own? Surely this is the Consul's job, surely we should be calling other people?"

Gale gave him a rueful look. "The Consul might have deliberately overlooked this. If we ask for help, it will generate news headlines about how I'm personally killing all these people. And then they'll die, because unfortunately it was too late to fix my error."

January watched them for a long second. Part of him said, *Don't do it, what you said yesterday is still true, you don't know what happened to Max.* But after talking to Gale in the night, he was coming, tentatively, around to the idea that though they very definitely might still murder him, it wouldn't be because he argued with them. Maybe if he found out something bad, yes, maybe if he tried to sabotage House Gale—but with a strange clarity now, he could see that the last thing that would upset them would be disagreeing. They *wanted* him to disagree.

Here we go then.

"Are you sure you don't want to go to the Consul because if they swoop in and save the day, you'll look incompetent?"

He had expected Gale to put him firmly in his place. But instead, he saw something that might have been close to happiness go through Gale's eyes. They were *pleased*. He had a fizz of answering happiness in his chest. "Let's call them and find out."

The Consul laughed at them and hung up, and about thirty seconds later, there was a sort of primordial howl from down the corridor, which was Mx Francis seeing the Consul post a recording of Aubrey Gale asking for help fixing a mess of their own creation on social media.

"Why do you even HAVE a press secretary!"

"Do you think this is rage that can be solved with cookies, or is it maybe more weapons grade?" Gale murmured.

January took his glasses off. "I'm so sorry," he said.

"I leave you alone for TEN SECONDS!"

"It was an experiment, Solly, we're sorry!" Gale called.

"I could get the dog elected Consul easier than you!" Mx Francis snarled from the doorway. "I can't believe I have to say this, but no calling the Consul, either of you! The Consul, remember, arch-nemesis Song who hates you?"

"It was my fault," January said in a small voice.

"It was not his fault, don't shout at him," Gale said.

"I'm going to work for House Shang," Mx Francis grumbled, off back down the corridor again. "They tried to head-hunt me. And you know what? Their offer didn't basically go, oh, Solly, you're stupid, come and work for a logarithm table that thinks it wants to be Consul . . ."

"Are they actually going to work for House Shang?" January whispered.

Gale waited till Mx Francis had definitely gone. "Born in House Gale, will die in House Gale. Anyway. If you were king of everything, with all the money in the worlds; what would you do?"

January shook his head, because he couldn't imagine for a second that anyone would do what he wanted. "Open the naturalisation centres.

Take the gates and the fences down, open it up to everyone who hasn't naturalised. No naturalisation, but—free rooms, free power, free food, for anyone in a cage, for the duration of the dust. The funds to do it already exist, but the uptake is really low and most of those rooms are empty. There can't be any fraud because it's obvious if someone's Earthstrong or not." He had to look away. "Otherwise people are going to go to the naturalisation camps *and* naturalise just so that they don't die of cold and hunger."

There was a terrible hanging moment in which he realized Gale would probably think that was ideal.

Gale was looking down at their own hands in their lap. He watched them without any hope. It was too much of an about turn. They couldn't campaign against cages and then say, oh, actually, it's fine, have some free stuff.

"Okay," said Gale. "Let's do that."

"Shut up," January said, and then clapped his hand over his mouth. "Sorry. No; why would you do that?"

"Rather than—letting thousands of people die?"

January waited. In his experience politicians were usually very happy to let thousands of people die if it was cheaper and easier.

Gale waited too, then looked indignant and punched him in the arm. "*You* shut up. Now come and be my human shield while I talk to the money people."

33

That evening, truck after gigantic truck arrived with building materials, and the great stretches of fallow land beyond the sun fields became a building site overnight, floodlit with halogens and powered by biofuel generators that rattled in the darkness. January walked out to see, along with a couple of drones. Even by the time he arrived, the work crews had marked out where the base of the tower would be, and they had begun to dig its foundations. It was the size of Songshu. He watched the truck lights flash and the cranes unloading rows and rows of steel cabins that would house the workforce. Thousands of people would be coming tomorrow; this was just the start.

Partly he was outside because he couldn't do anything useful inside Songshu. Gale was broadcasting the message about rolling power cuts.

The weather was turning. It was cold, really cold now. Perhaps it was that the dust had obscured the sun for long enough now that the ground hadn't soaked up any heat at all for the last few days, or perhaps there was always a cold snap toward the end of winter, but it wasn't safe to go outside without a heat suit any more. Counterintuitively, there was no frost. Not enough vapour in the air. As he passed a gigantic machine on caterpillar tracks, some people were checking the integrity of the steel.

Down in the Valley, below the dust clouds, the blackout started, and block by block, the city lights faded to nothing.

———

Half an hour later he was standing with the cameras while the drone operators took light levels, studying the script Mx Francis had written for him, dressed not in the spectacular new things that worked for business life at Songshu, but his own clothes, his old ones: jeans and a checkered shirt. The broadcast was going to be in English. He had never seen an official broadcast done in English. But when it went out, it would have the seal of House Gale.

". . . and therefore House Gale has deemed it appropriate to open the naturalisation centres for any Earthstrong person who needs a refuge whilst the blackouts occur; this will be complimentary, with meals and heat included, and no obligation to naturalise . . ." He trailed off and had to push his hand over his face.

"What's the matter?" Mx Francis said.

"I don't sound like this. Nobody sounds like this," he said helplessly.

"What do you mean?"

"I don't know, I can't explain!" He slid down the green screen wall and went head first into a bar of chocolate.

Mx Francis crouched down close by. "Are you okay?" they said.

"No. I'm going to need more chocolate," January admitted. "What if no one goes? There'll be all this funding and all this effort and it will be pointless and Senator Gale will think I'm an idiot and never listen to me ever again—what if Senator Gale throws me out and I'm eaten by a polar bear, Solly, why didn't we think of that?"

"I don't know, I think the bear would have trouble with the cage," Mx Francis pointed out.

"They're wily!"

Mx Francis patted him. "It will be fine. People will go. Or, you know, they won't, and someone will launch more missiles in through the window, but we serve at the pleasure of the House of Gale."

"Or everyone will think it's an evil plot to trap people in naturalisation centres and take their cages away," January said shrilly.

"*January*," said a Voice over the camera drone's speaker system. "*Can you put your microphone back on?*"

He dropped his scarf over the drone so that it veered around looking like a distressed ghost, and then put his microphone onto Kasha, reasoning that nobody could really fire him at this stage.

Mx Francis was looking worried about the chocolate bar. "Are you sure you should be eating that? It kills your pancreas. You know if you're addicted to sugar you can get virtual junk food, it's just protein and vitamins but it's engineered to taste exactly like—"

"Piss off with your engineered vitamins!"

"But look at the packaging, that's why it's got a picture of someone having their foot amputated on it."

Gale came in through a side door and folded down next to him. Confined to Songshu, they didn't bother with any of the Senate finery; just a plain green jumper and their hair coiled up without the official diadem or any of it, austere as a cleric. January looked over, surprised, and pleased. He wouldn't have pegged Gale as a sit-on-the-floor person.

"Could I have some? I'm down a whole leg already, I'm owed," they said.

The bescarfed drone zithered past, followed closely by Kasha, who was trying to catch it.

"I don't think this sounds right," January said, breaking the bar in half and showing Gale the script. "I don't . . . sound like this, this sounds like—I don't know, like a government official lying to someone."

"It's fine," Mx Francis said.

Gale glanced up from the script. "No, it isn't. He doesn't sound like this at all. It's all Latin and French."

Mx Francis's eyebrows went up. "I am ninety-nine per cent sure it's English."

"Which is made of four languages: German, French, Latin, and Greek, in ascending order of register. Germanic words usually sound simple and earthy, sometimes poetic. French and Latin are formal, which is why it sounds like a politician lying. Greek is scientific."

"Oh my God, it's happening again," Mx Francis said bleakly. "Do I even dare ask what you can possibly mean? Will I really regret this? Will I end up killing myself with my shoelaces to escape?"

Gale looked at January. "You know this, right?"

"No," he said, but although he didn't understand, he felt like the cavalry had arrived. "How does it work?"

"Every time you ask them anything about language, a fairy dies," Mx Francis told him, one hand over their face.

He tried not to be too aware that Gale was warm on his right side, or that he could feel them breathing. He wanted to put his head against their shoulder. Stupid.

"This is . . . why English has two or three words for everything," Gale said, as though they were worried January might feel the shoelace urge too. "You get yourself a drink, but a flight attendant offers you a beverage menu. Drink is German, but beverage is French; more formal. Half of English comes in pairs or triplets with the same meaning but different levels of formality."

"It does?" he said, to make them go on.

"It does. So . . . reckon is low register, consider is high. Watch is low, supervise is high . . . talk and converse, see and observe, place and location, shrink and diminish . . . what else?"

"Live and reside?" January said, starting to hear it, and fascinated. He knew the difference, but he would never have been able to explain what was behind it.

"Exactly. There's always one German, and one Latin or French." Gale was exuding apology. "This whole script is Latin and French. Complimentary, appropriate, refuge, obligation—even the words that aren't Latin are ludicrous. Deem? Solly, even I don't say 'deem' and I'm wildly pretentious."

"Sorry, I must have left my French and Latin dictionaries at home," Mx Francis said drily.

"How would you say it?" Gale asked January. "If you were just telling me over coffee."

January gazed down at the script. "I'd say . . . I'd say: at House Gale, we think the best way to keep everyone Earthstrong safe during the blackouts is to open the naturalisation centres. Nobody will have to naturalise. But you'll get a room, and all your food, and all your electricity, for free."

"That's great. That sounds like you. Say that." Gale looked sideways at Mx Francis. "Which is the French and Latin translated back into conversational Germanic root words, by the way."

"Just so you know, if I ever wanted to murder you in this election," Mx Francis said, "all I'd have to do is release a thirty-second clip of you doing exactly this."

"Solly," January protested, "stop shaming them for being clever. They're running for Consul, not Prom Queen. If I've got a choice between a relatable donkey and a stratospheric genius, I want the bloody genius, thank you."

"You can't call someone here a Prom Queen, January!"

He lifted his eyebrows. "I know. I didn't."

But Gale looked at him as though he had just held an umbrella over them in pouring rain, and a happy, warm, ashamed bubble swelled in his chest.

"Go and do your German speech," Mx Francis told him, flapping him with the script.

"Does this look okay?" January asked Gale, waving at his whole self. "And my English is Deep British. There are going to be Americans watching this going, *What's that funny noise he's making?*"

Gale thought about it. "Well, it—looks like Solly's dressed you up as a poor person and tried to make you cry."

"That's exactly what happened," January said, more reassured to hear the truth than, *Yes, definitely, you'll be marvellous.*

"But I think in this instance, it's what we need," Gale finished gently. "Are you ready?"

January nodded, and got up to stand where the camera people where pointing. He tried to breathe in deep. Even if he made the most convincing speech of all time, it would be tomorrow, or longer, before they knew whether or not people were going to the centres. At the end of the ad, they would put on a link for a virtual forum if anyone had worries or questions, and some of Gale's aides were ready to talk to people, but he seriously doubted anyone would bother until they had no other choice but freezing to death at home. Once he'd done this, there would be nothing to do except wait, and get on with planning ballet lessons people could do while they were trapped at home in the storm, when there was power, and keep coming up with silly things the reality show people could film him doing.

And hope Gale really didn't trap everyone in the naturalisation centres. He was only eight tenths convinced.

Gale was still sitting on the carpet, watching. When he caught their eye, they smiled.

"Five, four, three . . ." The camera drone operator counted down on their fingers, then made a spinning motion to say, *Rolling.*

January let Mx Francis's script drop to his side. "Good evening, everyone. I'm here to tell you what we want to do at House Gale to help Earthstrong people through the blackouts. It's going to sound a bit mad, but bear with me."

As soon as he finished, he crumpled down on the floor with Gale again, not nearly as relieved as he'd hoped. Gale put one arm around him. He hugged them back, tucked against their shoulder. It was a lovely feeling, but there were needles hidden in it, and he knew that if he relaxed too much, he'd cut himself. Somewhere upstairs, their real partner would be waiting.

"Don't be worried; I thought you were very compelling, for a cave person," Mx Ren said in passing.

Mx Francis was running through an amended schedule. A lot of charity and politics rallies and fundraisers were going to be cancelled because of the dust; there would be virtual events instead, so soon he needed to be in a virtual fitting for virtual clothes.

"Senator?" an aide said nervously from the doorway of the VR room. It was just a big blank space with padded walls so you could walk around while you were plugged into the internet and not hurt yourself. "Would you mind coming into the forum? There are a lot more people than we . . . er, expected."

Gale glanced down at January, full of wariness, and they both got up together. January pushed his glasses back on and Gale's eyes flared blue with the new connection.

The virtual forum was a lovely space. It was a forest glade, in golden sunlight and part shaded by the ruins of pillars bound up in red ivy. Statistically, Mx Francis said, people were calmer and you got more agreements and diplomatic treaties if everyone talked while they were outside, or at least, if they felt like they were. If January had had the haptic engines webbing across the right part of his brain like Mx Francis and Gale had, he would even have been able to feel the sunlight, and smell the warm pollen in the air. As it was, he was well aware of being in a blank dark room with rubber pads over the walls, but even just seeing the glade through his glasses was good.

It was full of people.

Hundreds and hundreds of people.

Naturalised people were there on behalf of Earthstrong friends who didn't want to appear even as an avatar; Earthstrong people using public VR access; staff from Songshu and the centres, marked out with red sashes and sparkling signs hanging above their heads that said HERE TO HELP.

There was a rush for January and Gale.

"That's them!"

"Is it really true that it would be completely free?" someone said.

"What's to stop you closing people in?"

"Is it okay to bring children? I have kids born here but I'm in a cage . . ."

January had never been so frightened that he had just made a horrifying mistake. Beside him, Gale was as luminous and warm as they always were in public, the calculating machine of their real character buried well out of sight, but now that he knew it was there, he couldn't unhear its ticking. They wouldn't consider it a reason not to lock people away just because some of them would suffer, or because he would be angry. Nobody had ever saved *them* from anything just because they would suffer.

He was still carrying the Consul's card in his pocket. He found himself turning it around and around between his fingertips.

34

The new tower climbed all through the end of November and into December[29] like an Advent candle in reverse. It climbed fast, too. Swarms of people were working on it, kitted out in heat suits and breathing masks against the storm. Through the blasting dust, all you could see of them from Songshu were the lights of the welding torches, whole constellations, through the day and the impenetrable nights. Sometimes, when the dust was dense enough, it caught fire, so that every torch had a brilliant comet-tail of burning particles downwind. Even in this gravity, the base of it was vast to support the weight. Twelve steel struts each the size of an oil rig held it up, and every day, more steel came, loaded on the trains from the Valleyside. Every foundry in Tharsis was going at full strength to supply it—even the blast furnaces that served the interplanetary shipyards.

Mars was rich because of its steel—it was iron that made the red planet red—but even so, January couldn't help wondering if the supply chain could keep up.

Not least because all those foundries used power that Songshu barely had.

From the Valleyside pinnacle, he could see down into Tharsis. It was dark for sixteen hours a day now. Almost all of it. Steelworks, Tereshkova

---

29 For January, it was November and December—for everyone else, they were rounding into the two hundreds of Winter. It was chance that his traditional winter and Mars's were lining up; of course, you usually got two Decembers in every Martian year, long as it was.

Wharf, and hospitals were the only exceptions. Schools were shut. Shops were shut, except for food. Offices. All most people could do was sit at home and wait.

Songshu wasn't any different. He had to sleep in his coat now. In the eight hours when there was electricity, the big screens in the dining room were permanently tuned to the news. It was full of stories about gigantic queues outside supermarkets as rationing kicked in, interviews with Earthstrongers who didn't dare go to the naturalisation centres in case Gale locked them in, with tailbacks of ambulances outside hospitals as cases of hypothermia rocketed. It was so cold that supermarkets didn't need power for freezers; they could just set up a stall outside and everything from vegetables to meat froze solid. Water rations were going out in slices of ice.

So that not everything broadcast from Songshu was doom and misery, January and Gale started filming little funny segments about culture differences; everything from how British English was different to Tharsese English, to things that made sense on Earth but not at all on Mars, like Lunar New Year, to how they felt temperature differently; Gale could hold their hand in ice for half an hour comfortably (which shocked Earthstrong people who were watching), and then there was some serious incredulity on Natural social media when January sat under a heat lamp in thirty degrees without catching fire. They did one about the genuine danger in coastal areas of being eaten by sharks, which of course to Tharsese people sounded like worrying about pterodactyls. It was only twenty minutes a day, but he looked forward to it, because it was the only time he heard Gale laugh their brilliant boiling-whisky laugh. He felt as though the two of them might be rebuilding their bridge, with more solid support pillars this time.

After a few weeks, he noticed he kept hearing about himself on the news more and more, to the point that it was a bit of struggle to sit in the dining room and go increasingly pink as the people around grinned and looked significantly between him and the screens.

There were analysis stories where social media experts were interviewed—

"House Gale really does seem to have tapped into some magic with January Stirling—what do we think is going on?"

"Well, I think what we're seeing is just appreciation for a really nice human being who's been put in the most extraordinary situation. I think a lot of us wondered what Aubrey Gale thought they were doing, but that Cinderella narrative is proving very hard not to like . . ."

And then there were political shows that seemed dedicated to picking apart every word to do with the election—

"Of course this sets up a problem for Senator Gale down the line: if they win this election, January Stirling is going to have to naturalise just like every other permanent Earthstrong resident in Tharsis, and a lot of people are feeling increasingly uncomfortable about the idea of making him do that . . ."

And even talk shows about daily life in the power lockdown—

"So something great happened to me yesterday. I live in a super mixed district in Dengta—we have one of the highest rates of accidental Earthstrong-caused homicide in Tharsis—and I have an Earthstrong neighbour. We've always avoided each other, but yesterday morning a mail drone delivered one of my packages to her, and she came round with it, when I opened the front door, she was kneeling on the threshold. I don't know about you all, but though I knew in theory that some Earthstrongers will do this if the situation might be dangerous, I'd never actually seen it before January Stirling knelt to Senator Gale, and I tell you, it just wiped out any fear I had right away. We laughed a lot and she came in for coffee, and I asked about whether she'd ever seen a jellyfish and she said no, I'm from Arizona, and anyway, long story short, we get together every second evening now to watch these crazy nature documentaries from Earth."

Mx Francis thought it was wonderful—apparently Fenhua's fashion house had started an affordable line of designs based on January's new clothes and the sales were ludicrous now that everyone had nothing to do but shop online, so now there were #EARTHSTRONGHONOUR T-shirts everywhere—Mx Ren thought it was hilarious (they wore the T-shirts under the pink dungarees), and January couldn't tell what Gale thought. They seemed pleased, but they didn't talk about any of it, probably because they had more important things to do, but he was worried there was a glassy, brittle edge to it. Maybe they were worried about a public backlash if he did have to naturalise in the end. In one way, that gave him a little slice of hope, but in another, it put a fearful knot in his stomach, because it would have been naïve to think that becoming briefly famous would stop Gale getting rid of him if he turned out to be more of a hindrance than a help. He didn't dare to ask. He was less scared of them lately—it was hard to laugh with someone about jellyfish every day and still be afraid—but playing like a drumbeat in the back of his head was, *You still don't know what happened to Max, you still don't know what happened to Max.*

Every night, Gale filmed a live update of the progress on the tower and the painfully slim intake of power from the solar panels for the day.

Despite all that public pressure, they didn't show any sign of being fuzzy or confused on the broadcasts. They looked very tired, January thought, but so did everyone. It was hard to sleep when the house got down to minus five indoors at night. And there had been no more midnight visits. He was beginning to hope that it had been a one-off.

Every day, the news reported the progress of the fleet from Earth, and the uranium it was bringing. Songshu wasn't the only place with a building project. Down in Tharsis, they were clearing people out of the converted nuclear towers, and getting those ancient reactors ready to fire again.

A hundred and eighty million kilometres away.

A hundred and fifty.

A hundred.

On Christmas Eve, the fleet and its uranium had only forty million kilometres left to come. They would cover that in two weeks, and arrive just after the election.

The tower was at thirty-eight kilometres.

As every single news programme and talk show pointed out, the person to win the election would be the one who could get their power to Tharsis first, and just now, the bookies were offering bang-on fifty-fifty odds.

35

People here didn't do Christmas. It existed, but it was a day when couples went out and had fried chicken, and the whole building site outside Songshu smelled strongly of it already, a day in advance. How Christmas had morphed from the original model to this one was lost to history and everyone had different theories, but the consensus seemed to be that somehow it was Tokyo's fault, though nobody remembered why. And for some reason, everyone kept giving him apples as if they were seasonally significant, and nobody explained why.[30]

After spending another morning filming another dance class—so many people were furloughed from shut-down industries now that they needed some kind of home exercise plan and it turned out, thanks to Mx Francis's advertising campaigns, that he was it—he felt coddled and pointless. He was dancing inside in the warm while a thousand people worked outside in minus forty degrees. A lot of them were Earthstrong. Most were commuting from the nearest naturalisation centre. It was close, right at the foot of the Valleyside, so it was just a train ride away, but he was worried. The centre was overcrowded already. He'd been

---

30 Mandarin was sometimes like a huge, industrialised version of Cockney rhyming slang. This was why the number four was unlucky ("four" and "death" were both *sì*) and why January's security codename was Railway; Jan, *zhan*, was "station." "Apple" was *pingguo*, and at Christmas, people wished each other peace and safety, which was *ping an*. Ping and *ping*. Peace apples.

down a lot, every third day, to keep checking that nothing horrible was happening, not that he had any idea what he'd do if it was. It wasn't, but things were creaking. It was six to a room already, pallet beds pin-neat just like on Crossing ships, and the longer the police didn't lock the gates, the more people came.

He was starting to hope that Gale didn't mean to do anything at all except let people live there for the length of the storm. It was a painful kind of hope though, the sort that was like a spider; it had spun a web across his chest and the web had turned so solid that it was hard to breathe past it. He couldn't help being vividly aware that Gale only needed those people while the building work went on. After that—well.

He was on his way down again, walking towards the train station with a drone and a polite security officer who stayed five paces behind him, when he saw a shadow in the dust that looked wrong.

He was nearly used to the dust tornados and the purple lightning that snickered inside them. They hadn't let up for a month. He was used to the breathing mask too, and how the lenses caught the dim light in a funny way and cast reflections that looked like ghosts.

But there was a shadow. It was big, very big, and not the right shape for a new tornado whirring in from across the Plains. It looked like a hill, but there were no hills here.

He stopped when the ground juddered. It was slight, but it was there. He glanced back at the security officer, because there were no earthquakes on Mars, and the security officer looked just as puzzled as he felt. The judder came again. He set one hand on the ground, trying to tell if it was something they were doing on the tower, drilling or something. Beside him, the little drone drifted up into the air to try and get a better view, but there was so much iron in the dust that its gyroscopes got seasick, and it wobbled uncertainly. The producers had been hurrying around with anglers' nets to catch them if they fell. Probably it was very stressful for the producers, but personally January felt you hadn't lived if you hadn't watched someone in designer shoes lunging after a queasy air-bauble with a big net.

The drone fell and he caught it, and he was still trying to see if it was okay when the sirens blasted.

Not the dust sirens. This was something else, a much more urgent wail, the kind of siren that something in his bones remembered from wars long since lost.

"January!" It was Mx Francis through his earpiece. "Get back inside! *Now!*"

He was going to ask what was happening, but there was no time before he saw exactly what was happening.

He had known that they existed here. To get ecosystems going here in the early days, the first colonists had introduced extinct cold-weather species, and so there were all sorts now. Tourists could go on safari looking for them, and souvenir shops in town sold fluffy toy versions, but somehow, it had never quite gone through his head that he might actually see one.

There were mammoths, on this side of the railway line.

He didn't know how big they had been originally, on Earth. In this gravity, they were bigger than he imagined even dinosaurs could have been. The looming shapes in the dust must have been at least a third as high as Songshu's main tower, titan things, and even though the sirens were still blaring and in his head somewhere he knew he should be running, he couldn't do anything except watch them plough through the young trees at the edge of the pine wood. One of them dipped tusks that must have been fifty feet long and ripped up a tree like it was a matchstick.

And they were talking to each other. It was so low he couldn't hear it, only feel it, a primal rumble that vibrated the roots of his teeth. When one of them trumpeted, it was deafening, even through his mask, and he had to half collapse with both hands clamped over his ears. They were starting to run—something had made them panic, maybe the dust catching fire from all those welding torches on the steel rig, or maybe the lightning in the dust—and under him, the ground jumped.

He realized what was going to happen a good few seconds before it did. Songshu was up a slope, and even in the dust, you could see the head-lamps of the cargo trains coming along the railway from the Valley. The one coming now had slammed on its brakes so hard the track was sparking, and just like the welders' torches, those sparks made the dust on either side catch alight in streams of wispy fire, and of course that scared the mammoths more than ever.

One of them ripped the train right off the track and *hurled* it.

The steel girders in the first cargo container spilled out and flew. He lost them in the dust, but he heard them land and slung himself into the roots of the nearest tree. There was a deep dull thump that must have been what a falling star sounded like as one of those girders drove itself ten feet deep into the ground, upright at a slant, right next to him.

And then the herd was gone, and all that was left were eddying dust-fires, puffing out nearly as quick as they started. He crawled out into the open again to see if the security officer was all right, the blood hammering at the inside of his skull and the need to just curl up and hide for *much longer* still more powerful than he'd ever thought it could be. They were; they were coming out from among the roots too, and together the two of them stood and looked at the wreckage.

The train track had been ripped up too. It was just a twisted mess.

It took a little while for that to sink in.

There was only one track, and one train, up here. One track and one train to bring a thousand Earthstrong construction workers every morning; one track and one train to bring the steel for the tower.

He had no idea how long it took to repair damage like this, but sure as hell it would be longer than two weeks.

36

Gale called a senior staff meeting in the dining room. Because Mx Ren was trying to run Songshu on as little power as possible, they were burning wood from the pine forest in the hearths now instead of relying on central heating. The hearths were glass, set at intervals all through the room, so you could circle them just like campfires, and as everyone sat down, January had a feeling that soldiers who had to camp on beaches in ancient wars who would recognise the scene exactly.

Mars was traditionally good at cold weather living, and there was plenty of provision for it. Now, everyone was wearing lab-grown seal-skin and polar bear fur, even the sixth- and seventh-generation Natural people. Inside, the temperature hovered around zero the moment you strayed away from the fires. The only reason there wasn't ice everywhere was that there wasn't enough water.

"Right," said Gale, who was reminding January more and more of those beleaguered generals who had to somehow get by with a fifth of what they needed, uncomplaining and flinty and always balancing on the edge of collapse. January had never met anyone who took disaster so steadily, and the more he saw it, the more grateful he was. It wasn't just courage under fire; it was showing the way. Everyone else was much calmer and more workmanlike than he would have expected as a result, himself included. His mind had changed gears to keep up with Gale, and now, if he personally wasn't right now on fire, he usually felt like he was having an okay-to-good day.

"Immediate problem number one: we have a thousand Earthstrong workers on the rig who can't get back down to the Valley tonight. We need to work out what to do with them before it gets dark tonight or we will—no longer have a thousand Earthstrong workers."

"Immediate problem number two," Mx Ren said, "the herd didn't just smash up the railway. They went through Fields Eight and Nine. Destroyed the salt towers. We're going to have to lose the internet in about—mm, six hours, or there won't be enough power to run Tereshkova Wharf."

There was a little quiet. The fire snickered. January stared at the floor, where there was a film of frost that disappeared only about four feet away from the fire. It only formed near people. It glittered, and between him and Gale, Kasha was patting at it curiously, making paw prints.

"Solutions to either one of those then please," Gale murmured.

"The last gravity train hit the Valley floor this morning," Dr Molotov said, shaking their head. "We have no reserve power left. All we have is the tiny amount coming in from the remaining sun fields."

"We can't lose the internet," Mx Francis protested. "Anyone who's grown up with implants—they'll go into shock."

"We don't have a choice. It's cut power to the servers or cut power to Tereshkova, which will explode if it's without power for the cooling towers for longer than ten minutes," Dr Molotov told them, with an edge.

Gale was staring into the middle distance, toward one of the fires, unblinking. January couldn't tell if they were even listening any more.

"Can we set up a temporary camp, for the Earthstrongers?" someone asked.

"With what? We're not the army, I don't have a thousand heat-sealed tents stuffed down my trousers, do you?" Mx Ren growled.

"There's a lot of horses on the farms up here," someone else offered. "We can get everyone to ride back. The funicular train down the Valley still works, so that's only a few miles."

"A few miles on horseback in minus forty degrees might as well be five hundred," January said, trying not to sound too frustrated. He had spent a lot of the last month trying to make people understand that even though a Natural person could happily go for a stroll in a jumper in minus ten degrees, anyone like him was going to be busy dying in a hedge. "You can't ask people to go on a gigantic hiking expedition just to get home—and then to do it again, twice a day every day, after a full shift at work. We literally couldn't eat enough calories to live through that. I need ten thousand a day just to function in this cold, and I'm struggling. I'm not being difficult, I'm telling you what we can and can't survive. I know no one's saying this because no one wants to think about it, but can I say the really obvious solution?"

All he got were blank looks. "What?" Mx Ren said.

"Songshu is enormous. We can bring them here."

It got a very deep silence.

"Any objections?" Gale said.

An appalled stir went through first the security people, then everyone else. In the end it was Mx Francis who sat forward.

"Er—*yes?* All they'd have to do is take off the cages and Songshu will immediately change hands. You're not talking about an ordinary work-force, Senator, you're talking about a thousand super-humans who all hate you. This is nuts!"

"They'd be filmed one hundred per cent of the time," January said, as softly as he could. "No one could do anything even if they wanted, not without immediately being shot."

"We all said that about Gagarin Square!"

Gale gripped the edge of their chair.

"Someone threw a *bomb* in through our window and we still don't know how she knew where you'd be!" Mx Francis pushed. "Are we genuinely saying this is a good idea?"

There was a surge of agreement from all round the fire. All the security officers might as well have just heard that Gale was planning to go swimming with some great whites who had promised that they weren't hungry.

Beside him, Gale looked ill. "Be quiet."

There was a strange, instant silence, because Gale didn't sound like the easily amused academic any more.

"The issue here is a thousand people who will die tonight if we don't help them, a thousand people who are working for us *despite* the reputation of House Gale among Earthstrongers. We are not going to let them freeze to death just because some of us wish to say that our varying anxieties carry more weight than a thousand lives. When I say, *does anyone have any objections*, I am not consulting you as your psychologist. I do not care if you have a vague sense of unease; I'm asking for numbers. I'm asking if we have the supplies and space to accommodate a thousand people. If it doesn't go on a graph, it is irrelevant. Does anyone have any objections?"

Nobody said anything. A lot of eyes were suddenly on tablets and styluses.

"Good," Gale ground out. "Make all the tower floors as safe for Earthstrong guests as they can be made, and get someone up to the building site to explain they will be welcome here. Dr Molotov, let the internet servers know we're going to have to cut power to them at night; it will go back on in the day. I'll tell people to make sure they're—that they're sitting down when it happens. Go to work."

There was a rush to get away. Gale was very still, and very pale.

A drone bobbed down to look more closely at Gale. January shook his head at it, but the operator ignored him and came nearer and nearer. He would have liked to throw it across the room, but then there would be a whole show about him losing his temper.

"Senator," he said quietly, "I'm not feeling so good, I think the altitude medication isn't working. I can't remember where Dr Okonkwo's office is; would you come with me?"

Gale stared at him for a second, but then nodded. "Of course."

He took Gale's arm and tried to make it look like he was the one who needed it. They made it to the lift, which was running on emergency power because of course Gale couldn't very well do many stairs, and he thought he might have misjudged, but as soon as it started to rise, Gale thumped the emergency stop button and stood more still than January had known a human could, soundless—he couldn't even hear them breathing, maybe they weren't—and tears leaking under their lashes.

January would have hugged anyone else, but he had a horrible feeling that getting close to him was the last thing Gale wanted. He pressed himself to the wall instead, out of reach.

"She didn't get very long in prison, did she," he said, in Mandarin so Gale wouldn't have to work so hard for it. "The woman who did it. I watched the trial. They said something about . . . I forget, but it meant she was a weapons-grade idiot who got all her news from social media and she thought she was on some kind of holy crusade, and it would be cruel to treat her as if she had a brain."

"Four years for assault . . . her lawyers said that if she'd been trying to kill me she would have. It was a very political trial. The point was to calm things down." They swallowed, and switched back into English. "And I think everyone agreed that I brought it upon myself."

"No," January said, very soft, so he wouldn't yell. "You said it already: this is Mars. It's cold here, and there's no water."

Gale looked at him for an expressionless age, and then stepped into his arms and locked their shoulders together.

"I'm sorry," Gale said tightly.

"What for?" January asked, hearing his own voice go high and tight, because his throat had constricted. "I'm so relieved you're a normal person, I've been going round terrified I'm married to the King of Sparta." He realized as he said it that Gale had no reason to know what Sparta was or that people from there were infamously war-loving crazies; not when most people here didn't even know what Europe was, except the funny bit stuck on the side of Russia. He had the familiar old tide of despair that he was never going to be able to talk to anyone properly ever again, not someone who understood straightaway everything he was likely to say, who didn't wonder if he was being strange or aggressive. He shoved it aside. He really needed to stop moping around feeling sorry for himself; it was getting on his nerves. "I'm not a Spartan, I'm a ballet hamster, I shuffle around complaining about opera scores that are played too fast."

Gale stayed bent forward against him. In a very deep-down simple way, it felt safe. He didn't mind being around people who were a foot taller than him at all, because he liked them all—except Dr Okonkwo, but probably even God didn't like Dr Okonkwo—but at some point in the last two months, he had got used to feeling a little bit uneasy, almost all of the time, because everyone's sight line went naturally straight over his head. People let doors go just before he tried to walk through them, he had to press himself to the wall in corridors as someone hurried by, and he had to keep stepping back from Mx Francis, who spoke with their hands once they'd got to know you, because his face was at exactly flailing level. Wrapped in Gale's arms now, it just—went away. He caught himself wanting never to come up. "Thanks," they said against his hair.

He pressed the emergency button again and the lift sighed upward. Gale tilted back against the wall, looking to the side as though looking at January would have been too much.

"Shall we hide in my room for a bit?" he asked. "I've got candles. We could tell ghost stories?" He thought about it. "But—not ones that are too good, or you might have to defend me from the thing under the bed."

Gale did look at him then. "With my shield or on it."

37

The whole of Songshu was a scramble for the next few hours; everywhere, there were people with drills and safety checklists going in and out of rooms, securing anything that could be secured against someone three times normal strength. Yellow tape went up, and signs that said

DANGER EARTHSTRONG ONLY

NO NATURALISED PERSONS BEYOND THIS POINT

or, around the production rooms and Gale's flat on the fifth floor,

YOU MUST WEAR A CAGE BEYOND THIS POINT

Tape went down in the dining room, the main foyer, spray signs went onto the floor, into elevators, and the big screens that usually showed interactive maps of the building flashed up reminders to keep right.

When the first people came in that night, they came slowly, looking just as uncertain as January had felt when Gale took him into the Tiangong. January stood in the entrance hall to meet people and direct them, and so did all the kitchen staff. They'd made vats of tea, coffee, and hot chocolate; toast, rice, fish, everything hot on open grills or sizzling in makeshift fireplaces. January went round as many people as he could to say hello, and make sure they had the right room keys. Songshu staff were in bright red sashes now so people could see them, although there was no real need, because of course they were much taller than anyone born on Earth.

Light gleamed on everyone's cages. The Natural people were doing good work of not looking obviously terrified, he thought. Gale was taking round a tray of hot chocolate and coffee. January had a twinge of painful pride.

Mx Francis coughed from behind him.

"Hot chocolate."

"Oh—thanks."

They hesitated. They were tying reef knots into the ends of their braids again. There were three that January could see already. "Are—are you angry with me, after the meeting?"

"Am I what? No?"

"Because—I know I'm the one who thought this was dangerous."

"It *is* dangerous," January said incredulously. "Of course it is. You weren't wrong." If Gale had been anyone else, he would have said, *Look, I know the Senator was scary about it but even they had a panic attack in in the elevator.* But even the idea of saying that felt like betrayal. He looked around for Gale again. Since the Earthstrongers had started arriving, a timer had been going in his head. A quarter of an hour, half, a whole hour, because what was right in the front of his mind was: *how long could I walk through a polar bear enclosure and keep pretending I wasn't scared?*

His heart stopped for a beat—it was unexpected agony, it had never happened before—when he saw that Gale was surrounded by bulky men in orange work jackets and cages dulled-down and scratched from labour work, boots still rusty with the dust of the site and clothes oil stained. But then while he watched, they all laughed.

Mx Francis shrank two inches from a relieved sigh. "Okay, good. Okay—and, and Jan—you haven't forgotten, have you?"

"Um—assume I have," he said, and wondered if there was a word for the feeling that uncurled when you knew for absolutely certain that you were about to be very embarrassed, because although it hadn't happened yet, there was no avoiding it.

"It's Sunday," Mx Francis prompted him.

"It . . . is?"

"It is, and remember a thousand years ago when we came up with a schedule . . . ?" Mx Francis said. They tied another reef knot.

January was blank for a good few seconds, and then his brain restarted properly and he couldn't believe he had forgotten. It was why he was here, after all. "Start of romance day."

"So don't scream and punch my boss please, it isn't sexual assault, it's scheduled, has been for weeks."

"I have never screamed and never punched anyone," January said.

"Only you kind of look like you have," Mx Francis said, sparkling tentatively. "Are we absolutely sure the Royal Ballet doesn't have its own haka?"

He nearly spat out his hot chocolate and Mx Francis laughed too, and neither of them said, *Christ, that came around quickly*. Start of romance day; when Mx Francis had given him the schedule, it had seemed so far away that you'd only need to worry about it imminently if you were a beam of light.

"With all this, is it really that vital?" he asked. His insides were tying their own reef knots.

Three of the Earthstrong construction men were telling Gale an involved joke, with gesticulating and one diagram on a notepad. Gale was giving it all their attention. Still all right. The Earthstrong men looked enchanted already. He didn't know why he was worried. Even if someone cut Gale off from all this money and power and dumped them in Americatown with short hair and overalls, he was nearly sure that they would have befriended the local gang, spell-checked the graffiti, and ended up being owed dinner by at least four different people by the end of the day.

A kneejerk instinct in him wanted to huff that if other people had had the kind of education Gale did, then they would have learned to do that too, so it wasn't so remarkable. But he didn't think that that was what was happening at all. It was—and he was askance with himself that he hadn't noticed this before—that Gale was a lot like Val. They basically liked ninety-nine per cent of the humans they met. He just didn't think you could fake interest in the weird and possibly indecent diagrams and still laugh like Gale was laughing. They could be afraid, or at moral loggerheads, or right at the other end of the political spectrum, *and still enjoy someone.*

That wasn't a class thing or an education thing. It was an intrinsic Gale thing.

"More than ever," Mx Francis said. They gazed around, and though they were trying not to let it show, they were thrumming with nerves. "Not just for the show. People need to see that the two of you are in this together."

"I don't understand."

"January," Mx Francis said, with an urgency that sounded like they'd restrained it so much only with great difficulty. "Look around. If the Senator wins the election, all these people are going to have to naturalise. Liking *you* is all that's between the Senator and a broken neck." A fleet of drones sailed past and both January and Mx Francis looked that way. "Oh, God. The Senator's about to do the broadcast about the internet. If this doesn't cause a riot, I'll wear that repulsive shirt of yours all week."

January lifted his eyebrows. "You sure? These stains are white spirit. I think this one is the Weird Mystery Sludge from when we cleaned out Silo 3."

"Weird Mystery Sludge and all," Mx Francis said, tying another knot as, between the willow trees at the front doors, Gale stepped up to the podium.

38

"In one hour from now, at eight o'clock, all internet servers in Tharsis will be powered down overnight. We do not take this decision lightly. But it's this, or Tereshkova Wharf.

"Everyone has been incredibly patient, and the building work on the tower is on schedule. This is a terrible but necessary step to take for the final two weeks. For those of you who have had haptic implants for many years, there is a high chance that you'll go into shock when the signal drops. Our medics recommend that everyone stay sitting down when this happens, and if you don't have anyone with you who doesn't have those connections, it is important that you find a neighbour who knows to look in on you. For those of you who do not have internal connections, please take care of those who do. Do not call the emergency services for anything less than life-or-death problems: they are already overrun. This is going to be very difficult. But it won't last long. The signal will come up again at nine o'clock tomorrow morning. Thank you."

Gale trudged down from the podium.

"Is it really going to be that bad?" January asked. He'd gone to the front to wait.

"Dr Okonkwo thinks so. We'll see in an hour." They sighed. "I can see you gearing up to draw something embarrassing on me in marker pen if I do collapse, but bear in mind that my revenge will be immediate and lengthy."

"Me? What? Why would you accuse me of something like that? I don't have anything behind my back. Sad."

Gale smiled, but they looked away suddenly, at nothing particular.

January claimed their arm and steered them away from that podium. It had its own gravity, and it only got heavier as the weeks ground on. Everyone was starting to look at it with a leaden dread. Gale didn't, but that was only because they could hold themselves too still for it to show. To walk up there every night and explain the latest horrible news was getting harder and harder, that was obvious, but Gale wouldn't let anyone else do it. If it all failed, they pointed out, it was going to be their face on that failure, not anyone else's.

"Let's go and see what horrifying news Dr Molotov has," he suggested. "I bet that'll cheer you right up."

Dr Molotov had two pieces of good news and one piece of horrifying news. The good news was that they'd worked out, to everyone's huge relief, that there was enough steel on site already to finish the tower, as long as some people could make the ride to the Valley for smaller parts like bolts. The second good thing was that if the Songshu pine forest were to be cut down, then that timber could heat a good deal of Tharsis for the next two weeks; people wouldn't die of cold in order to keep powering Tereshkova Wharf. When Mx Ren asked if the forestry equipment would still work in the dust, Dr Molotov brightened and said yes, of course it would, because it was built to withstand gales of sawdust. There were enough ranches on the Plains to requisition horses to get the timber to the train down the Valley. It would work. A little cinder of hope flared up through everyone.

"How far does that stretch the remaining power?" Gale asked.

"Another three days."

Everyone deflated.

"Yeah," Dr Molotov said, very quiet. "I'm sorry. Even at the rate we're going, even if we switch off the internet completely between now and then instead of just at night—Tereshkova Wharf will run out of power on Wednesday."

It was Sunday.

"Can the rig be finished any earlier?" January asked.

"No," Dr Molotov said heavily. "We need power to build it. To work the elevators. We're taking people forty kilometres up into the atmosphere. To use the equipment, work the cranes, power heat suits . . . and then to launch the fucking sun fields into orbit, don't forget that. If we could have unlimited power, the damn thing would be done in two days. The only reason it's taking this long is that we're rationing."

Silence around the fire. This time, Gale didn't ask if anyone had any solutions. If anyone had thought of anything, they would have said it. January watched the fire dance. Everyone had spent this last week hoping Dr Molotov's people would come up with something, maybe even feeling sure that they would. But even though the scientists had been pulling all-nighters, again and again, there was nothing.

Dr Molotov's voice sounded like they were having to pry it out of a wall with the end of a hammer. "I'm so sorry, but Senator . . . we need to look at evacuating the whole area around Tereshkova."

Gale was entirely still. January had to pull his hand over his eyes, as if not seeing would stop all this going any further.

"If those cooling pipes fail—the hydrogen explosion is going to destroy everything in Americatown, including the reactor building there, plus parts of Benin Gate and Dengta."

Gale nodded slightly. A month ago, January would have thought a savage part of him would set off streamers and do a happy jig at the sight of Aubrey Gale defeated, but he didn't feel that at all. It just hurt. And he knew why Gale was quiet. They were watching the future play out. Tereshkova would go off like a bomb. It would take out the old nuclear reactor building, which would destroy any chance of a swift power fix when the fleet from Earth arrived with uranium. Thousands of people would die in the cold and from thirst until the solar array was finally in the atmosphere and a working water factory was on its feet again. Which would be a hollow, awful victory, because by then, Gale would have been arrested for criminal negligence for letting the power to Tereshkova fail, and they would spend the rest of their life on a prison hulk orbiting Jupiter. It would be a short life.

"Could Earthstrongers lift the gravity trains?" Mx Francis asked January. "Nine hundred normal people, we said—that's only three hundred Earthstrongers. We have a thousand. What if we diverted them from the rig? Because—look, I know nobody wants to say this, but we are not going to get that array into the atmosphere before the fleet arrives from Earth. All we can do now is tide over until the uranium gets here, and make sure Tharsis is still in one piece when it does."

There was a ringing silence in which nobody said what that would mean, if Gale was right about Earth using the refugee fleet as a way to take over. Prison, as surely as if Tereshkova exploded.

"How would we hook three hundred people up to a gravity train windlass?" Dr Molotov said for him. "It would take longer to build something like that than we have. All we have, on site, are the cables from the trains, which are too big for a person to grip—even one link. Each one is the size of a person. The windlasses are *huge*, have you seen them? Maybe we . . . *could* find a way of hooking up enough ropes and—God knows. I don't know if we even have rope that could be used safely in these temperatures. Maybe. I'll look at it." But they didn't look hopeful.

More silence. Gale was frowning into the middle distance. If they had noticed that everyone was looking at them, waiting for them to say something, they didn't show it.

"Senator?" Mx Ren said, very quiet.

January touched their shoulder, trying to call them back from wherever they'd gone in their head. He couldn't imagine what it was like to stare down the barrel of all this and feel like it was your own fault. But he could see that everyone around the fire needed a reason to keep going, even when there was nothing to keep going for.

Gale didn't move.

Well, that was what consorts were for.

"Right, let's get the trees down," he said. "Dr Molotov; three days is ages for a genius. You'll think of something. Thanks, everyone. Ah—but don't go too far. We'll lose the internet in a minute."

"Which means stay sitting down," Dr Okonkwo said. "It's going to feel like the world has died. Does anyone here *not* have lenses and haptics?"

January was the only one with his hand up.

Dr Okonkwo looked bleak. "Well, Mx Stirling, if you could—you know, check nobody's choking on their own tongue then that would be great."

January had to catch himself before he said, *Come on, it can't be that bad.*

He jumped when a voice came over the house speaker system.

Internet going down in five, four, three, two . . .

Everyone collapsed.

January stood up slowly. He was the only one moving. There was no sound, no murmur of conversation, nothing except for the clicking of the fire and, from the kitchen not far away, the hiss of unattended grills. Away from the fire, the air was frozen, and winking with dust that found its way in from outside. He gazed around, half expecting to see thorns and vines climbing across everything, reclaiming it all like that cursed kingdom in the story, where everyone but the spiders slept for a hundred years.

He started to check pulses and breathing, and to help the people who were blinking and coming around again to sit up. But not many people could. Mx Francis was curled up on the floor, shuddering, and staring with an awful blind horror at the dim room, hardly breathing. January pressed a glass of water into their hands.

"It's okay," he tried. "You're safe, it . . . Just try and drink something."

"What? I can't understand what you're saying!"

He frowned, because he'd been speaking Mandarin. "You can. I have an accent, it's quite strong, but I'm not . . ."

"Oh my God, it's so . . . *quiet* . . . "

"God, is that how this place looks without any overlay?" said Mx Ren, managing to look disapproving. "What a dump."

January laughed, as much because it was an enormous relief as because it was actually funny. "Are you okay? Can you help check the others?"

"Oh, fuck, is that your *real* nose?" Mx Ren said to Mx Francis. "That's upsetting."

January wanted to applaud.

"You're—such—a bitch," Mx Francis whispered. They hadn't stopped shaking, but January didn't think a blanket would help. "Is the Senator . . . ?"

Gale was wrenching themselves upright. They were clearly a lot more annoyed about folding than the internet itself. "Well, this is illuminating," was the irritable verdict.

"Fire!" someone shouted from the kitchen. "There's a . . ."

January ran to help. It was only a little fire; someone had knocked a grill as they fell, and not far. He put it out, had a tiny moment of joy with the extinguisher, and by the time he went back to the others, some of them were starting to stand up.

"I don't—know the way back to my room," Mx Francis said, shocked. "Where do I . . . ?"

"It's that way," January said. "The elevator's just there, can you . . . ?"

"I can see, but I can't—make the house—make sense, is this how you live all the time?"

"Seventh floor, room seven two five I think," January said. "You turn . . . left, out of the lift at the top."

"How do you know that?"

"It's just above us now," he said.

"That's a sense of direction," Mx Francis said indignantly. "That's a myth, nobody really . . ."

"Let's go together, I'm near you," Dr Okonkwo said, limping. They always had a bad knee, but something must have twisted now. "Come on."

January knelt down to listen to Sasha breathe, because they were still flat on the floor. But they were breathing, and nothing seemed badly wrong. Maybe it was just too sudden a shock. He had no idea. He had never reacted to anything like this, and he didn't think he understood what people were losing.

Gale was upright and checking on other people.

"Are you okay?" he asked.

"I'm fine. Empty, but . . . fine." They blinked slowly. "It's so quiet."

January nodded, helping Dr Molotov into a chair. Dr Molotov was gripping his hands hard, not very steady at all. Their eyes flared as a call came in and for a second they looked relieved, but their whole expression crumbled after they'd listened for a second.

"It's my partner," they whispered. "But I can't—understand."

January sat down in the next chair. "What language do they speak?"

Dr Molotov stared at him drowningly. "I don't even know."

Gale folded down on their other side. "May I listen?"

Dr Molotov nodded and touched Gale's temple, which was a way to share the signal as far as January understood. Gale listened.

"Okay, that's . . . something Slavic but . . . right. That's Czech. They might know some Russian, shall we try . . . ?"

January left the two of them piecing things together with poor Mx Molotov and moved on to other people. A lot of them were having exactly the same problem. Some people were so confused they couldn't tell left from right. The most common haptic implant, he discovered, was a link to maps. Only you didn't *see* a map. Early models had worked that way, but it was more effective now. It just fired off the part of your brain that felt like it *knew* the right way. But if you'd had them since you were young, then your brain used the implant, instead of assigning space in its own matter for that kind of thing.

The kitchen was in disarray, because half the staff spoke Mandarin, half spoke Russian, and nobody spoke both. January had to translate a lot just to get the kettles going. It wasn't just that nobody understood. It was the shock of not understanding.

Even Gale looked the worse for wear when he went back out with cups and cups of tea for everyone. They were sitting with their forearms on their knees, hair in a heavy black rope over one shoulder, looking hard at a patch on the ground in the way January had used to do on the Crossing when he felt space-sick. "Thanks."

"How is it?"

"It's like being in a fever dream," Gale said reflectively. "It's not horrible, it's just—powerfully weird."

"You're not as confused as anyone else."

"Traditional education. I didn't have proper haptics till I was older than you. Just lenses. Most of my brain does what it's meant to by itself."

"How come?"

Gale smiled their real smile, the shy slight one. "Because that's what rich families do. River and I grew up like kids in the twentieth century. You know; wooden toys, running around outside, climbing trees, riding bikes. I didn't even touch anything electronic till I was five."

"Gross," said January, to see if he could make them smile more.

"I know, it's very punchable, isn't it, I'm sorry." They paused. "I feel like my English is—not so good, though, I don't think I realized how much I was using dictionaries, is it . . . ?"

January kicked their ankle. "Obnoxiously perfect. And shut up about dictionaries, I bet you don't even need a dictionary in Mammoth."

"In . . ." Gale frowned, and stopped.

"Are you okay?"

"I'm fine. I just—I have . . . River's old research gear."

"River's—what, the mammoth project?"

Gale nodded.

"We can talk to the mammoths?"

"I think so."

January tried not to disturb the idea too badly as he lifted it up. "How likely is a mammoth to agree to help turn a gravity train windlass?"

"I don't know, but—we could ask them?" Gale said.

39

The mammoths were scattered through five or six groves among the pines. A baby was hiding in a hollow log, and some of the others were trying to coax him out, reaching in with their trunks and stroking his head and making quiet rumbles that shook the earth. Above them, the trees groaned. The wind wasn't strong, but the cold was. There were fissures in the bark that whistled, and when the mammoths breathed out, there were no clouds of vapour, but ice crystals that made a shimmering sound as they fell. Under the permanent pall of the dust, Ariel said, the temperature was the lowest it had been on Mars since terraforming began. The mammoths were hardly more than silhouettes by the hazy light of the camping lanterns everyone had to carry outside now.

"Stay here," Gale said to January. "The big bull gets flustered easily, he's the one who tore up the train."

January hadn't realized that the bull was even there, because he'd thought what he was seeing was a tree. The bull was sitting on the ground next to it, very still, and looking miserable. A littler one, younger, was bustling around collecting pine cones, which it was stacking up next to him in exactly the same way a human might leave a plate of biscuits near someone who was having a difficult day.

The size of them wouldn't go through his head. They had been giants even at a distance, but up close, it was difficult to understand how something so vast could have working lungs and bones. Even the littlest of the babies was taller than Gale.

"Are you really just going to walk up to the one of them and hope it understands?" January asked softly.

Gale was carrying a bag full of equipment. It was, they'd explained, a halo, or a version of one with sensors designed to fit a mammoth. "That's the idea," they whispered. "They know me, or some of them do. River worked with this herd for years."

"That's great, but that was River," January whispered back. "What if they don't recognise you? I wouldn't recognise the brother or sister of some scientist I met once or twice for a couple of experiments . . ."

"It's true that elephants never forget," Gale said, and then they were walking out into the grove before January could argue any more.

"Are we about to watch them get gored?" January asked Sasha, who had come out too.

Sasha was strangely calm though. "No. I don't think so."

"Am I missing something? They're wild animals—we *just* saw them tear up a railway. And an entire train."

"Just watch," Sasha said.

For someone who had only ever seen a relative do the job, Gale seemed astonishingly certain about what to do. They were walking slowly, in full view, but not creeping; and they were going towards, not the big bull, but a smaller mammoth with a tawny coat. She was grazing quietly close to the others who were worrying about the baby in the tree trunk, watching them, but not involved. January had a strange feeling she was judging whether or not to tell the others to leave the baby alone for a minute.

When she saw Gale, she jumped. It was the way a human would have jumped if they'd seen an unexpected mouse right up close, not necessarily a horrible thing, just a surprise. Gale put both hands up slowly to show they weren't going to do anything sudden.

January was certain, *certain*, that the matriarch—that was who she was, he realized at a lag—was going to solve this human-mouse problem by crushing it. She had clearly had a long day. A frightened baby was hiding in a hollow tree. A gigantic bull had the worrying thousand-mile stare that veterans did. She wasn't going to be in the mood to deal with a mystery mouse that wanted things. He gripped Sasha's sleeve. The tendons of his cage gauntlet chinked against their watch.

"Do we even *have* anything that would deter a mammoth?"

"No. Quiet," Sasha told him, but not impatient. They were nearly laughing. "Just let them do it."

January had a flash of indignation. Sasha had spent weeks looking at him as if he might accidentally snap Gale's neck, but now here was a herd of ice age megafauna with tusks the size of buildings and somehow Sasha was the picture of Zen.

The matriarch didn't crush Gale. Instead, she dropped right onto her knees and made a sound that January couldn't hear, only feel reverberating in the spaces between the bone and cartilage in his knees, and even though he had never heard it before, and never met elephants before, never mind a mammoth, something right in his skeleton—maybe something left over from when human beings had first walked on the ice—recognised it. She was laughing. As if she knew exactly what was going on, she put her head right down, and let Gale reach up to put the halo sensors on her.

It was the most uncanny, incredible thing he had ever seen. She made Gale look tiny. Standing, she was about eighty feet high—her eyelashes were as long as Gale's arm—but she stayed still, and when the sensors were in place, she straightened up, unreadable, but calm. She was waiting. It wasn't like seeing an ordinary animal. She looked wise. This would be, he realized, how it felt when humans finally found an alien species. They would be unfathomably different, but unfathomably the same as well.

The halo feed appeared in January's glasses. It was a mind—that he could recognise—but he couldn't read anything in the patterns. It was like Gale's halo scans: there was clearly thinking going on, but how it worked wasn't clear at all. But what was obvious was that there was a *person* behind it. With opinions and feelings and memories.

"You have to *think* in Mammoth," Sasha explained softly. "They talk in two ways at the same time, like a piano, high and low. We can't make the right sounds, so that's why you need that machinery and the speakers."

The speakers made an unearthly sound. It was how mountains would have spoken to each other, and in January's glasses, the subtitles started.

Like Sasha had said, they were piano score translations, always two lines at once. Either one alone wouldn't have made any sense.

bad ⋆ lovely

weather ⋆ see you again

"Jesus Christ," he breathed.

Very, very gently, the matriarch lifted her trunk and brushed the top of Gale's head.

different ⋆ difficult

coat ⋆ day

"I don't understand," January whispered.

"They say coat when they mean clothes, on a human," Sasha explained. "She's saying it's been a hard day and the Senator looks different."

different ⋆ now

role

"They're saying they look different because they have a different job now."

now?

grandmother

"Like, in charge now. A senator."

"I got that one," January murmured, and then thought: hang on. Gale's been a senator for what, three or four years. River was doing this with Shang *when they vanished*, and that was less than two years ago; Gale would have been a senator already when this project was going on. It wasn't new, that they were the grandmother for their herd.

Or did she think Gale *was* River? Humans must all look alike. No; she hadn't even asked. She sounded sure.

There wasn't time to wonder about inconsistent timelines, but it stuck irritatingly in his mind all the same, like a piece of old thistle from a hay bale.

Right

Right

"It's emphasis if you say the same thing both ways."

"How do you know so much about this?"

"I live with the Senator," Sasha said tolerantly. "It would be weirder if I didn't know."

January shook his head, wondering how in the worlds Gale had had time, in life, to know any of this, when they also ran House Gale and the grid and all the rest.

The matriarch was still patting her trunk across Gale's shoulders. It seemed to January like a very close study.

why

coming?

"How in God's name are you supposed to explain electricity and power consumption and gravity trains to a mammoth?" January whispered to Sasha.

"I don't know," Sasha said, looking worried too. "I guess—this is where we see how good the Senator is."

As far as January could understand from the eerie two-tone sentences through the speakers, which seemed to separate out different parts of meaning in a way he could only just get his fingernails over,[31] what Gale said was something like this:

"You know how humans eat lightning? We can't make new lightning in the storm. Everyone in the herd is starving now, and soon, they'll die. Usually we harvest the lightning from the sun, but—there's no sun now."

---

31 River Gale had written the only extant pachyderm dictionary, he found out later. Lots of people had theories about the way mammoths divided up their speech, but what River had to say about it rang truer to January than anything else he found. The rule was, broadly: adjectives, descriptions, and very personal information above in the high strain, but actions and impersonal fact-type things in the deeper one. The reason (and River had asked several mammoths exactly this, because the best person to know why mammoths did things was a mammoth) was that the lower vocal range had evolved *so* low because the deeper the sound, the greater the distance it could carry. Mammoths could talk to each other across miles. But the kinds of things you needed to say to people over a long distance were different to the ones you said if you were snacking on pine cones with them. If you were calling over miles, what you were saying, usually, was something like: help, or come over here, there's water, or there's dust coming, or I'm on my way back now. What you did not need to say was: morning, how's your mother, isn't it lovely weather we're having. That would have been odd, and rude, because the whole herd would hear it—it was like talking on an open radio channel. Which had a knock-on effort into ordinary conversation: core information went deep, and embellishment came higher. You could switch things around, but it changed the meaning radically. Saying "happy" down low, for example, was a mammoth joke, because what it really meant was *I order you to become immediately happy.*

"We're hungry too," the matriarch said. "Everything is dying."

"I know. I can bring food for your whole herd, we have lots of mammoth food. You can have it no matter what you say next, but I was hoping you could help us too."

"I haven't got any human lightning." January had no idea how you went about reading tone of voice in mammoths, but he thought she looked wary.

"I know. But there is a way to make it, with the steel hills on the edge of the cliff. But they are too big for us to move. Even the strong humans can't move it. Only mammoths could do it."

"How?"

"There are big metal vines. If you pull them hard enough, the hills will move." The chains moved the windlasses. "Moving them makes the lightning." Lifting the trains made potential energy made electricity; January liked *moving them makes lightning* better though.

"Is that all?"

"That's all."

She was quiet for a moment. "How does it make lightning?"

January had no clue how to explain how a gravity train made electricity even if he was allowed to use normal ideas, never mind just the ones that mammoths knew.

Gale didn't even seem flustered. "You know when you pull your trunk down a tree really hard, it feels hot? That heat, that's a sort of baby lightning. When we move the steel hills, their counterweights drag down the cliff, and they make that heat too, a lot of it. That's all we need. Once we have that, we can make the lightning big, and we can feed everybody with it."

"You know, it would be much easier if you just ate pine cones," the matriarch said philosophically.

"I know," Gale agreed.

"The metal hills are very strange. Some of the herd are frightened of them. Too human. Is it safe to pull the metal vines?"

"Yes. We can use dead vines to fasten around you, so you don't have to pull with your trunk. It's safe. It won't hurt anyone. And if you don't like it, you can say, and we can stop."

Dead vines; that had to be harnesses.

"How long?"

"For one day. Seven of you, if that's all right."

"That's all right." She looked down at Gale for a long time, quiet. "It's very difficult to be the grandmother of the herd. Everyone always watching you. Bulls always chafing."

"Yes."

"You put your bull in metal vines," she said, and January realized with a shock that she was talking about him.

Gale laughed. "I didn't do that, he did. He chooses."

January found his fingers hooking under the cage's sternum, which they seemed to decide to do whenever he was feeling awkward. And he did feel strangely awkward. Gale had thought it was funny, but the matriarch seemed not to. She was giving him a long study that, even coming from a mammoth, didn't look very approving.

"Did he," was all she said in the end, and perhaps it was clunky translation, but it sounded doubtful to him. She paused. "We hurt your metal road and your metal monster. I'm very sorry. Everyone was scared of the fire. He panicked." She looked at the great bull who was still slumped against the tree. "Not his fault. Fear-mind not the same as calm-mind, especially for bulls. Cannot change. No metal vines for him."

January had a prickle of unease. *No metal vines for him*; she had phrased it in a way where Gale could interpret it as a bad thing, that was there was no constraining him, but something about the way she shifted, to put herself fractionally more between the unhappy bull and the humans, gave January a strong feeling that she didn't mean it like that. It sounded more like she meant: *Get away from him with your weird metal vines.* He tried to put it out of his head. He wasn't a Mammoth translator.

Gale, for sure, seemed not to read into it. "I know. I understand. It's okay. I can fix them later."

"This isn't a trick, for revenge about the metal road?" the matriarch asked gradually.

Just in the last minute or so, she had gone from being clearly pleased to see Gale, to much less trusting. She kept studying January and he couldn't help thinking it was because of him. She didn't like the cage, or she didn't like *him*, he couldn't tell.

"No." Gale paused. "The metal hills are near here. Everyone here will still be able to hear what's happening up there. I can leave some of my herd here with the rest of yours. You can kill them if it's a trick."

She thought about it, cast one last slow look over January, and then patted Gale gently. "Then we will help you make your lightning, grandmother."

And so Dr Molotov built mammoth harnesses from replacement chain for the trains—things they could get out of themselves when they wanted—and it was only early evening by the time they were ready. From what January could tell through the ribbon breaks in the dust, the moons weren't even out yet. He thought he caught a tiny shimmer that might have been the Pole Star.

There was no software that could translate from human to mammoth. The human had to do mammoth thinking and relay that through the halo and the speakers; even when Gale explained that the noises humans made among themselves was talking, the mammoths were sceptical and January had a feeling that they didn't see how it could possibly work. But Gale did teach everyone a few useful things they could all transmit through a halo, and there were plenty of halos when they raided a weary Dr Okonkwo's supply.

Mammoths had please and thank you like everyone else; they had pull, and stop, and now, but they were curious too, and like anyone else, they were wary about being involved until someone could show them how it worked. Unlike the grandmother, most of the others didn't like the idea of letting humans eat lightning, in case it hurt them, and because humans often didn't know how to look after themselves, and were they completely sure about this? If you found one in the desert, one of the young mammoths said seriously, they were always helpless. They couldn't find water or hunt or anything, they would just sit there and die if you didn't scoop them up and put them near to some other humans. The mammoth theory was that humans were so closely bound up in their herds that a single human alone was always going to be in danger. It sort of went mad—or, like bees, humans were a hive, and any single one didn't really have a considerable enough brain to look after itself. The living thing, the entity, was the swarm.

January thought that humans should ask mammoths their opinions about more things.

So it didn't work for Gale to explain. Gale was just one human; there had to be evidence that other humans in the herd agreed it was necessary, and it turned out, somehow to nobody's surprise except January's, that he was better at thinking in Mammoth than Mx Ren or Mx Francis and the others.

"You're closer to old ways of living," Mx Ren pointed out. "You still think in terms of bulls and grandmothers."

With Gale coaching him through, January had a go at explaining too. He had a feeling that it was *lightning* that was the problem, even though that was really the only word you could have in Mammoth for electricity. Lightning sounded dangerous, and the herd must have seen it hit the mountains, or even hit mammoths. But they weren't slow to understand ideas. They had huge ideas, and they used them, he was noticing, as metaphors even in ordinary conversation. When they said something was stupid, what they actually said was *bullthink*.

"They're so gendered," Mx Francis complained.

January took a breath to say that it might not be such a bad thing, a matriarchy, but he didn't have time, because Gale smacked Mx Francis over the back of the head.

"Do we have anything to make static with?" he asked Gale.

"Static. Ah . . . yes. Yes." They pulled off their coat, and took off the jacket they had on underneath. "This is silk."

January hesitated. "I might—get mammoth on it?"

"Are you seriously saying you believe I wouldn't rather be wearing tweed?" Gale asked.

A mammoth tapped him on the head to remind him he was meant to be explaining things.

As best as he could, he said what he was about to do, and then rubbed the silk on the trunk of one of the young bulls, so that the fur stood up on end. Everyone laughed, humans and mammoths. The little bull loved it, stole the jacket, and rubbed it all over until he was a giant fluff-ball.

"That's lightning too," January tried. "But little-lightning, instead of . . . sky-lightning. It does different things, depending on how much there is."

Gale helped him translate, and at last, it seemed clear that the humans weren't just doing something bullthink, even if it was odd.

Drones hovered; they were recording, for when the internet came back on. The producers, when they talked through the speakers, sounded like kids let loose in a giant sweet shop, and January didn't blame them. The footage would probably win them some kind of prize, later. Looking like joyful bubbles, the drones were swooping high, and out over the cliff, to watch the mammoths turn the windlasses; and down the Valleyside, the chains went taut, and the gravity trains began to rise. The mammoths didn't like electric lights—they had a belief about the two moons which Gale couldn't translate—and so it was all done by lamplight and the dim silvery glow that struggled through the dust. Each link in each chain was the size of a person. Everything was so gigantic that it made optical illusions. January's mind kept trying to tell him he was seeing something smaller, nearer to him, and so his sense of distance warped bizarrely, to the point that he couldn't tell how far away he was from Gale or the others.

Each windlass had a lock, so the mammoths could stop and rest, and eat. People from Songshu had brought crates of apples from the stores, and a cartload of raw corn from a farm further onto the Plains, for which Mx Ren had to trade five heat suits. Twice, the herd grandmother came out to see how things were going, and to take over if one of the others was tired.

Even in a heat suit, because heat suits were designed for Natural people, January was cold. The night had plunged down to minus thirty.

There wasn't anything real he could do, except be there and keep more important people company. He did the coffee runs and explained how things were going to the drones, interrupted once by the little bull with Gale's jacket, who used it to fluff up his hair and turn him into a dandelion. The bull was sneaking up on anyone too distracted to notice a sneaking mammoth.

But mostly it was watching, and standing still, and feeling slowly colder and colder. He didn't want to say anything. It was one of those experiences that, he could tell already, he'd forget later. Later, tonight would be only about the mammoths, about the raw awe and joy and worry of seeing such titan things moving among human beings and speaking, and the otherworldly creak of a windlass the size of a steamship turning and turning. Minds, or his at least, had a way of filtering out the uncomfortable dull in-between bits, especially when they came in among such spectacular things. Knowing that gave him a lot of patience with it. What he'd remember later wasn't the cold or being uncomfortable, but being here.

About halfway through, he had to turn back to Songshu for a bathroom break. Other people were just vanishing into the woods, but he couldn't even think about that; he was pretty sure he would get instant frostbite in places that he never wanted Dr Okonkwo to have access to.

Walking back was no problem, and he quite enjoyed how phantasmal everything looked in the dust; but walking back out to the gravity trains was a strain. The cage felt heavy, and it was an effort to keep putting one foot in front of the other. It was the cold: he had never realized just how much extra energy you needed to move about in cold like this, even with the heat suit. In theory if he just kept eating he'd have the calorie stores to spend on it, but he just couldn't eat that much. Maybe on Antarctic bases on Earth, someone had invented a clever super-drink or something that was the food equivalent of jet fuel, but there was nothing like that here, because everyone was genetically engineered to function normally on normal food. He had to stop near the mammoths' grove, leaning against the trunk of a giant dandelion. Everything ached. He felt like he'd been training for hours and hours. It was pathetic, but that didn't stop it feeling dangerous. He should never have set out like this on his own. It hadn't even occurred to him.

Someone tapped his shoulder and he looked round, and then squeaked and fell over, because towering above him was the matriarch.

She gave him what he was coming to recognise as the *really-I-think-humans-are-indoor-animals* mammoth once-over, and then without any more explanation, she picked him up like he was a little doll and carried him back to the cliff edge. He yelped, but he didn't think she heard. Her fur was so dense that he thought he might vanish into it. It was instantly warm, and despite the madness of what was happening—Jesus Christ he was *thirty feet off the sodding ground*—he was relieved, and he almost didn't want to go when she found Gale and dropped him on the ground next to them.

"Yours," she explained gravely.

Gale helped him up, then dragged over one of the translation speakers on its little wheeled tripod. "Ah . . . ?"

She didn't go. "The metal vines are hurting him. You must take them off."

Gale brushed him off, very light, and lifted some pine needles out of his hair. January swallowed, caught between a wild kind of joy at what had just happened—he defied anyone to be stolen by a helpful mammoth and not turn into the person-version of a pop bottle that had been shaken up—and feeling like a child for needing to be rescued. "No, they're keeping him weaker so he can't hurt anyone. He would be too strong. As strong as three people."

The matriarch gazed down at them quietly for what felt like a long time. "Bulls *are* strong," she said at last. "It is part of grandmothering to find a way to let them be. This—" she flicked January's cage where the high collar of it showed on the back of his neck, incredibly precisely, so that she only just bumped him sideways a few inches "—is *not* grandmothering."

Gale frowned. "I don't think I'm being clear. He would hurt someone accidentally—"

"And *you* are the grandmother," she interrupted sharply. She sounded like the beginnings of an earthquake. She pointed back to the grove, to where the big bull had been, when January saw him, nibbling his way through the pine cones, looking a little bit cheered up now, and entertained by a game the babies were playing with giant blow-up ball Gale had brought for them. "He is stronger than three humans? *I* am stronger than many humans. Will you bind *me*?"

"No, it's different," Gale said, but they looked thrown off, more than they ever had, even when the Consul had won the debate.

January had a bizarre out-of-body moment where a detached part of his brain said: *You're very cold, it's Sunday, and a senator is arguing about you with a mammoth. On Mars.*

"Not different," the matriarch said. "There is bull strength; this is small. There is grandmother strength: this is great." She looked down at Gale hard. "Bulls must not try to be more than they are, it is true. But grandmothers must never try to make them less."

"I see," Gale said carefully.

The matriarch said nothing more, but in her eyes was a kind of wry glimmer, and January realized she knew the cage would probably never come off. She dragged her trunk gently across him, and across Gale, then paced away to see the other mammoths who were harnessed to the windlasses. The ground shook.

January and Gale stayed there for a while after she had gone.

"Was I just schooled about the nature of good government by a mammoth?" Gale asked at last.

"I think that's what happened," January agreed, a bit numb.

Gale was frowning in the way they did when they were about to feed someone through an intellectual mincing machine.

"But look," January said quickly, because he was seeing a huge row hoving into view, and he desperately didn't want Gale to personally irritate a mammoth. "Don't argue with her. She doesn't understand what cages do, she's just seeing that you've tied someone up."

Gale was silent for so long, watching the mammoths heave against the windlasses, that January thought they weren't going to say anything, and he set out back towards the fire. But Gale touched his elbow to stop him.

"No, wait. You've been in the cage for weeks, you must need a break. There's plenty of space out here. If anyone's scared—it's more of a them problem than a you problem." They sighed. "And anyway, I think if she sees you in a cage again, she's going to take you away and have you adopted by some better humans."

"I like my current humans," January promised, and then faltered, because Gale looked at him as if he had just twisted a knife between their ribs. Whatever they were thinking, though, they didn't say it.

"You can get changed in the tea-and-coffee tent, there's a heater," was all they said, and they unlocked his cage.

"Just until we go back inside?"

"Right," Gale said, but they looked troubled, gazing after the matriarch, and he couldn't tell if it was because, again, they were terrified but determined not to let anyone know.

He had to get out of his heat suit, which was complicated and unpleasant when he felt just how cold the air really was, and then out of most of his clothes as well. When he unlocked the cage and pressed the release, he had the most incredible illusion of flying. If he'd shut his eyes, he would have thought he'd bobbed up to float around on the tent ceiling. It seemed insane to look and see he was still on the ground. If getting out of a cage after eight hours felt odd, then getting out of it after two months was a special genetically modified type of bananas. When he tried to step away from the open steel skeleton to get his clothes back on, he moved too strongly, and fell over—and then when he pushed down on the ground to try and get up again, it was too much and he sent himself jolting sideways.

"Are you all right?" Gale asked from outside. They must have heard a thump.

"Yep. Don't wait for me, this . . . might take a little bit of thought," he said to the tent wall. Very, very carefully, he eased his hands flat to the ground again, and pushed so delicately he was sure he wouldn't move at all, but it was enough to see him upright. Getting one knee under him and then standing up was tricky, but little by little, he got back into his clothes, and back into the heat suit. He cast around for something to throw between his hands, found an orange, and then had to explain embarrassedly to the cook why there was an orange exploded on the floor. At last, he edged outside and walked up and down until he was sure he wasn't going to rocket himself off the edge of the cliff. Not far away, Sasha was watching him hard, one hand resting on their gun, looking like they might be planning a brain haemorrhage.

Partly as way to stay warm, partly to show that, even though he wasn't in his cage for now, he wouldn't be moving about much, January stuck near the fire pit that was keeping the kettles hot. There was a windbreak that blocked most of the dust. He alternated between watching the mammoths at the windlasses, which was mesmerising, and watching the zithers of dust that did make it past the windbreak and caught fire in miniature comet-tails. Dr Okonkwo came out briefly to ask him how Gale seemed (fine, but how would he tell?) and overlapped with Mx Ren, who had watched a documentary about Antarctica and had taken it to heart about keeping your Earthstronger stuffed with enough calories in cold conditions.

"Nearly there," Gale said, emerging from the dust and radiating happiness. January had a pang, because he'd never seen them like this before. He wanted to hug them, but he was absolutely not coordinated enough to do that with any confidence he wouldn't break their ribs.

The mammoths had realized he was suddenly much stronger, because now he could work the locks on their harnesses without any mechanical help, and the little bull who liked static electricity had been challenging him to arm-and-trunk-wrestling contests. They were talking too quickly for the translation software to pick it all up, but he had a feeling that the mammoths had a betting pool going about the matches. Certainly there had been a delighted honk from one of them when he won, and the little bull dropped theatrically onto his back with all his feet in the air.

"Have you been talking to them?" he asked.

"Oh, don't let them start," Dr Okonkwo grumbled, hands shoved deep in pockets. "We'll be here till July on the construction of mammoth gerunds."

"You know nobody likes you," January said.

"God's sake, why does everyone keep saying that?"

"Wisdom of crowds, mate," said January, who had no idea who else had said that, but suspected he was destined to be their true love.

"They have *myths*," Gale said, pulling off their dust mask to drink some coffee. "It's incredible. And some of the stories are about things that—well, they know things they shouldn't be able to know. The species here is only two hundred and fifty years old, they were resurrected out of test tubes for Mars, so that's only eight generations of mammoths; but they have stories about a dream time when everything was heavier, and the horizon was further away, which does sound like . . ."

"Nonsense," grumped Dr Okonkwo.

But even Mx Ren looked intrigued.

"Earth," January said, and found himself smiling too, because if that was somehow true, then the worlds were subtly, quietly better than he had thought.

Gale gave him some coffee, glowing. He held his hands open so they could rest the cup in them without the risk of touching him, but they gave him that soldierly look that said *don't be ridiculous* and closed his fingers gently around it. He noticed himself grinning like a mad person, and reflected that he was really nothing more than a human-shaped version of Kasha: basically all he wanted from life was to play jumping and for someone to occasionally tell him he was a Good Boy.

"They're up!" someone yelled. "They're coming!"

Everyone ran to the cliff edge to see. Sure enough, the gravity trains creaked into view, and at last, they docked with their magnetic locks with a howl of freezing metal, and there was a human-mammoth cheer.

Because they were wild, though, the mammoths didn't stay. The grandmother looked at Gale and January for a long moment, unreadable, and turned away. They all walked into the forest, shaking the ground.

40

As they walked through the forest back to Songshu, they passed the work site where Dr Molotov and the grounds maintenance people were cutting down trees. Each one was so enormous that fallen, it reached all the way to the twisted wreck of the railway tracks, and as well as dust, the air swam with sawdust and old earth. A tornado was riding across the Plains, strobing maroon lightning that shone on the folds of everyone's sleeves, and on the surface of their masks. Up on the rig, the little fires from the welding torches still flew. The night shift had managed to come in partway on the train, and ride the rest of the way. They'd stay at Songshu too.

It seemed like something out of a dream, but the path back was full of horses. People from farms all across the Plains were bringing them, sometimes only one, a farm shire from one of the eco-establishments who never used grid electricity even at the best of times, and sometimes twenty from a training ranch. Tharsis horses were tall, just like everything else, but they were being corralled in exactly the same way they had been for hundreds of years; a couple of riders, a couple of fantastically trained dogs. They were getting ready to attach the horses to makeshift carts and wagons to get the firewood out to the train station and down the cliff.

The foyer was divided now into Natural and Earthstrong, so he followed the Earthstrong passage, which Sasha's team had separated from the Natural one with bulletproof glass. Gale walked on the other side, and with a playfulness he had never known from them before, trailed one hand along the glass close to him. He did the same, full of a fragile building joy.

They'd done it. No one was going to die. Tereshkova Wharf was going to have enough water. It wouldn't explode. The internet was coming back on. They might even get the array up before the fleet arrived.

And mammoths had myths about Earth.

People were hurrying up to ask how it had gone, if it had worked, was the power coming back on, was the internet coming back on.

While January said yes to as many people as could hear him, Gale went to one of the tannoy stations on the wall. "Good evening, everyone. It is my very great pleasure to announce that thanks to the local mammoth herd, all the gravity trains have been raised. This means that not only is there plenty of power for heating and internet, but also the solar rig is likely to be finished sometime in the next forty-eight hours."

As they said it, the electricity whirred back up, the lights glowed, the heating system made a wonderful singing noise, and a joyful cheer went right up and down the tower, from the dining room, up round the balconies to the Earthstrong floor, the glass-decked production room, and the scientists higher up. Someone had come prepared, because indoor fireworks started going off, bursting fantastic colours all up the tower. Gale laughed, looking more relieved than January would ever have expected given how calmly they had taken all the bad luck so far, the fireworks zinging mauve and amber lights across the black of their hair.

"We'll get changed and then champagne in ten minutes?" Gale said to January, who had never more wanted to throw his arms round someone, and never been so scared to.

"Oh, God, yes," January said, extremely ready to be drunk.

The third floor was given over to Earthstrong people now, and there was a strict no-naturalised-people-past-this-point rule, so that you could go about without your cage and not worry about hurting anyone. January glanced into rooms and coffee stations as he passed, checking that people were all right and, more tacitly, that nobody was deliberately destroying anything. Mx Francis had not been wrong to worry that somebody might come here with a grudge and a silent determination to start a riot. But so far, nothing like that seemed to be happening. He found a gang of hulking teenagers by the glass wall that looked into the hummingbird garden and looked over their shoulders, suspecting something terrible, but actually they had sketchbooks and they were all drawing the birds.

In one of his lenses, Sasha appeared too, to watch and sometimes to ask tersely for him to take a closer look at something. They had aged in the last day. It seemed insane to look at every shadow and oddly shaped bag, but he had a feeling Sasha would have a full nervous breakdown if he didn't. They were right. Anyone could have brought a bomb in here. Everyone had gone through a sort of airport-type security check on the way in, but even so. You could, Sasha said, going very high, print a sodding bomb out of carbon parts, and that wasn't going to show up on any scan.

"What are those men doing?" Sasha asked sharply.

"Those *boys*," January said gently, because they were only about eighteen, just old enough to work, "are playing conkers. All right gents?"

"All right Mr Stirling," they said happily. One of them was wearing a sparkly pink party hat.

"How do you even tell how old they are?" Sasha sighed. "They all look like they're forty-five."

"Practise," January promised, and turned sideways to let some very little kids zoom past. A lot of the contractors had brought their children with them to work; nobody liked the idea of leaving them alone at the naturalisation centre, just in case.

Everything smelled wonderfully of fireworks and beer in paper cups. Everyone looked happy.

Good; good. He went downstairs again once he was in fresh clothes and back in his cage—God, it felt stiff now—to the dining room, looking round for Gale, and feeling warm with knowing they'd be looking for him too, soon, and he wasn't just doing what he usually did, which was casting around for an unsuspecting victim to sit with. It was crowded. People were making the most of the heated floor, having picnics.

The only piece of strife he noticed was an older lady bothering one of the Songshu interns, who she'd cornered at a hot chocolate station.

"Come on!" she protested. "Why can't people say what they really are? All I want is a straight answer! Biology!"

"It's not about biology," January said, directing the intern away with his eyelashes. The intern bowed a little, irritated. "Look, asking people here that is like me asking you what your blood type is and then deciding what you should be like just based on that. It's no one's business except a doctor's."

"Nice of you to mansplain it to me," she snapped, with the whiplash of a person who had suffered because of someone who looked like him. "D'you have any idea how threatening it feels, not knowing? Any idea at all?"

He watched her for a second, thinking of those enormous dogs who had been terrorised by cats when they were puppies, and who still remembered being helpless and scared, even though they could easily have eaten a cat now. "You're three times stronger than people here. Who's threatening who?"

She slapped him, not very hard, but she was wearing gauntlets and it hurt, and he had to step right back and clamp down the instinct to hit back. She was smaller than him; for all he had got used to being little here, he was in fact six foot two.

"Do it again and you're out," he said wearily, and traipsed away with one hand over his cheekbone where it stung to see if there was any food left at the big buffet, which looked and smelled like the best kind of market grill. Around the room, the security people were scanning everyone, watching for anyone who'd forgotten their cage. Nobody had so far, at least.

"Again?" Sasha said to him, unimpressed. "We're just going to let her wander around harassing the interns, are we? Get rid of her."

He had to laugh, although not really with humour. "Sasha, come on. She's frightened of men in the same way the Senator is frightened of Earthstrongers. Probably one hurt her once, and now she thinks none of them should be allowed to walk around without a big sticker that says CAUTION, and ideally they'd be kept in cages all the time as well. I think

315

you'd want to know, if there was a secret Earthstronger in the room who *looked* like a Natural person? That's what she's seeing. I know she's wrong, I know there's no one here who could hurt her, but yelling at her won't help."

Sasha looked down at him, very hard. "That's the enormous difference though, isn't it: no one *can* hurt her. The Senator's fear isn't irrational."

"I didn't say it was," he said, regretting having said anything. Sasha was never going to understand. He pressed his hands over his eyes and wished there was a way to translate properly. He couldn't help thinking that that was most of the problem between Earthstrongers and naturalised people. People could say the same words, but they meant such different things.

After he poured himself some hot chocolate—he wanted to wait for Gale for wine, and he couldn't see them yet—he took off his glasses to polish them, and to give himself a break from all the glittering virtual overlays of art and artificial sky, all vivid and glorious and a little bit overwhelming now the internet was alive again. It seemed healthy to remind himself what was actually there. As he did, Kasha trotted by, wearing tinsel round her collar and trying to get into the pockets of Gale's real partner, who was dressed for outside, plainly hoping to persuade her to come for some exercise. January hinged forward awkwardly, a quarter-bow, not knowing if it was better to apologise for existing or to just be quiet. But they only bowed back, and then smiled when a very tiny person in a party hat asked seriously if Kasha would mind being made available for rides. Kasha, always thrilled with new humans, snuffled around and all but shoved the little boy onto her back, then ran away with him looking triumphant.

January wondered about the party hat until he saw people toasting.

Of course.

It was Christmas Day.

Hah.

He took his cup over to the piano. It was, as far as he could tell, only for show, because nobody seemed to play it; maybe they were embarrassed. He hadn't gone to an opera-ballet school for nothing, though. He tapped out the first few notes of "I Saw Three Ships" to remind himself where to start, then remembered after the first verse. He liked the piano; it was something you had to do with your whole mind, not just parts of it. Some of the children came to see what he was doing— some of them, maybe, had never seen a piano before—and then he leaned back a little to gave a drone space to skim along the keyboard.

A few of the children's parents came too, and he slowed down to let them sing along. He couldn't sing, but that was a good thing, because he had to teach the words to the kids, who wanted to join in but didn't know them. It made him sad in a papercut slice that they didn't know. Only brief. They learned fast.

Someone had brought a battered old violin and came in with him on the next round. By then it was loud enough for the naturalised people at the tables further from the fire to have noticed and begun to stray nearer too, he hoped not because they were worried something frightening would happen.

Because people had moved, he saw through them to Gale, who was sitting by the window with the angry lady from before. All his vertebrae seized up and he almost dropped everything, but Gale didn't look worried. They were showing her something on a tablet, and she was looking.

He forgot to explain what Bethlehem was to the children, because he was too busy praying the lady wouldn't get upset. If she hit Gale wearing the cage, she wouldn't hurt them, not really, but that wasn't the point. January didn't know how far a human being could go without having a nervous breakdown, but Gale must have been camped out in the precipice for a long time now, flicking pebbles over the edge.

"Is it to do with clothes?" a little boy asked seriously. He was about three or four.

In the time it took January to look down at him and think about it, Gale had crossed the room.

"It's a place in Israel," Gale said, settling on the piano stool, facing the other way to January, though shoulder to shoulder.

January breathed out. Thank God. Not beaten up: good start to the evening, very good.

The little boy went down to a hushed whisper. "Are you, are you a *princess*?" He was staring at the silver in Gale's hair, the Senate sigils. It was, January had worked out, mandatory for Gale to wear them when they were in public, and illegal for anyone who was not a senator to wear anything remotely like them. It was about making senators recognisable. He had an uncomfortable sense that it had passed into law after Gagarin Square. But if you were four, those silver sigils were a crown.

January saw Gale take a breath to explain senates and republics, but then let it out again. "Yes."

"Is this your *real* hair?"

"Yes," Gale said, as serious as they were with adults. They had gone still and terse. Not at home around little children.

"Can . . . can I see?"

January nudged the little boy. "Hey, little bear. Don't bother them too much, yeah?"

"Ah—no, it's all right," Gale said. They lifted the little boy into their lap, slowly, as though they were afraid of hurting him. In their arms, he was miniature.

The little boy looked delighted. Carefully, Gale lifted the silver sigil off—it was a kind of comb that sank into the base of a braid or a knot—and set it into the little boy's hair instead. The little boy bounced joyfully. Gale's shoulders tacked; he was stronger than they'd thought, though not strong. They caught him gently when he tried to lunge past them and bang the piano keys.

"Princesses keep still." It wasn't a command, just the quietest kind of suggestion.

"Mm," the little boy agreed, and sat perfectly still, tiny hands clasped over Gale's. After a minute, he twisted around to check, then straightened up too. January grinned and brushed his cheek.

"What's your name?"

"Yuan," the little boy said. "You're the dancing man."

"I am. January. And this is Aubrey."

Yuan smiled again and twisted away from him, embarrassed, and put his face against Gale's chest. Gale set one hand very lightly over the back of his head, watching him, not January. They looked—not sad, they were too controlled to seem sad—but muted. He had a feeling he knew why. It was how he felt here at New Year. It was all borrowed joy, from a culture that didn't belong to him. Because he was watching for it, he saw Gale decide it was time for them to get out the way and let the Earth people enjoy Earth things undisturbed by intruders, and he was in time to catch their wrist before they could put Yuan down.

"Stay," he said, and then realized what he'd done and let go; but when he met their eyes, scared they'd taken it as an order and not a request, Gale didn't look worried. Instead they held his shoulder as they shifted their weight off the prosthetic again and resettled Yuan. It put a happy fizz down his whole arm.

And all the souls on Earth shall sing; even though Earth was left behind now and for most people here there would be no going back.

As January let the piano fade away, Yuan said, quite clearly, "I want to be a princess too when I'm big."

People cheered, and one of the lumberjacks made a toast to a merry Christmas and a New Year that might be a bit above absolute zero. Gale opened a bottle of champagne, poured some for January, then passed it round.

"To mammoths," Gale said, just for him, under all the noise.

41

The carols went on into the night, and so did the wine. After January ran out of music he knew off by heart, the violinist took over and people showed no sign of wanting to go to bed. Yuan hurried away at last to his mum, who had been watching carefully from a bench near the fire. It hurt to see him run. He was so spindly he was nearly see-through in places, and he had the fragility of someone whose heart wasn't working properly. Born here, but first generation. January had a nasty feeling he wouldn't live long enough to marry into any sort of royalty.

"Merry Christmas," Gale said, tentative, like they'd looked up what to say. Of course they had.

He smiled. "Merry Christmas. I, um . . . I saw you talking with that lady. Are you okay, did she do something . . . ?"

"No, no. I saw your fight earlier, so I was showing her the comparative conviction statistics for sexual assault, America versus Tharsis."

"*What?*"

Gale pulsed that quiet embarrassment they did whenever they were caught going Full Academic. "Conviction rates are less than one per cent across most countries on Earth," they said, sounding guilty that they knew. "In Tharsis it's ninety-eight per cent."

"You were kept in a cellar and beaten with an abacus as a child, weren't you," Mx Francis said in passing. "Numbers were your only friends."

"I could fire you," Gale told them.

Mx Francis stuck their tongue out.

"Into space," Gale sighed.

"Ninety-eight per cent," January said, because he had stuck on it. "How? I'm not—sorry, you abolished gender, not sex, everyone's still a person with person-wants and some people in any society are dreadful, so . . . ?"

"Because it's taken seriously and well policed. There's a lovely historical graph actually. It tracks reported instances versus conviction rates after every major legal change in the field in the last two hundred years." They lifted one hand from their tablet to make the image project in three dimensions. The light made their eyes shine. "I love this correlation here. It's when marriage was reduced to a five-year contract rather than a permanent arrangement. The cases trail off within a generation."

"Why?"

"No one knows," Gale said, laughing a bit. "No one knows, but for my money; it's about taking away any sense that you can ever own someone. Make it normal for kids and hold it there; problem solved. Most elegant piece of legislation I've ever seen."

January looked across at them and had a strange, powerful feeling that it was a kind of magic, for any place to have produced a human being who confronted angry people softly, with a graph they looked at in the way most people looked at Renaissance paintings. "Did she believe you?"

Gale winced. "God, no. I'm a giant dork who accosted her with an unsolicited chart. But she knows where to find the data now, if she'd like to. What?" they added, because January hadn't looked away.

"I just . . ." He looked down. "Sorry, I'm not trying to start a fight."

Gale smiled. "Pick up your sword, Spartan."

"You're saying you legislated your way out of—everything she's scared of. But in the debate, you said no amount of legislation could stop violence against women. You said no one has ever succeeded doing that with legal systems, and the reason Tharsis succeeded was that you genetically edited people to make them more physically equal. Only it didn't work because of that, because if it had, you wouldn't have *needed* to make marriage last only five years to stamp it out." He swallowed. "Or am I getting the wrong end of the stick?"

Gale thought about it for a long time. "Huh," they said at last. "Okay."

"Okay what?" January asked, full of dread that he was about to be spectacularly demolished, and Mx Ren was going to have to sweep bits of him up off the floor all evening.

"Okay . . . I was wrong to say there was no legislative solution in either case," Gale said, starting slow and speeding up toward the end because, he realized, they had finished double-checking they had no counterargument.

"You . . . ?"

"See what happens when you fight?" Gale said, pushing him gently. "Sometimes you win." They were smiling as if they'd just seen January manage the most incredible spin in midair. "Ganbei."[32] They tinked their champagne glass to January's.

He had never felt so disconcerted about winning an argument. In fact, he was almost certain he had never won one before. What he'd had were rows with his father, who would usually say whatever would upset the other person most, no matter how insane, and then January would have to leave the house until the urge to murder someone went away. That was what his father had enjoyed calling *debate*. He had never just—had a conversation like a game of chess, and then watched the other person, entirely measured and courteous, lay down their king and say, good game.

"I—that was me winning? Then do you change your mind? You don't just want to ban Earthstrongers, you think there could be laws that would help, like with . . ." He waved incoherently towards where the angry lady was still sitting, only she didn't seem angry now. She had been befriended—and somehow he was seismically unsurprised—by Mx Ren. Gale glanced that way too, all alight, and very gradually, he managed to get his fingernails over the possibility that they weren't just making a show of good sportsmanship: they were honestly *pleased* he had learned to do what they did.

---

32 Cheers.

Not far from them, there was a little bout of laughter as Mx Francis almost bumped into an Earthstrong man, who went down quickly on one knee. Mx Francis bent to help him up and they went off together. The man had patent leather brogues on *without socks* and so January suspected that they were meant for each other.

He saw Gale's eyes snag in that direction too. They hid it well, but they did often flinch at big noises, even when it was laughter.

"I agree there is a possibility we could legislate our way to a far lower accidental homicide rate. I don't know what that legislation would be." Gale paused, and the light in them dulled down again. "And I doubt there's time to work it out before the fleet arrives."

"But—just—so we're very clear. I still won."

"You won," Gale agreed, with their slow, real smile.

A camera drone was focused on them. The production team were only doing their jobs, he knew that, but all at once he longed for a few seconds with Gale where he could tell, for sure, one way or the other, if they were doing what they were doing because they wanted to, or if it was acting for the bastard show.

He glanced sideways, hoping and not that Gale had forgotten what was on the schedule today. Gale was watching him back, just as carefully.

It was as good a moment as any. He dipped his eyelashes in the sketch of a nod to say, *yes, I remember.*

What filled his head was how bad he was at all this. He hated being flirted with but he fell in love all the time, and never with people who loved him back—generally the ones who would never have dreamed of flirting with him. He was like one of those cats that only wanted to be stroked by people who were allergic to cats.

Gale was so violently allergic to cats that they'd probably have to go and lie down for a few days after too close an encounter with one.

And so of course, of fucking course, he desperately wanted this to be real, that would have been wonderful.

It must all have shown on his face, because Gale covered his knuckles, without any pressure. It sent a crackle of electricity up his spine, enough to make him twitch. Too late, he realized it looked like a flinch. "It's all right. We're not doing that," they said, very quiet.

He sat still with his shoulder pressed to theirs, feeling relieved and robbed.

Gale bowed a little. "I think I'm going to have to go to bed. Good night, Mx Stirling."

God, he was useless.

42

He was too tumbled to think about sleeping. Instead, he pulled on a heat suit and went outside. The cold was stunning after being so cosy indoors, and he had to stand still just by the front doors for a second while he got used to it, even wrapped up in heavy-weather gear. But he needed to walk. Exercise, outside, because it would be so unpleasant he'd be hard put to think about anything else.

Like an ability even to *act* a scripted romance. What would the producers be talking about right now? Probably swearing up and down the production room, yelling at Mx Francis and demanding to know how House Gale had hired someone to do one specific thing he seemed absolutely incapable of doing. He had been warned about this weeks and weeks ago, he'd known it was coming and even then, *even then*, he had just frozen, and Gale had had to rescue him. Again.

He had no idea where all the idiot baggage had come from. He had a dull feeling it was just that he'd never learned how to do any of this properly. At school he hadn't gone drinking or partying or any of it, he'd just rehearsed and rehearsed, because he couldn't afford to screw it up. He'd had friends, but not relationships. As a teenager he'd been bewildered by them and by the time he was in his twenties it was obvious that none of that would ever come easily, which had been upsetting, so he'd tried, but what he got out of it was mostly crushing dread. He couldn't summon enough humour about it to even keep going to speed dating things. And now he was thirty . . . whatever he was, had he had a birthday recently? God knew: that was serious maths on a planet with no months. He was possibly thirty-four, and he'd had no practise, and no resilience, he felt raw trying to chase any of it down to real reasons, and he was, as bloody usual, falling in love with the nearest unsuitable older person who was kind to him.

What a joke.

He went slowly, feeling the altitude. It seemed to snatch at him in the evenings more than the day, but he couldn't have said why. Not sickness; but a fluttery anxiety, the feeling that someone bigger was following you down a part of the canal where the shopkeepers weren't paying enough protection money and the local gang had switched off the street lights.

There were bright lights in the forest; the logging crews were still working, and over the hum of the dust, the big machinery whirred and clattered. They were cutting up the felled trees. As January came into the haze of the lights, his shadow danced monstrous on the ground. Through his lenses, dim light trails highlighted where the paths were, and numbers moved in the air, telling him how fast the wind was, whether the dust was dangerous for machinery—there was a red warning—and the temperature. Hazy, because his mask was already dusty.

Someone took his hand.

He swung around, his heart lifting. But it wasn't Gale. It wasn't anyone. There was nothing there. Just the dust.

And then someone who wasn't there banged him backwards into a tree, someone a lot taller than him, one arm pressed across his chest to stop him moving, and there was *still no one there*, and he couldn't move, because whoever, whatever it was, it was pressing him flat to the bark, and then *Jesus Christ Jesus Christ Jesus Christ*, writing appeared in the dust on his mask visor, traced by an invisible fingertip, Chinese, mirror-imaged so he could read it inside the mask:

Find—tree—bear-carving—MAX—

He tore away and ran and ran, and didn't stop until he'd lost all sense of where he was.

He sank down between the roots of a tree so he was enclosed, back to some roots, roots around him, curled up small, his breath whistling inside the dust mask.

Max.

Tree—bear—what tree with a—

Max was at the tree?

Max, alive and well and about to—what, to tell him what had happened, clear everything up after all this time, but then, who was attacking him and telling him—

No.

He did know. He had seen that tree on the wedding day. He had stopped beside it and admired the bear.

He sat very still for a long time, scrubbing his hand again and again over the visor to erase the words like making them disappear could make the whole memory disappear, staring out at the dust, and not knowing what he was even looking for. He hadn't seen—whatever it was—even when it was right next to him. There was nothing now either, only the soft illumination of the trails in his lenses, and a sketch in light-lines that showed him where Songshu was. Around him, the trees groaned, an army of dying giants. Even with the heat suit, the cold started to press in on him, and so did the awareness that if you were out in the woods alone, you were supposed to have a rifle. There were bears. The building work would have scared most of them off, where the trees were being cut down, but he could well imagine the news story anyway. *January Stirling eaten by inattentive bear on mystery jaunt in the woods.*

Find the tree with the bear.

He had to make an effort to make his lungs slow down.

"What the fuck kind of ghost writes on . . ." He didn't know who he was talking to.

His lenses flared, because the messaging system was voice-activated, and the words appeared in a message alongside a helpful list of his contacts. Gale was Au for Aubrey, which filled his head with useless images of gold jewellery. *Send to Au?*

No.

Because what could he say? *Hello, me again, been attacked by a ghost who wrote a cryptic message on my visor for unclear reasons.*

Already, the memory of it was misting in the way strange things and dreams always did. He squeezed his eyes shut. Minds had walls that marked off *likely* versus *unlikely*, and the strange things and the dreams were outside, with no protection from the fierce solar wind that seemed to tear through the world beyond those walls. Already, it looked too bizarre to have happened. He had misunderstood somehow, not seen something, or seen something wrongly.

His lenses blinked the message at him again. *Send to Au?*

No.

No; he was just going to have to find that tree and see if anything was there.

The tree was gone.

He thought he'd made a mistake and lost his bearings until he understood what had happened. The loggers had already felled it. It was here: but it was stretched out lengthwise. The bear carving was just visible above the moss on the ground. He was lucky it hadn't been through the timber-cutting machine yet.

The roots had torn up from the ground and left a hollow. It was dark, away from the halogens; they looked gritty and dim, and he could only make out shadows. He fumbled through his pockets. He hadn't been using his phone; everyone was saving every scrap of power they could, but he did have emergency matches. Hunching forward to protect it from the wind, he struck one. Even like that, it ignited the dust particles around it in a soft, gunpowder flare.

And illuminated the body. Perfectly, beautifully preserved in the cold. Whoever it was might have died only a couple of days ago. But they hadn't. They weren't wearing enough. Just a jumper with the sleeves turned back.

There was a tattoo on the forearm, still clear. It was the army sigil, with SERVE THE PEOPLE in rigid Mandarin underneath.

That was the insignia of the marines.

Later, he tried hard to think that what he did next came entirely on instinct, that he just panicked, and it was pure helplessness, but the more he tried to convince himself, the more fake it looked. There was nothing instinctive about it. He sat still, looking at that sad figure curled in the hollow of the broken tree, for what must have been a clear minute, his mind ticking through consequences in the way he had learned at the Songshu meeting table.

If he went back inside and said to Gale, *So I reckon I've found Max*— one of two things could happen. One: Gale would turn out to be innocent. They would therefore call the police, all the proper procedures would be followed, and either the investigation would be inconclusive or there would be evidence on the body that Max had been killed by a random bear, irritable mammoth, or passing axe-murderer. Two: Gale was guilty, all footage of January saying anything would be scrubbed, the body would disappear, and if he tried to insist there *had* been a body, Dr Okonkwo would give him antipsychotics, because obviously he was having some kind of breakdown, and he would live the following five years as a heavily drugged zombie if he was very lucky; if not, like the Consul said, it would be death by garbage truck.

He wouldn't know unless he did it.

He wasn't doing that.

In English people said, *between a rock and a hard place*, which implied you were sort of stuck and mountain rescue might need to give you an embarrassing talk about being careful where you climbed. In Russian, though, they said *between the hammer and the anvil*. He felt like he was on the anvil now, watching the hammer come down.

He wrenched the Consul's card out of his pocket and held it in front of his glasses so that the software would read the number, and dial it.

The Consul answered on the second ring, sounding groggy. "January? Are you all right? It's past . . ." Midnight, it was past midnight, he was being rude.

"No," he said. "You were right, I need help. I'm really sorry. I think I've found Max." He flicked his eyes to the little icon that would share his camera feed.

There was a silence. "I'm coming."

43

Gale might have wanted to go in the direction of bed, but they'd been waylaid by Yuan, the little boy with royal ambitions, and Yuan had definitively won; when January came back inside, the two of them were sitting on the floor near a fire and playing with a marble run that someone must have unearthed from an attic. Yuan still had the Senate coronet, and he was explaining some complicated rules with the extreme seriousness known only to tiny children and professors. And Gale, with their ability to concentrate absolutely on anything at all, marble run or zoolinguistics, was listening just as solemnly, bent slightly forward to hear him, the ends of their hair pooling black on the floor.

January felt like his cage had clamped too tight around his ribs. He felt guilty all the time, he was English, he had a hair trigger for guilt—in the nuclear tower, because the lift opened straight out into people's living rooms, he'd felt guilty about accidentally seeing his own reflection in someone else's mirror when the lift doors opened on the way down to the ground floor, as though he had stolen their own personal light—but not like this.

He shouldn't have made the call. The Consul was going to crash through here like a mammoth, it was going to be public and horrible, and he *shouldn't* have bloody done it, he should at least have asked Gale what was happening, but—but. You could be gentle and kind and good with children and still a murderer. Everything he knew about Gale was clashing contrasts. A glamorous academic; an honourable CEO; a courteous demagogue.

Kasha nosed at his knees; she knew something was wrong. He stroked her ears, around the paper party hat she was wearing. Someone, with very great care, had stapled a ribbon to it and tied it under her chin.

It felt like a thousand years since the carols, but the last of the Christmas party was still smouldering, the smell of mulled wine rich in the air, and people's voices and laughter muted in the comfy way that happened late at night by firelight. Although most Natural people he'd met on Mars had no idea what Christmas was,[33] lots of Songshu staff had stayed up too. People were making friends.

Even though he was waiting for it, it was a shock when he heard the thunder of the helicopters.

The Consul brought at least thirty praetorians, who swept into the room in military formation, guns out and visors down. They surged past January. Gale started to stand up, clearly about to ask what they thought they were doing. January wanted to look away and couldn't. The praetorians slammed Gale flat on the floor and wrenched their wrists backwards into cuffs, scattering the wooden marble run, and marbles. Yuan stared, silent and frozen. So did everyone else.

It didn't look like an arrest. It looked like a black ops kidnapping. January heard himself yell at them to stop, but Gale didn't try to fight—they couldn't, not against three armed ex-marines—and then they were all gone, into the back rooms as if they knew exactly where to go. Yuan still hadn't made a sound, but he was crying and crying. Whoever had been looking after him before wasn't there now, so January scooped him up, while around him, alarmed people jolted onto their feet, slow from the wine and the warmth of the fires.

"Apologies for the intrusion," the Consul said to the room at large. They had come in after the praetorians, slow and steady, more like a

---

33   He had tried to explain to Mx Francis and Mx Ren that they'd got the wrong end of the stick, it wasn't about ritualised housebreaking that was legal as long as you dressed in a big red suit, and no, the random foliage people brought into their houses didn't really have anything to do with the dodgy supernatural thing that impregnated a teenager without her consent, please could they stop ruining it.

general than a politician. Which they had been, of course. More than ever now they were in a room full of Earthstrongers, they looked heroic and magnificent, firelight turning the consular coronet a brilliant gold in their grey dreadlocks. "We had an anonymous tip that a body was found in the grounds, and that's just been confirmed. A pathologist is examining it now, but it's a suspected homicide. Please do relax, nobody here is in trouble except Senator Gale."

With Yuan gripping his shirt, pressed against his shoulder, January looked back and realized people were turning towards him, as if it was up to him what to do. It broke over him only very slowly that they were right. The fires danced shadows over a lot of anxious faces. Nobody wanted to be Earthstrong and in a room with consular praetorians at the same time. He thought of all those cases where Earthstrongers had been shot just for sneezing at the wrong second.

"Okay, let's get everyone upstairs to bed and out of the Consul's way," he said, fighting to keep his voice level, and trying hard to copy Gale's way of talking in a crisis. "I'm sure it is safe but let's not tempt fate. Or the praetorians. I'll be up soon, I'll try and find out what's going on."

You know what's going on though, because you did this.

When he blinked, he saw the praetorians snatching Gale again, so rough it made him start to shake with something awful between rage and shame. What had he thought would happen? That they'd sneak in and ask for a quiet word?

"Why did you do that?" he said, turning back to the Consul, one hand over the back of Yuan's head and feeling very glad there was something between them, even if it was just a tiny boy. His voice came out strange and quiet. "We don't even know if it *is* Max yet."

The Consul tipped their head ruefully. "I did this so that we have lots of footage of a spectacular arrest in which my very dangerous opposition looks like the criminal they definitely are," they said, with an honesty that almost shocked his voice out of him. "I'm sorry, I didn't mean to upset the little one. What's your name, tiny person?"

Yuan hid against January's shoulder. He was still crying, in the terrible, silent way children cried when they didn't think anyone would care.

"Jesus, leave him alone, you're scaring him!" January snapped. "A bunch of *giants* just dragged away someone who was being kind to him, have some common pissing sense!"

The Consul blinked like a cat had just hissed at them for no reason, and dismayed, he realized that it had never occurred to them that anyone Natural might seem frightening.

"And now you're going to broadcast that I was the anonymous tip," January said, not quite able to believe he hadn't seen it coming. "Even better scandal. *Aubrey Gale given up to the police by new consort.* Right?"

"No, I'm not, because remember the garbage truck we talked about before?" the Consul said, quite gently. They glanced to the side as if they were hoping somebody would help them with him, but everyone Earthstrong had gone upstairs now, fast, and the only people left were a few praetorians stationed at the doors, staring straight ahead. "January . . . you were right to get help. If Aubrey is guilty—I don't think anything good would have happened to you if you'd confronted them alone."

"And if they're not?" he asked, his voice going high. "You just had them dragged off like they were waving a gun around—"

"I can see you don't want to hear this, but I am really quite confident that they *are* guilty." The Consul stepped up close to him and set both hands heavy on his shoulders. It made him flinch. They were huge, up close, and he had a nasty sense that they wanted him to feel it, rather than just notice it. He was about level with their breastbone. "I'm detaining the staff as well, as a precaution. You're the only person here who had nothing to do with Max, so—you're it, Jan. You're House Gale for now."

"Please stop touching me," he ground out. "I'm holding a toddler, for Christ's sake."

They looked genuinely taken aback, and took a little step away. "I'm sorry. I wasn't trying—"

"Do I have a choice about what I do with House Gale now, or will you shoot me if I choose wrong?" he interrupted tightly. In his arms, Yuan was reassuringly heavier than he looked.

The Consul looked like they were in pain. "We don't do things that way here. You know we don't." They sighed. "Look, if you don't want Aubrey to realize you're the one who called it in—I suggest you keep going with the tower, and make a good show of being furious with me. If they're innocent, great. If they're not; congratulations. House Gale is yours. The first Earthstrong senator, ever." They smiled, and he thought it seemed like a real smile. "Either way . . . I'll be delighted."

January stood still, fighting down the need to say, *Get out of my house.* He didn't know why he wanted to say that. It wasn't the Consul who had maybe murdered someone and fully endorsed locking up Earthstrongers. The Consul was annoying and theatrical and over-bearing, but they were here because he had asked them, and in the end, it was the Consul who wanted to help people instead of locking them up.

He couldn't stop seeing Gale hit the floor.

There was a word for that, when an idea made a kind of cross shape. When, for example, you had one person who was wrong but who was also endlessly kind, and another person who was right but also somehow terrible. Gale would have known.

He was saved from having to say anything, because a praetorian ghosted up to the Consul and murmured something.

"It is Max," the Consul told him. "They've just confirmed it. And cause of death is a gunshot wound to the head."

He had to shut his eyes for second. "Is there any way to prove who did it? A halo won't work on Senator Gale."

"We can try again." The Consul paused. "I was wondering if you'd ask the questions, actually."

"Me. Why?"

They shrugged a little, contrite, as though they really were worried he was going to get angry with them again. "It's harder to lie to someone you like."

He breathed out slowly. "Give me a minute to collect my thirty pieces of silver then."

"Sorry, what? Silver?"

"It's just an old story about someone who was a real bastard to someone who didn't deserve it," he mumbled.

The Consul caught his shoulder. "January. The chances are that they really, absolutely deserve it."

He nodded, and couldn't talk again over the noise in his head that was the consular campaign—and the whole of House Gale—smashing down around him.

Kingmaker indeed.

"Can I leave Yuan with you?" he asked.

"Oh, er . . . I'm sure we can find someone to look after them," the Consul said, not looking very confident. "It's probably dangerous for me to carry around an Earthstrong child."

January thought it was a joke and laughed, but then realized it wasn't, and the feeling that settled down over him wasn't a very good one. He didn't like words like "disturbed," because they were usually used by people who'd never seen anything more disturbing than a streaker on a football pitch, but disturbed was right; disturbed in the sense of water, and seeing something big writhe just under the surface which didn't move much, but did move all the same. "He's tiny. He couldn't break into a packet of biscuits."

"No, no, no," Yuan said suddenly. He must have realized what was happening. "No, they're scary, I want to . . ."

"*I'm* scary?" the Consul said, somewhere between tickled and incredulous.

January watched them for a second and almost said that Gale had been carrying Yuan around all evening, but he didn't. You couldn't control what frightened you. He was scared of spiders and it wasn't as though any of them were bigger or stronger than him, unless there was some horrifying low-gravity variety nobody had told him about.

Jesus Christ, maybe there were giant low-gravity spiders.

"I'll ask someone else to . . ." he said, then trailed off, because he didn't know who to try. If all of Gale's staff had been arrested, then everyone he was knew was locked in their rooms. Yuan was looking up at him with big eyes and no hope.

"I'll take them," one of the praetorians offered, with a smile that managed to be friendly despite all the combat gear. They bowed a little to January, careful and apologetic, just a normal person now that they weren't arresting anybody. "We didn't mean to scare you before, little person. We're really sorry."

January thought Yuan would only be more scared, but in fact, he straightened up speculatively. "In, in movies and things, soldiers have those things that go puff and then fireworks come out."

The praetorian thought about it. "Flash bombs?"

"Have you got any?" Yuan said hopefully.

January prodded him. "Okay, mate, no bombs for you, but . . . you'll be all right with the nice praetorian, yes?"

"Okay," Yuan said unwillingly.

"Who will definitely not set off some flash bombs outside and it definitely won't be massive fun," the praetorian said, doing an innocent face.

Yuan dived at them.

January took a breath, then decided that some things were out of his control, he wasn't Yuan's dad, and anyway, it *would* be massive fun. He wished he was playing with flash bombs outside. He bowed to the praetorian, who bowed back and gave him a little smile, one that promised they were just violent for a job, not as a person; as a person they had to go home and worry about laundry and running out of milk just like everyone else. He smiled too, knowing it was true even though every fibre in him howled that it couldn't be. The thing about fibres was that they weren't very bright.

The Consul gave him a strange look. "You are . . . a very graceful person."

"Sorry?"

"Nothing, really," they said, but they laughed, and he followed them, feeling confused.

Gale was locked in their own room on the fifth floor, just along from the production lounge. Two praetorians were at the door, one with a halo readout playing on a tablet. They nodded him through. When January went inside, Gale was sitting at the desk by candlelight, though there was power for the lamps now, writing on a tablet. Mammoth double-staves again. Someone had already been in and put a halo on them, a dim purple light just glowing against their temple from the reader. They watched him come in, but they said nothing. They looked afraid.

"Did you do it?" January asked. He moved a chair across and sat down in it, not too close. All his thoughts had turned sharp and serrated, and he was cutting himself whenever he tried to think.

"No," Gale whispered. They looked wrong for a murder suspect. Their hair was tied up in a knot with a white band, and they had on the same green jumper they slept in. It had holes in the sleeves where the weave was frayed, and around the hem where Kasha sometimes tried to get at their pockets for whatever interesting things might be in them. They straightened painfully, like they'd just been told they had to take the Senate floor. "They told me it was out in the woods." They tipped their eyelashes towards the door to explain who they meant. "The body. What happened, how was it found?"

Right. That was simple, at least. The razor-thoughts parted just enough to let him through. "One of the trees the timber people cut down tore up the ground and exposed it."

The sharpness came back to Gale's eyes and there was nothing soft about them any more. "They're felling half a mile from here, in the dark."

January couldn't quite believe that they could still be like this, even when they were staring down the barrel of life in prison.

"It was found, does it matter how?" It came out more snappish than he meant.

Gale let their shoulders drop a little and they lifted one hand an inch from the table before they noticed and pulled it into their lap again. People from Great Houses didn't talk with their hands. In one way it was infuriating to see them insist on that whalebone propriety even now, but in another, it was horrible. Things January was that compulsive about weren't choices, they'd been beaten into him by dancing masters with bamboo switches. "It matters that it happened now. Immediately after we got the gravity trains up, immediately after it became clear all this wasn't doomed, it's too . . ."

"Sorry, it's *narratively inconvenient* for us to find your murdered consort just now?" January demanded, so incredulous he'd gone all the way around the wheel and almost come right back to laughing.

Gale looked away, and January frowned, because he had never seen them struggle this much to say something. "I mean . . . did—did someone *take* you there?"

"Me?" he said, trying to tell himself not to panic. "Who said I found it?"

Gale smiled a fraction at their own hands in their lap. "You went outside, you were gone for half an hour, you came back looking haunted. I'm Schrödinger's cat; maybe it would have been all right, maybe it wouldn't, if you had come to me. You're not an idiot, so you called the Consul instead."

He pressed his teeth together until they hurt. "You don't think I've got other reasons to look a bit haunted? You know—worrying you're going to lock everyone in naturalisation centres, worrying what happens if you lose the election, and what happens if you win, and . . . ?"

"But did they?" Gale asked, black eyes coming back up to find his again, not angry, but not an invitation to try to evade the question again either. "Did someone show you where to find . . . ?"

He wanted to tell them. What had happened out in the woods was sitting in all his thoughts like a great lodestone, warping everything else that came near enough to feel the magnetism, and the closer he tried to get to it, the less sure he was of what had happened. Someone had grabbed him, someone had written on his visor, but he still didn't understand. He didn't know if he believed in ghosts. People said Songshu was haunted, and maybe it was, maybe there was a ghost who desperately wanted not to be stuck under a pine tree forever. It was crazy but he didn't know what else to think any more, and maybe . . .

He had a vision of Dr Okonkwo taking out the special inhibitor injection. God knew that would come straight out if he started talking about ghosts.

"No," he said.

Gale nodded slightly.

January was quiet for a second, but Gale didn't try to fill the silence. They weren't fighting. It was more disconcerting than a barrage of facts and reasons. "Senator, what happened to Max?"

"I don't know. I wasn't there."

January had no idea what he was doing any more, or what was going to happen, to Gale or to him. Gale knew he'd done this to them and there was no real way that he could see to prove what *they* might have done; maybe he was heading for a hole under a tree as well, not too long from now, or maybe the Consul would find something else to charge Gale with, or maybe . . . he just didn't know. The only solid thing in his mind was that he wanted to get as near to the truth as he could. He'd never met Max, but he *was* Max. He was another version of that figure curled up in the roots of the tree. "Look, halo scans aren't good on you and I bet you can warp them however you like, so probably you're not going to prison because there'll be no proof, but I'm going to tell you why I don't believe you and then you can tell me if it's unreasonable."

Gale waited. Dressed plainly, they looked a lot younger, and a lot less official. The white band in their hair made them look like a postulant at a monastery.

"You haven't asked me if I found River. So I think—you already know what happened to River."

Gale shook their head a fraction and he thought they would argue. "That's very reasonable."

"Are you going to explain?" January asked, frustrated. It was only then that he understood how badly he wanted them to have an explanation that wasn't the one he thought. "I mean—did River do it and you're covering for them and they're hiding at a lunar colony or . . . ?"

Gale was studying the edge of the table again like the answer might be written there; and then studied him in the same way. They were so good at letting questions bounce off them, January thought with a kind of hopeless admiration. They were a mirror person; the brighter the light you tried to shine on them see what was going inside their head, the more you got blinded. "I know you have no reason to listen me. But you need to leave. Now, tonight. I think something's going to happen. The Consul is going to find a way to start a fight, a bad one, and afterwards . . . they're going to find my body on a stairwell somewhere."

January felt like he had in his flat in the nuclear tower two months ago—Christ, it was only two months ago—when Gale had asked him to marry them. What they had just said was so divorced from anything he had expected that his brain didn't even recognise it as sentences with grammar at first.

"*What?*"

"This isn't about Max, this is about stopping me finishing the tower and moving the sun fields into the atmosphere, which is . . . why I asked if someone took you out there. This only happened once the mammoths helped us; before that, it looked hopeless, so there was no need. Now; we could actually win, we could get functioning solar power before the fleet arrives. The Consul needs me out of the way."

"No, what? They—can't, how could they even . . . ?"

Gale looked across at him for a hanging second, then pushed something into his hand, something small and cold and silvery. "Go."

It was the key to his cage.

The Consul was waiting outside, looking concerned.

"January—are you all right?"

He nodded, numb. He didn't know what to say, or what not to. Gale could have been lying to scare him or to make him doubt the Consul; he couldn't honestly claim to imagine they wouldn't do that. Of everyone he knew, Aubrey Gale was in runaway first place most likely to kill someone. They were exactly practical enough. And yet—now he'd spoken to them—he just . . . didn't . . . see it. He didn't see them shooting anyone, he couldn't imagine them making a mistake like that. If Gale wanted someone dead, they wouldn't be shrouded in interesting mystery inside Songshu's grounds, he realized suddenly. They'd be hit by a bus in town. Open; boring; no questions.

And, above all: no body. It was openly stupid to leave evidence, and yet, here it was. Gale wasn't stupid.

The Consul touched his shoulder. He wished they would stop doing that. Every time they came up close, they loomed. "What did they say to you?"

"They—said—you'd never let it go to trial. They said you'd find a way to start some kind of fight here and at the end of it, they'd be dead on a stairwell."

The Consul only sighed. "Yeah. Look. I shouldn't say this about my honourable opposition, but Aubrey Gale is a manipulative prick. You can see that, right?"

January nodded again, but it all felt wrong. His hand hurt and he realized the key to his cage was cutting into his palm, because he'd been gripping it too tight.

"Though obviously I would say that," the Consul said gently. "Hey. Come on. Let's go and have a hot drink and calm down a bit. I don't know about you, but I'm wrung out."

January looked up. "Consul—"

"For fuck's sake stop calling me Consul, my name's Guang." They bowed a little, like they were being formally introduced, which looked strange on them, because they weren't normally that polite.

And in the background, he had a familiar coil of anxiety that felt exactly how he did if someone banged on his door in the middle of the night. Not quite attacked, but . . . but.

"Jesus, are you flirting with me?" he asked. "What *for*? I haven't got anything you want."

The Consul laughed, a genuine merry laugh. "Phew, that was an insight into your lonely life right there, wasn't it? I mean—sorry, sorry. Don't be angry. I wasn't doing it to get anything, I'm just—you know, on a high because my arch-nemesis has just been arrested for murder and it's got away from me a bit. Forgive me?"

January bowed slightly back, keeping his back very straight, to rebuild the formal wall between them. "What did the halo show?" he asked, to move on.

"The analysts are looking at it now," the Consul promised. "You did well. They talked to you a lot more than they would have talked to an investigator."

He nodded, feeling disgusting. It was true, Gale *hadn't* asked what had happened to River, and he did find that very ominous indeed. But something was wrong, and he could see part of the shape of it but not enough to tell what was going on. He cast one last look back at the door as the Consul led him away towards the dining room, wishing he could be sure, one way or another, whether Gale was lying.

Certainly the praetorians scowling at the halo readout didn't look like they knew.

As he followed the Consul, Kasha bustled up to him and nosed hopefully at his pocket. Seeing her made him remember Gale's real partner—who undoubtedly hadn't the faintest idea what was going on, if they'd gone to bed already. Maybe the two of them pretended not to notice the other existed mostly, but that always silent figure had been kind to him when he needed it; and they were going to need it now. He rubbed Kasha's ears and started to take a breath to say to the Consul that there was someone he needed to find, and then stopped when he realized he had no idea where the person in the burnt-orange jumper lived, when they weren't with Gale. They hadn't been in the room just now. The Consul looked back, because he'd fallen behind.

"Everything all right?"

"I've just—this sounds odd, but Gale has a real partner who I don't . . . actually know, but I need to find out where they are." He frowned. "We should ask them about Max. I don't know how long they've been here, but maybe they know something."

"A partner? Really? Aubrey Gale has attracted an actual human? Are you sure they're not a cunningly disguised AI?"

January told himself to breathe twice before he said anything, but even after that, the glibness of it still needled at him. "Not to sound hopelessly square, but can you maybe not trash-talk the person whose life we've just destroyed, maybe for no reason?"

The Consul gave him a strange, sad smile, not at all as if he had told them off; more like he'd recently broken his arm and he'd shown them the cast. "Where do they live?"

"Not sure," January said, disconcerted and wondering what it was the Consul had seen in him just then. "I need to ask someone."

The Consul pointed to the production room and gave him a questioning look. *Will they know?*

"Right," he said.

On her way past, Kasha growled at the Consul. January patted her head, trying to project "good dog" without saying it aloud.

44

The production room stretched across the whole of the main tower, a sort of broad glass bridge that looked down into the dining room and the entrance hall with its streams and willow trees, and up to the dome thirty floors above. All of it was glass, the ceiling, the walls, the floor—he had thought initially that it was so that the producers could get a bird's-eye view of the drones that always operated on the ground floor, but now, he had more of a sense it was so that people could see in. If you were making a show like theirs, splicing footage, making stories, it would be very easy for everyone else to feel like it was a secretive process directed behind locked doors. All the glass was reassuring.

Incredibly, it was morning already, a few minutes before six, and through the glass walls, he could already see people zombily making themselves tea and coffee in the sleek staff kitchen. Up above, some of the Earthstrong people who hadn't stayed too late at the Christmas party were already up, getting ready for the day shift on the rig; he could see them on the balcony, not least because some people were showing their kids the production room, looking down at it through its glass ceiling.

He felt irrationally betrayed. It was just a normal morning. The normal schedule was happening: people were gearing up and going to work, the coffee machines were whirring. He wanted there to be some pause at least, or even a bit of chaos, but it was all gliding along as if nothing had happened.

The Consul opened the production room door for him with a little bow that seemed theatrically polite, as if they were taking the piss because he'd told them not to be rude about Gale. Up on the Earthstrong floor, someone exclaimed that that was the actual *Consul*. The Consul looked up and waved, and there was some embarrassed laughter as some teenagers waved back.

Inside, the production room was dimly lit as always, and everyone in it was either watching the drones' footage on the bank of screens, or splicing bits and pieces together for the show, which was going out— said a big timer on the wall—in twenty minutes. Everyone looked frazzled. Some of the praetorians were there too, looking at footage, and clearly directing what was going to go into the final cut and what was left out. January looked away when he saw the footage of himself. He looked tiny among the armed praetorians as they tackled Gale.

He hadn't been in here for a while, and there was a little stir when people saw him, the kind there had used to be at the backstage door after a show if he tried to escape to get a fizzy drink from the shop next door; it was how people were when they recognised someone they'd never spoken to, the awkward sense that they should say hello traced over the knowledge that of course it would seem very strange.

"Mx Gale," the senior producer said, and he actually looked back for Gale before he realized that meant him. It was the first time anyone had called him that. "Can we . . . do something for you?" They looked strained, and ill. Their eyes flickered to the Consul. "Um. Any coffee? We've just made some."

"I'm all right, thanks. I'm trying to find the Senator's real partner, do you know where they live?"

"The Senator's . . . real partner?"

He winced. Probably they'd all been sworn to secrecy. No, not probably: definitely. They probably had to scrub the person in the orange jumper from all their footage, so that the whole of Tharsis wouldn't see that the marriage and the romance was fake. "It's okay, you don't have to—I just need to find them."

"I'm—sorry, I don't know who you mean." They glanced up, seeming disconcerted, and when he did too, he saw why. On the Earthstrong

344

floor, quite a lot of people had come to the balcony edge to look down through the glass ceiling, pointing out the Consul to each other. It was strange to see the movie-star fizz around politicians here affecting even people from Earth, who he would have thought would be immune. Still, he could understand it. The Consul was just as powerful a presence as Gale, leonine and weather-beaten and good-looking even at a distance.

January dredged for more patience. He didn't feel tired, not in his bones and muscles, but he was fatigued. His brain was running low on Tharsese manners, and part of it was snagged anxiously with Gale, alone in their room. "Come on, you know and I know, and this is important. The Consul needs to see them."

"I'm not trying to be difficult," the producer said. "Can you describe them?"

"Er," said January, suddenly not sure he could describe someone who was just generic Tharsis Chic. "They're always in meetings, they're always with the Senator. Orange jumper, usually. They write things by hand in a book?" He was describing props, not a person. "Natural, sixth or seventh generation? Long black hair, Asian?" Like almost everyone else at Songshu. "They don't dress up though, they're always scruffy."

He wondered if his glasses could do some kind of image search on stuff he'd seen recently—he had a distant feeling that it was possible to do that, which now he was thinking about it was very creepy and meant that somewhere, everything he saw with them was being recorded—but he didn't know how, and part of him stamped its foot and said no, I shouldn't have to, this is stupid.

"An orange jumper? I'm not sure I . . ."

"We have footage of them," January said, beginning to feel like he was being messed around and not completely sympathetic, even given what was probably a ferocious gag-order situation. "When the Senator asked me to go to the fundraiser thing, their partner was in the room with them when I came in. They were combing the Senator's hair."

"Really?" the producer said, sounding confused. "Well—let's have a look . . ." They bent over a table-sized tablet and skimmed through a whirl of images, then brought it up on the big screens. The footage was from one of the drones, smooth and pin-sharp.

It was wrong.

It showed January coming to Gale's door, and inside, at the mirror, Gale was alone. They were sitting exactly like he remembered, bolt upright and terse, but the person with the orange jumper wasn't there. They weren't holding the silver comb, they weren't running it through Gale's hair. If he stared, then maybe Gale's hair moved, but it could have been the draught from the opening door.

"This has been edited," he said, caught somewhere between indignant and disbelieving that the producer was being so magnificently unhelpful over something so simple. "Where are they?"

"Uh," said the producer uncertainly, "we haven't done anything to it. We're legally obligated not to tamper with the footage in any way." They sounded stiff, and he realized they thought he was accusing them of something.

"Please. I saw them at the party with Kasha a few hours ago, I just want to talk to them."

Beside them, Kasha looked around, distracted by something that wasn't there. January had heard people say she did that, but he'd never seen it before. She held her paw up like someone was asking her to shake. The Consul was watching her too, looking puzzled.

"Mx Gale," the producer said, quiet and formal, "the Senator doesn't *have* a partner. They don't live with anyone. We'd know. There would have to be precautions taken, with the show, it would be—incredibly complicated, and we don't—"

"All right, whoever it is who's in and out of their room all the time then," January said, frustrated. "Look, I know you have to protect the Senator's privacy, but don't just lie to me, it's bloody aggravating."

Kasha held up the other paw to her empty space of air, panting happily. Up above them, some Earthstrong kids were looking down from the balcony, grinning. He could see why. Kasha was gigantic if you'd grown up with Earth-sized dogs.

"No, that's what I'm telling you. No one's in and out of their room."

"This is silly. Where's Solly Francis? They were filming too."

Not far off, the praetorians looked around with granite stares to warn him he had raised his voice and they didn't like it. Always on the lookout for drama, a drone lifted into the air to film it. He could see the person controlling it—they were in the corner, their lenses flaring green, silver gloves on their hands to direct the little camera's flight.

In the interest of not being rugby tackled, he held his hands up to promise he wasn't going to do anything sudden. To have something to do with himself, and to give him a second to think, he pulled his glasses off to polish them on the hem of his shirt.

The person in the orange jumper was right there.

They were playing with Kasha.

January pointed.

"The dog's always been a bit funny," the producer said.

"Not the dog, the—sorry, excuse me," he said to the person in the orange jumper. "I've been trying to find you. I know this isn't a very good time for an introduction, but—"

"Who are you talking to?" the producer said nervously.

The praetorians had just put their hands on their guns.

"No, there's—they're here," January said, stepping back from the praetorians, his whole brain freezing up. It was amazing how incoherent even the threat of a gun could make you and now it was happening, he could see exactly why people panicked and ran away, or did the wrong thing and ended up shot in the head for no reason. "Are you joking?"

The person in the orange jumper straightened up and bowed to him a little. They had their book tucked under one arm, and the pen stuck in their hair. As always, they looked carelessly elegant, in a tired sort of way.

"There is no one there," the producer said, in the very careful way of someone dealing with a mental patient. "Um. I think you might be having an altitude hallucination—"

"I'm definitely not! Look, I—" Without thinking about it, he put his glasses back on, and then stopped still, because the person in the orange jumper vanished. "It's a filter," he said, not loudly enough. "You can't see them through . . ."

"Mx Gale, we're going to have to ask you to step *away* from the Consul," one of the praetorians told him.

He only half heard. He took the glasses off again.

347

The person in the orange jumper had come right up to him in the few seconds he'd been seeing through the glasses. Now, they gave him an apologetic look, and shoved him hard, straight back into the Consul.

Even though the Consul was huge, January was too heavy, and the two of them went over backwards with a bang that smacked the air out of him, and ground the cage's ribs so hard into his real ones that he felt like they must have left a permanent dent. Yelling erupted everywhere, someone was dragging him to one side and then there was a gun in his face and a praetorian helping the Consul up, and someone else kneeling behind him to pin his wrists to the floor. Above it all, a drone hovered. Someone was shouting at the producers to stop filming. Somebody else was bundling the Consul out of the room. Way up above the glass ceiling, he could see people on the Earthstrong level's balcony still looking down, but no one was smiling any more.

"Stay still!" one of the praetorians told him.

"I am! I didn't do that, someone pushed me, you must have seen . . ."

He trailed off, though, because the person in the orange jumper had come up next to him. They bent slightly so he could see them properly, and then held up a sign they'd just written in their book, ink still gleaming. It said,

You seem great and this absolutely isn't personal; sorry!

It was the semicolon that made it insane, he thought manically.

And then, because manic thoughts have long tails, he thought: *What the fuck kind of sixth-generation Natural Tharsese person can handwrite* totally *natural English? Nobody. Gale and minus six people in a university.*

"What?" he managed, and at the most tremendous lag, he realized that this was what had happened to him in the woods—this *person*, whoever they were, had bodily dragged him and written on his dust mask visor to make him find Max—

He didn't get any further with the thought, because the person in the orange jumper gave him an apologetic wince and then kicked him in the stomach.

It doubled him up, which made him wrench his hands out of the praetorian's, and then there was more yelling and he heard a click that something right in the base of mind his informed him was the safety catch being turned off on a gun, and he tried to remember the Mandarin for "don't shoot" but it came out in English and then there was a noise like the bomb coming in through the window, and he slammed back into the floor so hard he thought someone had shoved him.

They hadn't shoved him.

They'd shot him.

He didn't understand until he saw the blood on the shoulder of his shirt. It didn't feel like he'd expected. It felt like being punched very hard, but it was more just impact than pain, or at least, right now this second it was. Something peculiar happened to his brain then. It sort of detached itself from the rest of him, and his thinking became perfectly calm, and clear. He might have been standing next to himself, not in his own body, just an onlooker, or at a cinema.

"I really don't think that was necessary, do you?" he said to the prae-torian with the smoking gun, and even as he said it, he heard how ludi-crous it sounded.

Everything was silent. Except, up above them, there was a noise that he'd thought was just ringing inside his own head; it was the people who had been watching from the balcony. There were a lot of them now. Some weren't wearing cages; it was still too early in the morning.

Later, he was almost sure it was one of the teenagers, just trying to express how unimpressed they were to have seen a soldier shoot someone who was flat on the ground. Certainly it could never actually have been dangerous. But someone threw a shoe. He saw, very clearly from where he was lying on the floor, that it *was* a shoe, not a brick, or a grenade; it had neon green laces. The praetorians, though, must have been trained to always expect the absolute worst, and what they did, of course, was fire up through the glass ceiling.

45

The bullets had fractured the glass, so it was hard to see up now through the webs of cracks. January shuffled backwards to get against the wall. The praetorian captain was snapping at the others to get up there and round everyone up—it sounded so casual but they were going with their guns out and Jesus Christ, if Sasha was anything to go by then they could barely tell the difference between fourteen-year-old boys and forty-year-old men. Very carefully, he pushed back against the wall and eased onto his feet, still struggling to breathe.

"Where do you think you're going?" the captain demanded.

"Out the way of the glass," he managed, edging towards the door.

The praetorian glanced up. "It's fine."

He didn't think so. Up on the fifth floor balcony, there were people whose kids had just been shot at, and maybe even hurt; and they knew, because they watched the news, that praetorians would be coming up to them now, and that those praetorians would shoot anyone who even twitched at the wrong moment. He didn't know what it was like to have children, but if he had been up there holding Yuan, who he had only met yesterday, he knew exactly what he would be considering very, very seriously just now. He would be looking at the distance between the balcony and the glass ceiling, and thinking it wasn't far to fall if you weren't wearing a cage.

They're going to find a way to start a fight, Gale had said, *and afterward, I'll be found dead on a stairwell.*

It was only a few steps back along the corridor to Gale's room.

"I said stop moving," the praetorian told him. He stopped. Reasonably they had no reason to shoot him again, but since Gagarin Square, he seriously doubted anyone had been training the praetorians to give passing Earthstrongers a reasonable hearing. The unspoken rule was shoot first, justify it to the lacklustre tribunal later.

"For God's sake, he needs a doctor," the producer tried.

"He—"

January twisted against the wall to get his arms over his face as the ceiling exploded inwards. It was safety glass, so there were no shards; instead, it shattered into little irregular cubes that smashed across the floor like a truckload of spilled beads.

Six or seven Earthstrong people had landed easily in the middle of the room, uncaged, the fall nothing to them, and all the praetorians swung that way. He heard the shots and heard someone scream but he didn't see what happened, because he was already on his way out the door.

He juddered the key into the cage lock, knocked the release, and stumbled out of the steel frame while it was still opening. Even after being out of it for a little while with the mammoths, he still smacked into a wall and had to slow right down.

The need to find a cupboard and hide it in was crushing. It shocked him as much as the gunshot. He was strong enough to hurl any one of those security officers aside, and naïvely, he had spent a lot of his life wondering why more people didn't just jump on terrorists when they pulled out a gun in a shopping centre. The answer was paralysingly straightforward. It was the visceral kind of fear he had never had before, never, not in the flood in London, not looking down the barrel of natu-ralisation, not once, because he had never once been about to die *right now* and that was as different from the dull constricting I-might-die-in-two-weeks fear as a dragon was from a snake.

As well as he could, feeling peculiar and swimmy now even though the gunshot wound still didn't hurt, he ran back along the corridor, towards Gale's door, wondering what in God's name he could say to the praetorians guarding it to convince them to let him through, all blood-soaked and cageless.

When he stumbled round the corner, only one of them was there. Just tilting open Gale's door, gun drawn, even though the door had been locked and no one was in there—no one *could* be in there—but Gale.

He had no idea what to do. Distract them? But then maybe he would get shot, again; but if he didn't, could he really move fast enough to knock out a praetorian in body armour? Probably it wasn't a fifty-fifty choice, probably there was a right answer, but there was no time and all he could think was that he was only thirty seconds out of the cage and uncoordinated. He had as much chance of ricocheting off a wall as doing anything useful. At least if he said something, and loud enough, Gale would hear.

"Hi!" His voice came out high and mad-sounding. "Are you moving the Senator to a safe room? Thank God. It's insane, someone opened fire, and now—can I come with you?"

It made the officer jump, and then there was an eerie lag in which they noticed he wasn't wearing his cage, and that he was already covered in blood.

The gun swung up towards him, but he had been watching for it, and he was quicker.

It was just a smack. That was all. He didn't close his fist, he was sure of it, even later when he went over it thousands of times.

But he was straight out of the cage, and you never knew what your strength was in that five minutes, and instead of banging into the wall like he'd wanted them to, the security officer smashed into it sideways. He swung away too slowly to avoid a spray of blood across his face. It froze him. He couldn't look. He would only have had to turn his head another inch to the left, but the bones in his neck wouldn't move, and a childish voice in the back of his mind said that if he didn't look it wasn't real yet, it couldn't be, you couldn't do a thing like that by accident, you couldn't.

On the floor, by his shoes, there were three teeth.

The door was half open. Gale came through it slowly, and didn't flinch. Instead, they picked up the security officer's gun, mimed to January to cover his ears, and then fired straight down into the body. He swung away so he wouldn't see, but he knew what had happened.

Evidence obliterated. It would look like a terrible gunshot wound now, instead of—instead of.

Gale turned the gun around in their own hands and pressed down hard on the barrel. He didn't understand, and then did: they were making it look like they'd taken the gun off the officer while the officer was aiming it at them. Fingerprints all in the right place. That was how you did it, wasn't it, you snatched the barrel and twisted it sideways and hoped to God you didn't get a bullet in the stomach on the way? He had no idea.

"Is that your blood?"

He still couldn't look.

"January," Gale said, very soft. They brushed his cheek. It was a powerful enough thing to snap him back into himself, more or less. Very lightly, they tilted him away from the body, and that just kissed his ribs against theirs. He turned to stone, terrified he was going to hurt them if he breathed, even while his heart swelled painfully with knowing that they didn't think he would.

"Yes," he heard his own voice say. "Um—I—some of it is."

"That's a gunshot wound."

"I can't feel anything."

"Shock," Gale agreed. They sounded level, but they looked worried. "That's going to wear off in about half an hour—"

"We need to go," he said, coming back to himself. "Jesus. It's *nuts* down there. The praetorians started shooting, people are out of their cages, and there's someone who's—"

"*This is the praetorian service,*" a voice said across the house tannoy. "*All Earthstrongers must report to the third floor immediately, wearing a cage. Any Earthstronger not wearing a cage will be shot. The exits are all blocked. Do not try to leave the building.*"

"Chapter Four of How to Do a Massacre," Gale snapped, more angry than January had ever seen them. "We have to get everyone out. Listen— funny question—say you fell out of a car at about forty miles an hour here. Would you survive it?"

"Sure," January said, not following at all but too shocked and too numb to do anything except answer the question. If Gale had asked him if he liked fish just then, he probably wouldn't have questioned why at all, he would probably have said, *Yes, I really like looking at tropical ones but I don't like eating any.* "I'd just sort of bounce. What—why?"

"The tower is five hundred feet high."

January took a breath to say *Say that again,* then understood. "Yes. Good idea." He didn't say that, his voice did. He'd heard the phrase before, *to be beside yourself,* but he hadn't ever understood how literal it was. He *was* beside himself. He felt like he was a few feet away, feeling his body do things of its own accord but without any instructions from the part of him that was him.

"Get on the tannoy," Gale said.

"Me?"

"Yes. No one's going to do anything I say, they just saw me arrested for murder."

"What about you, is forty miles an hour . . . ?"

Gale shook their head. "I'll find another way, I'll meet you at the big warehouse, where they keep all the heavy-weather gear."

"Um . . . have the doors open, and the lights on, so people can see where to go. It's cold out there," January said. He still couldn't quite fit himself back into all his true angles and edges. He was nearer than before, but he was sort of stuffed in, like when you hadn't put a glove on properly. Bits of him still didn't feel like they belonged. When he looked down at his hands, they didn't seem like hands but bizarre monster spider things. "I don't know how long everyone can survive without gear—maybe ten minutes?"

"I will."

He finally got himself to fit just about right, and thinking was easier. "The second I say that people should go up to the tower, all the praetorians are going to follow."

Gale nodded. "But it's hard to get a clear shot on the stairs, and if they want to keep people on the ground floor exits, they can't send many. There are only thirty of them or so in all."

"Are you going to be okay?"

"If I'm not, you're House Gale. Get the solar array into the atmosphere."

January stared at them. He had no idea what was happening any more and no idea what to think, except that there was someone *invisible* in the house doing God knew what and why, and all he could really understand just now was that Gale—who an hour ago he had been sure was a murderer—had faked a homicide to protect him.

"I will. Be . . ." He had been going to say careful, but Gale was always careful. "Be fast."

Gale gripped his hand, brief but hard. "And you."

January touched the intercom and took a deep breath. Gale glanced up and down the corridor, and then vanished around the corner. Despite everything, despite not knowing how to fit it all together, he found himself praying that it wouldn't be the last time he saw them.

46

The second after his message went onto the tannoy, the praetorians cut the power. No more talking to anyone; no more lights; no more heat; and no elevators. Too late though. People were already running up the stairs, Earthstrong people without cages, at least a hundred of them. It was a sprint up the tower, stronger people stopping on the landings to shepherd the frailer ones past. January, a broad Canadian blacksmith, and three women who had used to be triathletes at home went the whole way carrying the littlest children. Behind them, there were praetorians with guns, but exactly like Gale had said, not many, and they never had a good shot, though they tried. Without cages it was easy enough to outpace them, but not by as far as January would have liked. He had a nasty feeling that the strength differential between a consular praetorian and an older Earthstronger was much less than anyone thought. There was an elderly man who was only here because he depended on his son to look after him. The son was carrying him over one shoulder. Maybe a bit delirious now, January caught himself thinking he'd like to see what sort of polar bear that poor old man was equivalent to. Maybe an asthmatic cub.

"What are we even doing?" the Canadian blacksmith whispered. It was unbelievably dark; no moonlight got through the dust, no borrowed glow from the halogens that usually lit up the security perimeter around the house. Trying not to give the praetorians a target, nobody was even carrying a lighter or a torch. The only blips came from the emergency glow-in-the-dark stripes along the edges of the floor, and from the red wire-lines of the praetorians' gun sights, flicking a few floors below. "Is there a way down from up here—is there a helicopter?"

"No," January said. "We have to jump."

"*What?*"

They were at the top of the last staircase. The windows of the tower room were just high enough to catch the glimmer of the lights on the rig, from the welding torches. The night shift were still working.

What if people refused to do it?

He could try being very straightforward and calm. That worked.

Or, a fevered voice in his head clarified, *it worked if you were Aubrey Gale; if you looked like the emperor of somewhere and it was basically unthinkable to disobey.*

If you were just a January, it seemed a lot less likely.

Grandmother strength, that was what this required. He didn't have it.

He jumped when a message flared in his glasses. It was from Gale.

Livestream your feed. The news services need to see what people are being forced to do.

Right; right.

Way down the tower, perhaps even from the ground floor, someone was yelling in Mandarin to get the internet shut off. Someone else—who sounded a lot like Dr Molotov—was yelling back that it wasn't that simple, there were laws to prevent that if there was sufficient power to maintain the servers, and you had to get consent from Lao Zi, the AI who oversaw those servers, and Zi was emphatically *not* going to turn them off just for a politician's convenience. Their voices carried all the way up, pin-sharp.

"Then shut down Lao Zi!"

"You realize they can *hear* you!" Molotov shouted. "You'll be lucky if they don't lock you in a freezer! They have coding that allows for self-defence, you lunatic!"

January flicked his eyes into the corner of his right lens, opened a random Songshu social media account, he didn't even know which one, and started to film.

"Okay; break the windows," he said briskly, doing his best impression of Val. Val didn't look like the emperor of anywhere, but everyone always did what she said. "We're going to jump. We can survive a fall at terminal velocity here. It'll be a bang when we hit the ground, but not enough to break bones. The praetorians can't follow us. When you get to the ground, run for the warehouse; there'll be heavy-weather gear waiting for us. It's going to be really cold, but it won't be for long."

"Are you *sure* about this?" the young man with the elderly father said, gone shrill.

He kicked out the nearest window. He felt as though he'd barely touched it before the glass shattered and rained outward incredibly, delicately slowly. "It's this or get shot. I'm sorry, but we *have* to go."

Glass broke everywhere as people smashed through the windows. The wind and the dust and the cold poured in.

"Anyone in a cage, get out of it now," January said, having to call louder over the whistling. "You don't want to hit the ground still wearing one."

The last few closed cages shushed open, and people ringed the edge, hair spinning in the wind and clothes snapping. Instantly it was freezing, in the way that didn't just feel uncomfortable, but dangerous.

January looked back at the door. He could hear the praetorians on the stairs now. They would have heard the glass breaking.

Someone tugged his sleeve. He looked round, found no one, then looked down. It was Yuan. There was no sign of his mother.

From so high, he could see the mammoth roads in the forest. They went single file and threaded slim ways through the pines. Beyond them, the colossal skeleton of the rig stretched way into the sky.

Right across from him, the titan trees sighed.

He scooped Yuan up and let himself fall.

The tower was perhaps five hundred feet high. On Earth, it would have taken about six seconds, and he would have fallen at close to a hundred and forty miles per hour. But here, it felt like flying, and it felt like years in the air. There was time to be scared and then time left over to see that there was no need to be, and time still after that to feel like there was nothing else in the world but the air and the dust and the trees.

Even falling so slowly, the ground rushed up and smacked him hard. He rolled a few yards, trying to cushion Yuan, though he wasn't sure he was a very good cushion, and he was glad it was grass and not concrete. He skinned his knuckles and knocked chips out of his elbows and knees all the same. Around him, the ground juddered as the others hit it too. He saw one person break their ankle, but others stood up nearly straightaway. He hoped adrenaline wasn't masking a chest full of broken ribs and punctured lungs. No; no. He could breathe.

He looked up in time to see the last few people falling. They were points of light; because, he realized, they were filming the fall.

"Are you okay?" he asked Yuan, who was so tiny and so fragile it seemed impossible, but he uncurled and sat up in January's arms.

"Can we do it again?" Yuan asked joyfully.

January laughed a horrible not-laugh. "Maybe later, tiny bear."

He waited for the last people before he started running for the warehouse, but even in that time, the blood on his shirt had frozen. A bullet smacked into the grass next to him.

"The praetorians are shooting at us," he said, for the footage in his lenses. "We've got—ten kids with us, and six or seven old people who can't run fast. Uh—I don't feel too good, I've been shot . . . we're trying to get to the warehouse where the cold weather gear is, it feels a lot further away than it did yesterday." He had to slow down and stop talking, because his lungs hurt. The cold was too much. He'd read somewhere that in temperatures like this, you lacerated all the tissue inside your lungs and coughed them up after about five minutes if you were lucky. His shoulder was throbbing now.

He set Yuan down. "Run. Over there, to the light."

"What about you?"

"I'm right behind you. Go, go . . ."

Yuan didn't go. He was too little. He hovered anxiously, even though he had no coat and the cold was razoring.

Stars burst greenish over January's vision. At first he thought they were real lights somewhere up ahead, but then realized what was happening. He'd been running too fast and losing too much blood and not getting enough oxygen. You got blurry vision then, didn't you? And then . . .

He went down hard on his hands and knees. It jarred his shoulder, and slowly, he understood that he couldn't get up again. He coughed. The dust was getting into the back of his throat. It felt like it was making cement in his insides. He wanted to think he just needed to rest for a few seconds and then he could try again, but he could feel that wouldn't work. If he didn't get up now, he wouldn't get up.

"Jan, January . . ." Yuan was patting his shoulder.

He couldn't talk. He was going to be the death of a toddler because he couldn't *stand up* . . .

That had happened, part of his brain complained, stupidly quickly. He'd always thought he'd get more warning. Ten minutes ago he'd been fine and now he was dying. He blinked hard, trying to clear the green spots and get a message to Gale, but he couldn't see the letters inside his lenses any more.

Someone knelt down beside him and fitted an oxygen mask over his face. The green stars faded, and he could move again.

"Not much further," Gale said, and lifted him upright. They were already holding Yuan.

He'd never known what it felt like before to be willing to die for someone, but he would have done it now; if a praetorian had come out of nowhere, he would have stood in front of the bullet, even if it only bought Gale another couple of seconds. As Gale got one arm around him to help him along over the frozen ground, he had another of those out-of-body moments where he might have been looking at the three of them from above somewhere, and an entirely objective, detached part of him said: *Well, that's it then. You're just going to have to be in love with Aubrey Gale now, for better or—and this seems a lot more likely—worse.*

There were lights inside the warehouse, but dim; just lamps. The power was out here too. It was full of people, Earthstrongers—and Natural people. January jolted back without meaning to, vision still hazy and mind still sure that Natural must mean a gun, but Gale caught him.

"It's okay. They're just getting gear together."

They were. They were passing out backpacks with emergency supplies, and helping people into heat suits. Gale eased January down onto the edge of a crate near Dr Okonkwo, who winced at the gunshot wound and started to peel back the frozen bits of January's shirt to see. Gale tucked Yuan into a heat blanket.

Sasha was there.

"I will take that off you," Gale said to them when Sasha touched their gun.

"Do you realize what he did? He started all this, he called the Consul—"

"All right, hao de," Gale said, the mix of English and Mandarin the softest thing they could possibly have used, but Sasha backed down like Gale had slapped them. "We need to get into the forest, it'll be harder for them find us, and then we need to follow the railway."

"The railway—"

"Yes, we need to get down to Tharsis and somewhere safe. Maybe the naturalisation centre."

Sasha gave January one last homicidal look and prowled away.

Dr Okonkwo had got the bullet out, but January still felt hazy and strange. He wasn't sure he was going to make it so far as the railway, never mind Tharsis. It took him a moment to notice that Gale was watching him, plainly thinking the same thing.

"Leave me here," he said.

"Shut up," Gale told him.

"He's not going to be able to go far," Dr Okonkwo said quietly.

"We'll go as far as we can," Gale said. "I've got camping gear."

January swallowed hard and tried not to think what he was dreading more: the idea of slogging twenty miles to the Valley edge like this, or sitting in a tent in this weather. There was no use saying it, though, so he let Gale pull him upright, and zipped himself into the heat suit.

———

People scattered into the forest, following the mammoth roads. Sasha's officers were waiting at forks in the paths to keep directing people onward towards the broken railway, and it was just as well, because the darkness under the trees was deep. The dust was like brown smog even in the day, but at night, lamps barely did anything but show the patterns of the wind. The ground was thick with it even under the densest parts of the canopy, and their boots left deep, clear prints that started to wisp away as soon as they were made. That was good, at least. It would be impossible to follow them.

January couldn't decide if he kept hearing gunfire behind them, or if it was only the rattle of the trees way above. When he looked back, there was nothing behind them but the dark.

Dr Okonkwo had given him some anaesthetic and it was good, but he felt a lot like those dust-prints must have. Like the wind was hazing him away.

Sasha stuck close; so did Mx Francis and Mx Ren, and Drs Okonkwo and Molotov. January still hadn't seen Yuan's mother, so they had him too. Yuan was curled up in Gale's arms; he'd run out of steam all at once, while he was being wrapped up against the cold. January was worried about him. There were no toddler-sized heat suits, so he was tucked into Gale's sealskin jacket, with a blanket over that. And January was worried about Gale too. They were bloody fit—Sasha enforced a serious regime in the gym, January had seen that more than often enough—but fit wasn't the same as able to walk for twenty miles on a prosthesis that had only been fitted a few months ago. They wouldn't be able to walk on it for even half as long as it would take to reach Tharsis. He kept looking round and hoping to find a horse to snag, but even if a horse had passed within ten feet of them and stopped obligingly, fully saddled, he wouldn't have seen it.

He was about to say something when everyone else collapsed. They went down like marionettes whose puppeteer had just been called down to dinner. He yelped and managed, just, to catch Gale and Yuan before the two of them could hit the ground, then choked when it shot agony up his shoulder. He had to lever Gale down into the dust and the grass.

Yuan scrambled away, confused. January pulled him close, terrified of losing him in the dark, or of letting him get too cold again.

"What's happening!"

"I think it's the internet," he said, trying to make his voice come smooth and calm. "I think they've cut the internet so we can't keep broadcasting. Can you be super grown up for me and see if you can wake Dr Molotov up? They'll be really confused at first, so you have to explain that it was internet, all right?"

"Right," Yuan said firmly.

January didn't dare touch Gale. He wasn't wearing a cage and he hadn't done any of the exercises, and the thought of touching them made him hear the snicker of bones breaking and teeth skittering on the floor. "Aubrey," he said, close to them. He wanted to hold their neck and check for a pulse, because he couldn't see them breathing, at all; his fingers ached with it. "Aubrey, can you hear me?"

Gale breathed deeper, then sat up fast. "Suffering *Christ*."

Feverishly, January thought: *I say that. They're learning to swear in English from me.*

"What the hell was that?" Mx Francis managed, levering themselves up on both hands. "There's power from the gravity trains, why's the internet . . ."

January wanted to say it was the praetorians, but he couldn't gather up the words in time.

"That was the Consul," Gale said grimly. "They don't want any more footage getting out of their praetorians firing at people who are running away."

"Surely that screws up their own people?" January asked, horribly aware that they were all prone here in the howling cold.

"Soldiers train without internet. Hold that," Gale added, and gave him a loop of cord that was attached to something he couldn't make out. They walked backwards with it, unspooling the string and kicking old branches and gorse out of the way to make a clear space.

It was a tent. It didn't start out looking like a tent. It had fitted into a bag the size of a jam jar, but once Gale shook it out, it snapped into a tent shape, tall enough for January to stand in. Then you pulled the string, and there was a hiss, and it sealed to the ground, and January jumped, because it glowed inside. Gale held the flap open and saw him in; without discussion, the others came too. Incredibly, when January took off his dust mask, it was warm. He must have looked bewildered, because Gale pointed to a webbing built into the ground sheet that seemed to be glowing.

"Heat silk. The filament should be good for twelve hours." They breathed out slowly. "I'll be back in a second. I'm just going to see if I can find any of Sasha's officers. They're all separated out."

"I can—" January started.

"Stay where you are or I'll tie you to a tree," Gale said, and lobbed two more tents in their tiny packages to Sasha and Mx Ren.

So January, Yuan, Sasha, Dr Molotov, Dr Okonkwo, Mx Francis, and Mx Ren waited in miserable silence. Mx Francis was suffering the most. They were shaking and breathing too hard. Mx Ren looked ill. Dr Okonkwo seemed best off out of all them, and January wondered if that might be because they were the oldest; they must have been around for a good while before haptics were invented, or at least, before they were widespread. January kept both hands pressed flat to the ground sheet. It was hot. Yuan was flat on his front, soaking in the heat.

"Is this really happening?" Dr Molotov said finally. "Is the Consul really using an Earthstrong riot as cover to—to *assassinate* the Senator?"

"I guess it makes sense," Dr Okonkwo murmured. "The fleet is still two weeks away and against all expectations, we have enough power to finish the solar tower. Nobody could have foreseen that we'd get *mammoths* to raise the gravity trains. The Senator's going to win the election at this rate. They'll turn those ships around, or send them into the desert." They frowned. "Insane timing about Max really. Exactly when it would have . . . maximum impact."

Sasha shot January a black look. "Anyone would think it was on purpose."

"I didn't find the body on purpose just to screw up your campaign, Martinez," January said, and then had to put one hand over his shoulder, because despite the anaesthetic, it was hurting now. Beside him, Yuan settled down with his head on January's knee.

"Only it's funny how great it was for the Consul, just at that moment."

January had, suddenly and completely, had enough of trying to make himself little and obliging. "Okay, dickhead, so if you were married to someone whose last consort had vanished and whose excuses about it were all about as clear as a swamp, would you definitely trust that all was well and of course you shouldn't call the police when you found the sodding body?"

"Speak Mandarin, no one can understand you."

Dr Okonkwo sighed. "He said—"

"I know what he fucking said," Sasha snapped.

"Where's Kasha?" Yuan asked January, sounding scared he wasn't supposed to talk.

"I don't know, but she's a really smart dog, she'll be okay."

"Can you two not swear in front of the toddler?" Dr Molotov said at the same time, voice high.

Gale pushed the tent flap open. They were alone, and they looked defeated. Either they hadn't found anyone else, or they had and they hadn't been able to wake anyone. "All right, enough. Enough."

They all went quiet. It was like having the teacher back in the room.

"Sasha, it isn't his fault. He's right, he would have been demented to trust me. January . . ."

"Don't, Senator," Sasha said, very soft.

Gale brushed their shoulder and Sasha looked away. "January. You said—rightly—that the reason you didn't trust me is that I didn't ask if you'd found River. But I didn't need to. Because *I am* River."

"I'm too tired for weird Tharsese jokes," January said. "You're all super funny, ha ha, now tell me what's actually happening and stop taking the piss."

But Gale was giving him an anxious uncertain look, one that said they didn't know what else to tell him, and little by little, it settled on him that this wasn't a joke at all.

"Explain," was all he had it left in him to say.

47

The trouble with running around after mammoths with a halo and lots of recording equipment was that the mammoths found this very peculiar. Now that the dictionary was finally pulling together, River had confirmed a long-standing suspicion about all the recordings of the university's databases: they were mostly pachyderm conversations about what the funny little ape things were doing and whether perhaps they needed some sort of help.

There were ways to splice together recordings and come up with the Mammoth approximation of, *please would you talk to each other normally because I'd really like to eavesdrop for my research paper*, but after years of trying it, River wasn't convinced that mammoths always recognised Mammoth when it coming from one of the funny ape things with the speakers. They saw it in the way people saw parrots mimicking them. If it occasionally came out with something coherent, then the sensible mammoth wrote that off as a fluke. And that was before you had to try and explain what a research paper was, or what writing was, or why you liked to do it.

This herd, though, was used to its funny ape thing. They understood about research papers.[34] Except for the calves. If River stayed for long, they wanted to play football.

---

34 River had overheard one of them explaining it to her friends. Human writing, she said, was footprint marks that made talking sounds. Humans could discuss things with their special footprint marks, and that meant they could talk to each other over big gaps in time, as well as

"No, but the thing is," River said to the baby mammoth who was, right now, stealing the halo and holding it up, knowing very well it was out of reach, "this is important, because the Penglai mission is going to reach Alpha Centauri in three years, and you are our only realistic dry run at learning to talk to aliens before we actually have to. I know I look silly, but I mean it. People on Earth are trying this with elephants, but between you and me, you have bigger vocal ranges and you're less primed to gore people. So—no pressure at all, but—look, you can have a pine cone if you give it back."

The calf abandoned the halo and rooted through River's bag. Not far away, his mother made a deep amused rumble that was impossible to really hear, but thrummed up through the ground. It was such a wonderful noise. She was almost half as tall as the sequoia next to her; fifty feet away, River was still in her shadow, deep and cold. The calf's father, a bull who had uncharacteristically stayed with the herd rather than wandering off alone the way they usually did, had sat down not far away, clearly watching and enjoying himself. He had a gigantic stack of pine cones next to him. The whole herd had gathered them up and were snacking on them, very much, River was beginning to suspect, like humans ate popcorn.

"There's no football in there, you unholy terror."

The calf was very sure that there was, upturned the pack, and then triumphantly nudged the deflated beach ball over in River's direction. He honked in a way that very clearly meant, *Do the thing, do the thing.*

"I hate children," River told him.

"Moo," said the calf, unmoved.

There was a gunshot.

In the forest, it was a strangely unobtrusive noise. River swung around. The only reason to shoot out here was if there was a polar bear inside the perimeter.

---

big distances. It was like saying something today, and somebody hearing it next week. That was why several of the mammoths were convinced humans were time-travellers. River had tried to explain that they definitely couldn't time-travel, but the mammoths had said, *Well, but you can talk to someone a hundred years in the future, right,* and River had said, *Yes I suppose,* and the mammoths had gone off satisfied with a point properly proven, and River had had to stand there having an existential crisis.

No more shots. Either the bear was dead, or the person was.

River snatched up their own rifle. The baby mammoth prodded them in the back, interrogative.

"I'll be back," River promised. They were pretty sure the mammoths understood what that meant, even without speakers and a halo. The calf looked put out all the same.

The Songshu pine forest was the only place on Mars that had mist. Usually River was pleased about that, because it was a tiny link to Earth and the things everyone had left behind, but today, they would have given a kingdom for a clear desert morning. Instead, the vapour clung in rags among the great pines, and the ground was spongy and scattered about with tiny streams. Wonderful news for the ecosystem people working out of the Songshu greenhouses; less so if you were trying to find someone who was being eaten by a bear.

"Hello?" River shouted. "Anyone here?"

Someone smacked into them sideways, full of panic, and the two of them went down with a thump on the pine-needly ground.

"River! River, I've—I think—Max—"

"Aubrey! Are you hurt, where's the bear—"

"What bear?" Aubrey asked, voice wisping.

"I heard a shot, I—are you drunk?" River demanded, because they looked wrong, starry.

"No; no." Aubrey was staring at them. "No bear. I've . . ."

River frowned, because never once had they seen Aubrey incoherent. Aubrey was glamorous, confident, erudite, addicted to things River hadn't even heard of, but never lost for words. "Aubrey. Are you okay?"

Aubrey shook their head slightly. "I think someone's taken Max."

"What? Have you called security? We need to—"

"No, but I'm not sure, there's mist, can you—there was a gunshot, and then I couldn't find them, but there's blood, River, we—"

"Sasha needs to know even if you're not sure, it's a lot better to be wrong and embarrassed than right and letting someone get further and further away," River said, smacking the circuitry tattoo on the inside of their wrist. It was an emergency tracker, and a distress beacon, and plenty of other things. The insides of their lenses lit up with red, and immediately Sasha's voice came through the aural implants, too quiet for anyone else to hear.

River—what's happening?

"We think Max is missing, we need people to come out here and start looking. Aubrey heard a shot but there's fog."

We're coming.

It was just a flicker, but River thought there was something annoyed in Aubrey's expression; like River wasn't doing what they were supposed to do, even though they were, even though everyone in Great Houses did endless drills and training for this kind of thing, and even though it wouldn't have been the first time someone got into the grounds and tried to kidnap one of them. A furious ex-employee (there were plenty; Kali wasn't known for generous pensions and reasonable severance deals) had got in last year and snatched River at knifepoint not that far from here.

Not right, River's Aubrey-is-lying-to-me radar said, *not right*.

But what Aubrey said was, "Come on, help me look."

They took River's hand and led the way up a steep bank of roots, to a patch of open ground where ten or twelve confused llamas were standing around, looking at a lot of blood on the ground. It was already freezing to the grass. River swallowed hard. You couldn't lose that much blood and still be alive. It was everywhere.

It was on Aubrey too.

"Were you—close by?" River asked, trying to look at them more closely, but Aubrey was wearing black and it was impossible to tell. It was under their fingernails, and on the side of their neck.

"I fell over here," Aubrey said, and wrung their hands together. There was something actorly about it. They never usually moved their hands when they spoke. But then, it wasn't as though they usually had to talk over pints and pints of blood on the ground. "Come on, maybe we can find something in the mirrors . . ."

They were right at the edge of one of the sun fields. River had gotten turned around; they hadn't realized they were so far from the house.

The air was warmer here, as it always was in the fields, even on a drab day. It was why the mist was so much denser. Vanishing into the grey in either direction were ranks and ranks of solar mirrors, and way up in the air was a blinking amber light that marked the top of the salt tower for aircraft. It was an eerie, uncanny place, and River had a powerful instinct not to go in among the mirrors.

It would be very easy for someone to hide in there and shoot.

There was no blood trail. Whoever had done it was strong enough to lift a body and walk with it.

"Where were you, what did you see?" River asked.

"Nothing! Come on—"

"Hang on, hang on," River said, annoyed with themselves. Aubrey was scared: they wouldn't remember if they'd seen anything important. "Sorry. I've got a halo here. You might not know if you saw something, but it'll be on the scan if we can hook you up right away, while your memory's still clear. If you put it on—"

"I don't want to mess around with a halo, we just need to—"

"No, Aubrey, this is what Sasha will do in a second, come on, it's right here!"

Aubrey went quiet. Something in their face closed down, and went from urgent to . . . calculating.

River wanted to be horrified, but they just weren't.

Very slowly, with a feeling like egg fresh out of a fridge trickling down the back of their skull, came the understanding that there was nobody hiding in the mirrors.

Aubrey was more than strong enough to lift someone their own size.

Just too late, River realized they hadn't quite got control over their own face in time, and they saw Aubrey see exactly what was going through their mind.

It looked absolutely automatic. River didn't think it was even properly malicious. It was just a wild need to stop a problem. But it was a shock when Aubrey slammed the butt of the rifle right into River's chest. They fell over backwards and just for a second as their hands skidded through the grass, they were five years old again and trying to work out how to do cartwheels. They had to sit very still. It hurt, but that wasn't what was paralysing: Aubrey had never hit them before. Actually, no one had. They'd never been in a fight. More than the chance that Aubrey had killed someone, the understanding that there was no going back smacked into River. Something fissured right in the bedrock of their soul, something deeper down than they'd known they went.

A tiny child-voice in them said: *But if I haven't got Aubrey, then I haven't got anyone.*

Something similar must have shifted in Aubrey too, because instant regret flashed across their face.

"I'm sorry!" Aubrey gasped. "I'm sorry, I'm sorry, I didn't mean to do that!"

River looked up at them, and found themselves reflecting with a mad sort of calm that what you think you mean and what you mean can be very different things.

"Please don't look at me like that. Come on." Aubrey helped them up. "Are you okay?"

"I'm—yes, I'm fine." Grass stains on their elbows, just like being little again.

Aubrey pressed both hands over their eyes. "I don't know what happened. But I can't take a halo. I'm not—I'm not going to prison."

They sounded wild. Wild in the way of an animal that knew a hunter was after it, the kind of wild that would see a vixen attack a bear if it cornered her with her cubs, even though there was no possible way a vixen could win a fight with a polar bear. River had never seen it, but the mammoths said it happened more often than you'd think. It was a mammoth saying. When they said *vixen-and-the-bear*, they meant *really frightened people will hurt you if you give them no other choice, even if you're stronger.*

A very heavy thought dropped into River's head. It was that they'd dropped their rifle when they fell.

"Aubrey," River said softly. "If you turn yourself in—if you accept the sentence, you'll be out in half the time you're given, and it will be less if they find something went wrong in your head when—"

"Do you know what happens on prison hulks?" Aubrey demanded, and River took a step back without meaning to, and that scared them.

They'd never retreated from another person before. "If the prison company runs out of money, they just steer the ship too close to Jupiter's gravity and whoops, we all die of heart failure! Or they stop the air supply, or they let rations go down so badly the prisoners have to mutiny and then they're all shot on sight. And no one cares, because Tharsis doesn't have the resources to run a proper system. We all understand that prison means you live if you're lucky but otherwise it's execution in disguise, come on, I've been talking about this in the Senate for *years*, have you even listened to one debate?"

River had not. Aubrey had pet projects that were easy to talk about because you *had* to attend the Senate and you *had* to table a certain number of ideas per year if you represented a Great House. They had never once taken on anything that was difficult, or complicated, and they'd never got anything done either. Aubrey talked about the prison ships because it was an obvious problem, but they never pushed anyone to solve it, because then they'd have to come up with something new next time. So River never paid any attention. It was hard to cheer someone on when you knew they were being deliberately mediocre.

But they were right, about the prison hulks.

River's throat had turned into sandpaper. They were two miles from the house. It was at least a few more minutes before Sasha and the security people could arrive, and—oh, God, if Aubrey had managed to hide a body in the time between the gunshot and River arriving, they could definitely hide another one before Sasha got here. It was a crazy thought, it was insane to imagine being shot by your own Apollo, and yet; and yet, it was somehow not in any way surprising, it was somehow established in River's mind already, that maybe it would be like this one day.

"It was an accident," Aubrey said.

"I believe you," River lied. "I just don't know what to do. Someone's going to put a halo on you today."

They two of them stood staring at each other in silence, and in that silence, horribly, the internet glitched. It sometimes did, around the sun fields; it was the fog or the heat or something, River wasn't sure, but all their haptics shut off. The gentle, crowding shush of the rest of world vanished—the contented tides of the stock markets, the little bubble of joy that was coming from a high school where a movie star was visiting, the spikes of tension coming from the Senate, the strange void that was Americatown because nobody there had implants—and for a nasty second it was like going deaf.

And, in front of them, they caught a snatch of Aubrey's face; their real face. They looked very different. River hadn't seen them truly since the two of them were tiny. They had a broken nose that the filters corrected—when had that happened, why had they never said?—and a bolt of grey through their hair, and different teeth. Seeing that felt horribly like spying on them in the shower. That face, their natural face, was private.

River's own filters must have gone off too. They didn't use many, but there were some because, even for an academic, not wearing them looked somewhere between lazy and ill. Aubrey glanced away just the same as they had.

And then, right there, extraordinary but entirely simple, was the solution, and River had to stare at it to make sure that it didn't have any unexpected faults or fissures, but they stress-tested much bigger ideas for a living at the university and they could already see that however bizarre, this one was strong. Sometimes things really were simple. Sometimes your whole life was different because at exactly the right—wrong?—moment, you said five words.

Every day after, for a long time, River stared at the future that might have happened if they'd said nothing. There was pretty good visibility. What was there, was something that might be a fairy tale people on Earth told their kids a thousand years from now.

Once upon a time, there was a city. It was very rich, the richest city in the worlds, and beautiful, and emperors from far away were desperate to take it over.

The emperors promised to pay a universe of money to whoever could deliver it. In charge of the city was a wily general. Perhaps they wanted all that money, or perhaps they just really liked the emperors. In any case, they plotted and planned, but nothing came of it, because the city was too far from the emperors, and too strong.

Then one day, a foolish prince killed someone. Maybe it was an accident, maybe it wasn't; but that poor murdered person was from the wily general's family, and all at once, the wily general understood what to do.

The general promised to protect the foolish prince—*if* the prince gave the general their palace. At that palace, there were fields that harvested sunlight, and made power for the whole city. Now it belonged to the general.

The general sold it to the emperors.

Delighted, the emperors shut down the sun fields. Now, the city—which was in a very cold, frightening place—would freeze and starve unless *they* sent it fuel.

The taxes rose and rose, and more and more people from the emperors' country poured in, and the emperors put them in charge. The people who had lived there before either had to leave and go into the desert, or try to scrape by under new, unfair ways, getting poorer and poorer, and dying, until there were none left at all.

And that's how one foolish prince brought down a city.

"Halos don't work on me," River said.

Or was it, a little voice always asked, really because that joke Kali always made about you was true: you were born in the year of the dragon, but you spend your whole life trying to be a rabbit? Was it because after staying always hunched down and pretending to be little and fluffy, sweet harmless dorky River who'll never leave the university and never bothers anyone, you had to straighten up one day, and incinerate everything in front of you, not because it was right but because you wanted to see if you could?

"That doesn't do me any good!"

"No one knows what we look like. We both wear filters. All we have to do is swap."

Aubrey stared at them, and then half laughed. "You're right. Just until the police go away?"

"Right. And—Aubrey—will you promise to check into a treatment programme? You can't just kill someone and go back to your life—"

"No, no, I know. Of course I will. Of course."

That was a lie.

"What are we going to say has happened to you, meanwhile?" Aubrey said. They were looking earnest and deferential, which was also a lie.

River had to look at the ground. They couldn't look at Aubrey. If they looked at Aubrey, they'd believe it all. "Why don't we say that Max and I ran off together? Then no one's looking for me."

"That's good! How do we bring me back afterward?"

"I . . . don't know, we'll come up with something."

River tried to feel around inside their own soul, to see if there was enough iron in it to do—not the right thing, because they couldn't tell what right was, but maybe the just thing. They could see what was going to happen if not. Aubrey would refuse to go anywhere or change anything, and River would let them because they remembered being toddlers together, and then there would be another consort, and more rows, and more blaming everyone else, and perhaps one day there would be another body. And then that wouldn't be Aubrey's fault; that would be River's, because that was the law too. If you saw a murder happening and you did nothing, you were also guilty.

River could already see it, years away.

Not for the first time, they wondered bleakly if there was any true way to be clever and innocent at the same time.

"Should I show you where the—"

"No!" River half shouted. "I'm sorry. No. Halos—don't work on me *completely*, but something that . . . that serious would show up. I can't hide it if I've seen a body." They swallowed. "Just . . . just make sure it isn't where anyone can fall over it." *Ideally*, said part of their mind that was somehow fine with covering up a murder, *have it incinerated, don't leave it out here as evidence*, but there was no way they could set fire to anything without the security drones seeing it. The only reason any of this was viable at all was the fog.

Max deserved a lot better than an unmarked grave out in the Songshu woods. Most military people River had ever come across were dismissive of anyone who couldn't strip a rifle blindfolded, but Max had an inexhaustible courtesy, even when faced with an irritating university tweed-person. They had actually asked how the mammoth dictionary was going.

"I love you," Aubrey said suddenly, and hugged River hard.

They only ever said it these last few years when River did something useful. In a sensible world, River would have pointed that out and refused to have anything more to do with them, and maybe it would have been enough of a jolt to change the way Aubrey lived, maybe Max would be all right in that world, but River wasn't sensible in that way. Every so often, there was a flash of Aubrey-before-the-Senate, the old Aubrey who baked cakes at weekends and joked and who would sprawl on the floor with the dogs, and who squeaked unexpectedly and leapt onto haystacks. They were still in there somewhere, and River had never stopped hoping they'd come out again. Sometimes even now there were flashes—aurora flares, never for long, but bright and wonderful and worth the snarling and the temper.

Or, they'd always told themselves so.

"I love you too," River said into Aubrey's collar.

They agreed to give it a month, and Aubrey left for that month. They said they were going to a rehab centre, but River knew, because one of the security people followed, that they went to the Tiangong, enjoying their new filterless anonymity, and drank a lot.

It was painfully straightforward, pretending to be Aubrey. Aubrey handed over access to all their accounts, so River wore their filters, and they did look a little different over different bones, but politicians looked a little different all the time as trends shifted. River reported Max missing. Because it's always the consort, Sasha and then the police did indeed arrive with the halo test, and after puzzling over the bizarre readout for a little while, determined that no, however much River's mind writhed, they couldn't have killed anyone.

There were three mandatory Senate sittings in that month. River went to all of them, and sat silent in the first one, listening, heart thumping and waiting for someone who knew Aubrey well enough to say, *Hey, hang on a second, you're not the right person, I'm calling security*, but nobody did. Slowly, River realized that Aubrey knew other senators to nod to, but not really to have a conversation with. They weren't interested enough.

So before the second session, swearing inwardly that this was the test, and if this went wrong then it was over, River spent a few days canvassing law-and-order candidates, and having tea with people at beautiful clubs and saying simple things like, *We only need to shift a few million and lift the tax on air storage in shipping, and this prison hulk stupidness is done.*

Every time they met someone, it was with knots in their insides. Because Aubrey wasn't an idiot at all, Aubrey had been scholar before all this, and been lovely at it—and surely, surely it had to be more difficult to get things done than just charming some influential people. But one by one, the other senators sat back and said, okay.

"You know I really thought you just tabled this year on year so that the Regulatory Committee couldn't complain you weren't engaging properly," the Speaker said, creaking forward interestedly in the leather armchair. "But you actually want to get this done, don't you?"

"I do. It's a straightforward thing, why not?"

"Why not indeed." The Speaker watched them for a second. "Tell me what you think about this, I'm supposed to be tabling it soon. America and China are still issuing extradition orders on public figures they dislike. Our statehood is unrecognised on Earth, and so as you will have seen in the news, people are being arrested from ships in international deep space on the Crossing, and if they're naturalised, getting to Earth's orbit is immediately fatal. What would you do to stop that?"

"Doesn't the Refugee Act serve?"

"Sorry?"

"I'm not a lawyer, but doesn't the Act make it illegal to deport a refugee to a place where they would face physical persecution? Earth's gravity is physical persecution, for us. We don't need to be a sovereign state for that to apply. Do we?"

The Speaker smiled. "No. We don't. Listen. What would you think about spearheading a campaign to get more people arriving here to naturalise? It will protect them from extradition under the Refugee Act, but it'll be a hard sell, naturalisation being what it is."

River tilted their head. "And it doesn't matter if I fail, because I'm in an unelected seat which is safe as long as I technically do my job, and because I've been about as involved in the senatorial process before now as a very sickly donkey. You can pass it off as another Aubrey Gale dead end, nothing to do with you."

"I wasn't going to put it like that," the Speaker said, looking caught out in the way River found people always did with them, whether they were pretending to be Aubrey or not. It wasn't something they liked about themselves. They came across, if they didn't speak, as completely harmless; but then two sentences later, everyone realized that they weren't really talking to a person so much as some kind of threshing machine in a person suit. "And—naturally if you were successful, you'd make a lot of friends."

"No, it's all right. I like it." And, the mechanical voice that was so good at calculation said, it was supremely advantageous to help. The Speaker was Max's Apollo. When the questions and the rumours started when Max didn't reappear, it was going to be important to have Max's own Apollo consider them a friend.

You are a stone-cold sociopath, said another voice, a lot like Aubrey's.

River felt dirty. They had always been too calm under pressure, they'd never been panicky or scared or joyful even when they should have been, but until now it had been something between a joke and a disability. It had never clicked that in the right circumstances, this thing they could do was not a joke, but radioactive.

"You do?" the Speaker said.

"I do," River said, thinking.

The week before Aubrey was due to come home, River did the most insidious and despicable thing they had ever done and hoped they ever would do.

They got together with a lively, clever charity for young people, and launched a campaign about turning off your filters. On a livestream, River and two other senators, along with some actors and news anchors, all switched off their filters to show what they really looked like, and the footage and photographs sprawled everywhere. *Vogue* did a feature, and the fashion section of *Xinhua*. Then River bought some of the pictures from the charity, and used them for the posters of the new naturalisation campaign, with a new slogan.

No filters. Just the truth.

The head of security, a gentle veteran called Sasha who had always had a hell of a time with Aubrey, took River respectfully aside when they got back to Songshu.

"Senator, can I have a quick word?"

"Of course."

This was it. Sasha knew Aubrey more than well enough to know the difference.

Sasha shifted. "I just wanted to say—I've been with you a while, but I've never seen you work like you have this week. It doesn't mean much, Senator, but—we're all proud of you."

River stared at them. They would have been less shocked to get a punch in the head. "Doesn't mean—Mx Martinez. Thank you."

Sasha bowed. "Well. We all serve at the pleasure of the House of Gale."

"We all do," River echoed, suddenly on the edge of crying. They'd never understood people like Sasha, people who had been in the forces, who risked their lives all the time, and who then took jobs protecting senators and celebrities who must have driven them mad with all their naïveté and carelessness. There was an endlessly long-suffering nobility in it. When Sasha didn't straighten from the bow, River caught their arms and levered them upright again.

"I've—never really sat down with you, have I?" River asked, tentative, in case Aubrey had.

"Why would you?"

"Because you're interesting. I want to know about where you served, and . . . no, sorry. I'm chronically nosy," they said apologetically. It was something Aubrey snapped back with, every time River said they were being a dick. *When are you going to learn to have a normal human conversation instead of just interrogating people like you're an investigative fucking journalist on the scoop of the century?*

"Senator," Sasha said gently, "that might be the nicest thing you've ever said."

River laughed, and then stopped, because Aubrey had just burst through the door.

"What the fuck do you think you're doing?"

Sasha stepped in front of River, fast. Of course they didn't recognise Aubrey. "Step back please."

"Get out of the way, Sasha, what—River, if this is some kind of involved, insane joke—"

It was one of those moments where the world spun on a penny. Or rather, it spun on Sasha. They looked between Aubrey and River, and River *saw* them realize what had happened.

And then saw them decide to pretend not to.

"I'm afraid I'm going to have to ask you to leave," Sasha said to Aubrey, and guided them towards the door.

"Sasha, it's me, don't—*that isn't Aubrey Gale!* When people find out about this you'll be in prison for—I'm going to the papers!"

"No, you're not," River said quietly. "Or there will be two of us with things to say, and two of us under the halo."

Aubrey stared, and River's heart smashed under the jackhammer of that stare, because it wasn't angry any more. It was hurt and betrayed, and all the other horrible things they had hoped so badly not to see. Aubrey wasn't the foul-tempered senator now. They were Real Aubrey, the one who'd come to the university to look after River during flu season, the one who had propelled River into clubs and music festivals with all their popular friends and smacked down anyone who tried to say River was boring, who still insisted, even now, on cooking all the New Year food for the whole of Songshu together, just the two of them and the music on loud.

"You're free," River said, voice shaking too badly to control. They felt like they were falling. They'd been watching the cliff edge get closer and closer all this month, they had put on the gear to survive the fall, updated records, changed banking details, made sure that the DNA samples in the infirmary were switched, but now that it was here, the gravity was shockingly strong, and just for a few instants, they had a mad sense that they could just grasp a tiny corner of an understanding of what it must have felt like for those doomed people forced into the orbit of Earth or Jupiter on the hulks. "You can live however you like. You can be who you like."

"Fine," Aubrey said, very soft. Real Aubrey vanished again then. "I will. But one day, I'm not just going to kill you. I'm going to drive you out of your obnoxious righteous mind, and make you watch the world come down around you, I will burn this place down, and *then* I might kill you, if you ask me politely enough."

"Time to go," Sasha said, impossible to bypass.

River sank down into a chair and had to stare into space. Kasha snuffled up and put her paw on their wrist, full of sympathy. River hugged her. She was Aubrey's dog, and suddenly stealing even the *dog* was worse than anything. They had to sit and stare at her, and slowly get used to the fact that rather than having just planned and thought about doing a terrible thing, they had done it now. They were always going to have done it; they were always going to be the person who had it in them to do something so bad it sounded like it was from some medieval legend.

They hadn't left Aubrey with nothing. There was a bank account. They'd never want for anything.

Kasha tried to get into River's lap. River made a fuss of her, hoping that she wouldn't be too sad not to see Aubrey any more. Testing the halo for the mammoths, they'd had some good conversations with Kasha. She was very interested in how fish could breathe, and she was of the opinion that humans didn't really do life right, given how little time they spent chasing llamas.

Sasha came back and sat down, and handed River a cup of coffee. "Now," they said kindly, as if nothing remarkable had happened at all, "let's have a little coffee break and I'll bore you to death with navy stories."

48

After Gale stopped talking, there was a staticky silence in which everyone watched January like they were waiting for a mine to go off.

"Well—that's a relief," he said finally.

"It is?" said Gale.

"I'm not married to a murderer, I'm married to someone who gave up everything to do the least bad thing out of a lot of bad things. That's winning, sort of."

Gale nodded slightly and pulsed a certainty that they expected a horrible row about it later, once the others had gone.

January looked between them all and wondered if they would ever believe what he was going to say. Even knowing what they all knew, it was still insane, and of course, not a single one of them had seen what he'd seen.

"Kasha's had an imaginary friend for ages, hasn't she," he said, starting slowly, and not sure he had chosen the right place to begin, but it was too late now. "She plays with someone who isn't there, you all talk about it. But that isn't what I saw, before I had these." He touched his glasses. "She *was* playing with someone. They follow the Senator everywhere. They write everything down. They were at the Tiangong with us, they sat at the next table along."

Gale was frowning. "What?"

"You—I'm sorry, Senator, but can I ask *why* you set up the reality show inside the house? Cameras everywhere, thousands of people watching you all the time?" He begged Gale with his eyes to be honest. "You hate it, we all hate it, and I don't buy that it's just for the consular campaign. You could win without all this reality show rubbish. You didn't do it for that. Did you?"

Everyone looked at Gale.

"What's he talking about?" Solly Francis asked.

Gale nodded slowly. "No. I didn't. I did it so that—so that people would notice if I started to really lose it. And I hoped someone might see something," they said, nearly too quiet. "To show I wasn't going mad."

"I am so far behind the two of you I'm in a different time zone," Mx Ren said flatly.

"Sorry," January said. "No, it—so for a while now, you've had trouble sleeping, right?" he aimed at Gale, hoping for help. And under that, in the weakest, wintery sunbeam, a tiny warmth started to break across him when he realized what this actually meant. It meant Gale *didn't* have someone else. This marriage wasn't quite such a spectacular lie as he'd thought. All this time, it had been in good faith. He wasn't just an inconvenience to the side of their real life together with somebody else.

A bit wryly, he reflected that in the history of finding out an unwanted person was living covertly in your house, probably nobody had ever been as happy about it as he was now.

"You thought it was hallucinations, Dr Okonkwo thought it was trauma from Gagarin Square. But it's not like a real sleep disorder, you don't have any other symptoms and all the scans are clean. Because it's *not* a sleep disorder. There's—Senator, there's someone living in your room with you."

The others started to talk and ask questions, but January didn't really hear, because all he could really take in was Gale's expression. Gale had gone very still, their focus somewhere in the far distance, and he could see them listening to their own memories.

"They comb your hair," January added, very quiet.

"There was someone there," Gale said to him at last, more of a question than a conclusion. "They were—really there. You saw?"

"They've been there all along."

"I thought I was . . ."

"This is true?" Sasha asked, voice going high. "Senator! You've never said anything."

"No, because it would have sounded like I was convinced Songshu is haunted," Gale said.

January swallowed. "There's a bit more."

Incredulous looks.

"They showed me where Max's body was. I couldn't see them, I was wearing my glasses, but . . ."

Sasha had both hands clamped over their mouth. Mx Francis looked scared. Even Mx Ren shifted, uneasy. Dr Okonkwo had gone a horrible colour, and Dr Molotov was staring at the ground, fingertips twitching in a way that made January wonder if they might be doing some maths in their head.

"And it was them who shoved me into the Consul today. That was why the praetorians shot me, they couldn't see what had happened. That was why someone threw something, and . . . that was why they fired on the Earthstrong people."

"So it's Aubrey," Gale said at last, very quiet. They closed their eyes for a second as if seeing the world was starting to sting. "They even told me they'd drive me mad before they killed me."

"What—what I don't understand," Sasha managed, voice fraying, "is how the fuck they did this. I've been military since I was eighteen, I've never heard of anything like this."

"It's completely possible," Dr Molotov said. It was the first time they'd spoken, and as they always did if everyone's attention was on them, they pushed one hand awkwardly through their hair, clearly wishing there was a blackboard to hide behind. "The technology does exist; it's called the Hades filter.[35] It's top secret, but the marines use it to ghost security

---

35 The scientist who came up with it had actually been in the same Ancient Greek class as River as an undergraduate, and had felt extremely cool to have thought of a name that (a) sounded awesome and (b) was also technically accurate. *Hades*, the Greek word for the underworld, was actually a description, from *ha*, not, and *eido*, to see; Hades, *ha-eides*, was the Unseen.

cameras on black ops. I used to build this stuff for House Song. It's not even revolutionary, we could have made it a hundred years ago." They looked around at everyone else, nervousness seeping gradually away. "Basically, the only reason it hasn't been developed before now is that it only works if *everyone* is perceiving the world through lenses, you see? They're banned in a lot of countries, because obviously you need a heavily regulated internet in order for people not to go completely insane. Where they're not banned, most people can't afford them. If you're rich in Beijing or Lagos or Riyadh then sure, but filters like this are damn all use if you've got loads of people walking around *not* using lenses. Tharsis is . . . well. We're the only country in the worlds where *most* people use them."

"I feel like there's a lesson in this about getting too rich and clever for your own good," Mx Francis mumbled.

"It came from Max, right?" January said. "Max was a marine."

For the last couple of minutes, Sasha had sunk into a deep, painful silence, but now, they sat forward.

"Doesn't matter how, for now. While the internet's out—if you're right—then we'll all see them."

"If Aubrey wanted to kill you," Mx Ren said to Gale, "then it sounds like they could done it a thousand times over. Why haven't they?"

Nobody said anything.

"Anyway," Gale said after a long silence, "I don't know if the Consul can find a way to track us out here, but—we're going to have to hope that they can't. I know I can't go any further like this."

Everyone else looked some awful catch between scared and relieved. January drew his knees up and put his head on them. His whole arm was throbbing. He couldn't tell if that was just what happened if you'd been shot, or if, jumping off a tower and rolling around in grass and dust, he'd got something in the wound that he shouldn't have. It was only when he moved that he realized Yuan was tucked up against his left side, asleep, and still holding on to handfuls of his shirt.

49

The tent was so warm inside now that Gale was in shirtsleeves. Between the two of them, a little stove boiled some water, shushing cheerily and sending a soft glow around the silver walls. January was quiet, shifting a heat pack around and around in his hands. He was warm enough, but he couldn't put it down; he felt panicky whenever he thought about it, and not, he suspected, because he was scared of freezing to death. It was something to do with his hands and it stopped him disturbing Yuan, who was still asleep against his knee.

They had been sitting in exhausted silence. January didn't know what to say, except ordinary things like, *How does this stove work?*

It was settling on him slowly, like a bolt of silk thrown up into the air, that if the Consul's praetorians found them, they were going to die out here. It seemed mad, and he couldn't get his head round all the corners.

"How can they just—decide to murder us?" he asked, and then realized it had happened aloud. "I mean . . . people will ask questions if you just die, surely? Half of Tharsis wants you to be Consul, it . . ."

"It won't matter, as soon as the ships from Earth arrive," Gale explained. They didn't seem confused about any of it all. "I'll be very surprised if there isn't a legion of soldiers from Beijing on one of them. It will have been one of the Consul's conditions for letting them come."

"Soldiers from Beijing to . . . ?"

"Enforce the election result that China wants. A second term for Song."

"But that's a military dictatorship. The Consul—why would they want that? They don't . . . all right, confession: I've met them, and they're not a horrible person."

Gale was quiet for a second. "I think Consul Song really does believe that the best thing to do is bring half of Earth here and let Tharsis as we know it die. And I think they believe people who disagree aren't just different, but . . . evil. It's faith. To attack it is heresy. They're fine with killing me because I'm a kind of witch."

January wanted to say he couldn't imagine feeling that right about anything, but it would have been a failure of imagination. If he were living in one of those parts of Earth where women had fewer rights than guns and anyone like Gale who didn't do the whole "he" and "she" business was likely to end up in a mental hospital, he would sure as hell have wanted to stamp that off the face of the planet, because *anything* would have been better. A nuclear hole in the ground would have been better.

Which, now he was thinking it, was a terrible thing to think. It was a very *Consul-y* thing to think.

Gale met his eyes, just briefly, for all the world as if they were nervous of what he was going to say.

"There *are* evil things, though," he said at last.

Gale nodded. "Sure. I guess the problem is when you don't realize that someone who agrees with you can be doing something evil, and someone who's at total odds with you might be doing something good."

January had to stare at them for a little while, because they had just articulated what he'd been trying to for months. He was at odds with Gale *and* Gale was a good person. He agreed with the Consul, *and* . . . they weren't. It was that simple.

He wanted to say, *How are we going to get out of this?* But that was useless. Either the internet came back on and everyone became functional enough to move, or it wouldn't and perhaps in five minutes from now, perhaps in five hours, they would be rounded up and shot.

He was bleeding again. He could feel it soaking through his jumper.

"Look," said Gale.

He looked. They were holding an egg; it was frozen perfectly, still egg-shaped even without its shell, just a clear oval with the round yolk in the middle. Speculative, Gale dropped it in the boiling water and they both leaned down to see what happened. Almost too late, Gale got the lid over the little pan before the egg exploded. They both laughed.

There was rice and vegetables, a rich broth, and even meat, which wasn't normal here.

"Calories," Gale explained, and held out a chocolate bar. "Keep eating."

"You as well though?"

"I don't need to. The first generation of children born here were modified with . . . mm, no. You're never going to let me live this down, I don't want to say."

"You have to now," January said, aware he was being baited. He still couldn't tell how he felt about the story Gale had just told everyone. He had a sense that he should probably be scrutinising the right and wrong of it more, but he just—wasn't. Scary as it was, it sounded like a pretty sensible thing to have done, if you knew you had titanium nerves. Nicer than sending Real Aubrey to prison. Probably better for House Gale. Bonkers, but actually, typical Gale. They didn't let weirdness get in the way of an efficient solution.

Gale sighed. "Tardigrade DNA."

"The—super-cold-resistant microscopic bears that live in water?"

"Yes."

It did not matter that it was baiting. "That is the best thing you've ever said," January said. "You're right, you never will live it down. Are you okay with that pan, can your tiny paws cope?"

"Just get it all out at once—"

"Are you radiation-resistant? Could you survive nuclear holocaust? Vacuum of space? Moreover, when it's the full moon and you revert to your true form, how do you wear shoes—is it back two legs, all eight, or back six?"

"Yes, no, no, back six," Gale said. They sparkled at him, looking for all the world like they didn't at all mind the roast.

January reflected that he was the easiest person in the world to distract. Gale threw the chocolate bar at his head. He ate it slowly, watching the pan simmer, because even when it was obligatory, it still felt like luxury. Outside, the dust shushed over the tent walls. The horses were talking to each other, seeming not to mind the cold—perhaps they were part tardigrade too—and ambling close to the tent. He let himself tip sideways against his bag, woozy and hazy again. Keeping so still, he was cold again after a minute, but he didn't want to move and fetch his coat. Gale gave him a cup of the hot stew.

"Try and eat all of it."

"Thanks."

The exploded egg was surprisingly good, and even the rice tasted wonderful. Before long, he realized half of what he'd thought was just misery had been hunger, for all he had thought he'd been eating enough. After a little while, he risked a glance up.

"It's bizarre not to be filmed. We could say anything. I could say I hate rice and nobody will be offended."

"I could talk about Ancient Greek verbs," Gale said. They paused, and looked hunted. "I mean—I won't."

"Oh my God, tell me about verbs, quickly!"

Both of them were too excited; it woke up Yuan, who sat up and peered at the stew until January fed him some. Then he stretched tinily and trundled round to sit with Gale. Gale stroked his hair to make him look up and gave him some keys to play with. January wouldn't have thought keys would be very interesting, but Yuan looked fascinated, both legs out in front of him and the keys fanned out carefully on the groundsheet, where they winked in the light of the heat filaments.

"Have we ever been unobserved?" Gale asked. "Since the first day I came to your apartment?"

January tried to think. "No." He hesitated. "Hi." He bowed a little. "I'm January."

Gale did too, slowly. They looked scared, but not that he would do anything violent. Scared of—him, his opinion. "River."

"River," January repeated, and it felt right.

They were both quiet for a while. The little camping stove shushed. Outside somewhere, a long, long way off, there was a primal moan: mammoths talking to each other through the storm.

January wanted to take Gale's hand, but he didn't dare to touch them. He had his bearings back now, after an hour out of the cage, but that

didn't mean anything. Under his heat suit, his shirt was going unpleas-
antly stiff, and it kept sticking to him. He was trying hard not to think
about why. Under the part of him that was functioning quite well, given
that it hadn't slept and had been shot, he could feel a smoking void, and
the smoke was getting denser, and more dangerous. Soon it was going
to start choking off the rest of him.

He blinked twice and realized he felt the way he had before the altitude medicine kicked in; panicky, cold, full of broken glass.

"It's blood loss," Gale said. "Just rest for a little while."

He did as he was told, hugging his bag again. Gale put a blanket over
him. It was soft; sealskin, the expensive lab-grown kind that had always
been better than any new polymers. His shoulder was pulsing a nasty,
nauseous pain up through his whole chest now. He must have looked
ill, because Gale pressed one hand to his forehead. If he had a fever,
though, they didn't say anything about it, and only touched the side of
his skull to make him stay down when he tried to lift his head.

"I'm sorry," he said.

"For what?"

"For needing to be looked after."

"I'm the one who should be apologising. You were shot in my house."

"I'm very provoking."

Gale hummed, which might have been the start of a laugh or not.
They were quiet for a while then. He found himself tracing the patterns
in the heating filaments of the ground sheet, seeing—probably there
was a significant psychological reason for it—rabbits. Yuan curled up in
Gale's lap, still holding the keys. He hadn't asked where his mum was.
Maybe he knew; or maybe he was used to being handed around any
spare adults.

January hoped more people would find their way out of Songshu and
to the warehouse. Most Earthstrongers wouldn't be affected by the
internet outage.

"Are you okay with him?" he asked, because if kids weren't really
your thing, there was nothing more unpleasant than being saddled with
an unexpected one.

"Them," Gale said, sharp and incredulous, like January had smacked a stack of pornography in front of them, but it sounded like autopilot. They frowned. "I'm so sorry. I didn't mean to do that."

"No, it . . . you're right. It is weird to say that about a child." Actually it was horrifying, now he was thinking on it. "Are you, though?"

Gale nodded, still looking anxious that he was offended.

"Stop looking at me like I might shoot someone," he murmured. He had to put his hand over his eyes, because the light seemed too bright now. "It's just Tharsis. You can all bake amazingly, you're all obsessed with upsettingly dreadful folk music, and you don't do gender. Those things are on a level. No, I'm . . . lying, I care about the baking thing." He could feel his mind vapouring off in strange directions, but he couldn't catch at any of it, never mind scoop it back in. "I don't like the weird red bean paste everyone claims is jam, though. It's *not* jam."

Gale laughed low down in their ribcage and looked down for a little while at Yuan, who was asleep now, breathing in the snuffly way babies did. "I'm sorry about before, as well," they said. "I told Solly to change the script, the show psychologist told them too, but they wouldn't have it."

"What?"

"Today, earlier. By the piano. You looked scared. It's hard to convince Solly about . . . cultural differences."

He had to frown into the memory, because it didn't feel like it came from earlier tonight at all. It was a thousand years ago. He had some dim recollection of carols. "How do you mean?"

"Well, the . . . I was reading, and the consensus on Earth seems to be you need to know if someone's a man or a woman before—and keeping that from you is—something between deeply weird and quietly violent?" They sounded uncertain, watching him for any sign it was right or wrong.

"That definitely isn't the consensus, there *is* no consensus, that's . . . but you don't need to be reading *any* of it," January said, shocked that *this* was what Gale was worried about when, for all the two of them knew, the praetorians were minutes away from the tent. "It's a cesspool, just—don't—worry. All those things . . ." He shook his head a little.

"They're important at home, and there have been riots and laws and fights for centuries about giving people the freedom or not to choose one kind of human or another, but none of it was ever thought of with someone like you in mind. You're outside it."

"But you aren't." Gale hesitated. It was exactly the way January found himself talking to very religious people; wanting not to offend, but not understanding where the logic of offence might live, because if you weren't in it, it all sounded made up and arbitrary. "I can tell you. If it would . . . help."

"No. It doesn't matter." January pushed himself upright on his good arm. His head swam and reported he really shouldn't do that just now. "*Because* you don't even understand any of it. You're so clean. If you'd asked me two years ago I would never have been able to imagine—" He stopped himself before he could say what he had been going to. "I would never have been able to imagine someone like you. But now I'm here, and you're you—there's nothing better, honestly. I didn't look worried today because of any of that, I looked worried because I'm chronically scared of being flirted with, I always feel like someone's coming at me with a knife. I don't know why, I just always have been. Probably linked to my punishing issues about my dad and whatnot."

Gale gave it more thought than most people ever gave anything. They always looked down when they were thinking, and when their eyes came up, it was a good few seconds later. "What issues?"

January had a surge of love for them then. It was the contrast between who Gale was, and how they sounded. An annihilatingly clever scholar who had no self-consciousness at all about asking simple questions. He didn't know anyone else who didn't care if they sounded like they didn't know something. He'd *never* known anyone else like that.

"No idea, I don't need to be poking around in there."

"Mm. I'm sure there's a reason I'm an unfeeling drone but I don't need to know it."

"Never discuss it and hope it goes away by itself, it's the best way."

"It's fine."

"We're fine."

"Exactly."

They both laughed. It made something in January's head twang.

He was shivering, even though he could still tell, objectively, that the heated ground sheet was warm and the sealskin was doing its job. Gale must have seen, because they set Yuan gently aside and moved nearer, and tilted him half upright so they could sit behind him and he could lean back against their chest. He should have said no, because he still wasn't convinced he was very coordinated, but it seemed like a faraway concern, and all he could really do was sink into how much better and safer it felt to be cradled against someone so much taller. When Gale closed one hand over both of his, they were warm. He could feel them breathing. He'd always thought their bones must be fragile, but they lifted easily against his back for all he was heavy here, strong and sure. Then they pulled the blanket over him again, though that must have been far too hot for them.

He swallowed. "Thanks."

"How are you feeling?"

"Okay. Just cold."

Gale made a quiet sympathy sound and stroked his hair back. He shut his eyes under their hand, and his whole skeleton relaxed, even though he hadn't noticed he was holding himself tense. Part of him faded away with it. The world felt far off; the heat of the ground sheet, Gale's hand, the softness of the sealskin blanket catching on the new stubble under his jaw. He was seeing it from underwater. The cold was worse, but he minded it less, and all at once, despite the chaos of the night, he was so tired he couldn't think. But he was happy. Despite everything, he would have done it all again to be here, like this; no cameras, just them, and Gale's ribs lifting under his. He tried to gather up the memory so he could save it for later.

Gale was squeezing his hand, hard enough to hurt, but like the cold, the hurt didn't feel very attached to him. "January. January? Can you hear me?"

He wanted to say, *Of course I can hear you*, but his voice had shimmered off somewhere else in the cold ocean.

"January!"

"I'm okay," he said, or he thought he did. His voice sounded imaginary.

Gale tucked Yuan against him. "Would you look after him for a minute?"

Him; God, what grace.

He nodded, assuming they meant to go and find more water or something, and it was only once Gale had gone that it occurred to him they were doing their chivalric trick of making him feel less useless while they went to find a solution to the uselessness.

Only there wasn't one. Dr Okonkwo had done everything they could. All there was left now was to wait it out and hope the internet came back on.

Gale didn't come back, and didn't come back.

It was in stages that January started to see what they'd done. He snapped back awake as completely as if he'd dumped a bucket of water over his head.

"Sasha!" he yelled.

He heard a scramble in the next tent, and then Sasha pulled aside the tent flap. "What?"

"Is the Senator out here?"

"No, I thought they were . . . that's a lot of blood."

January swallowed. "I think they might have done something stupid."

Sasha stared at him but had no time to say anything, because the loudspeakers in the trees that usually sounded the mammoth siren blasted to life.

Everyone in the woods. It's safe. You can come back inside.

It was Gale's voice.

"Why would they go to the house?" Sasha said hoarsely. "Christ, why didn't you stop them? What did they trade, to get us all back in safely?"

Something they couldn't afford, January was sure.

Sasha caught the front of his shirt. "If we get back and find them hanged over the front door, I will skin you alive."

"Yeah," he whispered. "Fair enough."

Dr Okonkwo gave him more painkillers, and something in a very emergency-looking syringe that might have been adrenaline. It got him upright, and he felt normal again in a frenetic buzzy way, but they said it would only last about half an hour and then he'd crash. When he asked what happened then, they made an unwilling noise and said he'd better be close to a lot of medical supplies by then.

Sasha looked at him like they were happily anticipating watching him die in a ditch on the way, although it was important that he didn't, because he was the only one with any sense of direction left.

Yuan cried when January tried to hand him to Dr Okonkwo and even when he tried again with Solly, who was the friendliest-looking person in the worlds, and in the end, January had to carry him on his good side. Yuan stayed staunch even when Dr Okonkwo got cross with him.

"Leave him alone, he's scared," January said, too tired despite the adrenaline to be diplomatic. "You're all gigantic, you look scary even to me."

Dr Okonkwo bristled and Solly looked puzzled, just like the Consul had done. Feeling hopeless, he wanted to ask why everyone had such a mental block about understanding how a tiny child might think someone seven feet tall and brusque was alarming.

"Where's Senator Gale?" Yuan said miserably.

"Inside, little bear," January promised, hoping to God he wasn't lying. Then he hesitated, because it had just struck him how strange it was that Yuan wanted Gale, not his mum. "And your mum too, I hope."

Yuan shook his head. "She died when I was a baby."

January's brain felt like he'd accidentally dropped it in a washing machine. "Who was that lady you were with before?"

"That's Mrs Li. She looks after me sometimes. And Jenny. And Mr Hafiz." He put his head on January's shoulder and didn't elaborate.

January hugged him closer. "Then I bet Mrs Li and Jenny and Mr Hafiz are really worried about you."

"No. They don't love me," Yuan said, with the devastating clarity that tiny children sometimes have.

50

In the whirling dust, he caught snatches of things as they made the walk back to Songshu. Without internet, there were no highlights in his lenses to show him where the path was among the groaning pines. Once, he tripped into a mammoth footprint, fully five inches deep in what had used to be mud from a stream but was now solid, parched earth. Twice, people rode past their group on horseback, heading in the opposite direction, towards the wrecked railway track. Once there was a wagon. And in a fits-and-starts stream, people walking in heat suits, carrying kids and often carrying cages.

Even though he did know which direction he needed to be going, he lost the path twice. It was ludicrous: on a clear day Songshu would have been right in front of them all, obvious above the trees, but it might as well have been a thousand miles away in the roiling brown of the storm. Sasha had told everyone what to do if you got separated from everyone else—find a tree, find the markings on the trees, they all point towards Songshu, sometimes you have to feel for them—and shook their head when January protested that he could just use the compass on his phone.

"Mars has no north. Compasses point to Athena."

He could see it now, in the ribbon breaks in the dust way up in the atmosphere. Even from so far away, it was obviously not a natural moon. You could make out the hull and the great machinery that had been used to tow it into place.

He'd seen Athena on the Crossing, but he'd forgotten about it. Mars's core didn't spin, so there was no natural magnetosphere—and therefore nothing to keep the air where it was meant to be rather than floating off into space, not to mention no magnetic north and south. Until, that was, they built Athena. It was a gigantic electromagnet, and it sailed a planet-width ahead of Mars on its way around the Sun. Behind it, in an invisible comet-tail, its electromagnetic field hugged the world, and did exactly the same job a magnetosphere did. Without it, everything on Mars would die. Conspiracy theorists always talked about how Earth sabotage meant Athena might fail at any moment, but everyone else agreed it was good for about five thousand years.

Out here in the dust eddies and forming cyclones, he had a sudden feeling he could see exactly what it might be like after it all went wrong, after Earth was dead and civilisation here failed and people retreated underground to the hidden lakes way up by the pole, and all that was left of any knowledge of magnetospheres and electromagnets was a myth-memory about how there was no Mars without Athena.

And then finally, there was the front door. Gale wasn't hanging above it. They were waiting on the steps, with the Consul, and of all the holy things, a team of doctors, which was just as well, because right then his knees gave out.

He never lost consciousness, but he felt very, very spacey for a while until the blood transfusion started to make itself known in all those complicated halls in his heart. It was a peculiar feeling. He got sharper and sharper, and warmer, and even though Dr Okonkwo had been there all along putting a special kind of regenerative stitching in his shoulder—the first few stitches they'd done had already faded and made a wonderfully neat scar—he became aware of it properly for the first time after two or three minutes; and of the chaos swirling around them, the people trying to yell at Gale or the Consul or each other all at once.

He was under one of the willow trees in the entrance hall, and heroically, Dr Okonkwo was kneeling among the roots with their bad knee cushioned on a coat. Yuan was just next to him, snugged up close to

Kasha, who was panting joyfully, tail thumping. Dr Okonkwo kept having to pause to persuade her not to try and help with the stitches.

There were bodies lined up on the floor. Natural and Earthstrong. The power was still off. People were carrying lanterns, real ones with flame. Dust had burst in when the front door opened, and now the dim light made it sparkle.

"Ah," said Dr Okonkwo, sounding much gentler than usual. "Back with us. Can you tell me where you are?" For the first time ever, they spoke to him in English. He hadn't even known that they could. It wasn't American English. They had a beautiful, courtly Nigerian accent, the kind that made him think of the rich business types who visited Canary Wharf for the expensive diving trips, or the academics who all but lived on the excavations around Tintagel, being delighted by how weird sheep were.

"Songshu." He had to concentrate to speak.

"Good," Dr Okonkwo told him. "Now stay still or I'll sew your shoulder to your lung."

"Where's . . . ?" He had been going to say, *Where's the Senator?* but he could see now.

Gale was climbing stiffly up onto a table, above the yelling.

"Good morning, everyone." Even without any intercom or microphone, they could send their voice all the way up the tower.

People stopped and straightened to listen, and around the balconies, people came to the railings. Mostly they were just points of light and the sketched angles of faces and shoulders in the gritty dark.

"I know everyone is exhausted, and scared. I know none of you want to stay in a building with people who attacked you. If anyone wants to leave now and make the run to the Valleyside, my staff will find horses for you. That goes for Natural and Earthstrong alike. If you would like to stay until the police arrive—then you are likewise welcome. I have only two conditions. If you're Natural, you surrender your weapons. If you're Earthstrong, you must find your cage and get it back on as soon as you can."

January expected general disapproval from everyone, but instead there was a dead-eyed assent. With an odd drop, he came to the realization that the person in charge wasn't necessarily the person everyone trusted most—nobody here would trust Gale much at all, surely—but the one who got up on a table and talked like they knew what to do.

Which was, a sluggish part of his mind reported, *grandmother strength*.

He flinched when the needle bit too deep. Dr Okonkwo patted his good shoulder. The packet of blood hooked up to him was empty now. They put a new one up.

"The doctors will be in here; they'll see anyone who needs them. So will I. We're going to need to move the dead to an unheated room, but anyone who needs to sit a vigil, please ask for a heat suit. There are plenty to go around. If you need a priest, we'll do our best to get hold of someone—but bear with us, because in some cases we might have to contact Earth. The kitchens are making hot drinks and hot food; I know not everyone feels like it now, but I urge you to eat, particularly if you have no genetic modification for the cold. The police will get here as soon as they can, but it will be a while. Meanwhile—get some sleep if you can. If you'd like to talk to me, or if you have questions, I'll be here. The Consul and their praetorians will go back to their ship, which is in the grounds. It can't take off, there's not enough power, but we'll all be separate enough. Everyone is free to go wherever they feel safest."

They were quiet for a second. "All our cameras are running again, and the internet is okay. Power will follow in a few minutes. Everything from now on will be caught in panoramic detail, which seems to me to be the best way to prevent anything else boiling over. Consul?"

"Thank you, Senator. I'd like to assure everyone that the internet outage was an accident. The iron in the dust is disrupting the satellites. It wasn't an order of mine, or anyone's. Both of us feel terrible about all of this. Both of us will hold nothing back from the police, and we hope none of you will either. This was a horrible tragedy, and all of you have our deepest apologies."

January frowned. A united front; after everything. It seemed like the least likely thing in the worlds, but here it was, and the praetorians and the House Gale security staff were looking at each other with an uneasy kind of hope that nobody would pull a gun, and everyone else starting to lose the look that said they were ready to run for their lives.

Gale paused. "Now, this isn't the ending I wanted, but I don't think I can get down off this table."

Incredibly, people laughed. The Consul actually reached up and lifted them down. When their hair swung across one shoulder, the Consul grinned and tidied it back like they'd always been friends.

Something in January's insides twisted. Whatever Gale had promised to make all this happen—it couldn't have been easy.

Cages went back on. Someone even brought January his. It ached as it locked into place; even with all the painkillers, his muscles knew he was having a difficult time already, thank you, and they didn't much appreciate having to push three times harder than a minute ago. He was glad to get it back on though.

Guns went into a locked box in a safe. The power came back on. The internet was strong again. Soon, the night's footage was playing on all the screens as the news services sponged it all up. January saw his own fall from the tower eight times in one hour.

Every single report ended with the journalist or the news anchor wondering seriously whether there was any truth to the rumours that this had been an assassination attempt at the eleventh hour, now that, after the amazing mammoth stunt, Gale had overtaken the Consul in the polls. If seeing the two of them talk to the scared crowd inside had Songshu had been strange, it was utterly bizarre to watch them stand together in a live news interview and swear to the whole nation that it had been nothing of the kind, their relations were actually very cordial and sportsmanlike, and everything was okay.

January wanted to demand to know what the fuck was going on, but of course it was all being filmed and streamed and scrutinised by the whole country. And it was, in one way, clear what the two of them were doing. They were calming everything down and trying to avoid another huge riot. That had to be good.

———

He sat under the willows with Gale well into the morning, talking to anyone who wanted to talk. Mostly, they asked about immediate painful things. Someone needed white shrouds; could they have some spare sheets? Someone else was too old and fragile to sit outside with the body of his daughter; would anyone else be willing to sit the vigil? How were the bodies getting back down to Tharsis—or was it possible to bury people here? It was expensive to call Earth, but please could they try and get hold of the family minister in Utah? January called the minister, who was perplexed to find that the colony on Mars was real and not Chinese propaganda, which was what the U.S. news said.

January felt peculiarly detached from everything. He couldn't feel anything, not relief or worry. He wasn't wearing his glasses, and he was looking for anyone who was even a little like Aubrey, but even that didn't come with any fear or any tension. He was just—wrung out, and half waiting for the next disaster, even though he wasn't sure where he thought it might come from. Special forces weren't crashing through the windows. Nobody was shooting. Tucked against Kasha, Yuan was asleep in a little ball with his blanket. Mx Ren had investigated; Mrs Li was among the dead, and they couldn't find anyone called Jenny or Mr Hafiz. In their absence, Yuan seemed willing to make do with some Gales and a dog.

January kept hearing the snicker of bones breaking. It hadn't sounded like his bones would have. Just little snaps, like wood getting to know a fire.

Gale touched his arm. He surfaced and saw that for the first time in hours, no one was waiting to talk to either of them. "Come upstairs with me. I, er . . . need to stare at a wall for a while, I think."

What he meant to say was, *Yes, that sounds great, I'm so tired.* What came out was: "What did you say to the Consul, to make all this happen?"

Gale rubbed Kasha's ears and lifted Yuan up. "Can I tell you when I can think in a straight line?"

He nodded. He hadn't meant to ask in the first place. He was dreading finding out, and childishly, he wanted to put it off. Whatever Gale had agreed to, it was going to be horrible, and January would be angry and the two of them would probably have a huge fight, and he didn't have the steam left for that. He wanted to just pretend, for a bit.

Gale eased Yuan into Solly Francis's arms.

"What have you done?" Solly asked quietly. "How did we go from people trying to kill you, to you and the Consul being best friends?"

"I'll explain when everything isn't made of sandpaper."

"Do I need to be getting my résumé in order? Have you sold Songshu? Have you sold January? Firstborn child, kidneys, what?"

"I just—want a few hours where no one is yelling at me. Please?"

"You're a senator, it's your job to be yelled at!"

"Do not wake that child up."

Solly gave them a narrow look. "You *strategically* handed me a child, didn't you?"

Gale nodded.

"You're a bad person," Solly grumbled, but went away holding Yuan like they knew how to hold children, and January wondered suddenly if they *had* children. He had never asked.

He didn't know he was unbalanced until Gale took his hand. He had to concentrate to walk. When he blinked, he kept seeing teeth on the floor. He had to pull his hand over his eyes. The green flashes from the pressure looked like the muzzle flare of the gun. Kasha pushed her head under his hand and gave him a sympathetic look.

"*And meanwhile,*" said a news anchor on the screens, "*there seems now to be some order at Songshu, with footage from inside the building restored and joint statements issued from Houses Song and Gale calling for calm. How long that calm can last, however, is the question at the front of everyone's minds.*"

They really weren't helping, January reflected grumpily.

Back on the fifth floor, Gale pushed their door open. The lights were set low to save power, and so was the thermostat. It couldn't have been more than ten degrees inside. January had to lean against the wall. He wasn't in pain exactly, Dr Okonkwo's medications were doing wonders, but it was miserable to think how long it was going to take to get just a bit warm. He wondered about fetching his heat suit again.

Gale bent a little to catch his eye as they turned the thermostat right up. "You're still freezing," they said quietly. "Go through there, the water's hot."

"The water . . ." January trailed off when he saw. In the next room, beyond a glass door, there was a pool. "How do you have that much water all to yourself?"

"Same monthly allowance you have, but I couldn't stand up till lately," Gale pointed out. "Go on, I'll go and get some new clothes for you."

January had a horrible vision of that silent figure following them, walking next to them, invisible. "You shouldn't—"

"I've got the dog," Gale said gently. Kasha, who always knew when she was being talked about, yipped helpfully. "And—you need them."

January looked down at himself. He was covered in dirt and blood. Gale tilted the glass door open for him and then bowed a fraction as they went out again.

There were steps down into the pool, and a bench around the edge, underwater.

A little current tugged at the water—it was circulating from somewhere else, and somewhere close by, maybe under the floor, there was a thrum that might have been the hydraulics that filtered it. As he peeled off his filthy clothes he saw that the wall opposite was glass and beyond it was another of those fantastic, dense gardens, half lost in the gloom. He eased down the pool's steps into the water, sinking up to his shoulders, and watched hummingbirds flit between the blooms. He closed his eyes. Breathing was a lot easier in the steam. It felt amazing to be warm, *really* warm.

He pressed both hands over his eyes and stood still in the middle of the pool, concentrating on not letting his breath catch. There was probably a camera in here somewhere. He didn't need all of Tharsis watching him break down.

The door clicked. Gale sounded uneven on a hard floor; one step fast, one slow. He ordered himself to turn around, but a much stronger part of him didn't want Gale to see the tear-tracks. He was the big scary monster here. He shouldn't be crumbling. Gale had lost a leg and had made, as far as January could tell, anyway, less than zero fuss.

He heard cloth falling to the floor and still didn't look back; not until Gale touched his good shoulder.

"Don't—even with a cage I don't think . . ." he said incoherently.

Gale stepped away from him again and back to the edge of the pool to sit down. The water levelled at shoulder height for them. He tried not to stare, but it didn't work. They looked different to how he had thought. The way they dressed made them broader and more solid, but without the heavy dark layers, they balanced right on the knife edge between strong and fragile. For the first time since he'd known them, they weren't sitting bolt upright, posture just loosely bad in the way all tall people seemed naturally to fall into after a while, and it made them softer. There were scars that looked like claw marks across their shoulders. That must have been from Gagarin Square. And now they were studying him with the beginnings of a frown etched between their brows, the same one they aimed at reports about problematic taxes or mandatory minimum prison sentences. He had to pretend to be interested in the garden again. He was just beginning to grasp how he looked to people here; not wrong exactly, but a relic of something ancient, from a time and a world where everything had been feral.

He thought they would ask about Earth and what the gravity felt like, to hammer out human beings with forty-inch chests and bones that looked like they'd come from a foundry. He was wrong.

"You're covered in bruises," was what Gale said. "Where the cage is."

"I . . ." He was. "I've been wearing it for a few weeks now. You're supposed to take it off for a couple of hours a day, really."

"You—didn't say."

He shrugged, which ached.

Gale didn't have to lean forward much to touch the release. Then it was hushing open all around him, and he felt like he was floating, and he had to step back as his arms lifted of their own accord and the silver gauntlets slipped back from his hands. He froze, not knowing what to do, at all. He looked at Gale and there must have been raw fear in his eyes, because Gale held out both hands.

"Come on. Let's see what you've got."

He swallowed hard and had to talk himself into it. He hovered his hands over Gale's, staring down at the clear straight bruises that traced where the gauntlets had been. Very gradually, feeling exactly like he would have if he had been about to touch a hot stove-top, he flattened his palms to theirs. Gale pressed their hands upwards to make him push down. They were shockingly strong.

"Come on, more than that," Gale said, not seeming afraid at all. They pushed up harder, and January actually had to try to push back. There was no way he could have hurt them by accident.

Gale clenched both fists and pushed them against to his to let him push back. If it had been a real test of strength, January would have won, but it didn't feel like he had thought. If he'd closed his eyes, he would have thought he was pushing against a teenager new to the ballet corps. Someone slighter than him, but definitely not weak.

The last test, the one he had never done, was to lace your fingers through the other person's and squeeze.

They told you only to do that if you were thinking about living with someone.

"I'll break your hand," he said, not able to bring himself to exert even the slightest pressure.

"You won't."

He squeezed slowly, and Gale shrugged a little, and then more, and more, well beyond the point he would have thought it must hurt.

"There," said Gale, "that hurts." But they didn't pull their hands back. Instead they only kept his once he let his grip fade.

"Why aren't you scared of me?" he asked helplessly.

Gale had been studying his hands, but they met his eyes now. Theirs had stars in the black; the only light in the room was from the candles. "The Swan King is one thing at night, and another in the day. One is . . . wild, and one is familiar. But neither means anyone any harm."

He hesitated, then stepped into Gale's arms and kissed them, as light as he could and scared that that wasn't what they'd meant at all. He drew back again quickly in case, but Gale caught him.

He'd never been so relieved.

Or so hopeless, because not for a second did he really think it meant anything except that Gale was relieved too, to be alive. He wanted to ask how anyone was supposed to live like this and still tell acting from real, and how he was supposed not to feel devoted to someone who put hours of work every day into looking like they cared what happened to him and what he thought, but it would have been childish. His feelings weren't Gale's problem. All he had to do was keep them to himself. That was an old chore.

He didn't know what time it was when someone tapped on the door. He started to get up, but Gale touched the side of his skull and pressed to make him stay where he was. Then there was a tug round his knuckles and Gale made a quiet surprised sound, and had to unwind a ribbon of their hair from around his hand. Half awake, he remembered taking it so he'd know if they left.

"Sorry," he whispered.

Gale only kissed his knuckles, and then hinged his arm gently back against his chest.

"Senator," Mx Ren's voice said when Gale tilted open the door. They sounded strange. "We've got some news."

"The mammoths have taken over?" Gale said. "Someone else has been shot. The house is on fire. I'm on fire."

"No, no." When January sat up, Ren was grinning. "It's *good* news. The tower—it's above the dust. We can launch the solar array."

51

One of the meeting rooms was set up for surround-film calls, and by the time January and Gale arrived, the scene at the other end—at the control room of the interplanetary sky harbour in town—was bustling but calm. Everything was nearly ready, an engineer promised.

On a launch pad, a ship with a full cargo of photovoltaic panels was ready. The Songshu mirror array with its salt towers wouldn't work in the atmosphere, but these would. If this worked, and if the dust storm ever blew itself out, which January was starting to doubt, House Gale would be producing double the supply they had before. For the first time in history—news anchors were intoning this—the Tharsese energy supply would far outstrip the demand, and that would drive down energy prices, which would encourage new infrastructure projects. If House Gale could pull this off, it might be revolutionary.

Beside him, Gale let out their breath long and slow, both hands over their eyes. Around them, there was an ordinary stream of last-minute checks and safety protocols, and it felt like it went on for half of forever. Camera drones hovered everywhere, broadcasting live.

"The internet likes us," Mx Francis murmured. "All my haptics feel like I'm getting a big hug."

An engineer waved. They were wearing a halo that connected their haptics to the ship. As far as January understood, if there was anything wrong with the machinery, they would feel it just as much as if there were something wrong in their own arms. "Clear for takeoff."

Everyone went quiet to see the engines fire, and the docking clamps tilt away, and the ship rise impossibly slowly in clouds of flame that soared out on the dust streams.

There were newscasts up everywhere, here and at the sky harbour.

"*House Gale has said they expect the solar array to be fully functional in eight and a half hours. Good luck everyone.*"

The drones began to float away, and as the call ended, the image of the control room at the sky harbour faded and it was just a neat grey space with a picture window looking out towards the solar towers and the Plains. There was a kind of hiss as everyone breathed out, and then an awkward pause as they all realized no one had thought beyond this point. What were you supposed to do for eight and a half hours while everything lay in the hands of engineers working in the atmosphere? If this didn't work, House Gale was finished. If it did, they had to get ready to move to Jade Hill.

If January had been feeling a hundred per cent, he would have made the ride out to the part of the railway that wasn't damaged and visited the naturalisation centre to see how everyone there was holding up. But even thinking about walking as far as the front door made him feel tired.

Gale buckled down onto the floor. It was slow, not a fall, and so silent that January wouldn't have noticed if he hadn't been right next to them. He dropped onto his knees too.

"Okay?" he asked.

"Mei shi," said Gale, and then blinked. "I mean, I'm fine."

He wanted to hold their hands but didn't know if he should. He wasn't sure what yesterday had been, for them. Tiredness and relief, most likely. He couldn't go round assuming things just because he wanted them.

He looked around for the hundredth time. He hadn't seen the Consul yet, nor any sign of Real Aubrey, and that felt a lot more ominous than seeing them. His chest with tight with waiting for the other shoe to drop, and the certainty that it wasn't a normal shoe but one of those horrible iron boots they'd used in medieval torture chambers when someone thought you might be a witch.

"January," Gale said, holding his eyes properly.

"Mm?"

"What I promised the Consul."

Dread kept him still.

"It was me. I promised to step down from the election. I'll be in prison for the remainder of their consulship."

January set his teeth, because he had known it would be terrible; but not this terrible. "You can't just vanish, the Consul can't just . . . you're the favourite to win now, there'll be riots if you go to prison for . . ." January stopped, because Gale was watching him and just waiting for him to see it himself, without interrupting. "I'm missing something."

Gale nodded. "You know how we couldn't understand where Lucy Collins managed to get accurate information?"

January had to push his hand across his face. The gunshot wound was making him slow. He had *seen* that figure in the orange jumper duck out just before the bomb, and he'd even wondered why at the time. "Aubrey's working for the Consul."

"Right. No one will know I'm in prison, because the Consul is going to swap Aubrey back in. I imagine that in exchange for covering up what they did to Max, the Consul will get control of Songshu, and House Gale's vote in the Senate."

"River . . ."

"I have to honour this or we're both dead. If they think I won't, then we'll be shot behind the grain shed and they'll blame it on another flare-up of violence."

January dipped his eyes and nodded. Gale was right; it wasn't like getting in a fight with another politician. The Consul was the head of state and things had gone too far now to row back. "When?" he asked at last.

It was only then he realized there had been a pair of praetorians at the door for last couple of minutes. One of them, incredibly unusually for Tharsis, had red hair.

"Now," Gale said.

The praetorians made it look quiet, and ordinary. They led Gale away from everyone else, to another room down the hallway. Two more praetorians appeared on either side of January and ushered him through as well.

He had never known the room existed, never mind been inside.

It was four or five floors deep. There were two above and two below at least, and right through it ran a waterfall. Enclosed in glass, tropical plants and trees winked jewel colours, twining out of moss and flowers, without the tiniest gap of bare earth. Vines tangled above a smooth wooden floor, real wood, and couches as jewel-coloured as the plants. But now, the waterfall was frozen. The thermostat must have been turned off altogether. Frost glittered over those beautiful couches and cushions, and hazed the glass that protected the plants. A strange mist hung just above the floor, glowing in the lantern light. None of the electrical lights were on. January stared around, perplexed, feeling like he did in dreams when the dream took you straight from inside a building to somewhere wild and you didn't question it.

The Consul was sitting just inside; and so was Aubrey Gale, the original, in that same burnt-orange jumper as always. Only it wasn't as always any more. Everyone could see them. The Consul certainly could: the two of them were playing Cat's Cradle on a shoelace in the way of friends who had been waiting a long time and become distracted, as if, he thought furiously, they were normal people. River Gale could. They stopped walking, which made the praetorian with red hair jolt awkwardly.

All this time, they had been right here. If he had just said, that first day at the Tiangong, *and who are you then*, if he hadn't been so keen to pretend nobody was in Gale's room because he was scared of who they might be, this whole stupid thing could have been avoided. There would have been a confusing ten minutes where everyone thought he'd gone mad, but Gale would have believed him, because Gale wasn't the sort of human who thought people spontaneously started seeing things, and . . .

It made him so angry that he wanted to smack himself in the face, just from complete, stupid, powerless frustration. All this was happening for no more involved reason than that he was a coward who hadn't said, for months, *Hi, I'm January*. There had been endless moments where he could have but he just . . . hadn't. It was beyond stupid. If someone had told him about it, he would have scoffed and said, *That's dumb, that would never happen, no one is that much of a moron*. But here he bloody was.

Both of them stood up.

"Kali's old room," the Consul said cheerfully, to January. "Isn't it obscene? God knew what it cost to heat."

"A lot," murmured Gale, January's Gale. River. "Which is why I turned the power off." Their eyes slipped across to Aubrey. "You've been . . . staying here?"

"I knew you'd never let anyone come in, so."

Gale nodded once. January thought they were going to fight, or at least start buckling on armour, but when they spoke, it was quiet, and their voice had fissures in it. "But it's so cold."

"It's not like I deserved to be comfortable."

The two of them sounded incredibly similar, and they had the same straight bearing that said they wouldn't duck even if fire rained from the sky. They looked alike too—not in the way of real twins, but it was obvious they had grown up together. They stood in the same way, they paid attention in the same way. But they *seemed* very different, side by side. River was stark in their dark clothes, like winter walking; Aubrey, much more colourful, was golden and summery. They would have suited this room beautifully when it was still alive and all the colours were still bright and hot. The two of them stood looking at each other. They both looked tired, and emptied out.

"Are you okay?" River asked at last.

"Mm. Are you?"

"Yeah. I—I had a good run, didn't I."

"You did." Aubrey smiled a bit. "The thing with the mammoths and the windlasses was amazing."

"It was pretty fun," River agreed, and half-smiled too.

The Consul nodded to the praetorians, and they handcuffed River's wrists behind their back. Then there was something else. It was a device like a bracelet. Through January's glasses, they vanished. The praetorians looked like they were holding a patch of air. He tore the glasses off, fighting down the primal instinct that said Gale really *was* gone, lost into the winking motes of dust that still swam in the cold air. No. They were still there, eyes down, not meeting his.

He wanted to claw his own heart out. If they had been willing to let him die, then Gale would right now this second be the most powerful person in Tharsis. The election would be a dead certainty.

It was such a close thing he could taste that other version of now. Quietly and gently, Gale had left him behind to die in that tent, and taken the others and Yuan out to the train line. It would have been a slog, but without some idiot who'd got himself shot, they would have made it. They would have left Songshu to the Consul for now, because it didn't matter. They would have set up a little command room at the naturalisation centre, safely away from the Consul and the praetorians. The launch would have happened just the same. Sasha would have insisted on bundling Gale into some kind of safe house for the next eight and half hours, somewhere top secret, in case the praetorians were out for them with sniper rifles.

And in three days, Gale would win the election, the Consul and Real Aubrey would be arrested, and they would have exactly zero lethal problems.

But no.

He had never been so miserable and so angry at the same time. He wanted to yell that he had never heard of anything so patently, ludicrously, boneheadedly moronic.

The Consul opened their hands.

"January. We should have a chat, I think," they said in their friendly way. "You must be all at sea."

There was frost forming in his hair; he could feel how stiff it was. Part of him, though, was still petty enough to think: *Shut up*, all at sea. *There's no sea on Mars. You said that because you think it's culturally appropriate for me and it'll make me feel more reassured. Patronising fuck.*

The praetorians pushed Gale into a chair not far away and sat on either side of them. In the doorway, Kasha hurried through and stopped with her head cocked, clearly not sure about these new people. Yuan was with her. January clenched his hand, then held his arms out. Yuan looked relieved and ran across.

"Ah. Who's this fine young person?" the Consul asked.

"I'm Yuan, I'm going to be a princess," Yuan explained.

The Consul laughed. "Superb."

January, who had been wearing them for weeks now as a kind of talisman to remind him that he was House Gale but that he shouldn't get used it, unlooped the famous pearls and put them in Yuan's hands. "You have a look at those. I'm just going to talk to the Consul, okay?"

Yuan gasped. "Treasure!"

"You have to be super careful, they're Senator Gale's. They're real. They're worth more than I am."

"I will," Yuan promised reverently, and went to sit with Kasha.

The Consul looked. "He doesn't look too well."

"No, no cage," January mumbled.

The Consul nodded a little. If they'd chosen that moment to say, *You know he'll have one soon if I get my way*, January would have punched them. But they didn't. What they said was:

"I'm going to do a press conference. I'm going to say it's wonderful that the solar array has been launched, but that unfortunately Senator Gale has, in the light of the unrest here and how it's becoming increasingly clear that their own House security is responsible, decided to stand down from the election. The footage will show that it was Sasha Martinez who opened fire. Senator Gale presided over a massacre."

"That is not what happened and you know it," he ground out.

"Whoever wins is who writes the story," the Consul said, shaking their head, regretful, but he didn't think the regret was for what had happened. It was for him; it was regret that for reasons which perplexed them, he had reached the age he was without understanding how this worked. "And Senator Gale is going to agree, in order to live."

As they spoke, they looked past him, at Aubrey.

He understood. The switch would only work if he was in on it, because he could take his glasses off and see what they really looked like. Everyone else would see a filter. There would be no suggestion that this was a different person. He was the only bump in the road. If he helped, then he could smooth over any inconsistencies. Earthstrongers would see a different person, but only in real life: the filters would work if you were watching any kind of recorded footage, and how many Earthstrongers would ever get close enough to Aubrey to see them clearly? Not many.

If anyone did, well, probably there would be some story about an injury and plastic surgery. It would be silly, but people would believe it, because the alternative—there was in fact a different person running House Gale—was even sillier.

Of course, it would work without him. He could easily end up dead somewhere, whoops, tail end of all the riots and nastiness, very tragic, big funeral, job done.

If he played along, there would at least be time to think of something else.

"Who is this?" he asked towards Aubrey, to stretch things out, and because all his instincts howled to pretend to have no idea. He didn't know why. That part of his brain wasn't talking to him any more.

No; no. He knew why. Because if the Consul thought this was coming as a shock to him, and Gale had lied to him and never explained, then that was a reason to think he might genuinely want to help.

"I'm Aubrey Gale," Aubrey said, quite gently. "The person you've known lately is my Artemis. River. They took this House from me a year ago. I'm sorry I never spoke to you. I was worried you'd come up to me in front of other people."

No wonder. One hello would have undone everything.

"How?" he asked, even though he knew. He wanted the extra minutes. "Why are you even doing this?"

The Consul and Aubrey exchanged an awkward look. Neither of them seemed like maniacal conspirators. They were as clearly as uncomfortable with the absurdity as him. More, because they were the ones who actually had to do it.

Between the two praetorians, River was watching Aubrey.

"I can explain," Aubrey said.

What was dragging at him, painfully, was that they sounded just like River. They both had the same intonation, and the same smoke in their voices. If he'd had his eyes shut, he wouldn't have known he was talking to someone new.

52

Songshu, being a scientific research institute as well as the House Gale family seat, was full of physicists and engineers, and therefore its graffiti was of an unusual sort. On the kitchen doors, somebody had put a note that said *Beware*, followed by a wildly complex-looking chemical formula. It looked like it was warning you about some horrifying radioactive accident, but what the formula actually *said* was "exploding custard."

Which led Aubrey to develop the Exploding Custard Theory of Knowledge.

It went like this.

Sometimes, something scary-looking and incredibly complicated is in fact really simple. But because it looks so scary, it's hard to catch. Somebody can explain the actually-simple-thing to you in perfect detail, with graphs and lines and a helpful slideshow of evidence, and you understand entirely; for about twenty seconds, and then it kind of slithers away, because it *can't* be that simple, it *isn't*, look at the graphs and the slideshow, you wouldn't need those things if it were all just—custard.

The reason was pretty straightforward. Most people had an in-built horror of looking like an arrogant dick. You had to have an ironclad faith in your own brain if you could look at the graphs and slideshow and say, yes, that's just a stupid-complicated way of describing *this* boring ordinary thing. Most people assumed complicated meant difficult.

And the terrifying thing was: this process of doubt happened *even if right now you were covered in custard*.

A little while after Kali died and Aubrey took over House Gale, they sat down with the finance people and immediately fell victim to Exploding Custard Theory.

Because what the finance people said—they said it in the finance version of the incredibly complicated chemical formula—was that Kali had accepted vast sums of money from House Song to neglect the Songshu solar array.

The idea was simple. Kali was to drain it of funds, make solar power more expensive, more inefficient, make sure it was understaffed and undermaintained, and come up (preferably quarterly) with new reasons it was unfeasible to run properly or expand. All that, until the array wasn't fit for purpose any more.

When a flummoxed Aubrey asked why in the worlds anyone would want that, the finance people fidgeted with their tablets and said, well, this is what governments do when they want to privatise a beloved national resource: they make it terrible until the voters *ask* them to get rid of it. Probably the Consul wants to sell Songshu—probably to Beijing.

And to seal this, Kali had arranged Aubrey and Max's marriage.

It took Aubrey a long time—weeks and weeks—to understand what the underlying custard of the situation was. Because anything that vast and worlds-changing couldn't have a boring simple thing behind it, and when they realized that actually it *did*, they felt insecure, because like most people they'd been brought up to look carefully for nuance and feel suspicious about simple answers. Simple answers were usually to be had from zealots or morons.

But nonetheless, what it all added up to, when you got down to it, was a way to put the entire power supply of Mars—Songshu—into the hands of an Earth government.

"Is there any way to get out of this?" Aubrey asked. "Can we say no, new Senator, new arrangements, no more bribes?"

The lawyers looked uncomfortable. "Senator," someone said, very carefully, "House Song has some damaging material on you. Videos. They'll release those if you try to change anything. We can try to work out strategies to minimise that damage, if . . . ?"

Aubrey didn't even ask what video. There was probably a whole library to choose from.

"The other difficulty," said a second lawyer, "is that without House Song money, House Gale is bankrupt. Kali—was quite a big spender."

Custard.

"Did you know about this?" Aubrey asked Max about a season later. It took that long to winch everything up to a mental elevation at which they could actually articulate it. In that time, they had churned around, staring at accounts, trying to find a way out, and seeing there was no way out, and meanwhile they were going to the mandatory Senate sessions and voting with Guang Song. It shouldn't have been awful. Aubrey didn't care who had control of Songshu. That was big-picture stuff: mostly Aubrey's philosophy was that if you could pay everyone who worked for you fairly, you weren't currently in hospital with alcohol poisoning, and you'd managed to say hello to the dog in the last twenty-four hours, you couldn't really complain. But the more they thought about that money, and whatever video Song had, the more they felt—cancerous.

The two of them were on one of their walks through the Songshu pine forest. Because the project to introduce polar bears to the Plains had been too successful, it was now illegal to go out without a rifle, so they both had a semiautomatic propped against one elbow. The trees were groaning to each other in the deepening winter, and the husks of old dandelion seeds had piled up over the path in places, each one a big as a mortar shell. They were on their way out to Sun Field Twelve, because at this time of day, the heat bouncing around between the solar mirrors was just enough to be summery. If you sat at the base of the salt tower, you could have a respectable picnic and watch the moons rise.

Aubrey and Max didn't do this because they liked each other. They didn't. They did it because someone at the security office always leaked footage of them together, it did the rounds in the news, and it looked like they had a fairy-tale life and wasn't it romantic and don't you want to be sick in a bag.

Which was important, Kali had always said, because if the great aren't seen to be good (making their arranged marriages work, not complaining, showcasing their Family Values and Personal Integrity), that's when people get the guillotines out.

Especially, Aubrey thought feverishly, if you were swimming in dodgy money from Earth. Kali, though a giant cynic, hadn't been wrong. The one thing that set Tharsese Great Houses apart from repulsive megacompanies on Earth was their honour. Honour was everything. You didn't take bribes, you expelled anyone who so much as looked at an intern wrong, and if you were in charge you worked—above *all else*—for the benefit of those hundreds of people who worked for you. Nobody else. And that was right. Anyone who was as rich as the heads of Great Houses, and who did *not* have a crushing sense of duty, was in serious danger of turning into a proper despot by next Tuesday. If people thought for a second you might be despot material . . .

"I . . . went where I was told," Max said, which was military-speak for *I had a bad feeling about it but the consequences of asking too many questions would have been severe.*

"What do we do? This—I know I'm a useless socialite, but I draw the fucking line at being bought and paid for by Beijing."

Max thought about it. They were one of those old-fashioned strong-and-silent types, which was annoying, because they seemed to rely on you interpreting silence as deep feeling when as far as Aubrey could tell, it was just absence of feeling, and probably they were thinking about ramen recipes, or where the laundry had got to. "Would it be so bad to divorce? Let my House release whatever video of you they've got?"

"*What?*"

"Well, you hate being a senator, and you're shit at it." Max believed in saying what they thought. Aubrey always wanted to say, *That's fine, but then* you *have to accept that I believe in throwing those who vex me off the roof of the Tiangong.* "River would be brilliant. If your concern is House Gale, let it go to River, problem solved."

There were lots of things about that little statement that Aubrey wanted to smash with a hammer, but what their brain fell over was the last bit. "River doesn't want to be a senator, Max, it would destroy them.

They can only go forty-five seconds without lecturing someone about Oracle Bone Script or the formation of Ancient Greek participles."

"Okay," Max agreed, in the way that meant they didn't agree at all but, having come off a tour on Titan, didn't have the energy to fight unless someone was actually trying to stuff a hand grenade down the back of their shirt. They seemed to hear how annoying that was, and sighed. "Look . . . is it really that bad? You get lots of money from doing this, and you're not political. Is it really going to keep you up at night, to run the sun fields down? All that will do, really, is tie Tharsis to Beijing, which will make it—heaven forefend, I know—slightly easier for people from Earth to come here."

To some extent, Max was right. Aubrey liked having friends, and silly-luxurious celebrity parties with red carpets and press, and not being too bothered by politics. They didn't like people who ranted on one side or the other; those people always seemed to forget that you could solve a lot if you just drank a bottle of vodka with the other person instead of demanding they articulate mathematically the precise logic of their position and then destroying it with your superior logic, as if that had ever convinced any human in either world, in the history of anything, at all.

But they had never so immediately and so sincerely wanted to punch someone in the face.

"That isn't the point, is it, they're blackmailing me!"

"So just to be clear. You don't . . . care about unionists or nationalists or Earth or Mars," Max said, half laughing in exactly the way people laugh at a very small child which has just declared its aversion to spoons because a spoon once fell on its head. "You're angry because your personal dignity is being impugned."

"I care about someone holding some mystery tape over my head," Aubrey snapped. "And unless River can come up with a way to fund this House without help from yours, then they'd be no better than me anyway."

Speak of the devil; up ahead, there was a mammoth-sounding whoop, and a human laugh. River: playing with the mammoth babies, still invisible in the fog but probably only forty yards away among the trees.

Max lit up.

Aubrey was willing to admit that in theory there might exist, some-where, an actual human being whose definition of sexy was a person whose normal dinner conversation was a rant about an inaccurate academic article on grammatical gender in Indo-European languages, but it sometimes kept them awake at night knowing that somehow, they, Aubrey, were *married* to that person.

Aubrey didn't mind. You didn't get to run a Great House and marry for love at the same time. But it stung.

"Why don't we ask?" Max said. "I bet River has some ideas."

It was true, River *would* have some ideas. River was too clever to suffer from Exploding Custard Theory; they could recognise custard anywhere.

But Aubrey's whole soul locked up.

If they tried to involve River in all this, River would immediately offer to take over, because they were so sickeningly wholesome that nobody would ever be able to blackmail them. The only footage House Song would have about River would be of them making a flower crown for a llama, or being stolen by a baby mammoth, or talking happily to the Mormon gender extremists in that camp outside Jade Hill, so that the missionaries could practise trying to convert an atheist who *really* knew their Special Theory of Relativity.

And River would have no idea what to do when Guang Song found another way to get to them. Probably it would be easy. Probably all Song would have to do was yell. River had no idea what to do with someone who really was out to get them, not just someone who wanted to peacock about who had the more sophisticated understanding of the *Dao De Jing*.[36] River was surrounded by people willing to pretend that quoting Laozi and Dostoyevsky was standard human behaviour. Song would eviscerate them.

"No, leave River alone. I don't want them involved in all this," Aubrey said. "Five minutes in the Senate would just upset them."

Max gave them an odd look. "Funny idea of River you've got," they observed. "They talk to everyone. Even Kasha."

---

36 Quoting in the original unabridged version from 500 B.C., because—ha ha—anyone who needed a translation into *modern* Mandarin was basically a gorilla.

"About Ancient Chinese verbs, Max," Aubrey said, exasperated. "That's the opposite of social skills, that's *projectile* autism."

The odd look turned into a slow frown. "Aubrey—have you noticed how much you hate it when anyone suggests River is worthwhile? You act like there's something wrong with them because they don't have celebrity friends and they don't go out and get tanked every Friday night, but that's not really a them problem, is it? That's a you problem."

"And you know all about River . . . not at all because you've spent so much time spying on them in the sauna."

Max made an impatient sound and turned their head away. It looked like impatience, but it was shame too. "Nothing is going on."

"Of course it isn't!" Aubrey half yelled. Because River was a sweet, lonely robot that collected interesting things and kept itself busy and never complained, and absolutely did not notice when anyone had a crush on it. Aubrey had a terrible feeling that it was because River *knew* they were a robot and that nobody liked robots, so the sheer statistical unlikelihood of it became a blinker. An affair wouldn't even have occurred to River, and nothing Max could do would ever make it occur to them. Even if Max stood under the window and declared undying love to lyre music, River would just seek medical assistance, because the only possible explanation for this behaviour was that Max was having a stroke.

Which was heartbreaking. Aubrey wished they *were* having an affair. At least then two out of three people would be happy.

They hated getting angry like this. It was happening more and more since they'd taken over from Kali. Out of nowhere, they were just *furious* about things that didn't matter. Yesterday they'd blown up at a legal department intern for putting something in the wrong recycling bin, and last week they'd had to go for a ten-kilometre run in order to stop being so enraged about losing—of all the stupid things—a card game with River. And now River was avoiding all human contact, because that was what happened if your Apollo didn't just bite your head off for no reason but also mounted it on the wall and hung fairy lights on it.

"You know they're not ignoring you, right?" Aubrey asked after a while. "River, I mean; they're not trying to say no. They just don't think anyone would ever be interested. I don't think they have the right wires in their brain to even recognise what flirting looks like. You need to sit them down and talk to them. I don't mind. I wish you would."

"What are you talking about?" Max said roughly.

After you'd been promoted beyond lieutenant colonel, it became very difficult to have feelings, and Aubrey had a lot of sympathy for that, but it was still hard to watch.

In the following silence, which looked set to be one of those marathon silences that represented its country in the Silence Olympics and would be remembered by generations to come as a triple-gold-medal champion of all silences, the two of them reached the border between the forest and the sun fields.

It was a strange place, that threshold between the great trees where the mammoths grazed and the industry world of solar mirrors arranged in acre upon acre of concentric circles. Aubrey had always hated it. Something about gigantic stretches of machinery made the roots of their teeth prickle. It was worse now, in the mist and the fading light. The curving rows of mirrors vanished off in either direction, everything motionless, except for the tiny blinking lights of the security drones that floated overhead. Probably it had been a triumphant-seeming place once, the hope and independence of Mars: it should have felt like that now. But all Aubrey could see in those mirrors was Kali's neglect. The steel frameworks were worn and dusty, about one in six mirrors were cracked, the circuitry wearing away. What it was, was the slow ruin of House Gale.

Way over the Plains, a mammoth called. Aubrey had worked long enough on the translation project to know she was saying that there were bears. But it was impossible to tell how far away she was. Mammoth voices carried twenty miles.

Probably Aubrey should have said something, because if there were bears anywhere nearby then the two of them needed to go back inside, but just then, the idea of being eaten by a bear was quite attractive.

Max said, "Do you want to see something good?"

Aubrey looked up, because Max didn't do peace offerings. As far as Aubrey could tell, Max never felt bad enough about anything to bother, and to see it happen was a strange, important kind of revelation. "What?" they asked, maybe too soft, in case they scared it away.

"You can't tell anyone I showed you, but . . ." They took a bracelet from one pocket and clipped it over their own wrist.

And vanished.

Aubrey jolted back and almost fell over.

Max reappeared again, looking bashfully pleased, and with a dawning realization, Aubrey wondered if this was Max *playing*. If you'd asked ten minutes ago if they thought Max was remotely capable of that—aloof, elegant, definition-of-no-fun Max—they would have howled with maniacal not-laughter. "It's called a Hades filter. We're testing it at the moment. It makes you invisible to anyone or anything with an internet connection. Want to try?"

Aubrey did very much. They were at the edge of the sun fields by then, and Max guided them in front of a solar mirror and snapped the bracelet onto Aubrey's wrist.

Aubrey disappeared. It was so complete that even moving suddenly produced not the barest ripple in the air.

"If you hold something close to you, it goes as well," Max said, handing over a stylus, which also disappeared. "But if you hold it right out . . ."

Hazily, the stylus reappeared, floating.

"One bat, two bats, fifty bats, ah-ah-ah," Aubrey couldn't help saying in a Dracula voice, because really, what sort of human wouldn't.

"You know," Max said, starting to laugh, "the way out of all this mess with my House is really simple."

"It is?" said Aubrey, still invisible and playing with the solar mirror and the stylus. To the security drones, Max must have looked peculiar, talking to themselves. Actually, they wouldn't: the mist was too dense.

"Well," said Max, "the real problem is money. You could weather a scandal if you played it right. But you'd get all my money if you just bumped me off."

Aubrey laughed too. It was nice to laugh, even just briefly. "Who knows, maybe the next tour will get you."

"Or a wandering polar bear," Max said, smile fading and they gazed into the mist. "It's hard to see out here. I don't think this is a very good idea. There . . . could be anything between these mirrors."

Aubrey hid behind a mirror a few to Max's left. "Good for hide-and-seek."

But Max had had enough of playing. "No—I mean it. This is a security risk. Even the drones can't see in this. It only takes one crazy person . . . Aubrey. Aubrey?"

Later, when Aubrey tried to think about it, they didn't know why. But they didn't say anything. They just stood, silent, behind the mirror, watching. It was sort of a game, and it sort of wasn't, either. Max deserved to be wound up every now and then. Anyone did, who took themselves this seriously.

And who was complicit in horrible blackmail.

No, it was just playing. Looking back—which they did every day at least ten times—they had just been playing. They didn't mean anything malicious.

Max sighed. "Aubrey, come on. Sasha will crucify me if anything happens to you."

Aubrey ghosted another few mirrors along, so that if Max had heard them shifting, they wouldn't be on that spot any more. Max turned around, looking less certain that what was happening was a joke.

"Aubrey?"

Max was right, there could be anyone out here. A random crazy person. If you were in a Great House's line of succession, it was bound to happen at some point. Aubrey had once been bundled into the back of a van outside a club and rescued by a gang of unexpectedly kind Earthstrong drug dealers. River had been held at knifepoint in these woods.[37]

"Aubrey, you need to say something if you're okay," Max said, sounding urgent. "If you don't say anything I'm calling security."

It was a little bit satisfying to see Max get flustered.

---

37 By an unfortunate person who had not realized that River was on conversational terms with several mammoths, who had been pretty firm about getting their special talking ape back.

Leaning to the side to ease the muzzle of the gun up past the edge of the mirror, Aubrey sighted carefully, just as a thought experiment to see whether it would be difficult or not. It wasn't. Max was right there, bang in the middle of the iron sight.

The urge to pull the trigger was independent of their normal thinking. It was the same as that monkey need to jump off a cliff. They had to laugh at themselves. Imagine; wow. Imagine if they did.

They never meant to do it.

53

After River stole everything and threw Aubrey out of Songshu, getting back in was simple with the Hades filter. Aubrey walked straight back into the building and moved into Kali's old room—River had turned off the power, so the waterfall was frozen, but the cold felt like penance—invisible to everybody but the dog. Then they started what they knew very well might be a good week or so of following River about, learning who they'd spoken to and what they'd been doing this last month, and getting ready to switch back. It would be weird, a week being invisible. But it would be a week at most. At *most*.

On the first night, Aubrey stole into River's room behind the dog and stood still, heart galloping. River was at the desk, studying something from the Senate. Any second now, any second, they would look up and know someone was there.

But they didn't. They just worked into the evening and stopped at about ten. When they disappeared into the shower, Aubrey risked ghosting across to see what was on the desk, pulse throbbing in their temples, flooding with adrenaline-heat, and wondering if actually, now was the moment: if they should get to grips with what River had done for the last couple of days, then just—what? Knock them out in the shower and tie them to a chair until they changed everything back again? Say, okay, River, all the filters, all the DNA stuff, passwords, bank accounts;

you and I are going to go through it piece by tiny piece and change
everything back so I can have my name back and my life and everything . . . I'm . . . just going to have to trust that you'll get it all, because
I didn't

(this is why you won)

keep track of it all when we switched

because

I

fucking

trusted

you.

God, they'd have to threaten them somehow, which would be a farce,
because Aubrey was hardly military-grade interrogator material. But
they'd have to. If River wasn't scared, they wouldn't cooperate.

Deep breaths.

A call came through and Aubrey almost jumped onto the ceiling.

River came out of the bathroom, mostly dressed, hair in a damp rope
over one shoulder. When they answered, the Consul appeared in a life-
sized hologram.

"Aubrey! Bit early to turn in for you, ain't it?" they said, in their
cheery folksy way, looking over River's clothes, which were just the
plain things they wore when no one was around. Dark jumper, *never* any
bright colours, heaven *forbid*, typical academic. They might as well have
worn a sign that said ACTUALLY RIVER, but somehow, the Consul didn't
see it.

"Guang," River said, sounding genuinely pleased. "What's this
about?"

"You started on a gigantic repair program in the sun fields. You know
what that means, don't you? You know what kind of footage I have of
you?"

Aubrey, for all they knew they were invisible, found themselves
pressing back against the wall. They'd thought they wouldn't care, if this
happened. It was just a stupid video. People got famous all the time from
sex tapes and other kinds of tapes, and it was only terrible if you were
ashamed of it, but they *were* ashamed, far more than they'd imagined;

and somehow it was worse now that it was going to be aimed at River, who, if you put them in a room filled with prostitutes, would do nothing except suggest unionisation and appropriate sick pay. River would die of that kind of shame, and it wasn't even—

Well, they deserved it, but that didn't stop it being awful anyway.

River smiled. "Bring it on, Song."

Aubrey almost said, *What do you think you're doing?*

"Why are you so happy?" the Consul said speculatively, but they looked more intrigued than angry.

"You'll have to find out," River said, with every sign of joy.

Aubrey had never seen River alight like this.

"Hm," said the Consul. "Well. Watch this space."

River bowed, and cut the call.

Aubrey stood there feeling like they imagined people did when they could see an unsuspecting pedestrian standing right underneath a giant crate of bricks on a very frayed rope.

Maybe this would be easier than Aubrey thought. Maybe it would be a train wreck, and River would have to say, *I'm sorry, I need you to come back and sort this out.*

Relief washed through them. No threats, no violence. They could just wait.

What unfolded across the next week was extraordinary to watch from the inside. When every media outlet in Tharsis received leaked footage from the rehab centre where Aubrey had spent a month last year, River didn't even flinch. Instead, they looked like someone had handed them a big pile of presents. They did a live, televised drug test that proved not only was there nothing strange in them—but that there had *never* been. The halo could pick up addiction, even an old one. Clean. Of course. River wasn't even reliant on coffee.

Immediately House Song was facing a huge backlash for releasing what could only be faked footage.

———

And then, River dropped the price of energy. Drastically.

On a live broadcast, they explained why.

"Kali was overcharging. There was some well-hidden fraud in the House Gale accounts. Half of what taxpayers were paying for energy wasn't for energy at all, it was profit, and that's why Songshu is so grand. So House Gale is liquidating everything that that money touched. Every citizen in Tharsis will get their money back, in full." They didn't mention House Song. They didn't say where the money had really come from at all.

Between spikes of the urge to claw out their own eyes so they wouldn't have to watch what would have to be the total bankruptcy of House Gale in the extremely near future, Aubrey waited for the ensuing explosions. River should have been mauled for it. Senators always were, if they admitted making a mistake, or worse, admitted to fraud committed in their own House.

But somehow that wasn't what happened at all.

People were overjoyed with all the money they were getting back, and the new lower prices for power. Representatives of other Houses who tried to say that Aubrey Gale was clearly buying their way out of a scandal were just—not even shouted down. Attacked. People got death threats. House Gale was everyone's favourite thing in the worlds.

And insanely, the most insane thing of all—House Gale revenue went *up*.

Aubrey stole into the meeting where the engineers and finance people explained why. It was because, they said, a swathe of people who were usually priced out of using much power at all were now using it plentifully. It was Earthstrongers; suddenly, an extra two hundred and fifty thousand people were turning on the heating. Even with the new repairs to the neglected fields, which were now running at higher efficiencies than they had in the last decade, the array was struggling to cope with demand. No sooner had someone said that than River was ordering the construction of a new field. As if investing a billion yuan was an ordinary thing to do over coffee.

All the headlines, all of social media, all of everything, was suddenly about the new honour code that Aubrey Gale was single-handedly enforcing on Great Houses. Other Houses found themselves forced to invite people in to scrutinise their own finances. To no one's surprise, House Song were involved in much more fraud than House Gale. Millions that had been meant for its military defence contracts were being channelled to Earth. It was, the economic analysts said, the biggest money laundering operation in Tharsese history.

Consul Song had never been so unpopular.

The next day, River announced they were running for election.

Aubrey had to sink into a chair and stare at nothing.

They'd left it too late. They couldn't make the switch now. They'd end up stuck in the middle of a consular campaign. They couldn't make the switch and say, *No actually, I've changed my mind, I don't want to be Consul*; that was far too suspicious. They'd have to live with it for at least a few months just to protect the reputation of the House, and consular campaigns were punishing. They'd have preferred to live in a tent in the woods than live like that.

Kasha put her head on Aubrey's knee, looking sympathetic.

"No," Aubrey said to her, quietly, because they were in the dining room and people were everywhere, opening bottles of champagne to celebrate the launch of the campaign, which was apparently already wildly popular, "but—this is River. They can't keep this up. They'll screw it up. I just need to wait a few months. They'll drop out."

They will. The wise thing is to wait. You're not a coward just because you don't snatch it all back now. This is called prudence.

Though River would have taken it all back by now.

Kasha panted optimistically and took Aubrey to look at the fish in the entrance hall. River had put a halo on her once or twice and what they'd learned was that Kasha felt that most problems could be solved by the sufficient contemplation of fish.

Aubrey waited for a month with increasing nerves, and River failed to screw up with increasing confidence, when the riot happened at Gagarin Square.

Aubrey sat by River's hospital bed, watching them, and trying to come to terms with how there would no switching now for at least two seasons. They had listened to the doctors. It would be winter before the amputation site healed enough to start using a prosthetic. To use it with confidence, longer. However determined Aubrey was to get House Gale back, they were not willing to cut off a leg to make it look convincing.

They were trying, too, to accept that they couldn't keep up that early level of fury all the time. Sitting here, they didn't feel angry. They didn't even feel like River had got what they deserved. It was just horrible, and if they could have undone what had happened, they would have.

Because River was drugged with enough morphine for nobody to think it was odd for them to be hallucinating, Aubrey took their hand where it lay on the mattress and held it. River squeezed it.

"Hey," River said sleepily. "You said you'd kill me. Is that why you're here?"

Aubrey smiled a bit. They hadn't forgotten saying that. They had meant it; they still did, but differently. It was a serene iceberg of an idea that wandered through the archipelago of all their other thoughts. They would do it one day, but it wouldn't be today. Not like this.

"I don't need to, you're doing great by yourself."

"Yeah."

"This'll make you Consul."

"I'll screw it up, don't worry."

That brought Aubrey up short. "Why are you running then?"

"Prevent wholesale colonisation from Earth," River whispered. "Earth is about to catch fire. They need to come here. They will. Song thinks we should die for it. Noble cause. I'd rather not."

Aubrey snorted. "Don't be dramatic."

And because River was a machine, even lying in a hospital bed—because they didn't have the basic emotional intelligence to just say, *Yeah, you're right, I know I'm being annoying and exaggerating things for the sake of provoking people*—what they did, was think about it, and frown, and in that measured way they always delivered whatever loony conclusion they'd decided would be most irritating, they said: "Dramatic isn't the same as unlikely."

Aubrey walked away. If they stayed, they'd suffocate River right here and now, and it would be hollow and stupid and meaningless, because River still didn't understand *why* they were unbearable.

Still. River was right about the consulship. They were a maddening pedant. They weren't going to win any elections. One lecture about the etymology of "election" later and anyone in their right mind would rather eat their own eyes than vote in the obnoxious professor. And that was even if, after months of rehabilitation and struggling with the injury and a prosthetic, River even wanted to keep up the consulship bid.

It would be fine.

It would.

The spring and half the summer later, Aubrey let themselves into River's room after Kasha and folded into the spare chair, *their own* old chair, and put the screen on. River had done the rounds. Influencers, broadcasters, even newspapers, the serious-journalism ones. In a wheelchair, looking thin and battered and heroic and unbroken; and of course, what they were talking about was the naturalisation drive.

Cover of *Vogue*.

Aubrey veered between thinking River really believed in cage bans and closed borders, and being convinced they had just latched onto the big divisive issue that could propel them up to Jade Hill. Watching them, it was hard to tell. But whichever it was, losing a leg had done exactly zero to the campaign except skyrocket the poll ratings. It was official as of yesterday. Aubrey Gale was level with Consul Song.

Aubrey was fast losing faith in the voting public of Mars.

The door opened and River came in, looking exhausted. Solly Francis and that horrifying Ren creature were with them. Aubrey got up fast so that nobody would sit on them thinking they were an empty chair. Kasha bounded up and jumped into River's lap.

Traitor dog.

They were all talking about campaign things; ratings, how different issues polled in different boroughs of the city, a surprising uptick of newly naturalised voters in Americatown who thought the new House Gale policies were a brilliant idea. It was Last on the Bus syndrome. You jumped on just in time, and felt the most immense smugness at seeing the door slam in the face of the person right behind you.

Aubrey stood in the corner, making notes about what they said so they could review it later, and waited for Solly and Ren to leave. Then they waited some more, sitting on the floor, for River to take the evening dose of painkillers that would more or less get them through the night. And waited for them to go to bed.

Aubrey stood at the side of the bed, looking down at them. Awake, River was sharp, so sharp you tended to cut yourself trying to have a conversation. But asleep, Aubrey could see how they'd looked when they were little; when they'd been five or six and scared of Kali's evil cat.

Aubrey had never missed anyone more than they missed that child-River.

But there were two important facts here. One: the consular campaign wasn't going away by itself. Two: Aubrey could not be Consul.

You couldn't fight an election if you never slept and your staff thought you were going insane. So that was what Aubrey was going to make them think.

Hating it, hating how nothing stopped them and no thunderbolt blasted them through a wall and no angel appeared, Aubrey knelt on the edge of the bed and pressed both hands round River's neck. Very lightly, just enough to interrupt their breathing but not to hurt.

Of course they flew awake, and of course they could see nothing. River gripped at Aubrey's wrists, trying to tear them off, but they had only been out of hospital for two months, and they were weak from it. It was much harder to keep doing it than Aubrey had thought. They'd thought they were angry enough, after everything, but it was impossible to keep all the reasons front and centre. All they could see was River as a toddler, bubbly and happy.

Aubrey let them go after a minute or so—after that both of them were streaming tears—and then curled up in the corner as Sasha burst in, then Dr Okonkwo. Both of them listened to River's amazingly put-together account of what had happened, and exchanged exactly the concerned kind of look Aubrey had been hoping for.

———

The weeks dragged. Aubrey shadowed River everywhere, writing down every conversation and every meeting, all marked clearly by date, and cross-referenced with sticky notes. Because River would remember. River remembered the names of people they'd met once on a building site. So Aubrey filled notebook after notebook. It was better than taking recordings. To write, you had to rethink things, and re-remember.

It was exhausting and it was incredibly boring. Aubrey spent a lot of time staring hard at clocks, willing ten in the evening to creep round, because that was when River stopped working and went back to mammoth transcripts alone in the room, and that was when Aubrey could escape and go out for a proper walk outside with Kasha. People noticed that Kasha seemed to be going out by herself a lot, but she was an independent dog and she never misbehaved, so nothing ever came of it. Aubrey just had to be careful about throwing things for her.

The drones were a real pain. It was, however, a serious case of hoisted by your own petard.

After the fourth or fifth instance of faked sleep paralysis hallucinations, River had invited in the reality show cameras. Mx Francis was overjoyed, Mx Ren swore a lot, and Sasha seemed tentatively pleased, because more cameras meant better security. River never said it, not even to Dr Okonkwo, but it wasn't for the election. It was nothing to do with fame. It was that they were so pissing confident in the integrity of their own mind that despite everyone telling them otherwise, they weren't convinced they were hallucinating at all. The cameras were to see if anyone, anywhere, would see something strange.

And so Aubrey had to be more careful than ever.

Sometimes they had to open or close doors. Sometimes there was no one to follow, not even Kasha. It became well known that there was a ghost at Songshu. Some people murmured that maybe it was Max, maybe Max was dead; those rumours were everywhere, but in the face of no useable evidence from River's halo, all River had to do was shrug it off.

Sometimes it wasn't so straightforward. Getting food became a lot harder. It was one thing to sneak meals out of the kitchens in such a way that the cooks wouldn't notice there was any missing; in a place like Songshu it would have been impossible to keep track of exactly what five hundred people were eating. But there were permanent camera rigs in there now. You couldn't just open a fridge and take out some salad. Doors opening and closing was a spooky thing people could write off, but floating salad wasn't. Aubrey had to start putting duct tape over the cameras whenever they had to fetch anything. It was a shabby way of doing it, and of course the producers and the security office kept taking the cameras apart to try and work out why they kept blacking out for five or ten minutes, and then puzzling over the sticky residue, but Aubrey had no idea how to hack into a camera feed or loop footage or anything like that.

And then finally, finally, after River had been on the new prosthesis for most of the autumn, the ceaseless medical appointments faded away.

It was time.

There was a problem.

Aubrey hadn't talked to anyone for months. They didn't realize how debilitating that was until one Saturday, when River stayed in bed with a cold and Aubrey decided to have a day off and go down to Tharsis and not be invisible for a while. It was shocking how badly it went.

They didn't even get down the Valley. They were on the train when someone asked them, very politely and ordinarily, whether it was easy to get to Benin Gate from the station. The map haptics were always glitchy right by the Valley wall, something to do with satellite signals.

It didn't feel like being spoken to. It felt like being attacked.

To start with, Aubrey didn't even process the words properly—it was just an assault, and when they did ram it through their flurrying brain, they couldn't pull a sentence together. The part of their mind that did spoken words had—been buried somewhere, under the months and months of silence.

It shook them so badly they had to get the next train back to Songshu. They sat under the willow trees in the entrance hall hugging Kasha.

It was bad enough to find that they weren't functional any more, but what was mortifying was not having realized that that would happen. That was that kind of mistake River would make: assume people were machines you could leave in a cupboard for months and then brush off when you needed them.

Only, said an increasingly loud voice in their head, it *wasn't* the kind of mistake River made. *You've* spent so many years thinking of River as some socially inept, spectrum-straddling oddity that you keep assuming things about them that aren't true. You *assumed* that they would hate the Senate, you *assumed* they were such a cloistered introvert that it would be hell for them. You assumed they were such a machine that they would never make anyone like them. But that isn't River, is it? River—I mean, look at the polling results—is flying. That's *you*.

Horribly, Aubrey found themselves crying into Kasha's fur. By all objective measures, River *should* be the head of House Gale. Maybe even Consul. Sometimes people just took everything from you and there was no point in revenge. You just had to find a way to escape, and make a different life somewhere else. They should never have started any of this.

Maybe it was time to stop.

But there was nowhere else to go.

Aubrey went to the consular debate on automatic. They expected to see River wipe the floor with Guang Song, like they had been doing in all the news interviews until now, and when it didn't happen—when the Consul *won*—something in that despairing glacier started to shift.

Aubrey didn't really decide to do it. They just did. Deciding and doing happened at the same time, they put a portcullis down in their mind so they couldn't think about what would happen if it went wrong, and after the debate, they stole into the back of the Consul's car. They sat quiet for a while, watching Song read some worrying-looking documents that said big swathes of Earth were looking at terrible wildfires in a matter of weeks, and then, very quietly, said:

"Please don't be afraid. I need to talk to you."

The Consul looked up sharply.

"I think—you must have been wondering why Aubrey Gale has suddenly become so capable and so ambitious when they never were before. It's because that wasn't Aubrey Gale up there on the podium. Hasn't been for a year. That's River. I'm Aubrey."

"How are you doing that?" the Consul murmured, far too quiet for the praetorians in the front to hear.

Aubrey swallowed hard. "I'm wearing a military-grade filter which Max gave me. I'm—going to take it off. Can you make sure the praetorians don't shoot me?"

The Consul paused. "Folks," they said louder. "Don't panic. I've got a military agent in the back with me, wearing a filter. They're about to take it off. It's okay."

The praetorian in the front seat still swung round with one hand on their gun.

Aubrey turned the filter off and had to stare into the footwell. With three people watching them—the Consul, the praetorian, and the driver in the mirror—it felt like being crushed in one of those machines that destroyed suspicious packages at airports.

"Hey," the Consul said softly. They couldn't have seemed less flustered. "Can you explain what's going on?"

Aubrey poured it all out. The switch, this whole year, a lot of it incoherent to the point that the Consul had to ask them to double back and explain around things. About halfway, the Consul told the driver to do a big loop of the orbital road that led all the way around New Kowloon so there would be more time before they had to get out at Jade Hill.

"I'll take a halo," Aubrey finished at last, feeling utterly wrung out. "I know it sounds insane, but it's true, I swear, and the halo will . . . will prove it." It was an immense struggle to form longer sentences. Their voice kept shaking. It was appalling.

"So let me get this straight. River took everything from you because you killed Max to escape the influence of my House; but now you're coming to me, Max's own head of House, to escape River?" It would have been an accusation from anyone else, but the Consul looked merry.

Aubrey couldn't even choke out an explanation. If they could have, it would have gone something like:

I cared about being controlled by House Song a lot, before.

But it's amazing how your pride gets ground down after your twin has stolen everything from you, used your name—and God, every time Aubrey heard *their own name* given to River, it jammed another nail into them—and you've been literally invisible for almost a year.

The whole idea of being angry with someone for buying their vote seemed like a laughable privilege now. Imagine having a vote. Imagine existing. Imagine someone caring enough that you exist to bother blackmailing you. Luxury.

I'm just so tired now. Not tired like I've run a long way. That's nice tired. This is—filthy tired. It's in my bones. I just want it to stop, but there's nowhere to go. I can't take the fake name River gave me and make a new life as a schoolteacher or something—maybe I could have to start with, but now I can barely speak. I need someone to help me; but I have no one.

So what they said was:

"Yes."

"You're not worried I'll, you know, chuck you out of this car which is going at eighty kilometres an hour?"

Aubrey looked out the window, at the city strobing by, and the beautiful purple aurora that was the solar circuitry on the road charging the car. "That's okay," they said.

But the Consul didn't throw them out of the car. Instead, they watched Aubrey with an unbearable gentleness. It was how people—good people, kind people—looked at wounded animals.

Not how Aubrey did. Or River. Show either of them a wounded animal in the woods and they'd been trained to shoot it. Kindest thing, said Kali.

"I'm not going to do that," the Consul said. "Because that would be dumb. I'm going to look after you, and get you better, and then we're going to swap you back in. You'll have your life back, and House Gale will be friendly with House Song again."

Aubrey waited, because it seemed absurd that they would ever do that. They waited for the Consul to lunge past, open the door, and sling them out. Jokes! You're a splat on the road. Because Aubrey had just confessed to murdering a member of House Song. The obligation to get some justice—if that had been House Gale, the honour of the House alone would have made Aubrey publicly flay whoever had done it.

There was no lunging.

And that's because, said a little voice that sounded like River, *the Consul is a statesman, whereas you are a narcissist. You wouldn't seek justice because the person's family needed it. You'd do it because you would have felt dishonoured.*

"You haven't spoken to anyone for months, have you?" the Consul said.

Aubrey shook their head.

"Come here." They put one arm out and hugged them, and Aubrey juddered into tears they couldn't stop, desperately relieved, and desperately scared, because they honestly couldn't think of any reason why the Consul wouldn't just shove them in front of the national press and use them as proof that River was committing identity fraud, and then it would be a prison hulk, and one day they would die in one of those airless steel cells. But they couldn't think any more. They couldn't get further than knowing something had to change, for worse or for something else. "It's okay."

And so Aubrey was a guest of the Consul's at Jade Hill for the next two weeks. It was scary and balmy by turns. Words skittered away from them whenever anyone asked even a simple question like, *Are you allergic to anything we should tell the cook about?* If one of the praetorians opened a door for them, the fact of having been seen was paralysing, and it took every mote of courage just to walk through, even though, and this was maddening part, they couldn't have said what dreadful thing their stupid brain thought might happen.

They hadn't expected it at all—this was a business transaction, after all, and the Consul had no reason to care about Aubrey past their ability to take House Gale back from River—but the Consul came to visit every second day or so. When Aubrey had been there for a week, they appeared dressed up on the Friday night as a giant fluffy tiger with a bucket of sweets, and did a happy dance in the middle of the sitting room. Aubrey had no idea what was happening and said so.

The enormous fluffy tiger gave them a disapproving look. "It's the final. It's China versus India. Forget the election, this is the match of the century."

"The . . . ?"

"Soccer! I have brought you the necessary," the Consul said gravely, and handed Aubrey an Indian flag.[38] They had a Chinese one. They started a little flag sword-fight.

Aubrey considered. "We're going to destroy you."

Just for a second, the Consul looked delighted that they'd managed to think of a normal reply, but then danced away to put the big screen on, and did a sports-commentator voice. "Yow, fighting words from the underdog there, but can India really pull it off in the face of *the almighty—*"

"As the direct descendant of Kali, Destroyer of Worlds, I say the Celestial Empire can get back into the trash fire from which it emerged."

The Consul yelled the Chinese national anthem at them, and at the door, some praetorians had to try very hard not to look like they were laughing.

The Consul stayed in a good mood all week. River was being minced in the press over what had happened to January Stirling, and their polling looked awful now. Six months ago, Aubrey would have been hopeful that this was it, River had finally crashed, but they weren't so sure now. Now they were pretty certain that River was like a boomerang. You hurled it as hard as you could, but a little while later, it looped back and smacked you in the face.

It wasn't long after that that they both discovered River's boomerang plan. The Consul came in one evening with an intelligence services briefing file, looking speculative.

---

38 Aubrey was only Indian in the sense that they owned clothes paint-stained from Holi and had been forced to study Sanskrit. Nobody Natural in Tharsis was in any possible way Indian, or Scandinavian, or Congolese, or anything else. You were bolted together from whichever genes your parents thought looked cool at the time, and even if things hadn't worked like that, there was something embarrassing about trying to claim you were originally, say, Scottish, if even your great-great-grandparents had never seen Earth.

"So River just went to the Earthstrong block in Americatown where January Stirling lives. He's just out of prison."

Aubrey frowned. To anyone who didn't know River, it would be easy to assume they had just gone to apologise. But River never apologised for winning an argument. River believed in the survival of the cleverest. If you were a vole in the path of River's combine harvester of a brain, well, you deserved to be goo. "Why?"

"Not sure. There were no press there, so not an apology photo op. I wanted to ask you. Genuine apology?"

"Hell would freeze over first," said Aubrey, who was starting to suspect that something boomerang-shaped might be happening. They paused. "Let me go back to Songshu. I can find out."

The Consul's eyes ticked up and down Aubrey's whole self. "Will you be okay?"

If it had been just for the sake of learning River's ordinary day-to-day activities, Aubrey might have said no. But it wasn't. There was an innocent dancer standing in the way of a combine harvester. Someone had to make sure nothing horrifying was about to happen to him. River had cheerfully destroyed their own twin. There was no telling what they'd do to a stranger.

"I'll be fine."

Marriage.
    Boomerang.
    Pow.

"This is bad," the Consul said the afternoon after Aubrey had sat in on River's conversation with January at the Tiangong. They hooked a chair across with one ankle. They didn't ever just sit in chairs; it was more like a docking process. "If Stirling's got no haptics, he's not seeing the Hades filter. We can't swap you back in while he's at Songshu."

Aubrey thought about it, and tried to plan out what they wanted to say, to get it right. They were starting to think clearly again when someone spoke to them, which felt wonderful, but it was backfiring in that they were starting to get verbose just as a way of proving to themselves that they could. "He's being paid to do this. The—choice was this or naturalisation, and he's a dancer, I can see why he would . . ." *Stop letting it get away from you . . .* "He doesn't like River. He was being polite today, but he's going to hate them once he has to live at Songshu. Maybe—you can talk him round to your side?"

"I'm going to try," the Consul said heavily. "He might agree. We're about to get a lot of refugees, and I can't see him wanting to let River, or anyone, lock them out. Those wildfires that were forecast—they've started. It's going to be worse than they thought."

Whenever Aubrey saw footage from Earth, even when they saw people interviewed and convinced themselves for five minutes that such a place could possibly be real, it wouldn't stay in their head for long. It made sense, but it was one of those quicksilver ideas that danced away from you if you tried to hold it. The gravity, and the wars, and the floods—it sounded like something from a fairy-tale nightmare. It was difficult even to imagine wildfires. The hottest temperature ever recorded on Mars was twenty degrees Celsius, and people had lost their minds.

The Consul hesitated. "Anyway, I have an idea. But it depends on how you feel."

"I—sincerely doubt that it does."

"Okay." They hunched forward, hands clasped. "I have two problems. One, House Gale's anti-Earthstronger policies have taken off. There's a record clamouring from the general public for cages to be banned. Record hate crimes against Earthstrong immigrants too. Even if we fill the air with images of desperate refugees, we'll never get people to settle to the idea of bringing them here. Even though that's what this colony is for."

Aubrey nodded.

"Two, January Stirling, who could single-handedly derail your switch back into House Gale." They sighed. "So what I need is a way to get people to accept a flood of refugees; and I need January Stirling to *not* be the Senator Consort of House Gale. Do you know about Ariel, at the old weather station at Mount Penglai?"

"Sure," Aubrey said, puzzled at the sudden change of subject. They couldn't see what Ariel had to do with the politics of House Gale, or immigration rules. "The AI of the Met Office?"

"Mm. Ariel's been doing that for two hundred years. They were around in the old days, before the atmosphere was under control. Back when they were doing weather control experiments to try and make it rain."

"Didn't that just make giant dust storms?"

"Yeah. It did." The Consul gave them a long intense look, willing them to see without having to say it.

Aubrey inclined their head a little. "Sun fields can't operate in a dust storm. And our fields have had chronic underinvestment for the last twenty years under Kali. We couldn't cope with a period of prolonged darkness."

"Right. We'd need Earth to rescue us. Send uranium. Fire up the old reactors. It would take their ships a couple of months to get here, but— what's your assessment? It's nearly the end of winter, could River keep Tharsis alive until help comes?"

Aubrey gazed at the edge of the table, thinking. "There would be blackouts. A lot of people would die of cold. The poorest twenty per cent of Tharsis can only just afford electricity as things are."

"Okay, so some people die—actually that's to the good, because if they die without power, then that seems like River's fault—but the city as a whole, can it survive?"

"More or less," Aubrey said slowly. "It would be tight, though, even with blackouts. If the fleet from Earth were delayed, we'd be looking at thousands and thousands of deaths."

"But it's possible."

"Did . . . you hear me?" Aubrey asked, worried they hadn't articulated it nearly as well as they'd thought. "I wasn't exaggerating. A thousand deaths would be a *good* figure. We—I mean, House Gale—run simulations of power failure all the time, and it's pretty horrendous, even with short blackouts. And it would disproportionately affect Earthstrongers. They're not genetically modified for the climate here."

"I heard," the Consul said. "But a thousand deaths here in exchange for saving millions of people coming from Earth? I'm fine with that. Aren't you?"

Aubrey didn't know what they were fine or not fine with any more. They had spent all their time as a senator losing their temper over things that shouldn't have mattered, and failing to solve the problems that should have had their full attention from their first minute in office. If they had a moral compass, it was too wonky to be relied upon for decisions like this. Or any decisions.

"Even if something goes wrong, even if *most* people here die, that's still better than denying entry to the people coming here from Earth," the Consul pushed. "No?"

Aubrey had to look away. That didn't sound right. You couldn't always say that the greater number of people were always in the right. That was how you ended up with empires.

But they didn't trust that broken compass any more. The Consul was a kind person. You had to trust someone, and a kind person was a good place to start.

"And then any ships arriving from Earth will be able to land because— we'll need them."

"Right."

Aubrey nodded gradually.

The Consul hesitated. "What's your stance on Earth?"

"I haven't got a stance on Earth, it's a long way away and I don't know anyone there."

"Even after . . ."

"One lady rips one irritating senator in half and suddenly everyone's got an opinion," said Aubrey dully.

The Consul paused. "I can't tell if you're joking."

"I don't have a stance," Aubrey sighed. Their sense of humour was so off colour now that most doctors would probably have sent it straight to palliative care.

"You're so refreshing, have I told you that?"

"Do you mean unresisting?" Aubrey asked after a second.

"I do, that speaks poorly of my character, doesn't it? No: anyway, there's another step to this profoundly unethical plan."

Aubrey waited.

"The dust will wipe out all the security systems at Songshu, and nobody, *nobody*, will be surprised if some Earthstrong group sends a suicide bomber. We can make sure they don't succeed and no one's hurt—but we can also make it seem like they were talking to January Stirling. If you give us information about River's schedule, it'll look like it comes from him. It doesn't matter what his halo says, River won't want to defend him. They sent January to prison for nothing, they'll be expecting him to stab them in the back. All we have to do is convince them he has. He goes back to prison, and then we swap you back in."

Aubrey ducked their head. Now that it was possible—imminently, clearly possible—they didn't like the idea of putting River in the way of serious harm, even if the bomber had bad information or faulty explosives, or whatever. It was difficult to keep hating someone with enough passion to truly hurt them.

Aubrey breathed in deeper. "Either I agree to help frame January and then swap back in, or . . . you'll out me, won't you? Bring River down that way. Identity fraud. Protecting a murderer."

The Consul looked sad, and old. "Yeah." They didn't try to offer any reasons. They didn't try to say, *Look, perhaps millions of lives will depend on landing those ships here. The great purpose of this colony is to do that, and River is in my way.*

It must have taken a deep kind of restraint. Aubrey hoped they could be like that one day.

"Why haven't you done that already? It's easier and safer than dealing with the fallout of a dust storm."

"A dust storm is well worth the support of House Gale, once you're its senator again."

It was funny. They'd come full circle. They'd started out as a senator under the control of House Song, and now they would be again. Only this time, they weren't angry. Just grateful. The Consul was a safe harbour to shelter in.

"What happens to River, after we make the switch?" they asked at last.

"Prison," the Consul said sadly. They paused. "How do you feel about that?"

"I deserved everything I got. But River is as bad as I am. You have to be, to do what they did."

"They are definitely ruthless," the Consul reflected. They didn't sound like they were scared by it, only interested. "I am too."

Aubrey watched them for a little while. "Consul . . . when the fleet lands. What happens?"

They shrugged. "It'll be ugly. Probably a lot of Natural people will die. But there's five million of us and ten billion of them. There's no other way for this to go. No country in history has ever successfully resisted this kind of thing. Basically all we can do is keep people as calm as possible while Tharsis makes the shift to a majority Earthstrong population. But that's our duty now. The point of the vanguard is to die in the service of the many who follow, and if they turn round and decide they don't want to, well, it's the job of the general to *make* them."

Aubrey nodded slightly, and had to stare into space. They had thought River was being dramatic when they talked about all this; it had all felt too big and too complicated to be that simple, but it was simple. "Custard all the way down," they murmured.

54

As Aubrey stopped talking, January had to fight off a bizarre disappointment. He felt as if he'd been behind the curtain at a magician's show. To start with, it was thrilling and fascinating, but the closer you looked, the more ordinary the theatre was, the more you noticed the chips in the skirting boards and the peeling paint around the hot water pipes, and the dust on the red curtain, and how desperate it all was. He had wanted Aubrey to be someone hateful who he could just righteously resent, but the more they said, the more it slipped away.

He wondered what it had been like on the day of the bomb; when he'd helped Gale and Gale had helped him, instead of either of them doing what any thinking human would have predicted. Aubrey must have felt more trapped than ever.

They'd lost some of their carefulness after that, he realized. They had let him see them while Gale was getting ready to go to the Tiangong. They had been combing Gale's hair not at night when it might be a sleep paralysis hallucination, but at five in the afternoon. That tormenting of River had gone from strategic to something else.

"That was you," he said last. "The night we made the announcement about getting the sun fields into the atmosphere, you dragged River up to my door."

"I couldn't believe what they'd made you agree to," Aubrey said. "Helping to turn away your own people, I mean for fuck's sake." That last was aimed at River. "I shouldn't have . . . I was angry."

"You're angry a lot," January noted.

"So are you," they said, sharp. "It only took you a week to yell at River for the first time, imagine how I feel."

"That's—so the riot," he said, half to them and half to the Consul. "It was a way to kill us both and make the switch."

"It was," the Consul said heavily. "But you both got out too quickly." They smiled, and it looked like an honest smile. "I'm glad it didn't work. I'm glad we're doing this instead. Though I wish we could have found an easier way to it."

January honestly couldn't think of a way it could have gone more easily. Whatever you thought about Earth, whatever decision you made about the coming fleet, that decision would cost thousands of lives.

But he did think he finally understood what We Are Mars meant. It wasn't about Earth. It was nothing to do with wanting people to come here or not wanting them to. He knew River well enough now to know they would never mean that. What it *meant* was, it's fucking dreadful here, and in these conditions, there are no good choices.

"What happens now?" he asked.

"You stay with House Gale. You've done such good things here," the Consul said. "River will be safe. Not on a hulk."

They didn't say that those two things would be linked, but they didn't need to.

"I meant immediately, now," he said, a bit flat.

"Now you get on a podium with me and read your autocue," Aubrey explained.

The Consul tapped him and gave him a chocolate bar. "Keep eating."

It felt patronising, even though he did need it. "I'm not hungry."

"Tough. I watched a thing about how to look after your alien," they said solemnly.

He looked up at them, hanging over the edge of saying, *How can you possibly think I'm going to laugh at a joke after everything you've done.*

"January," the Consul said, intense and quiet. "I'm sure you're thinking of ways to screw me over, which is justified. I like you, of course I do, but I have to do what's in the best interest of my state. We're a city, which belongs to a country, and my country—China—wants me to take these refugees, because it is the bare minimum of humanity we can offer. I know it's hard to keep thinking that big when what you've got in front of you is a few rooms in a house on Mars, but that's what this is and I wouldn't be doing it if the stakes weren't so high. Do you—God, tell me you understand."

It was astounding how difficult it was to pretend to agree to something like that even when your life depended on it. He'd spent his whole life thinking what bloody idiots martyrs were—was it really so difficult to cross your fingers behind your back and say, ah, no, changed my mind, actually—but just now he could see vividly why plenty of people preferred to burn at a stake than swear to something when it wasn't true.

River tilted their head. *Don't be so stupid.*

He smiled. "No, I do. It's okay. Thanks for not just holding a gun at me. It's just—you know, I'm a bit tumbled. I feel like I've got jet lag, just with—events, instead of times. Plot lag."

They both laughed, and the Consul put one arm around him. "Okay. Let's get this done."

55

The praetorians set up lecterns in the foyer, in front of the main doors, between the two great weeping willow trees. People passing by noticed, and hesitated to see what was going to happen. Drones congregated too; and then more people when the House Song and House Gale seals went onto the lecterns. Nobody did that unless it was an important announcement.

All January could do was stand with Aubrey Gale, while River was still handcuffed beside a praetorian who, presumably, could see them. He found himself scanning the room for helpful things, as if there even existed a *thing* that would be helpful. Aubrey was bending a willow twig into quite a complicated pattern between their hands.

"Willow and leaving. *Liu* and *liu*," they explained when they saw him looking. "So you give someone willow when they're going away." They swallowed. "For River."

"Oh," he said. It was a lovely thought.

"Right, that's ready," the Consul said. "We'll do this live. All set?"

"Hang on," said January.

"Where are you going?"

"I feel sick, wait." He ran towards the bathrooms and, hoping to God they were out of the praetorians' immediate sight line, took Dr Molotov's arm and tugged them in gently but urgently after him. "Hi. Hi; sorry about this. Um. The Consul's just—just switched River and Aubrey back, and—how possible is it to turn off the internet in the house?"

"So people . . . see?" Dr Molotov said slowly.

"Can you do that? I know I heard you saying it isn't so simple, but . . ."

"January. You saw what happened before. A lot of people will go into shock, on no warning—people are going to be cooking, walking down stairs . . ."

"What if it was just a few seconds? Just a flash, so people saw, and then . . . ?"

"And then what?" Dr Molotov said carefully.

"I don't know, do I? I don't have any plans, but we can't just let the Consul drag River away." He glanced back the way he'd come. "They'll come and fetch me in a second, I have to—please? The AI who watches over the internet—what are they called, Lao Zi? Might they agree, just for a few seconds . . ."

Dr Molotov winced. "I made that up. It's just a switch in the boiler room."

"It . . . ?"

Dr Molotov tried to laugh. "I'll go now. January, I—listen. I know you don't think so, but you're as much a Gale as any of us now. You'll know what to do."

January didn't know what to say, except that he was very sure he had no idea what to do.

Dr Molotov bowed. "I serve at the pleasure of the House of Gale."

Stepping up to that lectern felt like climbing the gallows. By the time he did, there was a crowd of people watching, both in the foyer and around the balconies that looked down into it. The lights from the drones cut harsh across everything.

"All right?" the Consul asked him.

"No, but better. Thank you."

"Let's get going then," they said, and waved up to the production gallery.

On the live screens, the drum fanfare that came before consular appearances rolled out on all the live feeds, including the screen opposite. January breathed out as slowly as he could, thoroughly not liking the idea of having to look at himself while he talked.

Silence came down.

"Good evening," the Consul began. "As you have all seen on the news today, there have been some difficulties at Songshu. There was some unrest and, tragically, several deaths, both Earthstrong and Natural. In the aftermath, House Gale and House Song have come to a difficult decision."

There was a stir from the people employed by Songshu, and eyes slid towards January and Aubrey.

"House Gale would like to thank everyone who worked on the tower project," Aubrey said, sounding almost exactly like who they were meant to be. Off to the side, by the praetorian with red hair, River was staring at the floor. "And we're all overjoyed that the launch was successful. But given that it was my staff who started the riot here, I no longer believe it is in anyone's interest for me to stand in this election. I'm under an ongoing police investigation; that does nothing for Tharsis. I'm stepping down. I wish Consul Song the best of luck in their second term."

The stir in the crowd turned to something deeper, a kind of dismay that had nowhere to go.

It was January's turn. He put his glasses on to see the autocue that the Consul's people had written for him. By the praetorian, River vanished. He wondered what was taking Dr Molotov so long. It felt like hours since he'd spoken to them.

"House Gale will cooperate with the police investigation fully," he said, thinking feverishly that he sounded nothing like himself at all, that he never used words like "cooperate." "If the Senator is ever taken in for further questioning, which we don't expect, the House will continue to run as usual; we have an extensive, very capable staff."

"There won't be any questions for now, folks, the police have to get on with their work and so do the rest of us," the Consul said warmly.

Please hurry up please hurry up please hurry up.

"Thank you very m—"

The virtual overlays over everything in January's glasses vanished, and half the people in the room buckled as they lost their balance; even the praetorians.

He didn't know, until the praetorian with red hair stumbled, what he meant to do.

He slung himself off the podium and, while the praetorian was still trying to get their bearings, thumped into them sideways and tore the gun off them. River materialised again at the same time, and there was a collective shocked yell from the people who saw, but January ignored it, his whole weight on the praetorian's chest while he hunted through their pockets for the fob that unlocked the handcuffs. When he found it, he clicked it. River's manacles fell away, and after a paralysing moment where the internet came up again and they vanished, River appeared again and slung the bracelet onto the ground. They dragged January up and back to the lectern, where of course the cameras were still filming, rapt.

"That is not Aubrey Gale," River said, pointing at Aubrey, voice rich and steady and full of an iron authority that even the Consul didn't have. "I do *not* step down from this election, and I *will* be taking House Song immediately to court for kidnap. I was just abducted and held at gunpoint, and if anything at all happens to me today, please be in no doubt that it was murder."

"It's true, it's true," January said desperately. He smacked the release on his cage to put the praetorians off any thoughts of snatching River back. The silver skeleton hissed open around him. "*That* isn't Senator Gale, they're just wearing filters!"

"On the floor right now!" Different praetorians were yelling it, circling them both.

January stepped in front of River.

River touched his shoulders and moved him very lightly aside.

It was perfectly still. Someone with their eyes shut would never have known there were hundreds of people in the room.

January saw the Consul realize it was no good. His heart started to lift as their whole expression fell. They looked towards the head of the praetorians, and he saw them start to say, *Enough, we're going.*

Aubrey saw it too.

January was half waiting for it, which was why he noticed in time: Aubrey had a gun.

It surged through his mind that if he tackled them, he had no way of moderating the force of it. Either he jumped or he didn't, and at full strength, he would kill them. Live on camera, an Earthstronger murdering someone, and he would go to prison forever because there was no self-defence for an uncaged Earthstronger, no clause that let you defend someone else because it was *never* proportionate, it was like bringing a grenade to a knife fight, so—

But you couldn't think like that.

56

He wasn't going to watch the election results. They had it on in the canteen, on a big screen, and everyone was watching, and every now and then there was a yell from downstairs when a new announcement came from the polls. Every so often, the warden put their head round the cell door to ask, looking pained, if he was sure he wouldn't come down. Each time, they reminded him increasingly of one of those bendy dolls, because they didn't just stand in the door, but leaned sideways, like they were embarrassed about disturbing prisoners. He always said yes he was sure, and stayed propped on the top bunk with some Mandarin drills instead, because it didn't matter. Even if Gale won, nothing would change. Even if Earth invaded, won, overthrew the current government and brought in permanent cages, nothing was going to change. The law was the law. He was here for twenty-five years. He needed to learn to settle in.

There was another tap on the door.

"I know you're being really nice, but I mean it, I don't need to see who wins," he said, not to the door but the Mandarin character on his screen which he definitely *did know* but whose meaning was fluttering around the edges of his brain, just out of reach, like an especially annoying moth. "I'll find out in the morning."

"You'll find out in about half an hour, actually," Gale said. "I think they have to come and get me, either way."

He swung round. Gale rested both forearms on the mattress, tall enough to do that in a room for Earthstrongers without climbing on the bunk below.

"What are you doing?" January demanded. "How are—is this a publicity—you're going to be in so much trouble! I mean . . . hi," he trailed off.

"Hi," Gale said quietly. "How are you?"

"Good, I . . . how are you?"

"Nervous. I hoped you wouldn't mind. The warden said it would be all right, but—I'll go away." They frowned. "If you do mind, I mean."

"Of course I don't mind—hm." He had to look away, towards the wall. His eyes were flooding and there was a rock in his throat, which was infuriating. Gale came to see him every week and he had held himself together beautifully every time, but that, he realized now, was because he knew when it was going to happen and he could work himself up to it.

Gale touched his knee, looking worried. "What—is everything all right, has something happened?"

"No, everything's fine. Everything's fine. I'm happy." He pulled his sleeve over his eyes.

Gale stood back a little way and opened both hands. When he came to the edge of the bed, they lifted him down, so gently he might have been floating. The prison boiler suit wasn't unlike the factory one—maybe a little better—and he felt suddenly like none of it was real, he'd just come in a loop and everything from then until now had been a bright dream that didn't really belong to him.

Gale ghosted both hands over the ribs of his cage, and then hooked two fingertips under the collarbone. It wasn't difficult. "This is too big for you. Where's yours?"

"No, this *is* mine, I've just been—a bit off food," said January, which was a lie; he'd been completely off food. Whenever he even thought about eating, he felt weird and panicky. It was an oddly not unpleasant throwback to his early twenties, when he'd had to stay light enough for the then principal to lift, despite being a fair way taller. Since then, his brain had a switch about food. In times of proper anxiety it just went clunk, and he developed an immediate horror of toast. He was amazed it hadn't gone clunk before now.

"You've only been here a week," Gale protested.

He caught their hands. "I'm fine. Anyway, haven't you got bigger things to worry about tonight?"

"No," Gale said, nearly as a question, like they didn't really follow what he was talking about.

The noise from the canteen sounded louder and louder as they came down the broad corridor. There were flashes from that direction too, and in the air, drones floated to and fro. Like suddenly attentive bees, they looped down straight at him the second they noticed him. It made him jump. He sighed. It was possible the no-food thing was making him twitchy. He wondered tentatively about some rice, but the Swan King snarled that there would be no rice, only tea, shut up.

He saw it on the big screen before he saw it in front of him. The news anchor was already talking about the live footage.

". . . *in an extraordinary move, Senator Gale has taken their whole campaign team into Ares Prison, where January Stirling is being held for the mandatory minimum sentence of twenty-five years for uncaged manslaughter; already sparking opposition accusations of a publicity stunt to put pressure on the High Court to change the law . . .*"

Gale's whole staff was indeed here, set up on the tables along with the prisoners, none of whom seemed to mind, and some of whom were taking the opportunity to flirt with the beautiful rich people in the cheery way people do when they know they haven't got a hope. January would have been nervous in a prison at home, but none of these people really deserved to be here. All of them, in this wing, were in for the same thing he was. They had killed someone, always by accident. The ones who hadn't done it by accident were on the hulks around Jupiter. They were the unlucky one-in-two-hundred-and-sixty-sevens.

Mx Ren ducked through a knot of people to say hello, looking happier than he'd ever imagined they could possibly look. He had a sudden suspicion that actually they quite liked a bit of rule breaking.

"Will you not be in trouble for taking over a prison?" January asked them both, Ren and Gale.

"Trouble is how you get people's attention," Ren said, clapping his shoulder. "If we lose, we can still wangle you out of here. I mean, we'll be changing places with you for what will then be treason, but then it'll be your turn at playing with lawyers and negotiating with House Song."

So they all watched the news coverage together. Even the guards had come in from the staff room. A lot of them, he noticed, were wearing House Gale badges. Beside him, Gale looked serene, but he could feel them shaking. He slid his fingers through theirs, half sure they were going to push him off, but they only squeezed, hard.

"—in prison and even *I* don't think we should be allowed to walk too near Natural people," one of the other inmates was saying seriously to Sasha, who looked bewildered to find themselves roped into a heated card game about exploding cats with about eight other people.

"God, no, all this bringing new people into the city however they like is insane. The Consul's a nutbag. Gale knows what he's doing."

Sasha took a breath, but then held it, and nodded. "Well. I think so."

"Military, are you?"

"Oh, yeah."

"Me too."

"Whereabouts?"

"Ganymede."

"No!" Sasha laughed, pleased. "What base? I was at Jiangxi—"

"Jiangxi! We visited once and stole all your kiwis!" the Earthstrong man exclaimed joyfully.

"You bastards, I *wondered* what had happened!"

January glanced at Gale and grinned. "I don't know if you can hear, but I think an important thing is happening over this way."

Gale smiled too, and January tried hard to remember how they looked right then, in case he didn't have another chance for a while. As always, they were sitting very straight and still, the image of perfect Tharsese chivalry, hair loose in a heavy black spill sealed back with the senate sigils. Usually if they were out in public they dressed in House colours, but today it was white and a pale, rusty gold. It was something about dress code for elections, but it looked more as though the spirit of the winter had just stolen in to see what people did away from the frozen desert and the mountains.

"They're about to call New Kowloon," someone called suddenly, and there was a dead quiet.

New Kowloon was the biggest constituency in Tharsis. It would swing things definitively one way or another. With it, Gale's result would be too high for the Consul to catch up. Without it, they couldn't win.

"New Kowloon is the Consul's home constituency, isn't it," January said quietly.

"It is."

He drew his breath in deep. "I just wanted—I know I haven't said this to you before. But I didn't do it on the understanding that you'd swing something legal in the Senate. I don't *expect* you to be able to change anything. So just—whatever happens, promise you won't feel guilty. Or, you know. A flattering but not totally debilitating amount of guilt."

Gale looked down at him for a long second. "Please can you stop being so nice to me, please just fight me, not fighting feels like you don't like me enough to bother."

"What are you talking about? I can't stand you," January said.

Gale laughed.

On the big screen, the shot of the voting registry suddenly zoomed in on a steward who raised their hand. "New Kowloon calls for Senator Gale."

Being shot at had been quieter than the noise that erupted all around them. Someone threw glitter over them; when he twisted round, it was Mx Ren, actually, properly smiling for the first time since he'd met them, and then at least eight people were pushing Gale upright, up onto the table where everyone could see, and then they were on the screen as well as there in real life.

"Good evening. Well, first things first, right?" they said, and the whole room laughed. "January Stirling; by Consular Pardon, you are absolved of all charges against you. You're free."

Numbly, he wondered what it was he was free to do.

57

He wasn't aware of being ill, or even of feeling off. He was fine when the guards led him out of the prison, fine changing into some clothes that Mx Francis had brought especially, fine on the drive to Gagarin Square, where there was a secret back entrance to Jade Hill two streets away to avoid the crowds at the front. But he collapsed the moment he walked in through the door, and when he came around, he was in a room he didn't recognise, and Gale was sitting on the edge of the bed, reading.

They set the book aside and tapped their fingertips against the sternum of his cage. "Dr Okonkwo recommends that you eat something more often than once every five days."

"Yeah, I . . . that got away from me a bit." He swallowed, disorientated. It was a lovely room, all glass, with a view across Tharsis and plants tumbling down the walls, which looked alive. A little fountain bubbled in the corner. Kasha was there, studying what definitely seemed like a real iguana with her head cocked. He found his glasses; the clock in them said it had only been about twenty minutes. "When do I have to go?"

"Where?" Gale asked, with the carefulness of someone worried they were talking to a person gripped with delirium.

"The naturalisation centre. When are you—when are you banning cages, I mean."

Gale was quiet for entire seconds in which January's insides tied themselves up. Gale was going to say, *Now.* "We're not doing that."

It was too far from what he'd expected and he didn't understand. "What?"

"I can't. I can't send you to one of those places, it's brutal. And if I can't send you, then I can't send anyone. We'll have to come up with something else."

"People—voted for you to do that."

"No, they voted for me because I'm married to you and because the solar rig works." Gale smiled a little. "And—it's a less pressing problem than it could be. I have some numbers to tell you. The Office of Statistics released them just now."

"Numbers?"

"Yes, but it will be over soon. Lie back and think of England."

January swiped at them inaccurately.

"Since you swore the oath and gave me your key, the number of cage-related accidents has gone down significantly. People are giving their keys to their partners, or their neighbours, or their friends. There's a hashtag on social media, #EarthstrongHonour, and there are millions of posts. Where there have been non-lethal accidents—seventy-four per cent *fewer* victims are prosecuting than last quarter, because they say they can understand how it happened. The Earthstrong Rights group, which advocates never locking cages at all, has lost thousands of subscribers. The European Federation Embassy has opened a desk where people who live alone can hand in their keys, and people are starting to use it."

January stared at them. "But in your debate, you said—whenever there's a gigantic strength difference between two sectors of a population, what you get in the end is genocide."

"I did. But—as you said, I was forgetting how many kinds of strong there are."

He didn't know what to say, and so in the end, he caught the very ends of their hair around his knuckles and pulled gently until Gale leaned down to him. He touched their heads together. "Thank you."

Gale brushed his eyelashes. He didn't realize they were wet until then. "Promise you'll keep fighting me."

"Yes, Consul." He touched the new silver in their hair. "Isn't there a balcony you should be giving a speech from?"

"Yes, but I'm scared, so I was waiting for you."

"That's a lie, though, isn't it."

"Is it? Can you hear that noise?"

January listened. What he had thought was roar of the storm was—not. "Ah. Well. Let's not keep them waiting, then."

What he had thought was lightning far away were actually camera flashes, coming up from Gagarin Square.

"I'm not ready," Gale said, looking more anxious than they had when they had been facing straightforward death.

January took their hand and towed them towards the balcony. Outside, the lights across Tharsis were back on. Tereshkova Wharf showed water capacity at a hundred per cent on its neon sign. The Rings at the Tiangong were turning again. Gagarin Square was full of people, and like they always did after an election, they were holding paper lanterns, fires lit at their bases. As Sasha opened the doors, people started to let the lanterns go, and they floated up and up into the dust in winking swarms. "That's a good thing."

58

Three days later the fleet arrived from Earth. The air force escorted them down to a site twenty miles from Songshu, on the Plains. January had never seen so many ships in one place. There were tiny ones, ships that had been made with quick loops to the lunar colonies in mind, not the gruelling journey to Mars at aphelion. And there were the mighty Crossing ships, the ones so vast that if they ever landed, they would never take off again; they hung high above, their warning lights pulsing amber and glowing in the dust. Little shuttles struggled up and down, taking up supplies.

The dust storm was still howling, but that was to the good. It meant that no one could just wander off. It would have been difficult to anyway. The Plains altitude would knock most people flat if they left the pressurized cabins aboard the ships. The medication for it, the one Dr Okonkwo had given January, seemed not to exist on Earth—where, as Dr Okonkwo pointed out, it would be very difficult to travel from sea level to four miles up all at once.

With the leftover steel that had not been used on the solar rig, the same engineers and the same construction crews were putting up an old-fashioned biome, running in water pipes and power lines. Trenches were laid out everywhere the work was going on, the hexagon beehive skeleton of the dome was already half covering the site, and because cars were out of the question in the dust, teams of horses pulled carts loaded with resistance cages.

The army surrounded the whole site. Legions of tents stretched out in rows, and soldiers walked the boundaries. Searchlights powered through the dust haze.

"So far the Crossing ships aren't letting our inspectors aboard," a general told Gale as they rode together to the edge of the building work. January thought the wind might be dropping; he could hear them, even though they weren't yelling. "They say they're worried about names being taken, people arrested for extremism, human rights violations, all that crap. There are soldiers up there, not refugees, I'll bet you my boots."

"Why are you so sure?" said January. "It's a valid concern. I never gave my name to anyone either. If they wanted to invade, would we not have seen tanks by now?"

"Or," the general grumbled, "they're waiting to get a good clear shot at the Consul and save themselves a lot of effort. They didn't *request* that you came here, Consul, they *demanded*. No inspectors until they get a personal guarantee. That's going to be an assassination attempt. I still advise strongly against your being here."

The three of them, along with a lot of soldiers, were under a canopy that blocked the sight line of anyone not immediately ahead of them. It moved as they did, or rather, as the three horses did. Tharsis horses were tall, like everything else, and January was a long way off the ground. In front of him, though, Yuan seemed to be having the time of his life, twisting round to look at things and, when he wasn't doing that, telling the horse made-up secrets.

January had one hand clamped firmly on the back of Yuan's new cage. It was tiny and Yuan-sized, and he was struggling with it because of course it was making all his muscles sore, but he never wanted to take it off. It had little fairy wings on the back.

Gale had kept Yuan at Songshu after January was arrested. January hadn't realized until they got home and there Yuan was, zooming along the koi pools in the entrance hall in brand new shoes with wheels in the heels.

"Is there any evidence that there are military people in there?" January asked.

"Aside from the fact that it's clearly the most sensible thing to do? They don't get to buy their way into Tharsis with uranium, they must have had a plan B. They're not just going to sit here quietly, are they? They want to get into the city. I *really* advise you to send the child back," they added.

"That's speculation," said January, who was getting quite good at going Full Gale at people who vexed him. "What about evidence?"

Yuan looked up, aware he was being talked about. He was here because having a child with them was the easiest way to show this wasn't a war zone and they didn't expect it to become one. January was nervous, and he knew Gale was scared, but neither of them had even discussed leaving Yuan behind.

The general shut their teeth, annoyed. "No."

A small side ramp on the biggest of the docked ships was easing down, very slowly. It was just big enough for one person to come down.

"All right?" January asked Gale.

"Nope," Gale said lightly, knuckles white on the reins.

January knocked their shoulder. "If we're still in alive fifteen minutes, I've brought some yay-we-survived sparkle cookies. They're in my bag."

Gale laughed. "You're so smart."

Someone was coming slowly down the first ramp with the awkward rolling gait of a person not used to the cage or the gravity yet. January had a pang of sympathy nausea. It was absolutely weird, to step out of those ships and onto a world, but to feel instantly that the gravity wasn't what your body remembered gravity being on the ground.

When she was close enough to talk, January slid down from the horse, lifted Yuan down too, and went up to meet her. He shook her hand.

"Welcome to Mars, Ambassador." It sounded strange to say something formal and important in English.

She smiled a bit. She looked exhausted. "Oh, Mx Stirling. I can't believe the Consul let us land. We all thought we'd be shot down."

"No, ma'am. I know it's frustrating for people not to be able to get out yet, but we're doing our best, we really are."

"No, we understand," she said, sounding sincere, at least. "You—who's this?" She looked disconcerted to find a child here but, like January had hoped, halfway to being reassured.

"This is Yuan," January said, setting him down the ground. Yuan had never said as much, but January had a feeling he wouldn't like being carried around all the time instead of being allowed to walk if he were so small.

"I'm three," Yuan added seriously. He didn't speak English, but of course he knew what his own name sounded like.

"I'm fifty-one," the ambassador said, switching over, and January grinned. Educated in Beijing of course. He liked that about American diplomats. Despite all the rhetoric, all the rich families made sure their kids went to all the best schools. It was nice and human. "Good to meet you, Yuan. I love your cage. Are those fairy wings? I'm so jealous. It's . . . new, right?" she added, with an uncertain flick of her eyes to January.

Yuan beamed. "Brand brand new."

January glanced behind her into the darkness of the cargo bay beyond the ramp, wondering if hers was the sincerity of someone who understood but who also had five thousand marines waiting for their orders. There could be tanks in there, jets of their own, anything.

At the same time, she was gazing past him, at the horses and the people on them. "They're—so tall in real life."

"Yeah. You're going to feel little."

She glanced at him. "So: everyone stays here for three months while your guys bring teachers. I know I've said this before, but people are desperate to get off these ships, and there have been cultural classes on the way . . . is there really no room to negotiate here?"

He smiled too. "I know how you feel. But no. I had those classes too, but they're not enough. People are going to need a lot of practise, and a lot of time to learn, before they're safe to mix with the local population. I've done this and I'm telling you, ninety-nine per cent of people need it. It's not safe to learn on the fly. It's—like cultural quarantine. And I know it sounds like horrible segregation and as if we're going to turn this is into some kind of concentration camp, but I promise you. The Consul's a good person. There might be shortages of some things, and it will be difficult in this storm, but you're going to get absolutely every-thing we can give you, as long as you can promise your people will do as they're asked."

"Cultural quarantine. I like that," she said, unexpectedly light.

He had a little glimmer of hope. Perhaps there weren't tanks or marines. Perhaps there were just people. "Come and meet the Consul."

She looked honestly shocked. "The Consul *came*? We asked, but . . ."

"The general thinks you demanded."

"I think there might have been some translation issues," she said, with a nervous hunch of her shoulders. "We really didn't . . ."

"There'll be a lot of that," January admitted. "Chinese and Tharsese are getting really different. The same words mean different things, it's like the differences between British English and American English on a silo of cocaine."

She smiled weakly, plainly trying not to baulk at the scale of the climb ahead of her, and of everyone else. "Are you going to tell me that *please* means *immediately* or something awful?"

"It's probably just nuance," he lied.[39] "Anyway, they're here. Okay with the gravity?"

"It's so weird," she said, shaking her head, but she was laughing a little.

"We'll go slow."

Yuan broke away from him and ran back to the canopy, where Gale and the general were waiting.

He ushered her across. Gale slipped down to the ground. She was smaller than January, and she barely reached Gale's ribs. She stared, and then she did the most human thing he'd seen any politician do: she burst

---

39   The problem was that Chinese was one of those languages where verbs could be adverbs or adjectives or nouns if they happened to fancy it. It meant that different places could easily start to favour very different usages. In Mandarin, *gei ni* meant "here you go" or "for you"; in Tharsese, it had come to mean specifically "coming at you," as in "I've just thrown something at you." Gale had a theory that that was because of spacefaring. In zero gravity, you didn't hand anyone anything. You floated it to them. There were lots of things like that, and it all sounded simple enough until you turned around expecting to be given a pen only to have it smack you in the head.

into tears, and sank down onto the ground. January knelt beside her, wishing he knew what to say, because he knew exactly how she felt. It was joy for having arrived, and sorrow for having left, and fear and hopelessness, to be confronted with a human being who was just so utterly different there was no way to even pretend this was home.

Gale knelt down too, tips of their hair coiling on the dusty earth.

"It's all right. You're safe."

"Oh—my God, you speak *English* . . ."

"Apparently I've been picking up a British accent, which is very embarrassing, and you're going to have to help me get rid of it."

She laughed, sort of, a half-broken laugh. "Actually, to us it reads— rather well." She sat back on her heels, staring at Gale, while Gale looked back at her. It couldn't have been more than a few seconds, but it was eternity as well.

"We're hoping you don't have a tank regiment in there," Gale murmured, smiling just enough; their real smile, the hesitant scholar, not the film-idol smile from the campaign. "I know it's not a wonderful welcome, but would you mind if we have a quick look? It would reassure everyone. Nobody goes on any registers, no one is taking any names."

She hesitated, scanning them up and down, and he realized she was struggling to read them. Too foreign, even speaking English. January brushed her arm.

"It's okay," he said, because at least she would be able to read him. He hoped she could see he meant it.

She touched an earpiece. "Open the bay doors please."

Well. This was it.

Gale helped her up. January went round to stand with them, watching the bay doors creep down, very slowly, safety sirens singing. He watched Gale rather than the doors. If they were scared now, they weren't showing it. They were still and serene, straight and strong and fragile. All at once, all he could think of was turning over in bed this morning and seeing how the steel spine down his back had tattooed a perfect chain of vertebrae into Gale's chest.

Yuan, who was lovely with people who were upset, was holding the ambassador's hand.

"Oh!" the ambassador gasped, jumping.

Something had burst right next her, something big, and then something else, again, about the size of a snooker ball. January thought it was one of the drones at first, and for a mad, bewildered few seconds he was sure they were falling out the sky, because they were everywhere, falling that immensely slow low-gravity fall, but then he realized Gale was smiling.

"This is lucky," they said. "It almost never rains."

It was incredible, the rain; each drop fell so slowly he could see its surface moving and whorling, and when they splashed on the dusty ground, each one sprayed slow stars. Up ahead, the bay doors lowered, and lowered.

He breathed in, hoping.

ACKNOWLEDGEMENTS

Thank you everyone who was involved in the writing this book. That's a lot of people. That's all the students who have asked me worriedly over the years if it's okay to write fiction using they/them pronouns; that's my family; and my long-suffering friends, who let me show them linguistics graphs. That's also the teachers at Nihao Mandarin language school in Shanghai, publishing teams on either side of the Atlantic, and the excellent people at Bath Spa University who gave me a grant to study in China.

But I have to say a special thank you to three people. First is Jenny Savill, my agent. Despite having always been a historical fiction writer, I sidled up to her with this manuscript one day and in a very small voice said, "So, um, I've written a bonkers thing about Mars?" And instead of saying, "Get immediately in the bin, Pulley," she didn't complain at all, even when she got to the bit about the mammoths, and then marched off and sold it. That, I reckon, is properly good agenting.

The other two extra-special people are Grace McNamee and Gillian Redfearn, my editors. I didn't think this book would ever be published. My original UK publisher not only rejected it, but said they didn't want to hear from me again. I thought my career was over. But then along came Grace and Gillian, like actual knights on actual horses. I feel cosmically lucky. In fact, if you had a bit of a rubbish year in 2023, it's because I hoovered up all the available luck. Sorry about that.

A NOTE ON THE AUTHOR

NATASHA PULLEY is the internationally bestselling author of *The Watchmaker of Filigree Street*, *The Bedlam Stacks*, *The Lost Future of Pepperharrow*, *The Kingdoms*, and *The Half Life of Valery K*. She has won a Betty Trask Award, been shortlisted for the Authors' Club Best First Novel Award, the Royal Society of Literature's Encore Award, and the Wilbur Smith Adventure Writing Prize, and been longlisted for the Walter Scott Prize. She lives in Bristol, England.

The Rom-Commers

ALSO BY KATHERINE CENTER

Hello Stranger

The Bodyguard

What You Wish For

Things You Save in a Fire

How to Walk Away

Happiness for Beginners

The Lost Husband

Get Lucky

Everyone Is Beautiful

The Bright Side of Disaster

The Rom-

Commers

KATHERINE CENTER

ST. MARTIN'S PRESS
NEW YORK

First published in the United States by St. Martin's Press, an imprint of St. Martin's Publishing Group

THE ROM-COMMERS. Copyright © 2024 by Katherine Center. All rights reserved. Printed in China. For information, address St. Martin's Publishing Group, 120 Broadway, New York, NY 10271.

www.stmartins.com

Designed by Devan Norman

Endpaper plant illustration © flowersmile/Shutterstock.com

The Library of Congress Cataloging-in-Publication Data is available upon request.

ISBN 978-1-250-28380-1 (hardcover)
ISBN 978-1-250-36319-0 (international, sold outside the U.S., subject to rights availability)
ISBN 978-1-250-28381-8 (ebook)

Our books may be purchased in bulk for promotional, educational, or business use. Please contact your local bookseller or the Macmillan Corporate and Premium Sales Department at 1-800-221-7945, extension 5442, or by email at MacmillanSpecialMarkets@macmillan.com.

First U.S. Edition: 2024

First International Edition: 2024

1 3 5 7 9 10 8 6 4 2

For my dad, Bill Pannill,
who loves words as much as I do.
Maybe more.

The Rom-Commers

One

LOGAN SCOTT CALLED just as I was making dinner, and I almost didn't answer because my dad and I were singing along to ABBA's greatest hits. There were not too many people I'd interrupt ABBA for—but yes, fine, Logan Scott was one of them.

Logan was my former high school boyfriend, who still felt guilty about the way we broke up, and he dealt with that guilt by sending me job opportunities.

Not the worst way to handle it.

It was the penance he paid for his unscathed life.

Though nobody's life is truly unscathed, I guess.

His *less*-scathed life, maybe.

He was a manager. In Hollywood. For screenwriters. A very glamorous job.

Technically, he was *my* manager—although I'd never made him any money. I was kind of like his pro bono case.

It was fine, he always insisted. I'd pay off eventually.

I'd placed in two different screenwriting contests because Logan insisted I submit. He got me in the door freelancing for *Variety*. And all those movie reviews I got paid minimum wage to do? Courtesy of him.

He just kept sending me work.

I told him to stop feeling guilty. I was fine. But I didn't exactly mean it. Not if that guilt of his was going to keep paying my bills.

Some of them, anyway.

All to say, on this particular night, Logan had a doozy of an offer for me.

"Emma," he said. "I'm going to need you to sit down."

"I'm flipping pancakes-for-dinner right now," I said. My sister, Sylvie, was coming home from college, so I was making her favorite meal.

"You will definitely drop them all when you hear this," Logan said, like he'd pictured me *juggling* pancakes instead.

I covered the in-progress stack with foil, turned off the music, and gave my dad a "one minute" finger from across the room.

My dad nodded and gave a hearty thumbs-up, like *Do whatever you need to do.*

"I'm ready," I said to Logan.

"Are you literally sitting down?"

"No."

"I'm not kidding. You need to do that."

I walked to our dining-slash-breakfast table and sat down at my already-set place. "Okay," I said. "I'm literally sitting."

"I have a job for you . . ." Logan said then, pausing for effect.

"I'll take it," I said.

"Writing a feature film script . . ." he went on, stretching out the moment.

"Sold," I said, like *Moving on.*

And then he got to his grand finale: "With Charlie Yates."

Logan had told me to sit—but at the sound of that name, I stood up. Then I froze. Then frowned. Then waited. Was this a trick?

"Hello?" Logan finally said. "Are you still—"

"I'm sorry," I said, shaking my head. "I thought I heard you say Charlie Yates."

"I did say Charlie Yates."

I sat back down. "Charlie Yates?" I said, like there was room for confusion.

I could sense Logan nodding. "Yes."

But I needed more confirmation. "Charlie Yates who wrote *The Destroyers*? Charlie Yates who wrote *The Last Gunslinger*, and *Smokescreen*, and *Forty Miles to Hell*? The screenwriters' screenwriter, living legend, reason half the country says the catchphrase 'Merry Christmas, cowboy'—that Charlie Yates?"

"Uh-huh," Logan said, enjoying the moment. "That one."

I took a sip of the ice water in my glass—

"He's written a rom-com," Logan said.

—and I coughed it back out.

Logan waited while I recovered.

"*Charlie Yates* wrote a rom-com?" Now I was suspicious. A Western? Sure. A horror flick? Absolutely. A dystopic space adventure where the robots eat all the humans? In a heartbeat. But a *rom-com*?

No way.

"He didn't," I said, answering my own query.

"He did."

"Is it . . . good?" I asked, and then immediately shook my head to cancel the question.

Of course it was good.

I'd seen every movie Charlie Yates had ever written, and I'd read every one of his screenplays—produced or unproduced—that I could get my hands on, printing them off the internet and lovingly binding them with brass brads before alphabetizing them on their own dedicated shelf on my bookcase. And I didn't just *read* them. I highlighted them. Annotated them. Covered them with Post-its and exclamation points. *No question* it was good. Charlie Yates couldn't write a bad screenplay if you threatened to take all his awards away.

"It's terrible," Logan said then.

"What?" It couldn't be.

"It's so terrible, even calling it terrible is an insult to the word *terrible*."

I took that in. "You've read it?" I asked.

"My eyes will never be the same, but yes—I read an entire draft."

"You read a draft?" I asked. "How?"

How was my ex-boyfriend from high school just casually reading the private first drafts of the world's most beloved superstar screenwriter?

Logan paused for a second and then he said, "So, I've been waiting for the right moment to share this with you, but . . . I am actually his manager."

"*What!*" I stood up. Again.

"I've been waiting to tell you because I knew you'd freak out."

"I'm not freaking out," I said, but in truth I was now clucking around the dining table in a meaningless circle, headless-chicken style. I knew Logan represented some high-profile people. But not *that* high.

"Just from the way you're breathing," Logan said, "I can tell that you are."

"How am I breathing?" I demanded.

"Like a Charlie Yates superfan who is losing her shit right now."

Fine. He wasn't wrong.

I took a soothing breath, and then walked to our apartment door, stepped outside, and strolled deliberately down our fourth floor's exterior walkway. Calmly. Like a non-freaked-out person.

I tried again. "You're telling me in seriousness that you're Charlie Yates's manager?"

"Yes."

"Charlie *Yates*?" I asked, like he might mean another Charlie. Then, "*Charlie* Yates?" like he might mean another Yates.

"Yes to both."

I was baffled. "How long has this been going on?"

"About three years."

"Three years?!" I shrieked. Then, lower, "Did you just say 'three years'? You've been working with my favorite screenwriter *for three years* and you never thought to mention it?"

"It wasn't that I didn't think to," Logan said, trying to steer us to a calmer place with his voice. "I decided to wait until the right moment."

I thought about all the joy of being one degree of separation from Charlie Frigging Yates—joy I'd been missing out on for three years. Then I said accusingly, "You 'decided to wait'?"

"Yes. Because, as you already know, timing is everything."

Well. He wasn't wrong there.

I'd made it to the end of our walkway. I leaned over the railing and looked down at the evening lights over the parking lot, and the car lights on the freeway beyond that, and the downtown lights sparkling off in the distance. I knew somebody who knew Charlie Yates. Everything had a bright new shimmer.

"Fair enough," I finally said.

"I'm telling you now," Logan said, "because, like I said before, I have a job for you."

It all came rushing back. "That's right. You have a job for me—"

"To write a screenplay—" Logan said.

"With Charlie Yates," I finished, my voice glowing with awe.

"But *re*write," Logan said. "Ghostwrite. I need you to *fix* this thing—hard."

"It's a page-one rewrite?"

"Page *zero*," Logan said. "He's got a handshake deal with an exec from United Pictures that if he writes this rom-com, they'll produce that gangster thing he wrote that's been kicking around."

Was it weird that a screenwriter of Charlie Yates's renown had an unproduced screenplay lying around? Not at all. Most scripts by most screenwriters never saw the light of day, in fact. You can make a great living in Hollywood getting paid good money to write scripts that never become movies. But that's what made Charlie Yates such a legend. Getting anything produced was a feat. But Charlie sold script after script—that became movies, that won awards, that became classics, and that then had people quoting them verbatim year after year.

"I love that gangster thing," I said. I'd found a bootleg copy on the internet and used up a whole pad of Post-its admiring it.

And I didn't even like gangster movies.

I didn't like drug kingpin movies, either. Or prison massacre movies.

Or killer clown movies. Or sea rescue movies where everyone gets eaten by sharks.

Unless Charlie Yates wrote them.

He was that good. I loved everything he did, even though the only genre that I myself truly personally liked was . . . romantic comedies.

Which was the only genre he didn't write.

Until now, apparently.

That's how good he was. He forced me to love him—against my entire personality.

"He loves the Mafia thing, too," Logan said. "He spent months and months in Chicago for research and he wore a pocket watch the whole time. And he's hell-bent on getting it made, especially now that he's back from his"—Logan hesitated before finishing with—"hiatus. But that can't happen until he does this rom-com. And as I mentioned—"

"It's terrible."

"We're going to need a better word for terrible."

I gave it all a second to sink in.

"That's where you come in," Logan said, ready to move on to details. "It's going to need the mother of all rewrites. Uncredited, of course—"

"Of course."

"But for good money."

"How much money?"

"More than you're technically entitled to, Writers Guild–wise."

There it was. There were levels to how much you could earn, depending on how much success you'd had. And since I'd had—and I say this with great compassion for myself—almost no success, my level wasn't high.

Didn't matter. Who cared?

This was Charlie Holy Shit Yates.

"Send it to me," I said. There was nothing more to discuss. Would I uncreditedly rewrite Charlie Yates's incomprehensibly terrible screenplay? *Of course I would.* I'd do it for no money. Hell, I'd pay *him.* I'd already mentally opened a new file in Final Draft and saved it as CHARLIE F@$%ING YATES.

"There's a catch, though," Logan said next.

"What's that?"

"You have to come to LA."

Now I started pacing the walkway again. "Come to LA?" I echoed, like that was something no one ever did.

"Not *forever*," Logan said. "Just for the working period of the rewrite."

How long did a rewrite even take? I'd never done a rewrite for someone else.

Logan read my mind. "Six weeks," he declared next. "Possibly longer. This has to be an in-person thing."

"But—" I started, so many objections in my mind, it was hard to choose. "What about Zoom? What about FaceTime? What about Slack? Google Meet? Hell—even Skype! There are a million virtual ways to do it."

"He's old-school," Logan said.

"That's no excuse."

"And he's got a massive ego."

"He deserves that ego," I said, shifting sides. "He's earned it."

"The point is, he's Charlie Yates. He gets it the way he wants it. And he's never going to just accept virtual corrections from some unproduced writer on the internet."

"When you put it that way, I don't sound very impressive."

"I know."

"So I have to come out there and—what?"

"Woo him."

"*Woo* him?"

"Obviously not in the traditional sense of *woo*."

"I can't go to LA, Logan," I said. "I can't go *anywhere*. Remember my dad?"

But Logan wasn't deterred. "What about Sylvie?" he asked.

Dammit. He had me. "What about her?"

"Didn't she just graduate?"

"She did, but—"

"Wasn't that the plan all along? To get Sylvie through college and then let her take a turn?"

"That *was* the plan," I said, bracing myself against how right Logan was. "But she got a very prestigious summer internship with International Medical Aid—"

"Bullshit!" Logan shouted.

"Did you just shout 'bullshit' at me?"

"It's her turn," Logan said, mad at me now. "You've done everything for ten years—"

"*Just under* ten years," I corrected.

"—and the plan, all along, was for her to come back to Texas after college and take over."

"Yes, but that was before—"

"Call her," Logan demanded. "Call her right now and tell her she's coming home. You will never get another chance like this. This is the opportunity of your lifetime."

"I don't have to call her. She's on her way in from the airport right now. Remember the pancakes?"

"Perfect timing," Logan said then. "Tell her at dinner."

But I just leaned down and rested my forehead against the metal handrail as a garbage truck rumbled by down below. "I don't want to."

"Be fair to yourself, Emma," Logan cajoled.

Why were we even talking about this? I had things to do and no time for nonsense. "I'm not crushing Sylvie's dreams, Logan. That's not on my to-do list today."

"But what about you?" Logan asked. "What about *your* dreams?"

At that, I stood up. "My dreams," I said, like *We're done here*, "got crushed a long time ago."

Two

I DID *NOT* tell Sylvie at dinner.

It wasn't just the first dinner we'd had together in the months since she'd gone back to college last January—it was her graduation party. A graduation that, of course, my dad and I had missed, since he couldn't travel—and if he couldn't travel, neither could I.

This wasn't just dinner. This was a celebration. My glorious, brilliant baby sister had graduated summa cum laude and Phi Beta Kappa from the highly picturesque Carleton College—which, if you didn't know, is the Harvard of the Midwest—and she was now, among many other things, living proof that our family had overcome all of its tragedies and was thriving, at last. Officially.

We were celebrating, dammit.

I'd made a cake in the shape of a graduation cap and stuck sparkler candles in it. I'd festooned our kitchenette with gold streamers and sprinkled confetti on the table. I'd typed out little menus and rolled them up like diplomas.

I wasn't ruining all that by *moving to LA*.

You had to maximize joy when it fluttered into your life. You had to honor it. And savor it. And not stomp it to death by reminding everyone of everything you'd lost.

Sylvie showed up in a cropped tee with her fairy-tale straight blond hair billowing, looking like the personification of youth and beauty and hope—and lugging five hundred duffel bags of dirty laundry. And I hugged her around the neck with genuine joy and jumped and squealed and kissed her cheeks. And my dad met us at the door with his walker and we sang "Happy Graduation to You" to the birthday song tune, my dad adding some one-handed percussion with a maraca. And then we ate stacks of pancakes and sausages and squirted canned whipped cream all over everything.

We sat at our little dinette and chattered away and teased each other and enjoyed every second of being back together so much that I almost felt resentful in some tiny compartment in my brain that Logan Scott had called out of nowhere with that crazy Charlie Yates news and complicated things.

Today of all days.

The longer the evening went on, and the more we sat around chatting afterward, catching up and drinking root beer floats for dessert, the more the memory of that phone call faded for me. I felt a growing and peaceful sensation that the crisis had passed—that I no longer had to make any hard decisions, and life would continue on as predictable and normal and vaguely unsatisfying as ever.

I just wanted to be happy—simply, uncomplicatedly happy—for like *one evening*. Was that too much to ask?

Apparently so.

Timing really was everything, I guess.

YOU MIGHT BE wondering why my fifty-five-year-old dad had to use a walker to come greet my sister at the door. Or why we couldn't go to her graduation. Or why his percussion instrument of choice was *one* maraca.

I will give you the same vaguely cheery, deeply oversimplified answer that we always gave everyone: Just under ten years ago, my father had "a camping accident."

Pressed for details, I'll add this: He was hit in the head during a sudden rockfall while climbing in Yosemite and got a traumatic brain injury—which left him partially paralyzed on one side, a condition called hemiplegia, and also suffering from an inner-ear issue that profoundly messed up his balance called Ménière's disease.

That's the long story short.

I'm leaving out a lot here. I'm leaving out the worst part, in fact.

But that's enough for now.

That's why my dad couldn't be left alone. That's why he moved through the world like he was ninety. That's why I worried about him 24–7. And that's why writing a screenplay with Charlie Yates in Los Angeles was totally, utterly, entirely out of the question.

I wouldn't shirk my responsibilities.

I wouldn't abandon my dad.

And I would not, not, *not* eclipse my baby sister's potential by sticking her on medical duty in this six-hundred-square-foot apartment.

I wouldn't. And I couldn't . . .

Until I read the screenplay.

THE EMAIL FROM Logan with the subject "Apologies in Advance" hit my inbox just as Sylvie was settling in on the top bunk with Netflix and her headphones. Our PJs were on, the lights were off, and I stared at that attachment for a good long minute before finally giving in and clicking it open.

An hour later, I made it official:

Terrible.

We really would need a more terrible word for terrible.

First of all, it was—at least in theory—an updated retelling of the beloved rom-com classic *It Happened One Night*. Written by a person who had clearly never seen the movie.

If you haven't seen it yourself, please do yourself a favor: stop whatever you're doing and go watch it. This movie is ninety years old, and it still sparkles with life and vitality and charm. A down-on-his-luck newspaper reporter tries to help a runaway socialite travel by bus to New York in hopes of getting her exclusive story—and falls madly in love with her instead. Clark Gable is fan-yourself sexy, Claudette Colbert is sassy and gorgeous, and the romantic tension? You could *eat* it with a *spoon*. This is the road trip rom-com that launched a thousand road trip rom-coms—and it swept the Oscars, winning all of the big five categories, including Best Screenplay. It's a titan of the genre. It's practically sacred.

And Charlie Yates, my beloved Charlie Yates, my gold standard, my writer by which all other writers are judged, my absolute all-time screenwriting hero . . .

He mutilated it.

He besmirched it.

He *desecrated* it.

This thing he did—I don't even want to say "wrote" . . . It had no spark, no build, no banter, no joy—and no scenes that even resembled the original movie. The title was the same, and the character names were the same. But that was it. Was he *asleep* when he wrote this? Was he *in the middle of dental surgery*? How could someone so good and so masterful at writing—someone who could make you root for serial killers, and believe in ghosts, and genuinely *like* cannibal robots—take something that was already working, and had been working for ninety years, and chuck its charming soul into a wood chipper?

I mean, Clark Gable and Claudette Colbert had to be weeping up in heaven.

He had their characters going to a line-dancing competition.

A *line-dancing* competition!

Something was going on here. Did Charlie Yates have a stroke? Had a chat bot secretly rewritten the real script as a gag? Was Charlie Yates being held hostage somewhere and forced at gunpoint to write a career-endingly bad story?

But *career-endingly bad* didn't even capture it.

This thing was apocalyptic.

And there it was. Somehow *that* was the tipping point for me.

Real life was allowed to be disappointing. Heck, real life was *guaranteed* to be disappointing. Living alone in a tiny apartment with my sick father? Teaching community college freshman English so we could have health insurance? Denying my own dreams so my overindulged but lovable baby sister could live all of hers struggle-free? All fine. I didn't get to make the rules for reality.

But stories had a better option.

I was not letting Charlie Yates ruin this movie, his career, the romantic comedy genre as a whole, and *all our lives* with this nuclear-waste-fueled dumpster fire of a screenplay.

That was where I drew the line.

Nobody was dishonoring *It Happened One Night*. Not on my watch.

I didn't even make a decision, really. Just finished reading, clam-shelled my laptop, swung myself up to the top bunk, and stared at Sylvie until she took off her headphones and said, "What's up?"

"I've just read a romantic comedy script," I said, "that will destroy human civilization as we know it."

Half an hour later, she had the whole story: Logan's call, Charlie Yates's situation, my life-changing opportunity. And before I even knew what she was doing, she was typing out an email to withdraw from her summer internship, citing "a family emergency."

"You can't not go to your internship!" I said when I realized what she was doing.

"Sure I can," she said.

"It's a week away! You made a commitment."

"They'll pull someone off the wait list."

"But—" I shook my head. "But it's *very prestigious*."

Sylvie shrugged. "I'll go another year."

"What if they don't take you another year?"

"I'll go somewhere else."

But I was shaking my head—fervently. I mean, I recognized that I'd gotten this started. I was the one who'd climbed the bunk ladder and told her everything. She was a good-hearted person, after all. I could've predicted she might try to solve this.

But now that it was happening, I couldn't stand it.

What was she even thinking, giving up her internship?

Had I protected her too much? Had she had it too easy? Didn't she know how awful the world was? "I'm not sure you understand what a big deal opportunities like this are," I said. "You can't take them for granted. The world is horrible. Chances to shine don't just fall from the sky."

"You hear yourself, right?" Sylvie said. "Ditto—right back at you. Do you know what a big deal Charlie Yates is? We studied him in my film theory class."

"But you're . . ." I couldn't think of a justification. "You're *young*."

"You're also young."

"You're full of promise."

"You're also full of promise."

"But you're—just . . ." I shrugged. "You're Sylvie. You're my Sylvie."

"And you're my Emma."

I shook my head like that argument held no weight. "I can't take your chance away from you."

"And I can't take *your* chance away from *you*."

"But you've already said yes to your chance."

"But your chance is bigger than mine."

The more we argued, the more I had to pick a side. And of course, that side was always Sylvie's. She really was my Sylvie. I'd practically raised her. Between me and Sylvie, I chose Sylvie—every time. That was a given. I didn't know how to be her sister-slash-surrogate-mom any other way.

But Sylvie wasn't giving up. "Guess we'll have to flip a coin."

"I'm not flipping a coin, Sylvie."

Ugh. I'd created a monster. I used to win all our arguments—but now she was big enough to beat me.

"You know what?" I said. "Let's talk about it tomorrow."

"Too late," Sylvie said then, looking mischievous and defiant. "I just hit SEND."

"You *what*?"

She shrugged like she'd won. "I sent it."

"We weren't done talking!"

"I was done," Sylvie said. "You're going to LA."

"Write them back!" I said, grabbing at her laptop. "Say it was a mistake!"

But Sylvie clutched it to her chest. "Never!"

We were just starting to wrestle for it when our dad's voice came through the wall. "Girls!" he called. "Quit arguing!"

Sylvie and I froze and looked at each other like, *Now you woke up Dad.*

Then his voice sounded again, deeper this time—resonant and decisive, like the voice of God. "We'll discuss this in the morning like rational people," he said, in a tone that made it final. "And then we'll take a vote. And then"—he paused to be extra clear—"we'll send Emma to LA."

Three

ONE WEEK LATER, I was on a plane.

I could easily have taken *a month* to pack up my stuff, and organize my dad's medications, and label the supply shelves, and color-code daily to-do lists, and cover every surface with sticky-note reminders.

Taking care of my dad wasn't an art—it was a science, and it sure as hell wasn't for amateurs. Sylvie was a smart girl, sure, but she'd never had any training for this, and I felt like an astronaut handing over the keys to the space shuttle to a chimpanzee.

"He has to drink a minimum of forty ounces of water every single day," I told Sylvie as I marked water bottles in the cabinet with Sharpies. "And he won't remember, so you have to follow him around and nag him."

"Do I really have to nag him?" Sylvie asked, like a person who had never done any caretaking.

"If you don't nag him, then he won't drink enough water, and then sodium levels in his body will spike, fluid will build up in his inner ear, and he'll lose his balance, hit his head, and wind up in the ER all night."

"Ah," Sylvie said. "*Nag him.* Got it."

"It helps to keep a color-coded chart," I said, opening up one of the kitchen cabinets to show her where the last three months were taped up. "The blue boxes are for water. Yellow is for multivitamins. Red, purple, orange, and green are all for medications. And the unicorn puffy stickers are for sodium."

"Dad doesn't seem like he'd be motivated by unicorn puffy stickers."

"They're not for him. They're for me."

Sylvie squinted at the chart. "And how does the sodium thing work?"

Was it possible she didn't know this? Had I really sheltered her that much? "Milligrams of sodium" had been the organizing principle of my life for the past decade. "We have to keep Dad's sodium intake under a thousand milligrams a day," I said. "Which is not easy. One slice of deli meat has two hundred."

"But how do I even track that?"

I pulled out my frayed, dog-eared sodium guidebook. "You memorize it. Like a champion." I tapped the book with pride. "Learn it. Live it. I can tell you exactly how much sodium is in any food you ever name."

Sylvie looked at the book uncertainly.

"Seriously," I said, "that's true. Try me."

"Strawberries?" Sylvie asked.

"Two milligrams per cup."

"White rice," she tried next.

"Nine milligrams per cup."

"French fries!"

"Sixty-eight milligrams for a small bag."

Sylvie nodded in approval.

"Try to stump me," I said. "I dare you. I can go all day. Truffles. Pineapple juice. Beets. Mollusks."

"Sounds like you really know your shit."

I nodded, like *You know it.* "I will crush you."

The obsession with sodium, of course, was about trying to control the Ménière's disease.

Nobody knows exactly what causes it. But they do know it's an inner-ear disorder that throws off your balance. My dad's clearly started in the wake of his brain injury, and he had a particularly bad case that hasn't resolved over time. He would've been unsteady on his feet anyway, from the partial paralysis on his left side, but the Ménière's made it a hundred times worse.

More than just unsteadiness, though, he had a thing called "drop attacks" where he felt—suddenly—like he just got shoved to the ground. Or even sometimes like the room itself flipped upside down in one swift heave. And nobody ever saw it coming—least of all him. No warning at all. He could be sitting at dinner and just catapult out of his chair.

That's why we had carpet everywhere, and industrial pads on the kitchen floor, and foam bumpers on sharp corners. That's why he didn't drive anymore, or take stairs, if he could help it. That's why we were on a first-name basis with several nurses at the closest ER.

That's why I did not trust Sylvie to take over.

I wasn't sure I trusted her to run things for *six days*—much less six weeks.

And that's why, now, I couldn't sleep on the plane.

What was I doing? This was lunacy. I couldn't just leave my dad with a twenty-two-year-old. Even a college graduate with a Phi Beta Kappa key needed more than one week to prepare for this. Our widowed next-door neighbor Mrs. Otsuka had agreed to check in on them after she saw me burst into tears in the laundry room, but that would hardly be enough. Leaving—actually packing up and getting on my first flight anywhere in almost a decade—felt so astonishingly irresponsible, I couldn't believe I was letting it happen.

Sitting on that plane, wedged into a middle seat in the last row, listening to toilet flush after toilet flush, I realized I was shaking.

Like genuinely shaking. A lot.

Not just my hands, the way you might on a cold day if you'd forgotten your mittens. My whole body. From the core. And my heart was just thumping like a kettledrum—so big and so hard that when I looked down, I could see the fabric of my shirt vibrating.

Was it fear?

Was I afraid to fly? Afraid to leave my dad? Afraid of changing my narrow little life?

Sure. Yes. All of the above.

But more than that: I was going to miss him.

My dad wasn't just a dad. He was my favorite person.

He was everybody's favorite person.

He was a *delight*.

Sometimes a TBI will cause personality changes in people—you hear a lot about anger and depression in the wake of brain injuries like his, and reasonably so. But if it changed him, and I'm not sure this is even medically possible . . . it made him sweeter.

My dad was always the dad everybody wanted. If there were a dad store, he'd be a bestseller. They'd have rows and rows of him for sale, right up front. He was always warm and encouraging and connected and goofy—even before.

But now, in the wake of it all, he was something even more astonishing.

He was *cheerful*.

He lost everything in that rockfall—and he found a way to keep going. And not only that. He found a way to laugh. And sing goofy little ditties. And close his eyes and turn his face to the sun.

And he got me to do all those things, too.

How did he do it? How did he stand beside a personal Grand Canyon of suffering and manage to feel . . . *grateful*?

And how on earth would I cope out in the heartless world without him?

Who even was I on my own?

Before the rockfall, my dad was a cellist.

After the rockfall, he taught himself every instrument you can play with one hand—mastering the harmonica, the bones, the zither, the tambourine, the tin whistle, and the slide trombone. He also learned one-handed crochet, and potting on a wheel, and beading. "You pick the colors," he said, "I'll make the magic." He got so good at beading necklaces that he opened a jewelry shop on Etsy.

Which actually added a fair bit of cash to our monthly budget.

I would really miss him, is what I'm saying. And I found myself wondering, as we hit some turbulence and I white-knuckled the armrest, if maybe dreams were better off never trying to become reality.

Four

DON'T MEET YOUR heroes. Isn't that what they say?

Oh, god. They're so right.

Logan picked me up at LAX in his BMW SUV with a vanity plate that read KILL N IT. Which felt very LA.

Although apparently nobody ever picks anybody up at LAX.

I know this because it's the first thing Logan said to me as I got in the car. "I hope you're grateful," he said.

I was late to meet him because my enormous suitcase had gotten caught on the conveyor belt at baggage claim, and my carry-on bag had a broken wheel that dragged and squeaked like it was begging for mercy and slowed me down. Also because I'd stood so long in the airport bathroom trying to wrangle my curly red hair into something, um, *less curly and red* that I lost track of time.

I didn't hate my hair or anything. It was just . . . a lot.

It was the first—and last—thing you noticed about me. As my friend Maria once said about having curly hair: *You don't control it. It controls you.*

In the end I settled for the same thing I did with my hair every day:

pulling it back into a high ponytail that looked like a pom-pom and calling it a day. The other option was to leave it down—flowing out of my head like lava. But I had to consider poor Charlie Yates. That would be a lot to take in at a first meeting. Visually.

I didn't want to frighten the poor man.

I overthought my outfit, too, for the record. Jeans, and Converse low-tops, and a little boatneck printed blouse. Was this too casual? Too cutesy? Not badass enough? Should I maybe put on a gunmetal-gray suit and some aviator shades? How did one even dress for meeting the best screenwriter on the planet?

Logan, in contrast, knew exactly how to dress—a perfectly tailored suit so crisply pressed I was almost afraid to hug him. It was the first time I'd seen him anywhere but an occasional FaceTime in eight years, but he looked exactly the same.

"You haven't changed at all," I said as we buckled up.

"Are you kidding? I'm way cooler." Then he looked me over. "You're the one who hasn't changed."

So what if I was wearing the same hoop earrings I'd worn at my high school graduation? They were sterling silver.

I thought we might stop for lunch, or coffee, but Logan drove straight for Charlie Yates's house in the Hollywood Hills—no stopping allowed.

Guess this was happening.

"Hope you peed at the airport," Logan said, in a tone like *No turning back now.*

"Like a racehorse," I said, in a tone that I hoped said, *Bring it on.*

Yes, Logan and I had dated in high school—but we'd always been friends first. His very dashing father—American, and Black, and from Atlanta—had met his elegant mother—British, and white, and a TV producer—while working as a war correspondent overseas. Logan was raised mostly in London until his dad got a job as a nightly news anchor in Houston, and he showed up as the new kid at my high school.

We bonded because we were the only two students in our English class who thought Robert Frost's poem "After Apple-Picking" had to be about sex.

Also—even though he was tall and I was not, and even though he had a posh British accent and I just sounded like a plain old American teenager, and even though his complexion was a warm beige and mine was so pale and befreckled that a guy in my photography class kept squinting at me and saying he wished he could add some contrast . . . we had the exact same color hazel eyes.

Exactly the same.

And so we started telling people we were twins.

"Not identical twins, obviously," we'd say.

This game was so fun, and we got so good at it, sometimes people believed us. If they pointed out our obvious genetic dissimilarities, I'd say, "Genetics are complicated. Deal with it." And then Logan would add, "The eyes don't lie."

If a genius noted that one of us talked like the royal family and one did not, I'd wince as if pained by a cruel memory and say, "We were separated as infants in a tragic *Parent Trap* situation." And then Logan would lean in and say, "Please don't trigger her any further."

Our specialty was getting double free birthday desserts at restaurants.

Logan's family moved away after high school when his dad got an anchor job on the national nightly news—that's right: Logan's dad is *Malcolm Scott*—and Logan went on to graduate from Stanford and then seamlessly transition into a wildly successful career.

He didn't have to stay in touch with me, is what I'm saying. Me, stuck at home and not transitioning into a wildly successful anything.

But he did.

And, now, having not seen him in person since the night before he left for his freshman year of college—when he broke up with me, claiming, and I quote, "We both need some freedom"—I suddenly felt nervous.

He'd lived a whole lifetime since then—most notably, coming out in college, and calling me proudly to declare that I was the last girl he would ever date.

"I'm honored," I said.

"Right? Exactly. No woman will ever replace you."

I wasn't entirely sure what Logan's life was like these days, but I assumed it was full of awesome parties and awesome food and awesome people. So I was highly surprised when a decidedly *not* awesome guy named T.J. called on speaker before we'd even left the airport grounds.

"Lo! Gan!" This guy T.J.'s voice boomed, seeming to rattle the interior of the car. "What's up? Did you pick up that girl?"

"I have her here."

"Don't tell her she's a career-killer," T.J. said.

I frowned at Logan.

"T.J.," Logan said, "you're on speaker."

"I am?" A pause. "That's fine. I'll own it. The last thing the great Charlie Yates needs to do right now is to siphon off all his testosterone and write lady movies with the girls."

Logan poked at the controls on his dash and said, "You know what? I'll call you back."

But before he could hang up, T.J. added, "And by the way, this job should have gone to someone who's actually had some work produced."

"Bad connection!" Logan said, as he hit END.

Then a long silence as the seams in the concrete moved rhythmically under the tires.

Finally, I said, "That felt a little hostile."

"He's not even supposed to know about you. But my assistant has a thing for him."

"A screenwriter, I presume?"

Logan nodded. "He wrote and directed *Beer Tower.* And *Beer Tower II: The Reckoning.*"

I'd never heard of either of those movies.

"They were huge on YouTube," Logan said.

"Were they . . . good?"

"Hell, no!" Logan said. "But he synthesized a ton of horizontal integration. The sponsorship from Solo Cups alone put it in the black."

"How have I never heard of this movie?"

"You're not exactly the target audience."

"Did he want the Charlie Yates job for himself?" I asked.

"Can you blame him?"

"He just seemed douchey."

"He's not used to not getting things."

"Why is that again?" I asked.

"Because he's third-generation Hollywood royalty. And he's ridiculously well-connected. And *Beer Tower* made ten million dollars—
before *Beer Tower II* made twenty."

"And he just randomly calls you?"

"He's just one of those people who's everywhere."

Logan was acting cool, but it was a strange welcome to LA. I'd
barely left the airport and I already had an enemy.

Another little pause before Logan said, "You'll never see him. Charlie
can't stand that guy. He's a total dude-bro."

"But he's your client?"

"He's everything that's wrong with the world," Logan said. "But,
yes. He's my client."

BIT OF A rocky start there.

But here was the bigger, more important picture: I had a job working for Charlie Yates—whether dude-bro T.J. liked it or not—and I was
absolutely, undeniably on my way to Charlie Yates's house right now.

I'd never thought of Charlie Yates as even having a house before. I
assumed he just lived in some kind of ethereal writing-god plane.

"It's not exactly a house," Logan said. "More like a mansion. The
exterior was featured in a Nancy Meyers movie."

Why did that make it scarier?

"Maybe we should stop by the hotel first," I said.

"What hotel?"

"Am I not staying in a hotel?"

"Can you afford to stay in a hotel for six weeks?"

Wow. I clearly hadn't thought this through. "Am I staying at your
place, then?"

Logan burst out laughing at that and then explained his husband,
Nico, ran his own knitting-classes-to-the-stars micro-empire called Knit

& Bitch out of the guest room in their multimillion-dollar cottage in Santa Monica . . . and had filled all available space in their home with yarn.

Guess not.

"Where will I be staying, then?"

Logan shrugged. "With Charlie."

Like a reflex: "Charlie who?"

"Yates," Logan said, like *Duh.*

With Charlie Yates? I shook my head. "I'm sorry. Wait. I'm going to be *living* with Charlie Yates?"

"*Staying* with," Logan corrected, like that was different.

"This is way too close for comfort," I said.

"You'll never even see him," Logan said. "He's got, like, five guest rooms." He glanced over at my stricken face. "It's basically a resort."

How had I missed this basic information? Was I so starry-eyed at the prospect of going to Hollywood that I couldn't think straight?

"What other details haven't you mentioned?" I asked as Logan zoomed us through traffic like the other cars were slalom poles.

"Just go with it," Logan said. "Details are overrated."

Were they?

Logan glanced over. "You look a little green," he said.

"I'm out of practice with adventure," I said. "And you're a terrible driver."

"Being a terrible driver is a power move," Logan said. Then, from his place of power, he added, "Do you want some advice?"

"Not really."

"Don't sleep with Charlie."

"Don't *sleep* with *Charlie*?!" I shrieked, like the idea had never crossed my mind.

"I know you have a writer crush," Logan said. "But keep it at that."

"Are you insane?"

"You've got a photo of him on your bulletin board."

"I've got a photo of Kurt Vonnegut on my bulletin board, too."

"I'm not concerned about Vonnegut."

"Yeah. Since he's *dead.*"

"Since you're not *moving into his house.*"

"Well, whose fault is that?"

"I'm very *pro* the professional partnership," Logan clarified. "But I'm very *anti* anything more."

"Why are we even having this conversation?"

"You're lonely. He's lonely. It's like an incubator for fornicating."

"You're the one who set this up. I'd be perfectly happy to stay literally anywhere else."

"You'll write better in the house," Logan said.

I gave him a look. "As long as I don't *fornicate*," I added.

"Exactly!"

I was still a little motion-sick from the turbulence we hit during landing—and Logan's NASCAR-inspired driving wasn't helping. I hadn't eaten all day—or yesterday, for that matter—and I hadn't slept well the night before. I still had that heart-thumping thing going on inside my rib cage. Needless to say, this little fornication-themed heart-to-heart wasn't helping.

"All I'm saying," Logan said, "is don't even think about it."

"I wasn't thinking about it—until you got me thinking about it. Now I'm thinking about it."

"Stop complaining," Logan said. "I'm helping you."

"You're freaking me out."

"It's better if you're prepared," Logan said.

"Maybe you should stop talking now."

But Logan went on. "He's terrible in relationships! Why do you think his wife left him?"

He had me. "Why?"

"Because he did immersion research in Chicago for that Mafia thing, and he didn't call her one time in three months."

I felt an impulse to defend him. *He was working!* But then I said, "Okay, yeah. That's a long time."

Logan nodded, like we were finally on the same page. "Don't let those corduroy trousers distract you. You are here to get in, kick-start your tragically delayed brilliant career, and get the hell back out."

Five

YES, CHARLIE YATES'S house was an Old Hollywood–style mansion-slash-villa-slash-estate on a switchbacky road packed with mansions just behind Sunset Boulevard. *Of course he lives in a dream house,* I thought, as we stopped out front and Logan yanked up the parking brake. He was living the dream. And that's what the dream looked like.

After we parked, I dallied: I put on fresh lipstick, patted down my pom-pom, and pulled out a little mirror to spot-check—one more time—for pepper in my teeth. Even though I hadn't eaten any pepper today. That I knew of.

I'd already done all these things in the airport bathroom, but, dammit, I did them again.

I was about to stand before Charlie Yates.

I was about to come into contact with genuine greatness.

It wouldn't have entirely surprised me to find a throne in his living room.

I'd watched every video of him on the internet—most of them on stages at screenwriting festivals in front of adoring audiences—and practically memorized his remarks on structure, character arcs, and how to keep the mushy middle from sagging. I'd seen his face. I knew his voice. I knew that he was thirty-five, and a Gemini, and slightly duckfooted, and had an unwavering affection for flat-front, wide-wale corduroy pants. And while no one would accuse him of being movie-star good-looking, he had a kind of disheveled, no-rules, maverick appeal that I couldn't classify as anything other than handsome.

Also? He had a habit of grabbing the front of his hair while he was talking, and squeezing it in his fist so tightly that when he let it go, it was all pointing in another direction.

Come on. Irresistible.

It was the kind of thing I'd think about sometimes, idly, while making dinner. What was it about his face that I liked, exactly? Some hidden geometry that clicked with patterns in my brain? The plumpness of his mouth, maybe? Or the angle of his jaw? Or—and this might betray how many times I'd rewatched some of those videos—something about the shape of his nostrils? Is that a weird thing to say? That a man has appealing nostrils? But he did. Friendly, straightforward, symmetrical nostrils that kind of dimpled down a little when he was suppressing a smile.

Writers, in general, aren't exactly the best-looking subsection of humanity. Like if aliens came down and said, *Show us the most perfect physical specimens of your kind*, we wouldn't go searching for the coffee-stained writers of the world, hunched over their laptops in their basement efficiencies. The bar for writers, looks-wise, wasn't exactly high. Charlie might be a normal person's eight—but he was a writer's ten, for sure. That, plus his early success—the quirky indie movie that he made *in college* was a sleeper hit and launched his career—made him a media darling. Most screenwriters? No one's ever heard of them. But we all knew and loved Charlie Yates.

He had a perfect storm of talent, charm, and irresistible nostrils.

And I really, really hoped I would not accidentally say that out loud when I met him.

A nightmare vision of my pumping Charlie Yates's hand and gushing, "I love your nostrils!" flashed through my mind—and then, at the frozen horror of his expression, my trying to make it less weird by explaining: "It's that teardrop shape they have, and how they kind of lean back against that tippy-top part of your upper lip, like they're James Dean about to smoke a cigarette. You get it, right?"

Oh, god. I really was my own worst enemy.

Logan reached Charlie Yates's front door while I was still wincing at that, and so there was nothing to do but drag my suitcase and carry-on through the gravel of the driveway at top speed to catch up.

As Logan knocked, I tried to settle my breathing.

God, I was nervous. Should I visualize the ocean? Try a power stance? Do a quick meditation? I tried to assess how much time I had before Charlie Yates opened that door.

But he didn't exactly open the door. Not in the usual way, at least.

In response to Logan's knock, the knob turned a little and then the door cracked, leaving maybe a four-inch gap. It was clear from the voice inside that Charlie was wrapping up a phone call and not *answering* the door so much as just unlocking it. So Logan held his finger up at me, like, *Give me a sec*, then handed me his phone and keys to hold, and slipped inside.

Leaving me standing alone on the front steps with Logan's phone and keys, my bags, and my backpack full of favorite pens and notebooks.

Huh.

Looking back, Logan must've thought he shut the door behind him. But it didn't catch. Which meant, minutes later, I was accidentally eavesdropping on their conversation through the slit at the doorjamb.

A conversation that got very dark very fast.

"Got a present for ya, buddy," Logan said to start off, seasoning his voice with as much bro-ish camaraderie as the Queen's English would allow.

"What do you mean, 'a present'?" Charlie asked. His voice was more gravelly in real life than through my computer speaker.

"A writer," Logan said. "I've brought you a writer."

Charlie wasn't following. "How did you 'bring me a writer'?"

I tried to assess their relationship. There was something in Charlie's tone—nice, but not warm—that made it seem like Logan was trying too hard.

"Outside," Logan said. "A rom-com writer. To work on *It Happened One Night.*"

"You brought a writer here? To my house? Right now?"

And then I knew.

Charlie Yates had no idea I was coming.

Oh, shit.

Whatever was happening right now, it was not Charlie Yates approved.

I held my breath. Once I knew it, I couldn't unknow.

"Yes," Logan went on, clearing his throat like it was beading with flop sweat. "She's here right now. She's here—and she's ready to help."

I could tell Logan thought that if he made it all seem reasonable enough, it would actually just *be* reasonable.

But this was Charlie Yates. He wasn't going to be Jedi-mind-tricked by his manager. And he had exactly one syllable of response for this situation: "No."

"No?"

"No. I don't need help."

"Of course you don't *need* it," Logan backtracked. "Just to make things easier."

But Charlie Yates wasn't buying it. "Working with other writers never makes things easier."

"A consultant. Of sorts. It's my friend. The one I told you about last time."

"I don't need a consultant."

"Of course you don't. More like a secretary. A typist."

A typist!

Logan was trying to push past this initial resistance. "I'll just bring her in, and we can—"

"No."

"No?" Logan asked.

"No."

"Does *no* mean—"

"No means no. No, I don't want you to bring her in. No, I don't need help with the screenplay. Or a consultant. Or even a typist. I know how to type. And how to write a screenplay, too, by the way."

Yep. He'd offended him.

"I don't need anything," Charlie went on. "Not from you—or anyone. Especially not some amateur writer friend of yours."

Ouch. But fair.

"She may be an amateur, but there were circumstances—"

"No."

"No?"

"No. This isn't happening."

"I just think that if you—"

"Buddy. Come on. I'd be irritated if you showed up with anybody, honestly. But some random girl you had a thing with in high school? That's just insulting."

"I'm telling you, she's good."

"I'm telling you, I don't care."

"I'm handing you the help you need to get this done and move on, and you're throwing credentials at me."

"Credentials exist for a reason."

"Look, rom-coms are her specialty. They're her whole thing. She can recite every line of *When Harry Met Sally* to you verbatim."

"Please don't let her do that."

"I'm telling you, you'll never meet another writer who knows more about rom-coms. She's obsessed. And she's got nothing else in her life. No relationship. No kids. Nothing at all. This is *all she does.* Imaginary love is the only thing she's got."

Oh, god, Logan. You're killing me.

Then Logan made a fateful decision. He lied. To Charlie Yates. About me.

I can still hear it in slow-mo.

"She's read the screenplay," Logan said, "and she loved it."

What!

It was all I could do to physically restrain myself from bursting in and correcting the record. I did *not* love it! I *opposite* of loved it—times a thousand. I detested it. I abhorred it. I wanted to *scorch it from the earth*—and my own memory, and all of space and time.

It was one thing for Logan to humiliate me in front of Charlie Yates with true things about my actual tragic life. It was quite another for him to *defile my writing integrity with falsehoods.*

That's when Charlie paused. "She read the screenplay, and she *loved it?*"

I knew in an instant: Logan had *so* miscalculated.

Logan had made a guess that Charlie didn't know his screenplay was bad. That he couldn't help but love his own work. That if he told Charlie I loved his screenplay—the way he thought Charlie secretly loved it, too—that would put us on the same team. United against a cruel world that didn't understand.

"Yes," Logan lied.

No!

But it was the wrong call.

"Then she doesn't know shit about rom-coms. Even I know that thing is an insult to the genre."

Thank you!

Why did I feel so relieved that he knew that?

Logan registered his mistake now. Charlie Yates knew his terrible screenplay was terrible. Lying to him that I'd loved it was not *helping me* but doing the opposite. So he rerouted: "The point is, she's a huge fan of you, man!"

"Has she seen the original?"

"Only a million times. Seen it, read it, studied it."

"Then there's no way she loves what I just wrote. She's either a liar . . . or she doesn't know shit from a shoelace."

Harsh.

Harsh, but well-said.

She doesn't know shit from a shoelace. Did he just make up a new aphorism?

Logan was still trying to take the ego route. "I'm telling you. She's a Charlie Yates superfan. She's so excited to work with you."

That, at least, was true.

Next Charlie said, "Of course she is. Who wouldn't be?"

"You're being such an ass right now. I'm telling you, she's good."

"And I'm telling you to get her out of here."

A pause, where I had to assume they were staring each other down. Then Charlie said, "Wait. Hold on. Is this the same girl from the video you texted?"

The video? He texted?

I looked down at Logan's phone in my hand. I'd known his passcode in high school. I tried it, and it still worked. Triple O Seven. Guess some things never change. The screen opened to a text he'd just sent to Charlie saying, There in 5.

Above it, I could see the bottom section of the last thing he'd sent before that.

A video.

Standing on Charlie Yates's front steps, I tried to process the domino-fall of realizations their conversation had just set off in my mind: Charlie Yates had no idea I was coming. He had not consented to work with me—nor did he want to work with anyone. The job opportunity of a lifetime that I had abandoned my sick father for and robbed my sister of her future for and dismantled my entire life for *did not actually exist.*

To top it all off, my ex-boyfriend from high school had just both lied about me and told mortifying truths . . . and, apparently, sent Charlie Yates some mysterious video.

I stared down at the phone screen with dread, afraid to know for sure. *What video?*

From the format, I could guess that it wasn't the YouTube video of the writing talk I'd given for the library that now had almost three hundred views. Nor, clearly, was it the sample freshman English class that lived on our community college's home page.

No, this video was vertical.

This video was personal.

This video had come from Logan's phone.

And here I faced a choice that was really no choice at all. I *wanted* to stay and continue eavesdropping—since I no longer trusted Logan's relationship with the truth. But I *needed* to know which video Logan had sent.

Please, please, please don't let it be the bikini video, I begged silently as I snuck with my bags away from the door, out into the yard, creating enough distance to watch it without being heard.

The bikini video—that I'd regretted a thousand times. The bikini video from ten years ago that Logan had sworn he'd erased—but I never 100 percent believed him. The bikini video I'd recorded for him when he'd asked me to send him "something sexy" and so I'd gotten Sylvie to record me crawling through the surf and growling like a panther at the beach in my first—and last—bikini.

The bikini video that topped my list of Most Embarrassing Things I'd Ever Done on Purpose.

He wouldn't have. Right?

He couldn't have.

But now I knew something new. I really had no idea what Logan would or wouldn't do. If he'd trick me into flying out here for a job that didn't exist, he was capable of anything.

There was a bench in the yard, and without really noticing, I backed up and parked myself on it. Next, the fight inside the house now out of earshot, I slid the video into frame on Logan's phone and tapped PLAY.

It wasn't the bikini video.

It was a video I didn't even remember. Had possibly never seen before.

It was me. In high school. Laughing and walking away from Logan, saying, "Do it right this time!" I watched myself moving—walking the way girls walk when they know they're being watched. I wore cutoffs and a striped T-shirt. My red curls were longer and wilder then, draping down my neck like mermaid fire. I paused to tie them into a bun.

I'd forgotten that. My hair was so long in high school I could tie it in a knot.

Wow. That girl was like a stranger. Like some kid I'd walk past on the street.

She lifted her arms, stepped forward, and then kicked up into a handstand. And then she started reciting a passage from Shakespeare's *Twelfth Night* while upside down.

Oh, god. I'd forgotten all about this.

"O Mistress mine, where are you roaming?" the young me bellowed, walking on her hands. "O stay and hear, your true love's coming, that can sing both high and low. Trip no further pretty sweeting. Journeys end in lovers' meeting—"

As I watched, the poem was coming back to me, and I was just anticipating the next line when my dad—looking younger than I ever remembered him, with dark brown hair and broad shoulders—stepped barefoot into the frame and flipped up on his hands, too, and finished the line. "Every wise man's son doth know."

"Dad!" the other me complained. "This is for school."

It was this ordinary moment, but it was mesmerizing. There it all was: The backyard I grew up playing in. My mother's herb garden on the flagstone patio. The overgrown crepe myrtle tree we used to climb.

It wasn't *a video on a phone*. It was a time capsule.

A time capsule of everything I'd lost.

That's when I heard something in the video that stopped my heart.

Her voice.

My mom's voice.

She must've been standing right next to Logan as he filmed, because her volume was so loud—so much louder than everything else in the video, ten feet away—that for just half a second, it didn't seem like the sound was coming from the phone in my hand.

"Emma! Your shirt's coming off!" my mom called.

And it felt so much like my beautiful, long-lost mother wasn't *there*, but *here*, right here, in the present moment, beside me in Charlie Yates's yard, that I glanced down at my shirt to check it. For one heartbreaking instant, my brain thought she was with me here and now—and sent a spark of joy so bright it almost hurt.

But of course she wasn't here.

We scattered her ashes in the ocean nine years ago—as soon as my dad was healed enough to make the drive.

The spark faded. I came to my senses. The video kept playing.

"My shirt's not 'coming off,'" the other me corrected my mom. "It's just falling down."

"Either way, we can see your bra."

"It's not a bra," I said. "It's a bikini top."

"Well, it looks like a bra. Tuck your shirt in."

"I can't. I don't have any arms."

"You do have arms," my still-upside-down dad pointed out. "You're just using them as legs."

Just as Logan, still focused on the bra issue, offered helpfully, "It's nothing I haven't seen before, Mrs. Wheeler."

"That's not comforting," my mom said as she stepped into the frame. And then there she was—not just a voice, but a vision. My beautiful, ethereal, ordinary mother, striding across the lawn in a jean skirt and sandals toward her goofball daughter. She grabbed my shirt while I was still upside down and tucked it in while my legs went all cattywampus.

"That's better," she said, patting me on the butt. Then she continued off across the lawn and I tumbled down into the grass.

"Mom!" I shouted. "I was performing Shakespeare!"

"Perform with your clothes on!" she called over her shoulder, just as a spindly kid cartwheeled into the frame. Sylvie.

"I want to perform Shakespeare!" Sylvie said, her voice like a chipmunk's.

But I was up now—and running toward the camera with a goofy grin on my face. "Cut! Cut!" I called, making the "cut" gesture across my neck. And then, just as I collided with Logan, the video ended, going still at the last frame: my mom across the yard, on the back steps, with the door halfway open, heading into the kitchen to make dinner.

What did we have for dinner that night? I wondered, and it suddenly felt so heartbreaking that now I'd never know.

For a minute, there in Charlie Yates's yard, the phone lay quiet in my hand. I was somewhere out of time.

And that's when I realized I was crying. The ragged kind of crying that overtakes you without your consent.

I was just about to play the video again—sensing I could watch it forever on an endless loop, gulping down that forgotten moment non-stop without ever quenching my longing to see it again—when Charlie Yates's present-day front door slammed open, and the present-day Logan came charging out of it, yanking me back to present-day reality.

Which suddenly, in contrast, didn't seem so important anymore.

"Emma, you've got to—" he started.

But Logan stopped at the sight of me—at, I'm guessing, the gully washer of tears on my face. I looked back at him, blinking—my heart tied up in a fist, my throat thick, and my face overtaken with reawakened grief.

For a second, we were in a standoff.

And then I realized he must've been thinking I was crying like this over Charlie, over a person who, apparently, saw me as nothing but an amateur.

Which sparked me into action.

"This," I said, drawing an imaginary circle around my face with my finger, "is not about this"—and I drew a much-larger circle around Logan, and the house behind him, and—what the hell—the whole city of LA.

Then I held up Logan's phone to him—frozen on that final image—until he saw what this *was* about.

Logan's shoulders dropped. "Emma, I—"

Just then, Charlie barreled out the front door with an air like he was about to make a proclamation.

He was—and I realize this goes without saying—bigger in real life.

It was my first—and possibly last—time to ever lay eyes on Charlie Yates, and I confess, it hijacked my attention for a second. Because *there he was*. That was the hair he always grabbed with his fist. And those were the wide-wale corduroys I'd seen in so many videos. And there was one of his trademarked rumpled Oxford shirts. And that was the signature stubble on his neck that he forgot to shave more often than not.

He certainly hadn't been fretting over *his* appearance in an airport bathroom.

Of course, in his defense, he'd had no idea I was coming. But this, I knew from YouTube, was how he dressed all the time—whether he was on a conference stage or getting snapped by the paparazzi in a five-star restaurant. He was constantly showing up to industry events in flip-flops and shorts, or with bags of takeout food because he'd been writing all day and was famished. He once ate a cheeseburger and a large order of fries during a panel discussion at the Paley Center for Media—ripping little ketchup packets and squirting them onto a napkin on his knee.

That's how huge this guy was. Nobody cared.

Nobody even complained *in the comments.*

He was famously unorthodox onstage. He once took a nap during a roundtable. And it wasn't just forgiven *because he was a legend.* It was part of what made him a legend in the first place. Only later would I wonder if it was a power move. Like he was too cool to play by anyone's rules. Like *having to try* was a sign of weakness.

Point being: Here he was. Ten feet away.

At the time, all I could think was: *It's him. It's really him.*

And despite everything, seeing him in real life like that had a seismic effect on my body.

Like the nearness of him was causing fractures and fissures at deep, subterranean levels.

Like the presence of the living, breathing Charlie Yates was somehow . . . fracking my soul. Or something. The sight of him, for just a second, took me deep inside my own body. Where everything suddenly felt radically *different.* Like I might go to turn on some internal faucet and watch fire come out instead of water.

Am I overstating it?

Probably. But I know what I know.

The sight of me seemed to affect Charlie Yates, too.

What would Charlie have seen in that moment? A random, weeping female in his yard. Blotchy face. Eyes red from crying. Tear-smeared, shiny cheeks. Puffy pink nose. And so angry. Angry like a person with lightning bolts shooting from her eyes. Not to mention the hair: I always have to remind myself how carefully I had *definitely* clamped my hair back into a sensible pom-pom before we arrived—because my imagination always wants to say that, in Charlie's first-ever sight of me, I had fire-orange medusa snakes writhing around my head.

How often do you step out of your front door in life to find a sight like that?

Poor Charlie.

Even without the snakes, I'm sure I was a sight.

But before Charlie could react, or scream, or run back into the house and dead-bolt the door, Logan pulled us back on track. "I know what you're thinking," he said to me.

At that, my gaze shifted back to Logan. "Do you?" I demanded.

"My motivations were honorable!"

But I was shaking my head, Charlie Yates now forgotten. "My *mom* is in this video." I held out Logan's phone. "She's here," I said. "My *mom*. My *family*. How could you just . . . text it around? I"—and here I tapped my chest with my hand—"*I* haven't even seen this. How could you just send it to—to a stranger? It's my *mom*, Logan."

To be honest, I didn't even know what I was trying to say.

Rare for me.

Usually I started with words and found the feelings later, if that makes sense.

But here, all I had was a feeling. A feeling that this lost moment in time—these lost people, this lost family—was too precious to share.

Was it weird that Logan still had the video—much less that he would text it to his client without ever even showing it to me? Yes, of course.

But that's not what had me so appalled.

This was *my mother*. Her jean skirt. Her favorite sandals. Her warm voice like butterscotch. This was my beloved family. My unbroken fa- ther, my preteen sister, my forgotten self. This was everyone who was precious to me—captured just weeks before the end. It was everyone I'd ever loved, beautiful and hopeful and frozen in time. It was valuable beyond description. It should be nothing less than cherished. And it wasn't for anyone, even Charlie Yates, to watch on some phone while he was sitting on the toilet.

Or wherever Charlie Yates checked his texts.

"Emma," Logan said, "I get it. I'm sorry. But—"

I shook my head, busy forwarding the video to myself.

"Emma, look," Logan went on. "I was trying to get you this job."

"You told me I *had* this job."

"I was working on it."

"You lied to me."

"A white lie."

"Go ahead and tell yourself that."

"It was the best plan I could come up with."

"Well, it was a shitty plan!"

"I see that now. I definitely see that now. But he needed to meet you, Emma."

"There are lots of ways to meet people. Coffee! Brunch! Dinner!"

"Would you have flown all the way across the country for a coffee?"

"With Charlie Yates? *Yes!* Hell, yes!"

"Ah," Logan said. "Well, I didn't—fully—understand that. I thought you needed . . . a push."

Unacceptable. "You manipulated me." Then I added, "I gave up my whole life, and I left everyone I love for nothing. *Worse* than for nothing! For humiliation! For crushing disappointment!" I glanced over at Charlie. "For you to lie to this asshole about his apocalyptically shitty screenplay and tell him that I loved it!"

We all let that land.

Then Logan said, "You heard us?"

"The door didn't close."

Somewhere in the yard, a bird decided to tweet.

Then Logan said, "Just come inside and let's all talk."

But that was the other thing. Seeing that video made me overwhelmingly homesick. "I don't want to talk," I said. "He doesn't want me here, and you never should have brought me here." Then I added, "I just want to go home."

I pelted Logan's phone and keys onto Charlie Yates's lawn, and then I grabbed my bags and started dragging them away, the broken wheel on my carry-on screeching in protest.

"Hey," Logan said, following me. "You don't even know where you are."

I kept walking.

"Look," Logan went on, "I know I did this all wrong. But at heart, I'm right. Charlie needs you. And you need him."

"He already said no. Like fifty times. In no uncertain terms."

Logan nodded. "Okay, that's true. He did say no. But he can change his mind. And the only person who can make him do that is you."

But I just kept walking.

"Emma," Logan pleaded. "Help me do this for you."

"I don't want to," I said, keeping my eyes straight ahead. "And I'm not going to. I'm leaving. And then I'll find a fancy hotel that I cannot afford—and send you the bill. I'm going to take a scorchingly hot bath and eat everything out of the minibar. And then tomorrow? I'm going back home where I belong—to see if Sylvie can get her internship back. And then I'll start finding another career. Because you're the only person I knew in LA. And we're not friends anymore."

Six

THAT WAS A pretty strong exit. Right?

I spoke my piece, and ended on a zinger strong enough that they both mutely watched me walk off. I felt their eyes on me all the way down the street, as my broken carry-on wheel bewailed every step I took—and I held my head high until I was out of sight.

Though as soon as they couldn't see me, I felt the air that was holding up my lungs—and my posture, and my remaining shreds of dignity— release itself . . . and I deflated like a balloon.

That's how I walked after that: slumped, lopsided, lost.

I'll just call an Uber and go to a hotel, I told myself, in an attempt at a pep talk.

But I'd never called an Uber. I didn't even have the app on my phone. And I'd never been to LA. I hadn't traveled outside the five-mile radius of my apartment in almost a decade. How would I even find a hotel? I was alone, I had no idea where I was, and I was too humiliated to turn around.

I'd walked for about fifteen minutes—and was just starting to panic—when Logan drove up alongside me and matched his pace to mine. His window came down.

"Get in," Logan called.

I ignored him and kept walking. There was a pebble in my shoe, but I ignored that, too.

"He caved, okay?" Logan called. "He gave in. He says you can stay."

I kept walking.

"You got the job!" Logan shouted. "You don't believe me? I have the text right here."

He held up his phone, but I didn't look.

"You're not listening. I'm telling you it worked. He's in. It's happening."

My broken carry-on wheel caught on a rock, but I yanked it so hard I didn't even break pace.

"You should be thanking me!" Logan called next, a little louder. "It worked, didn't it?" He shook his phone at me. "He says, and I quote: 'Fine. Fuck it. She can have the guest room.'"

I didn't really know what to do in this moment. I didn't have a plan. All I knew was, I would not get in Logan's car. Nothing else was clear—at all—except that.

"Are you refusing to spend the night in Charlie Yates's mansion? Is that what's happening now? Because I'm telling you: He's got a wine cellar. And a pool. And a thousand-dollar coffee maker."

But the pebble in my shoe—or was it maybe a piece of glass?—and I just kept walking.

And walking.

Until finally, faced with my wall of stoicism, Logan gave up and drove off—leaving me behind, now more triumphant and more panicked at the same time.

Really? Was that all the penance he was going to do?

Fine.

How hard could it be to download the Uber app?

I stopped to pull out my phone, and that's when I saw the low battery alert.

Okay. No freaking out. If worse came to worst, I could find my way back to Charlie's house and borrow his phone. I turned back to study the terrain I'd just covered.

At least, I *thought* I could find my way back.

Probably.

If it didn't get dark first.

I turned back to face the way I'd been going again, scanning the horizon for, maybe, a luxury hotel that was having a 90-percent-off special.

What time did it get dark here, anyway?

On the heels of that thought, I heard Logan pull up alongside me again and idle. Without even looking to the side, or considering if this was the stupidest thing I'd ever do, I tilted my head to the sky and shouted, "Please! Just! Fuck! Off!"

"Really?" a guy's voice said.

A guy who wasn't Logan.

I turned, and instead of Logan Scott in a Beemer, it was Charlie Yates in a Chevy Blazer.

A cool, seventies vintage Chevy Blazer, by the way. Baby blue. Windows down. And Charlie Yates in aviators, regarding me and looking—*fine, whatever*—impossibly cool.

As impossibly cool as a guy in a rumpled Oxford could be.

Way cooler than any writer deserved to be.

I turned to face him. "Sorry," I said, vastly more polite now. "I thought you were Logan."

It wasn't Charlie's fault that Logan brought me here. Charlie wasn't doing anything wrong by not wanting to work with me. Yes, he'd said a few mean-ish things earlier. But I wasn't going to hold that against him. I wouldn't have wanted to work with me, either, if I were him. He could still be my favorite writer.

This was on me, really, for believing Logan's cockamamie story in the first place.

"Get in," Charlie said. "I'm here to rescue you."

"Oh," I said, still just wanting to stay as far away from both of these guys, and this whole experience, as possible. "It's fine."

Charlie leaned his head out the window then and checked the bright sky like an old sea captain reading the wind. Then he put the Blazer in park—just right there in the road—got out, and came around to face me. "It's not fine," he said then. "It'll get dark in a few hours. And that's when the coyotes come out."

"The coyotes?"

Charlie nodded, like *Yep*. "And the mountain lions."

"You have mountain lions?" I asked. "In the second-largest city in America?"

Charlie nodded. "Almost four million." Then he added, "People. Not lions."

He hadn't answered my question. "Should I believe you?" I asked, mostly to myself.

"I can't tell you what to do," Charlie said. "But I have yet to mention the bears."

"Seriously?" I said.

"It's cool," Charlie said then, calling my bluff. "I can tell you prefer to be"—he looked around—"alone."

"Wait—" I said, as Charlie started to walk back around toward the driver's side.

"You'll be fine," Charlie said. "Just a quick tip: If you do see a mountain lion, don't run."

"Don't run?" I echoed. Can you *lose* a conversation? Because that's what I was doing.

He shrugged. "You can't outrun a mountain lion."

"You know what?" I said. "I'll come with you."

"Naw," Charlie said, enjoying this now, "you don't have to."

"I want to," I said.

Charlie, like convincing me had been much easier than he'd expected, came back around to where I was, and, holding my gaze the entire time, stepped close and leaned in until there was less than a foot between us—close enough to spark a *What the heck?* question in my head—before I realized he was sliding my backpack off my shoulders and then picking up my bags.

He tossed both in the back of the Blazer, and then, when I still hadn't moved, he opened the passenger door for me. "I've got you," he said. "Hop in."

AND THAT'S HOW I wound up spending the night with Charlie Yates.

Although not like that sentence implies.

On the short drive back to his house, I tried to adjust: I was with Charlie Yates. We were in his very cool, vintage—reconditioned and now hybrid, he told me—truck. The Allman Brothers played on the radio. The windows were hand-cranked down. The famous zero-humidity LA air fluttered all around us. Charlie drove one-handed, his free arm resting out the open window.

Almost like I wasn't there.

I snuck looks at his profile. Had he really just agreed to work with me? Logan said so, but now we all knew exactly how trustworthy Logan was. Still, the dialogue "Fine. Fuck it. She can have the guest room" rang true. Logan could never write dialogue like that.

"Thanks so much," I ventured then, "for saving me from the mountain lions."

"Not a problem."

"I really am so sorry about all of this."

"It's not your fault. It's Logan's fault."

"It must have been so weird for you to see me standing at your front door with my suitcases."

"You have no idea."

"Logan just called me out of the blue and said he had a job for me."

"Right?" Charlie said, like *What a douche.*

"He's found me lots of jobs in the past, so it didn't seem all that weird. But it did seem . . . too good to be true."

Charlie nodded in solidarity.

"But I trusted him," I went on. "I took the summer off from my job. I left my family. I put everything else that mattered on hold, and I packed up my life and flew out here. With no idea that you had no idea."

Charlie shook his head at the situation, like he really got it.

"You *are* my favorite writer, though," I said next. "Logan wasn't lying about that. I love you more than Richard Curtis, and Elaine May, and Billy Wilder. I love you more"—and this felt so sacrilegious, like I might be smote by lightning at the words, but I had to make my point—"than Nora Ephron."

Charlie held kind of still.

Too much?

Then he gave a small, mechanical nod that read like *Got it.*

No doubt my cue to stop talking.

But I just had to know. I had to confirm. I decided to *proceed as if* and see where that got me. "So I just want to thank you. For this opportunity. It's not easy to change your mind. Especially not in the heat of a crazy moment. But I need to say that this is the hugest of huge deals to me." And then, realizing it might sound cheesy but unable to find any better words to capture my sincerity, I concluded with "I will do this work with my whole heart and soul."

I snuck a look at him.

He was frowning.

"What work?" Charlie asked.

"The rewrite?" I said.

At those words, Charlie positively detonated with laughter—the kind of *pah* you make when you are very surprised by something unspeakably ridiculous. Then he followed the *pah* with hooting, and chuckling, and slapping his hand on the door of the truck.

This went on for a while.

It was bitter laughter, I decided as he went on—but laughter all the same.

Anyway. I guess I had my answer.

"The rewrite?" Charlie kept saying. "The rewrite?"

I wasn't laughing myself, needless to say. "Logan told me you'd agreed to everything," I said. "He said you'd said, 'Fine. Fuck it. She can have the guest room.' He *showed me the text!*"

Like I might prove him wrong.

Charlie took a few deep breaths as he worked to settle. "I did say you could have the guest room. For one night. Before you fly home tomorrow."

"Ah," I said.

"It's so funny that you believed him," Charlie said. "Didn't he *just* lie to you?"

My shoulders hunched in my defense. "Yeah, but . . . he doesn't *always* lie. Most of the time he tells the truth." Then I had to add, "I think."

"Well, he wasn't telling the truth about that."

"Fine," I said. "Got it."

"I mean," Charlie went on, still marveling at Logan's gall and my gullibility, "I don't write with anyone. Ever. Logan knows that. And if I'm really your favorite writer"—he glanced at me like he'd caught me—"you'd know that, too."

"Yes," I said, mechanically, repeating the very famous story. "You once tried collaborating with Topher James Heywood, and it ended in a bar fight where you almost got shanked with a broken beer bottle, and then you never worked with anyone else again. I've seen you tell that story like ten times. Though sometimes it's a Heineken bottle, and sometimes it's Sam Adams."

Charlie nodded like I'd proved myself, and then he said, "I never should have named the beer. I keep saying the wrong beer and getting angry DMs about it."

"There's a whole discussion board on Reddit."

"That's disturbing."

"I'm on Team Heineken, by the way. But only because I like the label."

Charlie considered that. "Heineken it is, then."

That felt weirdly good.

But then something hit me. *Heywood.*

Topher James Heywood.

"Wait," I said. "Does Topher James Heywood also go by T.J. Heywood?"

Charlie flared his nostrils like he was not a fan. "Yes. 'T.J.' and 'Teej' and 'Trey' because he's a 'the third.' And also . . ."

"Also what?"

"He has another nickname, but nobody uses it but him."

"He has a nickname for himself?"

Charlie flared those nostrils of his again. "Yeah."

"What is it?"

Charlie hesitated. "Jablowmie."

"What?" I didn't get it.

"Because of the last name?" Charlie prompted. "Heywood."

"Jablowmie Heywood?"

"Flip it," Charlie said, and when I still hadn't cringed in recognition, he flipped it for me: "Heywood Jablowmie."

I dropped my shoulders, like *Seriously?* "That's the nickname he chose for himself? It's not even in the right order!"

"I'll be sure to mention that to him."

"Why were you even *trying* to write with this guy?"

"Well," Charlie said, like *Where to begin?* "He's richer than God, he knows everybody in this town, and he wields a crazy amount of power for somebody who wears a backward baseball cap."

"All because his dad is Chris Heywood and his grandfather was Christopher Heywood?"

"He's a classic example of failing to the top."

"But he *started* at the top."

"Yeah. That's how that works."

Of course it was.

"Anyway," Charlie went on, steering us back to the more pressing matter of why he couldn't work with *me*, "the point is, this you-and-me thing was never going to happen. And Logan should have known better."

"Agreed."

"I was never going to agree to anybody rewriting my script. Least of all some unproduced, underachieving, failed nobody writer off the internet."

Whoa. Could we go back to talking about Heywood Jablowmie?

I sat quietly and waited for Charlie to remember who he was talking to.

But he didn't.

"It's insulting," he went on. "It's ridiculous. It's utterly, comically out of the question. It's like hiring a crayon-toting kindergartner to repaint the Sistine Chapel! It's like hiring a toddler with Play-Doh to rebuild the Eiffel Tower! It's like hiring a teenager with a ukulele to rewrite Mozart!"

"Are you Mozart in this scenario?"

"Of course!"

"So your self-esteem is"—I tilted my head to emphasize the sarcasm—"healthy."

"I don't need self-esteem! I've got a whole drawer of Oscars!"

Ah. Sarcasm ignored. Oh, well. "I'd actually love to hear Mozart on the ukulele."

"You're missing the point."

"No," I said, with a little wry nod, "I think I got it."

"Because the point is, someone like you isn't even remotely qualified to work with someone like me."

"You've made that very clear."

"Someone who doesn't live in LA, who's never done any real work in the industry, and who placed in two film festivals, but didn't even go? No offense, but that's someone who clearly doesn't take her work seriously."

No offense? Everything he'd said up to now had been harsh, but not untrue. But "doesn't take her work seriously"? That crossed the line.

"I take my work very seriously," I said, feeling a sting of—you guessed it—*offense*.

"Incorrect," Charlie said.

"'Incorrect'?"

"Because if you were serious, you'd be taking every opportunity that came to you—and not just taking, *grabbing*. With both hands. Like nothing else mattered."

"But other things *do* matter."

"The fact that you think that is exactly why you're a failed screen-writer."

"I'm not a failed screenwriter!"

"Which part of your failed career gave you that idea?"

Whoa.

How to even respond? Finally I mustered a gritted "I *take* my career *seriously.*"

"Do you?" Charlie challenged. "Because the Warner Bros. internship isn't something that writers just ignore."

"Logan told you about that?"

"Do you have any idea how prestigious that internship is? How much it could have changed your life? It's unfathomable that you had that chance and didn't take it."

"I know exactly how prestigious it is, and I—"

But Charlie kept going. "Logan thought I'd be impressed that you won. But the fact that you turned it down tells me everything I need to know."

"Look, there were circumstances—"

"Fuck circumstances! That's what I'm saying. If you want to do this life, you have to eat it and drink it and sleep it, and it has to come before everything else. Family—friends—sex! Anything else is second best. Anything else is *not taking it seriously.*"

Turning down that internship had been the most agonizing sacrifice out of all my agonizing sacrifices. But if this guy really thought that my own personal writing goals should truly come before everything else, including my family—including my *dad*—then there was no use in trying to explain.

We'd reached Charlie's house. He swung us into the driveway, cut the engine, and stomped the parking brake.

"Is that what *you've* done?" I asked then, quietly. "Sacrificed everything?"

"How do you think I wound up all alone in this giant mansion?"

Was he saying that like it was a good thing? There was bitterness in his voice, and probably a whole story to excavate. But I had my own bitterness to cope with.

I'd already lost this fight, anyway.

I let out a long breath. "You must be right, then," I said. "By your definition, I guess I don't take it seriously."

"Thank you," he said, like he'd won.

"Pro tip, though," I said now, at the end of this endless day, not even able to disguise the exhaustion in my voice. "In general, if you have to add the words 'no offense' to something you're saying . . . it's probably offensive."

Charlie frowned at that. Like it registered. Like once the frenzy of trying to make his point had abated, he could suddenly see the wreckage he'd left behind.

"I'll find a plane ticket home," I said then, in defeat, hearing a threat of tears in my voice, "for first thing in the morning."

Then I pulled the door handle to get out.

But the door didn't budge.

"Oh—" Charlie said, remembering. "It's broken." At that, he leapt out and came around to my side. "I have to get it from here."

He opened the door, and I swung my legs out, fully intending to grab my bags, march inside, fire up the internet, buy a plane ticket, and then defiantly ignore Charlie Yates for the rest of my life.

But instead?

Instead, I fainted.

Seven

DID NOT SEE that coming.

One minute, I was fine—or as fine as you can be when your personal hero is telling you you're worthless—and the next minute, as Charlie held the car door, and I stepped onto the driveway, coming face-to-face with him by a matter of inches, close enough that I could feel his gaze on me like a breeze, I felt a swell of nausea, heard a rushing sound in my ears, and watched the edges of my vision go dark.

Next, I was coming to, flat on my back on the concrete, Charlie's face hovering above mine, frowning, his eyes dark with intensity. "Emma!" he was saying. "Emma!"

But the sound was muffled, and out of sync a little.

In slow-mo, Charlie moved his head away and pressed it to my chest. Was he listening to my heart? Checking my breathing? I can still see that chestnut-brown hair of his, as if my mind paused to snap a photo. He was on his hands and knees beside me, but next I saw him launch up and run—*run!*—to the back of his truck to grab my suitcase and drag it toward me. Then he was lifting my legs and resting them on it to elevate them.

Then his face came back to my face, peering close.

"Emma?"

I could hear him more clearly now.

He was handsome. To me, at least. There was no way around it.

Don't talk about his nostrils. Don't talk about his nostrils.

Thank god I was too nauseated to speak.

I started to sit up, but Charlie shook his head. "Don't get up! You're not supposed to stand. Give it a second."

I relaxed back against the driveway as Charlie wriggled out of his overshirt, wadded up a makeshift pillow, and tucked it under my head, cradling my face to his shoulder for a second to get it placed.

Dammit. He smelled good.

Whatever his deodorant was, it cured the nausea like a tonic.

I watched him rise again, and then come back from the car with a bottle of water. He squirted some on his palm, shook off the excess, and then smoothed the water over my forehead.

"What are you doing?" I asked, better enough at last to talk.

"I'm cooling you off."

"I'm not hot."

"The internet says to."

Fine. I wouldn't argue with the internet. It felt nice, anyway.

"You fainted," Charlie said, looking genuinely worried.

"I'm sorry," I said, closing my eyes.

"You scared me. You went so white."

"I don't think I've eaten anything today," I said. "Or yesterday."

"Nothing?" Charlie said, like *Why not?*

I didn't have the energy to obfuscate. "I was nervous to meet you."

"So nervous you didn't eat for two days?"

"Uh-huh."

"I'm not that scary," Charlie said.

But I shook my head. "You're scarier. If I'd known what it would actually be like, I wouldn't have eaten for a month."

Charlie was assessing me. "Your color's coming back," he said, nodding. "Are you okay to go inside?"

I started to sit up, but he stopped me again.

"Not like that," he said, and then I felt his arms slide under me and tighten as he rose and carried me toward the house.

I was still woozy, and the motion was a little *too soon*, so I curled against his shoulder to brace myself. My view from there was the stubble on his neck. And his square, way-too-appealing-for-a-writer jaw. And his Adam's apple.

My eyes wanted to close, but I talked them out of it.

How many people got *this* close to Charlie Yates's Adam's apple?

We walked through his front door and into a living room, where he set me down on a plush sofa.

"You leave your mansion unlocked?" I asked as he released me.

"It's on a remote," he said.

He turned now to other things: wedging a throw pillow under my head, and then grabbing a throw blanket off a chair, draping it over me, and heading off toward the adjacent kitchen.

I followed him with my eyes as he opened a cabinet, pulled out a glass, turned on the faucet.

He came back with the glass and knelt beside me. "The internet wants you to drink some water," he said, and then, with a tenderness I never would have expected from the person who'd just called me a "failed nobody writer," he worked his arm behind my shoulders to raise me up to take some sips.

"Okay?" he asked as I lay back down.

I nodded.

How long had it been since anyone had taken care of me in any situation? The last person to do it must have been my mom. Nowadays, it was me taking care of everyone else. When I got sick or hurt now, I just managed it on my own. Which I was fully capable of doing. But I'd forgotten what it felt like to be looked after. I guess I must have missed that feeling a lot—because tears kept rising to my eyes, and I kept blinking them away.

Or maybe it had just been a really long day.

✿   ✿   ✿

LATER THAT EVENING, as I lay catatonic on the greige-colored guest bed in one of Charlie Yates's many greige-colored guest rooms, I got a text from the man himself—across the house.

He'd ordered takeout for us, and I should come to the dining room to eat.

And so I did.

I was miserable, sure—but nowhere near miserable enough to reject dinner.

Charlie was there, seated at the table. And so was half the food in the city of Los Angeles.

Charlie saw my eyes widen at the sight. "I wasn't sure what you liked," he said, "so I just got it all."

I stepped closer to the table and took it in. Sushi, sandwiches, spring rolls, samosas, pizza, pastries, fried chicken . . . it was all there, and then some.

Charlie was chowing down on a big plate of everything, and he'd set a place for me to do the same.

I took one butter croissant and decided to start small.

Charlie watched me chew, and then asked, after a few bites, "How do you feel? Better?"

"I'm not sure how to answer that question," I said. Then I talked myself into a section of club sandwich, and a bit of fruit salad, and a few bites of strawberry shortcake before deciding I'd hit the wall.

Was he sneaking looks at me chewing? Was I being monitored? Did I eat like a failed screenwriter?

Just as I was thinking I'd make my escape, he said, "Can I ask you a question?"

"I guess so?" I said.

"What, exactly," Charlie asked, "didn't you like about my screenplay?"

Oh, god. "You know," I said, shaking my head, "I don't think we need to get into all that."

"I just . . . keep thinking about it," Charlie said.

"It'll pass," I told him.

Charlie tilted his head. "You don't want to tell me?"

"You've already explained to me in very clear terms that my opinion—in your opinion—is pretty worthless. So I just don't really see the point."

"What if I'm curious?"

"Why would you be?"

"It's just—it's that feeling—when you don't know something and you just really, really find yourself needing to know."

I knew that feeling. Of course I did. "An information gap," I said.

"Right," Charlie said, like he'd never heard the term before. Then, fainter, like he was mulling it over, "An information gap."

"Do you not know the term 'information gap'?" I asked.

"Of course I do. It's a . . . gap in information."

"It's a writing term for how to create curiosity in the audience by leaving out crucial information."

"Well, it works."

How did Charlie Yates not know this term?

"The point is," Charlie went on, "you information-gapped me—"

"You information-gapped yourself."

"—and now I need you to fill in the . . . information."

I gave it a beat. Then I said, "Why would I do that?"

Charlie shrugged. "Why wouldn't you do that?"

"Because," and I couldn't believe I had to say this out loud, "you didn't hire me."

Charlie nodded, like *Interesting*.

"If you had hired me," I said then, wanting to be totally clear, "I would happily do that right now." I gestured toward my backpack in the guest room. "I've got ten pages of typed, single-spaced notes. I've got Post-its all over the printed screenplay—and comments filling up the margins." Though, in truth, the margins mostly said things like *WTF??!* and *FFS!!!*—more of a chronicle of horrors than thoughtful commentary. "I spent every free minute," I went on, "from the time Logan told me I had this job until I got on the plane to come here breaking down that screenplay and figuring it out—time I will never be compensated for, by the way."

Charlie nodded, like he hadn't thought of that.

I went on, "I could spend *hours* explaining what I didn't like about your screenplay. I could go *all night*." Then I concluded with, "But *you didn't hire me*."

Charlie nodded, and said, "What if I hired you now—just for that?"

"What?"

"What if I hired you for a consultation? Just for tonight? Tell me what you think, and I'll pay you handsomely for your time and your thoughts and your trouble."

"Why would you do that?"

"Because you just taught me the term 'information gap.'"

Well, at least he could admit it.

He could see I was considering it. "What's your going rate? Two-fifty an hour?"

I had no idea what my going rate was. "Three hundred," I said.

"Okay. Let's cover three hours tonight, give or take, and whatever time you spent last week. Plus your time, your stress, your inconvenience, your fainting spell. How's three thousand dollars?"

"Five thousand," I countered, not skipping a beat.

That was reasonable, right? We were negotiating *in his mansion*, after all.

"Sold," Charlie said.

Wait—what?

Wow. Three cheers for information gaps.

"Sold," I echoed back. "You write the check. I'll get my notes."

Eight

ASTONISHING, REALLY—HOW A five-thousand-dollar paper check can perk a girl up.

The second Charlie handed it over, I tucked it in my bra for safekeeping.

Which felt like a power move.

We cleared the dining table, and then Charlie sat across from me with a fancy Moleskine notebook and a pen. Like he might—good god—*take notes* on what I was about to say.

Notes *for* or *against*, I wasn't sure.

He watched while I unloaded my backpack. My pen bag, my laptop, my stack of notebooks, my printed notes, all building to the grand finale of his screenplay, bound with brads and a card stock cover, absolutely bursting with Post-its, annotation tabs, and dog-ears. Not to mention a few coffee rings and a wrinkled corner where I'd accidentally dunked it in the bathwater.

A well-read script, for sure.

Charlie stared at it.

"Let me ask you a question," I said next when I was all set up. "Do you want me to be honest? Or do you want me to blow smoke up your ass?"

"I want you to be honest," Charlie said—no hesitation.

But that didn't mean much.

Writers always want you to be honest—but only if you love it.

"Because I didn't love it," I said.

"I figured that out when you called it 'apocalyptically shitty.'"

I squinted, like *I guess you heard that?* Then I nodded and said, "Can you handle it?"

"Handle what?"

"Not being loved."

"Sure. Easy. People *don't love me* all the time."

"Not like this they don't."

Maybe it was because he'd been so insulting and so dismissive to me back in the car. But now that I had some food in my stomach and some money in my bra, the idea of giving this guy a little comeuppance felt pretty appealing.

Did I want to tell him what I really thought about his screenplay?

Suddenly, I did.

"You sure you want to do this?" I asked him, in a tone like *Last chance.*

Charlie nodded, looking less sure.

I took a sip of my water and began: "Let me just start by saying that, up until I met you today, you were my favorite writer of all time. I've read everything you've ever written. I love your character arcs, your dialogue, your plot twists, your settings, your flawed heroes and heroines, your weirdly relatable villains, your timing, your redemption arcs, your sense of humor, and, maybe most of all, your catchphrases."

Charlie nodded, like all was right with the world.

"But this screenplay," I went on, "is a crime against humanity."

Charlie frowned.

"Still sure about doing this?" I asked, one last time.

"You've already put that check in your bra," Charlie said, gesturing in that direction before abruptly deciding that was a bad idea.

"Buckle up, then," I said, with a shrug.

The teaching rule I had for myself was to never criticize more than three things about a student's work at a time. If you hit people too hard with too much too fast, they shut down. They feel attacked instead of advised. It stops helping and starts hurting.

Three criticisms at a time was the magic number.

But was I going to follow that rule for Charlie Yates?

No way in hell.

He wasn't some beginner kid at community college. He was a ridiculously successful titan of the genre. With a mansion. And a "whole drawer" of Oscars.

He could handle it. And even if he couldn't—*all* writers are mushy goo, deep down—that wasn't my problem.

He was paying me handsomely to share my thoughts, and share them I would.

All of them.

And if they happened to crush him? That was just a bonus.

"First of all," I began, "this screenplay shouldn't even be happening. I want to register my objection at the outset. This movie is a beloved classic that brims with rare magic and its legacy should not be defiled by some appalling remake."

"Noted," Charlie said.

Now I began in earnest—and maybe I should have been intimidated to say all this to a writing god. But my outrage made me fearless. I had a higher purpose to serve. "Just for an overview," I said, "when I say this screenplay is 'apocalyptically shitty,' I mean that it has no tension, no character growth, no longing, no buildup, no anticipation, no banter, no fun, no play, and no shimmer."

"No *shimmer*?" Charlie said.

But I was just getting started. "It is a romantic comedy that is neither funny nor romantic. It doesn't do any—*any*—of the things that a rom-com is supposed to do."

"What's a rom-com supposed to do?"

"Great question. One you should have asked before you wrote this thing. But let's talk about it."

Charlie's pen was still lying idle atop his open notebook. He wasn't taking notes. But he was—and I'll give him credit for this—listening.

"The job of a rom-com," I said, "is to give you a simulated feeling of falling in love."

Here Charlie blinked, and I found myself wondering if this might be news to him.

I went on. "A rom-com should give you a swoony, hopeful, delicious, rising feeling of anticipation as you look forward to the moment when the two leads, who are clearly mad for each other, finally overcome all their obstacles, both internal and external, and get together."

Now I gave Charlie the stink eye.

"This is the first, most sacred rule of rom-coms," I said, in a tone like *You know what you did.* "The leads wind up blissfully together in the end." I paused for effect. "And you broke that rule when you made Claudette Colbert's character marry the wrong guy."

Charlie must have read my dramatic pause like I wanted an explanation. "It's more interesting that way," he said.

Ugh. The pomposity. "It may be 'interesting.' But it's not a rom-com. And when you rewrite the greatest rom-com of all time, *it needs to be a rom-com.*"

Charlie considered that.

And here I weaponized my encyclopedic knowledge of Charlie's body of work. "In *The Destroyers*, did the aliens win? Did they turn Earth into a desiccated hellscape and eject the little orphan boy into a black hole just so you, the writer, could do something 'interesting'?"

He didn't have to answer. Of course they didn't.

"Did the Navy SEALs in *Night Raid* give up after the submarine sank and let themselves drown in a watery tomb? Did the sleuth in *The Maharajas' Express* hunt down all those clues just to get to the end and say, 'Huh. I'm stumped'? Did the protagonist of *Live and Let Kill* just lose interest in solving his wife's decapitation and lie down on the guillotine?"

Charlie was watching me.

"Of course not! You know this! All genres have a promise. The Destroyer will save the universe. The soldiers will win the final battle. The sleuth will solve the mystery. The hunted, grieving husband will figure it out just in the nick of time. I can't believe I have to say this to you, but *the same is true for romantic comedies.* The two leads will wind up together. That's what the audience showed up for. The joy of it all. If you don't give it to them, it's beyond unsatisfying—it's a violation of trust. It's like sex with no orgasm! What was even the point?"

At that, I froze.

Did I just say the word "orgasm" to Charlie Yates?

Charlie looked like he was asking himself the same question.

But the point was valid. I decided to own it.

"A great rom-com," I said, "is just like sex. If you're surprised by the ending, somebody wasn't doing their job. We all know where it's headed. The fun is how we get there. Seriously—have you ever had fantastic sex that culminated in an epic orgasm and then said to yourself, *God, that was so cliché. It should've had a different ending?*"

Charlie tilted his head. "Do you want me to answer that question—or was it rhetorical?"

It was rhetorical, but I was so worked up, I said, "I want you to answer!"

Charlie gave a solemn nod as he conceded, "I have not."

"Thank you! Exactly!"

Safe to say, this little tangent had not been in my notes. I had a million legitimate, academic points I could have led with, and yet here I was, just minutes in, asking—no, *demanding*—to know about Charlie Yates's personal orgasms.

From Charlie's expression, he hadn't expected me to go there, either.

Though, if I'm honest, there was a brightness to his eyes like I'd surprised him.

The idea that I was seeing admiration from Charlie Yates gave me a fluttery feeling in my . . . everywhere.

I tamped it down. I had to stay focused. I wasn't here to make friends.

But that's when he picked up that pen of his and wrote, at the top of his notebook page, "Happy ending—essential." And then drew a box around it. Like he'd heard me, and he agreed, and he was ready to move on to the next point.

I needed to move away from sex talk. That much was clear.

I consulted my notes.

"Other problems," I said, in a tone like *Where to begin?* "I guess the next giant issue is that none of the things that happen in this script correspond to the original. At all. It's almost like you've never even seen the movie."

"No comment."

"Have you seen the movie?"

"Of course."

"Recently?"

"Not sure that's relevant."

"I think it's pretty relevant. You've got the characters going to *a line-dancing competition!*"

"So?"

"So there is no line dancing in *It Happened One Night!*"

Charlie shrugged. "They said to update it."

"With *line dancing?*"

He shrugged again. "It wasn't taken."

"It 'wasn't taken'?"

"All the other kinds of dancing have been done. Ballroom. Swing. Latin. Hip-hop. Dirty. Not to mention the whole *Magic Mike* stripping franchise."

"There was line dancing in *Footloose.*"

"But that's not a rom-com."

"You don't even know what a rom-com is!"

"I do now."

I gave him a look, let him have the point, and then said, "Disqualifyingly bad problem number three: there is nothing romantic here. At all. The leads don't even like each other, as far as I can tell."

"They like each other. What about when she falls on top of him?"

"That's an accident."

"Yes, but it leads to a sexy moment."

"Sexy how? She gets a concussion."

"But they gaze into each other's eyes before she passes out."

"I didn't read that as gazing. I read it as glaring."

"That's on you."

"No, that's on *the script*."

"I'm telling you, that's a turning point for them."

"And I'm telling you, that's not how that works."

"Fine. Fall on me sometime, and I'll show you."

"Fine. I will."

We faced off for a second until Charlie said, "The point is, people fight all the time in rom-coms."

"*At first* they do. But then it has to give way to something better. They can't just fight the whole time and then have hate-sex and call it a day."

"Don't knock hate-sex. It has its upsides."

"I'm sure it does. But it's not love."

Charlie paused to write "hate-sex = not love" in his Moleskine and box it.

I built on my advantage. "This'll take forever if you keep arguing with me. We'll be here all night."

Charlie frowned. I was right again.

"So," I went on, "I'm going to need you to just sit quietly and listen while I rip your screenplay to shreds. 'Kay?"

And here's the thing: he did it.

He really sat there quietly after that, while I earnestly went through every single sticky note on every single page of that script, enumerating every single way it was terrible—from structure to motivation and everything in between.

By the time we were done, it was after midnight, my voice was getting hoarse, and Charlie Yates had taken five pages of notes. And his handwriting wasn't large.

It felt like a triumph. Like this whole trip hadn't been for nothing. Like I'd maybe proved at least a few of his assumptions about me a little bit wrong.

Not that I cared, of course.

But as I repacked my backpack and Charlie read over his notes, I couldn't help but gloat a little to myself. *See that, Charlie Yates? I'm less worthless than you thought.*

Was that something to gloat about?

I would have loved to leave it there. But that's when I remembered I had to get myself to the airport in the morning. And thus I was forced to close out the evening by leaning over to Charlie and saying, "I'm so sorry. Could you explain to me how Uber works?"

Nine

THE NEXT MORNING, all packed for LAX, I tried to make myself some coffee in Charlie's kitchen.

Big mistake.

"Nope!" He came swooping in. "That's—You know what? Don't—" He placed his body between me and the coffee maker. "I'll get that. She's temperamental. Did you need some—some coffee?"

Huh. Okay.

"It's fine," I said. "I can get some at the airport."

"No, no—I'm glad to make it. I wanted to talk to you, anyway."

He set about turning knobs and running water.

"Latte?" he asked then. "Cappuccino? Macchiato?"

"Just—whatever's easiest," I said.

Charlie got to work, saying over his shoulder, "This is the only thing my wife ever let me cook." Then he corrected, "*Ex*-wife."

Was he making chitchat with me?

"So, you're all packed, then?" he asked next.

I frowned. I looked down at my stuff beside me. "Yep. The car comes in twenty minutes."

"And did you tell your"—he hesitated—"people at home you're heading back? Husband? Or whatever?"

What a weird question. Had Logan not told him even the most basic facts about my life?

I stood up a little straighter. "I don't have a 'husband or whatever,'" I said. "I live with my dad."

"With your dad?" Charlie asked, a hint of *Aren't you a little old for that?* in his tone.

"I'm his caretaker," I said.

Charlie turned around.

I met his eyes and went on, "He was in a camping accident many years ago, and now he needs round-the-clock care."

Charlie took that in. "Oh . . ." Then, "Who's with him now?"

"My younger sister." I did not add, *An amateur.*

I had no idea how they were doing. They'd forbidden me to call them or text them until I was settled. "Don't even try it," Sylvie had said. "We'll fully ignore you."

In the end, I hadn't had time to even think about calling. Instead, I'd woken up at four this morning, before my alarm even went off, because my heart was pounding so hard in my chest with so much anxiety about abandoning my dad, I swear it was causing ripples across the mattress.

Then I'd lain awake in bed, worrying.

Had I shown Sylvie where we kept the meclizine? Did my dad take his propranolol? What did they have for dinner? Please, god, tell me she didn't let him eat potato chips. Was she filling out the chart? Was he okay? Were they at the ER? Was everyone alive?

"So . . ." Charlie tried again. "Have you told them you're heading back?"

"Not yet," I said. And then I met his eyes, to be clear. "I can't quite face the humiliation."

Charlie nodded thoughtfully. "Because I was wondering if, rather than going back, you might . . . stay."

"Stay where?"

"Stay here."

"Stay here and do what?" Be his housekeeper? Mow his lawn? Refinish his yacht?

"Stay here and rewrite the screenplay with me."

I frowned. All I could think to say was, "Why?"

As far as I knew, this guy was dead set against me.

"Because of last night," Charlie said.

"Because I told you your screenplay was terrible?"

Charlie nodded. "That. And because you were right."

Huh. How about that. A pompous writer who could admit someone else was right. You didn't see those every day.

Charlie went on. "You were right about everything. I could see it so clearly after you said it. It's been a long time since I thought about writing from anyone else's perspective. It felt strangely good. Good enough that I stayed up half the night reading you."

That sounded odd. *"Reading* me?"

"Reading your work. Your writing. The stuff Logan sent and begged me to read that I never read. Your two screenplays and your submission to Warner Bros."

"He sent you those?"

"Multiple times. But you have no idea how many scripts people send me. Plus I was busy. And an ass. And I thought I knew everything there was to know." The coffee maker beeped, and as Charlie moved toward it, he added, "About screenwriting—not about life. And of course as soon as he said *rom-com* my eyes were rolling too hard to read anything."

I gave him a look. "Of course."

If Charlie registered the sarcasm, he ignored it. "But then, last night . . . You were just so . . ." And then he finished—with a little shrug like he knew the word was too much, but it was the only one that fit—by saying, "dazzling."

Dazzling. I tried to take it in as he poured the coffee. "You stayed up half the night reading my stuff?" It was so impossible. Charlie Yates . . . *reading my stuff.* And saying the word *dazzling.*

"And it was good," Charlie said.

"What was good?" He couldn't mean what I so badly wanted him to mean.

"Your writing."

Oh, god. *He liked my writing.*

"Really good. I mean, romantic comedies aren't exactly my favorite genre—"

"You've made that abundantly clear," I said.

"But it almost made me believe in love. And I don't believe in anything."

Charlie set our mugs down at the dining table, and I took a seat facing him.

"So . . ." I said. "You read my writing, and now you want to—"

"Hire you," Charlie finished. "For real. For the rewrite."

My brain quivered from the whiplash. As excited as I'd been when I arrived here yesterday, by this morning, I was feeling the polar opposite: desperate to get home—back to safe, friendly territory with people who didn't think I was worthless.

Like Charlie had.

But that was yesterday.

I tried to make the shift: today, apparently, he thought I was dazzling. And now, also, after reading my stuff: *someone he wanted to hire.*

"You want to hire me?" I asked. "For the rewrite?"

"Yes, but just for a week."

"A week?" I said. Logan had said *six.* "You can't fix that script in a week."

"I don't want to fix it. Just make it passable."

I shook my head, like *Doesn't compute.*

"Did Logan explain the whole deal to you?" Charlie asked then. "Why I even wrote this thing to begin with?"

I thought back. "It's like an exchange? With some executive? You write this for him, and he'll produce your Mafia script?"

"Yep. But it's not the exec who wants this script. It's his mistress."

What a weird, old-timey word. "His *mistress*?"

Charlie nodded. "She loves this movie, and she wants to star in a remake. She's pushy as hell, and she's been nagging him, and he wants something to give her."

"So you're saying it's not a real project."

Charlie nodded. "It's never going to go."

I stirred my coffee.

"It doesn't have to be good," Charlie said. "It just has to be good enough to pass her muster."

"Sounds like she didn't like your first version, either."

Charlie shook his head.

"So we're doing all this for a vanity project?"

"We're doing all this so I can get my Mafia movie made."

"Does the world really need another Mafia movie?"

"I don't know about the world," Charlie said, "but I know *I* need it." Then, leaning forward, like he was really sharing something tender and vital about himself, he looked into my eyes and said, "I just need to do something I'm proud of."

Right then, my phone dinged. I glanced down. My ride was outside.

Here's the thing. Honestly, in that moment, I just wanted to go home. "Charlie?" I said. "No."

Then I stood up and walked over to my bags.

Charlie followed me. "No?"

I slid on my backpack and grabbed my bags, lifting the broken carry-on so it wouldn't screech. "No."

Charlie took both bags and led the way out. "You're saying no?"

Was I saying no? To working with Charlie Yates? This was lunacy. But there it was. "I'm saying no, Charlie. I don't want to do this."

"You wanted to do it yesterday."

"You wouldn't even hire me yesterday!"

"I didn't know how good you were yesterday."

"Well, I didn't know it was a fake project yesterday."

We made it to the front walk, and when I didn't slow, Charlie dropped my bag, like *Carry your own crap, then.* I circled back and grabbed it, letting the broken wheel squeal and scrape toward the waiting Uber.

But Charlie kept following. "You don't want to work with me? It's practically free money! You're already here, anyway! This is an unbelievable opportunity for you! Let's make a few minimal adjustments to this shitty screenplay, collect our checks, and move on. Do you know how famous I am?"

I'd made it to the car. I turned around to face him. "How very inspiring."

"Inspiration isn't all it's cracked up to be."

The Uber driver popped the trunk and got out—but Charlie held up his hand like *Halt* and then turned back my way.

"Why can't you just help me?" Charlie asked, leaning in close.

I wasn't playing hard to get. The truth was—I really just wanted to go home. The mansion, the untouchable coffee maker, the fake project for some weird mistress. It just wasn't for me.

"Look," I said, hoping this would kill it for Charlie. "I live in a crappy apartment with my half-paralyzed father. I work all the time. I don't have money, and I don't have friends, and I haven't even made eye contact with anyone attractive in over a year. All I've got is my writing and my love of rom-coms and my basic human dignity—and I'm not sacrificing any of those things for this weird, sad project. I am *needed at home.* I was willing to leave for something big and inspiring. But I am not willing to abandon my family for some abomination of a screenplay that doesn't even matter."

That oughta do it. Right?

I turned toward the car, but Charlie grabbed my wrist to spin me back around.

"What do I need to do to get you to stay?"

And so I looked deep into his eyes and quoted Charlie back to Charlie: "I just need to do something I'm proud of."

To my surprise, that landed. Charlie blinked. "Fine." Then he started nodding. "Fine. Okay. You want to write it for real? We'll write it for real."

"I don't want to write it for real, Charlie. I want to go home."

"Name your terms," Charlie said then.

"What?"

"Anything. However you want to do it—that's how we'll do it."

I let out a long sigh. "Why are you doing this, Charlie?"

Charlie squared his shoulders like he was steeling himself to say something true. "Because last night, when I was reading your stuff, I wanted to work with you. And I haven't wanted anything—anything *at all*—in a very, very long time."

Ten

THE UBER DRIVER had just left us behind in Charlie's driveway when my phone rang.

It was my dad and Sylvie on FaceTime.

My first thought wasn't even a thought. It was just a stomach flip.

Did she give him the wrong medicine? Did he have a drop attack? Did he catch his walker on the carpet fringe again?

I answered right there in the yard, forgetting both my bags at my feet and Charlie standing beside me.

But as soon as the call started, it was just ordinary: my dad and Sylvie, heads together to squeeze into the frame, my dad playing "Good Morning" on the tin whistle, and Sylvie shaking his maraca as she sang the lyrics.

Panic gave way to relief, and I was so happy to see their faces that by the time the song ended, my dad leaned closer to peer at me, saying, "Sweetheart, what's wrong?"

Oh, god—was I crying?

I touched my face. It was wet.

"Nothing!" I said, smacking at my cheeks. "I'm just happy to see you."

I forced a big smile.

Nothing was technically wrong, right now, after all.

"And is that your writer?" my dad asked, pointing through the camera.

"*Dad,*" I said, like *Come on*. He wasn't *my* writer.

But as I turned, I saw that Charlie was closer than I'd realized, and as he shifted his attention to my dad's face on the phone screen, I realized what he was shifting it *from* was me.

Had he been watching me cry?

Bad to worse.

"Hello, sir," Charlie said, flipping his charm switch. "I'm so happy to be working with your daughter. She's a heck of a writer."

"Well, she certainly thinks the same about you," my dad said, "judging from all the"—he frowned at Sylvie—"what do they call it?" Then he remembered: "Fangirling."

"Dad!" I protested.

"I'm telling you, young man," my dad continued, "if I had a nickel for every time this girl read a piece of your dialogue out loud to me over dinner, I'd have a whole hell of a lot of nickels."

Charlie's eyebrows went up, like he hadn't realized my admiration for him extended to *reading dialogue from his works aloud*.

I wasn't even sure how to protest that. I mean, it was true.

"Tell Charlie Yates about your tattoo of his face!" Sylvie called then.

Charlie's look of surprise contracted into a frown of concern—but I shook my head, like *Hell no*. "She's joking," I said. Then, to be clear, "I do *not* have a tattoo of your face."

"You do have a photo of him taped over your desk, though," Sylvie said.

I should have denied that, too. "But that's for *writing motivation only.*"

"Sure it is," Sylvie said.

"How's the writing going?" my dad asked, like a proud parent.

"We haven't started yet," I said, grateful for the change of topic.

Charlie jumped in, "We're hammering out details."

I took the wheel of the conversation and turned the attention off myself. "How are you guys? How's everything there? What are Dad's sodium numbers?"

"I knew you'd ask!" Sylvie said, and then she held up a Post-it with the number *716* on it. "Grand total of milligrams from yesterday," she said, like *Boom!*, and then put her hand up in the frame for a high five.

I high-fived the phone.

"Stop worrying," my dad said then. "We're fine. Mrs. Otsuka's having us over for dinner tonight."

I pointed at my dad. "No soy sauce."

My dad looked insulted I would even say it. "I wouldn't dare."

"We're much more worried about *you*," Sylvie said.

"I'm also fine," I said then, not sure at all if that was true. And then, before I could decide, or god forbid *cry again*, a car pulled up in the driveway.

Logan's Beemer.

"What the hell is he doing here?" I asked as Charlie and I stared at it.

That's when my dad said, "We won't keep you! You've got a fancy Hollywood life to lead."

I blew kisses at the phone, and by the time I'd hung up, Charlie and Logan were staring each other down.

I walked up to them, and at the sight of my teary face, Logan said, "What did you do to her, man?"

"I'm fine," I said. "My dad and Sylvie just called."

"Is your dad okay?" Logan asked at once. He got it.

"All fine," I said. "It just made me homesick."

Logan got that, too. "Why didn't you reply to my texts yesterday?"

"Because I was mad at you," I said, like *Duh*.

"And what," Logan said, looking back and forth between us like he sensed a newly formed alliance, "is going on here?"

Charlie let out a long sigh, and then conceded, "We're working together."

"What!" Logan whooped out a big laugh, and then he started pumping his fist in the air. "I knew it! I knew it!"

"That doesn't make you forgiven," I said.

"Uh, I think it absolutely makes me forgiven. I think the words you're looking for are 'Thank you.' And to that"—Logan bowed—"I say, 'You're very welcome.'"

Charlie and I met eyes. Then Charlie said, "Your methods were extremely problematic."

"Yeah, well. I've got two problematic clients," Logan responded. Then he asked Charlie to confirm: "She's doing the rewrite?"

Charlie nodded. "She is. Unless she changes her mind."

Logan looked at me. "Do not change your mind. It just about killed me to make this happen."

"I'm not planning to," I said, lifting my hands. Then I added, "At the moment."

"Okay, then," Logan said. "Let's go."

Charlie frowned. "Go where?"

"To brunch," Logan said. "To celebrate." And then, when we hesitated, he added, "And to talk about the contract. Because there'll be no writing—at all—happening here until we make this whole thing legal."

WE WENT TO a fancy see-and-be-seen brunch place that Logan loved and Charlie hated (and that my airport-wear was hardly nice enough for), and the first thing I saw as the hostess led us in—and please just go ahead and take a deep breath right now to prepare yourself—was . . .

Jack Stapleton.

I'm not joking.

Jack. Stapleton.

A-list actor, Jack Stapleton. Sexiest Man Alive, Jack Stapleton. The guy on the billboard right outside the restaurant, Jack Stapleton.

Looking somehow *better* in real life? Wearing slacks with no socks and an Oxford shirt that fit him like it was spun from silk. And having brunch—I'm so sorry: if you happen to be holding a can of supplemental oxygen, please take a puff—with Meryl Streep.

The real people, I swear. In a real restaurant. Eating real food.

I'll give you a minute.

I needed a minute myself, to be honest, but before I'd even started to take it, Jack Stapleton looked up, saw Charlie, rose to his full height, and stepped over to positively *ensconce* Charlie in a full-immersion bear hug.

"Hey, buddy," Jack said warmly as he clapped Charlie on the back without letting go.

The hug lasted so long that the rest of us found ourselves looking around, and that's when I met eyes with Meryl Streep, still seated at her place.

"Hello," she said to me, lifting her fork in some impossibly cool hybrid between a wave and a toast.

Was that the most badass fork-based greeting I'd ever witnessed in my life? No time to ponder—because before I could stop myself, I was launching one big burst of nonpunctuated words: "Hello Meryl Streep I adore all your work and I am madly in love with you."

To which she said, "Thank you," as if people said that exact thing to her every day.

Which they probably did, right? Who are we kidding?

The full Yates-Stapleton hug shifted next into a side clamp, with Jack Stapleton, only a few inches taller than Charlie, tucking his head to try to ask a few private questions, even though we were all baldly staring. Everything he asked seemed like a follow-up to some other conversation no one else was privy to.

"How you holding up, man?" Jack Stapleton asked.

"Hanging in there," Charlie said.

"Everything still good?"

"Everything's still good. Yeah."

"You're following all their rules?"

Charlie nodded. "Trying to."

"How's the writing?"

"It might be"—Charlie glanced in my direction—"getting better."

"You know I'm here for you. Day or night."

"Back atcha, pal. Anytime."

Then another bear hug, more back clapping, and a totally surreal moment when Jack Stapleton turned to me, held out a hand, and looked straight into my eyes like electroshock therapy to say, "Great to meet you. I'm Jack."

And then there was nothing to do but sit blankly at our brunch table while Logan waved his hand in front of my face, saying "Hello?" before finally turning to the waiter and saying, "We're going to need another minute."

I was further—emotionally, spiritually, movie-star-wise—from my little apartment at home than I could even comprehend. Jack Stapleton just *shook my hand like a colleague*. Meryl Streep just *wave-toasted me with a forkful of fruit tart*.

It was another universe. One with too little oxygen.

Or maybe too much.

When the waiter came back, I still hadn't glanced at the menu.

Logan just ordered for me. The Arabian buttered eggs.

Then Charlie turned to me and said, "You okay? Meeting Jack is a lot."

I could have corrected him on feminist principle and said I was equally incapacitated by *both* world-famous actors. But I had more pressing business. "Are you friends with Jack Stapleton?" I asked. "Real friends?"

Charlie nodded. "I am real friends with Jack Stapleton."

"But—why?"

Charlie shrugged. "I wrote *The Destroyers*. Which—"

"Launched his career," I finished. "I know. But do all screenwriters become close friends with the stars of their movies?"

Logan snorted into his brunch sangria at that.

"He wasn't a star when I met him," Charlie said. "He was a strug-gling actor trying not to fumble his big break."

"But how did you become friends?"

"How does anybody become friends? He went through some hard times, and I showed up for him—and then I went through some hard times, and he showed up for me." Then he added, "We both like playing Warhammer 40K." Then, in case that wasn't enough: "Also, he didn't have a car for a long time, so he needed lots of rides."

Unbelievable.

"Did that really just happen? Did we just bump casually into Jack Stapleton and Meryl Streep having brunch?"

"This is LA," Charlie said. "You're gonna have to get used to that."

"They're filming a movie together," Logan explained. "A romance about a younger guy who falls for—and goes on an erotic journey with—an older woman."

"I will watch the hell out of that movie," I said.

But Logan shook his head. "No you won't."

"Why not?" I said, like *Don't tell me what to obsess over.*

"She gets run over by a bus in the end."

I made a growl of disapproval. "How do you know that?"

"The writer's a client."

"Great. Then can you please ask that person to *not kill off Meryl Streep?*"

"He says it's more realistic."

"*Really?*" I demanded. "How many people do you know who've been run over by a bus?"

That's when Charlie piped up. "Anyway, it's not a romance."

"What?" Logan said.

Charlie nodded, like *Yeah.* "Learned that yesterday," he said, cocking his head at me. Then, looking mischievous, he said, "It's not a romance unless everyone has an orgasm."

"That's not—" I started.

But Logan said, "Oh, I think that movie's got plenty of orgasms."

"If you don't have a *happy ending,*" I corrected. Then I felt the need to stress: "An *emotionally* happy ending." How was this conversation happening? To be extra clear: "An ending with the couple happily together. And Meryl Streep alive and well."

"How old is Meryl Streep, anyway?" Logan pondered.

I sat up straighter and declared, "She is timeless."

"The point is," Charlie said, "if you murder Meryl Streep, it can't be a romance—orgasms or no."

Logan frowned, like *Huh*. Then he turned my way. "I'll adjust my terminology. What is it, if not a romance?"

Were they teasing me? Either way, I stayed focused. "It's a tragic love story. Or a tragic erotic journey. You've got to warn people, so they know what they're getting going in."

"Real life doesn't come with warnings," Logan argued, half-assedly.

"That's why fiction," I said, "is *better* than real life."

We clinked brunch cocktails to that.

But just as we did, just as I was feeling a little bit valuable in the conversation, a guy in a backward baseball cap walked up to our table holding a Bloody Mary and raised it in a toast as he said, "Lo! Gan!" and then sloshed half a glass of tomato juice onto the white tablecloth.

Logan and Charlie glanced at each other, and somehow in that second, just from the vibe—and the backward baseball cap—I guessed who it was.

"Is this the girl?" Baseball Cap asked no one in particular, gesturing at me with that drink.

What was I? *Ten years old?* I waited for someone—Charlie? Logan? A waitress passing by?—to correct him with "woman," but no one did.

Not even me.

Next, he leaned in my direction. "You must be Logan's ex-girlfriend."

So I said, "You must be Jablowmie."

It was meant to be insulting, but he grinned. He swilled his drink, and then he raised the empty glass in another toast.

"Congrats on the new job! Isn't nepotism great?"

This from the grandson of Christopher Heywood and the esteemed auteur of the Beer Tower series. I cocked my head. "You'd know best."

He nodded, like *Touché*. Then he said, "I see you're already busy ending Charlie Yates's career."

Was this happening?

"Great hat," I said. "Where do you get those—with the brim on the back like that?"

"Okay, okay," Logan said, in a tone like *Cut it out.*

I looked down, a tiny bit scolded, wondering if I should've taken a higher road, but then I felt Charlie looking at me, and when I glanced his way, his eyes were smiling.

But T.J. wasn't quite done. "*This* is your romance expert?" he said to Logan. Then he looked me over. "No offense, but has she ever even been on a date?"

"That's it," Charlie said then, standing up and dropping his napkin on the table. "Knock it off."

Was Charlie taller than I'd realized?

It felt nice to be defended. But T.J. was actually right. I *didn't* have much experience with real-life romance. Even the quickest scan of my past made that painfully clear: The high school BFF I'd tried sex with for the first time—more like a science experiment than anything else—who later turned out to be gay. The fellow professor who I'd started seeing just as he left for a two-year sabbatical in Alaska—and who I got dumped by just as he returned home. A few attempts at dating that never got very far because I was always either tending to my dad, worrying about my dad, or on my way to the ER.

But that's not to say I'd never been in love. I was not stingy with my crushes. I had a thing for the guy at the meat counter at the grocery store, and the doc who'd stitched my dad up after his last fall, and a cute young maintenance guy who worked at our building.

I fell in love all the time. Just . . . nobody fell in love with me back.

Fiction really kind of was all I had in the romance department.

But that wasn't a weakness. That was a strength.

I had a theory that we gravitate toward the stories we need in life. Whatever we're longing for—adventure, excitement, emotion, connection—we turn to stories that help us find it. Whatever questions we're struggling with—sometimes questions so deep, we don't even really know we're asking them—we look for answers in stories.

Love stories had lifted me up, delighted me, and educated me on the power of human kindness for years. I knew a lot about love. A lot more, I bet, than all the people who took it for granted.

So it was fine. I knew who I was.

And I was not someone who could be insulted by some dude-bro named T.J. on his third Bloody Mary.

Though I did love that Charlie had just stood up for me. Literally.

Logan was busy shutting T.J. down. "Your table is waiting for you, Teej."

T.J. turned to look and, sure enough, it was.

When he turned back, he looked right at me and said, "Welcome to Hollywood." And then, before he walked away, he added, "You're going to need to get that hair straightened."

IN THE WAKE of that moment, Logan and Charlie pointedly shifted back to normal life, discussing the writing project at hand as if nothing had happened.

"We're going to need a serious contract," Charlie said. "I don't trust you anymore. I should probably get a new manager."

"It worked, didn't it?" Logan said, totally unworried. "You finally read her stuff."

"But what if it hadn't worked?" Charlie gestured at me. "You'd have crushed her."

"You think I don't know you? You're not as mean as you pretend."

"It was a risk," Charlie said.

"Everything's a risk. She needed a push. And so did you. And if you think I was going to let what happened just stop you from writing for-ever, you haven't been paying attention."

"What happened?" I asked.

The two of them looked at me, then at each other.

So I prompted, "You said you weren't going to let 'what happened' stop Charlie from writing. What was it that happened?"

Charlie frowned, like he didn't want to talk about this now. Or ever.

"You should tell her, Charlie," Logan said. "It explains a lot."

"It's not really brunch conversation," Charlie said.

"I can tell her later, behind your back, if you prefer," Logan said.

Charlie sighed. Then he turned to me. "I got sick a few years ago. And even though I really am completely—fully—better now, I haven't done much writing in the wake of it."

"Any writing," Logan corrected, gently.

"Any writing," Charlie conceded.

Logan leaned in, like he was sharing a dark diagnosis. "He's got the yips."

I frowned. "What's 'the yips'?"

Charlie grimaced like he didn't love hearing the term applied to him. "It's a sports term," he said, "for when an experienced athlete has a sudden, unexplained—"

"Performance problem," Logan completed.

Charlie looked aghast. "I do not have a performance problem."

Logan corrected: "An abrupt absence of skills."

"Oh," I said, like we were just learning vocabulary. "So it's like writers' blo—"

But Charlie gave me a hard look, like *Don't you dare.*

I stopped mid-word.

Logan jumped in to fill the void. "We don't speak the words for the writer's equivalent. We just say the yips."

"I don't have the yips," Charlie said. "I'm just . . . not writing."

"Not writing *at all*?" I asked.

"I've written one thing since I got sick four years ago," Charlie said, by way of an answer. Then he added: "The screenplay you're here to fix."

So . . . not writing at all.

Charlie added, "Everything that's come out in the past few years has been old stuff."

"Is that why you're trying to get the Mafia thing going?" I asked next. "Because you don't have anything else?"

"I also love the Mafia thing," Charlie said.

"Is that why the rom-com is so unbelievably bad?" I asked then. "Because you . . . forgot how to write?"

"It's bad because I didn't want to write it. And I don't like rom-coms."

"But you . . ." I scrolled mentally through a hundred different protests. "You can make *anything* good."

"Maybe," Charlie said. "But I have to believe in it."

Uh-oh. Please tell me I did not just agree to work on a rom-com with one of those men who do not believe in love. I almost couldn't ask. "Did you believe in cannibal robots when you wrote about them?"

He saw where I was headed. "No."

"What about aliens? Did you believe in those when you wrote *The Destroyers?*"

Now he was getting evasive. "I mean, the universe is a big place."

"I'm thinking of that one alien with the elephant trunk. Did you believe *that alien* might be out there somewhere, living its best life?"

Charlie took my point. "Not exactly, no."

"So what you're telling me is, you can take the imaginative leap to get on board with an alien from another galaxy that somehow managed to evolve a trunk that is functionally and visually identical to the elephants of earth, but you simply cannot fathom two ordinary humans falling in love with each other?"

I let us all sit with that for a second.

"It's just different," Charlie said.

Logan nodded to confirm. "He's lost his mojo."

"It's not lost," Charlie said, rapping on his sternum with his knuckles. "I just can't find it."

"Yeah," Logan said. "That's what 'lost' means."

"Right," Charlie said, "I was thinking of the 'dead' meaning of 'lost.' Like, 'lost at sea,' or 'I'm so sorry for your loss.'"

Logan shook his head and said, "Writers."

"Preaching to the choir," I said, all deadpan and relaxed. But inside, I was on high alert. Charlie Yates had lost his mojo? How was that possible? This guy was the king of mojo. Was this a sign of the apocalypse?

That's when I met Charlie's eyes and asked, "You're all better now health-wise, though, right?"

"Good as new," Charlie said.

"What were you sick with?" I asked.

Charlie looked down, like there was something on his shoe he needed to check out, and then, glancing off in the distance like he might see someone he knew, in a beyond-casual tone, as if whatever came next was so boring it couldn't even merit any follow-up questions . . . he said, simply, "Soft tissue sarcoma."

Eleven

GOING TO BRUNCH with Charlie Yates forced me to rapidly release the fantasy version of him I'd cherished for so long. Seconds after Charlie spoke the word "sarcoma," Logan had stepped away from the table to take a call, and the next thing I knew, Charlie was scooting his chair back and saying, "I'm gonna go take a leak."

Yeah. Exactly.

My *fantasy* Charlie Yates would never have said that.

Alone at the table, with no one to distract me, my heart decided to start doing that weird, violent thumping thing it was so into these days.

I tapped on my breastbone, as if to say, *Come on, buddy. You got this.*

But my heart was just insulted.

He definitely did not have this.

And neither did I.

Here I was—no thanks to Logan—in the fanciest brunch venue I'd ever seen, breathing the same air as Meryl Streep, with Jack Stapleton's . . . I don't know, *palm energy* still coating my hand from that bonkers handshake, and I'd just ingested a brunch cocktail with an edible flower in it, and my all-time greatest writing hero had just been teasing me about orgasms.

I mean. *Come on.*

I felt a rising surge of impostor syndrome, and so I stood up, just to have something to do, and started making my way toward the bathroom—stopping a waiter on the way to explain that we were not dining and dashing, no worries, and we'd all be back at the table shortly once we'd finished taking important business calls and peeing.

The waiter gave a deadpan nod. "I'll alert the staff."

And then I entered—I kid you not—the most opulent restaurant bathroom in history, complete with a water feature *and* a fire feature as well as a long, trough-like sink filled with black onyx stones. I was washing my hands and wondering how on earth the janitorial service cleaned all those rocks—*one by one?*—when I suddenly heard Logan's voice loud and clear, almost like he was in the bathroom with me.

"I knew you'd love her stuff," Logan said.

I turned. Looked around the ladies' room. Empty.

"I called it," Logan went on, just as loud, "and I was right."

"You called it," Charlie's voice agreed, "and you really were right."

That's when I realized that the trough of sink rocks wasn't just for the ladies' room. It was shared with the men's room. Below the mirror in front of me, I could see water running from the faucets on the other side of the wall. And Logan's hands, soaping themselves. And the pair of hands next to them that had to be Charlie's.

"Her dialogue," Charlie went on, "her verbal rhythm, her sense of structure. All amazing."

Oh, my god. Was I eavesdropping on Charlie Yates saying nice things about me?

I should pull out my phone to voice-record this moment—but I was afraid to move. If I could see their hands, they could see mine.

"And she's fucking funny," Charlie said.

Impostor syndrome solved. Charlie Yates, screenwriting god, had just used *a curse word as a modifier* to describe how funny I was.

Was this the best moment of my life? Should I steal one of these sink rocks as a memento?

But then Charlie kept talking.

"I only have one problem—" he said.

No, Charlie! Don't have a problem!

"The cheese."

I frowned. *The cheese?*

Just as Logan said, "The cheese?" Like he was frowning, too.

"Yeah, man. These love stories. They're so cheesy."

Oh, no. Best day of my life canceled.

"And not even like a self-respecting kind of cheese," Charlie went on, "like a Brie or a Gruyère. This is Velveeta. This is American slices in individually wrapped plastic sleeves. This is aerosol spray cheese."

Oh, god.

"The men in these stories?" Charlie went on. "They keep *crying*."

"Crying?" Logan asked.

"They cry a lot. Like, *a lot*. It's so weird, right? Men don't cry."

"I cry sometimes," Logan said.

"Do you?" Charlie said, like he was changing his opinion of Logan. "I can't stand these guys. I'm like, *Pull it together, man. Go chop something with an axe.*"

"Crying is good for you," Logan said. "It's cleansing. There's even a crying yoga now."

Long silence.

"Anyway," Charlie went on, shutting off his faucet. "I can't take her seriously. Why would anyone write about that?"

"Why would anyone write about anything?" Logan countered.

"I just think," Charlie said, "that our interests are . . . fundamentally different."

Logan sounded like he was frowning. "Does that mean you're not going to work with her?"

I held my breath.

"No, I'm going to work with her," Charlie said. "But only halfway."

"Halfway?"

"She wants to work on this thing until it's amazing. I want to work on this thing until it's passable. She wants this movie to happen. I want this movie to *never happen*. I want to improve it just enough to get my Mafia thing out of mothballs. And then I'll send her on her way."

"But weren't you both just telling me that you agreed to make it good?" Logan asked.

"Yeah, that's what I *said*," Charlie said, and then paused so Logan could mentally fill in *But that's not what's going to happen.*

"But that's . . ." Logan said.

What? I thought. *Lying? Cheating? Being a douchebag?*

Logan went on, "That's not what you promised."

"I'll wiggle out of it somehow," Charlie said.

"You have to tell her," Logan said.

"She won't stay if I tell her."

"Then I have to tell her."

"You won't be my manager anymore if you tell her."

"But this is . . ." Logan started.

A horrible betrayal?

"Not cool," Logan concluded. "Not cool at all."

"There are a lot of things I can't control about my life," Charlie said. "I could live to a hundred, or I could be dead next year. But there's one godforsaken truth I can guarantee you. The only thing I'm proud of is my career. And I will not frigging turn it into aerosol cheese by seriously writing a rom-com."

I nodded to myself at those words. *Okay*, I thought. *All right.*

Guess I was quitting, after all.

Twelve

HERE, I JUST have to pause for a second and tell you something genuinely sad.

I apologize in advance.

I wish I could spare us all the heartache. I do.

I promise, if there were any way to skip it, I would.

But you have to know what happened first to understand what happened next.

Until you know the before, you can't grasp the after. Why leaving my dad was so excruciating for me. Or why I never went away to college—getting a bachelor's and a master's online instead. Or why I'd squandered so much promise, or why I was willing—even *preferred*—to give up so much for my sister, or what a big deal it was for me to attempt to start my writing career in earnest.

Not to mention why it was extra-douchey for Charlie to refer lightly to my "failed career" as if his hot take was the only possible read on it. As if a cursory glance at anything could ever be the whole story. As if my life—my sorrow, my grief, my sacrifices—was something some ill-informed casual observer had any right to judge.

I have to tell you the thing I've been putting off telling you.

Stick with me. We'll get through it—and we'll be stronger on the other side, as all of us always are, for facing hard things and finding ways to keep going.

Plus: Bearing witness to the suffering of others? I don't know if there's anything kinder than that. And kindness is a form of emotional courage. And I'm not sure if this is common knowledge, but emotional courage is its own reward.

Lastly, I promise: everybody was okay now. Sort of. Mostly.

With obvious exceptions.

I was okay now, at least. Really. Honestly. Truly.

Okay *enough*, at least.

I'd had almost ten years to recover, after all.

Wow—had it really been that long?

Ten years since we took a family camping trip to Yosemite to celebrate my graduation from high school—and the writing scholarship I'd won to Smith College.

Ten years since the rockfall that ended our family as we knew it.

Ten years since I was sitting on an outcropping of rock while my dad belayed my mom, keeping the ropes on her harness tight while she worked her way up the rock face, and my sister, Sylvie, and I sunbathed—smacking on strawberry Fruit Roll-Ups as she begged me to tell her that seventh grade would be better than sixth.

But how stingy I was. "I can't promise that," I said. "Middle school is supposed to suck."

"Emma," Sylvie said, pouting. "Come on."

But I didn't give in. "Lean into the misery," I told her, feeling wise and grown-up and cocky. "It's good for you. It bolsters your emotional immune system."

So smug. So foolish.

That morning—the last morning of our normal lives—is weirdly vivid in my mind to this day. I can see the honeyed yellow sunlight falling across our legs. I can see the mismatched purple and pink socks poking out of Sylvie's hiking boots. I can see the frayed Band-Aid on her knee, and the Hello Kitty earrings I kept teasing her about, and the half-scratched-off hot-pink polish on her nails as she took a swig from her water bottle.

Such a goofy little kid.

I remember myself, too—that stranger I used to be. How the breeze was tickling my neck with escaped wisps from my ponytail. How I couldn't wait for summer to end and college to start. How my high school boyfriend—Logan—had suggested we stay together even after leaving for opposite sides of the country for school, and I told him I'd "think about it." How eager I was to grow up.

More than anything, I remember that feeling I kept carrying like a sunrise in my body that my life was really, genuinely, at last, about to begin.

I can place myself in the moment of that morning in vivid 3-D, as if it's still happening somehow, over and over, on an endless loop—my dad still holding the belay rope, and my mom working her way ever higher on the rock face, the sound of the wind high above in the background like a rushing river nearby.

All of us totally fine. Better than fine. Happy.

If my life were a screenplay, I'd end the story right there and roll credits—and then maybe rewind and watch it again.

But real life's not a loop, is it? There's always another moment that follows.

What I remember best after that is *sounds*.

A series of clacks coming from high on the rock face almost like fireworks.

Then an unearthly *clump* sound right at the base of the rocks.

I didn't see her fall.

I didn't see the rock that hit my dad, either.

The rest of the memory is built only with the scaffolding we pieced together afterward: A patch of rocks came loose—like a mini-avalanche. One of those rocks hit my father on the head before he even knew anything was happening, knocking him unconscious. As he dropped to the ground, of course the belay rope swished upward, out of his hands. And how high up was my mother then? A hundred feet, maybe? Sometimes I look up at the rooflines of buildings and try to re-create it. Was it three stories she fell from? Four? *Five?*

I'm sure my dad knows. But I'll never ask.

I didn't see it in slow-mo, the way you might in a movie, even though I was right there. It was over before I knew what had happened. And then there was nothing to do but run to the spot where they both lay, bleeding, unconscious, twisted like no bodies should ever twist.

I was back at the rock where Sylvie was sitting before she'd even moved. "Don't go over," I said. "Stay right here." We were too high for cell service, so I said, "I'm going for help."

But she wasn't listening. "Mom?" Sylvie whispered, staring in that direction.

I took Sylvie's face between my hands and turned it to mine. "Don't move from this rock. Don't go over there. And don't touch them, okay? That could hurt them worse."

"Okay," Sylvie said, still whispering, her eyes glassy.

"I'll be right back," I said.

Then it hit her I was leaving. Her voice wavered with panic. "But what do I do?"

"Talk to them," I said. "Just keep talking. Say I'm going for help. Say I'll be right back. Say it's all going to be okay."

It wasn't all going to be okay. That much was already clear.

"Don't leave me," Sylvie pleaded.

"I have to," I said. "Be strong. And just keep talking."

What else could I possibly do? I left.

I ran down the trail. Fully sprinted—no pack or supplies or water. I tripped on a root at some point but scrambled up to keep going—only discovering later I'd sprained my ankle and never even felt it.

I have no idea how long it took to make it to the trailhead—no sense of time—but when I found a lady with a working cell phone I was almost too out of breath to speak. "There was a rockfall," I panted, pointing back up the trail. "My mom was climbing. My parents are hurt." And then, as she was dialing for help, I heard myself say the only thing left that I knew for sure. "It's bad. It's bad. It's bad."

HERE'S A TRUTH that never changes: My mom didn't survive the fall.

The rescue workers said she probably died on impact. By the time they arrived, she was already gone—and my dad was critical. A rescue team strapped my dad to a backboard and readied him for helicopter transport to the ER. Another team—a recovery team—stayed behind to collect my mother.

They sent Sylvie and me with my dad. Decisions had to be made.

Sylvie didn't want to leave our mom. She screamed—feral with panic—and tried to go to her.

She was so enraged with me for that. For leaving our mom behind. Alone.

I asked her about it once, years later—if she was still mad.

"I was never mad at you," she said, like I was crazy.

"Yes, you were," I said. "You scratched me on the face."

Sylvie frowned, like that didn't sound like her. Then she said, "I don't remember anything about that day."

Maybe that's a blessing. I wouldn't wish those memories on her. The sound of my mother hitting that cliff base still woke me up in the night.

And then I always got up and went to check on my sleeping dad in the other room.

My kindhearted dad, who lived.

BEFORE THE ROCKFALL, my parents were both musicians. They played in the symphony together. My father was a cellist, and my mom played clarinet. At work, they were friendly and professional. At home, they teased each other and played duets all the time.

My dad survived that day, yes—but he never played cello again.

After almost ten years, and more physical and occupational therapy than any of us can fathom, there were two lasting effects he couldn't overcome: the hemiplegia on his left side, which never resolved. He could use that side, but only with difficulty. He could walk, but only slowly and mostly with a walker. That whole side—including the fingers that used to work the frets on his cello—stayed tight and jerky and full of tremors.

But that wasn't the condition that held us hostage. It was the Ménière's disease that messed with his balance, and the sudden drop attacks that slammed him to the ground out of nowhere, that kept me on high alert.

When the drop attacks happened, he went down hard—sometimes hitting his head. But even just off days could put him out of commission. He had to lie on his bed all day holding on to the edges because he felt like he was on a tiny raft being tossed in a vast, stormy ocean. Some months were worse than others, and sometimes he went long stretches when he felt fine. But he never knew when it would hit, which was why he didn't drive anymore, and he couldn't live alone.

He needed someone looking out for him 24–7, and—until I boarded that plane and flew to LA—that someone was always me.

The plan, as you've already heard Logan complain about, was for me to take the first ten years, and for Sylvie to take the second—and then to figure it out from there. Sylvie was twelve when we lost our mom, and the only thing I cared about in those early years—or maybe even my reason to keep going—was to give her the best childhood I could, despite it all.

To be as mom-ish as I could in our mom's stead.

I baked cookies. I drove her to parties. I took her for makeovers at the mall. I helped her fray her jeans. I supervised homework. I did laundry. I focused so hard on Sylvie and my dad that I almost forgot about myself. I just put my head down and kept going.

A relief, in a lot of ways.

I made my life about *Sylvie's* life.

Maybe staying so busy was a lifeline out of my own grief. But I willingly made myself a supporting character in my own story.

Sylvie was the star—and I was the dependable sister who helped her shine.

I wanted to shine, too, in my way. I didn't give up all my dreams. I kept writing, and kept studying stories, and kept fantasizing about some distant future where I would make it all happen. But I thought—and worried—much more about my Sylvie, and my dad, too, than I did about myself. And maybe, in a way, I started wanting my fantasies about the future to stay fantasies.

Right? Because if fantasies come true, they can't be fantasies anymore.

And then what do you have to fantasize about?

All to say, I got very comfortable living like that.

And everything that had happened since I came to LA? It was the opposite of comfortable. And it was certainly the opposite of fantasy.

Of course I should seize this opportunity. Of course I should be here and do this! Whatever "this" would turn out to be. There wasn't another reasonable choice. When you finally get your chance, you have to take it.

But it was one thing to live your dreams in theory—and it was absolutely another thing to clumsily, awkwardly, terrifiedly *do it for real*.

Thirteen

BACK AT CHARLIE'S house, I felt strangely elated.

I didn't have to do this. I could quit and go home.

Charlie wanted to get started at the table—but *one*, Logan had said not to do any writing until we had a written contract, and *two*, I was quitting.

I hadn't told Charlie that yet, of course.

Charlie sat down at his heavy, faux-farmhouse, designer dining room table, clearly thinking I would follow his lead.

But I didn't.

Instead, I walked around his living room, examining knickknacks and bookends and decorative ceramic bowls like I had all the time in the world. Which I did.

"Hey," Charlie said. "Can we focus?"

"This is a really nice house," I said. "You have great taste."

"It's not me. It's my wife. My *ex*-wife." Then a pause. "It wasn't even her, actually. It was her decorator."

"Well, then," I said. "My compliments to your ex-wife's decorator."

"Could you . . . ?" Charlie started.

But now I was opening a drawer under his TV console. *Empty.*

"What are you doing?" Charlie asked.

"I'm exploring my new workplace." I slid open a second one. *Empty.*

"Can we just get started over here?" Charlie asked.

But that's when I opened a third drawer. And this one . . .

This one . . .

Was full of Oscars.

I froze. Stared.

So . . . when Charlie had declared he had a "whole drawer of Oscars" . . . that wasn't a figure of speech.

This was a literal whole drawer of Oscars.

And not just Oscars, actually—all kinds of statuettes, jumbled willy-nilly like booty in a pirate's chest. Like they hadn't been *placed* in there, but maybe *dumped.* Or *dropped.* Or *chucked.*

"What's this?" I asked, in a tone like he was a naughty child and I'd found his box of stolen candy.

"Just . . . stuff," Charlie answered—*also* like he was a naughty child and I'd found his box of stolen candy.

I stared down at the contents of the drawer. Yes, there were actual Oscars—those unmistakable gold figurines. But also: the very recognizable Golden Globe awards that were literally miniature golden globes. Then, after that, a whole mishmash of silver and brass and crystal figurines engraved with words like HOLLYWOOD FOREIGN PRESS, NEW YORK FILM CRITICS CIRCLE, WRITERS GUILD OF AMERICA, HOLLYWOOD FILM FESTIVAL—that was just the top layer. Those were just the ones I could count.

I looked up. Charlie was watching me. "Are these your awards?" I asked.

Charlie nodded.

"Like, from the actual events? These are the awards you walked up onstage in a tuxedo and received from some world-famous actor?"

Charlie nodded again.

"What are they doing in here?"

Charlie shrugged.

"Charlie," I said, becoming more aghast by the second. "Why are the awards that most screenwriters would sell their organs for just piled in here like it's a junk drawer?"

"Just . . ." Charlie said, like he was trying to come up with an answer. "To keep them in one place?"

I shook my head. "In one place? This is the best you could come up with? How about a mantel? Or a bookshelf? Or an antique glass-fronted cabinet? Or a safe? How about anywhere other than shoved like trash into a forgotten credenza drawer?"

Charlie didn't answer, so I looked back down. Then I pointed. "This Women's Film Critics Association award has lost her little wing!"

Charlie had the good sense to look cowed. But then he said, "Look— none of this stuff means anything."

All I could do was blink.

"It's all just theater," Charlie said.

"Are you telling me," I said, "that you don't care that you got all these awards?"

"I do care," he said. "I just don't care enough to display them in a trophy case like a douchebag."

"So you're just going to shove them out of sight and break off their wings?"

"You seem to be taking this kind of personally—" Charlie started.

"I do! I do take it personally! Do you have any idea what I would give for even one of these awards? And you're just treating them all like they're garbage? Look!" I picked up an Oscar and held it out toward him. It was surprisingly heavy. "Look how scratched this is!"

"It doesn't matter!" Charlie said.

"It doesn't matter? It doesn't matter that you've scratched up the statuette of the highest honor in your industry? These things are made of solid brass and plated in twenty-four-carat gold! I watched a whole documentary about it! You don't even have the tiniest inkling of how lucky you are. I will spend my whole life writing and striving and obsessing over movies and I'll never even get close to one of these, and you . . ." I looked back down at the drawer, and words failed me.

"You want it?" Charlie said then. "Just take it! It's yours, okay? Now we're even!"

"But we're *not* even. Because I didn't really win it!"

"Nobody really wins anything!"

"Tell that to your thousand-dollar coffee maker!"

Charlie frowned, like he'd never made that connection.

Which just made me madder.

How dare he take his life for granted? How dare he stand here in a mansion full of awards and act like nothing mattered! "You want me to take it?" I said. "I'll take it! And I'll spray-paint it bubblegum pink and write my name on it in red Sharpie with little hearts! And then I'll tell everybody I won an Academy Award for a rom-com so rom-commy it was called *The Rom-Commers*!"

I wanted so badly to finish with "I quit!" right then—to charge out, Oscar and all, and never come back.

But I guess I wanted a chance to write with Charlie more. Because, instead, I just dropped that Oscar back in with the others. And then I walked myself out Charlie's back door without saying another word.

CHARLIE GAVE ME a minute—several, actually—to cool off. And then he quietly came outside, too, and stood beside me as I stared at his pool.

Finally, I said, "You've got a pool with a high diving board?" My tone was calmer now but still had insult-to-injury undertones.

"Yeah," Charlie said. "It came with the house."

"A *high dive* came with the house? Do they even make those anymore?"

"It's vintage," Charlie said. "This house used to belong to Esther Williams."

I turned to face him. "*America's mermaid*, Esther Williams?"

Charlie looked surprised that I knew who she was. "Yes. She lived here. In the fifties. And she put in that pool. You know who she is?"

"You could say that. I've seen every single one of her movies."

"For your mermaid rom-com?"

Ugh. Now I remembered: He'd read it. He'd read it *and called it aerosol cheese*. He didn't deserve to live in Esther Williams's house.

But stepping outside was restorative. It was a warm day—and sunny.

Maybe we needed a change of activity.

"We should go for a swim," I said next.

But Charlie shook his head. "I don't swim."

I turned. "Never?"

He shrugged, like he was about to tell me something fundamentally boring. "I had a near-drowning accident as a kid."

"Why do you own a house with a pool if you don't swim?"

"My wife wanted it. *Ex*-wife."

"Did she swim?"

"She didn't swim, either, to be honest."

"Why did she want a pool, then?"

"She liked the idea of swimming," Charlie said. "But she didn't like to mess up her hair."

I thought about my own hair—the fact that it was pre–messed up. Maybe that was a type of blessing.

I could feel Charlie looking at my curls, pulled back, as ever, in their little pom-pom ponytail. "I bet you don't have that problem," he said.

Was he complimenting me or insulting me?

"Swimming is my sport," I said, moving on. "I swim every day at home. It's the one thing I do for myself. Every morning at five A.M.—"

"Ouch," Charlie said.

"—I swim sixty laps."

"Every morning?" Charlie challenged, like I had to be exaggerating.

"Yep."

"Even on weekends?"

"Yep."

"Isn't it tiring?"

I shrugged. "Life is tiring. Swimming is just swimming."

Then I turned to head back inside.

"Where are you going?" Charlie asked.

I turned back. "To get my suit."

"You brought a swimsuit?"

"Yeah."

"Why?"

"To swim."

"How did you know I'd have a pool?"

"I didn't even know I'd be staying here! But I knew I'd find a pool somewhere."

"You can't swim here," Charlie said.

"Why not?"

"This pool's off-limits."

"Off-limits?" I asked.

"It's not for swimming," Charlie said.

"Your *pool* is not for swimming?"

"It hasn't been cleaned in a while."

I looked down at the water, sparkling like a mountain spring.

Charlie added, "And it's not safe. You know? It's not built to code. That diving board's a death trap."

"I think *Esther Williams* knew how to build a high dive," I said.

"She was a professional."

I sighed and put my hand on my hip. "Are you telling me I can't ever swim in your pool?"

"Pretty much."

"But why?"

"Because."

Nothing about this conversation made sense. But the idea of me in that pool clearly made Charlie unhappy. And maybe I was still mad about his whole Velveeta-themed comedy routine back in the bathroom, but the more unhappy I made him, the happier I felt.

I started walking toward the diving board at the far end.

"What are you doing?" Charlie called after me.

"I'm checking out the high dive."

"I already told you—no swimming."

"I'm not going to swim," I said. "I'm just going to bounce a little."

"You're going to *bounce a little*?" Charlie demanded, breaking into a jog to come after me.

But by the time he got close, I was halfway up the ladder to the platform. He grabbed at my ankles—but I kicked his hands away, and he stayed on the ground.

Once I'd passed his grasp, he said, "Come down from there. That's off-limits, too."

"I was a competitive swimmer in high school. I'm practically amphibious. Chill out."

Charlie watched as I reached the top and then walked out to the end, fully clothed, sneakers on. "Come down," he ordered.

But what could I say? That familiar bounce of the springboard always felt so good. Also, I really didn't like being ordered around.

Instead, I positioned myself backward at the edge, just my toes, heels hovering over the water, and got a nice rhythm going.

Charlie was halfway up the ladder, craning around the rungs in horror. "Please don't do that!"

"Why is this stressing you out? This doesn't concern you."

"Yes it does. Because if you fall in . . . I can't save you."

"I'm not going to fall in."

"You don't know that. That board hasn't been touched in a decade. It could snap like a toothpick."

"It's not going to snap," I said. "And even if it did, I wouldn't need you to save me."

"Not if you hit the water wrong. I've researched this. If you hit from high enough at the wrong angle you can pop your internal organs."

I kept bouncing. "Is that the technical term? 'Popped organs'?"

"And *I don't swim*," Charlie went on. "So if that happens, I'll just have to stand here and watch you drown. And I really don't feel like doing that today."

"If I pop my internal organs," I said, "then I've got bigger problems than you not knowing how to swim."

"I know *how* to swim," Charlie corrected. "I just don't swim."

"Same difference."

"Come down," Charlie commanded.

"No."

"It's my pool."

"They're my internal organs."

And that's when I saw Charlie's face adjust itself a little. "Fine," he said with a shrug, like he'd made a sudden decision not to care anymore.

"Fine?" I asked.

"Whatever," Charlie said now, almost like he'd shifted into a new character, and he started to walk back toward the house.

I didn't know if it was because I'd read everything this man had ever written, or watched every YouTube interview in existence multiple times, or studied the structure of all his scripts like a Shakespearean scholar might obsess over iambic pentameter . . . but bouncing there on Charlie's high dive in all my clothes, looking down at his suddenly totally disinterested face . . . an unbidden insight about Charlie Yates started rapping at my consciousness:

When Charlie Yates is scared of something, he pretends it doesn't matter.

I flipped back: He did it in his writing. His heroes were always unflappable, always totally unfazed by life's horrors—guys who'd show up for the battle, encounter the beleaguered company they were there to reinforce, be ordered by the captain to retreat, and say, "Retreat? Hell, we just got here."

His heroes were guys who got *cooler* in the face of fear.

He wrote guys like that, but he also *was* a guy like that. With reporters, for example, in interviews. If they got too close to a topic he didn't want to touch—his mother, for instance, asking for details about his parents splitting up when he was eight—he'd tilt his head with a half smile and say something totally blasé, like, "I must have been a pretty big pain in the ass."

He'd done it with his shrug just now when he'd talked about almost drowning, too, and he'd done it at brunch by looking at his sock when he casually mentioned *soft tissue sarcoma.*

Nonchalance as a weapon. Disinterest as a weapon. Aerosol cheese as a weapon.

Was I right? Had I just figured out something vital about Charlie Yates?

"Hey, Charlie!" I called.

He turned back, squinting up at me.

Right there, at the edge of the high dive, I sat down. Then I dangled my legs off the edge.

Charlie stared up, horrified. "What are you doing?"

"I'm sitting down."

"I can see that."

"I just want to ask you a question."

Charlie sighed. "What?"

I gave it a beat, and then I asked, "Why did your wife leave you?"

It was a hell of a question. The second I asked it, though, I knew I was right. His face shifted to extra indifferent. Then came the shrug. Then he said, "I guess she just got sick of my shit." Then he added, "And I don't blame her, either."

There it was.

Charlie Yates had a tell.

The things that he acted like mattered the least? Those were the things that mattered the most.

What would happen if I pushed past the nonchalance?

"Tell me about the day she left," I said.

"No," Charlie said. Then, "Why?"

"Because I'm not coming down until you do."

"Maybe I should just walk away and leave you there."

"Maybe you should. But then I will definitely do a swan dive off this thing. And maybe pop an organ or two."

Charlie squinted up to study me. Then he finally asked, "It has to be that? I have to tell you about that? There's no other way you'll come down?"

It felt so mean, but I had to know if I was right. Slowly, like there was no room for negotiation, I nodded.

Charlie sighed.

Then he looked around like he was checking for escape routes.

Then he frowned, and looked up at this crazy woman swinging her feet from his diving board . . . and then his face went extra nonchalant. He glanced off to the side like he was waiting for a bus or something, and then, in a tone like no one on earth had ever uttered a more boring statement, he said, "My wife left me on the day I found out I had cancer."

Fourteen

THAT WAS HOW I decided to stay.

More specifically, that was how I decided to try to convert Charlie Yates into a fan of rom-coms. A tall order. Maybe too tall. But that little epiphany about him changed everything.

Suddenly, I was curious about him in a new way.

Curious enough to stay.

I could give up anytime, after all. I might as well hang out for a bit in Esther Williams's mansion.

And so I climbed back down that high-dive ladder and followed Charlie to the dining table and sat across from him to start negotiations in earnest—from the new power stance of being happy to go home, but also willing to stay, if he'd give me enough of what I wanted.

Here's what I wanted: to do the screenplay right.

And seeing how aggressively indifferent Charlie was to the whole project . . . given his tell, I suspected that maybe, possibly, in some deep-down place he'd never admit to, he might want that, too.

And maybe—just maybe—in that same deep-down place we might find something more interesting and complex than just disdain. Something rich and nourishing enough to cure his yips. And jump-start my career in the process.

It was worth looking, anyway.

Was I dreaming too big? I knew too much about Charlie now to be overly optimistic. But I had a shot, at least. I'd just have to take it slow.

On the walk from the pool to the dining table, I'd decided on some long-term goals:

- Take Charlie on a journey of de-snobbification about rom-coms.
- Write a kick-ass screenplay together.
- Watch it get made into a great movie that would bring laughs and hope to folks all over the world.
- Not be a failed writer anymore.

And how do you reach your long-terms goals? With short-term goals:

- Don't get fired.
- Micromanage Sylvie from afar so well that my father survived the duration.
- Completely overhaul that appalling screenplay from the ground up without giving Charlie a chance to stop me.

Easy.

IF YOU'LL ALLOW me to skip to the good part: The negotiations went well.

I told Charlie—with the confidence of someone who was ready to just *walk right out*—that I would stay only if he agreed to: *one*, change his deeply uninformed and insulting unhappy ending into a proper, joyful, satisfying one, and *two*, actually research the crazy stuff he'd thrown into that script—the skinny-dipping, the line dancing, the kiss.

"Fine," Charlie said.

"Fine to what?"

"Fine to everything."

"Fine to changing the ending?"

"You've converted me on that."

"And fine to doing all that research?"

"Yes. Fine."

"You realize that means actually *doing* those things. With me. For research."

"I'm not going skinny-dipping with you," Charlie said then, like this whole thing might be an elaborate plan to get him naked.

"I'm not going skinny-dipping with you, either," I said.

"Good," Charlie said, a little too disinterestedly.

"And you don't have to swim," I said, "but you do have to get in the pool."

Charlie held still, like he was mentally scanning for an out.

"How long has it been?" I asked.

"Since I went swimming?"

"Since you got into any body of water at all. A bath, even?"

Charlie looked up, like he was calculating. Then he said, "Twenty-eight years. Give or take."

I nodded, like *Exactly.* "You can't write about being in the water if you can't remember what it's like."

Charlie's jaw tensed as he considered that.

I pushed on. "Rom-coms are about falling in love."

"I know that."

"And falling in love is about having feelings."

"I don't disagree."

"And you can't write about feelings—or help the audience feel them—if you can't feel them yourself." Note that I did not add, *You're also going to have to rethink your toxic and unexamined views that love doesn't exist.*

"I feel feelings," Charlie said.

"Great," I said. "Then this'll be easy."

In the end, Charlie agreed to all my demands—except for one. One that seemed like such a no-brainer I threw it in only at the end.

"And we have to change the title," I said.

But that was where he drew his line.

"No can do," Charlie said. "The title stays. That's the mistress's one requirement."

I didn't fight him. For now.

Logan had his lawyer draw up a simple, pretty standard contract—one that just basically said all I had to do was turn in a "finished work." It didn't have to be good—it just had to be finished.

"What happens if we don't finish?" I asked Logan.

"If you don't finish for any reason—if you leave, or he fires you—then it's a breach of contract."

"And I don't get paid?"

"And you don't get paid."

"That seems extreme. Given that he doesn't even want me here."

"It's pretty standard, honestly. What's extreme is Charlie."

"So I don't get paid until we're finished—and if we don't finish, I don't get paid at all."

Logan nodded. "Pretty simple."

"Simple?" I asked.

"Not easy, but simple," Logan said, with a shrug. "Just don't break the contract."

I wouldn't be breaking it, that was for sure.

We had six weeks to write this thing. Could I *not get fired* for six weeks?

We were about to find out.

THAT NIGHT, I should have slept peacefully, nestled under Charlie's ex-wife's decorator's million-thread-count bedsheets in his palatial guest quarters, with the new plan negotiated to my satisfaction.

But instead I woke up at two A.M.—shaken awake by my mattress.

Was it an earthquake? That was a thing in LA, wasn't it? But what did you do in an earthquake? Get away from the windows? Hide in a doorway? Run outside—flapping your arms like a flightless bird?

I had no idea.

I pulled on my cotton printed robe over my T-shirt-and-yoga-pants PJs—stopping for some flip-flops in case we had to dash to safety—and stumbled at top speed toward Charlie's wing of the house to wake him up and ask him.

But halfway there, in the dining room, there was Charlie. Awake. *Working*, from the looks of it. Not panicked at all—until he saw me, and then he closed his laptop a little too fast.

Okay. *That* got my attention.

"What are you doing?" I asked.

"Nothing," Charlie said.

"Your vibe is suspicious," I said.

"What are *you* doing?" Charlie asked then, bringing me back to the earthquake.

What *was* I doing? "I have a question."

"What is it?"

"Are we—having an earthquake?"

"Having an earthquake?" Charlie echoed.

I looked around. "I woke up, and everything was . . . shaking."

But Charlie frowned. "No earthquake," he said.

"No earthquake at all?" Maybe he was just used to them?

Charlie shook his head. "Nope. Nothing."

How mortifying. "Got it," I said, pointing at him like I was in on the joke. Though what that joke might be, I had no idea.

At that moment, I caught my reflection in the dark window—totally disheveled, robe askew, hair untied and undulating wild like some kind of angry jellyfish. My flip-flops, I now realized, were on the wrong feet.

"Maybe you dreamed it?" Charlie asked then.

We could go with that. "Sure," I said. "Maybe."

But that's when I heard a little trilling sound and looked down to notice for the first time a barn-shaped plush object sitting on the table next to Charlie's laptop.

"What's that?" I asked.

"What's what?" Charlie asked.

But I was walking closer now, following the trilling sound. And as I made it around to the barn doors, I saw a creature just inside. Looking out at me. A fuzzy little fluffball.

"What is that?" I asked.

"It's a guinea pig," Charlie said, like *Of course.*

But I wasn't sure. "Is it?"

My cousin had a guinea pig when we were growing up. This critter looked . . . different. And by *different*, I mean it looked like a dust mop. White and yellow with fur sprouting up and billowing down past its paws. Mostly fur, in fact. With two glossy brown eyes.

I stared at it.

"He's a Peruvian long-hair," Charlie said. "His name is Cuthbert."

"Is he yours?" I asked, in a baffled tone that might also have been saying, *What is an adult man doing with a pet guinea pig named Cuthbert?*

"Kind of," Charlie said. "Not really. Not anymore. He's my wife's. Ex-wife's. She rescued him and his brother back when we were still married—kind of without asking me. Then she took them when she moved out. Though we technically have joint custody."

I looked back and forth between Charlie and the guinea pig. "Has he been here this whole time?"

Charlie shook his head. "I'm pig-sitting. Just while my wife's out of town."

"Ex-wife," I corrected. Then I said, "Why is he in a tiny little fabric barn?"

"They like to hang out in little hidey tents. My ex has a whole collection. A circus tent, an igloo, a beehive. Even one shaped like an Airstream."

"But—doesn't he escape?"

Charlie shook his head. "He'll stay like that for hours."

"Did you say he has a brother?" I asked, looking around.

"His brother just died," Charlie said. "So he's pretty depressed. They're herd animals."

I looked at Cuthbert, and Cuthbert looked at me.

"Can I pick him up?" I asked.

Charlie shook his head. "They don't like the feeling of being lifted up," he said. "It makes them feel like they've been snatched by an eagle."

"How do you know how guinea pigs feel? About anything?"

That's when Charlie Yates, divorced custody-sharing guinea pig sitter, said, "I know what I know."

This was definitely a shocker. Charlie Yates with a pet.

But Charlie wasn't shocked at all.

He watched me watch Cuthbert for a minute, and then said in a stage whisper, "It's two in the morning. Go back to bed."

BUT I DIDN'T go back to bed.

Instead, I went back to my room, studied my bride-of-Frankenstein reflection in the mirror, and then tried to de-humiliate myself by putting my hair up, and brushing my teeth, and retying my robe—attempting to retroactively make myself presentable.

Somewhere in all that, I realized that the earthquake was still happening.

Everything was still shaking, I mean.

Except it wasn't everything. It was just *me*.

More specifically, it was my heart. Doing that crazy new thumping thing again. I put my hand over it and felt it hurl itself against my palm over and over, like I'd trapped some magical beast in there—and it desperately wanted to get out.

Without much hesitation, I shuffled back to where Charlie was. Flip-flops on the correct feet this time.

Charlie stood this time as I showed up again—as if *one* random middle-of-the-night interruption was tolerable, but *two* was cause for alarm. He was in sweatpants, I now noticed, and a T-shirt with a Stephen

King quote on it that said, THE ROAD TO HELL IS PAVED WITH ADVERBS.

Were those his pajamas? It was such an odd sight. But did I think he slept in an Oxford and corduroys?

"I'm so sorry," I said, making my way closer to him. "Can I ask you another question?"

"Sure," Charlie said.

I closed the distance between us—very glad now that I'd brushed my teeth and tied back my hair—and I looked up into Charlie's curious face.

I put my hand over my chest like I was about to start the Pledge of Allegiance. "Can you just put your hand here like this?"

Charlie nodded, and put his hand over his own heart.

"Not on yourself," I said. "On me." I clapped my hand against my chest to show him where.

Charlie's eyes widened a little. "You want me to put my hand . . ." His eyes dipped down. "There?"

"This is for medical purposes," I said. "I think I'm having a problem."

"Is it a problem we can use *words* for?"

"Yes," I said. "But I also need a physical assessment. If you don't mind."

He did mind. He clearly minded.

But he did it anyway, bringing his hand toward me with the energy of someone who has to reach down to fish something out of a garbage disposal.

He slowed as he got closer, like he might chicken out, so I grabbed his hand, pulled it the rest of the way, pressed his palm against my chest, and held it there.

"Can you feel that?" I asked.

Charlie looked a little panicked. "Feel what?" he asked.

"You tell me."

Charlie held still for a minute, his gaze resting on our two hands. Then he said, "Are we talking about your heart beating?"

Now we were getting somewhere. "Yes," I said. "Exactly. This is what woke me up."

"Your heart beating is what woke you up?"

I nodded, like *How crazy is that?* "It was beating so hard, it was shaking the bed."

"That's why you thought there was an earthquake?"

"But it's still going. You feel it. Right?"

"I feel . . . something."

"Do you think I'm having a heart attack?"

"I don't know much about heart attacks."

"Can I feel yours?" I asked.

"Feel my what?"

"Your heart," I said as I reached out to press my free hand against his chest.

Charlie blinked, like he couldn't quite catch up to what was happening.

"Your heart's beating, too," I said.

"Yeah, well," he said. "They do that."

"But I mean, thumping. Pretty hard. Like mine is." We couldn't both be having heart attacks, could we? That seemed statistically . . . improbable. Could we have been—I don't know—*poisoned*? Or something?

"It's thumping now," Charlie agreed. "But it wasn't. Before."

"Before?" I asked.

"Before you came in here like this in your robe with all your . . . hair, and—and put my hand on your chest. It wasn't. Thumping."

Oh.

"Just so you know," he added. "For medical purposes."

"I see," I said.

We should probably stop touching each other's chests now. That much was clear. But I couldn't figure out how to make the transition.

"Could you google it for me?" I finally asked.

"Google it?"

"The symptoms of a heart attack. For women."

I felt his lungs deflate with relief as he broke away to get his laptop. "Yes, of course."

"I'm not allowed to google medical symptoms," I said, to fill the silence as Charlie scrolled.

"Not allowed?" he asked, still scrolling.

"Back when my dad first got hurt, I developed a habit of frantically googling every tiny symptom that showed up. It kind of turned into a vicious cycle of hypochondria."

Charlie looked over. "Hypochondria? But your dad really was hurt."

"But I'd go down these rabbit holes. His shoulder would be aching, and I'd google 'painful shoulder' and two hours later I'd be convinced he had Parkinson's. And MS. And shoulder cancer."

"That's not your fault," Charlie said, going back to scrolling. "That's just because you're a writer."

I hadn't thought of that. "It is?"

"Believing in things that aren't real? Making something out of nothing? Connecting dots that don't need *or want* to be connected? That's what all the best writers do."

It felt weirdly good to hear Charlie Yates lump me in with *all the best writers*.

And it felt weirdly—unexpectedly—even better to know that I had just made his heart beat faster.

That's when Charlie stood up with my diagnosis. "The internet doesn't think you're having a heart attack," he said.

"It doesn't?"

"It doesn't. But it does think you're having anxiety."

"Ha!" I burst out. Then, at Charlie's tilted head: "This is the least anxious I've been in ten years."

No argument there.

"I'm a good person to talk to about this," Charlie added, "because I coped with a lot of anxiety when I was sick."

I frowned like he was bananas. "I don't have anxiety. I just worry all the time."

Charlie gave it a second and then said, "I'm just gonna let those words echo around the room."

Fine. I saw his point. "But only because I have actual things to worry about."

Charlie waved me off. "We don't have to label it."

"Thank you."

"The point is," he said, "the internet wants you to take slow breaths through your nose—five-point-five seconds in, and five-point-five seconds out."

"Five-*point-five*?" I confirmed. "That's what WebMD said to do?"

Charlie nodded.

"Can't fight the internet, I guess."

"True," Charlie said. "Now start breathing."

And then, after he'd watched me do a few breaths, he said, "The internet also wants you to ask me what I was hiding on my laptop when you walked in."

That was unexpected. I frowned at Charlie. "You don't have to—I don't really—" Then, "Do you *want* me to ask you that?"

Charlie nodded. "I suspect you'll like it."

I suspected I wouldn't. But okay. "What were you hiding?"

I edged around the dining table, and when he pulled a chair next to his and patted it, I sat beside him. Then he opened up his laptop and maximized the screen.

I peeked through squinted eyes, in case I needed to shut them again fast.

But it was just an illustrated image of a backyard.

"What is this?" I asked.

"It's a video game," Charlie said, "where you power-wash things."

Then he pressed some keys, and a jet of water started spraying in first-person point of view, as if he were holding a power hose.

Charlie turned the hose onto a dreary gray sidewalk, and as the water moved along, it left a bright clean section behind. The hose also made a deep, brown-noise shushing sound, and once all the dirt was gone, the game made a very satisfying *ding* sound and gave him some points.

"*This* is what you were doing when I walked in?"

"Yep."

"You were playing a video game where you virtually power-wash a sidewalk?"

"Not just a sidewalk," Charlie said, starting on the patio beside it. "The entire yard."

"But . . ." I started. And then all I could think to say next was, "Why?"

Charlie nodded, like *Fair question*. Then he said, "Because it's fun. And Cuthbert likes it."

Charlie started up again so I could see how soothed the guinea pig was by it. But glancing between the screen and the pig, I could see no discernible difference. Cuthbert was sitting there like a fluffball before Charlie started power-washing the side of that virtual doghouse, and he was sitting there like the exact same fluffball after.

"Are you sure it's Cuthbert who finds this comforting?" I asked.

"Does it matter?" Charlie asked, staying focused.

And before I knew it, I was hooked, too. I watched Charlie finish the patio, and then do the gutters, and then the wall behind the hedge, and then all the patio furniture . . . until deep into the wee morning hours—without noticing the time pass. I listened to the shush of the spray, and I pointed out when he missed a spot, and I sat companionably mesmerized beside the world's most beloved screenwriter while he finished off the whole rest of the yard and then leveled up.

That's when Charlie turned and took in the sight of both Cuthbert and me watching him.

"Good news," Charlie said then.

"What?" I asked.

"I think Cuthbert likes you."

Fifteen

WHEN I FINALLY made it back to bed, my earthquake had settled, and I slept hard—until I woke up again, at five, with a start.

And a feeling of dread that my dad might not be okay.

I know that's a pretty nonspecific worry: a vague sense that someone might not be okay. But I'd done a lot of worrying about my dad over the past ten years. It was like my heart had been cramped into a tight, worried ball all this time, and now—even with nothing particular to worry about—it couldn't unclamp itself.

I had officially handed my worrying duties over to Sylvie. I knew she was competent and mature. I believed she could handle things. Mostly. Sort of. I just didn't know how to not be the person who always worried about my dad.

Maybe that's what my heart was up to these days with the thudding. Trying to untie its own knots.

Or maybe I was just dying.

Maybe I should let myself google it, just this once.

That's what I was wondering—in bed, in the dark, at five A.M.—when my phone rang. And it was Sylvie—FaceTiming me.

"I knew it!" I said, sitting up in bed. "What's wrong?"

"Nothing's wrong," Sylvie said. There she was, inside the rectangle of my phone, her calm vibe validating her statement. She was in our room, sitting on my bottom bunk, with her hair pulled neatly back like she'd just washed her face.

My hair, in contrast—I couldn't help but notice from my own smaller FaceTime rectangle—had wiggled its way out of the ponytail I'd gone to bed in, and the alarm on my face plus the wildness of my curls gave me the look of someone who'd just stuck her finger in an electric socket.

"Nothing's wrong?" I asked. "Then why are you calling?"

"To tell you that."

"People don't call to say nothing's wrong," I said.

"*Normal* people don't call to say that," Sylvie said, "but this is me and you."

She had a point. "But it's five in the morning."

"It's *seven* in the morning here."

Another good point. Sylvie was sounding more reasonable by the second.

"Can we *not* FaceTime at this hour?" I asked next. "I am not camera ready."

"But I want to see you!"

Before I could respond, another face squeezed into Sylvie's frame. The face of her boyfriend, Salvador, with his ponytail mussed like he'd just woken up, too.

"I think you look great," Salvador said.

I'd FaceTimed with Salvador several times. They'd been dating since their sophomore year. "Hi, Salvador," I said.

"Hey, sis," Salvador said.

Then, to Sylvie: "Salvador is there? At our place?"

Sylvie took a minute to wave as Salvador left to go take a shower. Then she said, "He's staying with us."

I didn't want to feel alarmed. I liked Salvador. He was a great boyfriend for Sylvie—mature and thoughtful and supportive. He'd carved her a pumpkin last Halloween with teeth that spelled out I LOVE YOU.

But boyfriends sleeping over at our apartment was not part of the plan.

"I thought he was spending the summer in Brazil with his grandma," I said.

"Change of plans."

"Since when?"

"Since he got into grad school here."

"He's starting grad school?"

"Not till August. But he's taking prerequisites this summer."

And then, with dread, I asked a question I could already *sense* the answer to. "He's just staying there a day or two, right? Until he finds a place of his own?"

"Umm," Sylvie said.

"He can't stay with you there long term," I said.

"The point is, we have an empty bed," Sylvie said.

"That's my bed," I said.

"Yes. And as soon as you come back—whenever that is—we'll kick him right out."

But she was missing the point. I wasn't worried about my bed. "Sylvie, he can't be there," I said.

"Why not? Dad is cool with it. He loves Salvador."

"We *all* love Salvador," I said. "That's not the issue."

"Then what *is* the issue?"

"He's a distraction," I said.

"He's not a distraction," Sylvie said. "He's helping."

"He's too handsome to help."

"Can I just remind you that the master's he's getting is to become a physician's assistant? He's a medical professional."

"Not yet he isn't."

"The point is, he's a good guy to have around."

"Sylvie," I said, aware that I had no real power beyond a stern voice,

"Salvador can't stay there. Dad is a full-time, round-the-clock, twenty-four seven job. You can't *be in love* and do it right at the same time. Don't you think if there were a way to do that I would've figured it out by now?"

"Fine," Sylvie said.

I hadn't expected her to give in that fast. "Fine?"

"Sure—fine. We'll find Salvador another place. I mean, he's been doing morning yoga with Dad, and folding all the laundry, and taking Dad down to help Mrs. Otsuka with the community garden, but it's fine. Also he's been babysitting Mrs. Otsuka's grandson Kenji, who's visiting for the summer and kind of shy—and *adorable*. But it's no biggie. I'll just kick Salvador out."

"Good," I said. Guilt trip not accepted.

"Fine," Sylvie said.

"Great," I said.

"Perfect," Sylvie said.

Then, after a pause, to change the subject, she said, "I liked meeting your writer in real life yesterday."

"FaceTime is not real life," I said.

"It's close enough."

"And he's not my writer, either," I said.

But Sylvie ignored that. "He's cute!" she said. "You should marry him and have little writer babies."

"Sylvie!"

"They could smoke little pipes and wear tweed jackets and talk about metaphors."

"Sylvie—"

"I just liked his vibe, you know? And there's something about his face. A warmth. The way his eyes crinkle up at the corners."

"Sylvie, we are coworkers. Please do not mentally matchmake us."

"Too late," Sylvie said.

Now Sylvie lay back on her pillow. "Tell me about Hollywood," she said then.

"It's been . . ." I said, finally settling on, "a journey."

Then I filled her in on everything: Charlie not knowing I was coming, then not hiring me, then *taking notes* while I ripped his screenplay to shreds, then reading my stuff and accidentally liking it, then hiring me—but not exactly for real. I took her through every twist and turn, ending with the grand climax of shaking Jack Stapleton's hand and then holding my own hand up to the phone for proof. Sylvie frowned and gasped and cheered about all of it—and when we got to the hand part, she said, "You need to get a palm tattoo that says 'Jack Stapleton was here.'"

"Great idea," I said.

Next question: "What's it like living in Charlie Yates's mansion?"

I thought about it. "Quiet," I said. "Kind of lonely, maybe? I'm not used to all this space. And luxury. It's like a hotel. I had to put on a background podcast just to fall asleep."

"Tell me you're not homesick."

"I think I am a little," I said. "No one sings show tunes here. Or plays the zither. Or reads out loud like a human audiobook to entertain me while I make dinner. The kitchen in this house looks like it's never even been touched. It's like a model kitchen in a showroom. It's not . . ." I searched for a good word, and ultimately selected "fun."

"Maybe you'll just have to make your own fun," Sylvie said.

"Writing the screenplay will be fun," I said—but then I stopped. "Or a nightmare. I'm not actually sure which."

"How could writing a script with your favorite writer be a nightmare?" Sylvie asked.

"Well," I said, "it's looking like he's one of those guys who doesn't believe in love."

"Ugh," Sylvie said.

"And based on everything I can gather, before we even have a shot at writing something decent, I have to force him to take line-dancing lessons, cure him of his water phobia, and convince him that human connection actually matters."

"Piece of cake," Sylvie said.

"All," I added, "without his consent."

"You were born to do this," Sylvie said.

"Was I?"

"Just Sylvie him," Sylvie said.

"*Sylvie* him?"

"Just act like you're in charge. Like you always did with me."

"That's different," I said. "With you, I *was* in charge."

"But how did you get me to do all the things I didn't want to do?"

"I just proceeded like there was no other option."

"Exactly."

"He's not a kid, Sylvie. He's a full-grown adult. I can't just Jedi-mind-trick him into doing whatever I want."

"Everybody's a kid deep down," Sylvie said. "Use your teacher voice. I bet you'll be surprised."

AND SO I decided to give it a try.

Why not? I didn't have any better ideas.

By the time I'd hung up with Sylvie, it was six A.M. I put on my swimsuit and tied up my hair—and then I switched into teacher mode, strode confidently toward Charlie's bedroom, and knocked loudly on his door.

Charlie opened it a few minutes later with one elastic cuff of his sweatpants up above his calf, his T-shirt on backward, his hair pointing up and out every direction, and one eye closed like a sea captain.

"What the hell are you wearing?" were the first words out of his mouth as he looked me up and down. "You're practically naked."

Teacher voice. Teacher voice. "I am not naked. I'm wearing a swim-suit. To go swimming."

"Under it, I mean. You're naked."

"That's not news. Everyone is naked under everything."

"I'm not complaining," Charlie said. "That's just—a lot of arms and legs."

"What am I supposed to wear? An eighteenth-century bathing costume?"

"Maybe just go back to bed? Problem solved."

"You can't be this skittish about a one-piece Speedo."

"I haven't been around a live woman in a long time."

"That's not my fault."

"But it is your fault that you're standing here right now."

"It's time to get up."

"Why?"

Confidence! Teacher voice! Sylvie him! "Because that's the schedule. I swim first thing in the morning."

"I'm still trying to figure out what that has to do with me."

"You're coming with me."

At that, Charlie made a break for the bed. But I caught him by the arm and dragged him out—through the living room, out the French doors, to the edge of the pool.

"What are we doing, again?" Charlie asked, like I might've already explained it.

"Exposure therapy."

Charlie eyed the pool. "I'm not getting in there," he said.

"Of course not," I said. "*I* am. You're just going to keep me company and make a note of the fact that I am not drowning."

"What if you *are* drowning?"

"I'm not going to dignify that with a response," I said. Then I patted the lip of the pool at the top of the steps. "Sit right here and put your feet on the top step."

Charlie looked at me, then the pool, then me, then the pool. "Just the feet?"

"Just the feet."

"And I'm doing this why?"

"Because you can't spend your whole life afraid of swimming pools."

"Afraid of *water*," Charlie corrected. "Not swimming pools."

"And also because you agreed to. When we negotiated our terms."

"I did?"

Teacher voice. "You did."

Charlie sighed. And then, to my utter surprise, he just . . . *did it.*

Pulled up his sweatpants, then stepped in. Maybe he was too sleepy to fight me.

"Sheesh, that's cold," he said, sitting down anyway.

"You'll get used to it," I said.

"I haven't even had coffee yet," Charlie said. "I haven't even brushed my teeth."

"After," I said, not wanting to give him a chance to escape.

"I haven't even peed!"

"Permission to pee in the bushes," I said—and then I dove in before he could muster more objections.

Here's the thing: it worked. He stayed. He sat there the whole time, feet in the water, while I did sixty laps freestyle.

By the time I was done, he had two eyes open—but not much else had changed.

When I got out, I said, "How was it?"

There was that nonchalant face again. "How was what?"

Must've been stressful. "Spending time in the pool."

"I wouldn't call that 'in the pool.'"

"I bet your feet would disagree."

Charlie looked at me like I was totally insane.

"Anyway," I said, clapping the shoulder of his T-shirt with my wet hand. "Good job."

Sixteen

AND SO, THAT first week, we settled into a routine: swimming first thing, then showering, then coffee, then sitting across from each other at Charlie's dining table with our laptops back to back, surrounded by our various favorite writing accoutrements and good-luck charms—trying to ignore each other but not entirely succeeding. We found a sharing feature in Final Draft, which neither of us had ever used, and we forced ourselves to get acquainted with it.

My hope at the start was that we could just work quietly, like we were both used to, and send changes and questions back and forth via the internet without ever having to adjust our normal way of doing things. But of course that's not how it happened.

I mean, there was a guinea pig on the dining table.

Every morning, like a ritual, Charlie brought Cuthbert out of his cage and loaded him into the barn, where he'd settle in and spend the day alternating between lounging and napping.

"I think I'm going to find the rodent distracting," I said, the first time it happened.

"Don't call him a rodent."

I frowned. "Isn't he . . . a rodent?"

"The point is, he's going through a rough time right now."

But maybe Cuthbert was a nice mediator. Writing in the same room at the same time with another person was, for the record, not my normal way of doing things.

Not Charlie's, either. "I usually do this in complete human isolation," he said, at one point. "I always think that should be the title of my autobiography: *Alone Too Long*."

I nodded, like *Nice*. Then, wondering if all writers had a throwdown autobiography title, I went ahead and shared: "Mine is *Someday You'll Thank Me*."

Another human in the room. While I tried to write. So weird.

It felt a smidge vulnerable, for example, to pull out my lucky sweatshirt—which had a hood that made your head look like a big strawberry with little green leaves appliquéd at the top. When Charlie first saw it, he said, "That's—wow. That's really something."

"It's my lucky hoodie," I said, hoping he wouldn't point out that it hadn't brought me much luck. Then, quieter, I added: "My mom gave it to me."

"No judgment," Charlie said. "I have a lucky handkerchief myself."

I looked at his pocket, which was empty.

"For awards shows," Charlie explained, and touched the spot where I was looking. "My wife gave it to me before my first-ever nomination—and then I won. So I wore it again the next time, and I won again. And now I'm trapped. Every time I wear it, I win. So I have to keep wearing it."

"That's a powerful handkerchief," I said.

"Right?" Charlie agreed. "After she left, I thought I should get a different one—but I don't want to break my streak."

Other secret writerly behaviors that got exposed as we worked together: I feathered the corners of pages while reading. Charlie absentmindedly tapped his heel on the floor. Charlie wrote exclusively with Bic ballpoints, chewing on the caps and blowing through them, which—*who knew?*—makes a whistling noise.

Charlie turned out to be a blue-ink person, while I was exclusively black. FYI for nonwriters: blue versus black ink is an essential identity issue. Much like Coke versus Pepsi, or the Beatles versus the Stones, or college-ruled notebooks versus regular. You can be one kind of person or the other, but not both.

I couldn't help but judge Charlie a little—and I could feel him judging me right back.

I'll also add that he was a fine-point-pen person, while I had joined the bold-tip community years ago and never looked back.

One-point-six millimeters or bust, baby.

The idea that we might do all our writing in a sleek, virtual, digital, nonhuman way was not sustainable, looking back. It wasn't long before the dining table was covered with crumpled paper, marked-up printed scenes, snack wrappers, soda cans, spiral notebooks, water bottles, not one but two staplers, pencil pouches, a box of Kleenex, a printer attached to a long extension cord, various ChapSticks, highlighters, and old coffee cups—both paper and ceramic.

I personally liked it better that way. Visible signs of progress.

I got the feeling Charlie did, too.

And even though we both put headphones on, we pulled them off to talk almost constantly. I got to where I could sense Charlie pulling out his earbuds to ask a question or read a piece of dialogue. And can I just say? He had to really watch his pacing when he read to me out loud, because I'd get so caught up, if he slowed down too much, I'd jump in with what I imagined the next line should be.

And then Charlie would look up, and say, "No. But maybe that's better."

And then I'd wonder if I'd fallen asleep at the table or something. Because no writer ever thinks that what somebody else wrote *might be better.*

Astonishing.

The routine just evolved. We'd work all morning, and then sometime in the early afternoon, when we were both losing steam, I'd walk to the neighborhood coffee shop—just two blocks away, if you knew where to go—for a change of scenery and a little me time, and he'd field meetings and phone calls from a roster of Hollywood people that read like the invite list to the Oscars.

For the most part, we were surprisingly companionable. For a guy who didn't care at all about the project we were working on, he seemed to be enjoying himself quite well—enough to make me wonder if there might be an overlap in the separate-circle Venn diagram of our lives: the joy of messing around with words.

Maybe the project didn't matter.

Maybe the act of writing was so fun he couldn't help but enjoy himself.

I was enjoying myself, too, to be honest.

Being away from home was not as hard as I'd feared.

To no one's surprise, Salvador never managed to find his own place, and he and Sylvie FaceTimed me in their pajamas first thing every morning with the Dad Report: daily sodium totals, updates on refills, visual proof of color and sticker charts faithfully filled in. Salvador was taking my dad to the gym down the street twice a week for weight training, and he'd perfected a low-sodium artisan bread. Salvador also played the guitar—which delighted my dad—so the three of them were having nightly after-dinner jam sessions with Sylvie on vocals and tambourine.

I was forced to admit, as the days went on and the good reports kept coming, that two people doing all that caretaking was probably better than just one. More fun, too, apparently. The three of them even ventured to the farmers market one Saturday, bought a whole basket of organic veggies, and made pasta primavera from scratch.

Sylvie sent a group selfie of them slurping linguine at our dining table.

Knowing that helped me worry less. A little. And the less I worried, the more I realized how good it felt not to be worried. It was astonishing how quickly I adjusted to my new life of luxury in Charlie Yates's mansion. I was fine, they were fine—everybody was fine.

How hard is it to adjust to that?

The one thing I missed at first was cooking. Charlie was—how to put it?—not a foodie.

My second day there, I got the shock of a lifetime when I opened up his fridge—and there was nothing inside it but . . . luncheon meats.

Yep. Bags of shredded luncheon meats from the grocery deli.

I leaned against the open fridge door. "What's going on in here?" I asked, when Charlie looked over.

"In the fridge?" he asked.

"There's no food," I said.

"There is," Charlie said, walking a little closer. "There's pastrami. And corned beef. And Black Forest ham." He peered at the back. "And those are cocktail olives."

"You don't have anything else? That's it?"

"There's some beer in the door."

"But . . ." I just kept staring at all that meat. "What do you do with it?"

"I just eat it," Charlie said matter-of-factly, like that was a thing people did.

"Straight?" I asked. "Like, just . . . handfuls of meat?"

"Forkfuls," Charlie corrected, like he was offended. "Though, I do mostly eat them right out of the bag, if I'm honest."

"Charlie, this can't be healthy for you."

"It's fine," Charlie said. "The Maasai people of Kenya lived in perfect health for centuries on almost nothing but meat."

"But not *pastrami*, right?"

"Fair enough."

A pause.

"I also have cereal, if you want some," Charlie offered, nodding toward a small pantry in the corner.

"You don't have milk, though," I said, checking the fridge again. "What do you put on it?"

"Water," Charlie said. Like that made any sense.

I tilted my head. And then, trying to sound like his luncheon-meats-based lifestyle was just as valid as any other, I asked, "Do you mind if I—get some other foods?"

"Not at all," Charlie said.

"I cook a lot at home . . ." I said then, still trying to normalize it.

Charlie nodded.

"So I'll probably make dinner for myself in the evenings."

Charlie shrugged, like that was reasonable.

"And I'm happy to share," I added. "Unless you prefer—your . . . piles of meat."

And so that became another part of the routine—I started making dinner every night. And every night, Charlie hovered around, watching me, like *a person making dinner* was a total novelty. And he'd act all skeptical, adding commentary like "Don't cut yourself," and "I threw up after eating parsley once," and "Are you crying right now, or is that just the onions?"

Then, when the food was actually ready, he'd set two places at the kitchen table by the window, and fill up glasses of ice water, and say yes to everything I offered, and then chow down—making little happy noises as he chewed and swallowed and served himself seconds—like a person who . . .

Well, like a person who'd forgotten about the joy of the old-timey human ritual of *dinner.*

"You're an amazing cook!" Charlie would exclaim while chewing, over and over, like he just couldn't believe it.

It felt good to amaze him.

It felt good to do something that was so *appreciated.* My dad and Sylvie appreciated me, of course, and we all agreed that I could cook. But they were too used to me by now. The thrill was gone.

For Charlie, every bite was a novelty. Brand-new, and astonishing, and pure, gustatory bliss.

He took to accompanying me to the grocery store in the evenings, helping me find the things the recipes needed. And also purchasing little culinary delights for Cuthbert, like butter lettuce and bell peppers, to supplement his hay and pea pellets.

This Charlie was so different from the Charlie who I'd met on the first day—the one who'd so dismissively called me an amateur.

This Charlie was helpful. And eager. And grateful. And just—fun to pal around with. It got me thinking about how nice it was to do an ordinary thing like go to the market with someone and buy food for a meal you were about to eat together. The companionship and pleasant anticipation. The easy camaraderie. The incidental conversations about anything and nothing: songs on the speaker system, or the psychology of wine labels, or the social significance of Twinkies.

And can I just add? While I got dinner started, Charlie applied himself lovably and earnestly to the eternal project of trying to get Cuthbert to eat something.

Easier said than done. "He's off his food since losing his brother," Charlie explained early on. "Guinea pigs are very sensitive."

I looked at Cuthbert, perched under that unruly mop of fur like someone had dropped a toupee on him.

"He seems okay to me," I said.

"He should be devouring this bell pepper," Charlie said, and then we'd both look at the hunk of bell pepper sitting untouched in front of Cuthbert's nose.

And then I'd casually glance over time and again to see Charlie cutting the bell pepper into a star shape, playing Pachelbel's Canon through his phone speaker to get Cuthbert into an eating mood, and changing out plates because apparently the texture of Limoges versus Fiestaware can impact a guinea pig's gustatory experience.

"Sensitive" didn't start to cover it.

Sometimes I'd eavesdrop on their conversations. "I know you miss him, buddy," Charlie would say. "It's hard. I get it."

On a really bad day, Charlie might slice a carrot into thin sheets on a mandoline and form it into an origami-style carrot flower. Or hum "Bohemian Rhapsody" a cappella while he waited for the nibbling to start. Or both.

"You've got a great voice," I told Charlie.

Charlie shrugged. "He loves Freddie Mercury."

I don't want to sound insensitive, but at one point, I said to Charlie, "Won't he eat if he gets hungry enough?"

Charlie shook his head, like *Common misconception.* "If he goes too long without eating, his health can start to fall apart. And the thing about guinea pigs is that they're prey animals. So when they get sick, they hide it. Because the weakest of the herd are always the first to get picked off."

"Cuthbert," I said, in a tone of affectionate reprimand, "no one in this room is getting picked off."

We both gazed at Cuthbert. Then Charlie said, "I don't think he's buying it."

ONE NIGHT, WHEN I'd been there for more than two weeks and was feeling very at home, Charlie and I had just come back from another trip to the market when we heard the high beeps of Charlie's front door disarming and then a woman's voice calling, "Charlie?"

I'd been handing Charlie cans of crushed tomatoes to stack on a high shelf in the pantry—but at the moment her voice sounded, Charlie grabbed me by the arm and yanked me in with him.

Then he pulled the door closed until the tongue caught in the latch.

"What are you—" I started.

But Charlie shook his head like crazy and lifted a finger to his lips.

It was not a large space. We were corralled tightly by shelves of food, with only room for about an inch between our bodies. Which made me suddenly both exquisitely aware of the electromagnetic energy around Charlie's body . . . and aware that Charlie was also suddenly aware of mine.

I shifted to a whisper. "Why are we hiding in the pantry?"

"That's Margaux," Charlie whispered back.

"Who's Margaux?"

"My ex-wife."

Of course. Margaux. They'd been quite the power couple for a brief moment in time, the year when his movie *Forty Miles to Hell* and her documentary *Women Aren't Funny*—which was just an hour and a half of women stand-up comics being hilarious on the topic of that very thing—were both sweeping up prizes on the awards circuit.

I'd read a few features on her, in fact, over the years. My big takeaway—and please don't be alarmed—was that she, and these are her words, "didn't like fiction."

I'll give you a minute.

This lady, who was married to one of the most celebrated writers of fiction in the world, *didn't like fiction*. If I recall, she'd said that she "just couldn't get into fictional stories" because they "weren't real." One of the articles, in fact, ended with her rhetorical question: "It's all made up. It's all fake. How can it possibly matter?"

So, yeah. That marriage was probably doomed from Day One.

I don't know if they make red flags bigger than that.

Anyway—now she was here. In Charlie's house.

"What's she doing here?" I asked. Weren't they divorced?

"She's here to pick up Cuthbert," Charlie answered.

"She just comes into your house?" I asked.

"She still has the code."

That raised more questions than it answered, but okay. "I thought you guys weren't close."

"We're not."

Next, Charlie heard a sound that I didn't, and he stood up straighter, eyes wide, like *Oh, god, she's coming this way.*

Sure enough, as I fell silent, we could hear her. She must have been talking to someone on the phone. "His car's here," she was saying, "but he's not answering."

Then she called again: "Charlie? Are you home?"

I looked at Charlie like *Maybe we should just turn ourselves in.*

And he looked at me like *Never surrender.*

I heard the ex-wife drop her keys on the kitchen counter and then wander off to another part of the house.

As her voice receded, I whispered, "Maybe we should make a break for it."

"To where?" Charlie whispered back. "She'll be back any second."

"Text her! Tell her you've gone out."

"Just randomly text her my whereabouts?" Charlie said. "I *never* text her."

"Are you saying she'll get a text from you and think, *That's funny. He never texts me. He must be hiding in the pantry*?"

"I'm just saying it's weird."

"This whole thing is weird!"

Charlie capitulated and reached into his pocket for his phone. But after digging around a minute, he shook his head.

"What?"

"I don't have it with me."

That's when we heard the ex coming back. "He's definitely avoiding me," she was saying. Then, a pause. "But it's strange. The place is a disaster. There's stuff all over the dining table—like maybe he's writing again. And dishes in the sink. And—ugh—a box of Twinkies. How's he supposed to stay healthy if he eats like a middle schooler?" Another pause. Then, "This doesn't even look like his stuff, honestly. There's a *bouquet of flowers* on the kitchen table."

Charlie and I held each other's gazes, and our breath—united in the act of hiding—as we listened to the sound of her gathering her keys off the counter, and then her footsteps walking away.

The second we heard the front door slam behind her, we burst out of the pantry at the same time like bucking broncos out of the gate, moving too fast for anyone's good, and I'm not exactly sure how it happened, but somehow I managed to get caught in an overturned grocery sack on the floor just outside the door—one foot entangled in it, I think, and the other stepping *on* it?—just as Charlie turned back to ask me some question that will now be forever lost to history.

That's what I remember: Charlie turning around, just as I felt a sensation like someone had tied my shoelaces together—and I went jolting forward into his chest, knocking him backward.

And then we hit the ground.

Pretty hard, too.

I felt my knee knock the slate tiles like a hammer just as Charlie landed with a series of *oofs* and smacks.

And then he was rolling onto his side and pressing his hand on his tailbone, growling in misery.

I'd landed with my face in his armpit, so I hoisted up and over to get a look at his face.

"Are you okay?" I asked.

Charlie's face was red now, and his jugular was kind of pooching out, and all he could say was "Fuuuuuuuuuuuuuuck that hurts."

"Oh, god. I'm so sorry! Did you land on your tailbone? I did that once in Girl Scouts. This floor is not soft, either, by the way. No give there at all." I smacked the floor for confirmation. "Do you think you broke it?"

"The floor?" Charlie croaked, like I was crazy.

"Your tailbone!" I said, like he was crazier. "Should I take you to the hospital? What do they even do for a broken tailbone—right? They can't exactly put it in a cast."

Charlie had gone back to growling.

"Ice," I decided then, and I scrambled over to the freezer, returning with a bag of frozen veggies and pressing it to Charlie's butt.

"What are you doing?" Charlie asked.

"Just—move your hand," I said.

"Are you trying to put frozen peas on my ass?"

"It's *julienned mixed vegetables*," I said, like *I beg your pardon*.

"Get them off," he said, grabbing at the bag.

"We have to ice the area!" I insisted.

"Emma—cut it out. I'm fine."

"You don't sound fine."

By that point, we were basically wrestling for access to Charlie's butt, and I tried to snatch the bag away just as he got the bright idea to roll over to block me. The next thing I knew, we managed to rip the bag, scatter julienned vegetables across the kitchen floor, and, in the scuffle, I guess my elbow gave way because I collapsed on top of him—again.

In the wake of it, we waited a second—face-to-face, gazes locked, breaths intermingling, and expressions perfectly matched, like *Did that just happen—again?*

Then Charlie broke the silence. "You did all this on purpose, didn't you?"

On purpose? "No, I—" I looked around. "I tripped on a grocery bag."

I pointed at it, for evidence, but Charlie didn't even look.

I was still square on top of him, my arm pinned under his side. Charlie closed his eyes. Then he opened them and looked straight into mine. "Or maybe you just wanted to prove that there's nothing romantic about people falling on top of each other."

I blinked. "I don't have to prove that. It's just empirically true. It doesn't need proving."

But as soon as I said it, in that instant, I became aware of all the physical contact we'd just muddled through with each other—and how I was still lying flat on top of him. And then I suddenly thought about what my body must feel like to him, draped over his own like that. And how, other than maybe games of Twister or freak skiing accidents, there weren't too many situations in day-to-day life where people just lay on top of each other for no reason.

In any other situation, it would be a very different situation.

And once I'd thought *that*, I couldn't unthink it.

And if I was reading the room right—Charlie, suddenly, wasn't *not* thinking about that, either.

Questions started twinkling in my brain like stars. Did the room just go very still? Did my scraped knee just stop stinging? Was having our faces this close together causing some kind of chemical reaction in my body? And, maybe most important: Did Charlie Yates have the thickest, lushest eyelashes I'd ever seen on a man?

How had I never noticed those before?

Wait—

What was I thinking about?

Had I really been insisting all this time that there was nothing even remotely romantic about two people randomly falling on top of each other?

Because this was *working*.

Had I just proved myself wrong? In front of the Great Charlie Yates? This was not going to end well.

And then my weird heart took that moment to start doing its thumping thing again.

"Is that you or me?" I asked.

"What?" Charlie asked.

"The thumping."

"I'm not thumping," Charlie said.

I put my hand on his chest. "Yes, you are." Then, out of fairness, I shifted to my own. "But I'm thumping worse."

Why did this keep happening?

For a second, I got caught up in the scientific question of it all—but then I looked down to see Charlie shaking his head at me like I was the most exasperating person on earth. "Emma?" he said.

"What?" I asked, like it might be something important.

"Can you get off me now?"

Oh, god! His broken tailbone! What was I *doing*?

But before I could scramble up, from across the kitchen, we heard a sound that pinned us in place a little longer. A woman's voice like an irritated schoolmarm's, demanding: "What the hell is happening in here?"

And in the one second that followed—that felt like ten hours—I didn't even need to see the wry *Thank you so much for this moment* expression on Charlie's face to know that this was, of course, his wife.

Sorry—*ex*-wife.

AS CHARLIE AND I scrambled up—Charlie notably *not* clutching his tailbone now—she watched us, arms crossed, like she'd just discovered a pair of naughty teenagers.

"What are you doing?" she asked.

I knew her face already, of course. I'd seen her in many red-carpet photos with Charlie—always dressed in black and wearing superhuman heels even though she was tall to begin with, the two of them smiling like nothing, not even an insurmountable height difference, could scare them. With her straight dark hair slicked habitually back into a low bun, she was always then, as she was right this minute, tall and sophisticated and sleek as a mink.

The opposite of me, is what I'm saying.

I wasn't short—but I definitely wasn't tall. And you'd probably come up with a thousand words for me before you landed on "sophisticated." And if there was one thing I'd never, ever be, it was "sleek." My curls would make sure of that.

"We were just"—Charlie glanced at me—"doing research."

She crossed her arms and looked at the scatter of vegetables. "Is that what they call it?"

What was that expression on Charlie's face? I hadn't seen it before. Was he embarrassed? Guilty? Something was going on between these two that I couldn't read.

The ex-wife looked at me and touched her collarbone. "I'm Margaux," she said, like that should explain everything.

"I'm—" I started.

But Charlie jumped in. "She's just a writer. Here to do some—writing."

Huh. That smarted a little. *Just a writer.*

Margaux tilted her head, like *If you say so.* Then: "We were supposed to have dinner when I came to get Cuthbert tonight, Charlie. Did you forget?"

"Of course not," Charlie said.

Um, I thought. *We* were supposed to have dinner tonight. What was Charlie talking about?

"We were just finishing up," Charlie explained to Margaux, like we'd been hard at work doing something important.

Margaux nodded, with a vibe like *I'll allow it.*

Then she looked Charlie up and down. "We're already late," she said then, "so . . ."

"Right," Charlie said. Then he looked at me like he'd forgotten I was there. "You probably need to get going. I know your car had that . . .

that . . . flat tire. Why don't you just take my Blazer and bring it back for our—working day tomorrow?"

I guess we were hiding the whole *living together* thing from the ex.

"I can just get an Uber," I said.

"No," Charlie jumped in—weirdly eager to get rid of me. "The Blazer's faster."

"Okay, then," I said.

Why was I feeling so rejected? Charlie had a right to go out to dinner with his ex-wife. It wasn't like we had real plans. We were just eating together by default. And he certainly didn't have to tell her about every detail of his life—and maybe I was one of those details he didn't feel like getting into. That was fine. That was fair. And technically, he hadn't even said anything wrong about me.

I *was* just a writer.

That's exactly what I was.

So why was *me getting kicked out* so that Charlie could hit the town with this tall, slender, straight-haired woman with a perfect pedicure and matching manicure disappointing me so hard?

Oh, well. I could puzzle over that later.

They were waiting for me to go.

"I'll just leave most of my writing stuff here," I said, trying not to overact my part. "Since we'll be doing more writing again when I return—tomorrow." This was terrible dialogue.

"The keys are on the front hall table," Charlie said.

I knew that. But I said, "Ah," like that was news. Then I gave a little vague wave in their direction, the way I imagined someone who was *not* suddenly the girl not chosen might, and said, "See ya later!" with such forced cheer that I accidentally added a tinge of madwoman.

I walked out to the car before realizing that I'd forgotten my purse—so I U-turned back into the house, and I was seconds from snagging it off the dining table when I heard Charlie and the terrifying Margaux, still in the kitchen. Talking about me.

And get this: Margaux was pressing a bag of frozen corn niblets to Charlie's tailbone.

And Charlie wasn't resisting.

Guess he was fine with his wife's frozen vegetables.

Ex-wife's.

"That was definitely more than research," Margaux was saying, a hint of teasing in her voice.

"What would you know about research?" Charlie said.

"You don't have to be a writer to read that situation."

Charlie put his hand over the frozen corn to take over, and he stepped back to rest against the counter. "Don't read the situation, okay? Don't read anything."

"I approve. She's enchanting. I love that crazy hair."

"Don't call her hair crazy."

"The fact that you're so grouchy is just proving me right."

"You don't get to be right—or wrong—about any of this, Margaux."

"Look, I'm just saying you clearly like her."

"I don't *like* her!" Charlie said.

But Margaux's voice dripped with teasing. "Are you sure about that?"

"She fell on me, okay? It happens! Sometimes objects in space collide with each other!"

"Do they ever," Margaux said, just *luxuriating* in innuendo, clearly enjoying this.

"I didn't do anything!" Charlie said. Clearly not.

"I support you," Margaux said. "It's past time you released the ghost of our relationship."

"There's no ghost—and there's nothing to support," Charlie insisted, like he'd never heard anything more ridiculous. "She's nobody. Just a writer. A failed writer, in fact. A person with a tragic past who Logan asked me to work with. Briefly. As a personal favor. She has no job, no money, and absolutely nothing going for her. She's leaving as soon as we're done, and I'll never see her again. So don't turn this into a whole thing, okay?"

I held very still.

The words were bad, but the tone of voice was worse.

So eye-rolly. So devoid of warmth. So authentically dismissive. As if there were truly no topic less interesting and less important than me.

There was a good writing lesson in there—that being dismissed is worse than being scorned. In a different frame of mind, I might have paused to think about it: Of course *not mattering* is worse. It means you didn't even register. It means you're not even worth getting mad about. It means you're *literally nobody*.

Was this how Charlie really felt about me?

I thought about Charlie's tell—how good he was at pretending the things that mattered didn't matter.

I felt tempted to hope he was pretending.

But the thing was, he just didn't seem like he was.

More important: What was more likely—that I was important to Charlie? Or that I would engage in complex emotional gymnastics to wrongly convince myself that I was? Connecting dots that "didn't need, or want, to be connected."

This wasn't the first time he'd said these things, after all. He'd voiced all of this to Logan when I first got here. Nothing here should be a surprise. But that was before he'd read my stuff and then asked me to stay. Before we'd worked together. And lived together. Before he'd revived me from fainting, and googled my heart attack, and used the word *dazzling*. Had nothing changed for him? Had nothing shifted at all?

Just a writer. A failed writer.

If he was acting, he'd missed his calling.

One thing was for sure. I wasn't going to wait around here to find out.

Seventeen

THE NEXT DAY was, of all things, my birthday.

I woke up feeling deeply homesick.

I'd driven around until midnight the night before, in that hostile way you embrace your independence after you've been rejected: *Fine. Whatever. I never cared, anyway.*

I cranked the music up too loud. I left the windows down. I burned all Charlie's gas and did not refill the tank. I kept my phone turned off so that if Charlie wanted to find me, I was plainly unavailable.

I didn't turn it back on until I was crawling into bed.

And then only to check for texts from Sylvie, or my dad, or anyone I actually cared about. Though I did happen to tangentially notice in the process that nothing had come in from Charlie, either.

Not that I was looking.

It was all so odd. Charlie's saying those things should not have smarted so much. Three weeks ago, I didn't even know this guy. My life had been fine then, and—for the record—it was still fine now. In the big picture: *better than fine*, in fact. My dad was in good health. Sylvie was performing her duties respectably. I was in LA living a personal dream I never thought I'd get anywhere close to.

I was KILL N IT, as Logan's license plate would say.

Whatever *it* was.

I should be grateful! I should be delighted! I should be happy!

But as the morning light squinted in at me, I was the opposite of those things.

If I'd been home, I would've woken up early and gone for a refreshing swim by myself. Then I would've come home and made canned-biscuit doughnuts—our family's standard birthday-morning fare—with homemade chocolate glaze and sprinkles. And my dad would play some nutty rendition of "Happy Birthday" on some random assortment of kooky instruments, and then we'd sing it together so we could do some crazy, improvised harmonies.

Like we did every year.

Not a big thing. Just a pleasant little way to start off a birthday—one I'd never fully appreciated until I was all alone in Charlie Yates's mansion.

All alone and *just a writer.*

Anyway, I wasn't going to wake up Charlie for pool time this morning. He'd actually made a lot of progress—moving down to sit on deeper and deeper steps every time, until he shifted to standing, and then walking. That's what he was up to now in the mornings—walking waist deep, in the shallow end, edge to edge, back and forth the whole time until I was done with my laps.

I didn't even mind him being there. Most days.

But not today. Today, my present to myself was a morning swim on my own. If he could go on a date alone with his terrifying ex, I could certainly take a morning swim alone without his bothering me. No grumpy, pool-phobic writers with cattywampus morning hair allowed.

ON MY WAY to the pool, the first thing I noticed was that Cuthbert's barn was not on the kitchen table. Margaux had indeed taken him back.

Which made the day feel even sadder. It had been so weird at first that Charlie had a guinea pig at all—but now it felt weirder that he didn't.

Amazing how your perspective can shift.

The second thing I noticed was that Charlie wasn't sleeping in, like I'd assumed.

He was already awake.

And dressed.

And in the kitchen . . . cooking something.

He had an apron on. And he was heating frying oil on the stove. And there was powdered sugar spilled all over the floor like he'd ripped the bag open with oven mitts on.

"What are you doing?" I asked, walking nearer.

That's when Charlie turned in my direction, and I realized he was holding a cylinder of canned biscuits.

You know what I mean by *canned biscuits*, right? They're not really in a can. They're wrapped in a cardboard tube that you pop open with the side of a spoon. You've seen those? I'm only asking because I always thought everybody had seen those—until I beheld Charlie: tube of biscuits in one hand . . . and *a can opener* in the other.

A can opener—impaled in the metal lid of the biscuits.

When Charlie saw me staring, he held up the whole situation with both hands and looked at it, too. Then he nodded, like he was in full agreement. "Who designed these things, right?"

I tilted my head, like I just could not be seeing what I was seeing.

I mean, the instructions were *printed on the label.*

"I can get the tops off," Charlie went on, like he was truly befuddled, "but then I can't get the biscuits out." He turned to gesture to a counter's worth of biscuit corpses that he'd stabbed with forks and crushed with tongs—lying mutilated where they'd been slain.

"Is that biscuit dough on the pendant lamp?" I asked.

Charlie looked up somberly. "I had a leverage problem."

"It's a bigger problem than just leverage."

"There's gotta be a better way, right?" Charlie said—like a person who had no idea that, *yes*, there was, already, in fact, absolutely a far better way.

Reminder: this man had been on the cover of *Rolling Stone*. Twice.

He was frowning at the biscuit tube. "Maybe I should get an axe from the garage?"

"What's happening right now?" I asked.

Charlie paused. "I'm making you breakfast."

"Why?" I asked.

"Because it's your birthday," Charlie said.

"How do you even know that?"

"Your dad emailed me."

"How does my dad have your email?" Nobody had Charlie's email. *I* barely had it.

"He got it from Logan," Charlie said.

"But—why?"

"To send me this recipe. For canned-biscuit doughnuts."

Wait. Had my dad guilt-tripped Charlie Yates into making birthday doughnuts for me? Didn't he know that I was *just a writer*?

I shook my head. "Oh, god. I'm sorry," I said.

Charlie frowned as I stepped closer. "Sorry about what?"

"My dumb dad," I said, my throat feeling a bit tight. "He shouldn't have done that."

"Shouldn't have—?"

"Guilt-tripped you into making me doughnuts," I said, taking the canister out of Charlie's hand. "My dad just—loves me," I said, "and he assumes everybody else does, too."

I chucked the biscuits into the trash can. A three-pointer from across the kitchen.

"Hey!" Charlie said. "I'm doing something here!"

"Don't do anything," I said. "I'm shutting this down."

"But I bought three bags of powdered sugar," Charlie said, like that was some kind of counterpoint.

I was already walking away.

"Where are you going?" Charlie asked.

Um—I was in a swimsuit. Walking toward a swimming pool. But okay. "I'm going swimming," I said. "Alone." Then I gave the kitchen a quick glance, and said, "Just leave all this. I'll clean it up when I'm done."

CHARLIE DID NOT "just leave all this."

When I came back in from my swim, bundled in my terry cloth robe, my hair towel-dried and pulled back in a damp bun, and far less refreshed than I wanted to be—the kitchen was *worse*: sprinkles all over the counter, cocoa powder everywhere like the container had exploded, open biscuit cans and hunks of dough on every surface, and the remains of smoke in the air, as if Charlie might have set a thing or two on fire.

But on the little kitchen table, sure enough, there was a tidy plate of semi-successful doughnuts. With candles in them.

Mission accomplished.

When Charlie saw me walk in, he grabbed a box of matches and bounded over to light the candles—but I stopped him.

"Please tell me you didn't fish those biscuits out of the trash can."

"Nah," Charlie said, stepping over to the fridge and opening the door. "I panic-bought, like, thirty tubes."

Sure enough, lining the fridge shelves were enough cylinders of canned biscuits to keep us fed on doughnuts for possibly ever.

"Didn't I tell you not to do this?" I asked.

Charlie paused and studied my face. "You don't seem very happy. What's the story? Do you secretly hate doughnuts but you can't bring yourself to tell your dad and now it's become a whole thing?"

"I love doughnuts," I said, shaking my head.

"Is it *birthdays* you hate, then?"

"I love birthdays, too."

"So what's going on?"

"I just . . ." What to even say? "I just think we should get to work."

Oh, god—were my eyes tearing up? Over Charlie Yates calling me "nobody"? That couldn't be right. I had to be homesick. Or tired. Or maybe feeling the emotions that we all feel when we turn another year older and confront the relentless march of time and the inevitability of death. Right? This had to be just normal birthday weeping. Didn't everybody cry involuntarily on their birthday?

I needed to go pull myself together.

I turned to walk away—but Charlie grabbed my wrist and stopped me.

"Hey—" he said.

I looked up to try to drain the tears back.

"Is this about—" he started, but then he changed his mind. "This couldn't possibly be about . . . meeting Margaux yesterday. Could it?"

"I think I'm just homesick," I said, trying to gaslight us both.

But Charlie kept going, just in case. "Because that wasn't a date or anything. That was a meeting. It was a check-in. She forces me to do them every few months because she regrets how she left me—not *that* she left, but the timing. And she doesn't trust me to take care of myself and not get sick again—which is fair, actually. She shows up and drags me out and we sit at a table and she grills me to assess how well—if at all—I'm taking care of myself. She pulls out spreadsheets of health statistics and confirms that I've made all my checkup appointments. And none of it's about me. It's about her. Her guilt—and trying to find a way to feel better about her choices. I hate going. I dread going. My ex-wife and the fact that I got sick are the two last things I want to think about.

"But guess what?" Charlie went on. "Yesterday, for the first time, I didn't dread it." He shook his head in wonder, like he was telling me something impossible. Then he said, "I completely forgot it was even happening. I was just hanging out with you, strolling around the grocery store and teasing you about never having eaten Frito pie—and then we were putting away canned goods in the pantry in that ordinary comfortable way, and I was just . . . I don't know. Happy? I think I was happy. Then she showed up like the buzzkill of all buzzkills. *That's* why I yanked you into the pantry. *That's* why I hid. And when she came back in and found us, and I pretended like you were just some random coworker—it was only because I didn't want how I feel about you and how I feel about her to get mixed up with each other. Does that make sense?"

I wasn't sure. Did it?

Charlie nodded, like not getting it was valid. "I don't know how to explain it. But one thing's for sure. I'm not making you birthday dough-nuts because your dad guilt-tripped me. I'm making you doughnuts because I'm grateful that you're here—for whatever you being here is doing to my life. And I genuinely want you to have a happy birthday."

Ugh. One of those unwelcome tears of mine spilled over.

And Charlie, like a reflex, reached up and wiped it away. Like you might do for someone you cared about.

"Also," Charlie said, "I burned a hundred canned biscuits before I got the hang of this, so these little guys really are miracles."

I gave Charlie the wobbly smile that happens when you try to shift emotional gears.

Something was making me feel shaky. Maybe that I wasn't just a writer to him. Or that he was glad to have me in his life. Or that I was doing things to him—just like he was doing things to me.

"You have to eat one," Charlie said then, putting his arm around my shoulders and turning us both toward the waiting doughnuts. "So many canned biscuits gave their lives for this moment."

And now I really smiled. Despite myself.

I sat down at the table. And I let Charlie sing me an off-key, cater-wauling version of "Happy Birthday." And I blew out the candles. But it wasn't until I took a polite bite of one of the doughnuts that I really felt better . . .

Because that doughnut . . . was *good*.

"Charlie, this is perfect," I said, mouth full, shaking my head in dis-belief.

I wasn't lying. The outside was crispy, and the inside was fluffy. It was the perfect mix of doughy and oily, soft and crunchy, sugary sweet and bready.

It was like taking a literal bite of comfort.

"Is it?" Charlie asked.

"How did you do this?" I asked.

Charlie looked just as surprised as I was. "Your dad said it was easy," he said, "and after five hundred tries, it was."

"You nailed it," I said, taking another bite.

Charlie sat up straight and watched me chew, like he was very proud of himself. "This is the first thing I've ever cooked from scratch."

I tilted my head. "That's not what 'from scratch' means, but I'll let it go."

"Now you have to cook these for me on my birthday," Charlie said.

"When's your birthday?" I asked.

"October," Charlie said.

I shrugged. "I'll be long gone by then."

Charlie nodded, like that was a good point. He looked me over for a moment, and then, like he was making a suggestion, he said, "I'll be cured of cancer before you go."

I tried to understand that. "You'll be cured of cancer? Before I go?"

"A few days before you leave is the five-year anniversary of my last treatment," Charlie said. "And that's when I can officially call myself cured."

"Oh," I said, nodding. I hadn't realized he wasn't already cured. Five years is a long time.

"Better than a birthday, really," Charlie went on. "Every time I go for a checkup, I keep expecting bad news—that it metastasized, that it's back somehow. But I keep on being fine. It seemed impossible that I was sick then, and now it seems impossible that I'm well. That's what Margaux was here for—to make sure I didn't miss that final checkup."

"You won't, right?"

He shook his head. "I won't. I'm ready. I've been thinking about how to mark it. Some people take vacations. Or plant a tree. One guy I know got a tattoo. I was wondering if I should do something really wild. Go cliff diving. Or bull running. Or shark-cage snorkeling."

"That's a lot of choices."

He met my eyes. "But now I wonder if maybe I just want to hang out here. And eat homemade doughnuts."

Were we still talking about doughnuts? Something about the way he was looking at me made it feel like he meant something else.

"Oh, god!" Charlie said then. "I forgot the whipped cream!"

He grabbed a can of Reddi-wip out of the fridge and shook it as he walked back to the table. "Your dad said this was essential."

He popped the top off and brought the nose of the can over the plate of doughnuts.

"That's not what that's for," I said.

Charlie paused and looked up.

I stood and took the can from him. Then I squirted a dollop of whipped cream on the back of my hand and set the can down. "It's for doing this," I said, and I brought the hand with the whipped cream up just as I smacked down on my wrist with the other hand. The dollop of cream launched up in the air, and I opened my mouth, positioned myself under it, and caught it as it came back down.

For a second, I swear, Charlie had a look on his face like I was the most amazing woman who ever lived.

And I kind of agreed.

Then he grabbed the can off the table and copied what I'd just done—launching the whipped cream just fine, but overshooting it so it blopped on his ceiling instead of coming back down.

"Softer," I said.

He tried again and this time got a nice arc, but the cream missed his mouth and hit his cheek instead. He wiped it off and licked his finger.

"Keep your eyes on the puff at all times," I said, sounding like a coach. "*Be* the dollop!"

Charlie tried again and missed again—hitting the floor, the counter, the tabletop, and somehow the window before getting close to his face again.

I did a few more demonstrations: "It's all in the timing," I said. "As soon as it launches, you need to be moving into position. Head back! No fear! You're a champion!"

When Charlie finally got one, he was so excited, he hugged me. And then he offered to squirt some straight out of the can into my mouth.

An offer I graciously accepted.

We were sticky, the floor was sticky—even the ceiling was sticky. But we'd clean it all up later. Life felt suddenly impossibly bright—the kind of bright that feels like it's going to stay that way forever.

It was my first birthday away from home. Charlie had made me doughnuts because *he was grateful I was here.* He was almost officially cured, and we were covered in whipped cream, and these doughnuts were so much more delicious than anything cooked by a man who thought you opened canned biscuits with a can opener had any right to be. And right there, in a moment of ebullience, with no sense at all that I might ever regret it, I said, "Why don't we make a whole meal out of it?"

"A whole meal out of what?"

"Your cancer-free-iversary. Why don't I make a big, fancy dinner to celebrate, and we can eat doughnuts for dessert?"

Charlie picked up his half-eaten doughnut for a toast. "It's a date," he said.

So I clinked my half-eaten doughnut to his, and said, "It's a date."

Eighteen

AFTER FOUR WEEKS of living with Charlie, day in and day out, I had to make it official: We were good together.

Good at writing together, and good at living together.

Given how everything started, I might've expected the whole rewrite process to be endless clashing, and arguing, and insulting each other. Charlie could so easily have chosen to be offended by some nobody from nowhere trying to tell him what to do. He could have dug in his heels and fought me on every single thing.

And yet—he didn't.

I had armored up for a field of battle—and somehow we wound up in a field of daisies instead. Having a picnic.

I worked out many theories to explain it. Maybe Charlie really did understand that his version of the script was bad. Maybe he truly had liked my honesty when I ripped it to shreds. Maybe he was telling the truth when he said he liked my writing. Maybe his ego wasn't as immutable as everyone claimed.

Maybe I'd fallen madly in love with his writing for a reason. Maybe we shared some kind of essential linguistic rhythm, or some comic outlook, or some moral framework that made it easier to be friends than enemies.

Or maybe we both just really loved writing—in the exact same way.

Maybe writing was our shared love language.

There's a joke that writers "don't like to write—they like having *written*," and that must be true of some writers. But it wasn't true of me or Charlie. We liked the process. We liked the words. We liked playing around and trying things. We liked syllables and consonants and syncopation. We liked deciding between em dashes and commas. We liked figuring out where the story needed to go and then helping it get there.

It wasn't easy, exactly—but it was fun.

It was work that felt like play.

Which is all to say that one day, when we should have been writing, Charlie wanted to take me to a farmers market off Mulholland Drive instead—and swore that we would definitely get work done by talking about the story nonstop there and back, and I believed it. That was absolutely what we would do.

Except we never made it to the farmers market.

The road was windy and breathtaking—built in the 1920s as a scenic drive and strung with the hidden driveways of world-famous people—and Charlie seemed more than happy to tool along it with the windows down and his shades on and the radio blasting 1970s music.

I, in contrast, was terrified.

I didn't know who designed this road—but it must have been before the invention of safety. *Or road shoulders.* This thing slalomed back and forth between a steep valley on one side and a low canyon on the other, and only at the most lethal points were there any guardrails. Over and over, we rounded curves where the edge of the road kissed hundred-foot drop-offs. I started gasping and wincing.

As we weaved along the two skinny lanes, I found myself getting motion sick. The ups, the downs, the side-to-sides. It was a lot for my inner ear to handle. Charlie drove it fearlessly—one hand slouching on the wheel—like he drove it all the time.

Which I guess he did.

When Charlie happened to glance over and see me bracing against the door in fear, he said, "You don't like the Hollywood Hills?"

"I come from a town that's elevation zero," I said.

"Don't worry. I drive here all the time."

"Why aren't there more . . . guardrails?"

At the question, Charlie scanned the road and noticed its very weak guardrail game for what seemed like the first time.

"People are just careful, I guess," he said in a tone like *Huh*.

We'd curve one way and get a glimpse of a deep ravine to the right, then curve the other way and see the LA valley on the left. Through it all, I braced against the dashboard and jammed my foot over and over on a nonexistent brake pedal.

"You're a terrible passenger," Charlie said.

"I'm a fine passenger," I said. "On a normal road."

"Try to enjoy the view. We just passed Jack Nicholson's house."

"I'll enjoy it later. After we've survived."

"You want to know why you shouldn't be worried right now?"

"Why?"

"Because the bad thing you're worried about is never the bad thing that happens."

I took that in.

"It's always some other bad thing you're not expecting. Right? So the fact that you're worried we're going to plunge to our deaths off the side of this road means that there'll definitely be an earthquake instead. Or a drone strike. Or Godzilla."

"So you're saying something terrible is a given."

Charlie shrugged. "Pessimism's always a safe bet."

I was just about to argue with that when—right then—an orange cat scrambled full tilt out of some low bushes by the edge of the highway and shot across the road in front of us.

We were edging along a section of the drive that had a steep hill to our left, and, um—how to put it—*nothing at all* to the right. Just a curving road with no shoulder that dropped off so dramatically into a canyon that you couldn't see any edge at all.

With only a laughably low aluminum guardrail to protect us.

The cat dropped out of nowhere from the hillside, skittered across the road, and shot under the guardrail to disappear. Charlie touched the brakes, but the cat was gone in a flash—but before we could even exhale, that's when, from the exact same place in the exact same low bushes, another, much bigger animal leapt out.

I thought it was a dog at first. It was the size of a yellow lab.

But it wasn't a yellow lab.

Charlie hit the brakes for real this time—hard enough for me to slam forward against my seat belt like I'd been smacked with a wooden board.

And then the chaos started.

The second animal was gone as fast as the first one was—but it had been much bigger, and faster, and closer, and if Charlie hadn't jammed on the brakes, we would've hit it for sure.

Who knows—hitting it might've been worse.

But it was bad enough, either way.

We were on a curve so sharp that stopping short made the back wheels spin out. And then the whole lumbering seventies Blazer started fishtailing into a 360 across the pavement like we were on a carnival ride.

The worst carnival ride ever.

I remember Charlie and me—both screaming—as the world outside the car blurred past the windows and Charlie desperately worked the wheel to try to regain traction. I remember the exact pitch of the tires wailing across the asphalt. And I don't know if it was Charlie's maneuvering or just an accident of physics, but as the car straightened itself out, I realized we were now lurching toward the guardrail.

The measly, maybe two-foot-high, definitely not-to-code guardrail.

Which was the only thing standing between us and a deep ravine that dropped off to nothingness past the edge of the road.

Everything disappeared except for the rail itself, and it felt more like it was coming toward us than the other way around.

And then we hit it. Front wheels crossing the white line painted at the edge of the road head-on like a finish line—just as the snout of the

Blazer hit the metal railing with unholy creaks and deep groans like thunder as the metal bent with the force of our impact.

The front axle of the Blazer went fully over the edge of a berm of dirt before we stopped.

And I immediately felt terrible for underestimating that poor guard-rail.

It caught us. God bless it, it caught us.

We fully snapped two of the posts as we went over them, but the horizontal belt caught us like a muzzle and didn't let go.

In the silence that followed, with the wind whistling through the axle underneath us, I pieced together an understanding of our position: the back tires were still on the road, the chassis of the Blazer was resting on the berm, and the two front wheels were fully over the edge.

In front of us, and all around, was only a vast empty sky, with a valley that I couldn't really see—and didn't dare to look for—down below.

As an aside, I'll mention that the view of the sky was breathtaking—electric blue with stippled white clouds.

"Did that just happen?" I whispered out loud.

"I guess the good news is," Charlie said, "we didn't hit the dog."

"That wasn't a dog, Charlie," I said.

"It wasn't?" Charlie said. "I thought it was a Great Dane. Or maybe a deer."

"It was a bit too *mountain lion shaped* to be a deer."

"A mountain lion? That's crazy!"

"You're the one who told me about the mountain lions!"

"Yes—but I was just trying to scare you."

"Mission accomplished."

At that, the car shifted a little.

We both froze, holding each other's stares, like *Did we just imagine that?*

Then quietly, in a whisper, Charlie said, "I think we must be teetering on the axle."

"Let's get out," I whispered back. "Can we get out?"

Almost imperceptibly, Charlie shook his head. "There's no getting out. We have to call for help."

"Where's your phone?" I whispered.

In slow-mo, Charlie reached up to slide it out of the breast pocket of his Oxford and dial 911—and I listened, frozen still, while he calmly explained all of our details to the dispatcher.

After Charlie hung up, he said, "Ten minutes or so," in a non-whisper that I suspected was meant to signal somehow that we were okay enough for full volume. Then, when I didn't say anything, he added, "Lucky for that guardrail."

"Charlie," I said, also making the choice to not whisper, but not 100 percent sure that the vibration of my vocal cords wouldn't be enough to shift our position. "That thing could give way at any second."

"All we have to do," Charlie said, keeping his voice as smooth as chocolate milk, "is wait for help."

But that's when, as if to undermine all his efforts, Charlie coughed.

And then he coughed again.

I wasn't sure if the coughing was rocking the car or if it was just my imagination, but I said, "Don't cough, Charlie."

In response, Charlie coughed again.

"Hey," I said. "Are you trying to get us killed?"

"It's allergies," Charlie said.

"What are you allergic to? Plunging to our deaths?"

"We're not going to plunge," Charlie said, like I was being far more ridiculous than I actually was. "And we're not going to die."

But in the silence as we waited for him to cough again, I wondered.

Finally, I said, "I have this worried feeling like I might freak out."

"Freak out in a *still* way?" Charlie asked. "Or in a way that will rock the car?"

"Unclear," I said. "But the waiting is definitely getting to me."

Charlie studied me for a second. And then he said, out of nowhere, "My first kiss was in the seventh grade. Did you know that?"

I frowned, like *How would I know that?* And then, additionally, *How is this relevant?*

"She was a friend of my sister's, at her birthday sleepover," he said, and then in a tone like just speaking the name conjured up a whole world: "Mary Marino. She had, and I say this with so much reverence, *legendary* boobs."

"Why are we talking about this?"

"She left the party," Charlie went on, "and asked me to take a walk, which I did. And we made our way to an empty park and sat side by side on a bench and talked, but I have no idea what we talked about. All I remember is that she kept leaning close to me, and looking at me, and kind of puckering up her lips. I was not getting the message. I kept wondering if her braces were bothering her. Finally she turned to face me like I was the biggest pain in the ass in the world and said, 'Are you going to kiss me or not?'"

"I love this kid," I said. "She's a role model for us all."

"So I kissed her," Charlie said. "And then she said, 'That's it?' And I could tell she was disappointed, but I had no idea how to do anything differently. And while I was thinking, she told me she was going back—and to wait ten minutes so nobody would catch on."

"Did you ever figure out what you did wrong?"

"I think I just kissed her like you'd kiss your grandma."

"Oof."

"What was your first kiss?" Charlie asked.

"Second grade," I said. "The boy across the street. I made him climb up onto the top shelf of my bedroom closet with me, pecked him on the cheek, and then swore him to secrecy forever."

"And? Did he keep the secret?"

"Does it count if he forgot about it entirely?"

"Okay. Next question," Charlie said. "Ask me something interesting enough to keep us distracted."

And so I just said, "Tell me about your cancer."

It was a wildly inappropriate question. One I never would have asked if we hadn't been teetering above our deaths.

"Sure," Charlie said, extracasual. "What do you want to know?"

"What happened?"

"I had a lump on my forearm, which seemed like an odd place for a lump. I asked the doc about it at a checkup—but more just making conversation than anything else. I still had that thing back at that age where you think you're invincible. But just from his frown as he started looking at it, I knew."

"You knew you had cancer?"

"Yeah. I'm a pessimist, though, so I didn't trust myself, either. I always start with death in every situation and work my way backward."

"Are you starting with death now?" I asked.

"No."

"Why not?"

"Because you're here. And you're gonna be fine. And if you're gonna be fine, then I'm gonna be fine. So it's not even a question."

"That's the worst logic I've ever heard."

"The point is, I thought for sure I was only worried because that's just what I do. Not because there was actually something to worry about."

"But then you turned out to be right?"

Charlie nodded. "The biopsy came back malignant. So starting with death turned out to be the right approach."

"But you didn't die."

"Not yet. Give me time."

"And that's when your wife left you?"

"Yeah," Charlie said. "On the day I got the biopsy results. But she'd been planning it for weeks, if that makes it less bad."

"She was planning to leave you while you waited for biopsy results?"

"In her defense, I didn't tell her about the biopsy."

"You didn't tell her anything? Not even about the lump? Or that you'd gone to the doctor?"

"Nothing," Charlie said.

"Why not?"

"It just felt . . . personal."

"But wouldn't a wife be someone you're supposed to share personal things with?"

"This tells you a lot about our relationship."

"Were you not close?"

"Our lives just didn't intersect as much as they should've."

"Isn't that the point of being married, though? So you can intersect?"

"I guess that's why we're not married anymore."

"So—" I was still trying to wrap my head around it. "You told her you had cancer, and she told you she wanted a divorce?"

"Kind of. But not in that order. When she got home that night, I said, 'I have something to tell you,' and she said, 'I have something to tell you,' and then we did a 'you go first; no, you go first' thing for a while, and then finally we decided to just say our things at the same time. So I said, 'I have cancer,' just as she said, 'I want a divorce.'"

I swallowed. "Brutal."

"Yeah."

"She tried to take it back after that, but I said, 'You can't take it back. It's already out there.'"

"So you just—went through everything alone?"

"My sister came to stay a couple of times, but my dad's not in great health and couldn't make the trip. Logan helped out. And Jack and I played a lot of video games."

"What about your mom?"

"She left when I was a kid." And then, like he was putting something together for the first time, he frowned and said, "When I was sick, actually."

"When you were *sick*?"

"I never talk about this."

"Why?"

"Because it makes my mom sound so awful, what she did. But my dad wasn't exactly a dream, either."

"You don't have to tell me."

Charlie looked at me like he was deciding. "I'll tell you. Just don't, like, retell it in an interview."

"Nobody's interviewing me, Charlie."

Charlie tilted his head. "Yet," he said. Then he said, "I was eight, and I was obsessed with Harry Houdini. I'd seen that movie about him— you know the one where he unties all the ropes underwater?"

I nodded.

"My sister and I were making a kid version of that movie on our dad's camcorder, and I was going to do that trick, and she was going to film it. We'd studied the scene and taken notes, and I'd practiced untying the knots like five hundred times with a stopwatch. And so one night we tied my hands and feet and I jumped into the pool, but we'd used the wrong rope, and it plumped up once it got wet, and I couldn't get the knots undone. My sister had a timer, and when I hadn't surfaced in twenty seconds, she ran to get our dad—but our parents were having this epic fight, which they did sometimes, and she couldn't get their attention right away. By the time our dad pulled me out, I'd inhaled a bunch of water and I was pretty hysterical."

"Wow," I said. "No wonder you don't swim."

"After a few minutes, I was okay, and they put me to bed, but later that night I woke up and couldn't stop throwing up, and it turned out I had this thing called 'secondary drowning' where your lungs have kind of a delayed reaction, and I had to spend the night in the pediatric ICU getting fluids and supplemental oxygen. But the thing was, my parents weren't just fighting that night. They were breaking up. My mom was leaving. And so when I woke up that night, and only my dad was there, I kind of knew."

I felt a wave of indignation. "Wait! Your mom left your dad *on the night her child almost drowned*?"

"In her defense, my timing wasn't great."

"But . . . how *could* she?" I protested, as if that moment had been written wrong and we needed to revise it.

But Charlie was coming to a bigger realization. "Maybe that's why I didn't want to tell Margaux I was sick." Charlie looked at me, frowning. "Could that be it?"

"Uh, yeah. Hello. That is textbook subconscious nonsense. Didn't you take psych in college?"

"So . . ." Charlie said, still snapping the pieces into place. "My mom left when I was sick, and my wife left when I was sick."

"But now you're *dying*," I said, gesturing at the valley below with my eyes. "And another woman in your life"—I pointed at myself—"is not going anywhere."

I lifted my eyebrows, like *How 'bout that?* Like by breaking the pattern, I'd fixed him.

But then Charlie said, "Only because you can't get out."

"You don't know that."

I gave Charlie a minute to process. This had been a very productive near-death experience so far.

Then, to keep the distractions going, I said, "I don't have a mom, either."

Charlie met my eyes. "She left you?"

"She died," I said. "In the same camping accident that injured my dad."

"Oh," Charlie said then, his voice low and soft like a hum. "I'm sorry."

"You know what?" I said. "It's okay. I'm okay. I remember my dad saying, over and over in the years after she died, 'We're going to be okay. We know how to do this.' And he wasn't wrong."

"How to . . . grieve?"

"How to let go."

"That's not easy."

"No. And it takes a long time. My dad kept promising that grieving was a natural process—part of being human—and that we'd be okay in the end. I didn't believe him at first. But he was right. It's okay now. It doesn't make me sad to remember her now. I miss her, but in a way that doesn't hurt. You do get there, eventually."

"Your dad sounds very wise."

I nodded—just barely. "I won the dad lottery, for sure." Then I added something that I'd never said out loud before—something that was so scary to verbalize that it made my feelings about the situation we were currently in—teetering above a vast valley below us, held only by a ribbon of guardrail metal—seem almost cute. "The camping trip was my choice," I confessed to Charlie then. "Everybody else, my mom included, voted to go to the beach."

Nineteen

IT FELT LIKE ten hours before the first fire engine got there—but it was only ten minutes.

Nothing like perching above your imminent death to bend the space-time continuum.

Once the firefighters arrived, they talked to us through our open windows, explaining that they were going to stabilize the Blazer by running cables around the axle at each back wheel and winching it to the engine. Once it was stable, they promised, they'd get us harnessed and help us climb out.

All in all, once the professionals took over—things got pretty easy. We didn't have to make any decisions after that. We just had to follow instructions.

Which we did. Gratefully.

Minutes later, we were out of the car, safe and sound.

The Blazer was pretty unscathed, considering—but a wrecker still hauled it off to a body shop to get checked out. The cops gave us a ride back to their station, where we could call a ride to pick us up.

Once we were officially not dead, I felt a gale-force euphoria that had me thanking everyone, and shaking hands, and giving hugs.

It happened. We lived. And now we had a story to tell.

But Charlie didn't bounce back so fast.

He'd been so personable in the car trying to keep me calm. But once we were rescued, he got all quiet and frowny and didn't want to talk. He stayed like that all afternoon, and after we got home, and all during dinner.

He kept coughing after that, too—like it was his new thing.

Which felt a bit stubborn.

All I wanted was to feel better—and all Charlie wanted, apparently, was to feel worse.

I kept trying to talk and joke around and just kind of celebrate the fact that we hadn't died.

It was a safe bet that he'd forgotten we had signed up to do research at a line-dancing class across town tonight, and in his current mood, I wasn't sure how to remind him.

Finally, I just decided to pretend we were all on board.

"Come on," I said to Charlie after dinner.

Charlie was clearing plates from the table. He read my body language. "Come on where?"

"It's line-dancing class tonight," I said.

"Line-dancing class?"

"For the script."

But Charlie shook his head. "Nope," he said.

"Yep," I countered. "I put it on the digital calendar."

"We are not going to line-dancing class tonight," Charlie said.

"Why not?"

"Because we almost died today!"

"Yeah, okay," I said. "But we didn't. And it's not as easy to find line-dancing classes around here as it should be."

I waited for Charlie to capitulate. But he didn't.

So I added, "And it starts in an hour, so we probably should have left already."

I tapped my wrist to emphasize the time pressure.

But Charlie didn't get swept up in my momentum. He gave me a look. "I'm not going to line-dancing class," Charlie said.

Dammit.

"Why not?" I asked. Classic tactical mistake: giving him a chance to solidify his objection.

But he didn't take it. "Because."

"Why are you so mad right now?"

"Because I almost killed you today!"

"That's not my fault!"

"You're not the person I'm mad at!"

"Look," I said. "It's over. We lived. Let's celebrate and go dancing."

"I'm not going anywhere."

"What? Ever again?"

"I mean—give me a day or two."

"But the class is *tonight*."

"I don't care."

"You have to go!"

"I don't have to do anything."

"But that line-dancing scene sucks."

"You're forgetting that this project is never going to go."

"You're forgetting that you promised you'd make it good, anyway."

"It's good enough."

Was he really going to refuse?

I pointed at him. "Are you a—" I couldn't find the term I needed, so I had to make one up: "A *promise breaker*? Is that what you are? You said you would do research."

"I can watch videos on the internet for research."

"Watching videos is not the same thing."

"It's close enough."

"Why are you fighting this? You love immersion research. You've done it for every script you've written. You did a cattle drive in Montana for *The Last Gunslinger*! You lived in a bunker for three months when you were writing *Forty Miles to Hell*! You got so nauseated doing zero-gravity training for *The Destroyers* that you threw up three times!"

Charlie looked impressed that I knew all that. "Three times *that you know of.*"

"That's exactly my point!"

But Charlie shook his head. "Those were all different."

"Why?"

"Because those movies mattered."

That smarted, I'll admit.

I would've expected a comment like that back when I first got here. But we'd been working on this thing for weeks. Talking about these characters like they were real people. Writing scenes that were genuinely funny. Having fun. The scene where they fall on each other that we'd rewritten *after we actually fell on each other* that now incorporated frozen veggies? Pure delight.

Doesn't delight matter?

I guess not.

I sighed. "This, right here, is why your screenplay sucks."

"Because I don't want to go line dancing?"

"Because you don't believe in love."

Charlie snorted a laugh. "Do *you* believe in love?"

"Of course I believe in love. It's the best thing humans ever invented. There are *books* about this." And then, like books weren't enough: "There are TED Talks!"

"If you really believe that," Charlie said, "shouldn't you be married with like ten kids right now?"

That was so low. "I have to take care of my dad. I *can't* get married and have ten kids."

He clearly wanted to win—and settle this once and for all. "But doesn't love conquer all? Doesn't love find a way? Shouldn't some cartoon woodland animals show up and help you find your Happily Ever After?"

My eyes flashed. "Don't use a romance term against me!"

"You're the one who taught it to me!"

"Are you really this cynical?" I asked. "Do you really think that love doesn't exist? Or are you just saying dialogue that sounds good? Because if you really think love is something Hallmark made up to sell greeting cards, then we should just burn this screenplay right now. The last thing the world needs is another shitty rom-com. Produced or unproduced."

"I believe *hormones* exist," Charlie said then. "And I believe kindness exists. And affection. And altruism, sometimes. And longing. And I believe that every now and then those things can show up at once and knock you out of your senses for a while. But it's random. It's like the weather. It's not something we all should be aspiring to. Or counting on. It comes and it goes, whether you like it or not. And then one day, you tell your wife the results of your biopsy, and she tells you she wants a divorce."

Oof.

"So you're bitter," I said.

"Yes. Absolutely. But I'm also realistic."

"And you're lonely."

"No argument there. But I'm also honest. And I'm not going to get out there and spin cotton-candy fantasies for gullible people who don't know that's not how life works."

"How does life work?"

"People love you for a little while—when it's convenient for them—and then they move on."

"Not everybody's like that."

"But there are no guarantees."

"There are no guarantees for anything!" I said. "Would you rather cancel hope altogether than risk the possibility of being disappointed?"

"The *certainty* of being disappointed," Charlie corrected.

I sighed. "But don't you see how if you decide that's the way it is, then it can't be any other way?"

"I don't make the rules."

"We all make the rules—all the time."

"I just can't make myself believe in a total fiction like that."

I felt so baffled. "But you're—*a fiction writer.*"

"Not that kind of fiction, I guess."

"Then you should write something else."

"I can't write something else! I can't write anything at all."

"That's your problem, right there."

"Don't tell me what my problem is."

"*Your problem,*" I said, "is that you can't say no to everything," I went on, "and say yes at the same time. You can't cancel one emotion without canceling them all. You can't *hate love*—not without hating every other feeling, too. Stories exist *for the emotions they create*—and you can't write them if you can't feel them. This screenplay is a chance for you. You can make *anything* good"—I was almost pleading now—"but you can't make it good without believing in it. You can't bring this story to life without coming to life yourself."

This was my bid. This was my shot.

But I missed.

Charlie refused to take my meaning. His response just off-gassed disdain. "And you want me to come to life by *line dancing*?"

Why was contempt so hard to counter?

All I knew was that had been my best, most heartfelt argument.

If Charlie couldn't hear *that*, then there was nothing left to say.

"Fine," I said. And looked down. And sighed.

Charlie watched me.

"You don't have to go," I said. "You can stay here and . . . do whatever it is you do in this big mansion all alone. But *I'm* going." And then, on the off chance that it might make him even the tiniest bit unhappy, I added, "I'm going. And maybe I'll find a six-foot cowboy—with a horseshoe belt buckle and one of those perfect square man-chins with a little dimple in it—and let him buy me beers all night. And maybe he'll even have a big, crazy Sam Elliott mustache and a whole tragic past full of heartache, and maybe the two of us will just comfort each other all night long till the sun comes up."

Weirdly, it worked.

Charlie's eyes went dark. "Don't you dare."

"Try and stop me," I said, striding toward the front door. Then, over my shoulder, grabbing a set of keys off the key hook: "And I'm taking a random car out of your garage. And I'll see you tomorrow. Maybe."

But I hadn't even made it to the entryway when I heard Charlie's footsteps clomping after me, fast and hard. Then he blew right past me, grabbing the keys out of my hand as he went, spinning back to glare in triumph as he raised them high above his head.

I jumped for them but couldn't reach.

"You're an asshole," I said, shifting tactics to open-palm smacking at his shoulder. "Give me the keys!"

I smacked him a few more times, and then when he didn't budge—and when hitting him also didn't make me feel any better—I gave it up.

I pulled out my phone in defeat. "Fine, I'll get an Uber."

But that's when Charlie let his arm down, and I looked up to see him holding the keys out—also in defeat.

"I'll go," he said then, in a quieter voice that sounded like surrender.

But the change was so sudden, I had to ask for confirmation. "Go where?"

He closed his eyes like he was sealing both our fates and said, "Line dancing."

And then, before I could decide if I should thank him or hit him again, he opened his eyes, leaned in close, pointed at me, and said, "No six-foot cowboys for you."

Twenty

THE INSTRUCTOR TURNED out to be a six-foot cowboy.

When Charlie saw him on the tiny stage at the back of the bar—in Wranglers and boots with an actual straw Stetson hat—I heard him say, out loud, "Oh, god. He's a hillbilly."

"I don't think he's a hillbilly," I said. "I got propositioned by a hill-billy at a wedding once, and he had a very different vibe."

Charlie eyed me. "Did you?"

"A groomsman," I confirmed, with a nod. "Want to know what he said?"

Charlie squinted. "Do I?"

"He invited me to his hotel room and said, 'Red in the head—fire in the bed.'"

"Please tell me that didn't work."

I gave Charlie a look like *Come on*. "I politely said, 'No, thank you.' And then he shrugged like it was my loss and said, 'You're missin' out on the ride of your life.'"

"I bet you really were," Charlie said.

"Not in a good way."

"You've got to admire his optimism, though," Charlie said.

"He also passed out in the women's restroom that night," I added. "And got into a fistfight at a bowling alley. And propositioned the bride's mother."

"You *do* have experience with hillbillies," Charlie said.

After we signed in at the bar, got informed of the two-drink minimum, and knocked back two shots called Silver Bullets, we made our way to the crowded dance floor.

The instructor was getting ready to start, messing with the sound system and wearing his Wranglers like they were shrink-wrapped.

If this guy was a hillbilly—I looked around the room—at least we could all agree he was a *hot* hillbilly. Possibly an out-of-work-actor hillbilly just waiting for his big line-dancing break. Which I suddenly realized might actually be *me and Charlie*.

I elbowed Charlie. "We should cast this guy in the line-dancing scenes."

Charlie, whose face was busy personifying misery, said, "Writers don't cast actors in movies. That's what *casting agents* are for."

"I bet *you* could, though," I said, "if you wanted to."

"This guy's not an actor," Charlie said. "He's somebody's inbred cousin."

"Chalk one up for inbreeding, then," I said, letting my eyes float back in the instructor's direction.

"Are you ogling him?" Charlie asked.

Yes. Yes, I was.

"Unbelievable," Charlie said. "Didn't we just agree *no cowboys*?"

"Look," I said. "I didn't *request* a . . ." I glanced back to the instructor for reference and then got stuck. "A six-foot-three backwoodsman with a butt like a quarterback wearing a longhorn belt buckle and ostrich boots. But it happened. What am I supposed to do?"

"My opinion of you is plummeting," Charlie said. "*This* is your type?"

"I have lots of types, thank you. Sexy cowboys. Sexy lumberjacks. Sexy werewolves with tragic pasts. Sexy ghosts."

"Sexy *ghosts*?"

"That's the only kind of ghost I like."

"What about sexy hicks?" Charlie said, tilting his head at the instructor. "Or sexy corncob-pipe smokers? Or sexy mouth breathers?"

"That man can breathe all he wants," I said.

But this was really bothering Charlie. "This guy," he said, "is not sexy. He drove to LA on a riding lawnmower eating fried butter and squirrel nuggets."

"I don't think you can knock his food choices, pastrami man."

"Have some respect for yourself," Charlie said.

I glanced back at those Wranglers. "I think I'm respecting myself just fine."

That's when our instructor, ready at last, adjusted his headset mic and turned to face the audience. And then he started speaking. And it turned out he wasn't a hillbilly at all.

He was Italian.

"*Ciao a tutti*," the instructor said.

Charlie and I looked at each other, like *What!*

Then we both peered over at the easel with the class poster. It had the instructor's picture. His name was Lorenzo Ferrari. And he was from Venezia, Italy.

"Did he just get *handsomer*?" I asked, looking around at all the women in the room who were asking themselves the same question.

"You've got to be kidding me," Charlie said.

But this really was a game changer. Our instructor wasn't a hillbilly. He was a gorgeous Italian dreamboat *cosplaying* as a hillbilly.

"Welcome," Lorenzo said next, in a perfectly delicious accent.

And then, even as he launched into explaining the class, and how we'd learn three simple dances tonight—he'd do a "teach" first, and then he'd turn on the music and we'd do it for real—I couldn't concentrate. His voice was like a deep-tissue massage.

Had I brought Charlie all the way here to prove to him that line dancing wasn't sexy?

Can't win for losing, I guess.

I blame Italy.

"Try to focus," Charlie said, punching my shoulder to break my trance.

But I'll tell ya: Line dancing is not as easy as it looks.

I'd always kind of harbored a suspicion that I might be a secret dancing savant. Not *line dancing* per se, but just—from all the moves I'd busted in the kitchen while cooking over the years—I'd nursed a secret fantasy that maybe, if I ever *really* tried to dance, I'd astonish us all.

Ten minutes into that chance, I stood corrected.

I was not secretly awesome.

I was terrible.

We'd need a more humiliating word for terrible.

As Lorenzo led us through the steps of the first dance, I could follow pretty well as long as I could see him—but as soon as we all turned to face the next wall, which happens a lot in line dancing, I forgot everything. My mind went blank. I'd wind up craning my neck over my shoulder to try to keep him in my sights.

Which didn't work too well.

I'd get all pretzeled up, and then I'd step on my own feet, and then I'd slam into Charlie. Sometimes hard enough to get him coughing again.

"Don't keep looking backward," Charlie said.

"I'm a visual learner."

"Just watch me. I'm right here."

"But he's the *instructor*," I said. "And he's Italian."

We were learning a dance called the Canadian Stomp, which started out easy—a heel touch, a toe touch, and then a very satisfying stomp—but then devolved into lots of fluttery grapevine-ing that flummoxed me. And also forced me to confront that I'd never fully mastered my left from my right.

Was I the worst person in the room?

By a mile.

I was like a bumper car gone rogue, colliding into everybody—especially Charlie.

Every time I slammed into him, he said, "Oof."

"Sorry," I'd say, and pat him at the place of impact.

I was bad enough that Lorenzo himself eventually came down from the stage to help me. But having that face and those shoulders and that belt buckle in close proximity only made me worse.

"It's a scuff with a quarter turn into the jazz box," Lorenzo said pleasantly, like he was clearing things up.

I'd have to google "jazz box." "My legs keep getting tangled," I said.

At that, Lorenzo—*good god!*—looked down at my legs.

I held very still.

Then he said, "You should tie your shoelaces," in a voice that made me feel pretty certain I'd never think about shoelaces in the same way again.

For a half second, I wondered if Lorenzo Ferrari, line-dancing Adonis, might actually kneel down and tie them for me.

But that's when I looked down to realize Charlie was already there.

Charlie Yates. Had dropped down on one knee. In front of me. On the floor of a honky-tonk. And was now tying my sneaker laces in double knots with gruff but unmistakable affection.

Not gonna lie. As much as our instructor was objectively, legitimately, inescapably sexy, and as much as I'd enjoyed teasing Charlie about it . . . No amount of ogling Lorenzo Ferrari did even a fraction of the things to me that the sight of Charlie Yates tying my shoes did.

Right there, for a second, it felt like the music disappeared, and Lorenzo disappeared, and all the other dancers did, too, as Charlie held my gaze and I held his right back, and something happened in my chest that was the opposite of all the thumping and thrashing my heart had been doing lately.

Something, instead, that was like . . . a sigh.

Like my heart itself might be letting out a five-point-five-second breath.

Something that was absolutely, undeniably romantic.

Even though what he was doing was completely obvious, I said, "What are you doing?"

I expected some brush-off response, like, "Tying your shoes, dummy." But instead, he said, "I'm apologizing."

"For what?"

He tilted his head back in the direction of his house. "For being a dick before."

"You're apologizing? In a honky-tonk bar?"

This was the moment we'd come here to find. This was the real moment that would bring the fictional one to life. This was the difference between imaginary things and real ones.

Case closed: we'd have to put this in the screenplay.

Just as soon as I could figure out how to explain that to Charlie without completely confessing what he'd just done to me.

As Lorenzo moved on to the next waiting female who wanted help, Charlie stood back up, shook his head at me, and said, "Double knots—not just bunny ears." As if he gave me shoe-tying tips all the time—but I never listened.

He bent at the waist and pulled up his pant legs to show me his own laces, with their own double knots, as examples to strive for.

I peered down, and that's when I realized we were both wearing the same shoes. Black Converse low-tops. "We match!" I said.

"You're not very observant," Charlie said. "We've been matching this whole time."

"Have we?" I asked, feeling absurdly charmed by that fact—like it was some kind of fate.

But then a woman in a fringe pearl-snap blouse leaned in and pointed at our feet. "You can't spin in those," she said.

We both looked up.

"The rubber soles," she explained. "It'll twist your knees."

"Do we need different shoes?" I asked her, strangely dismayed at the prospect of no longer matching.

But the woman shook her head. "Just cut up some old socks," she said, "and stretch them over the balls of your feet like leg warmers."

I turned to Charlie, like *Brilliant.* "Shoe leg warmers!" I said, holding up my hand for a high five.

But no high five from Charlie. He just shook his head.

"I'll do this research," he said then, "and I'll let you slam into me a hundred times, and I'll watch you ogle that Italian guy, and I'll double-knot your laces all night long . . ."

Just then, someone behind jostled us into each other, and Charlie's eyes roamed my face for a minute, adjusting to the closer distance, before he finished: "But I will never"—he paused for emphasis—"*ever* put leg warmers on my sneakers."

HALFWAY THROUGH THE lesson, Lorenzo gave us a break, and Charlie and I found ourselves at the bar.

"So what's the verdict?" Charlie asked. "Is it?"

"Is it what?" I asked.

"Is line dancing romantic? Now that we're actually doing it. Is it?"

"What do *you* think?" I asked.

"I don't know. I'm not sure I know what that word means."

"You don't know what *romantic* means?" I asked. "Be serious."

"I think I am being serious. It's like I can't quite remember it."

"You can't remember *the feeling of love*?"

"You know how you can have a sense memory? Like if you try to imagine what it feels like to put a spoonful of ice cream in your mouth, you can summon up a mental experience of that feeling?"

"Yeah."

"Can you do that for love?"

"Of course you can!"

"But—how?"

Was this a real question? "Just . . ." How did you do it? "Just think of someone you love, and you . . . feel it."

"What does it feel like?"

"Are you asking me what *love* feels like?"

"I'm just wondering if it's the same for you as it is for me."

He looked earnest—like it was a real question. I could have shamed him for even attempting to write a romantic comedy *if he couldn't remember what love felt like.*

But I decided to be earnest back.

I imagined my dad and Sylvie and Salvador sitting at our dinette table, and then I just took in the sight in my head. "It feels warm," I said, eyes closed. "It feels hopeful and kind. Sunshiny. And soothing." And then, knowing there was a chance he'd scoff at me for talking about "the heart" and call it a cliché, I went ahead and said: "It feels like your heart is glowing."

Because that's true. That *is* what it feels like.

Sometimes clichés are clichés for a reason.

I waited to hear something cynical from him.

But when I opened my eyes, Charlie was shaking his head. "I can't feel my heart."

And then, maybe because it was the only response I could think of, I lifted my hand and pressed it against his chest. "Can you feel it now?"

"Yes," Charlie said. "But it's not glowing."

"What's it doing?" I asked.

Charlie let his eyes drop, like he was really thinking. "You know when birds commit suicide?"

I frowned. "I don't think—that's a thing?"

Charlie regrouped. "You know. When a bird sees its reflection in a window and thinks it's another bird and so it dive-bombs the window over and over, trying to attack, until it injures itself so badly it dies?"

Ah. Huh. "Kind of?"

Charlie nodded. "I think my heart is doing that."

Twenty-One

IT'S SO HUMILIATING to admit this, but the next afternoon, when Charlie had a meeting with the mistress we were doing this screenplay for and he told me to make myself scarce, there was no mistaking it—I was oddly jealous.

"I can't stay for it?" I asked.

"Trust me, you don't want to stay."

"You don't know that."

"This woman would eat you alive," Charlie said.

"She doesn't eat *you* alive."

"No," Charlie agreed, "but she flirts with me. Which is weirdly similar."

We were entering our sixth and final week of writing—which meant I'd only known Charlie for five. Five puny weeks out of my whole lifetime. Why did the idea of some mistress flirting with Charlie bug me so much? "It seems like we should both be here," I said.

"The thing is," Charlie said then, "there's another issue."

"What?"

"The mistress," Charlie said, with an apologetic shrug, "happens to be T.J. Heywood's stepmother."

I frowned. "The mistress—?"

Charlie nodded. "—is married to T.J.'s dad and cheating on him with this United Pictures executive."

I took it in. "The mistress is Mrs. Jablowmie?"

"Mrs. Jablowmie *Senior*," Charlie corrected. "There is no current Mrs. *T.J.* Jablowmie."

"Shocker."

And then I couldn't help it. I pulled out my phone and googled T.J.'s father "+ wife"—and got a thousand photos of a woman who looked like she might still be in high school.

"How old is she?" I asked.

"She's younger than T.J., actually. He brings it up a lot."

"Wow," I said. "No wonder he hates women."

"Does he?"

"Doesn't he?"

Charlie thought about it. "Yeah. I guess that's right."

"So . . ." I said, still processing. "This teenager is married to the directing legend and very middle-aged Chris Heywood, but she's also sleeping with this even *more* middle-aged executive who wants to make your Mafia thing—at the same time?"

Charlie nodded. "That's pretty much it."

"And everybody's fine with it?"

"As fine as it gets in this town."

I nodded. "She must be a hell of a multitasker."

"So that's the hesitation," Charlie said. "It's possible T.J. might show up at the meeting."

"Ah," I said. And suddenly, Charlie was right. I didn't need to stay. "But why do you have to meet in person? Can't you just email?"

Charlie shrugged. "She wants to come by the house," he said, like that was that.

It bothered me. A lot. "She's not going to try to seduce you, is she?"

"What!" The very notion prompted a coughing fit. "No!" When he recovered, Charlie said, "Turn off your brain, and go down to the coffee shop. Maybe you'll run into Spielberg."

The first time I'd ever gone there, Charlie had said, "That place is crawling with industry people," and every time I'd gone since, I'd expected to see somebody, *anybody*.

It had become a little joke. "Who'd you see?" Charlie would say whenever I came home.

"Alfred Hitchcock," I'd say. Or Robert Altman. Or Fellini.

And we were so deadpan, we didn't even laugh.

In truth, I'd never seen even one industry person there—and I'd wondered if Charlie had made it all up.

But it turned out, Charlie was right.

That day, while Charlie was hobnobbing with Mistress Jablowmie— and possibly even Teej himself—and I was at the café, working on my laptop and quietly demolishing a banana muffin, who should walk in but the reigning queen of all industry people . . . the one and only Donna Cole.

I'm not kidding. Donna Cole!

Donna Cole. Director of *Time of My Life*. And *The Lovers*. And *Can't Win for Losing*.

Donna Cole, whose most famous wise quote—"The most vital thing you can learn to do is tell your own story"—was the centerpiece of my vision board back home. Right next to the iconic red carpet photo of her in a white Wayman + Micah gown with her natural Afro high and bold and stunning like she was the patron saint of fashion and wisdom and rom-coms all rolled into one.

I'd loved her so long—and so madly—from afar.

And now here she was. Up close.

Very up close.

So up close that I stopped breathing when I saw her and didn't remember to start up again until I began to feel woozy.

To be honest, my number one fantasy about coming to LA was that I might run into her by pure, nonstalkery accident, get to pleasantly chatting, give her the elevator pitch for *The Accidental Mermaid*, and then, when she looked intrigued, just happen to have a copy of it in my bag.

This is a common fantasy for aspiring screenwriters on the outside of the industry: running into their own personal Spielberg by accident. Common, but also impossible. A moment like that would absolutely never happen.

But . . . what if it did?

It wouldn't. It couldn't.

But that didn't mean I hadn't carried a copy of that ninety-three-page script in my backpack with me everywhere I went ever since the day I'd finished it—just in case it happened anyway. Like impossible things were more than welcome to do.

The worst-case scenario, I'd decided early on, wouldn't be me carrying the script everywhere like a deranged hope junkie for years without ever getting the chance to hand it over. The worst-case scenario would be me *actually running into Donna Cole* but not having my screenplay with me because I'd given up too soon . . .

And then missing my chance.

Holding out hope for too long was one thing.

Giving up too soon was quite another.

You know what an elevator pitch is, right? It's the one-line description of your screenplay that you prepare in case you ever run into your dream director in an elevator.

I wasn't sure how many elevator pitches actually happened—in elevators, or anywhere else—but I did know they were crucial to write. And memorize. There were whole chapters devoted to them in screenwriting books.

I mean, if *you* couldn't sum up your screenplay, who the heck could?

Here was my elevator pitch for *The Accidental Mermaid*: A woman doesn't know she's a mermaid until she falls off her mean new boss's boat and sprouts a tail; now she must navigate her new identity, keep her dream job, and get her boss to fall in love with her before time runs out and her legs disappear forever.

You'd watch that, wouldn't you? As long as I could guarantee that no Meryl Streeps would be harmed?

And Donna Cole could make that movie *in her sleep*. Pop Jack Stapleton into a slim-fit business suit and slap a tail on Katie Palmer—and Wah-lah! Your next summer blockbuster.

Actually, it's mostly only Marvel movies that are blockbusters these days.

Maybe better to say: Wah-lah! Your next low-budget, moderately successful, character-driven comedy beloved by a not-small half of the population.

That wasn't dreaming too big, was it?

Maybe it was.

Because even after all that vigilant, relentless, almost masochistically deranged hope I'd refused to let go of for so long . . . on the day I actually got my impossible chance?

I'd left my backpack at Charlie's.

I forced myself to take a five-point-five-second breath.

Donna Cole.

She was here. I guess the impossible made its own rules.

I'd cried my face off watching *My Beloved Stranger*. And I'd practically memorized *Good as Gone*. And I adored her sexy remake of *The Best of Things*—damn all those snooty critics.

And *here she was* in the real world. Shorter and yet somehow so much taller than I'd ever thought possible, otherworldly and yet totally normal, divine and yet so human—and wearing a casual-yet-classy Dior wrap dress and surrounded, of course, by a gaggle of important-looking people.

What was my elevator pitch again? I'd practiced it so much, it was practically tattooed on my brain.

I rummaged through my memory. But the pitch was just . . . gone.

Time to think fast.

I pulled out my phone, nice and slow, keeping an eye on Donna Cole at all times like a wildlife photographer might track a rare bird that could flap away at any minute.

HEY, I texted Charlie. You busy?
His reply came right away.

>   What's up?

Emergency

>   What's wrong???

Need my backpack—Can you bring?
URGENT

>   Where are you?

Coffee shop

And then . . . nothing.

Had he gotten another phone call? Lost interest? Fallen victim to Mrs. Jablowmie's predatory behaviors?

Was his meeting over—and now he was coming? Or was the meeting still going—so I should try to sprint to his place and back here before Donna Cole escaped?

I closed my laptop and capped my pen. And then I hesitated—not sure what to do.

Minutes went by. Donna Cole ordered at the counter, then took a seat at a banquette around the corner.

More minutes went by.

Then more.

Maybe Charlie wasn't coming. Who knew what the mistress might be doing to him by now.

I stood up. I couldn't stand it. I had to do something.

But that's when the coffee shop door swung open—and it was Charlie. Hair wild, shirt untucked, my backpack over his shoulder, out of breath like he'd been running. He scanned the room until he saw me, and then ran—*ran!*—over. "Here," he said, shoving it at me. "Does it have"—he shook his head—"an inhaler or something? What's going on? What do you need? Are you hurt?"

Ah. He'd thought I was having a *medical* emergency.

Oops.

"Nothing like that," I said, waving my hands to help him regroup. "It's just got my screenplay in it."

Charlie coughed at that. "Your what?"

"My mermaid screenplay."

He shook his head. "*That's* your emergency?"

"Yeah." I pulled the zipper and yanked it out.

"I thought you were . . ." Charlie said, still breathing hard. "Hurt or sick or something."

At the thought of that, Charlie coughed some more.

"Shh," I said, glancing Donna Cole's way. "What is it with you and the coughing?"

"I'm not doing it on purpose," Charlie said.

"It feels performative."

"This from the woman who just made me abandon my meeting to sprint over here."

That felt oddly touching. "You abandoned your meeting?"

"I thought you were dying. I was picturing you like a fish flopping around on dry land."

I tilted my head, like *Odd visual.* Then I said, "I'm fine."

"Clearly."

I glanced Donna Cole's way again. I could explain all this later. Then, real quick: "How do I look?"

Charlie shifted from puzzled to baffled. "How do you *look*?"

I patted around on my head. "Is everything—battened down? Pom-pom all in order?"

"You look," Charlie started, and then he reached out to tuck a little curlicue behind my ear before finishing with "lovely, actually."

"I will settle for *not crazy*. But 'lovely, actually' works, too."

I targeted the banquette like an action hero. Time to do this.

"Thanks again so much, Charlie," I said, and then, in my excitement, I accidentally bounced up on my toes and kissed him on the cheek—only realizing halfway across the café that it might not've been appropriate. "Sorry," I called back then, giving him a *scratch that* wave as he stood blinking after me. "That was an accident."

And then I rounded the corner and landed smack in the legendary presence of Donna Cole—and a table of industry people. When had all these other folks showed up? The memory's a bit of a blur, but Katie Palmer was there. And that girl who starred in that thing about the trapeze artist. And that actress who always played the wisecracking best friend in everything. Dammit—what was her name? I loved her!

That's when I noticed, nestled in among them, of all people: T.J. Heywood. Backward baseball cap and all.

How *dare* he sit at a table with my favorite director?

Something about the sight of him with his big dude-bro energy smacked me with reality like a board.

Oh, shit.

This was not some fantasy version of my life. T.J. Heywood could never even get a bit part in that. This had to be reality—where T.J. got to go wherever he wanted.

What could this group possibly be meeting about? Making an all-female, beach-bikini *Beer Tower III*?

No. Donna Cole would *never* let that happen.

One thing was clear, though. These people were all really here. At a table together. A table that T.J. Heywood had clearance to join. And I did not.

I froze.

Miscalculation.

I want to point out that, with the exception of T.J.'s hat, no one here was doing anything wrong. These people were just having coffee.

I was the one in the wrong.

In that moment, I switched sides.

All the glee I'd been feeling one second before just disappeared into the realization that, yes, Donna Cole was here in this café, and yes, I was *also* here in this café—but I had zero actual reason to talk to her. She had no idea who I was—nor would she care if she did—and, like everyone else at the table, had no interest in being accosted by a sad and desperate writer.

Ugh. Who did that pathetic writer think she was?

Wasn't there a famous story of a nine-months-pregnant Amy Poehler falling asleep on the subway and waking up to an unsolicited screenplay teetering on her belly?

Oh, god. Was I that subway person?

I couldn't be that subway person.

But I couldn't let Donna Cole just walk out of my life, either.

There was an awkward grace period while the whole table ignored the figure standing cringily beside them with a screenplay in her hand. A moment when I should have spun a 180 on my heel and escaped.

But this is true: my feet couldn't move. It was like they'd been soldered to the floor with a blowtorch.

Then, the grace period expired. The conversation stopped. And this veritable party bus of Hollywood royalty all just turned my way and waited, like a silent chorus of *Who the hell are you?*

A burning humiliation that started at my feet filled my body. My clothes felt hot. My collar got damp.

Time to say something—anything.

"I'm so sorry to interrupt," I said.

Then I faltered as I caught a fleeting glimpse of Donna Cole's expression, perhaps best described as: *Seriously? What the hell?* And I saw Katie Palmer with a similar one. And then I saw T.J. indulge in a little triumphant smile, anticipating how satisfyingly this moment was going to confirm every mean thought he had.

No way out but through. I pushed on. "I just wanted to . . ."

But what *did* I want to do? Foist my unwanted screenplay on Donna Cole? Beg her to love me? Burst into tears? Dissolve into fumes of shame? *Perish?*

"I just wanted to—" I tried again. Then, "I really don't mean to—"

"Do you need something?" Donna Cole asked.

Oh, god. Oh, god. What had I been thinking, coming over here? Humiliation clutched at my neck. My lungs withered.

Eject! Eject!

I so badly wanted to turn and sprint out of there, leaving only cartoon streaks of shame behind. But my feet still wouldn't move. And I was just wondering if my only option was to drop to the floor and crawl out on my hands and knees . . . when Donna Cole's gaze shifted to the side and her face broke into a smile.

I turned, and there was Charlie. Hands in his pockets, hair pointing in ten different directions, demeanor all *aw-shucks*—but smiling big, like he knew exactly how cute he was.

"Charlie!" Donna Cole said, standing and reaching out for a hug.

"Donna," Charlie said, leaning in to kiss both of her cheeks. "Radiant as ever."

"Aren't I?" she said, shrugging with pleasure. She took in the sight of him. "You look adorable."

Charlie nodded. "I've taken up line dancing."

"I love it," she said. Then, leaning closer, she said, "What are you writing these days?"

"I'm writing a rom-com," Charlie announced, loud and proud.

"What!" Donna Cole gasped—total surprise with a splash of delight.

Charlie nodded to confirm, like *Yep.* And then, god bless him, he yanked me sideways, put his solid, nothing-can-ever-hurt-you-again arm over my shoulders, and said, "Under the tutelage of this one."

Charlie, I could kiss you. Wait—oops. I already did.

I felt all eyes shift to me, now under the loyal protection of Charlie Yates's arm.

"But," Charlie went on, "I guess you already know each other."

Donna Cole looked me over with new eyes. "We were just . . . meeting."

"Great!" Charlie said, making everything okay with his big we're-all-impressive-people-here energy. "Emma Wheeler, meet the legendary Donna Cole. Donna Cole, meet my new favorite writer, Emma Wheeler."

Donna Cole tilted her head. "Your new favorite writer, huh?"

I did *not* glance over at Jablowmie for his reaction to that pronouncement.

Charlie gave Donna Cole a lifted-eyebrow nod, like *You better believe it.* Then he said, like this was not an opinion, but a fact: "She's good."

Donna Cole looked back and forth between us. "Is she?"

Another nod from Charlie. Then, "Like I haven't seen in—" He stopped and thought a second. "Nope. That's it. Like I haven't seen."

Donna Cole looked at me, like *Interesting.* Then she scooted over at the banquette and patted the seat next to her. "Join us."

"Nope," Charlie said, clamping me tighter. "She's mine today. But Logan Scott can set you up."

Donna Cole squinted in approval. "Good to know."

"Anyway," Charlie said, looking around the table. "Great to see all of you."

And then a funny thing happened: T.J. stood up, clearly wanting to emphasize his only-other-bro-in-the-group status, and leaned across the table in a burst for a fist bump—but he lost his balance and it turned into something Charlie had to dodge.

As the fist flailed toward his face, Charlie jerked away to the side and wound up smacking his forehead into my cheekbone.

Not that hard. But, yes—it hurt.

I made some kind of *oh* noise and dropped my face to my hands as Charlie turned toward me.

"Whoa—whoa—whoa—are you okay?"

Charlie was peering in now, touching at my hands, nudging them to move so he could get a better look.

"I'm fine," I said, head down. "It's fine."

"Show me," Charlie said, his voice soft, like there was no one else there.

I let him move my hands away so he could get in close for an inspection as T.J., who had just jostled and spilled every coffee on the table, went around apologizing and mopping up the table with paper napkins.

When the crisis was over, Charlie made his next and final move. He took my screenplay out of my hand and tucked it under his arm possessively, like it was something precious and thrilling and intended for him only—and he'd been waiting in agonized anticipation all day to get his hands on it.

Next, he pointed at me with impatience: "Did you say that quick thing you wanted to say?"

The question was like telepathy. I got exactly what Charlie was telling me. It was, I suddenly knew, *not* okay to hand Donna Cole a script out of nowhere, but it was fully okay—extremely okay, in fact—to tell her that you loved her work. Later, I'd thank Charlie a hundred times for helping me find my voice in that moment.

Of course, of course: it made so much sense.

Your first meeting with someone should never be an *ask*. It should be a *give*.

There wasn't much I could give Donna Cole but admiration. But I genuinely had that in spades. I met her eyes. "I just wanted to say that I'm a wild, adoring fan of your work." Then I added, "The peanut butter sandwich scene in *The Lovers* is the best thing that ever happened to me."

I was right. Donna smiled at that. Her first real, non-Charlie-related smile this whole time.

And then, as Charlie started to steer us away, Donna put her hand on my arm. "Stay behind for one quick second?"

I looked at Charlie, like *Do you mind?*

And he nodded, like *Go ahead.* Then he glanced over toward my table and said, "I'll be waiting over there."

Take that, Hollywood. I was someone Charlie Yates would wait for.

Donna Cole waited until Charlie was out of earshot. And then she said, "Quick question."

I nodded. "Of course. Anything."

Then she tilted her head and said, "Is Charlie Yates in love with you?"

"What?!"

Donna Cole just watched me, like *We both just saw the way he touched your cheekbone*, and waited.

"No!" I finally said. "We're just—just—writing colleagues. Doing—writing stuff together."

She nodded, like *Got it*. But then she said, "I've just never seen him touch a woman like that, or look at a woman like that, or *rescue* a woman like that." Then she thought about it. "Actually, I've never seen him rescue *anyone*. In any way. For any reason."

"We're not—" I said. "We're just—"

Donna looked around the table. "You heard her, folks. No rumors."

But of course nothing creates rumors like saying "No rumors."

Judging from the way the table was smiling at me now, being the rumored love interest of Charlie Yates might not be a bad thing—if you weren't too fastidious about it not being true.

"Okay, then," I said. "Well. It's so great to meet you."

She reached out and took one of my hands in both of hers. "It's actually great to meet you, too," she said. "Any friend of Charlie's truly is a friend of mine." And then, before she let go, she gave my hand a warm squeeze, pulled me close for a kiss on the cheek, and whispered, "Don't break his heart, okay? He's much sweeter than he seems."

Twenty-Two

"WHAT," CHARLIE WANTED to know on the walk back to the house, "could you possibly have been thinking?" He was ahead of me, calling back his questions in astonishment. "What the hell was going on in there?"

I didn't know how to answer.

"Donna Cole," he went on, "is brilliant, and accomplished, and at the top of her game—and she also won't think twice about ripping out your beating heart and squeezing it like a sponge in front of you before you die."

"Really?" I said. She'd always seemed so supportive in the red carpet photo on my vision board.

"Not really. But she's not someone to mess around with, either."

"I wasn't messing around."

"You weren't messing around?" Charlie challenged, slowing to let me catch up. "You walked over there on a whim—manuscript in hand—with no plan, no strategy, no forethought, and no idea that T.J. Heywood Jablowmie the Third might be sitting at her table, and then you lingered beside her like a lunatic stalker—and that *wasn't* messing around?"

By the end, we were face-to-face. "You sound kind of mad at me," I said.

Charlie tilted his head like he hadn't noticed. Then he started walking again. "I guess I am kind of mad at you."

"I was trying to seize the moment," I said.

"That is not how you seize the moment," Charlie said.

"That's not how *you* seize the moment," I said back.

"You can't accost Donna Cole in a coffee shop, Emma. That's not how that works."

"I couldn't do nothing," I said.

"Yes, you could."

"I had to take a shot," I said.

"But that's not how it's done."

"It's not how it's done *for you*," I said. "You're famous, and dashing, and beloved."

"Did you just call me *dashing*?"

"The point is, there are people walking around this town right now wearing T-shirts with your dialogue on it. You have directors begging you for scripts. Donna Cole lights up like a marquee when she sees you. You're on easy street—and you have been from the very beginning. Do you know how lucky you are that a script you wrote *in college* took off ? Or that *The Destroyers* catapulted you to screenwriter stardom? Nobody has it that easy! You're a damned unicorn. We don't play by the same set of rules. I can't just have my people call other people's people and say *c'est la vie* if it doesn't work out. Nothing has ever been easy for me. I have to hustle. I have to wrench something out of every opportunity."

"But you don't."

"I beg your pardon."

"You got that Warner Bros. internship and you didn't even go."

"I didn't not go because I didn't know how to hustle," I said. "I *couldn't* go. Because we found out right after I won that my dad needed another surgery that nobody had seen coming, and there was no one else to look after him."

Charlie looked down then, and I could see him regretting assumptions he'd made about me. I wished I could send a little snippet of this moment to the me from weeks ago, freshly arrived in LA, trapped in Charlie Yates's car as he berated me for not wanting success badly enough.

"Ah," Charlie said, humbled in a satisfying way. "I didn't know that."

"Of course not. How would you? You were too busy stuffing awards into that awards drawer of yours."

Charlie gave me a look.

"The point is, you've had it too easy. I heard you once took a phone call onstage—at an awards ceremony—while receiving an award!"

"That was a really important call."

I glared at him.

"It was also an accident," Charlie said. "I left the ringer on."

"But you *answered*!"

He gave a half shrug, like *Fair point*. "That might have been a questionable decision."

"I'll say. And that didn't even surprise me. Because I saw that interview you did with Terry Gross at the Kennedy Center where you were drinking a smoothie the whole time."

"Should I have been hangry instead?"

"You should have respected the audience! And Terry Gross, for that matter!"

"I offered her a sip," Charlie said.

I let out a growl of frustration.

"The audience thought it was funny! And so did Terry Gross, by the way. You can get away with anything if everybody has already decided to like you. People love it when you break the rules."

"Everything you're saying here is validating my point."

Charlie decided to get us back on track. "What I don't understand about that whole Donna Cole debacle back there is why you didn't just ask me to introduce you."

I paused.

Now Charlie had to listen to *my* silence.

That idea had never occurred to me.

Finally, I said, "I didn't realize that was an option."

"Why wouldn't it be an option?" Charlie asked.

"I guess I'm used to just—going it alone."

"But you're not alone," Charlie said.

I shrugged. "Maybe not right here, right now. But in general, in life, I am."

"You have your dad," Charlie said.

"My dad's not a writer."

"The point is, I was standing right there."

This seemed like such an odd thing to be irritated about. "Look," I said, "I'm just hoping you don't fire me before we finish rewriting the script that you keep insisting doesn't matter."

Charlie frowned at that.

"We're done next week, anyway," I said then.

"You think we're done next week and then we're . . . just done?"

"Of course," I said.

"How could you think that?"

"Well," I said, "for one thing, I overheard you in the bathroom."

Charlie frowned. "Whatever that means, it can't be good."

"Back on the first day—at brunch with Logan. Through that weird lava-rock sink basin. You said this screenplay was doomed from the start. I know what happens once we're done here. You give the new version to the mistress, she green-lights your Mafia thing, the world adds one more movie with seventies mobsters in tan bell-bottoms to the pantheon, and I take the express train back to obscurity."

Charlie frowned, like he wasn't sure which part of all that to object to. Finally, he said, "You heard that—but you stayed, anyway?"

"Yes."

"But—why?"

I shrugged. There was no other answer. "Because I just—love you."

Oh, god! That came out wrong!

"Not *you*!" I corrected fast, my voice pitching up with panic. "Not

you—like *you* you. *You* meaning *your writing.* You—like what you *do.*
Your work. Stories! Your genius. Not *you*! Obviously! Of course!" And
right about here, I gave up and let my voice drop into a sigh of defeat.
"You know what I mean."

"I get it," Charlie said. "Don't worry."

"Also," I added, just to shift topics, "I was hoping I could change
your mind."

"About what?"

Um—about all of it! Hope! Love! Human kindness! "About rom-
coms," I said.

Charlie didn't respond to that. Just kept walking. Our feet were exactly in sync now, tapping the asphalt at the exact same time, and Charlie's place was in sight. But next, before we reached the house, Charlie
said something so odd, I'd wind up thinking about it for days.

Charlie said, apropos of nothing, "I heard what Donna Cole asked
you, by the way."

"What Donna Cole asked me?"

"Right at the end. When she asked if I was in love with you."

"Ah. Yes. That was awkward."

"Don't worry. It means she liked you."

"It does?"

"Yeah. It was on purpose. She was making the whole table curious
about you. Making you a person of interest. Turning you into a bit of a
mystery to solve."

"Huh," I said.

"She was doing you a favor. Status-wise."

"I thought she was just messing with me."

"Maybe a bit of that, too."

In front of his house now, Charlie kicked a rock and watched it skit-
ter down the road.

"I'm not, by the way," he added.

"Not what?"

"In love with you."

"Oh," I said. Then, in case my voice sounded weird, I added, "Of course not!"

"I googled it," Charlie continued, "and I'm not."

"You googled whether or not you're in love with me?"

"I googled how long it takes to fall in love."

"And?" I asked. "How long does it take?"

"Eighty-eight days," Charlie answered, definitively. "And we've only known each other for thirty-one. So. Problem solved."

Why was Charlie googling this? And what nutty professor came up with that number? And what problem, exactly, were we solving?

"I wish I'd known that back at the coffee shop," I said then. "That would've been a great comeback."

THE NEXT AFTERNOON, we made it to Act Three, and there were only two—huge, insurmountable—things wrong with Act Three: The ending was 100 percent wrong, and the kiss was terrible.

We were almost done with the rewrite. In a week, I'd pack up all my office supplies and head home. We were galloping toward the finish line now. But I'd saved the hardest part for last.

And by "the hardest part" I meant *the kissing*. All the physical stuff, really. Charlie had done it so wrong, it felt like there was no way to explain to him how to do it right.

"It's fine," Charlie kept saying.

"It's not fine," I kept insisting. "All you wrote is, 'He storms in. They kiss.' That's it."

"That's plenty."

"It's really not."

"I'm not telling the director what to do."

"I get that it's not our job to get in there with blocking. But you have to give them something." He knew this already. A good screenplay had to make readers see it in their minds. And a good rom-com screenplay had to make readers feel it, too.

I grabbed my laptop and plunked it down in front of him.

"What are you doing?" Charlie started, but then he saw all my open tabs up top with rom-com after rom-com. "Are these—?" he started.

"Compilations of movie kisses," I answered, like *Of course*.

"Where did you find these?" Charlie asked.

"On YouTube," I said, like *Duh*.

But Charlie shook his head.

"You know—best-of compilations," I prompted. "'Best Movie Kisses Ever'? 'Swooniest Kisses in Movie History'? 'Most Rewatchable Kisses of All Time'?"

"Rewatchable?" Charlie asked, like he couldn't fathom what that meant.

"The kisses that you rewatch over and over."

Charlie just frowned.

"Kisses so good, you'll watch the movie again just for the kiss."

Charlie shook his head.

"Kisses so good, you'll rewind them a few times before you even finish the movie."

Now Charlie looked at me like I was fully bananas. "Nobody does that."

"Hello? *Everybody* does that."

"I have never rewatched a kiss."

"That's because you refuse to let yourself be happy."

Charlie sighed.

"This is important," I said.

Charlie narrowed his eyes. "Is it?"

"There is exactly *one kiss* in your screenplay as it stands, and it's the tragic Charlie Brown Christmas tree of movie kisses."

Did I have a full, curated collection of dramatic kissing clips from around the world bookmarked on YouTube?

Yeah. Doesn't everyone?

I don't want to show off or anything, but if these clips had been artworks, I could have started my own very impressive museum.

I had clips from all over the world: Turkey and Japan and Azerbaijan and Iceland. It was almost an anthropology project—curating the best human efforts at kissing. I'd subdivided them into categories of style, too: Accidental, Gentle, Drunk, First, Pretend, Angry, Practice, Stolen, Forgotten, and Goodbye. Not to mention Kisses on Horseback, Rooftop Kisses, and Wall-slams.

Through it all, Charlie sat very still, like a captive.

"Why are you fighting me on this?" I asked.

"I'm not fighting you," Charlie said. "I'm just not writing a whole, big, ten-page love scene."

"*One* page," I said.

"You do it," he said.

"We're supposed to do it together."

"I'll rewrite the ending at the wedding," Charlie said, like he could escape.

"Uh," I said, "that's *also* going to have a kiss in it."

Charlie dropped his shoulders, like *Seriously?*

"Yeah," I said. "This first kiss gives us a sense of what's possible—but they don't get their happy ending until they get their happy ending."

Charlie shook his head.

"Just pay attention, okay?" I said. "You might learn something."

I pulled up a chair next to him and made him watch them all. The waterfall kiss in *Enchanted Forest*. The in-front-of-a-whole-stadium kiss in *Can't Win for Losing*. The rooftop kiss in Donna Cole's magnum opus, *The Lovers*. We watched the scenes on my laptop while I physically leaned up against Charlie, trying to pin him in place. We watched people kiss in lakes, in snowstorms, in burning buildings, and while transforming into werewolves. We watched lens flares and misty mornings and pouring rain. We watched slow, tender kisses that felt like melting candle wax and passionate wall-slams that felt like possession. We watched mouths and hands and tilted-back throats.

Then, for a grand finale, I made him do a close read with me of Ji Chang Wook executing a perfect Korean drama cool-guy kiss—slowing the clip down frame by frame and pausing to point out "nuances, subtext, and emotional body language of the kiss journey."

By this point, Charlie was too exhausted to fight me. "First he pretends to tease her," I said. "Then he puts his hands in his pockets and strikes a conversational yet masculine pose. Then she steps closer, and then he steps closer. And the whole time, he's acting like he's not all that interested. But now look: he's stepped so close that his thighs are touching hers, and his torso is touching hers—but the genius is that his hands are still in his pockets."

Charlie looked at me like *Why could that possibly matter?*

"There is nothing sexier than a man starting a kiss with his hands in his pockets," I said, like *Hello?*

Charlie frowned.

"The snug turtleneck also helps."

"Ah," Charlie said—sarcastically.

But I had the moral high ground here. I was saving the world one kiss at a time. "Look at how he leans in," I said, as Ji Chang Wook bent his head lower. "Pretty sure that's the exact geometrical angle of maximum yearning."

"How many times have you watched this clip?"

But this wasn't about me. This was about the craft of writing—capturing human emotion. Did Charlie *not care about craft?*

"Do we need to watch it again?" I asked.

"Nope," Charlie said. "I think I got it."

But he clearly didn't.

Because if he *got it*, he wouldn't have argued with me when I said we should use a pockets kiss for the grand finale.

"It's not our job," Charlie kept saying, "to tell the director how to block the scene."

"We won't tell him *or her* what to do," I kept saying. "We'll just write it so vividly that she, or he, will naturally do it right."

"You don't understand how movies work."

"Well, you don't understand how kisses work."

We wound up arguing about it all through the end of the writing day, all the way through our trip to the grocery story to get ingredients for dinner, and all the way home. We argued while we cooked, Charlie standing next to me, bringing up counterpoint after counterpoint like he was never going to give in.

It was like he liked teasing me. Like he liked getting me worked up.

Like maybe he didn't even *want* to finish the screenplay.

"You know what you need?" I finally said as I peeked into the oven to check the readiness of the roasting chicken with herbes de Provence. "You need to kiss someone."

"What?" Charlie recoiled physically like he had to dodge the words.

"Yes," I said, clanking the oven door closed. I liked the notion more spoken out loud. "You need to remind yourself what kissing is."

"I know what kissing is," Charlie said, now shifting from offense to defense.

"What it *feels* like," I said, feeling more and more pleased with how right I was. "Of course you can't write a totally immersive kissing scene! Not if your heart is a suicidal bird."

"Now I'm regretting telling you that."

"Who can you call?" I asked then, raising myself up to sit on the island countertop, ready to get to work on this idea.

But Charlie just took in the sight of me sitting on his kitchen island. "Margaux never let anyone sit on the counter."

I nodded like this was good. "We're breaking all the rules tonight, Charlie. We're leaving our old limitations behind. Now give me some names."

"Names of what?"

"Of people you could kiss."

Charlie blinked. "People I could—?"

"Kiss, kiss," I said, in a tone like *Get with the program.* "There have to be women in your life who could help you with this. Friends from high school. Divorcées. Or—what about some of the actresses I've seen you with on the red carpet?"

Charlie was totally aghast. "You want me to kiss real people—in real life?"

"All you need is one. What about Liza McGee? She's cute."

Charlie could not disguise his horror. "She's, like, nineteen!"

I shrugged. "That's legal enough."

"You can't be serious. I *work* with these people."

"Charlie, this *is* work. This is research." Then, before he could brook another protest, I said, "What about Brooklyn Garcia?"

"She just had a baby! And she hates me."

I saw a pad of paper at the far end of the island and stretched way over to grab it.

"What are you doing?" Charlie said.

"Making a list," I said.

"Of women for me to proposition?" he said.

"Of potential sources," I said, like this was Woodward-and-Bernstein-level stuff.

I wrote down BROOKLYN GARCIA and LIZA MCGEE and then crossed them out. Then I held my pen to the pad. "Let's brainstorm some potentials."

"I'm not doing this," Charlie said. "I'm not going to call up random women and ask them to kiss me."

"For *research*!" I said, like that made it better.

"It's creepy."

"It's for the sake of art."

"This script is hardly art."

"It could be. If you would take it seriously." Then I had an idea. "What about your ex-wife?"

"What!"

"You've kissed her before," I said, like *No big deal.*

"You have lost your mind."

"I'm just trying to get you past this mental block."

"This is not the way to do it. I'm not going to proposition random actresses, or—god forbid—my ex-wife, to do something that literally nobody on earth could possibly even start to understand except for another writer."

It was meant to end the argument.

But as soon as he said that, we both knew who my next suggestion would be.

"That settles it, then," I said.

"Settles what?" Charlie asked. "How?"

"Me," I said, without even stopping to think.

"You?" Charlie asked.

"I'm another writer."

"I didn't mean—"

"You just said nobody would understand this except for another writer. And I think you already know this, but, just in case"—I pointed at myself—"*I* am another writer."

If I'd paused to think it through for any length of time, I would never—never—have suggested it. But I was caught up in the momentum. We'd been arguing all afternoon. He'd been pooh-poohing kissing, and me, and *love itself* all day. I wanted to get past this. I wanted to shake him out of that stubborn head of his. My kissing-for-research idea was a good one—though I could also see how, for anyone else in the world, it might seem a bit bananas.

In truth, I *was* kind of the ideal person for this job. I did a ton of research. I understood how important it was. Plus, this circumvented the whole creepily-propositioning-a-random-woman issue. *I* was propositioning *him*.

This was the perfect answer.

If the last person Charlie had kissed was the wife who'd left him when he got cancer, maybe he needed something—anything—else to replace that last association. I was no pinup dream girl, fine. But I had to be better than cancer.

I would've told him to go find a girlfriend—but we didn't have time for that.

I could do in a pinch.

"This is a great idea," I said to Charlie.

"Absolutely not."

"This is the breakthrough you need."

"I don't need a breakthrough."

"Yes, you do."

Charlie was backing up now. "Emma, this is nuts. We work together."

"Exactly," I said. "That's why it's perfect."

"This doesn't—" Charlie said, shaking his head. "This isn't—"

"I can do this. I took two weeks of scuba-diving lessons to write my mermaid screenplay with a very handsy instructor named Karl. Five minutes of kissing is nothing."

"*Five minutes* of *kissing*?" Charlie said, like I'd just proposed we run a marathon.

"The point is, you're right."

"I'm right?"

"I really am the best person for this job. And I'm fine with it. So let's go."

But Charlie was shaking his head with a frantic *no way in hell* vibe.

"It's not a big deal," I said.

"We can't," Charlie said.

"We *can*."

I took a step toward him, but he took a step backward. Then I stepped closer, and he stepped back. "Emma? Don't. Hey—this is a bad idea. Hey! I'm serious."

At that, Charlie reached for a pair of tongs on the counter, and he held them up like a weapon.

A weapon of self-defense.

Something about that visual stopped me.

I suddenly saw the scene from a different vantage point: a predatory female writer advancing on her coworker as he defended himself with kitchen utensils.

Wow. He wasn't kidding. This guy *really* didn't want to kiss me.

Like, at all.

To the point where he would brandish a pair of kitchen tongs.

The sting of rejection hit me, and I held still for a second, not sure how to respond.

I dropped my eyes. Then, to the floor, I said, "You really are horrified by this idea."

"Not horrified—"

"Repulsed, then, I guess."

"No, I—"

I couldn't meet his eyes. I squinted at the window, instead. "I had no idea that I was such a revolting option."

"Come on, Emma. That's not it."

But it really did seem like it *was* it. At least, it felt that way.

"Okay," I said, feeling everything in reverberations. "That's fine."

I turned around and started walking away.

I didn't even know where I was going, to be honest.

Hell of a rejection, huh?

Charlie didn't even want to kiss me for research.

How unappealing are you, exactly, to not even qualify for a research kiss?

How stomach-turning must you be for a man to take up arms against you?

I could dwell on feminist-y questions like why the hell Charlie Yates of all people got to be the *arbiter of my personal appeal* later. Right now, only one thing was clear: I'd been fully willing to kiss him. And Charlie Yates—most definitely, most emphatically—had *not* been even the tiniest bit willing to kiss me.

Fine. Fine.

The rejection descended into a burning humiliation. All I could think of to stop it was to flat-out flee the room. I wanted to pretend that I didn't care—but I felt so rejected, I couldn't even do that.

"Emma," Charlie said, following me.

"I get it. It's cool," I said, walking faster. "I've just gotta—I just need to—" But my mind was jumbled. What did I need to do? What out-of-nowhere pressing issue could serve as the pretend reason I was leaving?

There was nothing. Nothing convincing, anyway.

"Emma," Charlie said, with a tone like *Don't.*

Don't what? Don't get your feelings hurt? Don't overreact?

Don't walk away?

Charlie was gaining on me, and I wasn't sure what I would do when he caught up.

I just needed a minute to regroup and hide all my feelings behind a mask of indifference—a minute that Charlie wasn't giving me.

Which seemed wildly impolite.

A minute to hide! Was that so much to ask for?

But that's when Charlie caught my arm and tugged it.

I stopped and let him turn me around.

I could have ripped out of his grasp and taken off sprinting, I guess. But the game was already up. I was a writer, not an actor. My hurt and disappointment and infinite vulnerabilities were plain to see in every possible way.

The sight of my face just confirmed it all for Charlie.

I watched him reading me in real time.

"Did I—disappoint you just then?" Charlie asked.

I looked down. "No," I said. But it was an obvious *yes.*

"Did I hurt you?"

I shook my head, but I didn't meet his eyes.

"Did you *want* to do that research kiss?"

"No." Not convincing.

"Emma . . ." Charlie said, taking in all this new information.

Finally, I brought my eyes up.

Charlie was leaning in with concern. And intensity. And maybe a whole new understanding of who he had become to me.

He took a step forward—and then it was my turn to take a step back.

"Are you pitying me right now?" I asked.

He took another step closer, and this time, I backed into the kitchen doorjamb.

"It's fine," I insisted. "I don't care." But I was such a bad liar.

When he took a final step, there was nowhere for me to go.

He closed the gap and leaned in closer. "I didn't want to kiss you—" he started.

"Yeah. I got that. Thank you."

But Charlie gave a sharp headshake, like I hadn't let him finish. "For research."

I held very still.

"I didn't want to kiss you *for research*," Charlie said again, watching me to see if I got it.

Did I get it?

Neither of us was sure.

Charlie gave it another second—waiting for my expression to shift into understanding.

But I was afraid to understand. What if I got it wrong?

So Charlie gave up on the waiting.

Instead, he cradled my face in his hands and tilted me up to meet his eyes.

Then he shifted his gaze from my eyes to my mouth, and he wasn't just looking, he was *seeing*. It was like he was taking in everything about my mouth—from color, to texture, to shape. It was physical, like it had a force, and I swear I could feel it, like he was brushing the skin of my lips with nothing but the intensity of his gaze.

And then he leaned in closer, staying laser-focused on this one place right in front of him.

The anticipation was excruciating.

I watched his mouth as he leaned closer.

And then, just as we touched, he brought his hand into my hair to hold me close.

And I stretched my arms up around his neck.

And the kiss just took over.

His mouth felt smooth and firm and soft all at once, and the warmth and tenderness of it all swirled together with my dawning understanding that *this was happening—Charlie Yates was kissing me*. And a dreamy euphoria hijacked all my senses, and I felt like long grass billowed by the wind.

I was just sinking into it when Charlie pulled back a little and opened his eyes to check my reaction, like *Was that okay?*

Um. Was that even a question? We'd need a better word for okay.

I reached up behind Charlie's neck to pull him back.

Had I been ragging on Charlie for forgetting what kissing was like? Because I'm not sure I ever knew in the first place.

There's something about a kiss that brings all the opposites together. The wanting and the getting. The longing and the having. All those cacophonous emotions that usually collide against one another teaming up at last into a rare and exquisite harmony.

I remember pressing my mouth to his, and plunging into a feeling of being lost—submerged in touch and closeness. I remember our arms wreathing and entwining around each other, and pulling tighter and exploring. I remember how my palms wanted to feel everything they could find: the sandpapery stubble on his neck, the muscles across his shoulders, and his solid torso under his T-shirt.

He felt real.

But more than that: he made me feel real.

The kiss lit a warmth that spread through me like honey, softening everything tense, and soothing everything hurt, and enveloping everything lonely.

I'd dated other people before. I'd had a few mild relationships. But I'd never felt anything like this.

And then a thought hit me: *This might be love.*

Oh, god. This really might be love.

But then, before I could decide if that was a good thing or a disaster, the oven timer for dinner went off.

Loud. Off-key. Insistent.

We ignored it until we couldn't ignore it anymore, and then we broke apart—him looking exactly as disheveled as I felt.

I walked over to the stove, but then it took me a second to find the oven mitts that were on the counter right in front of me. I pulled dinner out, and set it on the stovetop for a second while I tried to pull myself together.

I guessed Charlie was doing the same.

Because just as I turned to him, unsure of how to shift gears from *whatever that just was* to doing an ordinary thing like eating dinner . . . Charlie said, with a slow nod, "I get it now."

"Get what?" I asked.

Charlie met my eyes. "Why we're rewriting this story."

Twenty-Three

THE NEXT MORNING, on FaceTime, Sylvie and Salvador were a little dismayed.

"You had a totally epic kiss," Sylvie asked, more than once, "and then you just ate roasted chicken?"

"With herbes de Provence," I said, in our defense.

"You didn't . . . I don't know—confess a bunch of feelings?" Sylvie asked.

"Or have a night of passion?" Salvador suggested.

"No!" I said. "No. It was a first kiss!"

But Sylvie was calling bullshit on that. "You've been living together for weeks."

"But as professional colleagues."

"So . . ." Sylvie said. "Was the kiss real? Or was it research?"

"It was real," I said.

Sylvie and Salvador looked at each other like I was some kind of love weakling. "Are you sure?"

"It was real for me," I said. "And for him, too—I think. Just based on nonverbal cues."

Sylvie frowned.

"He said he didn't want to kiss me for research—and then he kissed me. So that implies it wasn't research."

But Sylvie kept frowning.

"What?"

"Could that have been part of the research, though?" she asked. "To pretend it wasn't research?"

"No!" I said. "That's crazy!" But was it also a good point?

Now we were overthinking it.

"This is ridiculous," Sylvie said at last. "Just go ask him."

"Ask him?!" I gasped in horror. "I will never ask him!"

"You don't want to know?"

"I desperately want to know," I said. "But I will just privately obsess over it, like a normal person."

"Why can't you just have a conversation? Tell him you like him and see if he likes you?"

"Please," I said. "If human relationships worked like that, I'd be out of a job."

Sylvie thought it over for a minute before saying, "Guess it's time for Plan B."

"What's Plan B?"

"I'm FedExing you my slinkiest slinky dress and my strappiest strappy sandals."

"For what?"

Sylvie leaned into the FaceTime camera, like *Duh.* "Put them on and see what happens."

"Just put on a slinky dress for no reason and walk around his house like a lunatic?"

"Like a *sexy* lunatic," Sylvie corrected. "It's a maxi dress with a plunging V-neck made of silky fabric printed with giant tropical leaves. You've never worn anything like this in your life. You're going to discover a whole new side of yourself."

"What possible excuse would I have for wearing something like that?" I demanded.

"You're a writer," Sylvie said. "Make something up."

✿ ✿ ✿

UGH. LEAVE IT to me and Sylvie to overthink that lovely kiss and drain its afterglow with overprocessing.

Had it just been research?

I hadn't thought so at the time. But the fact that it hadn't led to anything else seemed to refute that view. We had a mad kiss—and then ate dinner. It hadn't seemed strange at the time, but the more I over-thought it, the less sure I felt.

Maybe I didn't really want to know.

I sent Charlie an overly cheerful text that said, Day off from swim-ming today! Enjoy sleeping in!

And then I took a shower and did the best I could with my hair and put on just a hint of eyeliner and lipstick—enough to try to look better without looking like I was trying. And then I tried on ten differ-ent outfits to wear before deciding to go with my usual writerly duds under my usual strawberry hoodie so that if that life-ruining kiss last night had, after all, only been research on Charlie's end, I had plausible deniability.

It hadn't been research for me.

But I would never, ever admit that—unless it hadn't been research for Charlie, either.

I showed up at the writing table and couldn't decide if Charlie had put product in his hair—or if it was just wet. If he was wearing after-shave—or if that was just his deodorant. If he was glancing my way more than usual—or just the regular amount.

One thing was for sure: There was a bouquet of peonies on the table.

"Nice flowers," I said, sitting down.

Charlie looked over, like he hadn't noticed them. "Yeah."

"Were they there yesterday?"

"Don't think so."

"Any idea how they got there?"

Charlie nodded. "We were out of coffee this morning, so I had to hit the store."

"Peonies are my favorite flower."

Charlie looked up at that. "Are they? I wondered."

"You wondered?"

"Yeah. Because you always look at them longingly when we're at the market, but then you never buy them."

I wrinkled my nose. "They're like nine dollars a stem."

"So you want to buy them, but they're too expensive?"

"They're just not the kind of flowers you buy for yourself."

Charlie was quiet a second, and I realized he was suppressing a smile. "I'm glad I bought them for you, then."

WE WORKED ALL day, and I can't vouch for Charlie, but I had a buzzy feeling of anticipation the whole time. The kiss yesterday, the peonies, the way he kept glancing at me over his laptop screen—these things fluttered around my consciousness like butterflies of hope.

All signs pointed to *not research*.

It's a wonder I could concentrate at all.

But then, in the late afternoon, Charlie got a phone call.

His phone started ringing, and he looked down at it for a second before he answered.

"This is Charlie," Charlie said.

And then, I swear, he'd been listening only a few seconds when, in response to whatever he was hearing, he launched into a massive, hacking coughing fit—almost like a reverse spit take.

He had to set the phone down—that's how all-encompassing it was.

"Sorry," Charlie said, when he'd calmed down enough to bring the phone back to his ear. "Could you repeat that?"

Then he listened for a good minute—and as he did, his face went grayer and grayer, and I found myself at full attention, trying to figure out what the caller was saying. But nothing on Charlie's end gave me any solid clues. "Yes, I did," Charlie said, standing up now and starting to pace. "It was just for—" he started, and then followed that with "That's right." Then his whole body seemed to sink before he said, "You're kidding me, right?

Please tell me you're kidding." And then he made his way toward the French doors and—there's no other way to describe it—hurled himself out to the yard.

I didn't dare follow—just watched from inside.

I was engulfed in curiosity about what was going on, but he'd gone to the far side of the pool to pace, so I couldn't hear anything. All I could do was watch his body language and try to read his lips.

Neither of which yielded results.

Was he arguing with someone? Trying to talk someone out of something? Working very hard to stay calm—but not succeeding?

More important: What was it all about? Was it the exec's mistress saying she no longer wanted the screenplay? Was it the producer himself saying the Mafia thing was off? Was it Charlie's ex-wife? His accountant? Some relative with bad family news?

I'd never seen Charlie act remotely like this.

The more he paced and argued, the more he coughed—as his breaths caught on each other and tripped over themselves. When the phone call finally ended, and he dropped his arm and let the phone fall away from his ear, he stood there, churning in the aftermath . . . and then he took his top-of-the-line phone and fully pelted it across the yard.

Then he paced the side of the pool again, grabbing his hair and letting it go, turning one way and then turning back, not seeming to see anything around him.

Whatever it was, it wasn't good.

And just as I'd made up my mind to go outside and ask if he was okay, Charlie came crashing back into the house, plowed straight over to the liquor cabinet, poured himself the biggest glass of whiskey I'd ever seen, and downed the whole thing.

"Charlie?" I said. "Are you okay?"

What a question. He was not.

Charlie turned at the sound of my voice, like he'd forgotten I even existed, and then came straight at me so fast I took a few steps backward, before he grabbed hold of me in a suffocating hug—and held on and didn't let go for a long time, pulling in big breaths and pushing them out—that felt more like he was clinging to me for dear life than anything else.

And that's when I suddenly wondered: Was he sick again?

Before I could ask, he'd gone back for another drink.

"What's going on, Charlie?" I asked then, from across the room. "Is it— Are you sick? Is that what it is?"

This question really pissed him off. "I *told* you," Charlie growled. "It's *just allergies.*"

"No," I said. "I mean *sick* sick."

Sometimes you intuit a thing on impulse and you turn out to be right.

This was not one of those times.

Charlie gave me an Olympic-level eye roll that involved not just his face, but his neck and shoulders, too. Then he said, "Not everybody is dying all the time, Emma."

There was a bitterness to his voice I hadn't heard before. "I know. I just—"

"Let's not add your paranoid hypochondria to this situation, okay? It's bad enough without you backing up a whole dump truck of crazy."

I blinked.

This wasn't about me, of course. I'd just walked into Charlie's own personal mysterious bad moment and suffered some collateral damage. But the meanness still stung. I withdrew a bit, and then I said, "I just want to know if you're okay."

"Guess what? You don't have to know everything. Yes, you're living in my house, and yes, we're spending a lot of time together, and yes, we get along almost stupidly well—but that doesn't give you the right to pry into every nook and cranny of my existence. Sometimes I'm going to have shit to deal with that's none of your damn business."

"Fine," I said.

"Great," Charlie said.

"Don't tell me, then," I said.

"I'm not going to."

"I just wanted to help."

"There it is, right there," Charlie said. "I don't need your help, and I sure as hell don't want it. So why don't you just back off?"

HE MARCHED OUT after that, and I didn't see him again until after midnight.

I spent the day "working," but was totally unable to concentrate, walking to the front door every time I heard a car go by. He'd left without his car, and he'd also left his cell phone in the backyard, and I just couldn't imagine how a phoneless, carless person could be gone so long in LA.

If it wasn't that he was sick again—what was it?

I called Logan, but he didn't know. I called Sylvie to process, but we were just like loony birds trading nutty theories. Could he have a secret love child? Could he have been falsely accused of murder? Could his financial advisors have stolen all his money?

"My bet's on the ex-wife getting remarried," Sylvie said.

But I wrinkled my nose. "He doesn't even like her. I'm telling you this was something big. Something *catastrophic*." But what?

I WAS ASLEEP on the sofa when Charlie finally got home—and rang the bell twenty times.

I heard the sound in my dream for a minute before realizing it was real. Then I shuffled to the door and opened it.

I think he kept ringing the bell even after I'd answered, but all I remember was the sight of his face—covered in blood. One swollen purple eye, a split lip, and a veritable goatee of blood that had gushed from a recently punched nose.

"Charlie!" I gasped at the sight. "What the hell happened?"

But Charlie just squinted at me. "What happened to what?"

"To your face! You look like somebody beat you with a two-by-four."

Charlie touched it, like he needed to jog his memory. "Oh," he said. "Bar fight."

"Bar fight?!" I demanded, like nothing could be more ridiculous. Writers *imagined* bar fights. They didn't actually *do* them.

"Why aren't you sleeping?" Charlie asked then.

"Because you just woke me up."

He turned around like he was looking for himself. "I did?"

I sighed. "Yes. When you rang the bell for ten minutes straight."

"I'm the worst," Charlie said, remembering. "Another reason to stay away from me."

"Who gets into a bar fight?" I demanded. "That's a TV thing. That's not a real thing that real people do."

Charlie shrugged. "Some guy called Jack Stapleton an overpaid hack."

"So you just *hit* him?"

"I meant to *verbally spar* with him," Charlie said, "but he wasn't much of a wordsmith."

"You tried for a battle of wits in a bar."

"It escalated quickly."

"Charlie," I said. "You're such a dummy."

Charlie nodded in agreement. "It's possible I was spoiling for a fight."

"You're way too famous to be getting into bar fights," I said.

"This wasn't a paparazzi kind of place."

Charlie had wedged himself against the doorframe while he was ringing the bell—and as soon as he tried to unwedge himself to come inside, he stumbled forward, attempted to catch himself, and wound up draping himself over me and collapsing.

"Hey!" I said, buckling under his weight. "Get off!"

From the crook of my neck, he tried to bargain with me in a muffled voice: "Thirty seconds." Then he lifted his head to check my reaction. "Okay?"

He was looking at me intensely, waiting for an answer.

Or maybe it wasn't intensity. Maybe he was just trying to focus his eyes.

"Let's go in, Charlie," I said. "We need to figure out what to do with your face."

But Charlie didn't move. "You always say people falling on each other isn't romantic—but then it always is."

His bloody face. His puffy eye. The scrapes on his cheek. The smell of liquor and other people's cigarettes. "Nothing about this is romantic," I said.

But I wasn't sure if I was telling the truth.

"That's debatable," Charlie said, tripping a little over the syllables.

I shifted into action, strapping my arm around his rib cage to haul him toward the kitchen, but as soon as I did, he started coughing deep, heavy coughs—and I wondered if he'd broken a rib.

I made him work on drinking a bottle of water while I pressed all around on his torso to see if anything felt broken or tender. "I'm fine," Charlie kept saying. "Nothing's broken."

Next, I went through like a whole roll of paper towels to clean the blood off his face. He watched me the whole time.

"Sorry that this is gross," he said.

"I'm wondering if we should take you to the hospital."

"Over my dead body," Charlie said.

"That's the whole question," I said.

"I hate hospitals," Charlie said.

"That's not relevant," I said.

"It looks worse than it is."

So I googled "How to know when to take someone to the hospital after a bar fight" and discovered that many of the symptoms for a worrying head injury are the same as just being stupidly drunk.

"I'm not going, anyway," Charlie said. "This is gratuitous googling."

"I'll decide if you're going," I said, busting out my in-charge voice.

"I'll do that thing where protestors lie down on the road—and then you'll have to drag my two-hundred-pound ass the whole way."

"Maybe I will."

"Yeah, good luck."

I'd dragged my dad many places for many reasons. "I'm stronger than I look."

"Actually," Charlie said, his voice softening, "I believe that."

BY THE TIME I was done cleaning up his face, Charlie looked a lot better. He had a cut on his swollen eye where the other guy's fist had popped the skin. I leaned in close to peer at it. "You should get stitches for this."

"Nope."

"It might leave a scar."

"There are no words for how much I don't care."

I sighed. And then I just kind of gave up. Yes, I'd helped my dad many times—but my dad had *wanted* me to help him. It was one thing to drag an incapacitated man to the hospital. It was quite another to drag an unwilling one.

"Drink," I urged, filling Charlie's water glass.

To my relief, he did—big, sloppy gulps that sloshed out and ran down his neck.

I found some Neosporin and a Band-Aid. Then, while I took my time applying both, I asked, "What was that phone call, Charlie?"

When Charlie didn't respond, I prompted: "Earlier today? The phone call?"

Charlie shook his head. "I can't tell you."

"You can, though. You really can."

But he shook his head again. "That's need-to-know info."

"Why?"

"Because it'll ruin your life."

"It'll *ruin my life*?" Just how drunk was this guy?

"Or maybe it's *my* life it'll ruin. But you won't be too pleased about it, either."

Once the Band-Aid was on, I shoved myself up under his armpit like a crutch, then half walked, half dragged him toward his bedroom.

At his bed, he collapsed backward across the comforter.

"Do you want to put on pajamas?" I asked.

Charlie kept his eyes closed and shook his head.

His feet were still flat on the floor, so I knelt down to untie his shoes and take them off.

When I finished, Charlie was sitting up—and looking down at me.

"I think," he said, surprisingly lucid for a moment, "that you're my favorite person I've ever met."

"Oh," I said, looking back down. "That's very nice of you."

"And I've met"—and here, less lucid, he made a big, drunk gesture—"everybody. In the world. And you're my favorite. Out of all seven billion."

What did words like that mean coming from a person in this state? I had no idea.

"How crazy is that?" Charlie asked, leaning closer to study my face, like he might find the answer there. "I've known you six weeks, and I already can't imagine my life without you."

"Six weeks can be a long time," I said.

"Not quite six weeks," Charlie corrected then. "Thirty-seven days."

"How do you know that?"

"I just know."

"You're weirdly good at counting, for a writer."

But Charlie didn't respond. He just let his gaze travel from my eyes to my chin to my cheekbones to my mouth and back again, taking in the sight of me like he might never see it again.

For a second, I wondered if he might kiss me.

But then, instead, he clutched me to him in a tight hug.

And before he let go, he whispered, "What am I going to do, Emma? You're going to hate me so much tomorrow."

Twenty-Four

CHARLIE WAS RIGHT.

By the end of the next day, I really would hate him.

But I didn't believe that at the start.

At the start, I couldn't even imagine not liking him. In forty-eight hours he'd kissed me madly like I'd never been kissed before, and bought me peonies, and then gazed at me longingly in a drunken state. Other than the whole mystery phone call—followed by the storming out and the bar fight—all signs were good.

All signs about me, anyway.

So when Charlie finally emerged from his room the next day around noon, I had already resolved to talk to him.

I'd expected to find him looking rough. There was no way he wouldn't have a brutal hangover. But he showed up at the dining table shaved, showered, and as neat and tidy as writers ever get. Looking quite dashing, in fact—aside from that shiner on his right eye and the little Band-Aid trying to cover the cut. Even his split lip managed to look rosy. How could he look so good today—after yesterday?

I walked closer and intercepted him at his chair before he could sit down.

"Can I talk to you?" I asked.

Maybe the slight wince that crossed his face should have been a red flag. And maybe it's never a great idea to proposition a hungover man. But I'd been up since six, and I'd changed outfits three times, and put on mascara, and I was nervous and ready to get it over with.

Timing was never my thing, anyway.

"What is it?" Charlie asked, not meeting my eyes.

"I woke up thinking about how you told me last night that I was your favorite person—" I began.

"Did I?" Charlie interrupted.

That threw me a little. Did he not . . . remember? "Yeah," I said, peering closer for a sign of recognition. "You told me I was your favorite person. In the entire world."

"That doesn't sound like me," Charlie said.

"Well . . ." I said. "You said it."

"If you say so."

This conversation was already off the rails, but I was so focused on the plan I'd been formulating all morning that I couldn't seem to shift. I just kept churning forward on the thing I'd decided to do. Which was to confess to Charlie that I liked him.

"Anyway," I said, "I keep thinking about how much I've loved getting to be here with you, and work with you. But it's not even just the working. It's everything—you know? The grocery shopping, the morning swims, the . . ." I was starting to lose my nerve. "The shenanigans."

Charlie frowned like he didn't love my word choice. "The shenanigans?"

I nodded. "And the thing is, when you kissed me the other day—I was just flooded—just overtaken, really—with this feeling of infatuation. At first I thought it might just be hormones or, you know, just a chemical reaction to being kissed after"—I hesitated, and then finished with—"kind of an epic dry spell in the love department."

The *love department*? Oh, god. This was not the elegant soliloquy I'd written in my head.

"But the thing is," I went on, taking a breath. "The thing is . . . it didn't go away."

Charlie shook his head. "What didn't?"

I took a deep breath for courage, and I held his gaze. "The infatuation."

Charlie's shoulders dropped.

Which didn't seem like a good sign.

But I'd started this, and apparently I was going to finish it.

I went on. "I seem to have—kind of—developed a thing for you. A strong thing. A distracting, preoccupied, swoony, crush-like thing."

Charlie closed his eyes, like *Fuck*.

Up until I'd started confessing, I'd felt strangely sure that he had a thing of his own for me. But as I stood there, in real time, I could feel that hope blowing away like dandelion seeds on the wind.

But I kept going. "Over and over, since you showed up in my life, you've helped me and looked after me and been a genuine source of strength. And I don't know what happened on the phone yesterday, but I do know one thing for sure. I want to be a person who does that for you, too."

Charlie dropped his head and pressed it against his hand, like I'd just said the last thing he wanted to hear.

"Whatever's going on," I said, "I want to help."

At that, Charlie lifted his head back up, and he had a new expression: a combination of determined and stoic and fully uninterested. "That's not a good idea."

"It's not an *idea*," I said, like maybe I could win with a rhetorical technique. "It's a feeling."

But Charlie just shook his head. "Emma, you can't."

I shook my head back. "I can't?"

"We're not going to have that kind of relationship."

"But," I said, "the"—I wasn't sure how to describe it, but I finally went with—"kissing thing that happened?"

Charlie straightened his shoulders. "That was a bad call."

A *bad call*? What was he—a referee?

I felt like I needed to stand up for that best-kiss-of-my-life kiss. "I thought it was a good call."

His voice was a monotone. "I shouldn't have done that."

I really wasn't following. "Why not?"

"Because we"—he gestured between us—"can't start anything."

"Too late!" I said. "It's already started."

"Then it needs to stop."

"What if I don't want to stop?"

"That's not relevant."

"It is to me!"

"I'm sorry," Charlie said. But he didn't sound sorry.

Was this a version of his tell? Was he pretending not to care *because he cared so much*? But why would he do that? There was no reason to.

"Charlie," I said, meeting his eyes and taking a step closer. "What's going on?"

"Nothing," Charlie said. "I just—don't like you like that."

I could feel my throat tightening with disappointment. "You don't?"

"I don't."

"Not . . . at all? Nothing?"

Charlie just watched me.

"Okay," I said. "But . . . so . . . why does it feel like you *do* like me like that?"

Charlie shook his head. "Maybe it's because we've been living together. Maybe it's because we found a great writing groove. Maybe you've been alone too long."

"I've been . . . *alone too long*?" That was *his* autobiography—not mine.

"I don't know, Emma!" Charlie said, like something had just snapped. "It was a mistake. It was a fucking mistake!"

At that—at Charlie Yates *using the f-word* against our beautiful, ethereal, life-changing kiss—I stepped back.

But Charlie was worked up now. "We don't know what's happening!

We don't know the future! All you want is answers—but I don't have any! I could move to Alaska tomorrow! I could sail around the world!" Charlie threw his hands up, like *Who knows?* "I could get back together with my ex-wife."

At that, I started coughing for no reason. As soon as I'd recovered enough to talk, I said, "Who did you just say you're getting back together with?"

"Could," he corrected, like that was an important point.

"Get back together with—?"

"My ex-wife," Charlie said, without blinking.

"The mean one?" I said, like there might be other choices.

Charlie nodded, but he said, "She's not actually mean."

"The ex-wife who left you on the day you got cancer?"

He gave me a look. "Yes, but—"

"The ex-wife you don't even like?"

Charlie made a weak protest: "It's complicated."

"You hid from her in a kitchen pantry like she was some kind of banshee!"

"That happens in a marriage sometimes," Charlie said.

"You're not even married!"

What was happening? What was going on? I was so confused. Ten minutes ago I'd been floating on an afterglow of a kiss for the history books from a guy I was 99 percent sure was exactly as into me as I was into him . . . and now he was *thinking of* getting remarried—to a person he couldn't stand?

Unbelievable! But maybe I just didn't want to believe it.

Maybe I really had been alone too long.

"Are you dating her?"

"Who?"

"The mean ex-wife."

"Not yet," Charlie said. "But we could start. Any day now."

What?

"I've heard a lot of crazy things in my life," I said then, "but this is the craziest."

Charlie nodded like he agreed. Like we were *both* baffled.

But I guess the takeaway here was that Charlie had said no. Charlie had said he wasn't interested. Charlie had said it was a *bad call*.

That wasn't confusing. That was simple.

I felt things for Charlie, but Charlie—apparently—felt nothing for me. So that just had to be the end of that.

Twenty-Five

WHAT HAPPENS NEXT—AFTER a famous writer has given you a hard pass in his dining room at the start of your writing day together?

You, uh . . .

You just, uh . . .

You just get back to work.

You nod for a few seconds, blankly, letting it all register . . . and then you take a long, slow walk back around to your own side of the table, sit primly in front of your own laptop, and place your fingers on your keyboard.

Did I want to storm out of the house and never come back—possibly swiping one of his drawer awards on the way out?

I did.

But I stayed. For the contract.

Going through all this and then forfeiting the money at the end would just be bad to worse. If I had to stay until the end to get paid, then I'd stay till the end to get paid.

A display of strength, if nothing else.

A decent person would prorate my pay. I'd gladly leave for 90 percent of the total. I'd give up 10 percent in a heartbeat to get out of here.

But *was* Charlie a decent person?

I honestly wasn't sure. About anything.

Three more days. We had three days and a good chunk of Act Three left before we were done. I wouldn't leave. I'd finish my work here like a non-crazy professional, and then coolly collect my check and go home.

The best thing to do after a person flat-out rejects you is, of course, to never, ever see that person again. But since that wasn't an option, I had to figure out how to cope.

With Charlie "Bad Call" Yates.

It was the imbalance I hated: we both now knew for sure that I thought he was special, and desirable, and lovable—and that he did *not* feel those things about me. Lots of people didn't think those things about me, I pep-talked myself, and it was fine. And I'd had unrequited crushes before, too, and survived them. But it was the combination that was so lethal. Him knowing that I liked him—and still not liking me back.

Charlie had rejected me—and that was a fact. Nothing could change that.

But how I responded to it? That was my choice.

I could let it totally destroy me—sit across the table all day, staring forlornly at Charlie with tears dripping off my face. Or I could pretend it wasn't a big deal.

It *was* a big deal.

To me, anyway.

But if the last ten years had taught me anything about myself, it was that I could survive anything. Or at least—I could survive being rejected by a man who couldn't remember what love felt like.

But how was I supposed to work like that?

That was the question I couldn't answer. How could I think about dialogue and commas and character arcs now? How could anything going on with imaginary people even compare to the humiliation that had suffused my entire emotional landscape like a fog? And how, exactly, was I supposed to craft the last thing on my to-do list for the screenplay: the *happy frigging ending*?

I'm glad you asked, because I googled it, and now I have many tips for how to transition from a soul-crushing rejection right on over to a productive writing day with a coworker: Make eye contact, because that's what alphas do. Stand up tall, because it summons a sense of pride. Keep your movements simple and direct to show that you aren't flustered. Lift your eyebrows so you look unconcerned. Take deep breaths because they inflate your chest and hide your collapsing soul.

I wrote down a cryptic list to remind myself: Stand up. Lift. Breathe. Inflate.

And then, past the crux of it, I gave quiet thanks for how disappointment so easily gives rise to contempt.

Really? *This guy?*

I snuck a look at him as we got to work. His hair part was all zigzaggy, like no one ever taught him how to do that. His collar was half-flipped, he'd missed a button, and that Oxford was redefining the maximum limits of rumpled. And while I'd always seen Charlie's can't-be-bothered-to-do-laundry vibe before as proof positive that he got to make his own rules, today it just seemed pathetic. *Really, dude? You're in your thirties and you can't iron a shirt?* Also—his shoe was untied, his fingernails were chewed, and he'd never learned to type. For real. He hunted and pecked. Remarkably quickly, but still: If you're going to be a writer, shouldn't you at least learn to type? Wasn't that the bare minimum?

See? He wasn't so great.

I was fine.

This was freeing, in a way.

I could go home with no attachments when this was all over and return to all the many, many delightful activities I did back at home.

Whatever they were.

Maybe I'd take up line dancing for real and astonish us all by getting so good that I went to the Olympics.

Did they have an Olympics for line dancing?

Maybe I'd start one.

Point being: only three more days.

Be strong, I told myself. *You're fine.*

But my eyes betrayed me. Every other part of my body was being utterly obedient: my body was neat and composed, my fingers were typing busily—even if only the *asdf jkl;* keys over and over—and my heart was trudging along numbly but steadily. Only my rebellious eyes were acting out—so much that I had to pretend to sneeze over and over so I could wipe them.

"Allergies," I told Charlie.

"The worst," Charlie agreed.

Eyebrows up. Sit tall. Deep breath.

Don't collapse. Don't collapse. Don't collapse.

WE WORKED ALL day, and after a while, in that way that stories can save you—it started tugging me along like a little paper boat in a stream. The pull of that familiar current helped a lot.

Here's another tip for being okay when trapped in a small space with the man who rejected you: Play loud music in your earbuds like an angry teenager.

Loud, *cool* music—because you are a cool person and no guy who doesn't appreciate you can touch that.

I had a playlist called "Coolness," in fact, and I just let it rip. The bands were cool, the songs were cool, I was cool for listening to it—and Charlie Yates could go to hell.

Needless to say, there was not much reading aloud of dialogue today.

No sharing snacks, no chatting, no collaborating.

I never took my headphones out—worked for six straight hours without touching them. Even wore them to the bathroom.

As we worked, I vacillated over whether or not to cancel the dinner I'd promised to cook Charlie—*tonight*—for his five-year-iversary of being cancer-free.

On the one hand, why on earth should I cook for him? I should leave him alone with his meat bags and go out to a fancy restaurant by myself.

But on the other hand: I *was* a very good cook. Reminding Charlie of all the endless culinary delights he'd given up by having no interest in me seemed like a good idea.

Also: he was officially cured of cancer. That was bigger than my feelings about some petty rejection. Whatever Charlie Yates might mean to me personally in this moment—I could appreciate the bigger picture of what he meant to the world in general.

Yes, I detested him. But I was still *glad he was alive.*

Maybe "glad" was a bit strong.

I broadly supported the concept of him continuing to exist.

Also? Sylvie really had FedExed her tropical-print spaghetti-strap maxi dress and her strappy sandals to Charlie Yates's mansion. The package arrived while we were working, along with a note from Sylvie with no greeting or signature that said, simply: "Make him regret he was ever born."

I liked the look of those words.

I liked them so much, they answered my question for me.

I'd make Charlie dinner tonight, and I'd wear that crazy tropical dress, and I'd celebrate his good health like a virtuous person, and I'd save face at last by cooking something so delicious, it would haunt him for the rest of his life.

And through it all?

I would wear that dress.

WHEN CHARLIE HEADED out in the late afternoon, I was so relieved that I didn't ask him where he was going because I officially didn't care.

Nor did I check in with him about what time he'd be back.

Yes. Objectively, on a night when you're cooking dinner for someone, it is helpful to know what time that dinner should be served.

But asking seemed . . . needy.

Who cared, right? *Whatever.*

We usually ate around seven, so I just planned for that.

I went to the store alone and bought the ingredients for a beef Wellington—which was, everyone in my family at home agreed, the most mouthwatering, buttery, comforting, life-altering entrée in my very large repertoire—as well as vegetables for roasting and a bottle of real champagne from the actual French region of Champagne.

Also, I abandoned the doughnuts-for-dessert concept—trading it out for a snazzy lemon and rosemary tart, instead.

While the beef Wellington was in the oven, I dressed with a distinct *getting ready for prom* energy. I even googled a tutorial for an "Inside-Out Ponytail Updo" and tried to wrangle my hair into submission. I FaceTimed Sylvie so she could walk me through the process of putting on eye shadow—and voilà: three attempts later, I had eyes that were, both Sylvie and Salvador agreed, "at least ten percent sexier than usual." The sandals were half a size too big, but it was fine. I wasn't going to hiking in them. And then, the dress: miles of voluminous, foliage-printed fabric from the empire waist down—and almost nothing from the string-bikini-style top up. The spaghetti straps held up two simple triangles and then crossed over a nakedly open back.

Basically, the top would've been racy even on a Saint-Tropez beach, and the bottom was like I was wearing one of Maria von Trapp's curtains—*as a curtain.*

But somehow it worked?

Did it feel soul-tinglingly vulnerable to wear a garment that left whole sections of my body exposed to the open air? It did. But was it also kind of a power move to be so fearless that I didn't even need clothes?

Weirdly, yes.

Let's just say it was a far cry from my strawberry hoodie.

Sylvie made me send a mirror selfie to our group chat—and when she saw it, she texted immediately back: That's a life-ruiner.

Perfect. Exactly perfect.

I wasn't trying to change Charlie's mind about me.

I just wanted to ruin his life a little.

And so I set the patio table with his ex-wife's decorator's fanciest cloth napkins, and a little army of candles for mood lighting, and I figured out how to work his stereo system for a little background music, and I got everything ready just in time for the sun to set and Charlie to come home and find it all waiting for him like a glorious gift that he could not keep.

I took the beef Wellington out of the oven to rest and took off my apron, and I sat down at the patio table, struck a pose of nonchalance like I wore tropical-foliage-print maxi dresses all the time, and waited.

And waited.

Seven o'clock came and went.

By seven thirty, I was feeling pathetic enough to open the champagne as a gesture of defiance—so that when Charlie got home, at least I'd be doing something fun.

I was pleased to discover that I'd accidentally bought a sweet champagne.

It was, in a word, yummy.

Too yummy. By nine o'clock, I'd accidentally imbibed the entire bottle.

Oops.

I'll note that I wasn't a big drinker, and I hadn't touched any food all evening, so a full bottle of champagne on that empty stomach was— *how to put it?*—way too much.

By the time I realized I'd emptied the bottle, it was too late.

The world looped and undulated, and my limbs felt rubbery. I remember thinking I had to be careful with Sylvie's favorite dress—but then I couldn't quite remember exactly what "careful" meant.

It hit me that *I was drunk* right around the same time it hit me that *I'd been stood up.*

Stood up by Charlie Yates.

Stood up for a dinner that I'd prepared only for revenge.

As the minutes had crawled past, I hadn't texted Charlie on principle.

I refused to seem like I cared. Whatever, whatever. He could show up or not—it was all the same to me.

Though, of course, it wasn't.

I had needed a triumph tonight. That's why I'd gone to all this trouble. To prove to the world—and mostly myself—that despite everything, I was still awesome.

But this wasn't a triumph. It was the opposite.

And somehow, just as I was thinking that, I noticed the high diving board watching me from across the pool.

I was weaving toward it before I'd even made a decision. My brain was so far behind my body that I think I was halfway up the ladder before I realized what I was on my way to do.

A swan dive.

Charlie had said I couldn't. And so now, to punish us all, I would.

There was nothing more awesome than a swan dive.

I'd done them all the time in high school. Not usually in a backless dress and strappy heels after a bottle of champagne, but still. This was in my skill set. Charlie had forbidden me to dive off that board—*forbidden!*—but Charlie wasn't here now, was he? If he really wanted to keep me off it, maybe he should show up for dinner.

It was just the rebellion I needed.

And I was just thinking that as I reached the top of the ladder and stepped onto the board to see Charlie stepping out onto the back patio, gawking up at me as he took in what was happening.

"Emma, what are you doing?" Charlie called up—raw panic in his voice as he moved closer.

"I'm swan diving," I said, my lips feeling a little useless.

Charlie made it to the edge of the pool, staring up. "Emma, come down."

"I don't want to," I said.

But Charlie started moving now—reaching the ladder and starting to climb.

"You stood me up!" I shouted toward the sky.

"I stood you up?" Charlie answered from the ladder.

I turned around to face the ladder and wait for him. "For your five-year-iversary dinner. Your cancer-free-abration. Your perfect-health blowout bash. Your not-sick-anymore jubilee."

When Charlie reached the top, he said, "I didn't know that was still happening."

"Why wouldn't it happen? We put it on our digital calendars!"

"Yeah," Charlie said, "but that was before."

"Before what?"

"Before the whole thing about me possibly getting back with Margaux."

"You think I'm that petty?" For the record, I was totally that petty.

"No, I—"

"You think just because I like you—*liked* you—and you have absolutely zero interest in me at all that I can't be happy that *you're not sick with cancer?*"

"I guess I just—"

"Where were you?" I demanded.

"I was visiting Cuthbert."

I gave it a beat so we could all take that in. "You stood me up for a guinea pig?"

But Charlie refused to be cowed. "He's off his food again."

"So?"

"So Margaux asked me to sing to him."

Seriously? I was all for humane treatment of animals, but *come on.* I flared my nostrils at Charlie. "I've been waiting for you for three hours while you were serenading a rodent."

"That's an unfair spin."

Fine. Whatever. "I made you a beef Wellington!" I shouted. "Do you have any idea how much those cost?"

"Let's go eat it," Charlie said, clearly hoping to inspire me to come down. "Let's eat it right now."

"It's cold now," I said. Then, "It's ruined."

"Cold beef is a delicacy," Charlie said, reaching his hand out like I might take it. "People eat cold beef all the time."

"Feed it to Cuthbert," I said, bouncing on the board.

"I don't— That's not—"

"The point is," I said, turning back to face the pool, "I've moved on."

"Emma, come back this way—*please*," Charlie said, and I could hear genuine fear in his voice. Of course, that didn't mean much. I'd heard plenty of things in his voice.

"The beef Wellington was going to be my swan dive . . ." I said.

"Do you mean 'swan song'?"

I gave him a look, like *Don't tell me words.* Then I ignored him. "But now I guess the swan dive will have to be a real swan dive."

"Emma—do *not* do a swan dive!"

"Charlie—do *not* tell me what to do!"

"Emma, I'm begging you. Come here. You look very unsteady."

"It's the shoes. They're too big."

"It's not the shoes. It's the wine."

"Champagne," I corrected.

But, just then, Charlie took a step out onto the board. I felt his weight register.

"What are you doing?" I asked.

"I'm coming to get you."

"Don't do that, Charlie. You're afraid of this thing."

"I'm more afraid of you falling off it."

"I'm not going to fall."

Charlie started edging his way toward me.

"Cut it out!" I said. "You're scared of heights."

"I'm not scared of heights. I'm scared of water."

I pointed down at the pool. "What do you think that is?"

"I can't just leave you up here. I have to come get you."

"That's ridiculous! You can't even swim."

"I *can* swim. I just *don't* swim."

"Get down," I told him. "Leave this to the professionals."

"The *drunk* professionals? In evening gowns?"

The evening gown. I'd almost forgotten. Then, just because I suspected he'd say anything I wanted him to right now, I said, "Don't I look amazing in this thing?"

And then Charlie surprised me by saying, "You look fucking incredible."

Wow. Okay. That was better than I'd hoped for.

"Emma," Charlie said. "Please come here. You're so drunk."

"I'm not drunk," I said. "I just drank too much."

"That's the literal definition of being drunk."

"Why are you so argumentative?"

"Why won't you come here?"

"Because," I said. "I don't want to."

It felt good to defy him. And upset him. And worry him. Was this what all the parenting books I'd read while raising Sylvie had meant by "attention-getting behaviors"? I never understood it until now. It did feel good to have someone's full attention—good or bad. Especially someone who already had yours.

I wouldn't notice this until I thought about it later, but that thing Charlie was so good at where he pretended like things didn't matter? He wasn't doing that right now.

He was the opposite of nonchalant.

He wasn't pretending not to care. He was openly caring. Very much.

Maybe I liked that, too.

Charlie had made it halfway out on the board—to the part where the side rails ended. He was clutching the railing with white knuckles as he stretched his other hand out to me. I looked at it. It was trembling.

Huh.

I could scare the hell out of him on a high dive.

Maybe that was enough for me. Or maybe I'd sobered up a little. Or maybe I just didn't want to ruin Sylvie's dress. But I decided to come down.

"Fine," I said. "No swan dive."

I *felt* the sigh exit Charlie's body. "Thank you," he said, leaning farther out.

But why did walking back feel so much harder than walking out had been?

Maybe because I'd realized Charlie was right.

I *was* more drunk than any person on a high dive had any right to be.

This *was* a bad idea.

Bad ideas are a lot scarier once you realize how bad they are.

I took a step, and then bent my knees to absorb the bounce of the board.

I took another step, and did it again.

And then I took a third step . . . and it was probably the alcohol, but the too-big shoes certainly weren't helping: the board under me bounced a little, and I guess it pushed the heel sideways as it came up, and the too-big sandal was loose enough that the whole shoe rotated under my foot . . . and then, to sum up: I tripped.

And fell. Into the pool.

Twenty-Six

IT WAS BASICALLY a belly flop—but onto my side.

I tripped on that crazy shoe—and then I went over. Not gracefully.

Whatever I did on the way down, it was—I think we can all agree—*not* a swan dive.

The specifics are a bit blurry, but there was flailing involved. And thrashing. And screaming. And then a shatter like a shotgun as the side of my body smacked the surface of the water so hard that it popped the side seam of my sister's maxi dress.

It hurt like hell. And it knocked the wind out of me, too. And all I could do was sink downward for a minute, hopelessly tangled in Maria von Trapp's curtains.

In that moment, I felt so bad for what I'd just done to Charlie.

Poor, aquaphobic Charlie. He'd shimmy back down the ladder as fast as he could and then call 911 as he paced back and forth at the edge, watching me undulate beneath the surface—helpless to save me.

Oh, god. I was a goner. They'd never get here in time.

This was it. I'd die in Esther Williams's pool and become a footnote on her Wikipedia page: *A failed screenwriter drowned in the *pool of her second mansion after getting stood up by a man who couldn't swim. Her last words were: "Cold beef Wellington is not a delicacy!"*

What *were* my last words? Were they guinea-pig related?

Now we'd never know.

A fitting end for me, in a way. Maybe my mermaid screenplay would sell now—with the macabre addition of a real-life aquatic tragedy to the story.

No matter what, Charlie would carry the crushing guilt of this moment for the rest of his life. I'd wanted revenge, yes—but not this much.

Poor guy.

But then, before I had the chance to list any more regrets, or feel thankful for my blessings, or start writing my mental obituary, something clamped around my waist and started yanking and tugging me up toward the surface.

Charlie.

Charlie's arm, to be specific. Clasped tight around my waist as all his other limbs propelled us through the water.

Huh.

Charlie was not panicking at the pool's edge. He was underwater with me.

He really could swim.

As soon as we reached the surface, I coughed and sputtered and gasped, and Charlie rotated me onto my back and tugged me by the shoulders, his legs scissoring beneath us, to the steps at the shallow end.

He propped me on the second-to-top step and I draped over the pool rim, both of us breathing and coughing as Charlie clapped his hand on my wet shoulder, lacking any other way to help. We stayed like that for a few minutes, just trying to regulate our breathing. My side was stinging like hell from ankle to shoulder where I'd hit the water's surface.

Heck of a way to sober up.

But I was alive. I should be good-and-drowned right now, not suddenly hyperaware of the wet smacks of Charlie's bare palm as he patted my naked shoulder.

"Are you okay?" Charlie asked then.

I turned toward him. "I'm okay," I said. "Are *you* okay?"

In response, Charlie coughed some more.

"Oh, god," I said. "You're half-drowned."

But Charlie shook his head. "I'm fine." As he settled, he turned to inspect my body. "But you really belly-flopped."

"I *side* belly-flopped," I pointed out, like that was better.

"You can break a rib hitting water from that height. You can—"

"I know, I know. Explode your internal organs. You told me."

Charlie met my eyes. "Did anything explode?"

"Just my dignity."

"Well," Charlie said, a microscopic glint of affection in his eyes. "That's nonessential."

"Tell me about it."

We kept breathing for another minute before Charlie said, "I knew this was going to happen."

"Did you? I didn't."

Charlie tried to shake some water out of his ear. "I knew from the very first day you came here that some way, somehow, you'd make me go off that high dive."

I frowned. "Did you go off the high dive?"

Charlie nodded.

"Just now? You jumped in after me? That's how you wound up in the water?"

Charlie nodded again.

Why was that so touching? "I'm very impressed, Charlie," I said. "High dives are scary even if you *aren't* afraid of water."

"I agree."

"But you jumped in, anyway."

Charlie was looking into my eyes now.

"That was genuinely courageous," I went on. "You saved my life. You performed *a water rescue.*"

There was something electric about it all. The way he was leaning in close, and examining me, and dripping wet—but somehow so aware of me he didn't even seem to notice. Focused on me like he couldn't see anything else.

"Thank you," I said, and I really meant it.

But it was all too intense. Charlie had to break the moment. "Couldn't you have tried to die in, like, *any* other way?"

I wrinkled my nose. "I prefer the worst possible way. That's just my style."

Charlie shook his head at me. "Anything except water next time, if you don't mind."

"But," I pointed out, "I did give you a chance to conquer your aquaphobia."

Charlie smiled and looked down. "You're such a pain in the ass."

"What I'm hearing," I said, "is 'thank you.'"

At that, a breeze came through the yard and Charlie saw the shivers on my arms. "You're cold," he said.

He looked a little blue himself. "So are you."

"Come on," he said.

"Where?"

"Inside. To dry off."

As he said it, he brought his arms around to gather me up and hoist me out of the water like he was some drenched, bedraggled, corduroy-clad superhero.

"This feels like something we should be writing about, not doing," I said into Charlie's neck as he carried me up the steps and back to dry land.

But Charlie just said, "I wouldn't even know where to begin."

Charlie carried me straight to his room, wrapped me in a towel as big as a sheet, and sat me on his bed while he rifled through his chest of drawers to find us some dry clothes. I was genuinely shivering now, so I just held very still and waited.

"I'm going to change first real quick," he said from behind me, "and then we'll deal with you."

"Okay," I said, teeth chattering a bit.

"Don't look," Charlie said. He was just feet away—in easy looking distance.

"You don't have to tell me that," I said, squeezing my eyes tight.

And then there was a notable silence where I heard brushes and slaps and squelches as Charlie—presumably—stripped down out of his sopping clothes, toweled off, and replaced them with dry ones.

I wasn't looking. I would never have looked.

At first.

But then there was this moment when I guess Charlie must have been closing a drawer and he pinched a finger, maybe—because next, I heard him yelp, and when I looked over, he was hopping around and shaking his hand.

Shirtless.

He'd achieved full pants status . . . but he hadn't even started on the shirt.

It was a bit of a shock, to be honest.

We'd done lots of swimming together, of course, and so I'd seen his chest and his shoulders and his whole . . . upper half before. Maybe it was the context this time—in his bedroom, me still somewhere south of sober, him *very recently naked*.

"You *looked*!" Charlie said, like I was a cheater.

"You *yelped*!" I countered, like he was a troublemaker.

"I was fine."

"I didn't know that."

"Close your eyes again," Charlie commanded.

"Put your shirt on," I commanded back.

But I closed them. And waited. Poutily.

By the time Charlie arrived in front of me with a set of sweats for me to use, I was semi-determined to never open them again.

"It's fine now," Charlie said.

"I don't trust you."

By the time I finally peered out through my lashes, Charlie was wearing a hooded sweatshirt printed with the words I'D RATHER BE WITH MY IMAGINARY FRIENDS.

"Who's that quote by?" I asked, dropping all pretense and frowning.

"Me, actually," Charlie said. "I said it to my sister at a family dinner once, and she got it printed on a hoodie."

Then he held up the one he'd grabbed for me: WRITERS DO IT ON THE PAGE.

I met his eyes, like *Seriously?*

Charlie shrugged. "My sister keeps giving me writer-themed work-out gear."

"That one is . . . humiliating," I said.

"I agree," Charlie said, pulling me up into a standing position so we could get started. "But it's fleece-lined."

I was shivering too much to argue. "Fine."

"Here," he said, holding out the set.

But I shook my head. "I'm too cold."

"You won't warm up until you're dry," Charlie said.

I *was* shaking. That much I knew for sure.

Charlie must have looked at this wet, shaking, still-drunk human in front of him and decided we had nothing more than a medical situation on our hands. He didn't hesitate. "I'm going to help you, okay?" he said.

"Help me do what?"

"Change."

"What! No!"

"Look," Charlie said. "You can't stay like this."

"I'll do it," I said, reaching out a shaky arm for the hoodie.

But then, I dropped it. We both looked down at where it landed.

"Somebody's got to get you into some dry clothes," Charlie said, picking it back up. "Just pretend I'm a doctor."

"But you're not a doctor."

"You should've thought of that before you catapulted off my diving board."

I really was quite cold.

"Fine," I said, not seeing a viable way to argue. "But you have to close your eyes."

"How am I supposed to do that?"

"Echolocate," I said. "Like a bat."

"Emma," Charlie said. "That's not—"

"There's no way in hell I'm letting you *see me naked*," I said, in a tone like I would gladly die of hypothermia before I ever let that happen. "And I don't think that mean ex-wife girlfriend of yours would be too thrilled about you doing that, either."

"Fine," Charlie said. "I'll close my eyes."

"Fine," I said. "Don't peek."

Had I been thinking that Charlie seeing my shivering, wet, quasi-hypothermic, goose-pimpled naked body would be too erotic for either of us to handle?

Because whatever I'd just insisted on was worse.

Charlie did close his eyes—and I never saw him try to cheat—but that meant he had to put his hands all over me to figure out how to peel that wet, tangled maxi dress off.

"I think it ripped when I fell," I said.

"It definitely did."

"How can you tell?"

"You don't want to know."

Oh, god. What had Charlie seen?

At least for now, he wasn't looking.

But since he couldn't *see* me, he had to *feel* me. All over. In places I'd never even really noticed or thought about before—from the inside of my elbow, to the crown of my hip, the soft pooch below my belly button, to my . . . withers. And everywhere else, too. I'm telling you, those hands were *omnipresent*—as he untangled knotted wet cloth, and moved limbs for better positioning, relentlessly feathering accidental brushes and strokes in unexpected places that gave me a whole different kind of shivers.

I clutched the loose sweatpants and sweatshirt to guard my front like a protective barrier between us. But it was no match for the touching.

I was too cold to enjoy it, of course.

Mostly.

Once the dress was in a sopping pile on Charlie's floor, he had to come back up halfway with his hands to find my underwear elastic on my hips and then roll those down to my ankles so I could step out of them. And then he had to come back up and reach around behind my waist to unhook the low-back strapless bra, the mechanics of which totally threw him.

I guess he could have turned me around to work on the hooks. But he didn't. He just encircled me with his arms, and I shivered nakedly there while he tugged and yanked at the hooks, the stubble of his jaw brushing against my cheek as he made almost imperceptible breaths of frustration into my ear. What did he smell like? Some kind of classic barbershop shaving cream, maybe? Sweet, and a little salty, too. Whatever it was, I wished I could steal some to take back to Texas.

"I hate this contraption," Charlie said, in apology for taking so long.

I really was freezing. "Push and *then* pull," I said, through trembling lips.

Once every wet thing was off, I handed Charlie the sweatpants while retaining the sweatshirt—carefully positioned in front of my torso like a polyblend shield. He bent down and arranged the sweatpants so I could step into them and then worked them up my legs to my waist.

"Better?" he asked.

"Getting there," I said.

Then, eyes still closed, he held the sweatshirt open like an O so I could slide into that, too.

As soon as I was in, Charlie opened his eyes.

"Hey," I said. "I didn't say you could open your eyes."

"You need socks," Charlie said, all business. He grabbed a thick pair from his drawer and squatted down by my feet to put them on. I braced myself against his shoulder for balance.

As he finished with the socks, he looked down at the wet, empty dress as if that, of all things, was stumping him.

"Just throw it away," I said.

"It's a hell of a dress," Charlie said, in protest.

"It's ruined now," I said. In more ways than one.

Charlie didn't fight me. He tossed it toward his trash can, but missed.

"I can't believe you just made me do that," Charlie said then.

"What?" I asked. "Throw away my dress?"

"Change your clothes with my bare hands."

"Stop complaining," I said. "You're fine."

But Charlie wasn't about to stop complaining. "Classic Emma," he said. "Everything that you say is not romantic *is* romantic. You said it's not romantic for people to fall on each other, but then you fell on me and it was. You said line dancing isn't romantic, but then we went there and you ogled that Italian guy and I thought I was going to lose my mind. And here you are telling me to strip you down naked with my eyes closed, like if I can't see you it'll be PG-13, but instead I'm having to put my hands all over you—and it's not better, it's *so much worse*."

By the time he was finished, he'd stood back up and was face-to-face with me.

His eyes were dark, and he looked kind of mad.

"Are you mad at me?" I asked.

"No," Charlie said, still looking mad.

"I thought you didn't feel feelings like that," I said. "I thought your heart was a suicidal bird."

"I feel feelings, okay?"

"Yeah, but not *those* feelings. Remember? I had to explain to you what love feels like. And you don't even like me like that, as you've explained in very clear terms. And you're getting back together with your mean ex-wife. Nothing about any of this should be a problem for you. There should be nothing going on here but mechanics and knitwear."

Charlie was frowning hard now, like he had fifty different things he wanted to say but couldn't decide between them.

I waited. Frowning back.

Finally he said, "I'm not getting back with Margaux, okay? That's not happening. That was never going to happen."

"You said it was."

"I said it *might*."

"Are we parsing verbs now?"

"The point is—" Charlie started, but then he stopped himself.

I gave it a second, then I said, "What? What is the point?"

His voice quieted. "The point is, we should find you a blanket. And dry your hair."

"I'm not cold anymore," I said.

"Yes, you are."

"No, I'm not."

Charlie dropped his gaze to my mouth. "Your lips are blue."

I dropped my gaze to his. "So? Yours are, too."

"I'm not the person who was just shivering too much to put on my own clothes."

"Well, I'm not the person who's super mad about nothing."

At that, we stared each other down. What were we even fighting about?

I looked at his bluish lips again, and he looked at mine.

And then there was only one thing to do.

I grabbed a fistful of his sweatshirt right at the neck, and pulled him closer into a kiss.

For the record, he kissed me back.

With enthusiasm.

The second our mouths met, he was clutching me to him, and I was clutching back and we were devouring each other like hungry animals. Maybe it was all just physical. Maybe this kind of thing was bound to happen if you made any man peel off your wet dress and slide you limb by limb into a set of his own fleece-lined sweats.

But I didn't care.

He didn't like me like that—but I didn't care.

I was leaving in two days—but I didn't care.

His heart could only attack its own reflection—but I didn't care.

This moment, right here—no matter where it came from, or what it meant, or what it would or wouldn't lead to—was worth it.

He clutched me tight with his arms, and I ran my palms over his jaw and into his hair. There were so many questions whirling through my head that I couldn't even pay attention. Was this kiss ruining all other kisses that had ever existed—or *would ever exist*? Was there some way to crawl inside his body? How, exactly, could I make this go on forever?

I wasn't cold anymore, that was for sure.

I took a step back toward the bed, not breaking the kiss, and Charlie followed.

Then I took another step, and he followed that one, too.

Then, when the backs of my calves touched the bed frame, I tightened my arms around his neck to hold on as I climbed up onto the bed—never breaking the kiss—and tried to pull him there after me.

But as soon as Charlie realized what I was doing, he pulled back and broke away—leaving me kneeling there alone.

He took a second to collect himself, breathing hard. Then he said, "Emma, we can't."

"Sure we can."

"We already said we weren't starting anything."

"But we seem to keep doing it anyway."

"Emma, we agreed."

"*You* agreed," I said.

But now he was returning to his senses.

He shook his head. "We have to stop."

"Why?"

"You've been drinking, for one."

"I am totally sober."

"That's exactly what a drunk person would say."

"The belly flop sobered me up."

"That's not how that works."

"Maybe it's the hypothermia—"

"You do not have hypothermia."

"—or maybe it's the adrenaline. Who knows what kinds of chemical reactions go on inside the human body? But I'm fine." I touched my pointer finger to my nose a couple of times for proof. "See? Easy! We're good. I could walk a straight line right now. I could do a cartwheel. I could take the SAT."

"Emma," Charlie said, "there's an empty champagne bottle lying on its side in the flower bed."

"I admit that's a large quantity of alcohol," I said, trying to sound extra sober. "But I drank it slowly and responsibly over a long period of time. Like a grown-up." Then, for added panache: "Like a *French* grown-up."

"Emma . . ." Charlie said, shaking his head. "You are not in a state to give consent—to anything."

Ugh. Now he was throwing *consent* at me?

How was I supposed to argue with that?

Maybe I could use my feminine wiles.

Did I *have* feminine wiles?

I decided to find out.

"Come here," I said, waving him closer.

Charlie leaned cautiously in.

"I'm leaving in a few days," I said conspiratorially. "We'll never have to see each other again. And so I'm wondering if you'd be willing—just real quick"—and I still can't believe I suggested this—"to go to bed with me."

"What!" Charlie yelped, pulling back.

"I think it's a great idea," I said, refusing to participate in his drama.

"Emma," Charlie said, shaking his head. "Do I have to explain what consent is to you?"

"I won't tell anyone," I stage-whispered.

"There will be nothing to tell," Charlie stage-whispered back.

"Look," I said, changing tack, "I have never in my whole life had the chance to sleep with someone who I really, really wanted to sleep with." To be clear, "really, really wanted to sleep with" was a euphemism for "was hopelessly half in love with."

Maybe more than half.

But that was need-to-know information.

"And," I went on, "I would really, really like to sleep with you. Specifically."

Charlie closed his eyes with a *What a nightmare* sigh.

But I kept going. This was my shot, and I was taking it. "I don't live a life where chances like this come along very often. I may never get a shot like this again. So you'd really be doing me a favor. I'm not saying we should date—or even stay in contact. Just for fun, huh? Just a little treat. All the good stuff, and none of the angst. My life doesn't have time for real romance anyway. My schedule's too booked with"—I couldn't think of what it was booked with, and somehow I finished with—"worry and stress."

There it was. That was my pitch.

For a tiny second, Charlie held very still—and I wondered if he was tempted.

I studied his earnest, writerly face and felt a little buzz of hope.

But that's when Charlie said, "Absolutely not. No way in hell."

I gave him a second to change his mind.

Then, when he didn't, I asked, "Charlie?"

"What?"

"Why don't you like me back?"

Charlie blinked, like he never in a million years saw that coming.

"Is it my hair?" I asked, already agreeing. "Is it the frizz?"

"No!" Charlie said. Like he was offended by the question.

"Is it the color?" I pulled one of the corkscrews straight to take an appraising look. "I get it. The way it scratches the backs of your eyeballs. It's a lot."

Charlie shook his head. "No," he said. "I love your hair."

Huh. Okay. "Is it my strawberry writing hoodie?" I asked. "I know it's crazy. But my"—my breath caught unexpectedly here—"my mom gave it to me."

"Your strawberry writing hoodie is adorable," Charlie said, his voice softer now.

But I was searching for an answer. "Is it how I ripped your screenplay apart when I first came here? That couldn't have been fun for you. Or how I mocked you so much for trying to open biscuits with a can opener? Or how I keep rolling my eyes at your Mafia movie? I could revise my opinion on that. Maybe I haven't been giving leather bell-bottoms a fair shot. Am I too chatty—is that it? Too opinionated? Too direct? Maybe if you tell me what it is, I could try to fix it."

"Stop talking," Charlie said. "You're making me mad."

"So it's . . . not fixable. Is that what you're saying?"

"You don't need fixing," Charlie said. "I'm the one that needs fixing."

There was such impossible finality in his voice.

"You're asking me what's wrong with you," Charlie went on, "but you should be telling me what's wrong with *me*. I am not a catch, Emma. I'm an insomniac. I'm a misanthrope. I like imaginary people better than real ones. I haven't folded laundry in, like, four years. This isn't a rejection for you. It's a lucky escape."

What was he doing? Trying to argue me out of liking him?

None of those things were deal-breakers, but okay.

None of those things were deal-breakers . . . but maybe *the fact that he was listing them* was. How fully, incontrovertibly, utterly uninterested in me must he be to construct a whole case against himself like that—to my face?

I took a five-point-five-second breath.

"Okay," I said, nodding.

"Okay, what?"

"Okay, I get it."

"You do?"

I nodded. "You really don't like me." I nodded some more. "I'll stop bothering you. I got carried away. I've never had a writing partner before. Or lived with a guy. I must have"—and here I quoted him again—"connected dots that didn't need or want to be connected."

Charlie glanced away.

"I kept thinking we must be having a misunderstanding. But there is no misunderstanding. Is that right?"

Charlie nodded and met my eyes again. "There is no misunderstanding."

"You know I like you, and you know I am *propositioning* you," I said. "And any feeling I keep having that you like me, too, is just wishful thinking bending my perceptions—because you are clearly, plainly saying no."

Charlie nodded, like he was really sorry about it.

Then he said, "I am clearly, plainly saying no."

Twenty-Seven

I NEVER GOT the chance to wake up—as I should've—just *marinating* in humiliation.

I never got the chance to open my eyes and feel horrified beyond description that I had drunkenly fallen off of Charlie Yates's high dive, and then drunkenly forced him to rescue me, and then drunkenly tried to coerce him—a man who was clearly *so not interested*—into bed.

It was enough to keep my head churning shame like butter for years.

But there was no time to even begin.

Because before my alarm went off, I got a call from Sylvie.

Not one of her fun FaceTime calls. A real, old-fashioned, middle-of-the-night emergency call.

At three thirty A.M.

"Sylvie?" I said, as I fumbled with the phone in the dark.

"It's Dad," she said, and the panic in her voice told me everything. "He fell down the stairs."

"Which stairs?"

"To our apartment."

"The *concrete* stairs?"

"He's in the ICU right now. He won't wake up. It's bad."

"How bad?" I demanded.

"Emma. You need to come home."

My mind ground like it was in first gear on the freeway. "Okay," I said. "I'll—I'll change my ticket."

"No," Sylvie said. "There's no time. Send me your flight info. Salvador's mom works for Southwest."

"Okay, okay," I said, opening my laptop and looking for the confirmation email. I forwarded it, and then I said, "Done. Now what?"

"Now go to the airport," Sylvie said. "Right now."

I DIDN'T EVEN shower—or change out of Charlie's WRITERS DO IT ON THE PAGE sweatshirt. I brushed my teeth, raked my hair into its pom-pom, stuffed everything I owned into my suitcase and still-broken rolling carry-on, ordered an Uber, and left.

No time for a note, even.

Charlie was still asleep, of course.

As I climbed into the back of the Uber, Sylvie was calling me with an update. "We got the flight switched," she said. "How fast can you get there?"

"How fast can we get to the airport?" I asked the driver.

"Hour and fifteen," he said, "on a good day."

"This flight's at six," Sylvie said.

"That's not enough time," I said.

"Just try," Sylvie said. "There's not another open seat until the red-eye."

She did not say, *And by then it might be too late.*

Then, feeling semi-ridiculous, I said to the driver, "I'm so sorry, but do you happen to know any shortcuts for getting there faster?"

He kept his eyes on the road. "Not really."

"I'm cutting it very close for my flight," I said, like we might team up for a Formula One–style race against the clock.

"They know you're coming," Sylvie said. "Maybe they'll hold the plane for you."

"Airlines don't hold planes for people, Sylvie," I said. "They have regulations. And rules. And requirements. And other passengers!"

"But maybe," Sylvie went on, unfazed by reality, "given the whole situation—"

"What *is* the whole situation? I have no idea what's going on."

Now that we had a minute, Sylvie took a deep breath. "He had a drop attack on the apartment stairs and took a very hard fall."

"He knows not to take those stairs!" I said in protest.

"The elevator was out of service," Sylvie said. "He must have thought, *It's only one flight.* He must have thought, *What are the odds?* But it happened. He fell all the way to the landing. His face is all cut up and swollen, and he had to get stitches on his forehead, and he doesn't even look like himself. I took a picture at the ER, but I can't even bring myself to send it to you. If I could unsee it, I would." Sylvie's breath sounded ragged. "He lost consciousness when he hit the landing, and he hasn't woken up. Mrs. Otsuka's seven-year-old grandson called 911 right away, and they stayed with him the whole time."

"The *seven-year-old grandson* called 911?"

"He's very mature."

I sent a silent thank-you to Mrs. Otsuka's grandson.

Sylvie went on. "The scan of Dad's brain showed a subdural hematoma, which is bleeding between the brain and the skull. But the skull doesn't have any give. So when bleeds happen there, there's nowhere for the blood to go. If the pressure builds up too much, it can cause brain damage or even death."

"How bad is Dad's bleed?"

"It's . . ." Sylvie hesitated. "It's not good. They showed us the CAT scan of his brain, and the blood is pushing his entire brain off-center. I mean, the doctor circled the pool of blood on the image with his pen and said, 'This is the blood,' and I was like, 'Dude, even I can see that.'"

"So what do they do? How do they get it out of there?"

"Surgery," Sylvie said, giving the short answer. "He's in right now. Basically, as soon as they saw the scan, they rushed him to the OR. It's called"—I heard paper flipping like she was checking her notes—"a 'burr hole.'" Now she sounded like she was reading: "They drill a small hole in the skull to siphon out the blood."

"He's in emergency surgery right now?"

"There wasn't time to wait."

"Are you in the waiting room?"

"I stepped outside. Salvador says that thing about cell phones messing with hospital equipment is real."

I had so many questions, I didn't know where to start. The biggest, loudest question, of course, was *Will Dad be okay?*

But Sylvie didn't have the answer to that question.

So I went with the next one that came to mind: "Why was it Mrs. Otsuka's grandson?"

"What?" Sylvie asked.

"Why was Mrs. Otsuka's grandson the one who called 911—not you or Salvador?"

A weird pause.

"Sylvie?"

Then a quiet answer. "Because we . . . weren't home."

"What!" I shouted—so loud the driver swerved. Then, quieter: "Where were you?"

"We were at the beach," Sylvie said. "On a date."

Worse and worse.

It's pretty rare for me to be totally speechless. But I was.

When I finally found some words, all I could do was repeat: "You were *at the beach*? On a *date*?"

At that, Sylvie burst into tears—her voice thick and trembling. "Dad *told* us to go! He *insisted* we go! He practically forced us!"

"So you left his life *in the hands of a seven-year-old*?"

Sylvie couldn't deny it.

I went on. "You can't go to the beach when you're Dad's caregiver!

You can't go *anywhere*! Why do you think I haven't had any fun in ten years? Do you think I just have a bad personality? That I don't like fun? What part of all the medicines and the charts and the hemiplegia and the five books I handed you on Ménière's disease gave you the idea that you could just take off for the beach? Would you like to know how many times I went to the beach in all these years? Zero! Zero times! You've been at it six weeks—and you decided to just *take a vacation*?"

"We weren't taking a vacation," Sylvie said. "We were getting engaged."

I stopped.

Then I said, "Engaged? Like, to be married?"

"To be married," Sylvie confirmed. "Salvador asked Dad's permission last week, and then the two of them cooked up this whole scheme—and they were so excited about it. Totally in cahoots. And Dad was having so much fun and really bonding—not that they needed to bond. They're already like BFFs. Dad's teaching Salvador how to play the harmonica, and they've set up a dartboard in the living room—"

"That can't be a good idea—"

"—and Salvador loves Dad, and he's so good at looking after people—just such a nurturer—and so he's got this whole dream for us that we'll get married and build our lives around Dad, and family, and being the best caregivers ever, and so that's what we were trying to do: just take another step forward into our lives together and making it all happen."

"And then you went to the beach," I said, in a tone that clearly sounded much more like *And then you killed our dad.*

Which—granted—was maybe a bit harsh.

Sylvie descended into sobs.

But I didn't care.

For maybe the first time ever, I wasn't on Sylvie's side first.

I wanted to empathize with her, I really did.

Objectively, their little fantasy was lovely. Who wouldn't get excited about building a little health-and-wellness-themed life with Salvador—

kids running around and trips to the farmers market and cutting-edge therapies to help our dad live his best possible life?

In another frame of mind, I might have jumped on board, too.

But as it was—in traffic while rushing to the airport with our dad in emergency surgery, still wearing Charlie's humiliating fleece-lined sweatshirt—I was having trouble accentuating the positive. All I could see in Sylvie and Salvador's plan was selfishness. Selfishness and hubris. They wanted to *go to the beach*? How dare they?

Didn't they know that if there was some way to make life with Dad *charming and delightful* I would have found it already?

"You left him," I said, feeling a howl in my chest that I now recognize as ten years of unspoken resentment. "To go to the beach! And he fell down the stairs. And now he's on the brink of death getting a hole drilled in his head. That's all there is to it. Did you think what I've been doing all these years was easy? Did you think I just hadn't been creative enough in my approach? Did you think I didn't go to the beach because I didn't want to?"

Sylvie didn't answer.

"I *love* the damn beach!" I half shouted.

Sylvie was still crying, but I didn't care.

"I would've given *anything* to go to the beach! But I didn't! Because I knew that I—I alone—was the only thing standing between the only parent we've got left and this exact situation! You knew that, too. You couldn't have not known. But I must've ruined you. I killed myself to give you everything you ever wanted and I guess I taught you that's how life is. But I was lying the whole time. That's the opposite of how life is. You don't get everything you want! You get a few tiny, broken pieces of what you thought you wanted and you tell yourself over and over it's more than enough!"

"I'm sorry," Sylvie whispered.

But I was revved up now. "It's so tempting to blame myself," I went on. "That I set you up for failing me by never asking you to sacrifice anything or think about anyone else, *ever*, other than yourself.

I'm so tempted to say *That's on me*, like I always do. But you know what, Sylvie? This one is really on you. This wasn't complicated. This wasn't confusing. You were told what to do! Never let Dad out of your sight! Simple! Not *easy*, but simple! I did it day in and day out for ten years—and all I needed from you was six pathetic weeks. But I guess I can't have them. You can give up your internship and act all self-sacrificing and do this grand gesture of telling me to go off and live my dreams—but if you can't do the job right, then I can't really do it, can I? If you leave Dad alone and he winds up in the ICU and I have to race home to Texas at the crack of dawn without even telling Charlie what happened and I wind up breaching our contract and not even getting paid—that's the same thing as not letting me go at all!"

But as soon as I heard those words, I had to correct them. "No! Wait!" I went on, my voice starting to tremble. "It's *worse*! Because you got my hopes up. And it's so much more agonizing to hope for something and not get it than to never even hope at all."

"I'm sorry," Sylvie rasped out.

But I was so angry I didn't care. "I don't even know what to do right now," I said. "But I know one thing for sure. If Dad dies? If your *trip to the beach* kills our father? You will never see me again—guaranteed."

But I guess Sylvie had had enough of being called a murderer for now.

There was a funny half pause. And then Sylvie said, "If my trip to the beach kills our father," Sylvie said, "we'll be even. Because your trip to the mountains killed our mom."

"OOF," THE UBER driver said as the line went dead. "That was harsh."

Guess we'd been on speaker. And in the long, disconnected silence that followed, I wondered if I'd ever forgive her.

Even with family—people you're presumably trapped with for life—there are deal-breakers. I'd loved Sylvie all her life unconditionally. But

I guess there were some conditions I hadn't thought of. Because I never could have even imagined her saying what she just said.

But she'd said it. She spoke my worst fear about my life out loud.

And now I wanted to punish her by never speaking to her again.

I let that stand as my tentative plan: We were done—forever.

But I also gave myself permission to recant. Because yes, cutting Sylvie off forever would punish her. But it would punish me, too.

I was mulling that over when the driver hit the brakes so hard that my phone flew off my lap and smacked the seat back in front of me— and then we came to a full stop on the highway. A full stop at the start of what looked like miles and miles of traffic ahead.

"What's going on?" I asked.

"Looks like some traffic," he said.

"I see that," I said. "But what's causing it?"

"Not sure," he said.

"Don't you have . . ." I started, but then I wasn't sure what he might have. "A walkie-talkie or something?"

"A *walkie-talkie*?" he asked, giving me a look in the mirror.

"Or—some way to get the inside scoop?"

He shook his head as we both looked at all the red, glowing brake lights. "This is the only scoop I've got."

"Is there—some way around it?"

The driver scratched his ear. "Probably not."

"Can we drive on the shoulder or something?"

"That's illegal," he said, like *Case closed.*

"I have to get to the airport," I said. "Urgently. My flight takes off in less than an hour."

He sucked in a judgmental hiss. "That's really cutting it close."

"Yes," I said, like *I know.* "I have an emergency. A medical emergency."

Why was I explaining all this? He was just as powerless as I was.

"It'll probably clear up soon," the driver said then, like that might cheer me up.

But it didn't.

We made it to the airport with twenty minutes until takeoff, and
my flight was already boarding. I got my boarding pass, checked the
suitcase, and took off running at a full sprint, dragging my squealing
carry-on behind me, for the TSA line.

When I got there, the first line—to show your ID—wasn't too bad.
But the second line—to get scanned—was worse than the freeway traffic.
An infinite number of miserable people and squirming children, coughing and staring into dead space in a purgatory-like queue that seemed to
fold endlessly in on itself like an Escher drawing.

I'd never make it.

But what else was there to do? I got in line.

And then I took off my shoes. Like being five seconds ahead of the
game might make the difference.

And then I waited in line to wait in the next line.

I craned my neck around the endless room for someone who looked
official—someone human I could talk to. Someone who might—bless
them—solve all, or even *any*, of my problems.

But in this giant, overflowing room of people, no one seemed human, somehow.

My hope was eclipsing.

I was going to miss this flight. And then not get home until late tonight. And by then—and I hated myself for even having this thought—it
might be too late.

I was panting—hyperventilating, really. How long was a breath
supposed to be? Five-point-five seconds? I couldn't even make it to
one.

My father might be dying—and that was the only thing that mattered.

But all around that one solitary horror was a cacophony of other
losses: I was bruised where I'd hit the pool water, I was hungover, I was
still wearing Charlie's sweatshirt. I was alone in a feedlot of soulless travelers with a broken bag and no chance to make my flight. I'd broken my
contract with Charlie, and given up all the money I'd worked so hard
for, not to mention any chance I had of reaching my potential. My baby
sister whom I'd sacrificed everything for had just said the meanest thing

anyone had ever said to me, besides myself, and I was so incandescently angry that I couldn't imagine ever feeling anything but anger again. And I was still cringing in shame at the memory of begging my writing hero and desperate crush to take me to bed . . . and receiving the hardest of hard passes.

That's when the tears came.

Are tears supposed to make things better?

Because these definitely made things worse.

People started turning around to look at me. Children started pointing. A teenager lifted her phone and took a video. And *no one* offered to help.

Not that there was any help to offer.

This was the real world. This wasn't some Richard Scarry picture book of police dogs riding motorcycles. Mister Rogers wasn't going to step out from behind a kiosk with his zippered cardigan and help me out.

I already knew how this would end.

I'd miss my flight. No one would care. And all that perky, chirpy, optimism-themed nonsense I'd always clung to would come back to bite me in my contemptibly naive ass.

BY THE TIME I made it to the ID check, my diaphragm was absolutely spasming with sobs. Still, I stepped up to the booth at my turn—still barefoot—and slid my ID through the window. A lady agent picked it up and peered at it. Then she peered at me. Then she grabbed her handheld radio, pressed a button, and said into the receiver, "TSA to command. Requesting the supervisor."

Oh, no. No, no. I didn't have time for a supervisor. Was my license expired? Had I broken some unknown rule? Was sobbing in the TSA line a security red flag?

"I'm sorry—" I started, but she held up a finger to quiet me.

Was I in trouble?

I didn't have room for any more trouble today. I was over capacity as it was.

A stocky Black TSA officer with no-nonsense dad energy showed up, and the agent held out my ID for him to inspect.

"Emma Wheeler?" he asked, comparing me to the license photo. "Flight 2401 to Houston?"

"Yes, sir," I said.

"I'm the supervisor. Please come with me."

"Sir, I'm—I'm very late for my flight. They're taking off any minute—"

But he was already walking away.

I had no choice but to follow, my bare feet slapping along the industrial floor and the squealing wheels of my carry-on bewailing our plight.

We rounded the mosh pit of travelers, and he took me to a room with an AUTHORIZED PERSONNEL ONLY sign.

This couldn't be good.

I'd managed to snuff out my active bawling on the walk over, but now I wondered if I'd have to start up again. Had things just gone from bad to worse?

But once we stepped inside, I saw a bag scanner there, with a female agent standing at attention behind it. Once the supervisor closed the door behind me, he put my carry-on on the conveyor belt. Then he ushered me to stand on a spot marked with two footprints, requested I hold my arms out, and while he checked me with the wand, said, "We got a call from Southwest. The pilot's holding your plane."

Did I just hear that? "He's—what?"

The supervisor did not choose to help me with my verbal double take. He went on, "But he can't hold it long. No longer than time he can make up in-flight."

I was still back at: "The pilot is holding the plane?"

"So once you're clear," he went on, "I'm going to need you to run to the gate."

Run to the gate? My brain tried to catch up.

"Got it?" he asked, standing straight to meet my eyes. "When I say run, I mean 'sprint.'"

I wasn't sure. But I said, "*Sprint.* Got it."

"It's Gate 30, at the farthest end of the concourse," he said. "So I hope you're in shape."

"I hope I am, too," I said.

The female agent handed me my bag, and the supervisor opened a far door on the concourse side, and as I passed through it, I met his eyes and said, "Thank you, sir"—hoping he could see how very much I meant it.

"You're welcome," the supervisor said, with a voice so gruff it verged on tender. Then he said, "Now get moving."

So I did. I clutched my shoes to my chest, clamped a death grip onto my banshee of a carry-on, and sprinted.

Barefoot.

Past the Brookstone and the Dunkin' Donuts and the Starbucks. Past burger joints and taquerias, bookstores and duty free, fast food and hipster bars—dodging my way around strolling passengers and moms with toddlers and grandparents in wheelchairs. My legs pumping, the soles of my feet slapping, my breath tearing in and out of my lungs— and my screeching wheel turning every head I passed.

The first thing I saw as I approached the gate, gasping like a person who'd forgotten how breathing worked—was the digital sign with my flight number and the word DEPARTED.

I slowed.

Did I miss it?

Did I run this far this hard—and miss it?

But that's when I saw a pilot—straight out of Central Casting, with a salt-and-pepper mustache, a crisp white shirt with epaulets, and a captain's hat—round the gate kiosk and take an at-ease position to wait for me.

I picked my speed back up, and as I got closer, he said, "Emma Wheeler?"

There was nowhere near enough air in my lungs for talking, but I forced out, "That's me."

The captain nodded and said, "Let's get you on board."

"Thank you so much, sir. I thought for sure I was too late."

He looked up at the DEPARTED sign, and then glanced out at the waiting plane on the runway. Then he passed my scourge of a carry-on bag to a waiting gate agent, gave me a nod, and said, "They weren't taking off without me. And I wasn't taking off without you."

Twenty-Eight

MY FATHER DIDN'T die.

Maybe that's a spoiler—but we've all been through a lot so far. If you were anywhere near as worried as I was, I thought you might need some good news as soon as possible.

The surgery was successful, and once the pressure in his skull was relieved, he made a brisk recovery—all things considered. All signs indicated he'd be back to his old self in fairly good time. Or as much of his old self as he could be with a hole in his head.

We owed it all to Mrs. Otsuka's grandson's quick thinking and calm presence of mind.

What a blessing of a next-door neighbor.

If they hadn't shown up when they did—if we'd lost any more time than we had—I might be telling a very different story.

I said this to my dad over Jell-O in his room that evening, when he'd been out of recovery several hours. Sylvie was in the room, too, and I averted my eyes from her presence so relentlessly that she finally excused herself to go look for a cup of coffee.

My dad's sweet face was bruised and swollen and cut, and his head was bandaged and partially shaved, and it was hard to look him in the face. Instead I just kept squeezing his hand and thinking about how I'd know it anywhere.

He had a fuzzy blue blanket Salvador had brought from home on his lap, and he said, "I'm so sorry I scared you, sweetheart."

"Thank god Mrs. Otsuka found you."

"Mrs. Otsuka didn't find me, she was *with* me."

"I thought she discovered you just after you fell."

My dad shook his head. "She was beside me when I fell. We were taking the stairs together."

This seemed like a pretty fine point, but okay.

"You know those bedraggled teachers on the first floor who have eight kids?"

"I think they have *three* kids—but okay."

"Kenji was with us because we were dropping him off to watch cartoons at their place for the evening while we went for a bite of dinner."

I nodded agreeably, like that was a pleasant but not super-relevant detail.

But then my dad gave me a funny little smile that flipped all the lights on in my brain.

"Wait!" I gasped—raising both hands to my mouth. "Were you—?"

My dad didn't say anything, but his eyes twinkled.

"Hold on! You're saying—?"

This time, a pleased-with-himself shrug.

"You?" I asked. "And Mrs. Otsuka?"

My dad tapped his nose, like *Bingo.*

"You were going on a *date*?" I asked. "With each other?"

"Yep."

"You're dating? You're, like, boyfriend-and-girlfriend?"

"More like late-in-life companions," he said, "but that's the basic gist."

"When did this happen?"

My dad kept wrestling with insuppressible smiles. "Well," he said, "you know. She lost her husband a few years back."

"Yes," I said. "I know." Then, for proof: "Mr. Otsuka."

"Exactly," my dad said. "And ever since then—over a respectful time frame, of course—we just kind of developed a little flirtation."

The pieces snapped together in my mind. "Is that why you've been teaching Kenji how to play the harmonica?"

"He's been a little homesick."

"And that's why she kept having everyone over for dinner?"

"She's a phenomenal cook."

"And that's why she kept stopping by with flowers from the community garden?"

Now the smile he'd been suppressing broke through. "It's not her fault," he said. "I'm just so irresistible."

"Dad!" I said, nodding. "I'm very impressed."

"Still got it," he said, with a little wink.

"I love this for you," I said. And I did.

"You know what I keep thinking?" my dad said then.

"What?"

"Your mom would love her."

My eyes sprung with tears.

Then he added, "And Kenji, too. He's a great kid. He wants to be a magician."

"She would love them both," I said. "And she'd be happy for you."

"I think so, too," my dad said, nodding like he'd given it some thought. "Good people have to stick together."

IT'S HARD TO maintain the silent treatment with your sister when you're the joint guardians of a parent in the ICU, but I was up to the challenge.

I directed all my questions to Salvador, like he was my translator, and whenever Sylvie was in the room, I averted my eyes. Through Salvador, we agreed to trade off nights at the hospital until our dad was ready to transfer to rehab. I insisted on taking the first shift that first night—still unshowered, and still in my WRITERS DO IT ON THE PAGE ensemble, which allowed me to extend the enjoyable feeling of having been wronged. Not only was Sylvie guilty of attempted patricide *and* saying the meanest-thing-ever to me, she *also* wouldn't let me go home to take a shower.

What a monster.

The next day, after Sylvie relieved me of my shift, I was heading home to change clothes after more hours than I cared to count, when I arrived at our apartment door to see someone sitting beside it, elbows resting on knees, head bent, like he'd been there a while.

Charlie.

As soon as he saw me, he scrambled to his feet and came as close to me as he dared, an intense, just-flew-to-Texas-without-telling-you-and-showed-up-on-your-doorstep expression on his face.

My first horrified thought was that I was still wearing his ridiculous sweatshirt. And I hadn't showered. And I still had no underwear on. And my hair probably looked like I'd been electrocuted.

How humiliating.

But my second, more forceful thought was: *Wait a minute. Who cares?*

"Hey," Charlie said then, with a little wave like he was striking up a conversation.

We were *not* striking up a conversation. "What are you doing here, Charlie?"

He looked at me like there were a hundred things he desperately wanted to say—but he couldn't say any of them. He hadn't shaved. His hair was mussed at its maximum level. He was also—I now realized—still wearing his same sweats from the last time we saw each other.

It was a basic question, but he couldn't answer.

It's kind of excruciating to watch words fail a writer.

But I let it play out.

Finally, Charlie bent down to unzip the backpack by his feet. He rifled through it, pulling out my strawberry hoodie. Then he stood and stepped closer.

"You forgot this," he said, handing it to me.

Why was the sight of that red, fuzzy old friend so comforting? I took it, of course. But I said, "You came here to bring me my lucky hoodie?"

"I thought you might want it."

He thought I might want it? So he flew halfway across the country? Wasn't that why they invented FedEx?

"Why are you really here, Charlie?" I asked.

"When I woke up and found the house empty, I thought you'd left. *Left* left—for real. But then I heard from Logan about your dad."

"I meant to text you," I said—trying to stay explanatory instead of apologetic—"but things have been really crazy."

"Of course—of course," Charlie said. "I get it. I was just worried about you."

"You were worried about me, so you flew to Texas?"

Charlie nodded, like *Yeah*. "You weren't answering your phone."

Of course not. "I was at the hospital."

"How is your dad?"

"He's fine," I said. Depending on how you defined *fine*. But that was my story, and I was sticking to it. "He's fine, I'm fine, everybody's fine," I said. Then: "I don't understand why you're here."

"I just wanted to—check in."

"Ah," I said, in a tone like flying halfway across the country to check in like this was patently bananas. "Well, then. Mission accomplished."

"More than that," Charlie corrected. "I wanted to comfort you."

"Comfort me?"

Charlie nodded.

"You can't."

Charlie frowned. "I can't? That's it?"

I shrugged. "That's it."

"But you're having a tough time," Charlie said.

"I'm aware of that."

"I can't just let you go through all this alone."

"Sure you can."

"But," Charlie said, "I don't want to."

"Look," I said, too tired to help him work through his thoughts on this—but somehow forced to do it, anyway. "I said I liked you, and you said no. I blatantly propositioned you, and you said no. At every chance, you've made it clear that you want to remain work colleagues *at best* with me. That's fine. I'm not fighting you. But work colleagues *work* together. They aren't friends, and they aren't confidants—and they sure as hell don't fly across the country to bring each other sweatshirts. We're not in a relationship where we fly anywhere for each other. And we're not in a relationship like that"—I paused for effect—"because *that's the way you wanted it.*"

"But that was before your dad got sick."

"Why does that change things?"

"I don't want to not be there for you."

"That's a heck of a double negative."

"I hate the thought that you're suffering."

"People suffer all the time, Charlie."

"But it's *you*," he said, like I was something special.

"Sure. Fine. It's me."

"There has to be something I can do."

"Yes," I said. "You can leave."

But Charlie shook his head at that. "I can't. I don't think I can."

I met his eyes. "You have to."

"But don't you—need someone right now?"

"Of course! Obviously! Anyone—and everyone! Just not you."

Charlie frowned, like that made no sense. "Why isn't *someone* better than *no one*?"

I sighed. Did I really have to explain this, too?

Apparently so.

"I really liked you," I said. "And you hard-core rejected me. So seeing you doesn't make me feel better. It makes me feel *worse.*"

I watched the understanding overtake him.

"There's nothing I can do for you." Charlie said, trying on that idea for size.

"Nothing," I confirmed.

"Nothing," Charlie agreed. "Not even"—and here he cringed a little, anticipating my answer—"a hug?"

I gave him a look. "To quote a famous writer we both know: 'Absolutely not. No way in hell.'"

Charlie nodded, like *Got it*.

But he was still lingering there. Like despite it all, he couldn't bear to leave.

To be honest, I lingered, too.

Would I have liked Charlie to stay? Could I have used that hug? Was I tempted beyond description to just bring him inside and swaddle myself in his arms? Did I wish like hell that I could still feel about him the way I did before I knew how he felt about me?

All yes.

But there was no misunderstanding. I had fully, unabashedly offered myself to him, and he had clearly, plainly said no.

"The only thing you can do for me," I said then, "is to get out of my sight and stay there."

AND SO CHARLIE left.

He left, and I got back to my life.

Almost—*almost*—as if those surreal weeks in LA had never happened.

Back at home, in our apartment, with my dad to look after, and Sylvie to ignore, and Salvador still living with us (now banished to the couch), and a whole new relationship to begin with Mrs. Otsuka, I was able to keep busy.

LA started to feel more like something I'd dreamed.

My dad spent a full ten days in the hospital, and—*yes*, I can hear how odd this sounds—it was a surprisingly pleasant time. That hospital was really a remarkable place. We got a surprise upgrade to a VIP room, for example, because my dad's surgery was the ten-thousandth one they'd performed. And that room was part of some ongoing study about the impact of foliage on surgery outcomes, and so his windowsill was filled edge to edge with jade plants, and aloe vera, and bromeliads and prayer plants. Not to mention a gorgeous leafy shrublike beauty that exactly matched the fabric of Sylvie's tropical maxi dress called *Monstera deliciosa*.

They asked us to keep them watered, so I got a little misting bottle and made one of my signature sticker charts.

And I guess this is VIP life, but the nurse's station brought in astonishing, delicious food for lunch every day and insisted that we share with them. "It's too much," they insisted. "It'll go to waste." And so we were forced out of politeness to down steaming bowls of gourmet ramen, crunchy catfish po'boys, juicy gourmet burgers, gyros dripping with aioli.

I'm telling you, this hospital ward ate like takeout food *royalty*.

"Isn't this expensive?" I kept asking.

"It's the administrators." The nurses would shrug. "They pamper us so bad."

And who was I to argue?

My dad and I had spent a hell of a lot of time in various hospitals over the years. I could describe some of them down to the ceiling tiles. But we'd never seen anything like this before. Plants? In a hospital room? Free-roaming massage therapists in the hallways? Ice cream delivery on a three-wheeled scooter?

Insane.

But we sure as heck weren't complaining.

Mrs. Otsuka stayed for hours every day, fussing over my dad, and reading to him from his new book on Norse mythology, while Kenji and I made origami animals to put on the shelves among the plants—frogs, foxes, whales, pigs. He had a whole zoo's worth memorized, and he patiently walked me through the folds—his turning out like something you'd see in an instructional tutorial, and mine a bit more like wadded-up gum wrappers.

Even still, he kept saying, "You're definitely getting it," and I let myself feel encouraged—though I didn't care too much about being terrible at origami. What I cared about was the companionable feeling that sitting together making things gave me. Comforting in the way that having a project with someone is comforting. Safe in the way that gathering with others always makes you feel safe. The way that being together was just, on some fundamental level, always better than being alone.

It was the most family-like vibe I'd felt in years.

Not to mention, there are conversations that happen sometimes when you're waiting around that would never happen if you were just scurrying from errand to errand like we all do most of the time. There are conversations that can happen only after waiting has slowed things down.

One night, late, after a nurse had checked my dad's surgical dressing and his vitals and then left the two of us alone, I had the bright idea to show my dad the video of us that Logan had sent to Charlie, way back when all this started. I thought at first that we'd find it funny, and we did—me and my dad doing our handstands, Sylvie's little chipmunk voice, my mom scolding Logan—but by the time we'd finished laughing, all we were left with was tears.

"I'm sorry," I said, as we both pawed at our cheeks. "Maybe that was better left unexcavated."

"No, no," my dad said, his chin still trembling a bit. "I'm glad I got to see it."

I put my phone away.

Next, my dad reached up to touch the bandage on his head. "This wasn't Sylvie's fault, you know."

He was looking for emphatic agreement. But . . . I mean, it kind of *was*.

When I didn't answer, he turned to meet my eyes.

"It wasn't her fault," he said, leaning forward a bit for my full attention, "any more than the rockfall was yours."

My eyes stung at that, and I looked down at my lap.

"Things happen, Emma," my dad said, reaching for my hand. "Nobody can see the future."

I kept my eyes down. "But—" I said. I felt a tightness rising in my throat, and then, without, of course, needing to specify who *she* was, I spoke out loud the one little sentence that had been haunting me in whispers for ten years: "But she wanted to go to the beach."

This was the thought that woke me in the night. If I hadn't been selfish—if I'd just given my mom what *she* wanted instead of being all about me—she'd have been on a striped beach towel with a book at the shore a thousand miles away on the day that rockfall happened. She'd have been nowhere even close. Our lives would've continued blithely on. Everything would've been different.

She wanted to go to the beach.

My dad squeezed my hand.

"I want to ask for your forgiveness," I said to my dad then.

He looked at me. "You can't have it."

"What?"

"I won't forgive you," he said. "You only forgive people who've done something wrong." He tugged my hand a little closer and shook his head at me. "Emma. *You never did anything wrong.*"

But I argued with him. "Sylvie said I killed her." Was I trying to get her in trouble?

"When did she say that?"

"As I was racing to the airport."

My dad studied me. "And you're going to hold her to it, huh?"

He had a point. Was I going to clutch onto something mean she'd said in a moment of panic forever? What would be the point? It didn't seem like a choice that would benefit anyone. And yet: She'd said it, and I'd heard it.

I wasn't sure where to go from there.

I lowered my voice. "She's not wrong, though." And then I said the thing we'd all been thinking all along. "I wanted to go rock climbing. I *insisted* on going. If it hadn't been for me, we'd have been nowhere near that rockfall. If it hadn't been for me, she wouldn't have died."

But maybe it wasn't the thing we'd all been thinking—because my dad sighed like he couldn't even follow my reasoning. "That makes no sense, Emma," he said. "Mom could have gone to the beach instead and drowned in a riptide. Or been run over by a drunk driver on the sea-wall. Or hit by a stray firecracker. Or bitten by a snake near the dunes."

I frowned.

"There is absolutely no way to predict the infinite random forces in the world any of our choices will expose us to. How paralyzing would it be to even try?"

And then there was a seismic shift—for both of us—in our thinking about me.

Was that what I'd been doing? Trying desperately to predict the unpredictable and avoid the unavoidable? Was that why I'd been so willing—or, if I'm really honest, *relieved*—to stay home all this time? Had I decided in some place deep below my consciousness that the best way to avoid disaster was to just never do anything?

"You can't live like that, Em," my dad said.

I could have denied it, I guess. But it was late. And quiet. And we were already telling truths.

"I don't know how *not to*," I said.

He studied me. "I think California was a start. In more ways than one."

At that, I let down the bed railing so I could scoot closer and lean in to rest my head on my dad's chest. I could hear his heart beating a soothing rhythm, and I listened for a minute before I said, "How do you do it?"

"Do what?" my dad asked, his voice muffled through his ribs.

"How do you find a way to be okay?"

"Well," my dad said, frowning. "I had to be, didn't I?"

He squeezed my hand.

Then he said, "Things were very dark for me after Mom died. But I knew you and Sylvie needed me to find the light somehow."

"I didn't know things got dark for you. You always seemed . . . okay."

"It was my job to seem okay."

"You didn't want to talk to me about it?"

"You were a kid."

"Sylvie was a kid," I said. "I was—"

"A girl who'd just lost her mom."

Okay. That wasn't wrong.

"I decided that if I just held on, things would get better. I wasn't sure how much better, but better. And when you've seen *worse*, better is good enough."

"But how? How did you hold on?"

"I just got up every day, and went to bed every night, and tried to be a good person in between."

"That can't be all there is to it," I said.

My dad took a slow breath, and then he said, "Somewhere during that time, I got very lucky and I accidentally figured something out."

"What?"

"Whatever story you tell yourself about your life, that's the one that'll be true."

I lifted my head to give that idea my full attention.

My dad went on, "So if I say, 'This terrible thing happened, and it ruined my life'—then that's true. But if I say, 'This terrible thing happened, but, as crazy as it sounds, it made me better,' then *that's* what's true."

"You believe you're better? Since the rockfall?"

"I know I am," my dad said, with so much conviction I had to believe him. "I'm wiser, I'm kinder, I'm funnier, I'm more compassionate. I can play at least ten instruments one-handed." He held up his good hand for us both to look at. "I'm more aware of how fragile and precious it all is. I'm more thankful, too—for every little blessing. A ladybug on the windowsill. A succulent sprouting a flower. A pear so ripe it just dissolves into juicy sweetness in your mouth."

Maybe this wasn't polite, but I really wanted to understand him. "But don't you miss Mom?"

My dad gave me a sad smile. "I do. Of course. And would I give up *all* this personal growth to see her again for even an hour and just clamp her into my arms? In a second. But that's not a choice. All we have is what we have."

"I miss her, too," I whispered.

My dad squeezed my hand. "It's okay," he said then. "Here's another thing I accidentally figured out: happiness is always better with a little bit of sadness."

BY THE TIME my dad was in a pretty stable place with his postsurgical health, Sylvie and Salvador decided to make an announcement: they were getting married.

A surprise express elopement. In twenty-four hours. *In Dad's hospital room.*

"We're eloping," Salvador explained.

"But we're just doing it here," Sylvie added.

"We don't want to wait," Salvador said.

"We just want to start our lives together," Sylvie said.

"Sooner—not later."

Of course they did.

"Works for me," my dad said.

I wasn't sure if it worked for me. And I was just wondering if there were a way for me to call in sick to this particular family event . . . when Sylvie asked me to be her maid of honor.

"What?" I said, as she dragged me out of the room to the hallway.

"You have to let me apologize to you," Sylvie said then.

"You've already apologized like ten times."

"But you never accept it!"

She wasn't wrong.

That's when Sylvie burst into tears. "I don't know what else to do," she said now, her face getting blotchy and her voice starting to rasp. "I didn't mean to say it. I was just—I don't know—scared and exhausted and trying to defend myself. I don't think that. Nobody thinks that. It just popped into my head and I said it—more because it was mean than because it was true."

"Does that make it better?" I asked.

"I regretted the words even as I was saying them. There's no excuse. I don't know how to make it right. But I'm begging you to forgive me.

Please, please! You're my favorite person. You're my hero! Please tell me that I didn't ruin our relationship forever in one stupid moment."

I mean, I had figured I'd have to forgive her at some point. I just thought I'd give myself a few years.

But now she was suddenly getting married. Tomorrow. And if I didn't let this all go, we'd spend the rest of our lives knowing that I was mad at her *at her wedding*.

What choice did I have, really?

"Fine," I said. "I forgive you." And as soon as I said the words, I felt them.

Sylvie threw her arms around me.

"But if you ever say anything like that to me again, I'm moving to Alaska. And I'm taking Dad."

It was that easy.

Because she was the only baby sister I had.

Anyway, we had a sudden surprise wedding to plan.

It gave us a project, honestly. Twenty-four hours to hang some twinkle lights and fluff some tissue-paper roses. Mrs. Otsuka offered to make Sylvie's bouquet with zinnias from the community garden, and Sylvie cried and hugged her.

We got grocery-store cupcakes and sparkling cider and asked my dad to play "Here Comes the Bride" on his harmonica.

Sylvie wore the dress our mother had worn at our parents' wedding—not a wedding gown per se, but a simple white dress she'd loved—along with her favorite cowgirl boots. Salvador wore a ruby-red tux they'd found while thrifting. We got Dad a little tweed driving cap to cover his surgical dressing, and he put a gray jacket over his hospital gown and tied a silk scarf like an ascot. Kenji arrived in a little suit and clip-on tie with an origami flower pinned to his lapel for a boutonniere, and Mrs. Otsuka wore a salmon-colored pantsuit that was the exact color of love. And I let Sylvie put me in a chiffon bridesmaid's dress with bell sleeves she'd found for three dollars at the Salvation Army.

The hospital chaplain performed the ceremony—which was mercifully short and very sweet—and we lit a candle beside a photo of our mom on the hospital tray table. Our dad "walked" Sylvie down the aisle by joining the couple's two hands together. Sylvie and Salvador wrote their own vows, and read them aloud . . . and I didn't even judge them.

I just took the high road right past all those mixed metaphors and clichés.

Love is love, after all.

Even for nonwriters.

And as those two kids kissed each other and pledged an astonishing, gorgeous, hope-filled promise to take care of each other *for the rest of their lives* . . . even though I never cried at weddings, I wept like a deluge. I wept because it was all too much—but in the best way. I wept with gratitude and grief and joy all at once—and because my mom would have done the same, if only she could've been here. I wept because my sister had found a genuinely good-hearted man, and because Mrs. Otsuka sensed halfway through that my dad was thirsty and slipped over to bring him some water. I wept because there was nothing cuter than my dad in his jaunty little cap—smiling through his bruises like a man who'd never seen a day of sorrow. I wept because halfway through the vows, Kenji slid his hand into mine in that sweet, unselfconscious way that little boys do. I wept because the nurses were all weeping, and because it was such a miracle to have something to celebrate, and because we were at a wedding right now instead of a funeral. I wept for luck and for beauty and for kindness—and for the magic of being alive.

And then we had a dance party.

Right there in the hospital room.

It was all just starting to wind down when one of the nurses stepped out into the hallway—and started shrieking like a teenager at a Beatles concert.

And we all rushed out . . .

And I know you'll never believe me . . .

But there, looking around the empty nurses' station—in a pair of Levi's 501s and a T-shirt that could just as easily have been body paint—was Jack Stapleton.

The guy on the billboard outside the hospital. *That* Jack Stapleton.

I knew, like everybody knew, that Jack Stapleton lived on a ranch outside of town. And he had a well-publicized history of randomly showing up to serenade healthcare workers of all kinds in gratitude for the good work they do in the world. So it wasn't an utterly impossible coincidence.

No more impossible than other impossible things, anyway.

Jack Stapleton randomly showed up at my sister's last-minute hospital elopement. And then he stayed. He sang karaoke with every single person there, and he toasted the bride and groom, and he took a hundred selfies—even one with me.

He didn't seem to remember me, but it was fine.

He might not've been quite as starstruck to meet me that day in LA as I had been to meet him.

And then, after Jack Stapleton had taken off, leaving a trail of swooning nurses in his wake, and after Mrs. Otsuka had taken Kenji home for bedtime, and after the bride and groom had waved and hugged their way down the hallway . . . just as my dad was about to turn in for the night, he squeezed my hand.

"That was fun," he said. "Who's next?"

"Not it," I said.

"How's your writer doing?"

"He's fine," I said. And then amended: "I assume he's fine."

"Not still in touch with the writer?"

I shrugged. "He turned out to be disappointing."

My dad nodded. "Most people are."

"I liked him," I clarified. "But he didn't like me back."

My dad was appalled on my behalf. "Then he's much worse than disappointing! He's *a dolt.*"

I'd never really appreciated the world *dolt* before. "Thanks, Dad."

"We'll find you somebody good, sweetheart," my dad said.

"We definitely will," I said, not believing it at all.

And then my adorably out-of-touch-with-pop-culture dad gestured with his thumb at the door that Jack Stapleton had walked out of not fifteen minutes before and said, "How about that Jake Singleton guy? He's not bad looking. I think he's got a future."

Twenty-Nine

TWO WEEKS WENT by.

Sylvie and Salvador took a forty-eight-hour mini honeymoon on Galveston Island.

Kenji started a marine biology summer camp at the science museum.

My dad left the hospital for a stint at an inpatient physical therapy rehab to strengthen his limbs.

And I . . .

I didn't do much. I'd taken the summer off from teaching when I got the Charlie Yates gig. So, when I wasn't visiting and fussing over my dad . . . I binge-watched TV. I ate scoops of peanut butter straight out of the jar. I slumped by the window like an unwatered houseplant.

Any day now, I'd start figuring out my life. Any day, I'd start feeling better and come up with a future I could get excited about.

I was a little disappointed in myself, to be honest.

Was all this hopelessness really necessary?

I'd had an adventure. I'd seen a bit of the world. Experienced a little heartache. And now it was time to learn from it and move on.

But if I'm honest? Really honest? Honest in the way you can only be when you know for sure the person you're telling won't judge you?

(Don't judge me, by the way.)

I missed Charlie.

I knew it was pathetic. I knew it was indefensible. I knew that moping over a man who didn't appreciate me was ridiculous. I didn't *want* to miss him.

Wasn't that the number one rule of standing up for yourself?

Don't like people who don't like you.

It wasn't complicated, I told myself over and over.

It was just hard.

Because everything had been better with him somehow. Swimming had been more fun when he was sitting grumpily on the steps. Writing had been more fun when I was sparring with him about love. Grocery shopping had been more fun when he was making me watch him juggle oranges. He just . . . lit me up.

And I missed that light so much.

But I guess this was a teachable moment.

If you wait for other people to light you up, then I guess you're at the mercy of darkness.

I WAS LYING on the living room floor of our apartment, watching the ceiling fan blades spin and avoiding cleaning the bathroom, when I got a call from Logan.

"Are you sitting down?" Logan said.

"Even better," I said. "I am *lying* down."

"Brilliant," Logan said. "Brace yourself."

I flattened my arms against the floor. "I'm braced."

"Donna Cole," Logan said, "wants your screenplay."

I sat up. *My screenplay? What screenplay? "The Accidental Mermaid?*" I asked. I never even gave it to her.

"*The Rom-Commers,*" Logan said.

"Okay, there's been a mistake," I said. "I haven't written a screenplay called *The Rom-Commers*."

"Yes, you have."

"How? In my sleep? I'm telling you, I didn't."

"It's the one you wrote with Charlie."

"But that's not called *The Rom-Commers*. It's called—"

"He changed the title," Logan said.

"But—"

"And the plot."

"Apparently."

"Now," Logan said, "it's about two screenwriters who write a script together and fall wildly in love."

I ignored the funny flutter those words prompted in my chest. "That's crazy," I said—though, actually, it was kind of a great idea.

"And guess what?" Logan said. "It's good."

"Of course it is. It's Charlie Yates."

"Spoken like a person who called his last rom-com 'a crime against humanity.'"

"Everybody deserves a mulligan."

"I love your loyalty."

"Charlie Yates *the human* is complicated," I said. "But Charlie Yates *the writer* is the love of my life."

"You say that like they're not the same guy."

"When did he have time to do this?"

"After you kicked him out of Texas."

"That was fast."

"He's fast when he's obsessed," Logan said. "And thank you for your service, by the way."

"For my service?"

"You cured him of the yips."

Did I?

"He's the opposite of blocked now," Logan went on. Then, like he was reading a marquee: "Charlie Yates is back."

My heart stung at that. Charlie Yates was back.

"I'm sending it to you," Logan said. "Read it. You will lose your mind with joy. It's a love letter to fun. And to love. And to you, I think."

"It's definitely not a love letter to me," I said. "That much I know for sure."

"Guess who it's written by?"

"Is this a trick question?"

"Check your texts," Logan said.

A picture came in of a title page. There, in classic screenplay Courier font:

THE ROM-COMMERS

WRITTEN BY

EMMA WHEELER & CHARLIE YATES

"But I shouldn't have a credit," I said. "I was the ghostwriter."

"Stop talking," Logan advised. "Let yourself have this."

I stared at the photo.

"Charlie finished it and sent it to Donna Cole that same day, with a note that said, 'Present for you!'—and she texted him within the hour and said, 'I want it.'"

"She wants it?"

"And she wants to meet with you both. In LA. On Thursday."

"In LA?" I echoed. "On Thursday?"

Guess I was going to LA.

So much for never seeing Charlie again.

Thirty

THE MEETING IN LA with Donna Cole went very well.

And by "very well," I mean: I sat nervously in an original Mies van der Rohe chrome-and-leather chair next to Logan while an icon of modern filmmaking rhapsodized for an hour about a surprise screenplay I barely knew I'd written—and then offered me six figures to buy the rights.

That kind of "very well."

Her office was bigger than my family's entire apartment, by the way. And she had a Georgia O'Keeffe painting—an original painting, not a poster from a museum store—on the wall behind her desk. And she was terrifying.

Terrifying in the most fantastic way.

I didn't wind up seeing Charlie, though. Donna Cole is an exceptionally busy woman, and the only hole in her schedule happened to be just when Charlie was headed to the Biltmore hotel to receive a screenwriting award.

Another one. He was gonna need a bigger drawer.

Oh, well. So much for the crown braid, mani-pedi, and new moisturizer I'd invested in before leaving town. Not to mention the three different outfits I'd panic-bought—settling on a crisp blue shirtdress and some sandals that actually fit—for nothing.

His loss, I guess.

At the end of the meeting, as Donna was dismissing us, she gave a pretend pout: "I can't believe Charlie Yates picked getting another award over seeing me."

"Lunacy," Logan agreed, as Donna air-kissed him goodbye.

Then she turned her attention to me, and said, "Don't ever let Charlie write anything again without you."

"I'll see what I can do," I said, feeling like a liar.

Her assistant was waiting for her, but Donna stopped us at the door.

"I almost forgot," she said.

Logan and I turned back.

"It's not official, but we've got Jack Stapleton attached to star."

"Jack Stapleton?" I asked. "Attached? To star?"

Logan was smiling like this wasn't news to him.

"That was all Charlie," Donna said.

"But," I said, and this I'd learned from Charlie himself, "I thought only casting directors chose the actors for movies."

Donna gave a nod like *Of course* as she said, "Unless the writer and the star happen to be in cahoots."

"Are they?"

"Jack will do anything for Charlie," Donna said, nodding at Logan for confirmation. "Didn't he just go to a hospital in Texas to serenade an old man?"

Logan did not meet my eyes.

Donna was still trying to remember the details. "The man was very sick—just out of the ICU. And Charlie couldn't stop worrying about him, so Jack offered to pop in randomly—like he's famous for."

I looked at Logan.

He looked at Donna.

"And then," Donna went on, squinting at Logan, like he would probably know, "didn't he take the nurses aside afterward to say, 'Please take extra-special care of my dear friend'?"

Finally, Logan glanced my way. "Something like that," Logan answered. "Yeah."

THE SECOND WE were in Logan's car, I said, "Was she talking about my dad just now?"

Logan pretended to be busy with his seat belt.

"The old man in Texas? That had to be my dad, right?"

"I'm not at liberty to say," Logan said, starting the car.

"Logan," I said, dropping my voice. "You were *my* friend first."

Logan considered that as we pulled out of the garage. "Fine. Yes. He asked Jack to pop in and make it look random."

"Jack Stapleton didn't *pop in*. He can't *pop in* anywhere. It was total mayhem. One of the nurses fainted."

"Wouldn't you?"

"The point is, you're making it sound like it wasn't a big deal when it definitely *was* a big deal."

Logan nodded for a minute, and then he said, "Charlie wanted to look after you, but you sent him away."

"This is my fault now?"

"Look," Logan said. "Charlie agreed with you. He didn't think you should have to see his face, either. So he worked from behind the scenes."

"Worked to do what?"

Logan steeled himself to break a confidence. "To do nice things for you."

"Like what? What kind of nice things?"

"You know," Logan said. "Like upgrading your dad's room."

Now I turned to really look at him. "They said we won that upgrade! They were celebrating their ten-thousandth surgery."

"I can't believe you fell for that."

"He told the hospital to lie to us? And they just did it?"

"He also made a sizable donation."

This was an outrage. "He tricked us into being upgraded? I thought we'd won that VIP room randomly—like decent people."

"Also," Logan went on, "all those fancy lunches every day."

"That was Charlie? That wasn't just . . . life on the VIP wing?"

Logan shook his head. "That was all Charlie. He got a hotel room after you told him to get out of your sight, and he stayed close by until he knew your dad was okay."

"Why would he do that?"

"Why do you think?"

"I honestly have no idea."

"He also did the whole thing with the plants."

"The *plants*?" I demanded, like now this had gone too far.

"Why are you so mad about this? Those plant studies are real. Charlie can recite the statistics all day."

"It wasn't his place to do that stuff."

"It wasn't his place?"

"Yes," I said, doubling down. "That's totally inappropriate behavior. Would you secretly upgrade a work colleague's father to a VIP room?"

"If I were in love with her, I would."

I blinked. "He's not in love with me," I said. "He told me he wasn't."

But as we pulled up to the Biltmore valet, Logan just said, "I can't believe you fell for that, either."

I THOUGHT LOGAN was just dropping me off at the Biltmore, but as I got out—still a little dazed—he handed his keys to the valet.

"You're—coming in?" I asked.

Logan nodded. "I'm headed to the ballroom."

I frowned. "What's in the ballroom?"

Logan met my eyes. "Charlie."

"Oh," I said. "This is where the awards ceremony is?"

Logan nodded.

"Did you know Charlie would be here tonight when you booked a room for me in this hotel?"

Logan nodded again.

"Are you tricking me into going to the ceremony?" I asked.

"Not unless you want me to," Logan said.

"I don't want you to," I said.

"Even after finding out about the VIP upgrade?"

"I didn't ask him to do that," I said. "I asked him to leave me alone."

"You should come with me," Logan said, gesturing at the ballroom. "It would mean a lot to Charlie."

I flared my nostrils. "Charlie doesn't care about me—or awards. Don't you know he keeps them all in a drawer?"

"Yeah. But that's only because he smashed the glass-front antique he used to keep them in."

"What do you mean, *smashed* it?"

"He pushed it over, and it shattered," Logan said. "On the night his wife left him."

I took that in.

"He does care about those awards," Logan said. "And he cares about you, too, by the way."

But it all felt like too much. "I'm going to pass."

Logan nodded, like *Fair enough*. Then he said, "I'm going to send you a three-minute video now, and I want you to watch it right away."

Logan had a checkered past with sending videos. "What kind of video?"

"A video that I wanted to send sooner."

"That's not really an answer."

"I don't actually have permission to send it even now," Logan said.

"That's never stopped you before."

Logan ignored me. "It's got some information on it I think you should have. I've been hesitating, with your dad being sick. I know you're going through a lot. But I think you'd rather know than not know."

"I'd rather know than not know what?"

"It's a video for you. *To* you. From Charlie."

"For me?"

"It's a video he sent me to send to you—but not yet. Only later."

"Only later when?"

"Later . . ." Logan said—and then finished: "After he's dead."

Dead? "Logan!" I said, like *What the hell?* "What are you talking about?"

"Just watch it," Logan said. "Go up to your room right now and watch it. And when you're done, I suspect you'll have a change of heart. I suspect you'll want to see Charlie, after all. If I'm right, come down to the ballroom. I'll save you a seat."

WHAT ELSE COULD I do? I went up to watch it.

I sat at my hotel room desk, opened my laptop, double-clicked the file. And there, on my screen, appeared a video of Charlie. The second I saw it, I knew from his beat-up face exactly when he'd filmed it: it was the night he'd had that bar brawl and come home completely pummeled. The same day he'd gotten that mysterious phone call he'd never explained. He was seated, hunched, on the side of his bed, filming into his phone, rumpled as ever, and exactly as many sheets to the wind as I remembered.

"Emma," Charlie said into the phone. "If you're seeing this right now—if Logan sent it to you to watch—then I'm . . ." Charlie shook his head, like he couldn't believe the words. "It sounds like the worst kind of bad movie dialogue . . . but if you're watching this, then I'm already dead."

He nodded, like he was letting the idea sink in. "I don't know why it's so weird to say that. Everybody winds up dead eventually. What's actually weird is the way we all think we're gonna last forever." Charlie looked up at the ceiling like he was blinking back tears. "I would have liked some more time, though. To be honest. I barely found you. I *just* found you. Right?" Charlie closed his eyes and made a fist in his hair before going on. "So . . . it's late. And you just cleaned up my face and tried to tuck me into bed. But I can't sleep. I can't sleep until I say this." Charlie took a deep breath. "At my well checkup this week . . . I got a positive screening for metastasized lung cancer."

Charlie grabbed a fistful of hair and squeezed his eyes closed for a second.

"There are more tests to do and questions to answer," he went on. "But I've been down this road before. And no matter how I turn it around in my mind, the only good place for you . . . is *as far as possible* from me."

He looked away, sucked in a deep breath, held it, then pushed it back out—and as he did, he started coughing.

Hold on—was that why he'd been coughing so much? Not allergies— but *lung cancer*?

"You're not going to believe this," Charlie went on, "but I knew on that first day that I was going to fall for you. You hadn't been yelling at Logan in my front yard for even sixty seconds before I knew. I felt it. I called it! It was so predictable."

He took a minute to rub his eyes. Then he went on, "I like you like crazy, Emma. I didn't even know it was possible to like another person this much." He shook his head. "And up until today, I wanted nothing more than to make you like me, too." He frowned, like he was think- ing. "Maybe this is my punishment. Maybe you were right about self- fulfilling prophecies. All I know is, I really don't want to die. And the reason I don't want to die is because I just want more time with you."

Charlie paused to cough again.

Then he went on. "That's the only thing I want. That's the only thing I can *think about* wanting. But guess what? I'm going to rise above that. I'm not going to ruin your life. For once, I'm going to put someone else first." He grabbed another fistful of hair. "I can't believe your life. You've spent ten years taking care of your dad—and you gave up everything to do it. All this time, you've kept a lid on that Spindletop of talent you've got. It's so wrong that it happened."

Charlie slid down to sit beside the bed.

"I lied to you today," he went on. "And I'm going to keep lying to you. I'll never tell you about any of this. I'm going to push you away for your own good while I'm still strong enough to do it. And you know why—and you know I'm right. If I don't, you'll take care of me just like you did with your dad—and I refuse to be another thing that stops you. You need somebody in your life who lifts you up—not drags you down.

Trust me on this. I've been through it all before. It's shitty, I know. But every option I have is shitty. At least this one sets you free."

Charlie stopped talking, and put his head in his hand, but the camera kept filming.

When he looked up again, he peered straight into the lens.

"I'm so sorry, Emma," he said then. "I would write a hundred happy endings for us if I could."

Thirty-One

I SHOT DOWN to the ballroom so fast after that, I don't completely remember how I got there. I mostly remember crying. Crying in the elevator—riding eight floors down with two kids who faced backward and stared at me the whole time. Crying while giving my name at the sign-in table. Crying as I slipped through the closed door at the back of the room.

My thoughts somersaulted unintelligibly around in my head—mainly denial-themed, if I recall. Charlie was sick? But he didn't look sick. I'd seen plenty of sick people. He looked great! He looked healthy! This was unacceptable! He'd just had his five-year-iversary! Hadn't he been through enough? This couldn't be right! He was *Charlie*!

The ballroom was dark and the crowd was on its feet, cheering as Charlie took the stage. The sight of him captured my attention—and the crying trickled to a stop.

He was here. He was alive. He was just across the room.

Charlie, you astonishing dummy. How could you ever think that pushing me away was a good idea?

I wanted to run right over to him so bad—and wrap my arms around him and refuse to let go—but I held myself still and just focused on him in the spotlight. He walked up to a clear podium and squinted out at the audience.

Charlie, in a tux.

Someone had done his hair so it was all spiking up in the same direction. He was as close to picture perfect as I'd ever seen him. Until I noticed his green-and-white pocket square.

It wasn't in the square shape he usually wore—but a fanlike triangle.

It wasn't hemmed, but ripped at the edge.

And it wasn't even a handkerchief, it was—oh, god.

I held my breath.

It was a piece of that green-and-white fabric from the tropical-print dress I'd almost drowned in. As if maybe, instead of throwing it away, Charlie—without even bothering to find scissors—had ripped a piece of it free with his bare hands, folded it, and declared it to be a handkerchief.

But the effect was oddly charming—almost like he had a pocket full of greenery.

Maybe he'd start a trend.

The crowd settled down and took their seats. I looked around for Logan and saw that he had, in fact, saved a seat for me. But T.J. was sitting on his other side.

Was T.J. wearing a backward baseball cap in the ballroom?

I think you can guess the answer to that. But in the interest of journalistic integrity, I'll just go ahead and say yes. Yes, he was.

I decided to pass on the saved seat and just stand at the back of the room.

Up onstage, Charlie cleared his throat.

Just when we thought he'd start his speech, he pulled his cell phone out of his pants pocket. Then, flipping on the ringer at the side, he leaned into the microphone and his voice filled the room. "I'm expecting an important call," he said, and the crowd melted into warm laughter.

I thought about Charlie saying, "You can get away with so much when people have already decided to like you."

Had I already decided to like him?

I had.

"I'm serious," he said to the crowd, setting the phone smack in the middle of the podium. "I've been waiting on this call all day. And if I miss it now, I'll have to wait until morning. And I'm just not gonna do that."

More warm laughter.

"It's not going to ring, of course," he said. "It hasn't rung all day, and I'll be up here—what?—twenty minutes? Thirty if it's going well?" The crowd watched, still not sure if he was joking. "But if it does ring," Charlie said, eyeing the audience like he meant business, "I'm answering." He checked his watch. "They're open late on Thursdays, so I've still got an hour."

More laughter.

With that, Charlie settled in, repositioned the phone on the podium one last time, bent the mic closer, put his hands in his pants pockets, and then peered into the stage lights.

We all waited for whatever might be next.

He sure knew how to command a room.

"I had a whole different talk planned," Charlie began at last. "But I lost interest in that talk. Tonight, the only thing I want to talk about is the very maligned, highly ridiculed, generally dismissed concept of love."

The crowd felt his vibe and waited.

"Eight weeks ago, I was one of those douchey guys who thought love was made up by Hallmark to sell greeting cards. I thought it was an emotional Ponzi scheme. I thought it was a fiction we'd been tricked into believing by the animators at Disney. And I thought our only hope of escape was to unplug from the Love Matrix and see our true dystopic loveless hellscape for exactly what it was."

Charlie looked around while the room waited.

"And then," he went on, "I met a woman who disagreed. Really disagreed. Loudly—and often. Like, she made me watch a TED Talk about it."

The crowd chuckled agreeably.

"She argued with me," Charlie went on, "and she made fun of me, and she told me I was wrong so relentlessly . . . that of course I had no choice but to fall in love with her."

More chuckles.

"Her name is Emma Wheeler, by the way. And she's about to be a very successful screenwriter. And before I met her, I thought the only stories worth telling were the realistic ones. You know—like ones about zombies."

A good rumble of laughter from the crowd.

"I don't know how I let myself get so cynical," Charlie went on. "I've been wondering about that a lot. All I can figure is this: it hurts to be disappointed. It hurts so much, we'd rather never get our hopes up. And it's humiliating, too—right? How foolish are you to hope for the best? How pathetic is it to try to win after you've already lost? How naive must you be if you don't know that humanity is dark and vicious and totally irredeemable? But the argument Emma's been making this whole time—and I'm paraphrasing here—is this: If those are the only stories we tell about ourselves, then those are the only stories we have."

Nods and murmurs from the crowd.

"And that's kind of where I've landed, after taking her crash course in why love matters. Humanity at its worst is an easy story to tell—but it's not the only story. Because the more we can imagine our better selves, the more we can become them." Charlie nodded, like he was really siding with himself now. "It's cooler to be jaded. It's more badass to not care. But I just can't stop thinking that it's kind of chicken, too. If you try to write stories about love and kindness, you really are risking being ridiculed. Which might be the worst form of social death. But my friend Emma kept insisting that it was really important to be brave and try. And I'm here to say, after arguing with her from every single angle, I've decided at last that she's right."

Was this a whole speech about how I was right?

I would have thought, *Popcorn, please,* if I hadn't started crying again.

But then, before Charlie could go on—his phone started ringing.

He looked down.

"Oh, god," he said. "There it is. That's the call." Then he looked up at the crowd. "I'm so sorry," he said, holding up a finger. "I wasn't kidding. I really do have to take this."

And then, in front of three hundred dinner guests, he picked up the phone, and, without thinking to step away from the podium—or the mic—put it to his ear and said, "Hello?"

Then: "This is Charlie Yates. Yes."

Then a pause while he listened.

Then: "Oh, god. How is that—"

Then: "You're saying—three weeks ago—?"

Then: "I understand. Yes. Okay. Thank you."

And then Charlie turned off his phone, dropped it back into his pocket, put his head down on the podium, and cried.

For a good while.

Charlie Men-Don't-Cry Yates . . . *cried.* At a podium. In a tuxedo. In front of three hundred people. Hands clutching either side of the dais, shoulders shaking, breaths and chokes and cries finding their way straight into the microphone and filling the room with the amplified sounds—making it feel strangely like it was happening to all of us, too.

Like we were all crying, in a way. But only one of us knew why.

I took a few steps closer to where Charlie was, entering an aisle between the tables that gave me a straight path to the podium.

But I stopped when he finally lifted his head, remembered the crowd, rubbed the many tears off his face with his tuxedo sleeve, and then took a deep breath to say, "I have an announcement to make."

The whole room braced itself. Something real was happening here.

"I, apparently . . ." Charlie said, taking in another deep breath, "had bronchitis three weeks ago."

The crowd burst into laughter and applause, like this had to be a punch line. And Charlie was laughing, too—but he also kept frowning and wiping at his eyes like he was still quite shaken.

"To be clear," Charlie went on, "up until three minutes ago, I thought I had metastatic lung cancer."

A murmur from the crowd as the laughter receded.

And then, still watching, a bit hypnotized by everything that was happening in front of me, I took a few steps toward him down that center aisle.

"But it was just bronchitis," Charlie said next, shaking his head. "And now it's already gone. Hell of a twist."

The room chuckled. I took a few more steps.

"Turns out," Charlie went on, "on a screening test, it's hard to tell the difference between a 'concerning mass' in your lungs and plain old everyday congestion. That's the news I just got. Better imaging gives a much clearer picture. But my second test with better imaging got postponed because, like a genius, I went to Texas, instead. I skipped my follow-up. Which was worth it, by the way."

He nodded as he thought about it.

"Bronchitis," he said next, shaking his head. "I'm not dying, after all."

Charlie took a deep, five-point-five-second breath.

"And now I can't even remember why I'm up on this stage. Or what I was talking about. Was it about how we should tell ourselves better stories about who we are? About how we shouldn't rob ourselves of hope and possibility? About how light matters just as much as darkness—maybe more? Or was I maybe just rambling on about Emma Wheeler? Because, honestly, she's—"

Right then, I stepped into the reflected stage lights—close enough that he could see me.

Our eyes met.

And Charlie lost his train of thought.

Charlie just stood there staring down at me, and I just stood there staring up right back.

"Because, honestly, she's . . ." he tried again, quieter, like he wasn't even listening to himself anymore—his eyes fixed on me like I might disappear.

"Because," he tried again, "honestly, unless I'm hallucinating right now . . . she's here in this room."

The crowd all craned to look.

"Are you really here?" Charlie asked into the mic then, his voice low and private, like we were the only two people around.

I nodded.

And then Charlie looked up and seemed to remember where he was. He lifted his award statuette off the podium. And then he said, without pauses or punctuation, "Thank you for this incredible award I'm more honored than I can say and I'll never forget this night."

Then he walked straight to the front of the stage, and, without ever taking his eyes off me, he jumped right down.

It took him about ten strides to reach me, and when he got there, he let his award hang forgotten in one hand, like the coolest of cool guys.

The whole room was watching, and now flashes were going off.

I glanced down at the award. "Another award for the drawer?"

But Charlie, never taking his eyes off mine, shook his head. "There is no more awards drawer."

I waited for clarification.

"I took them all out, one by one, and polished them, and apologized to them, and put them on a shelf, like a person determined to be grateful for his blessings. And I even glued the angel's broken wing back on."

I kept my face deadpan. "The Women's Film Critics Association will be very pleased."

"Did you hear that just now?" Charlie asked, tilting his head to gesture back at the stage without breaking eye contact.

I nodded, and stepped closer.

"All of it?" he asked.

I nodded again, and took another step.

"Specifically the part about how I'm not dying?"

One more nod. "So that cough that you thought was allergies—it was actually bronchitis?"

"That's right."

"So you were sick when you had your screening test? But by the time you went back for the real test, you were well?"

"Exactly."

"So," I said, "just to confirm: You're not dying?"

Charlie nodded in awe, like he could barely believe it himself. "Not at the moment."

I let that sink in.

"What do you think?" Charlie asked next.

"I think you'd rather feed my heart into a wood chipper than tell me you were sick again."

"Correct. And I'd do it again, too. Because I was *not* going to be another person ruining your life."

"You really don't understand how life-ruining works, do you?"

"You can't be trusted to do the right thing for yourself."

"For the record, I would never have left you because you got sick."

"I know that. That's why I had to leave you first."

But I shook my head. "Logan sent me your video. The one I wasn't supposed to see until you were dead. And I came down here ready to force you to let me be with you—no matter what."

"That's a hell of a decision."

"That was a hell of a video."

"But I'm not sick. So it doesn't matter now."

"It matters that you lied to me," I said.

"I misled you," Charlie said, like that was different.

"You said I was a hypochondriac."

"You *are* a hypochondriac."

"But you said it in a mean way."

Charlie lowered his head. "I'm sorry."

"You shut things down with me. You said there was no misunderstanding."

"There *was* no misunderstanding. Not on my end, anyway."

"You said you didn't care about me."

Charlie took exception to that. "I *never* said I didn't care about you."

"You said, and I quote: 'Absolutely not. No way in hell.'"

"I was trying to do you a favor."

"That's a shitty favor."

"It was a shitty situation."

"But it's better now."

"Yes," Charlie said, frowning like he still couldn't believe it. "It's better now."

"More proof for my theory," I said.

"What theory?"

"Sometimes things get better."

Charlie nodded like that was a bit of a revelation. "I guess sometimes they do."

Then he leaned down to set his award respectfully on the floor and stood back up to meet my eyes.

"Did you hear the other thing I said up there, too?"

"What other thing?"

"The part about how I'm in love with you."

"That does sound familiar."

"Is that okay?"

I nodded. "It's okay." Then I added, "Better than okay, in fact. Because now we're even."

At that, Charlie put both of his hands in his pockets.

I looked down at one, then the other, then back up. "Are you Ji Chang Wook–ing me right now?"

"I don't know who that is."

"The guy in the turtleneck. Who perfected the pockets kiss."

Charlie smiled in that way that made his nostrils dimple. "Then I guess I must be."

"Did I ever tell you," I said then before I could stop myself, "that I really love your nostrils?"

Oh, god. It had to happen, I guess. A Chekhov's gun moment: You can't forbid yourself from mentioning someone's nostrils in Act One without finally doing it by Act Three.

Or wait. Maybe *this* was Act One—and we were only just getting started?

As if to answer, Charlie stepped closer, hands still in his pockets like a champion, and completely closed the gap between us—pressing his thighs to my thighs, and his chest to my chest. Then he tilted his head until his mouth was just breaths away from mine.

"How's my angle?" he asked, like he really wanted to know.

"You're a remarkable student," I said.

"Are you kidding me?" Charlie said. "I'm the best."

And then he pressed his mouth to mine, and as he did, he slid his hands out of his pockets so they could skim around my waist to hold me right there.

Not that I was trying to escape.

I think the whole ballroom broke into applause—but I can't say for sure. And I feel like a live camera fed the moment to the jumbotron up front—but I'm not positive about that, either. All I remember for certain was the feeling of my heart unfolding to its full wingspan in my chest, like a bird that had decided to stretch out wide at last and absolutely soar.

Was this a happy ending?

Of course. And also only a beginning. In the way that beginnings and endings are always kind of the same thing.

I had no idea where we'd go from here, or how we'd manage it all, or where the future would take us. But it was okay. We don't get to know the whole story all at once. And where we're headed matters so much less than how we get there.

Charlie was here right now. And I was here, too.

And that was enough for now.

"I'm so in love with you," Charlie said then, his breath against my ear. "It's terrible."

And so I said, "We're gonna need a better word for terrible."

Epilogue

SO MY DAD was right, in the end.

We all really did manage to be okay.

And it only took us ten years.

But what does *okay* even mean? Life is always full of worries and struggles, losses and disappointments, late-night googling of bizarre symptoms—all tumbling endlessly over one another like clothes in the dryer. It's not like any of us ever gets to a place where we've solved everything forever and we never have another problem.

That's not how life works.

But that's not what a happily ever after is, anyway.

Poor happy endings. They're so aggressively misunderstood. We act like "and they lived happily ever after" is trying to con us into thinking that nothing bad ever happened to anyone ever again.

But that's never the way I read those words. I read them as "and they built a life together, and looked after each other, and made the absolute best of their lives."

That's possible, right?

That's not ridiculous.

Tragedy is a given. There is no version of human life that doesn't involve reams of it.

The question is what we do in the face of it all.

AND WHAT *DID* we do, our little family?

We did the only thing we *could* do. We made the best of things.

Sylvie and Salvador both wound up working in medicine—him as a physician's assistant, and her as a nurse anesthetist. They stayed with my dad in his apartment for two years after their elopement before Mrs. Otsuka got the bright idea that maybe my dad should come live next door with her.

My dad loved that idea—but he said they should get married first.

Which Mrs. Otsuka was happy to do.

And so they had a little ceremony in the community garden, and then Salvador helped my dad move all his instruments next door—and Mrs. Otsuka didn't even have to put foam cushions on her sharp corners, because by that point, my dad had been spending so much time at her place that she'd already done it.

She took on a lot of caregiving, marrying my dad. But she told me once that it's worth it. He cures her loneliness. He shines light on her shadows. He makes her laugh all day long and into the night. That's how she sees it: she takes care of him, but he takes care of her, too. And it's so plain to see that they have much more fun together than they'd ever have apart.

My dad started learning Japanese, by the way. Turns out, he has a knack for languages.

And he also has a great tutor.

Sylvie and Salvador turned my dad's old room into a guest room. Sylvie also decided to redecorate the apartment in her spare time—dismantling our childhood bunk beds, and wallpapering an accent wall with tropical flowers, and filling up the windowsill with succulents in bright painted pots. She made a Pinterest page and everything.

Now Sylvie and Salvador are working hard, and saving up, and hoping to buy a house big enough for all of them, and a gaggle of kids, at some point. Sylvie even googled our sunny, rambling childhood home to see if that might be an option—but it had been bulldozed to make way for a megamansion.

"Maybe it's better this way," I said as Sylvie ranted about it on the phone. "Maybe life is telling us to keep moving forward."

Kenji continues to come visit every summer and go to camps at the science museum. And it turned out, he has twin younger sisters, who started joining him when they got old enough. My dad loves it when all the kids show up at the apartment and fill it with life and scampering and giggling, and he's taught them all how to play the harmonica.

"It's a *lot* of harmonicas," Sylvie says. "They could start a Bob Dylan tribute band."

AND ME? WHAT became of me?

I moved to LA and kept writing.

I got my own tiny apartment for a while, right above a tattoo parlor.

It did just happen to be walking distance from Charlie's place, but I swear that was a coincidence. Mostly.

It was my first time living alone in my life, and I did some hard-core nesting—amassing a block-printed cloth napkin collection, stocking up on kooky coffee mugs, and diving full-immersion into a throw-pillow lifestyle.

"What is it with women and throw pillows?" Charlie asked when my bed got so laden with them, it was hard to find the mattress.

"I think the words you're looking for are 'thank you,'" I said.

Charlie fully supported my commitment to independence.

But, even still, every single day . . . he asked me to marry him.

Which I loved.

Even though, every day, I also evaded the question.

A smile would take over my face, and I'd say, "You don't have to be married to be happy."

And Charlie wouldn't disagree.

"I just want to belong to you," he'd say. "And I want you to belong to me."

And then I'd push him down into all those throw pillows in a way that left no doubt about who belonged to whom.

But I still resisted saying yes—in that way you can when absolutely everybody knows you *want* to say yes. And you *will* say yes—eventually.

And anticipation is half the fun.

One great thing about being writers is that our jobs are portable. So we spend summers in Houston, in Sylvie and Salvador's guest room. It's a total circus: Sylvie, Salvador, their two golden retrievers, our dad, Mrs. Otsuka (who, once we were family, encouraged us all to call her by her first name, Mitsuko), all three of her grandkids, and Charlie and me. All of us just back and forth between apartments, and sharing food, and babysitting, and helping out, and working in the community garden, and buzzing with kinetic energy in that cheery, noisy way that happens sometimes when families are piled into close quarters.

Sometimes we even add Jack Stapleton and his cute wife, Hannah, into the mix, and we all squeeze in around the dining table, grandkids on various knees, and have little impromptu sing-alongs after dinner.

Though my dad has never stopped calling Jack "Jake Singleton."

And Jack never corrects him.

DID CHARLIE AND I wind up going to the Olympics for line dancing and taking the gold for the USA?

Well, since there is no line dancing at the Olympics, and since it's much more cooperative than competitive, and since it's not exactly a thing you can win—unless you count just *being there* as winning—and since I just recently pulled a muscle while executing a sailor step into a coaster step . . .

Not exactly.

But we did keep going to lessons.

Though, in an effort to minimize any and all six-foot cowboys, we signed up at the senior center nearby, where eighty-year-olds danced circles around us. The instructor herself was eighty-six—and still going strong in a pair of red rhinestone boots and a fringe jacket. We went every week, faithfully. Charlie was universally adored, and I was routinely pitied—but with a warmth and compassion that made it okay.

"Oh, sweetheart," they'd say. "That's not a rumba step."

And then they'd show me. Again.

It's fine. A little humiliation gets you laughing like nothing else can.

And I have begun to master *right* versus *left*.

And, for the record, I never mind having a reason to bump into Charlie.

DID CHARLIE AND I keep writing together? We did.

And did writing "lady movies" tank Charlie's career, as Jablowmie had prophesized? Would Charlie have been better off lending his talents to the string-bikini reboot of *Beer Tower III*—or whatever project T.J. was meeting Donna Cole about at the coffee shop that day? A project she declined to work on, by the way. Which wasn't my fault—though T.J. still insists that it was.

"You sabotaged me," he said in a lowered voice the last time I saw him at an awards show—just as Charlie broke in with "You sabotaged yourself," and steered me off to visit with someone else.

I won't name-drop who the *someone else* was . . .

But let's just say her name rhymes with Sheryl Sheep.

Was that enough comeuppance for T.J.? Not getting what he wanted *one time*?

Probably not. But it's a start.

If you're wondering how *The Rom-Commers* did, I'll let the legendary box office numbers answer that. And all the headlines that included the term "surprise blockbuster." And also that piece in *The Atlantic*, "How Charlie Yates and His Writing Partner Are Resuscitating the Rom-com." True, my name is missing from the headline. But the full-page photo is of me, filling up most of the frame, with my curly hair puffed out to maximum dramatic capacity by a makeup artist who also does shoots for *Vogue* and who made me look a thousand percent cooler than I am in real life. And Charlie, in profile and half out of frame, gazes at me admiringly.

When I saw the photo, I said, "This is the only time I've ever liked my hair."

And Charlie said, "That's okay. I like it enough for both of us."

Also: During the interview for that piece, Charlie deferred to me at every question, and then, when the writer turned for his response, just nodded and said, "What she said." Every time. Making sure, in his friendly way, that I was quoted—heavily.

All to say: Charlie's doing just fine.

As am I.

I did eventually give in and marry Charlie, by the way. And I did transfer my mug collection to his mansion. But I am still, to this day, not allowed to touch the coffee maker.

AND THAT'S HOW this story comes to an end: with a total of not one, not two, but three weddings.

Do you have to get married in life to be happy? Of course not.

But it's certainly one way to go.

My dad got certified as a reverend online for thirty-five dollars, insisted we all start calling him Reverend Dad, and then served as our officiant. We all gathered once again in the community garden, surrounded by a bumper crop of Mitsuko's dragon's egg cucumbers—just a year to the week after my dad's own wedding in the same spot.

I carried a bouquet of marigolds, which were my mom's favorite flower, and which the lovely Mitsuko had planted and grown in anticipation of the big day. We also pinned them to the guys' white guayabera shirts—it was far too hot in June for jackets—as boutonnieres.

This time, in his official capacity, my dad had some things to say. Leaning on his walker, he told us the smartest thing he knew about being married:

"People say 'marriage is hard' all the time." He looked around the small crowd—which included our family, Jack Stapleton and Hannah, Logan and his husband, Nico, Mitsuko's family, in town for the summer drop-off, and all the members of the community garden.

My dad went on, "But I disagree. I don't think marriage is hard. I think, in fact, if you do it right, marriage is the thing that makes everything else easier."

My dad let that sink in.

He went on. "Now you're wondering how to do it right—right?"

We nodded.

"Well, you're lucky. Because love is something you can learn. Love is something you can practice. It's something you can choose to get good at. And here's how you do it." He let go of his walker to signal he meant business: "Appreciate your person."

He looked around.

"That's it," he said, like we were done. Then he added, "Well—first, be sure to choose a good person." He evaluated the crowd to make sure we'd done that. Then he said, "But we're all good people here."

Bashful smiles all around.

He went on: "Choose a good, imperfect person who leaves the cap off the toothpaste, and puts the toilet paper roll on upside down, and loads the dishwasher like a ferret on steroids—and then appreciate the hell out of that person. Train yourself to see their best, most delightful, most charming qualities. Focus on everything they're getting right. Be grateful—all the time—and laugh the rest off."

My dad smiled at us, and then put a hand back on his walker.

"And that goes for kids, too, by the way—and pets, and waiters, and even our own selves," he said. "There it is. The whole trick to life. Be aggressively, loudly, unapologetically grateful."

My dad nodded at us then, like *You're welcome.*

Then he concluded with, "Now let's get these two kids hitched."

ALL TO SAY . . . yes. This *was* and *is* a happily ever after.

Even though I still—always—miss my mom. Even though my dad

continues to struggle with his balance, and just got seven stitches after slipping in the shower, and still keeps his unplayed cello in a corner of the room where he can see it. Even though Sylvie and Salvador have been trying for a baby for two years and haven't had much success. Even though I still google "elbow cancer" in the middle of the night, and I don't make it home nearly as often as I'd like to, and feel, honestly, a little jealous of Sylvie sometimes, now that she's taken over. Life has no shortage of disappointments. Mistress Jablowmie got vengeful when she didn't get her screenplay from Charlie, and now his Mafia movie may never see the light of day. T.J. Heywood continues to menace me every chance he gets—stubbornly refusing a redemption arc. The lovely Mitsuko has an irritating new neighbor who keeps spraying insecticide on the butterfly weed she planted as food for the monarch caterpillars. And Cuthbert the guinea pig never did conquer his melancholia—and eventually followed his brother across the rainbow bridge.

That's just life.

Tragedy really is a given.

There are endless human stories, but they all end the same way.

So it can't be *where you're going* that matters. It has to be *how you get there*.

That's what I've decided.

It's all about the details you notice. And the joys you savor. And the hope you refuse to give up on.

It's all about writing the very best story of your life.

Not just how you live it—but how you choose to tell it.

Acknowledgments

I always panic when it comes time to write acknowledgments because I'm always terrified of leaving important people out, and then I always do. Whoever you are, thank you—and I'm so sorry I forgot you!

Before I go any further, let me be sure to thank the lovely people of Macmillan Audio for their support and hand-signed holiday cards over the years. Warm and grateful thanks to Emily Dyer, Katy Robitzski, Amber Cortes, Matt DeMazza, Guy Oldfield, and Michelle Altman. I've been so lucky that Macmillan has found two wonderful narrators for my books—Therese Plummer and Patti Murin—and that they've so warmly let me record stories and notes for them over the years. I'm so grateful to be a part of it all!

The Rom-Commers is a story that combines a job I know better than any other—being a writer—with a job I know very little about: screenwriting. The biggest, warmest thanks to two friends who consulted with me about screenwriting life: TV writer and producer Alison Schapker (*Alias, Brothers & Sisters, Scandal, Westworld*) and feature screenwriter/director Vicky Wight (*The Lost Husband, Happiness for Beginners*) for taking the time to give me a sense of what it's really like.

Thanks to Dr. Lindy McGee and Rhonda Sherman, Ph.D., for helping me think through some medical questions—and to Dr. Mark Brinker for diagnosing Charlie with bronchitis. I'd also like to thank Dr. Jocelyn Abrams for much wisdom she's shared with me about how anxiety works.

Thanks to our dear family friend Nelda Jasper for introducing me to the joys of line dancing, and many grateful thanks to Britt Beresik of Cross The Line Dancing Houston for not shaming me in her class—because, like Emma, I am comically terrible at line dancing. Thanks also to my daughter, Anna, for taking line-dancing lessons with me one summer on a whim, and not letting me quit when I realized I was bad, and to my friend Laura Laux, who started coming with me to class after Anna went back to college. And speaking of joy, I'm so thankful to Janis Goldstein and her daughters, Bailey and Emery, for letting me spend some time with—and teaching me a lot about—their guinea pigs, Oli and Apple. I also need to thank my brother-in-law, Matt Stein, for his help with research on Japan. And much gratitude to my dear friend Maria Zerr for our deep and resonant heart-to-heart about the joys and perils of our curly hair. Maria, I dedicate Emma's pom-pom to you.

Some great books influenced my thinking while I was writing this year. *The Grieving Brain: The Surprising Science of How We Learn from Love and Loss* by Mary-Frances O'Connor and *The Power of Fun: How to Feel Alive Again* by Catherine Price both gave me a lot to think about. I also love Judson Brewer, M.D., Ph.D.'s practical and helpful book, *Unwinding Anxiety: New Science Shows How to Break the Cycles of Worry and Fear to Heal Your Mind.*

I also need to thank an unnamed Southwest Airlines pilot who once held a plane for a passenger in much the way that it happens in this book. I read an article about it years ago and it's stayed with me all this time—just knowing that it can happen and has happened, even if it hardly ever does, adds a little brightness to the world for me.

I've already thanked Vicky Wight for letting me interview her about screenwriting for this book, but I have to thank her again for turning my novel *Happiness for Beginners* into a movie for Netflix. Thanks also to

Melissa Ryan at Netflix for all her amazing publicity for the movie—and for making sure to include the book so prominently! I'm so overjoyed that this book got a second chance to find its readers years after it was first published! Thanks also to Stephanie Hockersmith of Pie Lady Books and Katelyn Cole of the Bookcase Beauty for coming to Houston to celebrate!

I can't even believe how lucky I am to get to work with some of the all-time greats of the publishing world. My agent, Helen Breitwieser of Cornerstone Literary, has been with me from the beginning—and never gave up. Much gratitude and many thanks to the good people of St. Martin's Press who work so hard to help my books find their way in the world: Christina Lopez, Katie Bassel, Erica Martirano, Brant Janeway, Kejana Ayala, Lisa Senz, and Anne Marie Tallberg. Thanks also to cover designer Olga Grlic and illustrator Katie Smith for all the beauty they create. Heartfelt gratitude, especially, to my brilliant and inspiring editor, Jen Enderlin. I wish I had a bigger word for grateful.

So much love, at last, to my awesome family: Lizzie and Scott Fletcher; Shelley, Matt, and Yazzie Stein; and Bill Pannill and Molly Hammond. Many thanks, also, to my nephew Wiley Fletcher and his bride, Courtney Tee, for asking me to officiate their wedding on a Colorado mountainside. Some of what I said that day made it into this book. And at last, I am beyond grateful to my hilarious kids, Anna and Thomas, my legendary mom, Deborah Detering, and my absolute dream of a husband, Gordon Center, for making the best of every single day.

And you. Of course: *you*. If you're reading this book, thank you. You make it all possible. People are always leaving me comments like, "Keep writing!" And I always think, *I definitely will—as long as you keep reading*. Right? I get to be here only because you're here. I get to write books only because you read them. So thank you for reading, and thank you for being here. I'm so endlessly grateful that we have each other.

About the Author

Skylar Reeves Photography

Katherine Center is the *New York Times* bestselling author of eleven novels, including *Hello Stranger, The Bodyguard, Things You Save in a Fire,* and her newest, *The Rom-Commers.* Katherine writes "deep rom-coms"—laugh-and-cry books about how life knocks us down, and how we get back up. The movie adaptation of Katherine's novel *Happiness for Beginners,* starring Ellie Kemper and Luke Grimes, became a Netflix movie in 2023 and hit the Global Top 10 in 81 countries around the world, and the movie of her novel *The Lost Husband* hit #1 on Netflix in 2020. Katherine lives in her hometown of Houston, Texas, with her husband, two kids, and their fluffy-but-fierce dog. Join her mailing list at KatherineCenter.com!